CHRONICLES OF TARC

545–9

NIGHTWALKER KING
AND QUEEN OF NIGHT

Jiryü Räsen

FIRST EDITION

PUBLISHED BY J. KASSEBAUM

October 10, 2025 First Edition.
Paperback ISBN 978-1-949359-20-6
eBook ISBN 978-1-949359-21-3
© **Jiryü Räsen**. All rights reserved.
Published by J. Kassebaum, Indianapolis.
Cover background ©Sumners Graphics via Canva.com.
#NaNoWinner2021, #NaNoWinner2022

Historian's Note to the Original Chronicle

Having been commissioned by Their Royal Excellencies, the Grand Duke Ore Melick and the Grand Duchess Ilena Polov Touka, to be the Royal Chronicler and Historian of the Grand Duchy of Tarc, I, Baron Reynold Tennyson, have set my hand to accomplish the task.

As of the end of this work, I believe I've finally caught up to the present time. It's been quite difficult here at the beginning, trying to get my research of Tarc written so that I can set that chapter of my life behind me while at the same time trying to begin the new one. I've been told that the way the first few volumes were written leaves the reader to believe it was written by a foreigner. ...I suppose I am. Having lived so many years with the Tarc, speaking after the manner of the men of Ryokudo is hard. So is writing in my native language. Many times I slip back into the Tarcian patterns.

I'm afraid that most of the works through even this one suffer from the fact I'm quite far behind. I had to go back and get anecdotal stories from those who lived during the time I was doing double duty and sometimes triple duty as I also was needed in the Ministry of Intelligence during the early very stressful time. My notes are sketchy at best from that time, I'm afraid. I was paying close attention to the partnership issues wanting to understand that better along with Justinian, who also remembered those parts best. I was able to write quite knowledgeably about the Marluk'nak' of Chaos and Change, having been present for that one.

When I finally submitted the previous works I was taken a bit to task. The Historical Department of the Ministry of Scribes let me know when they returned my early manuscripts that I could review what they'd written down, but they'd taken license to make it more readable for Ryokudan minds. That work is quite sterile and much abbreviated. I could only relent once I'd confirmed they hadn't changed history in that action.

I've kept the originals, seeing they're bound so that I can enjoy them myself. I'll continue to keep my notes bound for myself and summarize them the way the court historians want me to before I send written things over there. It's better to anyway. I like to record things that the Immediate Family finds important, but many of those things are or should be kept secret for this current immediate time. (The beginnings of the Toukas' movements against Brulac and the actual doings of the nightwalkers of Nijoushi being cases in point in these notes.)

Apologies aside, although I suppose they aren't really needed for documents only I'm likely to ever read, I shall now allow any reader who might find these works in the future to continue their study of the history of the Grand Duchy of Tarc and the Immediate Family of Princess Ilena Polov Touka.

-Baron R. Tennyson

Contents

CHAPTER 138 Returning to Nijou

In the city of Nijoushi, capital seat of the Regent of Suiran, spies of the various nightwalker Houses were kneeling in front of their Heads. "The House of the Queen of Night is returning," was their message. Equally unanimous, those spies then sighed in resignation. "The Queen of Night passes on a message." They winced as their Heads went stiff and began to grow cold.

These spies had been sent to join her forces in Tarc. It hadn't been a pleasant job. After being ignored and treated like members of the Queen of Night's House the whole time, they'd been approached directly at the end of it. With deep breaths, her message was passed on: "She'll come speak with you before the Winter Solstice. You can face her with blades and die, or welcome her to the negotiation table to see if you might live. She'll make her proper place in Nijoushi this winter."

The Heads asked in cold tones if her word was good. Every spy told their Head of the strength of the men of Tarc, who as a whole nation and people were as the nightwalkers, won to Ilena's House in only one week. Every spy told their Head of the cunning of the Queen of Night, how well she was protected, and shivering gave their witness to her speed and skills.

"The rumors of the House of the Green Dragon were true," they said in whispered, fearful voices. "She killed everyone in the House with her own hand for daring to touch the Consort." Then those spies pulled in on themselves even more, to have to report the final news: that her House had named Ore King of all Nightwalkers. Heads declared angrily to the members of their Houses that were listening to the report that he'd never be allowed to hold on to that title.

The wisest and most cunning of the Heads sat mused on the words they'd heard. "What's her gift?" the Head of the House of the Rose Flame asked her spy after thinking about it for a while. Her eyes pinned her spy to the wall where he was resting.

He swallowed, thinking of the summary. "She... can motivate nightwalkers, on a very large scale, and still keep them under control."

The Head nodded thoughtfully, then said, "But how?"

He blinked at her. "She's a Touka princess and a nightwalker herself."

The Head sat up and scowled. "A *royal* nightwalker?" she spat. "An *enemy* can make everyone forget who the enemy is and lick the ground she walks on?"

The spy sat up straight and stiffly, silently scolding his Head, making her back down and consider it more deeply. She finally waved a dismissive hand, but the scowl stayed on her face. "Even the despised nightwalkers wish to be given regard by those who lead their nation. Weaknesses like that are why the lot of you will never be Heads."

The spy rose to his feet and looked back at her soberly. "And thus why you and they will never be King and Queen of the Nightwalkers. You've only understood the part you despise."

Her eyes went wide. "And have even you already turned traitor and become theirs?"

He paused in his walk to the door. He shrugged and answered her simply. "How many of your own House had you already lost long ago to the rumors you sent me to confirm? I've confirmed them. What do you think?" He didn't make it out the door, for the thrown blade that pierced his heart from her hand. It was a hand that shook, though, as none of the other nightwalkers in her house would meet her eyes. *

-o-o-o-

Hello Elder Brother,

You may end the war games and return your soldiers to their places. Peace has been settled — for at least a year. Likely it will stay that way. Ilena's Children are watching to make sure.

The reports will be forthcoming. Sorry to make you come up in time for the winter snow to have just begun, but given when the council of clans was there wasn't a better time.

The clans understand the hierarchy sufficiently and the two crown princes are supporting Ilena, seemingly content with the offices she's given them. Your two thousand should be heading home after a month. I want them to be seen a while longer by those two, who feed their horses close to the border. They also understand that if we have to take soldiers back in, it will be to cleanse the land of Tarc of all humanity.

Ilena was wondering if it was originally a penal colony. It feels like it. Do we have any ancient records in Ichijou that would say? None have been found in Nijou. Bring them when you come. I have other theories I want to check.

The Dance of Joy is certainly a sight to see. It was rare to see all the clans at once dance it. But Ilena's version is more ...thrilling. Watching the Naluk' in her own element makes it impossible to not let her go back. The Marluk' even said so himself.

Well, we'll see you soon, I'm sure.

Rei (Who <u>might</u> be the All, but I'm not saying it — it could be you.)

---

*The wise nightwalkers understand that the nation at peace brings them more profit and their own peace. They don't and won't ever trust those who lead them who are set on tearing down leaders that promote peace within their own nation. For all there are those who have no loyalty, are sociopaths, or are fully chaotic evil, they are not the majority.

Sasou Touka barked a laugh into his hand upon reaching the end of the brief notification that his family was safely out of Tarc and back at the northeast garrison. He was sure Rei would rather Sasou took on the highest office of Tarc, but he'd let his little brother hold the title for now.

"It looks like they passed," he waved the message at his Minister of Intelligence and top aide to let him know he could come take it to read for himself. "Let Aryana know we'll be leaving in roughly twenty days." Michael Barret took the letter and bowed. "Ah, and let her know we may be *snowed in*."

Michael sighed. "At Nijou Castle? Really?"

Sasou waved a hand. "Somewhere along the line," he said distractedly as he rose and went to his personal bookshelf and pulled down three old, worn books, the pages very yellowed with age. He set them carefully on the outer corner of his desk where he'd remember to see them and take them with.

Michael wasn't fooled. The King was ready for a vacation and the Queen was from the north and loved the cold snows. Even if they didn't torture the younger brother and his castle, they wouldn't be coming back for a while. It was really more an order to let the rest of the castle know — at least those who'd be most needed to keep it going. "Yes, Sire," Michael answered and returned to his desk to write up the notices to send by paige, reading the letter on the way.

But then.... He paused. *...It might be the other castle.* He nodded to himself. That was a lot more likely. Sasou had already said he didn't want to stay long at Nijou since they'd just been there (for only three days). Some peace and quiet was more likely it. He'd send the notice to Sasou's personal castle, then. "Do I have to be snowed in also?"

"Hmm?"

Michael looked up at Sasou and pursed his lips. His eyebrows and eyelids dropped just enough to get his message across.

"I don't need to see your face *that* much," Sasou answered, then promptly went back to his work.

Good. Michael was going to get a vacation as well. He'd let Ilena know to save some time for him, and then he'd disappear for a while, too.

-o-o-o-

"It is rather cozy and nice now, isn't it?" Rei said approvingly, having finally been able to review the new updates to his living quarters in the Old Regent's building of Nijou castle.

"Yes. I do like the wood burning stoves, too," Mizi said. "They contain the smoke but heat the room very nicely."

"It only takes a few logs at a time," Rei's manservant Rutherford commented helpfully.

"Really?" Rei frowned at it in concentration. "Then why aren't they used everywhere, if they're better than fireplaces?"

"They're a new invention," Delia said as she passed the two desks on the far side of the front sitting room. She was just done in the bedroom with putting away the clothes from the trip to Tarc. "I guess Mister Balar thought they'd work well here since he couldn't find the fireplace flues."

"What?" Mizi and Rei both raised eyebrows. "There really weren't any fireplaces in this building?"

Delia paused in the doorway to the hallway. "I don't really know, but I do know he decided it wasn't worth it to knock down the top level walls. The pipes bend above and still let the smoke outside. Fireplace flues have to go straight up. Plus, these are a bit safer, since they also contain the sparks."

"They keep most of the warmth inside as well," Rutherford said in approval.

"Until little fingers touch them, it's fine." Maria stood at the door to the bedroom clenching her skirt in one hand. She was eyeing the stove warily. The maid had been putting out their bed clothing but now moved to pass the stove at a careful distance.

"I suspect that could be trained, though...." Mizi frowned as she tucked a stray lock of golden-red hair behind her ear.

"They're already going into the new Regent's building, Princess Mizi," Tanner reassured her from his chair in the corner of the sitting room near his and Rutherford's bedroom door. "Mistress Ilena will let you know officially, I'm sure, or she's waiting to hear you want them. It was her home that was burned, after all."

"True," Rei nodded. "Now you're too many. Get out." Four people bowed. Two left and two went to their own room. He breathed again. "Well, now I know my limit, anyway. I wonder if it's any different, though?"

"Probably not," Mizi said. "That was mine also."

It was nice to be back in the old Regent's suite from the aspect it was home and not Tarc. It was better now that it was renovated so that the whole household wasn't sleeping in each other's laps. It was still too small and closed in to have all the servants and staff gathered into one double room ...and four had been the usual minimum.

Maria and Delia, as Mizi's personal maid and hairdresser, split duties to keep the numbers of people hovering minimal, unless Mizi was to be presented formally. Tanner knew very well how to be invisible, until he needed to speak as Mizi's secretary. Rei wouldn't accept more than the one manservant, but didn't need more than that, particularly now that the maids had come when he and Mizi had gotten married four months before. Rei really didn't need to be remembering having all the guards in this same space as well just before they'd left.

Rei stood from the couch in the comfortable sitting area of the room and stretched. "Now that they're done in the bedroom, shall we?" He held out his hand for hers and they walked into the new bedroom. His head turned as he took in the whole of the room again now that it only had the two of them in it. "Still too big, but it's better." The large bed was still swallowed up by the rest of the open space. With one wardrobe, a small dining table with two chairs, a cabinet for his most important papers and not much else save the rugs around the bed, it still seemed more than he'd ever need.

"Really? I thought it was a nice size, except for being lonely," Mizi said.

Rei thought about it. "Maybe you're right. I'll decide in the morning. It's just the same size as my room before, and that always felt too big. With both of us here, maybe it will be okay." The bedroom was a little cooler than the inner sitting room because of the painted glass windows, but it was still better than outside where winter's cold was settling down to warn that the snows would be on their way soon. Looking up, Rei could see the pipe from the new stove in the sitting room crossed overhead to pass through a small hole that had been cut into the outside wall over the windows. Perhaps some heat was being added to the bedroom from that.

It really was bad timing. The winter snows would start about the time Sasou arrived for the investiture but Rei wanted his Minister of Intelligence. Ilena needed the power of her new titles behind her as soon as possible, in his opinion. He wanted her to help him with punishing the other ministers. They'd used Rei's absence to try to steal more from the castle coffers for projects rather than figure out reasonable ways to earn the money for them.

Speaking of said punishment.... "Mizi," Rei paused in taking off his second boot.

Mizi answered as she came out from under her overdress. "Yes?"

"We'll be sleeping in tomorrow morning, and doing nothing but wandering the castle all day. I'd like to go and see how the new building is coming along, and just put my ear to the ground, so to speak."

Mizi's eyes widened a little. "Alright," she agreed. "...Would it be okay for us to stop by the medical department so I can check in with Ryan? I'll try not to get lost in my research, but I left an experiment running the day you called me. ...Maybe an hour at most?"

Rei pulled off his boot, then nodded. "Okay. That will give me time to get a good look around, and maybe talk to Doctor Elliot as well. I want to check up on his research also."

He watched Mizi pull off the underdress until she was only in her shift. Her cheeks pinked up when she saw him watching her. Rei's heart thumped and his body went warm. His eyes widened, though, when she walked up to him, the hem of her shift swaying around her knees. She helped him out of his clothes, all while kissing him. That was new, but he didn't complain.

When she had trouble with a buckle, the corners of his lips turned up. He licked her lips that had paused their kissing. That made her freeze briefly, having the distraction while trying to do something complicated without looking. His hands caught hers and brought them up between their chests. "So...," he said teasingly, not letting go, "for what purpose are you being forward tonight?"

Mizi's cheeks went redder. *Thought so*, he grinned a little wider, showing his teeth a little. He let go of her hands, but quickly wrapped his arms around her so her hands were still trapped between them. "I don't think so," he said softly in her ear. "You still owe me most of the two years you and Sasou stole from me." Mizi moaned and dropped her head onto his chest, giving up quickly. "I'll take the offer, though," he said.

"But, Rei," he knew she wouldn't give up without some resistance, "what else am I supposed to do for you next?"

"Well, first off," he leaned back a bit to look her in the eye, still holding her, "you should've asked that to begin with."

"Oh." She dropped her gaze.

"And second, what you've already been doing. For all that time you're mine, and mine alone. I'm not sharing, not even with children. After all, they'll be in the way for the next twenty years or more after that. It can wait." They were only nineteen. They had a long time ahead of them before needing to worry about heirs.

He didn't wait any more, though, and soon enough they were christening the newly–renovated bedroom, where they were blissfully *not* under ear or eye of too–close servants. The tent in Tarc had been worse than the previous version of the Old Regent's building as far as marital bliss went.

-o-o-o-

Ore and Ilena were in complete agreement. Solid walls were better than cloth ones. "I'd forgotten how beautiful the new bedcloths were." Ilena ran her hands over the bed covering, feeling the smooth texture and the raised needlework.

Ore ran his hands over her to hold her close and kissed her ear. "Still not as beautiful as my wife," he said, "but —" One hand was getting tangled up in her long black hair at the nape of her neck as his kisses moved down the side of her neck.

After a long while Ilena asked, "But what?"

"Hm?" His golden eyes looked into her matching golden eyes blankly for a second. "Oh." He turned her and encouraged her to get in bed, then joined her. "But better than how it looks is how soft it is. I'm quite done with sleeping on mattresses on the ground." Cuddling her closely he asked softly, "It's about time, isn't it?"

"Yes," she answered softly back. "Mina's agreed also."

"Hoh?" he breathed.

"For the rest of the port, she sold him," Ilena referenced Mina's husband Andrew. That almost ruined the mood for Ore who laughed, hard. Mina was hard to win over in the court games. Ilena was the only one he knew that could do it. Ilena only smiled with him.

"How long, do you think?" he asked after he finally recovered.

"Before?" she asked.

"We'll know if it works? Can we tell which month you're on, yet?" He meant the month she had a potential to get pregnant in. She was only able to every other month because of her surgeries to repair her broken hip that had allowed her to walk again.

"Sadly, no." Ilena looked into the distance of her thoughts as she somewhat absently ran her fingers through his short black hair. "There's a little bit of a bet, too. She said she'd be first."

"Which makes the competitive Ilena want to be first, just because," Ore commented wryly.

"Well..., yes, though it's a vain thought, I suppose, and not necessary, really." She admitted to him, "I'd like to have their and our children be born close together. They'll need to train together to be prepared to stand together. It's easier if they're the same age, as close as possible."

"What if one's a girl?" Ore asked.

Ilena shrugged a little. "Who cares? Both sets of parents are mixed." Ore and Ilena walked at Mizi's back to protect her the same as Andrew and Mina did for Rei.

Ore raised up a bit and furrowed his brow at her. "True, but what if *Master's* is a girl?"

"All the better. Our sons will have more time to figure out how to work together before they have to help the son."

"You're incorrigible!" Ore protested. "You'd leave the little Princess to have no one?"

Ilena's expression and tone went very dry. "Rei will be so overprotective of her that he wouldn't let any of our sons near her."

Ore turned away and laughed into his hand. "*Pft!* Are we so untrustworthy, then?" He tried to give her a high and offended look, but he was also hiding his smile behind his hand.

Ilena shrugged. "I think it's all the teasing and threats of kissing him that's done it, Ore." She pulled him to her to kiss him. "After all," she purred, "he'd see red if he even thought your son and his daughter spent a moment like this."

Ore put his head down on her chest and laughed heartily for a solid minute.

The next morning was a quiet recovery morning for those who'd been out of the castle for just over three months. Their heads were still spinning with the work they'd done on the progress around Suiran and the intense month in Tarc. One day of rest would bring more benefits than a day of ragged efforts.

As Rei and Mizi walked the castle pathways arm in arm it wasn't surprising to Rei to be accosted by Marquis Preston, Regional Minister of Natural Resources and Trade and "head nursemaid" by his own pushy behavior. Really, it was good Preston did show up first, as far as Rei was concerned. To have the nag be the first to learn who the Regent was, now that he was ready to let them know, would calm the weight on his shoulders. They shivered under the awful burden of having to be pleasant to the overbearing man for so long.

"Your Highness." The firm expectation in Preston's voice interrupted Rei in the middle of his sentence to Mizi. Rei ignored Preston and finished his sentence, and didn't stop walking.

Preston had to restart with a blink at being ignored. His voice was louder and more insistent as he called Rei again, "Your Highness!"

Rei continued to ignore Preston long enough he had to start moving his feet to keep up. "Prince Rei! I have a thing I must speak with you on, please!"

Rei paused and turned to look at Preston with cold stoniness for being interrupted by a vassal. The man barely noticed. "I really must protest at the laxness with which you run your office. How can the full depth of requirements be met to a Region when the main office is full of amateurs and leaves questions in the minds of all the lords of it?"

Rei went colder and colder until there was space for him to speak. "I do wonder why," he mused quietly, "the man who stands outside my office for weeks at a time believes that he can rant at me about a thing he has no capacity to perform himself?"

Preston's mouth snapped closed. Rei didn't think he'd really heard the whole of the comment, it had been said quietly enough. More loudly, Rei finally deigned to speak with the man. "I appreciate that I had the opportunity to interview your daughter, Lord Preston." Preston froze slightly. "Do you think she has the capacity to learn a new language sufficiently quickly?"

Preston's mouth gaped open as his brain tried to change tracks. "I – I should think it shouldn't be too much trouble," he spluttered. His hands were suddenly being wrung together.

"Good." Rei began to turn away. "I've suddenly a need for an alliance with a foreign nation. I believe she'll be the best available candidate for the position." Preston was already behind him and his entourage, sweat beginning to bead up on his forehead and his face going pale.

Rei slightly looked over his shoulder to speak to Ilena. "I'm terribly sorry Ilena, but I'll have to have her sent to your office for her lessons. Only there can she learn the language she needs to know. I know your Ministry is going to be terribly busy, but I hope you can fit her lessons in around the edges."

"Yes, Master Rei," Ilena murmured with a submissive bow of her head.

When Preston finally unfroze and caught up to them, Rei merely lifted a hand to Mina without any other acknowledgment. Mina slipped out of her position behind him to intercept the minister. "I'm sorry, Minister Preston," Mina said quietly, keeping her hand on the panicking man's arm to restrain him, "Regent Rei has returned, but all castle business is still postponed at this time. I'm sure the Rose office will be contacting you when there's time to fit an appointment with you into his schedule again."

Preston could only give up at that point. Still, his protests made it to Rei's ears before they were too far to hear them. He continued to ignore them. He'd let them swing in the maelstrom of fear for a while, Preston and his daughter who'd attempt such underhanded tactics at their interview as to even try to undress before him.

It would be a fitting punishment to the father to believe his daughter was to be sent to the backwater nation of Tarc. The actual location she'd be sent to would be a fitting punishment for her being obedient to her father to that awful a degree. The two other lords' daughters who were of proper caliber would be going to more useful alliances closer to home. Those offers of proposal had already been sent by him to the parties in question.

-o-o-o-

The new Regent's building, under construction, was visited and admired. The foundation was completed and the framing for the walls was going up now, with some exterior sections already being bricked in. Plumbing pipes stuck up out of the ground making the whole look odd, but exciting the owners with the potential that was visible. Mister Balar, the construction manager, entertained his guests with explanations and answered questions until the expectant residents were satisfied. A few modifications were requested as well, but that was to be expected.

As they left the construction site, Ilena, Ore and their guards excused themselves to run the roofs for a bit of exercise, and to let all the guards of the upper levels know they were back. Rei knew they'd tease as much as test and hoped they'd find the right balance to not make the guards upset with them.

A few courtyards over, Rei's eyes were caught by another minister he was seething with anger against. He'd told Ilena to see that the Region's

Minister of Public Works was on his pathway for a brief conversation. He caught the eyes of Eadsley so that the man couldn't leave his slightly hidden position in one of the joining outdoor walkways, where he was watching the Regent's entourage from.

Not in a hurry, but not letting the man escape, Rei approached him, still holding his wife on his arm and trailing those of their guards he'd been willing to put up with this day. "Minister Eadsley." Rei greeted him almost casually as the man bowed to him with a slight hesitancy in the motion. "I'm pleased Princess Ilena was able to clear your name."

Eadsley relaxed slightly. "Thank you, Your Highness. It was very relieving to have my irritating cousin ratted out."

Rei nodded absently and turned his gaze away from Eadsley, allowing it to go distant. Keeping his tone distant as well, Rei added, "While I have you here, please let Lord Hubert Riley know that I'll be expecting him in the Rosebud office daily from tomorrow. Lord Nedlow has completed the training of the under–staff and is ready to train his assistant."

He only waited long enough for the stiff late–to–come bow to follow the blood that left Eadsley's face, then turned on his heel and continued his slow walk of the castle. It would be Eadsley's problem to figure out how to replace his most competent and useful undersecretary on such short notice. The Region's Ministry of Finance would be Rei's last stop. That would be delicious payment to exact.

-0-0-0-

Ilena stopped her run across the roofs of the castle buildings to breathe for a bit. She ran her hand over her head and sighed, the middle of her long black braid unconsciously ending up in her hand to just be held onto, like a knight would rest his hand on his sword hilt. Ore watched her as he walked towards her from his landing on the side of the same roof. He'd been staying back to follow her and judge her capacity now that they were back where there were roofs. He wanted to know what the final healing of her hip in Tarc had done for her.

Like she'd hid, fought, and run in the plains against the Tarc without thought or reminder of her injury since the last of the hitch in her stride had been worked out there, she'd run this morning without much thought to it. Running without thinking was a necessary thing for today, Ore thought. It had been making her twitchy to walk with the angry Rei, so time not being with the other half of the royal family in Nijou was also rather necessary.

Having her usual guards from a long time ago run with her close enough she knew they were present but not pushing her had kept her relaxed. Thayne had motioned for Ore to keep up with her and kept himself and Petroi back quite a ways, saying only it would be a familiar enough pattern.

When Ilena's shoulder twitched upon Ore's closer approach, everyone froze. When Ilena's head turned slightly towards Ore, he continued on to reach her side. He slipped an arm around her waist while staying standing next to her, having placed that Thayne and Petroi had reached their closest limit she'd tolerate.

That was still rather far: about five city houses' distance. Here in the castle that was a landing on the next building back's roof from the previous building. Henry and Marcus, the closer pair of guards, hadn't moved from that twitch, even so. She'd only asked for the presence of one so wouldn't tolerate more than that at the moment.

"Is it too much to be in the castle today?" Ore asked Ilena quietly.

She was quiet while she changed her thoughts to answer the question. "It's sufficient to be up for a while," she answered, meaning up on the roofs where the sky didn't pen them in like walls did. Her eyes were still focused into the distance, though.

Ore wouldn't mind having the excuse for time outside the castle walls, even though they'd been gone long enough he didn't feel closed in today. His eyes looked for what was in the direction Ilena was looking. "It's made you think of business?" he asked, almost smiling about it except today wasn't supposed to be a business day.

Ilena's tawny eyes swung around to look into his, a little wide. She slumped a little to lean on his shoulder. "Yeah," she admitted more as a sigh than a word.

Ore considered options, then offered, "We could go visit Garen in the name of being welcomed home."

Ilena's wide eyes turned to him again, then she smiled her small smile. "Okay. That sounds good. If I can wiggle my way to where I want to be, we'll do that, too." Ore smiled back as she gave him a quick kiss on the cheek then pulled away. He was a little surprised when she caught his hand and pulled on him to stay with her.

They ran down the long side of the roof in the direction that Henry was waiting in and jumped hand–in–hand to the next building over. It was a long jump compared to the houses in Nijoushi, and certainly more distance than in Kouzanshi. There in the northwest university city the buildings were very close together because they had to squeeze inside the city walls against the mountain. Kouzanshi's houses and buildings were taller for that reason also, like here in the castle. Nijoushi's houses didn't have to be quite so tall nor close together since they were outside the castle walls and not so close to the mountain's side.

Ore was pleased that Ilena was strong enough on the take–offs now for castle distances. That had been her weakness before they'd left the castle for the progress. She'd run the roofs a little in Kouzanshi when they'd been there, but he'd not let her do the longer cross–street jumps there. It had been enough strengthening exercise to make the climbs instead. The exercise of riding for the entire time they'd been gone had helped also.

Their feet landed simultaneously on that next roof, then they were sprinting down that roof to turn, dash, and jump to the next building over. The next jump put them on top of the roof of the medical building, but that wasn't their goal. Between the medical building and the garrison was one covered walkway. Their guards caught up to them on the medical building roof over the surgical wing so they could cross the covered walkway in more of a cohesive group.

Petroi and Thayne walked across it first. On covered walkways their footsteps would echo down into the space below so they took them softly, if swiftly since they were also more likely to be seen on top of them. As soon as they were across and guarding the passageway, Ore and Ilena took their turns, still holding hands. Marcus and Henry stood guard at the back side of the passage while waiting their turn.

Ore and Ilena were half–way across the walkway when four guards popped up from the other side of the roof peak over the garrison. One of the farther out guards made a motion and two more arrived over the peak. They were spread out along the entire roof top and moving to cut off any thought of continuing forward.

"You will allow the Princess and her Consort to continue," Petroi ordered, the steel of his blade in his voice.

"If the General approves the reason," the closest guard replied. "He's ordered for the roof passages to be guarded most strenuously."

Ilena tipped her head in curious thought. "Any reason why?" she asked innocently.

"You'll not be the first to come this way in the last several weeks," she was answered. The guards refused to say more and refused to allow them entrance to the garrison.

Ilena pulled a little on Ore's hand, leaning towards him. He gave her his ear. It was only show since she could whisper and he could hear at a quiet enough level the guards wouldn't know they were communicating. "I think we'll need to let the House know that to attempt to rescue Lieutenant Danel is to volunteer for the next big job out–country. I suspect Garen hasn't let any of those caught back out again."

Ore gave her a small nod. That would be his job, to make sure they knew. He'd send Petroi and Thayne into the city to pass that message on. They could be spared that long while he couldn't. Ore would be chained to his desk for at least a week while they tried to get caught up from being gone for more than three months. And that much business was more business than he wanted to think about.

His grip on Ilena's hand tightened at the thought, even. She gave him a sympathetic and grateful smile. She also wouldn't like being chained to hers any more than Ore would. Thus why staying away from even this hint of business would've been good. They both took simultaneous breaths for patience and to stay still. Now that they'd called Garen out it wouldn't do to disappear and waste his time.

-o-o-o-

Danel lay on the floor of his small private cell and held his arm tightly against his side and chest. His eyes shut tightly against the pain, his usually lazy expression twisted to hold the coughs in, he could only groan to himself. "Are ya gonna make it, Chief?" the member of the House on the other side of the cell bars from him asked. Danel gave a slight shake of his head. It was almost too much to talk anymore. The man reached through the bars to give him a squeeze of the arm.

Danel had been put in the farthest back cell, one of the two at the end of the hall that were solo cells. The rest were big enough for four to six prisoners, eight if squeezed in tightly. Because they were all injured, they'd been placed no more than six per. Lying down was rather essential, as was room for the medics to work.

There were a few prisoners from before they'd gotten there. Even with them added the cells weren't full, but then this wasn't the only block of cells. It was only one hallway of the third floor in the prison that had five floors and who knew how many basement levels. With no windows it barely mattered they weren't in the basement, other than the relief they'd felt deep down that they weren't in the torture chambers, if such things existed.

The chill of nightwalkers going still and silent in the face of a threat wrinkled its way down the hall until it reached Danel's cell. The hand on Danel's arm tightened as the man turned to look toward the door. Danel didn't bother moving or opening his eyes. It was outside normal times for them to be visited, and every nightwalker in the room still believed in his heart that Danel would be taken and executed. Before he died on his own would be more likely than after and they knew he wasn't doing well.

Danel. The name whispered down the hallway before the hall door was even unlocked. Every member of the House drew in a silent breath — silent because they were all still in hiding even though in plain sight in this room of only bars. Danel relaxed, his body going limp in relief to hear his mistress' voice finally.

That panicked the man who had hold of Danel, enough to make him hiss at Danel and shake his arm. Danel clicked at him to shut him up. He needed to listen through the pain, which was difficult enough.

The door opened and the sound of eight people walking into the hall came to Danel's ears. That was understood automatically underneath his listening. That number wasn't surprising since the four who'd come would need to be matched at a minimum. To tell the Princess she wasn't trusted by bringing along over an equal number would be very insulting to not only her but the Prince and King.

Ilena was taking her time, pausing outside every cell. Danel thought at first it was because she had a lot to tell him. At the third pause of the walking feet, however, Ilena interrupted her secret words to him. "General Garen, that one is a spy of another House, and those two are from other nations. You may remove them immediately." The room went a bit tense and more sets of feet entered the hallway. *They were to be removed immediately?* It didn't really help the group as a whole that those three weren't the only ones to be removed from the cells and the hallway.

The extra coming and going had calmed down by the time the footsteps reached Danel's cell. The hand on his arm was gripping him rather tightly by then. Nightwalkers didn't do well when generals of the King's army had eyes on them. The chill coming from the Queen of Night didn't help, except that it might relieve the nightwalkers of her House that were worried about Danel. "What's been done?" Ilena asked, her quiet ice in her voice. "No judgment's been made yet."

One of the soldiers set over this wing answered her. "He's been given the medication to keep his lungs from filling as required, and has been obedient in taking it." The guard swallowed slightly and added, "He's been getting weaker daily, and his coughing less and less."

"You know that's bad for lungs that are filling up?" her scowl was very much in her voice. "Allow me in to see to him, General Garen."

Keys jangled as the cell door was unlocked. These doors squeaked when opened, but not because they weren't maintained. It was because they'd been made to warn the guards at the end of the hallway if the lockpicks had decided to begin an insurrection.

The hand on Danel's arm was removed as warmth arrived close in front of him. A hand just as warm was lightly on his brow, brushing it as if to brush away the pain that creased it. "Danel," Ilena called to him quietly.

Ah. This is all I needed. A tear slipped out from under his eyelid to roll down sideways on his face towards the floor.

"Have they been giving you all your medicines?" Ilena asked him. Danel gave a slight shake of his head. "What's missing?"

Danel carefully put his body into a state it could answer without coughing. The answer came out in a bare whisper. "Pain ...kill ...er."

"*Ah,*" Ilena sighed. She shifted slightly and her voice was directed towards the hallway again. "A man with this sort of wound requires the painkiller in order to be able to keep his lungs clear. See the guards who order and dispense the medications are changed out and punished. They'll end his life before the Regent can choose his punishment."

Danel caught her sleeve and shook his head. "Rather ...die ...first, if ...it's my ...turn."

"You know that it'll cause great political troubles between my department and the garrison, to allow that inconvenience." Her scold made him smile. The sudden tension in the two guards from the garrison who'd been feeling sullen until then brought out Danel's desire to kick them again, but he let it fade quickly. He didn't have the energy for it and the Missus was doing it for him anyway, like she always did when they were lying dying in the street.

"It's ...alright." Danel pulled her hand to his mouth to kiss the back of it. "Thank ...you ...for ...coming." The final word was barely a whisper as he faded to darkness.

CHAPTER 139 Returning to Nijoushi

After dinner Ore apologized to Petroi and Thayne. "I'm sorry to make you work on our one vacation day, but given how restless the House is you need to go tonight."

Neither one was surprised and both bowed. "It is certainly better sooner than later," Petroi agreed. Upon getting Ore's nod, they turned for the glass door to the patio.

Ilena said quietly, "Not in the castle uniform. Get a feel for the undercurrent of the city as you go. I expect it will be just as unsettled, if not more."

They turned hurt looks on her. "It *was* a rather forceful declaration, Mother," Thayne complained at her. He'd worked very hard to make her Head of all of Kouzanshi. She'd likely made their job twice as hard as it needed to be here in Nijoushi.

Ilena leaned forward, resting her forearms on her knees. She was sitting next to Ore on one of the couches that bordered the long edges of the low table in the room. "The city as a whole needed to be stirred. It's become as much a cesspool here as it's been anywhere, not having been poked to proper vigilance for a very long time. We'll face them properly once they've sorted themselves out." The partners blinked at her, then bowed their heads to her and continued on out the patio door.

Petroi and Thayne leaped up to the second floor balcony and entered the common room of the Upper suite. Their room was to their left over Ore and Ilena's. When they'd changed clothing to comfortable nightwalking clothing they were headed back out again the same way they'd come in. They didn't talk to each other until they were through the Cat gate that was just outside the courtyard to the Department of Intelligence wing. Thayne gave a large sigh. Petroi glanced at him. "That wasn't really the answer you wanted," he said, rather pragmatic.

Thayne glanced away, over the rolling hills to their north. The lane here was mostly untraveled so they had it to themselves. "No, not really. She's become quite impatient compared to how she moved as a teen. We had two years to win all of Kouzanshi for her."

"Well," Petroi mused as he looked towards Nijoushi, the city rising up from behind the castle wall as the road they were on curved around to be able to see it. "I suppose she feels a bit late to some degree, but it hasn't hurt for her to move fast on occasion." He gave a bit of a teasing lift of his lips as he looked at Thayne from the corner of his eye. "The city would probably rather she move faster. They have been wondering what she was going to do with them since she was announced after all."

"But to throw down the gauntlet before we were home, even," Thayne moaned. "We're likely to be jumped just getting close to the city." He glared at the buildings they were coming up on.

"Like that is new?" Petroi raised an eyebrow lightly at him.

Thayne had to give him that. "Well," he finally sighed, "at least it's better now than it would've been before." Petroi's questioning eyebrow came again. Thayne clapped his hand on Petroi's shoulder. "I have your back so you don't have to face the city alone. If they do decide to test us, it's *us* not just you."

Petroi chuckled slightly. "That is definitely better," he agreed. "Your youth and my wisdom might keep us alive." He was silently laughing at Thayne.

Thayne returned the favor. "Indeed. If Master Ore hadn't assigned me to walk with you in your old age, you'd have to retire tonight."

Given Petroi was only in his lower thirties, he wasn't old yet, but in the world of nightwalkers he was getting there. Most didn't survive past their forties, even if they were in the top levels of their Houses. Petroi was at the top in Nijoushi, being the Queen's Messenger of the House of the Queen of Night in the city, or the equivalent of her Voice to the House. Thayne was considered in the prime of life for a nightwalker, being in his mid–twenties.

They slipped into Nijoushi in a different location than they usually entered it, knowing that at least a few spies had seen them on the road. Given they weren't uniformed it would be assumed they'd been given the night off — once their requirement to meet with the House was over. It was their first requirement to confirm the House was still loyal to the Queen of Night, as it would have been for any House whose Head had been away for a time.

They didn't go straight to the main safe house. One: nightwalkers never went straight anywhere unless it was to the morgue. Two: they wanted to hear what they could on the street. They were a little surprised to see positive responses from nightwalkers not affiliated with the House of the Queen of Night. A few nightwalkers gave them carefully neutral looks, marking them as spies who wouldn't attack them in their own territory. They chose to leave them alone.

One approached them. They let him come, staying wary. The nightwalker spy put his hands on his hips and looked them over, taking his time. "Why has the House named the Consort the 'King of all Nightwalkers'? My Head demands to know by what temerity the House has done it."

Petroi blinked and Thayne's mouth fell open in shock. Thayne was stunned enough he let Petroi take the responsibility for answering, not just because it was Petroi's to answer regardless. "I think perhaps there has been a misunderstanding?"

"Not likely," the man disagreed. "The Queen's message wasn't unexpected, but that news has been the buzz of the town."

Petroi paused, then answered, "Well, I don't have an answer for it yet, being on my way for the first time since returning from Tarc myself. I will look into it. It has gone through the whole city, you say?"

The man scowled, "And beyond by now."

Petroi gave a thoughtful nod. "It wasn't official from the Heads, I do know that much. If it was the House that has done it, I will see what it was." He moved to continue on to go do that. "The House has been waiting for him to be official for some time. Perhaps they are just happy to finally have the Heads married?" He flashed a small smile at the man as he passed him, "Who else marries a Queen but a King?"

Once they'd moved on, Thayne scolded mildly, "I'm not sure you wanted to support the rumor? Master Ore already struggles with that title."

Petroi gave a slight shrug. "It also explains why the House members would have picked it." Thayne sighed. He wasn't sure this had gone in a way Ilena had expected it to. It certainly had been a surprise to him.

-o-o-o-

The main safe house was full. The nightwalkers of the House had arrived before them, the word they were on their way spreading through the streets faster than they'd walked them. Within the room the atmosphere was more somber and tense than it had been outside of it. It couldn't be a surprise given that the House was worried about Danel. They'd also be wondering why Ilena had been so openly confrontational to the rest of the city, bringing on them greater pressure from the other Houses. The latter would be tempered by their own interest in seeing they became a stronger House if she could make it happen.

Petroi walked the narrow passage between people from the door to the raised stand at the back of the room the two Lieutenants were sitting on. He stepped up onto the dais and faced Landras and Barakka, his heart suddenly sad even while his stance was firm. They looked at him solemnly. "Have you reconfirmed the House for the Queen of Night?" he tested them verbally. The room was so quiet the question carried to all the corners of it.

Both men bowed before him. "We have, Messenger," Landras answered. It was good to know the House was still loyal to Ilena.

"But they're more loyal to the King," Barakka said.

Petroi pondered on that for a moment. "You will explain that to me." Barakka's hair over his ear was beginning to grow back in, but was still the reminder that Ore required the obedience of all of the House to the Queen of Night's orders.

Barakka rose from the bow to look into Petroi's eyes. "Those who've come from Tokumade have always recognized Mister Ore as their proper master." Petroi understood that. Ore was the heir of that House, even if the land was now under the lordship of a newly assigned Earl. "He won for himself many hearts when he was a freelancer, apart and separate from what Missus Ilena has done. Those of the House who knew him then are happy to have him over them. He's won for himself in his visits here those who didn't know him."

Barakka blinked at Petroi, then added, "However, it was the happy noise of the House in celebration that put the title into the ears of the spies that were allowed to go with us into Tarc. They're the ones who've put the claim in the ears of the other Houses and the nightwalkers on the street. We need instruction. How many shall we allow into the House now that he's been named King? We're being asked daily by many to allow them in so they can follow him."

Petroi slumped internally. Thayne's warning had been right. It was going to be more than Ore would accept. It sounded like they might not be able to turn aside the movement. Such things entered into the minds of so many individuals at once were nearly impossible to change or root out once they chose as a group to move on them.

"Allow none for now," he answered. "We will take the word to the Heads and see what they will do." He pursed his lips slightly then added, "And you two do not need the added burden at this time."

Barakka put one hand down on the surface of the platform as his back tensed. His lips pursed and his eyes narrowed. "And will you also leave us?" he asked softly. The attack came as Petroi had been waiting for. He didn't let Barakka win that battle any more than any of the many before, but by the time he was kneeling on Barakka, his hand to Barakka's throat holding him still, tears were slipping down his cheeks.

Barakka's eyes were quite wide to see that. "What is it?" Landras asked in concern from his position that he'd not left during the battle.

Thayne stepped up onto the platform and faced the silent nightwalkers, allowing Petroi to continue to keep holding Barakka down. Solemnly he said, "Before our eyes — we who are the two Messengers of the House of the Queen of Night — we watched Lieutenant Danel die to his wound received in Tarc. He managed to live until he could hear Missus Ilena call his name one last time." The silence in the room buzzed as the many people took in long breaths at the news.

Thayne turned to look Barakka in the eye, the man seeking for the second confirmation. "The House is ordered to not attempt any retribution against the garrison. He'd been given and was taking the medication prescribed by Princess Mizi herself. We all understand a lung wound is difficult at best. When delivered by a Tarc, it would be surprising for anyone to survive it."

Petroi swallowed to find his voice again. "It isn't because we won't come when directed, or needed. It is because you are short a partner who is necessary and needed to the running of the House." Barakka relented in sorrow. Petroi let him return to his place on the dais.

"Seek for a replacement when you can see through the grief. With Missus Ilena moving in Nijoushi this winter, it will be even more important for that seat to not stay cold." It would be particularly true because Danel had been in charge of training new members. "It is very regrettable that he should fall at this time." Barakka and Landras both gave nods of accepting obedience.

It wouldn't be easy. Ilena had trained all of the Lieutenants of both cities at Tokumade and they'd been loyal to her since they were all much younger. Petroi had already been trying to pick one person out of the many in the city and had been having troubles with it. He'd welcome their input when they were ready to give it. In particular it would need to be someone who was devoutly loyal to the House as a group and an institution. There were a few among the young who might fit that requirement, but they were still perhaps too young to fill the seat of a Lieutenant.

-o-o-o-

Petroi sat in his place on the dais where he could speak with the Lieutenants. Thayne joined him, sitting just a little behind him in the guest or guard position. "Tell me what the message sent to the other Heads by Missus Ilena has done to the underworld," Petroi requested.

While normally the Lieutenants would answer most questions, this was one of the rarer times where they turned to the room as a whole. One of the older and well known information brokers of the House rose to stand forward. "The city's agitated, with most of the spies who went into Tarc dead by the hands of their own Heads, for all the Heads ordered it to begin with."

Noses were wrinkled the room over in distaste for such behavior by those Heads. The average nightwalker of the city as a whole would be discontent with those Houses with just that much. It would be another reason for so many asking to join with the House. The House of the Queen of Night was known to be reasonable, if strict. Obedience wasn't rewarded with death, regardless of if the news was disliked or greatly appreciated.

"Several Houses have already fallen, or been weakened enough to be overtaken by those around them." That was surprising to have it happen so fast, but those would likely have been the Houses the nightwalkers already had no true loyalty to.

"Messengers have been sent between many smaller Houses to see if alliances to join into medium Houses can be won. Most of those negotiations seem to have failed as more recently those same smaller Houses have been sending to the medium Houses that already exist. So far the larger Houses are holding back, waiting for the Queen to arrive back again to see what actions she'll choose to follow up her words with." The informant sat down after getting nods of gratitude from the leadership up on the dais.

Another nightwalker stood. "Many on the street who want to join with the House are asking to join because they've heard that Mister Ore has been named King. They won't necessarily be fully loyal to the House of the Queen of Night. There are others who come from those Houses that've already fallen, angry at the deaths of the spies. They'll be loyal until that anger fades. Then who knows?" he shrugged. "Perhaps most of them'll settle and be good additions because they understand what it was to be where the Head didn't understand the heart of the Suiran nightwalker."

Nightwalkers the whole room over nodded, agreeing with that understanding. It was in large part why they stayed loyal to the House to begin with. Having an honorable Head did that: held them. They would've left long ago if Ilena wasn't since she didn't force her people to stay as many of those would have. It was actually one of the main reasons the House *could* be spread over the whole of Suiran and even into other nations.

The man rubbed his chin and continued a little slower. "Some who ask to come in seem to be spies from the other Houses, but that can be hard to be sure on. It feels like they're feeling out what the Queen and King will do and allow. Almost more as if their Heads want to know if we'll take their members in if they capitulate instead of fight." He scratched his head and looked around the room. "Has anyone been approached with actual requests for that yet?"

The people in the room shook their heads. "It is perhaps too early, then," Petroi mused. "They also are likely waiting to hear now that we have returned. Asking that much lets us know that there are those who would be approachable in that way." The informant gave a nod of agreement. Petroi considered it, then said, "As I said, there isn't an answer to it yet, but I will take the question back. Don't discourage them yet, as I am sure Missus Ilena would rather the peaceful options wherever possible." Thayne nodded his agreement to that statement. The informant gave a sharp nod and sat down.

One of the older teens rose to his feet. He blinked at the men up on the dais, but stood facing them with a straight back and sure shoulders. A fist clenched and his shoulder twitched. A bit of a scowl came on his face. "The pressure the other direction has gotten rough outside the House boundaries." The teen listed off those territories where the members of the House of the Queen of Night were chased out or beaten. Petroi carefully memorized that list. Those were the territories likely to fight them, or at least the changes that would come to the underworld of the city.

When he sat down, another nightwalker rose and gave the report of those alliances that had already been formalized. Then he listed those alliances that were likely to fall in the near future if Ilena didn't move fast enough to make those alliances solidify against her. Many Houses had such different ideologies and purposes that any alliance beyond very temporary fell apart, or one by subterfuge would oust the Head of the other, taking all of the nightwalkers that would stay as their own.

When no one else stood up to speak, eyes turned to Thayne. They all knew he'd been in Kouzanshi for the consolidation there. He straightened his spine and shoulders and faced the room. "Continue to watch, but don't act or say anything yet. This early posturing and self–cleaning is helpful. It isn't worth bringing in the Heads until there are Heads worth talking to.

"Continue to report on those Houses that have been attacking us." His eyes were on the teen who'd reported. "It's okay for us to begin with those Houses to remind them we won't be bullied into submission by the insects of the city. We found in Kouzanshi that was rarely necessary. Those became the first pickings of those looking to more firmly solidify their own positions and strength. Because they knew we were getting angry, they moved before we could take more territory early."

"Don't we want the territory before they steal it out from under us?" one asked, a bit confused.

Thane's lips smiled just enough to show his canines. "Oh, it won't be theirs for very long, most likely. It just removes the insects so we can focus on those with teeth." He shrugged, "It might be that those who move do so because they believe we'll be more lenient out of 'gratitude' that they stepped in and 'protected' us." His predatory look didn't change. "That never works with Missus Ilena. ...But you already know that." There were mirthless chuckles throughout the room. "Still, for now, be neutral to them until they're too prideful. Then let the Lieutenants know that they need to be taught a lesson."

Thayne paused, then somewhat apologetically added, "If the Messenger of Nijoushi will forgive me for saying it out of place, this is also the time for you to begin to hunt for other Houses to be in if this one hasn't been what you really wanted." Petroi blinked at Thayne, but decided to let him finish what he had to say, for all that had been rather forward and perhaps somewhat damaging.

Thayne bowed his head slightly, looking into painful memories as he looked at the space in front of him. "You know the Queen kills traitors, for all she isn't generally heavy–handed." The room went rather still. "Before she's told any of us what's in her mind is the time to move to any other House you'd rather support. She'll allow you to go, as she would anyway, but once she gives out her orders: to leave the House will mark you as a traitor." He soberly blinked at the room. "Don't die."

"But..., if all of the Houses become hers?" one asked a bit brusquely.

Thayne shook his head. "Many Houses in Kouzanshi were only required to swear fealty to her, being obedient to her as they were obedient to their own Heads. She's Princess there as she is to Ryokudo, and they're vassal as the lords are to the Regent. She'll do the same here, but to what degree we don't know yet." That settled the House, to understand that piece they hadn't before. It would help to not have the House diluted by those who wouldn't care for the same things they did.

-o-o-o-

Released from guarding requirements after dinner, Henry took Marcus out of the Department of Intelligence wing and over the top of it to head towards the northeast corner of the Nijou castle complex. He'd been reminded of a job he'd been ordered to see to. There was a task that needed doing this night or he'd regret not doing it.

"Can't stay inside even for all today's walking?" Marcus half–teased him. Likely that was because Henry wasn't treating it like the stroll he could've been. He slowed down and shoved his hands into his pants pockets, his shoulders rather automatically rising up towards his ears.

Henry rolled his eyes at Marcus, who linked his hands behind his head and was looking out of the side of his eyes at Henry. "I'm only bringing you because I'll get into trouble to walk without you."

"You know it!" Marcus threatened Henry. He'd be in trouble with Marcus before he'd be in trouble with Ilena. It wasn't that they didn't on occasion do things apart, it was that they'd gotten too used to watching each other's backs from the time they were young children. Things usually got difficult, crazy, or very dangerous if they didn't have eyes on each other. Having to be apart so much in Tarc had been rather hard for that reason. Getting to be together at the Northeast garrison for a week had helped, but they weren't quite settled to being alone just yet, particularly for walks across the castle grounds.

Well, this was across the roofs since Henry had taken them up. It was the fastest way to the medical building. They went from the roof of the Intelligence wing, two more residential buildings' roofs east, then to the wide defensible wall where they greeted all the guards who patrolled it. Then they went back down to the roofs of the various smaller buildings and sheds around the medical building, then back up on top of the medical building, over it and down to the ground in the inner courtyard.

Marcus raised his eyebrow at Henry. "Why back here?" They'd spent a good portion of the afternoon there already, watching over Ilena. The other royals had been there with Mizi as she'd worked on catching up with her current experiment. Ilena in particular had caught up with Ryan, finally admitting to him she was the one who'd spent time with him at his family's home when he was very young. She'd also warned him to hire more assistants to help him soon because of the upcoming audit.

"Need to talk to Mister Ryan," Henry said shortly, and slightly bitterly. Both of Marcus' eyebrows rose, but he kept his mouth closed. That made him an even better person to have at Henry's back. He'd stay the quiet background support, which Henry needed to do this task.

They wandered into the infirmary, tipping their heads at the guards on the door and letting themselves in. When they were first hired into the castle as paiges they'd made sure to be seen by all of the guards so they'd be recognized as messengers generally. "Are we the Nijou Messengers now?" Marcus had asked, tongue–in–cheek, when they'd finally managed to get all of the guards to relax by the beginning of the third week of work. They'd always been Ilena's runners and messengers — usually to the Family or directly to the Messengers of Kouzanshi and Nijoushi — but being officially in the castle and working with her directly now it seemed even more so.

Henry paused to answer the curious head that looked at them. This was the main entrance, and thus the main place people looking for healing walked in. "We're just here to see Mister Ryan briefly. Won't trouble you." He got a nod back and that person went back to their studies. The interns usually got the night shifts, so usually had their heads in books when they weren't helping late night sudden difficulties of castle staff. Henry didn't envy them.

They took themselves through the side door into the depths of the wing where the offices of the staff were. Ryan's was fairly close to the patient receiving area so if there was a medical emergency he could come quickly to their call. He was still on the floor writing on what looked like at least a tenth–for–the–day sheet of paper. Ryan was just as odd as Ilena most days. He lay on the floor in the office to write his notes and wrote in his created language they'd learned a long time ago for Ilena's sake. They paused to watch him, having learned from watching Ore, Mizi, and Ilena approach him.

Ryan reached the end of a line, set his pen in the inkwell, sighed a bit and shifted to read the paper to review what he'd written. Henry still wasn't quite sure what to say so waited for Ryan to set the paper with the others near him. As he sat up to shuffle the papers into an order, Henry quietly said, "Hey, Mister Ryan. It's after dinner–time. I hope you weren't going to forget again tonight."

Ryan's head swung around to look at them. He blinked owlishly at them, his short black hair standing up in the front from being pressed back out of his face by his off hand so he could see his work. He was four years their junior but they'd been following Ilena around so knew to be respectful of his skills and office regardless of age (and short size). "No, actually," he said in his soft shy voice. "Having all of you visit earlier has made me remember. I was just going to do that."

"That's good," Henry encouraged him kindly. "We're on break for a bit. Can we keep you company? We've already eaten, but it's never hard for a prior nightwalker to put down just a little more just in case." He winked. "That's a hard habit for us to break. We'll be stout, then fat before we know it."

"That wouldn't be all bad," Marcus mused to keep the flow going as Ryan moved to put his papers on his table in the room. "I might like to end up a fat, lazy lower lord with all the comforts of home. That's good payment, actually."

Ryan's lips turned up as he turned to head for the door and the food cart that would have been delivered at the normal dinner time. "While that might be good, I think Ilena won't let you get lazy for a long time. As long as you're chasing her, being fat would be a great detriment, I think?" Henry and Marcus both laughed and followed him into the next room over where the cart was waiting for Ryan.

"Well, you'd be right about that," Marcus slumped and moaned as Ryan picked up a plate to fill. "I can just see me huffing and puffing, trying to catch up to her and having to lose her in the crowd." He bent over and put his hands on his knees, "huffing and puffing" as if he were doing it now and trying to recover. He looked up pleadingly and raised a hand of entreaty to the invisible pretend Ilena. "Mistress! If you don't wait for me, I won't get to watch you beat them up for me when you get attacked!" They all laughed at that.

Ryan went thoughtful. When he was done filling his plate he went to the table. Henry wasn't hungry so didn't bother to pick anything up, but Marcus grabbed up a small sweet roll to munch on slowly for something to do mostly. They joined him at the table. Ryan's dark eyes came to them and he finally asked his question they'd been letting him formulate and work up the courage to ask. "I know that royalty need to have guards, but why do you follow Ilena? She can protect herself quite well. Ore, too. Is it just for show to the castle?"

They both shook their heads. "There's actually lots of reasons," Henry said gently. "We don't usually openly tell people about most of them, since it's better to let people believe whatever they want to believe. The main one is that they both need the company. They were really lonely a lot of the time until they found each other again."

Marcus nodded soberly, swallowing his bite of roll. "The other main reason is because they want to know someone they trust is watching the back of the other. They're afraid to lose each other now that they're together again. We watch over Mistress Ilena for Master Ore's sake. Sir Petroi and Thayne watch over Master Ore for Mistress Ilena's sake. Then they don't have to worry."

Ryan gave an understanding nod and looked down at his plate. Softly he said as he picked another bite to eat, "I can understand not wanting to be lonely." He didn't look back up while he chewed that bite and the next.

Henry sighed to himself and firmed up. He couldn't help Ryan with that. He'd been given orders to the contrary, as much as he didn't want to have to step in. He took the conversation the direction he preferred it to go. "It must be lonely to not have Master Ore and Mistress Mizi in the wing so much anymore."

Ryan glanced up at him, then gave a small nod. "I'm hoping now that the progress and Tarc things are done, she can come work more on her experiment. She's also agreed to help me find and test some new interns. We need a few more, plus to bring on one or two more who already have the experience. I'd like her help with that for this first time I do it as Department Head."

"You really value her opinions and thoughtfulness, don't you?" Marcus rested his chin on his hand, his elbow already on the table from the eating he was done with now. Food didn't go down all that slow no matter how much they tried because food eaten slow had always been food that could be stolen. "She's very good at such things."

Ryan gave a nod as the fork was just coming out of his mouth. They let him get the food eaten and swallowed. He didn't add anything, just kept eating. They understood. Once food was going in, it was hard to pause until the stomach wasn't quite so pinched. It looked like he was working up to the next question anyway.

Some people who were like this they could joke and play around to fill the spaces so the person wasn't uncomfortable with such a large thing as silence. Ryan, however, needed to not only have the quiet to get the questions formulated, he needed to have space already waiting for him to fill. He was very bad at interrupting to say what he needed to say. They'd learned early that Mizi always let Ryan have the space to say what he needed to say, and Ryan was always grateful for it, rather than embarrassed. Ore only ever added the bantering *after* Ryan had embarrassed himself in some way, to give him the time to recover.

"Why've you come?" Ryan asked. It wasn't particularly abrupt, but it was for him. It could have been because he was embarrassed to ask the question, but Henry thought there was something behind it, actually.

He didn't answer that question just yet. Instead he leaned on his fist now. "You know, Mister Ryan? We watched you a lot. We got to be some of your guards while you and Mistress Mizi were at Kouzanshi. Mistress Ilena wanted to make sure you both stayed safe from the nightwalkers there, and that you were both happy.

"Some days she could come visit there and she'd watch the two of you herself." He gave a soft smile to Ryan's very surprised stare, the food paused and forgotten for a moment. "There were some days you were both stuck on a problem and we had to take her out so she wouldn't break her hiding to help you. That was very hard for her. Probably half of the books you found to get you out of sticky problems were put where you could by us, since she couldn't read them but could tell us what to look for."

"She can't read?" Ryan's brow furrowed up in worried confusion.

"Only your language," Marcus explained quickly. "Letters don't hold still. She has to work very hard. She loves your language because it holds still for her."

Ryan blinked, then cautiously took the bite waiting for him, his eyes staying on them. "We learned it for her, too, and we learned to read so we could read the words out of books to her. That was faster than her trying on her own," Henry added.

They let him have space again. A few bites later he asked, "She knew from that long ago. She's been watching from then."

"Probably before then, but yes, she was able to see you with her own eyes then, for the first time in a long time. She's missed you a lot," Henry said with great sincerity. "I'm sure she's looking forward to the time she can relax in here with you and Mistress Mizi again, helping where she couldn't before."

Ryan studied Henry's face, then sat up straight and rested his eating hand on the table. Henry waited, then gave a nod confirming what Ryan wasn't saying. "She can't just yet, even still. They're going to set her and Master Ore over Tarc. She still has a report to finish writing and send to the Regent and King. Then she'll have to be preparing for the investiture. Master Ore has required a one week vacation before then, to mourn the death of his freedom." Ryan's face fell in a bit of sorrow for his friend, understanding that Ore would find it difficult to be a high lord, for all he'd be a good one.

Henry sighed out loud. "I'm afraid it's even worse than that, though, because afterwards we all have to figure out how to be a Ministry instead of a Department, plus handle the census and financial stuff." He gave a significant look at that last one, knowing Ilena had told him about it. Ryan thought through that list, then slumped. Henry gave him the positive last. "We'll let you know as soon as they aren't under such pressure and stress that visits again would be welcome, but it really would be wise to give them at least until after the investiture, and then maybe a week of figuring out how to be high lord and lady and Minister and Assistant Minister."

"That's not likely long enough," Ryan said dryly. Since he'd been given his post as Head Healer of the Nijou Department of Medicine only a year ago, while only seventeen, he had the experience to know how hard it was to step into higher places than one felt ready for. He sighed a little sadly, and took one of his last bites. "I'll wait to hear, then." His look back up at them was rather pleading.

"I promise," Henry said. "We won't forget. Captains don't forget anything. We'll remember to come and let you know when they need your soft friendship again. They won't be able to be soft for you until then. We all want to protect you and see you happy."

Ryan shifted a little uncomfortably. "Could Rio come here for lunches, to pick back up my training?"

Henry paused, considering Ryan. "Have you been practicing while we were gone?" he asked, to test that much. Ryan gave a perfunctory nod. "Well, if she gets to be less stressed out than Mistress Ilena and Mrs. Leah, we'll send her over. Or if she needs to not scream at Master Ore." He smiled a small smile. Ryan grimaced slightly but accepted that answer.

-o-o-o-

Henry made their excuses to Ryan when he was done passing along his message and he and Marcus were back outside. This time Henry took them at a slower stroll on the ground. He needed time out of the wing to relax again after that, relieved it had gone well enough. He tucked his thumbs into his pants pockets and sighed with a little slump. Marcus patted his shoulder, then sighed also. "It was good to remember that warning," he said softly. "Even if you didn't like why you had to do it."

Henry glared at Marcus from the side of his eyes. He still hadn't said it, so it shouldn't be thought of or mentioned out loud. He wasn't ready to have to step into Rio's life, nor did he want to change her happiness as it was. She had her own growing up to do and her own strengths to learn still. For her to spend time alone with the gentle Ryan was something new for her. That wasn't a strength to prevent her from learning. It was Ryan that Henry had to step in front of. By his order he wasn't allowed to let Ryan think he could have Rio as a wife. It was going to be a difficult thing for a while.

They walked in silence for a while then heard voices coming their way from a side direction. They slowed down just a little, having recognized one of them. They listened, trying to make out the words. They watched as Mitchel Barkley walked into view talking to another man likely in his upper twenties to lower thirties. They had similar brown hair and walked similarly.

Henry and Marcus followed them a little bit, not going too far out of their way and not wanting to be caught by them. Mostly it was curiosity. Mitchel was being far softer with that man than he usually was with most people. It was in the softer expression on his face, the more thoughtful voice, and in Mitchel's shoulders and back. He was the most relaxed they'd ever seen him, actually. With a glance at each other, Henry was calling in the department's coded whisper, *Who is it that walks with Minister Barkley tonight?*

It took a bit for the answer to come, and it came from towards the gate as if the Minister had gone to pick the man up and bring him into the castle. *Carl Stern. He visits occasionally, sometimes coming a few days in a row, but his home is in the city.* Henry and Marcus looked at each other, then turned for the wing the castle paiges were in to get some in–castle gossip on the man.

As they left that research detour behind them to return to their own quarters, Marcus said, "I think we might have found our other assistant."

"Perhaps," Henry answered. He sent out an information request to the Family in Nijoushi asking for any information on Carl Stern. If he really was an outside spy who came in to make reports, and might even be in a minor to middle staff position, that would be rather perfect. Even more so that the Minister, whom Ilena was going to get herself, liked him enough to relax with him around. That might be important in the office, too.

When they reached their wing they were on the roof again, that being the easiest way to access their room. Henry paused, snatching at Marcus' jacket to get him to pause. Marcus settled down to wait. Henry took in a breath, knowing Rio would hear, and Ilena as well. *Henry to Delia.* Marcus blinked but waited with Henry to receive the word back she was paying attention and could receive the message. It really was very convenient to be able to talk in the secret whispered–sung language of Ilena's information network. They didn't have to go the even longer distance to the complete opposite corner of the castle to talk to Delia.

It took a bit longer than if she'd been outside. Likely she'd been in her room, or finishing up helping Mizi and Rei get ready for bed. Her room had no window so often a castle Child had to go into the Old Regent's building to fetch her out. Her ears weren't quite so good as to hear through solid walls like Ilena could. She heard better when in the Regent's suite of rooms because there were windows there.

Delia to Henry. Continue.

Henry to Delia. Mother has promised Ryan that he can be trained to Agent. Rio had been training him during the lunch hour until we left. He's been practicing faithfully while we've been gone, but our office will be too busy for the next while to be able to pick it back up. Will you please take on the responsibility until we get ourselves figured out again, or until he passes to Agent, whichever comes first? Her lunch–time duties were usually quite light, so it shouldn't be a burden for her. It would also keep Ryan's lessons "in the family" since the Regent's household counted in that umbrella for Ilena.

Henry's head turned and Marcus' eyes as well as they heard a window being opened below them. Rio was on the roof with them before they received Delia's response, but Henry ignored her for now. That much was understood. A long–distance conversation was still a conversation to not interrupt nor intrude on. *Can do. Starting when?*

At your earliest convenience, please. Thank you. Henry sent the end–of–sending code and waited. They didn't hear a response, so he turned to face Rio. Her scowl was on, and a fist was clenched along with her teeth. No words would come out in that state. He sighed at her lightly. "You can still go to him when the office becomes too much. There isn't anything to prevent you when you need to escape Mistress Ilena or scream, or to not strangle Master Ore." He gave her a gentle smile.

It wasn't quite enough. Her scowl stayed but her eyes dropped from his. As softly as he could speak, Henry whispered, "I'm protecting him, Rio." At that her eyes widened, then her head dropped. Henry very lightly put his hand on top of her head until her fist and jaw could unclench. Then with a breath Rio was gone, down to her room again. They heard the latch catch as they turned to head for their own window and room. She only ever unlatched windows for them.

Petroi and Thayne's window was the one directly across from Rio's. Theirs was the farther down top floor bedroom on that side. They made the usual automatic check that no one was watching them, then they were down the side of the wall and opening their own window to enter their room. Their window was never latched. It had always been their escape route from buildings and rooms: unlatched windows.

Henry couldn't keep the scowl off his face any longer. "Is it so hard?" Marcus asked quietly. They'd both immediately gone to getting undressed. They might get more hours of sleep in the castle than in the cities, but as many as they could get were required to keep up with their days and not get overly grumpy.

Henry didn't answer until his jacket was hung over his chair next to his bed and he was unlacing his boots, his sword and belt now on the bed next to him rather than around his waist. He did like being able to sleep with it next to him. It helped him sleep a little more deeply during the hours he'd normally lie awake to be the one on watch over the two of them. "It's not like I've ever considered it before," he grouched quietly. "What nightwalker thinks of the luxury of having a wife unless he's survived into his thirties and managed to save up enough treasure to retire to that kind of life?"

Marcus sat up from taking off his second boot and blinked in surprise at Henry. Henry scowled again, slipping his boot off to hold it. "I understand *you*. That's always been a goal of yours, to live the daywalker life." He held the scowl and boot for a bit longer then set the boot by his chair.

Marcus had to admit that much was true. He considered Henry's mood while pulling off his pants. As he lay them out on his chair, he said, "Master Ore always had that goal in mind, though."

Henry shook his head and rose to take off his own pants. "Freelancer's different. They've got goals they're reaching for. Nightwalker's goal is to survive to tomorrow, knowing that tonight might be their last today."

He lay his pants neatly out on his chair. They were so used to wearing only one set of clothing until it was so worn out with holes that they only changed out the uniforms once a week. The extras were in the wardrobe. Leaving the ones they were currently wearing set out on the chair made it that much faster they were dressed in the mornings. Or in the middle of the night if they were called up in an emergency.

Marcus had had to work very hard to train Henry that all of this was okay. In the past they'd slept in their clothing, only loosening the boot ties and buckles on their jackets. Otherwise they'd lose them if they had to run, or were attacked to have them all stolen from them.

Marcus thumped down into the middle of his bed, his nightshirt on. Henry pulled his on over his head, then sighed as he sat down on the edge of his bed. "There's plenty of time," he whispered, almost more to himself. "She's got a lot of strength to earn for herself first. Here's a good place to do that."

"And maybe you'll have grown into it by then," Marcus teased with a wrinkled nose. "Although, I suspect I'll have to drag you kicking and screaming into that just as much as any daywalker thing you've had to learn to do."

Henry glanced at his clothing on the chair next to them. "Well..., maybe. Old habits that kept one alive are hard to change. It's rather frightening, you know, most of the things I've had to give up here." He looked towards the wall the door was in, seeing the one desk they shared. It was used more as a surface to put things on like combs and the polishing set.

"That won't be the same. That's taking on a responsibility that's rather large." He gave a dry teasing look from the corner of his eye at Marcus. "More like how hard it was to want to have you but to work up the courage to actually act on it. I knew how hard I'd have to work to train you up so we both stayed alive."

Marcus laughed at him. "She already knows how to survive and live. Mistress Ilena's paying you plenty enough to support the both of you, and that's a life–long job you won't have to worry about anymore." Henry glared at him, already knowing that much. Marcus' look went to a kind one. "All it means is more warmth, Henry, having someone to love and love you back."

"And if I die?" he snapped back.

Marcus shook his head. "We all do eventually. It's the days we had to share that make it worth it, regardless." His face was as soft as his voice was warm. "I'm grateful we've already shared as many as we have. I wasn't sure we'd be able to at the beginning, I was so scared. Thank you for keeping me alive and by your side until now, Henry." He paused, then added, "When you're ready for that step, you'll see. That reward will be just as good."

In the bedroom across the suite from them Thayne silently held his weeping partner. He understood. He treasured his warm memories of his mother the same way. He was sure Petroi also treasured the warm days his wife had been alive. He hoped Marcus' words to Henry could help Petroi heal just a little more from that time of losing her.

-o-o-o-

Petroi and Thayne reported to Ilena and Ore the following morning after breakfast. Petroi started with the issue most concerning Ilena. "The House will obey and grieve Danel without retribution." He read the small signs from her that said she was relieved to be able to set that burden down.

He followed that with the report of what the city had done since receiving her message to the Heads of the Houses of it. She was content with the level of chaos that it was at currently. She was also satisfied with the report of what Thayne had advised the House to do. It was relieving that she verified Thayne's assumptions of what she expected.

"Keep me informed when you begin to hear of Heads that rise above. I'll want to keep track of their progress. Some may reach out early to negotiate. Gather as much information about their Houses and reasoning for why before bringing me their requests as I'd like to be able to know enough to make quick decisions. Some will need to be respected that highly." Petroi accepted the order humbly.

She shook her head at her two Messengers. "While in Kouzanshi I did need to rule, here I won't. Here it will be a council. The city needs to rule itself as much as possible, but to also understand it's also my home now. That's what I'll be looking for: who rises to the top that can be relied on to see that Nijoushi remains a place Suiran can be proud of. Be my eyes and ears to learn it so we make wise decisions." Both Thayne and Petroi bowed to her.

Petroi then turned to Ore. "There has been an unexpected occurrence, brought about by the desires of the nightwalkers both in and out of the House. You likely won't be pleased."

Ore's expression went both surprised and trepidatious as his shoulders hunched. Petroi tried to drop the news on him gently. "You are a popular man among the common folk. The spies brought back the House's desire to call you King and all of the city has become embroiled because of it." Ore's face was turning to horror and Ilena's was going a little pale. "The numbers of nightwalkers wishing to join with your House is a daily request. The Lieutenants wish to know if they should allow them to enter the House or refuse them. A number of the Heads are threatened by the news and displeased, wishing to know if you will actually claim the title of King of Nightwalkers yourself."

Ore's head was already shaking itself in firm denial. Ilena swallowed slightly and she turned to look at Ore, taking in his dismay. "Ore," she said almost timidly for her, "while I did know it and try to warn you, I didn't expect them all to move in such a way. I'm sorry to not have protected you properly in the matter."

He blinked at her. "Well, I suppose, but you'll still have to help me fix it. I really don't want to have every Head in Suiran challenge me. And if that title gets south of Suiran, I may have to defend myself even down to the coast. They're already upset enough with me there."

Ilena put her hand over her eyes for a moment, then took a deep breath. "You don't need to have any of them in the House for them to proudly claim you as theirs. They already do anyway. They just need to be kindly discouraged from joining the House, being reminded that you began as and always were a freelancer. It's part of your charm and legend. If that's emphasized, they won't be upset with the refusal of the House to accept them as formal members and you won't have to have any of the duties or responsibilities."

"Yes, let's do that," Ore answered, almost automatically. He paused, then said, "But that's only for the nightwalkers. What about the Heads?"

"Well, they'll settle the same, once their own nightwalkers decide to return to them or stay regardless. It's the ones who are too insecure in their positions that won't relent. Most of those will be removed by the actions happening in the city now, without our involvement. I think once that's resolved, we'll have resolved that issue for at least Nijoushi. Word should go from here to the rest of Suiran and then Ryokudo." She slumped. "However, there will likely be the testing and posturing at least once everywhere we go."

Ore put his hand over his eyes now in resignation. "I really didn't want it," he complained quietly.

"I know," Ilena answered. "I'm sorry."

He looked back at her again. "And will King Brother want to kill me now, too? Or imprison me?"

Ilena slumped a little more. "I suppose Sasou might be a little miffed. I think he'll laugh, too, though." She looked off into the distance, then said, "I'll ask him. If he hates it we'll work harder to quiet it down."

-o-o-o-

Flynn, Head of the House of the Gold Lion, shook his head, his wild mane of dark auburn hair brushing his shoulders as he did so. "We won't go take the territory?" his Lieutenant asked in surprise.

Flynn looked at him out of the corner of his eye, but didn't answer for a while. He made the kneeling messenger in front of him wait while he thought it through one more time. *"The House of the Rose Flame has removed from it its Head."*

He wasn't surprised. That one had always been a little too strict, a little too worried about her position to relax enough to just let the nightwalkers be. Still, she'd had a very strong following and the loyalty of her "ladies of the night" because she'd been willing to help them as fellow businesswomen, giving them a respectable House to work from. That had never been his business, since he didn't need to encroach on the Rose Flame as his neighbor and thus have House battles constantly. Power struggles of those sorts weren't in anyone's best interest.

The power struggle that was coming whether they would or no — apparently — was another matter. He'd been trying to decide just where he was going to settle. The difficulty in this case was that he was rather sure that the Queen of Night wouldn't take in the ladies, even if she'd respect their individuality. He'd been pondering it nearly constantly since the message had come from her. Flynn sighed. It was time to move whether he would or no, now that the individual nightwalkers had started to move on their own.

"Send a messenger to the House of the Queen of Night." The messenger in front of him tensed, but Flynn had been talking to his Lieutenant. "We both border that territory. I'll not offend her early by just walking in and taking over. If the Rose is dead by her nightwalker's hands, there's already loyalty to Ore in that House. To offend those won't do either, or there'll be battle in those streets regardless — to our detriment." The messenger in front of him relaxed a little.

This messenger was one of those ladies, her clothing made to tempt, particularly when in such a formal kneeling and bowed position, but Flynn wasn't going to be won over by that. They also likely already knew where the Queen of Night stood, and had chosen him instead. He supposed he ought to be flattered that his reputation for being a calm Head of some level of wisdom, relaxed in his place, had made them decide it.

"As for you," he said to the messenger, his sharp look coming to rest on her, "if you ladies truly wish to join to my House, knowing what's coming in this city, you must prove yourselves." The messenger blinked at him, but wasn't surprised. He pursed his lips, then gave her the orders he'd already considered.

It would change the focus of his House, but all of the prostitute Houses in Nijoushi were small and scattered. There actually wasn't a big market for it in this town. Ichijoutsu had only one prostitute House from long ago (although lots of houses in it) for being a coastal city with many sailors and international travelers in it. Kouzanshi was smaller, but also had only one consolidated House to meet the needs of the soldiers at the barracks, minor lords, the few internationals that visited the university there, and insular scholars who hadn't the time for spouses but still were men and women.

If the ladies of the Rose Flame did his work for him, to recruit the rest to the House of the Gold Lion, that would clean up the minor Houses. It was already his thought that they were likely to fall early, leaving the prostitutes of the city to become fodder for whomever picked them up, killing them in the main over the next few months, and potentially letting someone whom the Queen of Night *should* kill off pick the rest up.

Really it was personal survival to make the move. He figured if he cleaned up that part, stayed a reasonable and (mostly) relaxed sort of Head, and showed he was willing to negotiate with the House of the Queen of Night, he might just end up at the top of the city. That would be fine by him. More gold was more gold. He ended his orders to the messenger with, "If the ladies agree, have the ma'am you all trust the most come speak with me here. She'll keep her job and train me to it."

The messenger gave a small smile. He'd won her over with that. Now to see if it would win the rest. He sighed to himself as she rose to her feet, tipped her head in a bow to him, and left the house. At least the ladies already had a house to work from. The nightwalkers who wanted to follow Ore might not have it so easy in that part of living.

-o-o-o-

Landras blinked at the messenger from the House of the Rose Flame in front of him. He wanted to say, *what'd you go and do a stupid thing like that for?*, but knew it wasn't what Ilena would want him to say. It wasn't helping them that Danel was the one missing. He was the one who knew best how to keep the House together, and how to have new people come in — particularly when it was a group of them all at once.

Barraka — being the opposite of Landras — was nodding knowingly, as if it was a given that the nightwalkers would rather have Ore as their Head than the Rose Flame. He'd already let them just come on in. Landras scowled, trying to hold him back even just a little. "And we're supposed to fit just *how* many new nightwalkers into the building all at once in the next month?" he complained at Barraka. That made him pause better.

Landras glared at the nightwalker in front of them. He was trying to be humble, but was obviously not one of those that could really do it. Most from that House couldn't, having to push back against the Rose Flame on a regular basis to be allowed to just breathe. "And do the ladies agree?" he asked, also needing to know that part.

The messenger hesitated, then shook his head. "They've disagreed." His tone went a little apologetic. "The reputation of the Queen of Night in that regard is already well known. ...And Ore isn't much different," he tacked on as an afterthought.

"Well, that's true," Barraka agreed and settled back to think properly.

Landras was still waiting on the messenger. He had to raise his eyebrow at him to get him to think and properly finish the answer he was waiting for. "Ah..., they've gone to petition the Gold Lion."

Landras gave a satisfied nod of his head at that. At least they were all thinking properly, instead of just being random. That was a good sign they might all be worth taking in — on both sides. He was fairly certain Ilena would allow that alliance. Barraka had paused at that answer, though, and seemed to be in some minor disagreement. The furrow on his brow had deepened.

Landras blinked at him, then clucked his tongue. "You can still go visit your favorites over there." Barraka was headed for a scowl, but Landras wasn't done. "And having to *pay* for them keeps you kind and reasonable. Getting more than your fill of 'free' women would make you lazy and completely useless. Like a regular Grouse clansman." Barraka looked away, refusing to answer to that insult since he knew best what that meant.

Landras ignored him and turned to the messenger again. "As a freelancer, Ore isn't inclined to Head a House like that." The messenger shook his head and said the nightwalkers wouldn't be swayed and would only take Ore as their Head. Landras frowned, then finally sighed and said, "We'll let the Heads know you've asked. We'll try to have an answer for you before the heavy freeze. Do your best to stay at your own safe house for now." He waved at their assistant who sat just at the outer corner of the raised dais they were sitting on. "See he knows which building it is and we'll see if we can purchase it, if Mister Ore agrees. It won't be wise to have you all in here this winter. We're already rather full."

The messenger scanned the room again and had to agree. More bodies meant more warmth, but also meant less floor space for sleeping and more fighting. Barraka, as the one who made sure there was just enough order in this house, finally said something useful: "How is everyone right now? Are they infighting yet, or is it still uneasy truce?"

The messenger shrugged. "The few who don't want to follow Ore have moved on, hunting for a House they can bear to live in. We were just done with her tight rein and the ladies mostly self–sufficient as it was. It's not like there's a lot of us. There's enough space there to sleep without killing, so the truce should last until the winter hard freeze. After that, people will assume the King's unwilling."

Both Landras and Barraka nodded understanding to that. Wait too long and they'd be just as angry with Ore at his silence and for him ignoring them. He wouldn't have to go himself for a while, but he did have to answer them and give them the leadership they needed if he agreed to Head his own House.

When the messenger had left, Landras sighed. "And then there's the matter of territory. Who's going to see to that sector? Do we just let Gold Lion have it and let the new ones fight for places in ours? Or will he let those who know those places continue to work in those zones? That's going to be complex." Half of the nightwalkers were the salespeople for the ladies, bringing in the work for them, but they still didn't want to walk behind anyone but Ore, apparently.

They didn't have to wait very long to get their orders back. *Ore isn't ready to consider it. If it happens, no nightwalker who swears allegiance to only the King will learn the codes. I'll handle territory negotiations. He'll handle the nightwalkers.* Well, that was about what they'd expect to hear from Ilena. Those nightwalkers wouldn't listen to her anyway. It was nice she'd take the load off them for the Head side of the equation, if it came down to it.

Second Son to the Lieutenants. To help them keep the peace in their house for now, call up the squad leader over those who protected the King in Tarc to go sit as their house captain. We're tight on coin at the moment, so they'll have to continue to pay for the building. Tell them the usual tax — they can pay that much — then take donations. The more they help the sooner they can rest assured they've got a warm place to sleep.

Both Landras and Barraka had to assimilate that for a moment. It should have come from Petroi. They both slumped around the same time, too. "Because he's already had to do it once before — in Kouzanshi," Landras said.

Barraka agreed. "Likely he'll be talking a lot more for a while for that reason." He grimaced.

"Likely," Landras agreed. He sat up straight, stretching his spine. There was going to be a lot of work from now on. If the nightwalkers were moving on their own, they couldn't just sit back.

-o-o-o-

Michael Barret sighed to himself and rose to his feet. He didn't often make reports to the King from the more formal position of standing in front of the King's desk, but the message he'd just received through the patio door from Ilena's contact rather demanded he at least be where he could watch Sasou's face.

Sasou set his pen down and looked into Michael's eyes. The brilliant blue eyes were questioning at the moment. He'd heard the report being given. Michael was glad most times that Sasou wouldn't learn Ilena's secret language. It was often best for Michael to retranslate messages into the words Sasou needed to hear to keep the impetuous youngers of their generation from setting him off when he was stressed out. Sasou wasn't at the moment, which was good enough.

"Princess Ilena and Lord Ore have came up for air just enough to send out the Messengers. Lord Ore was quite dismayed to learn what the nightwalkers came home saying about him." Michael paused as Sasou's brilliant blue eyes went very piercing, the look of the great eagle suddenly seeing potential prey. Sasou had already been keen to know where that rumor would lead.

Michael didn't flinch from Sasou's eyes. He'd seen all of the expressions of the King since he was very young, many of them directed at him, and he never flinched from them. Keeping calm always helped Sasou get to the emotion he wanted to be at eventually. Not that Sasou was often wild in his emotions, but Michael had seen the deepest griefs, the greatest fears, and the slow unstoppable anger.

The anger of most Toukas was sharp and cold. Not in Sasou. He used that as a feint. The anger of Sasou was hot, slow and thick, like lava coming up from the ground. It didn't explode out. It rose, slowly increasing in quantity until it finally climbed out and moved to squash everything he was angry at, burning and unrelenting until it had been satisfied, cooled enough by being exposed to the air of action to be pushed back down into the ground. He changed things when that happened, just like cooled lava changed the face of the earth it had crawled on and stayed upon once cool. The fight against the Doll House had been like that. Sasou's fight to free Ilena from Tokumade had been as well. Michael had learned to watch for the beginning of that one. He usually had a lot of work to do once it started.

Since this hadn't been that yet, Michael continued on, "Specifically, Lord Ore apologizes for the incorrect message brought out by the spies allowed to travel into Tarc. It seems to be a side effect of the pre–war party that has gotten out of hand. Lord Ore was apparently really unaware of his popularity in Suiran." His lip quirked up slightly.

Sasou acknowledged the humor of the blindness of the man who didn't want popularity, nor even a noble honor of any kind, yet wanted to be spouse to a princess. He sat back in his chair and thought about it. "We'll let him sweat just a little longer, I think, but it would be good practice for him, like it's been for Ilena." He pondered a bit longer and added, "I think it will be very interesting to see how he handles it, actually, once they make him take King of Nightwalkers for sure."

Sasou went quiet and into his own thoughts. He blinked a few times, but didn't come out of his introspection. Michael interrupted to get out of him what was going on inside. "And will it eventually offend you that he's called King, even if it doesn't now?"

Sasou's focus came back to Michael, his lips pursing just a little. "That depends, doesn't it? As long as it stays the way he wants it today, that's fine. It can't stay in the family after him, just like his children won't be princes or princesses of Ryokudo. *He's* not proud nor greedy in those ways, but his children are another thing altogether. If one is steady enough to run the

House, that can stay in the family, but King of Nightwalkers will have to go."

Michael was pleased when it went from the firmness to a shrug of the shoulder. "But the nightwalkers themselves won't be able to accept it that long, either. They'll take it back from him eventually. I expect Ilena to make that happen quietly and in the right way as they age, like she made it explode now while she can control it." He picked up his pen again. "Make sure to remind her if she needs it as that time comes," he ordered Michael as he bent to his work.

"And what message shall I send back to Lord Ore?" Michael wasn't going to have that left in his own lap.

Sasou paused just long enough to compose his desires into words. "See you don't forget, but as long as you're taking that hat for Suiran, I don't have to wear it."

Michael pursed his lips at Sasou and didn't move except to rest his hand on his sword hilt. Sasou raised his head to look at Michael. He blinked mildly, then said, "He's my brother–in–law. Why treat him any different than I treat Rei?"

Michael slumped and sighed at Sasou, a long–suffering sigh. "Fine. See you keep it that way, then."

Sasou snorted and turned back to his paper again. "Like the wild falconess will let me be otherwise? I've no wish to make him an enemy when he doesn't want to be one." Satisfied, Michael returned to his desk, passing along the message to the contact still waiting outside the office. He made sure that messenger had left the premises before he returned to his work. They were loyal, but to Ilena first and Sasou second.

Michael's responsibility was to the King first. He never forgot it. Not since Sasou's father had died and Kata had confided in him, "Tell no one, including Sasou, but my husband has died at the hands of an enemy nation. They'll take Sasou next in order to take Ryokudo and enslave our people. Keep Sasou alive, no matter what. If I give you an order, follow it without fail, or we'll all fall."

The years from when Sasou had been one month away from thirteen until he was nineteen and come into his own adult strength and had finally trained enough hidden guards to keep him protected had been hard years. Sasou had survived those years because Michael had been faithfully obedient to his orders. In his eyes, Kata would be the least well known but best strategist of all Toukas of Ryokudo.

CHAPTER 140 Beginning to Pick the Work Back Up

Rei strode into the Rose office. He stopped rather suddenly. His eyes swept around the walls of the room. He'd forgotten that it was going to be updated while they were gone. His brow furrowed a little at the fact the walls had been painted a blue color. He really did prefer white to help lighten the room up and found it the most calming color. He was rather used to it from Ichijou where there weren't any colored paints on the walls. The gold roses were pretty, though, and done very well.

He finished his walk into the room slowly, taking in the doubled size to his left where the wall had been removed. That was nice and made the blue walls a little more tolerable, to have all that open space. It was rather undone by all the tables, but those got to be more spaced out now, too. He wasn't surprised they were set at the far side and the desks were still in the original Rose Office space.

Because he'd moved his desk to be on the right wall, facing that now-long space, they'd just moved all the aide's desks and the tables to face his desk. As if he wanted to be at the head of the room and lecture from his desk. He sighed a little to himself. He just might, actually, without really realizing he was. Since he was already exploring with his eyes, he passed by his desk and on to the double glass doors to the balcony. The new curtains were heavy, nicely done in the Regional gold color, and stately as befitted the Regent's office. He'd have to ask what had happened to the guards that were supposed to be on the balcony doors.

Whomever had come in to start the fire in the new fireplace had pulled the curtains back from the glass doors and tied them open to let the light in like he preferred. That patio hadn't changed and it was cold outside, so he didn't open the door. Instead he turned left and walked to the fireplace. The mantle was of a dark wood, intricately carved with vining roses to match the gold ones that ran around the top of the walls and down in a few places to give variety to the walls.

Rei ran his hand over the mantle. It had been polished to a nice smooth finish and was of a good long size so that the fire could be made large enough to heat the double space. The fire wasn't overly large today, it still not being as cold as it would get, but it was popping nicely. It must have been stirred up recently, then. There weren't too many ashes in it, either, so it was a morning tending, likely.

He passed on to the next set of doors. They also had the curtains pulled back. That let in twice the amount of outdoor light, but he wasn't sure that helped brighten up the room. He might have to call the painter back, but he'd wait to see if it grew on him first. It would be rude to not enjoy their effort and desire to please him long enough to show some appreciation. That patio was also a short one, left alone in the renovation. He wondered why. Maybe Ilena could tell him.

He moved on to walk back up towards his desk between the two rows of desks and tables. The farthest back set of tables was mostly clear with very few stacks on them. The next several sets each had stacks neatly set on them and waiting pens and inkwells. Empty report folders and blank sheets of paper were sitting to the side waiting to be used. There were four of those tables total.

Then it was the aide's desks, six of those now instead of four. Rei paused, then backed up to the farthest back tables with stacks. He picked up the top folder from one of them and reviewed what was in it. It was rather old, actually. The stacks on all four of the tables were. The stacks on the first set of desks from the back were recent. The stacks on the next pair were from a little farther back but not too far out of line. The stacks on the front pair were shorter, but of a different kind of content and need.

Rei gave a contented nod. They'd put the aides in ranking order. Likely that had been Lord Aiden's decision. Andrew and Mina would still have the desks closest to his, then it was Tairn and Dane, then Aiden and Brianna. He did wonder who handled the tables, then? He took the top folder from the left corner on his desk, opened it to review the contents, then smiled. This side was Mizi's side. Her neat lettering was easily recognizable. He'd let her sort through those stacks and give him what he needed out of them, if anything.

The four stacks on the right corner were his, rather obviously by the first one. That whole stack was message folders tied with ribbons, making them for his eyes only. Those that had been most important had been waiting for him at the Northeast garrison when he'd arrived there. He'd have to figure out how to delegate those kinds of reports to the aides this time around. Maybe Ilena could help him get over his insecurities at having people other than himself see the dirty laundry of the country. It wasn't like they didn't already see it and have to deal with it after all.

He paused then decided that at the least if he ever had to call Ore into the office he'd train him to it. Ore was *supposed* to be handling things like that, under Ilena's direction. Not like he really wanted to add more to Ore's plate right now. Now wasn't a good time for that. Maybe once they'd settled to their new positions.

Rei looked out the window and sighed. That was going to be hard. Tying Ore down was a harder thing to do than tying Ilena down. Ilena expected it. Ore wanted to be obedient, but he didn't want to rule. Rei's face went sad for a moment, but he let it go. It was necessary and Ore could do it.

"Good morning, Rei," came from the door. "You're here early..., and before anyone else?" came the surprised query.

Rei turned to smile at Aiden. "Good morning. Yes, I ran away this morning. I wanted to approach the office today on my own two feet instead of feeling like I was being dragged back to the mines against my own will. They'll be scolding me most likely when they all get in." He'd also needed to let Lord Nedlow know he should be expecting his new assistant for training this morning.

Aiden nodded wisely, understanding it. "Well, if you managed to come back to it on your own, that's good strength to have learned, and a lot less stressful." He smiled a small smile.

"Yes, I thought so, too," Rei stretched his back out a little, then leaned back on his desk. "How have you been holding up?"

Aiden paused to consider his answer. "It's certainly helped to have Tairn and Dane return recently. Knowing the rest of you weren't too far off has as well." He waved at the piles on all the desks and tables. "We've tried to sort it appropriately so people only need to get started." He looked a little sympathetically at Rei's piles. "I'm afraid some of yours we couldn't sort for you, so you'll likely have the most catching up to do."

Rei shrugged a little. "Probably, but that's normal. It's helped to have you and Brianna added in, as well as all the other help. ...And learning to delegate." He smiled and Aiden smiled in return. It did seem that Aiden had relaxed a little. At least he wasn't in a hurry to end the conversation and get right to work. "Before we all get to work, however, we'll be having a little meeting about what we're going to do in the near future. It'll keep the waiting stacks waiting longer, I suspect; although, we'll hopefully get to fit some of them in around the edges."

Aiden's eyes went to his desk, then returned to Rei. Rei suspected he'd instantly thought of all the reports that were marked in his head "to do immediately". Rei nodded at the desk. "If you want to get started on settling things into a state they can pause briefly, go ahead. I'm interested in seeing who's going to show up today and where they're going to sit." He grinned a little and the twinkle of a tease came up to wrinkle the corners of Aiden's eyes. Aiden was quite relieved to be allowed to get to work, though, pulling three folders down to the working surface of the desk right away.

Rei turned his attention away from Aiden and looked towards the door. Once one of them arrived the rest usually arrived fairly quickly thereafter. He wasn't at all surprised when it was everyone at once. Everyone else came from the same place he did, and he'd snuck out early, as he'd said. As they flowed into the room, he was met with a mixture of glares, looks of relief, and hidden smiles. He wasn't surprised the last was from Mina.

"You're all late," he said smoothly to them, stopping the complaints before they could come. He waved at the places in front of him. "We've a meeting to have before we get started." Andrew still wanted to complain, but Mina put her hand on Andrew's arm and he puffed out a sigh of frustration and let it go. *At least he came straight to work,* her touch said. Andrew couldn't complain when it was that.

Rei watched with interest as the desks were filled the way he expected. The new thing for him was to watch all of Mizi's guards head to the tables behind the desks, each one knowing which was their's already. The very back two tables were left alone. He wondered what the reason for that was. Mizi chose to stand at the corner of his desk, near her stacks. Since she likely sat there and it was his chair and he was here now, they'd need to work out an arrangement for the both of them.

As his eyes turned to her, she jumped a little. "Ah! Rei, I've been meaning to ask it since I got here after the progress and things would chase it out of my head." She waved at the wall behind Rei. "Can we put a door to the Lotus office in? Then I could use my desk in there and come and go without being accosted in the hallway. That was quite annoying when I needed to go between the offices."

Rei smiled. "Let me consider it. I'm not sure if I'll get a scolding for putting another door at my back when I was just ordered before we left to not have one there." Mizi's face fell since she hadn't thought of that, but she understood. "I'd be just as happy having your desk in here next to mine," he added, making her pink up like he knew she would.

He turned his attention back to the room, having everyone's attention rather quickly. "Welcome back to the castle," he said to everyone. "I'm sure we're glad to be here in once piece, alive, and no one harmed — in the main. For the next month or so we'll be training the castle staff who the Regent is and what he expects from them, now that I understand who they are and where things stand in the Region as a whole.

"I do need the final data points of the census and the financial audit to be able to make the changes we need to see to make everyone content again, but I think if they know those are coming they'll be patient enough to wait that long." He shifted to rest one foot on top of the other as he leaned back a little on the desk, his hands resting on the edge of it. "I need to have a long meeting with Ilena and General Garen, but that's after I have the scolding audience with all of the staff of the castle."

His eyes looked to Andrew. "We'll be going over that in detail today, to get ready for it." His eyes turned to Dane and Tairn. "It would be good to have the brothers in on that so they learn what a high formal court is like and how to prepare for one. Once it's planned everyone will be helping get it set up." Andrew drew in a breath of surprise and a fist clenched on the desktop, but he gave a nod. Since Toukas generally hated high functions, for Rei to say he was going to have one without shuddering was a surprise for sure.

Actually, Rei didn't mind the courts and formality. They brought to his mind the solemn responsibility that he and his family held to the people of Ryokudo. They were supposed to, in his mind. They were for a purpose, told messages to everyone who participated, or who knew they were going on. In this case, he had a very specific message to send and a high formal court would tell the castle his message very clearly, leaving no question behind. People could choose to pretend or turn a blind eye to it afterwards, but in the moment and to his face they'd have little excuse.

He turned his mind to another court. "Until the investment court is completed, I don't think it's worth letting either of the pairs go home. I'm going to need all of you to help me hold those two in place until it's done." That got resigned comprehension. "Then, if I remember rightly, it's Dane and Tairn's turn to be at Nakaba and my turn to have Mina and Andrew, finally."

He looked down at the space in front of his toes for a moment, then looked back up at the people in the room. "Ore's asked for a week of vacation for the whole of the Immediate Family. I'm minded to give it to him. He'll need the time of relaxing with them to be able to come to the crown. They'll all need it in order to face what's after that. Timing will depend on when Sasou expects to arrive."

Rei's eyes went to Lord Aiden. "I'll rely on you to continue holding Ore's hand, particularly after the investiture. If you can find one of the other lords who can be trusted and that he gets along with well enough, he'll need a Voice to lead him through the learning phase of wearing one. Until one is found, that's you."

Aiden's shoulders slumped just a little, but he gave a nod. "There are a few who've been sufficiently impressed with him in our training sessions before now that he seems to get along with well enough — to their faces. I'll test him on them to see which ones he can actually put up with, without telling him the reason until afterwards. He'll not like the feeling of a restraint beforehand."

Rei agreed with a shake of his head. That wasn't really what he wanted anyway. Ore needed someone to help him learn he could walk through all the formalities he'd run away from so far. Someone who'd lead and encourage gently until Ore understood for himself.

Rei focused on Mina. "After the scolding audience I'll have you teach Dane how to get the castle prepared for a visit from the King. He was here last time, but not as involved as he'll need to be if you aren't here at all. You coach, he'll do the work." Mina gave a curt nod.

Rei looked between Andrew and Tairn. "Which one of you has the schedule?" Tairn put his hand down on a folder on the side of his desk. At Rei's distant look Tairn opened it and prepared his pen. "Formal high court in three days. Call for Lady Seraphina to come immediately. I have a rush order for her." Dane was already doing so. "Ultra formal guard uniforms for Mina, Andrew, Ilena, Ore, and their four, to be ready by then." Mina went a little pale, but her pen was already moving to write up the requisition to the castle tailors.

"Intelligence and security meeting between Garen, Ilena, and myself at her office in four days. It will take at least all morning." Andrew and Tairn both blinked, but it went on the schedule. "I'll take Andrew and Mina to that one." They gave bare nods.

"Mizi, there'll be no meetings with claimants for at least a week. It's possible if the message of the court doesn't get across I'll make them wait until after the investment court, but I don't think that will have to happen." He turned his head to address her directly. "You and I will have a meeting to discuss what I'm doing there after this meeting is done."

"Yes, Rei," she bobbed a small curtsy.

His eyes still on his strategy board in his head, he turned back to Tairn. "I expect the security meeting to interrupt Ilena, but for her report to go out at least one or maybe two days after that. They'll disappear for potentially a full week, then we'll have a short window of final preparations for the investment court and the arrival of the King. As soon as I receive Sasou's letter, that'll set the remainder of the schedule firmly. Please be sure Ore hears what amount of time he's allowed to have at Falcon's Hollow as soon as we know. Ilena knows we'll send the garrison after them if they don't come back." Mizi paled and a few in the room shuddered, but he'd only said it as part of the walk–through of the plans.

His brilliant blue eyes bored into Brianna's surprised grey ones. "We'll set you to be a lady–in–waiting for Ilena for the time Sasou's here. I'll have you go introduce yourself to Leah today. She won't be as busy now as she will be once Ilena's report is done and ready for transcribing."

Rei tapped the edge of the desk, thinking through the plans in his head one more time. "I'm still not available to any lord or staff member until at least after the scolding court. I'll let you know when that changes. The Rosebud office is an exception. They're *my* staff." His lip twitched up briefly.

"Are you going to do battle with the lords?" Andrew asked cautiously.

"No," Rei looked back at him calmly. "I'm going to train them after giving them the clear education they apparently need to understand." He stood up on his feet again. "Well, Andrew, start with Tairn and Dane while I meet with Mizi. I'll join you in progress. Dane, let me know when Lady Seraphina's on castle grounds. We'll want to meet her at the tailors so she can see the expected color scheme."

"You'll pay her fees for the new formal?" Mina asked, wide–eyed.

Rei looked back with his calm, bland court face on. "Yes."

Brianna rose to her feet to go be obedient to her order immediately. Mina handed her the requisition, asking her to pass it to a paige on her way out.

She quietly agreed and took it in hand. Aiden hesitated, then rose to his feet. "I'll go with you and speak with Ore for a bit as well," he said.

Rei was content enough with that as he turned to Mizi. He turned back to request over his shoulder, "Do have the paige stop by the Châtelaine's office and request another desk be set next to mine for Mizi. Today if at all possible." He got a positive response and turned back to Mizi. Her eyes were wide. "We'll go with that for now, until I have the time to think of your request," he said. "I should discuss the full ramifications with Ore and Ilena." He frowned at the still–unguarded patio doors. "I need to talk about more than that, apparently."

Mizi looked where he was looking, then raised a hand. "Ah..., that was me. ...And Tanner. It was too much to have them looming over me all the time, when I already had a room full of guards who don't let me go anywhere without them and don't have anywhere else to go anyway. The guards on the roof were enough with them here. I'll let General Garen know to send them when our meeting's over."

Rei considered that, then shook his head. "Until we're thin in here again, it's fine. I also don't need more than necessary." He'd take the option he preferred, and her logic wasn't wrong. He had to send his aides out all the time — like he'd just given them orders to. Hers would stay put and Tanner had already been silently and invisibly standing at that doorway anyway. Rei figured he usually did when Mizi was in the room. He gave a pointed look to the man and received back a bare raised lip of a smile.

-o-o-o-

"Brianna, I'm sorry to continue to keep you from work today, but would you please come with me to the Lotus office for a bit?" Mizi asked at the end of lunch in the Rose office that same day. Rei had raised his eyebrows to learn that the back tables were kept bare to be the lunch tables. They filled them now that they were finally all present. Mizi hadn't let him keep the two of them separate from everyone else. There really wasn't a better place to eat, when onc wanted to keep paperwork clean of the meal, and they were all family now anyway.

Brianna glanced at her desk, but bowed her head to Mizi. "Of course, Mistress Mizi." She and Aiden had spent most of the morning at the Intelligence office so the waiting work was likely worrying her some.

When they were seated in the Lotus office, with Tanner standing silently nearby as he always was, Mizi pulled out several sheets of paper she'd written her notes on. She drew in a breath and faced Brianna candidly. "I think perhaps you've been given a lot more work suddenly than you might have been expecting." She smiled slightly. "I'm afraid I wish to add even more to it. Rei has said that if it's too much, then for the next while you may lessen your duties to the Rose office. There's enough of us right now that you could pass along some of your stacks."

Brianna's eyes were a little wide. Mizi plowed ahead. "While I'm sure some of your time will be taken up with answering to Rei's request of you this morning, and you're likely already working hard to catch up to who the rest of us are given I've asked you to be the matron of the household, I need to monopolize you for a bit."

Mizi placed her hand on top of the papers in front of her. "Rei has said that we won't be working on having children for a few more years. Thus, I'd like to continue moving forward on my lessons in being a princess of Ryokudo. Ilena's taught me what she can, but there are some gaping holes in her own education that I feel should really not be in mine." Brianna blinked.

"We of necessity focused on allowing the lords to understand who I am to Rei, and what my capabilities and qualifications are. At this time, I need to be able to understand the ladies of the court and my role as regards them." Mizi wasn't looking forward to it, honestly. These lessons were rather difficult generally, and even more so when it came to the ladies who'd only been jealous until now. "I'll be relying heavily on you for those lessons.

"I've already begun going to a few teas that I felt I had the level of capacity to go to, making sure that Maria and Leanna went with me. I had to postpone an invitation when Rei called me away, and have recently received a re–invitation to it. I'd like to be sure you and I have discussed the expectations of those who'll be there as to what a princess of Ryokudo should and should not do, as well as — if you know — how the Toukas will expect me to present myself." She sighed. "I'd like to ask that of Queen Kata, but I expect she'd rather test me at the end than give me any helpful suggestions or training."

Brianna smiled sympathetically. "I think that could be arranged, in a rather Ilena–like way, actually, but we'll wait to get there."

Mizi blinked in surprise at Brianna, then gave a nod. "I'd appreciate that, actually." She glanced through her notes. "While I have all sorts of simple questions that will certainly show what a common dolt I am still, I also need to learn such things as what activities is the princess expected to hostess and how often, what sorts of things do princesses do to support their husbands and the region, and how much of the activities of the other ladies of the court am I expected to participate in? I know that many more invitations are sent than I need to accept, but I need to know which ones shouldn't be ignored and how to know when to reward those who can be."

Mizi wanted to slump just a little. She was glad she'd already known before the invitations started arriving that to ignore them altogether until she was properly trained and ready to face them was not only fine, but expected. It really was good she'd learned those finer points from Ilena. If she hadn't she would've already gone absolutely insane trying to go to all the things she was being invited to.

Her list in front of her really did have a lot of seemingly inane questions, but she still had them and they still needed to be answered. She needed to know things like: what sorts of things do the ladies learn while growing up? Because she was a researcher, she hoped they got to have formal educations. She wasn't sure they did. In her questions of this sort she really wanted the crash course in growing up a young lady of the court, since she hadn't.

While she'd been on Rei's arm at the Lord's teas and other such functions, she'd come up with a few questions from those. What were the expectations of the ladies when they visited with each other as just ladies? Did any of the other ladies play the court game when it was just them together? (She was pessimistic about that one. She rather thought they would and wished it was otherwise.) She also wondered what the ladies were expected to do when they were with their lord husbands (or fathers) at court functions? Did they visit with each other or were they just flowers on arms? Were they expected to participate in the conversation their husband was engaged in? By how much? How much of the court game was played by them then?

Mizi lifted her eyes from her papers and handed them over to Brianna. "This is the full list, like I made one for Ilena when we were working on the first part of my lessons. I'm sure it will be very overwhelming, as I find it to be so now that I've put it all down on paper. I'd greatly appreciate it if you could fit it into a set of lessons, personal and then practical practice, a little at a time. I'm willing to work as hard on this as I did to become Princess to begin with. I want to be able to fulfill all of my duties and not continue to have half of the court completely upset with me, when half of the other half is already enough."

Brianna smiled kindly. "I think, Mistress Mizi, that if you already wish to face the ladies of the court with kindness, you're already very much on your path. There hasn't been a Touka princess in Nijou for several decades. Most of the ladies of the court haven't got any idea of what you're to do either. You'll be able to make your own decisions as to what you'll do, in the main. We'll work on making those decisions as we have the personal lessons."

"Oh, good," Mizi did finally slump. "I already have so many things I wish to be doing, and need to do for Rei, that I can't really afford to add too much more after the lessons are completed." She pondered that, then said, "However, that means Queen Kata has left me a lot of work to do to get any of them to accept that I might be more friendly than a Touka, but that at the same time I won't be cowed by them any more than by the lords." She wrinkled up her nose to not let a few tears out. "Do keep the lessons easy here at the beginning, please. I'm not ready to face the worst yet."

"I understand," Brianna said gently. "Give me until tomorrow to read through your list and set my desk in the Rose office in order. Then we can come up with a lesson schedule."

"Thank you, Brianna," Mizi said gratefully. "We'll meet in the Regent suite's office after breakfast. I won't be needed over here until after the investiture, so we'll just stay there for now, now that it's much more comfortable to be in." She rose to her feet so the two of them could return to the Rose office for the rest of the day. She took a deep breath and set it firmly into her heart again: she was Rei's princess and she'd do everything she needed to do to support him from that position.

CHAPTER 141 A Stern Liege

Rei walked into the throne room with calm purpose. Today he owned his mantle and this throne and it showed in his bearing. If those watching him from the full audience of the court lords and staff in attendance were looking to see anything other than his age, they'd see that mature bearing in his shoulders and back. Andrew wondered if any of them would bother. It was rather sad that so many people chose to be close minded and blind. It would get them into a lot of trouble with this member of the Touka family, who was actually the easiest to get along with.

Rei walked to his throne and sat in it without any tension to him, letting the court see his calm confidence from the beginning. He was dressed to tell his message, not just say it with words. The shirt, jacket, and pants were crafted from fabrics of Touka gold and brilliant blue that made a larger statement today than Rei usually wore. The blue was *his* blue, not the blue of Suiran. They were perfectly tailored and accentuated his Touka height. Lady Seraphina had come herself to Rei's call and worked quickly to deliver excellence with exactness.

Rei was also wearing the pale gold cloak of the Toukas lined with ermine that was typically only worn to winter high national state functions. His First Prince's medallion and pin were both on, the medallion under the cloak but obviously visible across his chest that was broadening out nicely and the pin on the left breast. His crown had been polished to a near–blinding gleam and his hair combed, then jelled just enough to make it stay tame but beautifully and lightly curly for the whole court — a vanity Rei had never moved to take before. It wasn't a vanity for him, but part of the statement of the whole. The only bow he'd taken to the Regency was to sit the Regent's throne (another part of the message) and to wear the Regent's signet ring (also polished to be gleamingly obvious).

Andrew had stopped at his proper location where he always stood, to Rei's left, in front of the level of the throne one pace. Mina had stopped in her place, to Rei's right, a single step from the back and arm of the throne. Both had been told to also come properly dressed to represent the Toukas. Thus they were in the ultra formal black uniforms with dark gold piping in the seams. Their black boots, swords, and sheathes were polished to shining. The mark of the Toukas in gold gleamed on the leather sheaths.

Personal knights to Touka always wore short waist–length cloaks so they could move to fight. This time he and Mina were wearing the formal ones: fine black wool on the outside, dark gold lining inside in satin to match the piping on the jacket and pants. The embroidered badge of the Toukas on the left breast of the cloaks matched that on their sheaths. Rei had asked Mina to also wear her pin of heir to Earldom Yosai. That was pinned to the right breast of her jacket, under the clasp of the cloak, as perfectly placed as she always dressed. She'd made her and Andrew's hair perfect as well, this time. Andrew wasn't liking the jell in his hair, but he wouldn't complain knowing what statement Rei was trying to make. It would take all this and more to get the blind to pause and maybe really listen this time.

The room had gone quiet as Rei and his guards had settled into their places, but Rei wasn't in a hurry to start the court. He wanted everyone to have the time to properly place the people they were looking at. Many eyes were glancing now to the one place that was still empty. Andrew only smirked inside, keeping his stern look on the outside. Rei had left Mizi in the office. The court wouldn't get to see her for a while still, having not earned that privilege of having an advocate with the Regent yet. Nor was she worthy of the scolding that was going to come. It didn't need to blister *her* ears.

Eyes looked for, and heads turned even, to see if they could find one more expected person. Ilena was present, but not where anyone expected to see her. She, Ore, and all of their guards were lined up along the back wall, having come in while the court was distracted by the arrival of Rei. Ore and Ilena were centered, directly across from Rei. Their personal guards were to either side of them.

There were other guards in the room, the usual soldiers in their white formal uniforms and cloaks, placed regularly around the perimeter of the room and on the doors. Ore, Ilena, and their personal guards were in the Touka formal guard uniforms. Today they represented Rei in that way. Ore was wearing his Consort to the Second Princess pin on his right breast and on his finger the signet ring of Count Falcon's Hollow. Over Ilena's shoulders, under the black cloak, was her golden Second Princess' medallion. Her white–sheathed sword and knife fastened to her white belt stood out as usual on the black, but everyone was starting to get use to it, Andrew felt. If nothing else, it did give people pause and remind them that there was one who wouldn't hesitate to use the blade in defense of the Prince, the nation, ...and herself.

Rei shifted slightly, lifting his left hand at the fingers only. He was resting comfortably on the throne, both arms relaxed on the arms of it. He actually fit it fairly well, being of adult size even if only the beginning of that in age. Andrew drew in a breath. Formal meant formal in the speaking, too: "You stand before the First Prince of Ryokudo, Rei Touka, Regent Suiran. Do him honor and homage as your liege acknowledged by the Crown of Ryokudo." Andrew kept his tone sober and a little lower than he usually spoke.

Everyone in the room that wasn't a guard or Rei bowed, held it for two seconds while chanting, "Hail Prince Rei," then rose to standing again.

Andrew continued, "Prince Touka has returned from successfully sub-duing all of the nation of Tarc under him. Praise him." It wasn't like Rei needed or liked such things. Perhaps some would accuse him of holding this formal court just so he could gain the accolades and have his nonexistent ego stroked. In this case it was to remind the court that Rei was quite capable regardless of what they thought. Rei was also supposed to report on such actions, regardless.

"Praise to Prince Rei for his successful campaign," the court responded, many actually relieved. That campaign being successful meant less cost to the Region in money and personnel than it could have. Not to mention everyone knew it would be difficult if war had come to Suiran soil itself.

"King Sasou Touka, long may he reign, has declared that Tarc shall be considered a Grand Duchy of Ryokudo, under the supervision of the Regent of Suiran." There was some stirring, but not much surprise. The gossip would be wondering who it was that would be placed over Tarc: Rei or Ilena. To not be told right off who it would be meant that Ichijou was unsettled as to the final selection still. If it was Ilena, the lords of Nijou would consider it a good punishment for her rather than a reward. Of course, for any of them to be made to rule Tarc would also in the end be considered a punishment, so they didn't want it for all their envy made them two–faced about it.

"Hear and attend to the voice of your acknowledged Liege Lord," Andrew said. He paused, then stepped back to stand to the left side of Rei's throne, level with Mina. The court was suddenly holding their collective breath.

While Rei often spoke on his own in casual settings, if not often to this particular group of people, it meant something different in a high formal court. Any word of the person on the throne, when spoken by themselves in a high formal court, was considered law and was required to be obeyed. Given the room was full of all ministers, directors, their staffs, all the department heads and their staffs, and anyone with any authority in the castle at all including Rei's own staff, it was even more important.

Rei drew in a silent breath and began speaking. At times throughout the entire speech Andrew could hear the suppressed anger, and sometimes the couched pleading, but with Rei they were always smoothed over by the overarching tone of firm command. "Having spent the last thirteen months studying, testing, and being tested by the court of Suiran, I have come to the conclusion that some are confused. We will clear up those confusions today." That was the thunderclap to the lightning statement of the whole formality presented in this court.

The stunned looks and body language minutely changed in everyone and the three up on the dais took note of who went to resignation, who went to irritation, who went to fear, and who went to anger. It was a relief very few went to anger. Those were the ones to remove immediately. The rest were expected, as they already knew these men now. The court masks and stillness were back on the members of the court rather quickly, but it had been enough.

"It is my whole desire and wish to be known as a wise and just ruler," Rei began. "Because that is what I am, it is necessary to make sure you understand what I require of you so that you don't stumble in your efforts." He paused to emphasize that he was expecting everyone in the room to listen well to his following words. "The ruler of the land is required to see to the peace and prosperity of it, so that the citizens of the nation may live their lives as contentedly as they possibly can, thus providing for the prosperity of the nation as they ought. It is the responsibility of the lords and administrators of the land and nation to support and strengthen their proper liege with strict loyalty so that the joint goals of all citizens may be seen to."

Rei paused and pursed his lips just ever so slightly. Andrew knew he was having to control his anger to not just scold fiercely at this point. "It is *not* proper for the lords or administrators to assume the power of the Regent. You will not have it as long as I sit the throne and have the approval of King Sasou to sit it. Nor is it proper for the subordinate to order the superior. I have already removed from the court those who proved through their own visible actions and back room voices that they would not be loyal to the authority placed over them, nor see to the proper prosperity of the Region but to their own selfish desires for wealth or acclaim.

"For those of you who remain, I will be clear in what I require." His piercing blue eyes looked directly at the members of the court in the room as he slowly scanned through them. "I have either placed you where you are, or have accepted your works in those places until now. I expect that my trust in your loyalty will be returned with obedience. Only in this way can the works of the Region and the administrators thereof become the sum of peace and prosperity for it. It is the same regardless of what position or office you hold. Obedience to your immediate superior is obedience to me. Only in this way can the whole be made to work together smoothly for the benefit of all." Andrew was rather amazed at how many of the court got Rei's point this early, and actually agreed with it.

Rei's eyes went from piercing to more blazing. "This includes those whom I have placed in positions they are most competent to perform. It is a waste of everyone's time for people to be put into a position they cannot accomplish properly. When you have learned this lesson, then I will allow my Assistant over petitions to reopen her office to hear wiser voices than you have given to me until now, because what heed you give to her you give to me, the same as I said before." He particularly glared at Eadsley and Hulmer, the Minister of Finance. A few of the lords in the room shuddered at Rei's look, and a few others drew in breaths to firm themselves.

Rei released the room once he felt he had some understanding of his requirement by closing his eyes to near–half–lidded. With a Touka that was sufficient. When fully open, the piercing blue was difficult to turn away from or escape. Sasou hid his with his bangs on a regular basis, but Rei had always kept his hair short. He'd learned to do it with how open his eyes were, and if he looked directly at a person or not. "It has been my relief that many of you at all levels have sufficient wisdom in you for your tasks. It is also appreciated that you are willing to share with me what I need to know when I come to you with questions. Such things allow me to help your work go smoothly so that the work of all of us can do so as well."

Rei's eyes opened a little more again, but only to his usual calm level. "When things become troubling to you, report it immediately. Small troubles dealt with early don't have to become large troubles. The work is hard enough without adding such things." Many of the lesser staff in the room relaxed fully into Rei's camp at those words. Andrew hoped they understood the unspoken part of that which was related to the first. Troubles should be said to immediate superiors, and immediate superiors should deal with them properly as if they were Rei, only bringing to him what was necessary to be fixed at his level. Rei would train that, too, if he had to, though.

"I have been considering the troubles already brought to my attention, both here in Nijou and by the landed nobility during the progress just past. While the workload will perhaps be a little heavier in the near future, the goal is to relieve unnecessary pressures and discover untapped resources. A proper alignment for today's Suiran will relieve many and rebalance the requirements of all." Rei lifted his hand and closed his mouth. His gaze went slightly sharp as he waited to see the reaction to the next words Andrew would speak.

Andrew stepped forward to the position of Rei's Voice and opened his mouth again. The room was perhaps slightly more respectful now. They were certainly paying attention. "As the landed lords complained both that they had too many or too few people on their land, and that the taxes seemed unbalanced, a census of all peoples of Suiran will begin King's Day 1 After Dark in the 546th Touka Year. It is to be concluded within one year with the summary report to be given to Prince Rei's office within three months of conclusion." It had already been announced in the Ministry meeting, so wasn't really a surprise to anyone. It was just formally announced now and bounded in time.

"As the number of complaints of a lack of funding for necessary projects has been at the forefront of all court meetings, Prince Suiran has requested King Ryokudo that a formal audit of all Ministries, Divisions, and offices of Suiran be taken, to be completed if at all possible within that same time frame." The majority of the high level staff in the room stiffened.

Andrew kept going. "With the data from both actions, it is the hope of the Prince and Regent that a proper rebalancing of people, projects, and funding can be found both within the castle and within the lands of Suiran. His office will submit a report of the findings and resolution to the presented problems to all offices of Suiran and to King Ryokudo. It is anticipated that report will include a request to the King that the taxes on Suiran be reconsidered to more appropriately reflect the current capacity of the citizens of Suiran and the burden they already must bear to support the Region."

The room was buzzing with the whispers of the attendees to their neighbors. It was going to be a difficult thing to add in that burden to the things they were already doing. It was going to be worse because they'd all begin to quickly protect their favorite money–wasting projects. Rei was determined to dig those out altogether. He'd be pushing them hard to chose between favorite unnecessary projects and essential ones. It would be the final testing. If they couldn't give up their selfish desires for the good of the Region, they were unworthy of their positions.

Andrew waited for everyone to get that stress out of their systems just a little and return respectful attention to him. It took shifting just slightly to remind them where they were. "While the Regent and his respective offices will do their best to assist and attend to their regular duties as well during this coming year, it is expected there will be one requirement on his time in the middle of the summer by King Ryokudo. It is expected that the chosen Grand Duke and Grand Duchess of Tarc will also be required at Ichijou at that time."

Andrew saw Ore's face go rather pale. Ilena's lips tightened, but she managed to restrain the rest of her reaction. Andrew didn't envy them. He was glad his testing by that body had been merely by observation and a few sudden personal interviews by those most interested in being busy–body interferences. Ilena and Ore would be going through much more formal and intense testing. Similar to but likely worse than what Mizi had gone through, actually.

"Give honor and homage to your liege and lord, First Prince Ryokudo Rei Touka, Regent Suiran," he intoned. The room bowed and said the same words as at the opening. Rei rose to his feet and walked to the back of the room to exit it. Andrew stayed where he was as Mina followed Rei out. When Andrew received the nod from Marcus that Rei was out of the room, Andrew turned and followed his liege and partner. That released the lords. The hum started quietly but was plenty loud by the time he made it through the door in the back of the room that led to a small royal office.

Rei sighed as Andrew walked in. "They'll run tonight if they're going to," Mina said quietly. Andrew nodded in agreement.

Rei looked away from them, a little pensive. "Well..., I'll hope they won't." He looked a little sad. "I'd miss them, you know."

"Yes," Mina nodded. "You like getting to share the burden now that they've come to do that for you."

Rei glared at her, a little put out, but he couldn't deny that he did. "Who'd make me laugh?" he asked sourly. "You can't and Andrew won't."

Andrew looked away, then sighed slightly. "Well, that's true. No one quite has Ore's lightness of being." He hesitated, then said quietly, "I hope he's allowed to keep it." It would be sad to see the carefree thief buried by the bitter careworn high lord.

Mina looked away at that, then shrugged a little uncomfortably. "I think we'll see them fight this winter as they learn how to deal with the winter stresses, but I think when Ilena isn't overwhelmed by herself she'll be the first to make sure he returns to the balance he needs to stay happy and her proper support."

Rei sighed at them both, then got the look on his face that said he was seeing the board in his head and the players on it. After a bit of considering that board, he said softly, "And that's why they have the Seconds they do. Half of their supporting staff is the lighter side to bring them back to it."

Andrew and Mina considered that as Rei turned for the door to leave the throne room office and head back to the Rose office. "See that you watch Marcus and Thayne. If they begin to need support and help, be sure you let me know immediately, or we'll lose the whole ministry and half the Region."

Andrew gave an obedient nod. Mina said quietly as they stepped into the hallway, "I'll speak with Justinian. He'll be a willing spy for that requirement."

Andrew's lip turned up at the corner and Rei's shoulders relaxed just enough. Justinian instinctively knew when the right touch of interference was needed, and would take that particular duty quite seriously. He loved both Ore and Ilena too much to see them fall that far.

-o-o-o-

Garen seated himself at the far end of the table, opposite Rei, in the Lower office of the Department of Intelligence. David stood behind Garen in his usual place as his aide. Ore and Ilena were in their usual positions next to each other on the couch to his left. Marcus and Henry were behind them with Petroi and Thayne on the wall to the right in their usual positions. The couch to his right was usually empty for these security meetings. He was quite relieved it was the first meeting Rei had called for after the scolding full–Nijou high court. His men were still rather anxious.

Rei began the meeting as soon as he was seated, with Andrew and Mina standing behind him. Rei started out with a request of gossip and information on the few lords he was currently punishing and how their offices were doing. Ilena included the feel for the other lords of the castle. The whole had become quite tense, actually, just like the garrison was at the moment. Like everyone was balanced on their toes, just waiting to make the quick move forward, left, or right, or even in retreat at whatever the next move might be.

"Most of the comments after you left the high court were heavier towards the positive from the lesser staff and lords. The higher lords know that adding both the census and the financial audit will add to their own workloads more than they'd like. At the same time, the moderates and reasonable lords didn't oppose their lesser staff's comments to the fact that even they'd be helped if there was a better balance of understanding what the financial needs were."

Ilena ran her hand over the top of her head to grasp at the back of her braid for a moment. "Because we've already gotten rid of the worst of the corrupt lords, and those who've replaced them are trying to understand what they've been given, I think they'd be rather relieved to have the help getting unnecessary projects off their plates.

"It's the ones who've been in their places the longest and aren't unloyal that we'll have to dig into the hardest, I think. I've asked the few agents I have in their departments to be watching for certain projects to be buried and hidden, if they can. They'll do their best to keep their Heads honest when it comes time for that."

Garen wasn't surprised that Rei gave Ilena a few names of people to watch more closely than others. He always had a keen eye and had likely seen things from the throne in that room the rest of them hadn't from standing in the audience (himself) or in the back (Ilena and her people).

When Rei was satisfied with his current concern, he turned to Garen. "How were things while we were gone?" he asked.

"Fine," Garen answered. "The scolding removal of Princess Mizi was — as expected — taken with some derision for all I and the Rose Office most firmly held to your words. Eventually, most settled regardless. I was getting a few frustrated visits in the last few weeks by those who wanted their projects moving faster. I suspect those same lords are still frustrated you haven't moved on them even still."

As expected, Rei asked for that list. Garen gave it to him. It was lords already on the list of those who didn't like to be obedient to their liege and preferred to make demands. It looked like, by Rei's faint expression, that they'd get to practice both patience and obedience longest of all the lords.

"It's more what's happened because of the Tarc conflict," Garen continued, taking the topic to where he was most concerned. Rei's eyebrow lifted in slight surprise and Garen pushed firmly forward. "The garrison soldiers have become rather concerned and are uncertain." At that Rei's eyes went wide.

"To have nightwalkers who served the region faithfully to great injury, and then have them brought to be incarcerated in the castle garrison rather than a city prison is rather concerning. Until Lady Ilena came to settle the greatest difficulty on her first day back, we had to have a roof–top watch all around the garrison night and day." Rei blinked and sat back in his chair, slightly defeated it looked like. "I'd like to have you decide their sentences within the week or less, please, Master Rei. Knowing that you've properly attended to them will help the soldiers calm. As long as they think the nightwalkers have been forgotten by you, the soldiers will continue to worry."

Garen turned to Ilena. "I think in large part it's because they still don't know how to face you when it comes to your position in the Department of Intelligence. You came strongly against — for all in the behalf of — the garrison as your first action for them to really see you. Then you became a princess rather suddenly and surprisingly. You're still an unknown." Garen turned back to Rei, and somewhat to Ore. "In order to have them become more comfortable with what and who you are, I'd like to have Lady Ilena come practice on the field at the garrison so that the soldiers can learn who she is," Garen said.

Rei perked up. Andrew did, too, but with a concerned look. He was shaking his head and opened his mouth. "Kishi Knight's School was begun by the first peace king of Ryokudo — The Strategist — after he came to sit on the throne. One of the rules for royalty he set in the charter there, and at all castles, is that they must only practice in private lists. I was one of the few fortunate allowed to practice against then–Prince Sasou in the private list when he was there for his studies, as I was close to him in capability at the time.

"I wondered then why it was a private list only, as that seemed a bit lonely. Everyone would have liked to have seen him more while he was there, and it seemed to me that it would've helped them to get to know him like I was able to. So, I went and did a little research. Most people don't know that it's because his father — the last war king that united the north with the south of Ryokudo — died from a 'friendly fire' wound at the end of the battle against Kouzan.

"The Strategist was grieved at the loss of his father and realized that the open practice field, like the open battlefield, was too great a risk for royals. Practice swords can still kill. An open field can have an assassin's weapon thrown across it and no one able to find the assassin." Rei glanced up at Andrew, his eyes a little wide.

"Rei goes to visit at the garrisons, but it's never in the open practice fields. We only go to the off–duty common rooms where there are no weapons, or to the places where swords are kept sheathed and the spaces aren't crowded *and* open. Open with few people is acceptable but we're extra mindful then. When he must be presented to crowds of people it's from a very high height and distance. Thus the viewing stand above the practice and parade ground for addressing the soldiers, and the tower in the wall for public events." Garen was blinking at Andrew, who was quite serious.

Andrew continued, "Now that Ilena is openly acknowledged as a Touka princess, she also can't go into the open practice field of the garrison. When we tested the guards before the wedding ceremony, she wasn't originally in the field with us, nor was Rei with us. She also wasn't known to anyone save we few. It's different now. You'll have to think of something else." The room was a little colder for the saying, but it was hard to refute the logic of that long–ago many–greats–grandfather. Garen frowned a little as they all considered what other possibilities there were.

Ilena moved first and Rei raised his eyebrow at her. "Perhaps it would work a little better, regardless, if they heard it from those who've already seen it. You could transfer some of the soldiers from the Northeast garrison to the castle garrison, and some from here to there." Ilena turned to Garen. "While that might be the rule for those locations, it was necessary for me to be in the open fields to train the soldiers and common men what to do to face the Tarc. It was true that they weren't to have weapons flying around in the areas I was in."

She mused a little. "I'm not sure the soldiers saw quite so much of what I actually did while in Tarc —"

Rei was already shaking his head. "Yes, they did: during the Hunt." His brilliant eyes turned to Garen. "That's actually a very good alternative, and perhaps we can come up with more. The soldiers that were part of that offensive saw how she was as a field commander, and then as a tactician and soldier herself." He paused in a little surprise, then slumped slightly. "Ah, I guess Ore was right in the end, and you, too, Ilena." He was a little rueful. "Not only was it important for the Tarc to see you fight, but even for our own to see and understand."

Garen was somewhat satisfied with that as a workable solution. "I'd like to see other possibilities and opportunities taken that arise, but that would be a good next step to what we've already begun doing."

"I do want for the military to understand they're to work with the Ministry of Intelligence, and to be able to have faith in the Minister's sincerity. That said," Rei sat back with a sigh, "I think I'll have a more difficult time getting them to believe it than otherwise." He glared slightly out of the corner of his eye at Ilena. "As we found in Tarc, the soldiers and nightwalkers already don't trust each other, save with a very tenuous truce."

Ilena smiled slightly and shook her head. "Actually, I'm having the same troubles you are here in Nijou. I wasn't ever allowed into the castle. Or, rather, my people weren't in the main. Thus I wasn't able to establish a relationship with them. Half of those soldiers were from southern Ryokudo, sent by Sasou. They also don't know me and mine." Her expression went to a happier almost–grin. "You didn't hear any of the others on the progress complain did you?" Rei's brow furrowed and he shook his head.

"That would be because the rest of the garrisons in Suiran already know my people." Rei and Garen both had eyes that popped opened wide. "We've worked hard to have a working relationship with them. While there were the few witnesses I was saving for you and the Lord's Court against Pakyo, that wasn't the only thing the Family and House were doing. We regularly took our information to the local garrisons. We've been helping them to keep the crime down everywhere."

Ilena went sober. "It was particularly Sasou's fight against the child slave House, the Doll House, that cemented our alliance. He ordered the garrisons to faithfully look into every piece of evidence that we brought to them, and to help us gain it. He knew that it was as pervasive as it was and that he'd need everything he could get to bring all those minor, middle, and even the few high lords down. My people handled getting the evidence for both sides when possible, and we had to take out the nightwalker House. His soldiers handled getting the evidence we couldn't on the lords, and helped us take out those places we didn't have enough hands to do ourselves."

She shook her head. "There were a few garrison commanders in the back pockets of the corrupt lords, too. We couldn't do anything against them without getting into a lot of trouble, so we worked in concert with the more honorable of those garrisons to see they got the evidence to take out their commanders." She sighed a little to relax just a little. She'd tensed up at having to talk about that time. "The progress might've been the first time most of those garrisons saw me in person — other than Osterly — but they understood as soon as I let them know who I was to them."

Rei blinked at her, rather stunned. Ore was nodding his head. "When we first rescued Ilena and brought her back to Osterly, the soldiers of that garrison already knew she was the one who'd been giving them the hints they needed to keep even Pakyo's corruption in check as much as it could be. I'd asked in disbelief that she could still be uncorrupted herself, being Pakyo's steward, and they scolded me rather severely."

"Then, why—?" Rei asked Ilena, confused.

Ilena shook her head. "Tarc was the first time the nightwalkers worked with *those* soldiers, and usually the fighting is separate. The soldiers of Ryokudo and Suiran can't *actually* fight the lords and people of Ryokudo. They gather complaints, evidence, and make arrests. When they fight, it's against other nations. It's the natural part of things for nightwalkers to police themselves with battles like that, as I've told you before. Many have been the battles of my House against the worst of the corrupt Houses that needed to be taken down.

"We don't fight those who are only housing, feeding, or clothing those who are the poorest, most down–trodden, and hardest to deal with." Ilena pointed at Rei with some intensity. "I realize that those who live those lives are on that line. I'm certainly not going to defend those who are captured and the evidence is overwhelmingly against them. That's another way the nightwalkers are policed, after all, and I can't do it all myself, nor my Houses. However, as I said at the beginning, none are allowed into either of my Houses if they don't already love Touka and Ryokudo. That's *both* of my Houses. They might've done things worthy of prison time before they come in, but after that it isn't acceptable."

Garen's mouth dropped open. "But..., all of those in the prison now.... You're saying, ...what?"

Ilena shook her head at him. "Most of what the soldiers will tell you is rumor only. In some cases, yes." She sighed. "It's hardest for my Lieutenants. They had to follow Pakyo's orders first, over mine, until I was able to free them. They've been quite relieved to not have to continue racking up points against themselves."

"So...," Rei mused, "I really only need to absolve them of the deeds done long enough ago that a short payment wouldn't be out of line?"

"Correct," Ilena answered.

"That's helpful, then," Rei said. "Saying the slate can be swept clean because they were willing to put their lives on the line in Tarc will work, then. I'll do a posthumous pardon of Danel, and write in that he was also a witness against Pakyo so received grace for his willingness to do so." Ilena gave a grateful nod.

Garen had been tapping his finger as he was thinking hard. "I think..., we might want to bring soldiers from multiple garrisons here. Not a lot, but a few. ...Could we have a few–week–long to month–long military conference here in the near–ish future? If the soldiers from here can hear it from many places, and I'd think those coming from those far places would be curious to hear how Lady Ilena is here at this place.... Enough conversations would take place during that time, I think the garrison would settle."

Ilena had frozen. Rei was nodding thoughtfully. Garen's eyes sharply pinned Ilena. Her mouth opened, but nothing came out. Ore looked between the two keenly. Rei finally caught it and looked at Ilena as well. Then his gaze became that of the hawk. "It would be a thing you'd have done regardless?" he asked.

Ilena blinked, sucked in a large breath, then said. "Ah..., yes. And before it looks like we're actually preparing for war. To have the opportunity for a secret meeting with all the garrison commanders, or even their seconds, would be of very great benefit."

"Wonderful," Rei said firmly. "Garen, see to it. Make up a reason and bring it to me. We'll see if we can make it work sufficiently to seem a reasonable purpose." Garen wrote it in his meeting notes of things to do as Rei added rather firmly to Ilena, "I do hope you're going to tell me soon about this next war you keep dropping hints of."

Ilena bowed her head humbly. "When Sasou comes, I'll request he speak on it. As I've already said, he needs to tell us why he allowed the second son of Altherly to enter our nation secretly."

Rei blinked at her, then gave in and moved on to his next point of business. "Garen, who of the ministers and their subordinates that were taken to the prison after the Lord's Court against Pakyo receive regular visitors, or at the very least letters?"

Garen rubbed his chin as he considered the answer to the question. The answering list was rather small for visitors, a little longer for letters that came and went. "And you're reading the mail?" Rei wanted to check.

"Yes," Garen answered soberly.

Rei tapped his finger on a list in front of him, then handed the sheet of paper over to Garen. "Don't let the lords know of this action. I'd prefer if there's substitution so that they believe those who were 'deserving' of death were the ones who received it." Rei frowned as Garen looked up from glancing down the page, his face kept smooth of a reaction. "I don't need the lords mistrusting me, but I need the prison cleaned out as much as the court and the castle. It's expensive to have this many prisoners, and those men don't get pardon — ever." His blue eyes were very sharp and his voice firm.

Garen hesitated, then asked, "Have you the roster of those who've been in since long ago?"

"No," Rei answered. "I'd like to have it sent today, with the date of offense, what the offense was, the sentencing and who ordered it. If you need time to pull it together, then by two mornings from now, please. We'll have you do them all at once to confuse the issue while at the same time explaining it properly."

"I'll see to it," Garen answered. He wouldn't mind having that cleared out as well, during all the cleaning Rei was doing. It cost him in manpower, not just the castle in food costs, and Rei had quite filled up a number of cells just on his own since Ilena had come.

"Feel free to add comments and opinions to the list as well," Rei said as he looked to his next piece of paper and topic he wanted to speak to. "If there are a few that I should visit myself, I can probably work in some time, but I'd rather not completely fill up my schedule with it."

"Understood." Garen slipped the list he'd been given into his folder behind his notes. Ilena made a request related to that topic that they discussed briefly, then moved on.

Rei referenced his notes for the meeting, then asked Ilena, "Tell me of Lord Odle. Has he been keeping his word to me since then? And the others, too."

Ilena smiled. "He has been, actually, and the others to the best of their abilities. Sometimes I have to frown at them when I've heard they might be slipping. He in particular, though, I haven't heard concerns about."

Ore raised his hand. "He's actually come to me on a few occasions to ask questions to confirm rumors, or words from supplicants. At least one of the times was to ask me if what he was thinking of would be acceptable to you or not. I've answered him as best I could and from what I hear he's followed through rather admirably."

"Good," Rei was pleased. "I'll be able to use him as my next lesson to the court, then. Please continue to watch the others, or let me know of those who are already loyal that have needs that I can meet for them. I wish for the lords to begin to understand that I reward the obedience and loyalty I require. Rewards must balance out punishments and we've not had much opportunities for that yet." He gave a slight grimace. Garen could understand.

"However," Rei added a warning, "I don't reward with coin. Gratuities only lead back to the graft we wish to prevent now that we've weeded out the worst of it. I reward with easing the burdens of those who are placed to do the work. I think now that we've added burdens it's a good time to teach both things at once." He gave a small smile and the others agreed knowingly.

"And thus why Ilena rewards with dreams fulfilled instead of coin," Ore said.

"And head rubs and hugs," she agreed. Garen sighed to himself as Mina rolled her eyes slightly. While those might be appreciated at the appropriate times, most people didn't consider those "rewards" in the same way. It was good she at least understood that she had to pay coin for honest work done for her. At least, he assumed she was paying her staff and had paid the nightwalkers for their efforts in Tarc. That might be worth confirming outside of this meeting.

Rei moved them on to a review of the security processes that would be implemented when Sasou arrived at the castle again for the investment. That was much easier to do this time around, having had the lessons and practice once. "I'll set our own guards to line the passage from the carriage into the castle, Garen," Ilena informed him. He gave a nod and noted it. It meant she likely had an ulterior motive, but he didn't really care one way or the other. He'd put the most trustworthy on the walls around the courtyard.

"Are there any particular places other than the ones last time you'd like me to set guards?" Garen asked both of them.

"Yes," Rei answered rather quickly. Garen raised an eyebrow at him. "I'll be making him spend time with the lords this time. He'll be wanting to test what state they're all in now, and who's remained after my cleaning them out. He was too curious about Ilena last time to do it then. See that the extra guards are set in the gathering places of the lords. He already knows where they are. He had to live here with Mother for his own training." He glanced at Ilena. "That was at the time he moved against the Doll House."

Ilena didn't look at him and the flash of pain on her face made Garen pause. He glanced at her guards and the pain was on their faces and in their hunched shoulders as well. It hadn't gone well, then, that battle, for all the whole of the nation knew it had been successful in the end. He wasn't too surprised to see Rei reach out a hand for her. She handed him her hand and looked into his face. "Thank you, Ilena," Rei said gently. "Thank you for helping him and all the children of Suiran."

Her eyes brightened with unshed tears and she could only nod back at him. He held her hand until she was able to let go and relax. Garen thought the gratitude from a crown had helped her recover from those pains somewhat. Likely she'd not reported her own losses to Sasou, knowing that the deaths of nightwalkers wasn't important to lords. They'd certainly been important to her. The tenderness she'd shown Danel had loudly spoken to the care she held for them. So had the stories of Elandra and the other nightwalkers that had been taken to Falcon's Hollow. He'd have his soldiers read those stories if it would make sense to, but it didn't.

Rei moved on to let her finish recovering. "What was the report on the paiges in retraining?" Ilena had as ready an answer for that as for anything. Sometimes Garen was rather amazed at the Department. "Pick two who need strict supervision but could be moved up on a trial basis. See they're sent to Lord Odle. He sounds like he's still aware and concerned enough he'll see to their training strictly."

Garen and the others smiled as Ilena bowed her head in acquiescence. Her glance at her guards said that Henry and Marcus would take care of it. "If there are several that are ready to move up, all the middle offices lost a lot of people during the cleaning out. They have the funds to hire replacements. See they're sent to the appropriate offices." He glared slightly at Ilena.

She smoothly answered, "Those that need help and have earned it." Rei gave a firm nod. She bowed her head to him. "What about the newest office that needs people: the census takers?"

"Those are coming from your people," he said without looking at her. Ilena froze slightly, then sighed quietly. He raised an eyebrow at her. "Running out of people already?"

"Well, it's not an infinite number," she scolded slightly. "If you'll take them from the nightwalker half, I'm sure some of them would love real pay and real jobs for a year."

"Fine," Rei answered, but he glanced at Garen, "as long as they aren't well known and on the most-wanted lists. I don't need more soldiers wondering if I've lost my mind. Besides we'll need people in each area, not just here in the castle."

"True," Ilena said and rolled her eyes to look at Ore. He sighed and gave a nod. They'd just had one more thing added to their already rather full plates.

Garen was sure the Region's soldiers would also be called on in the end for the census jobs. "That wouldn't be bad, to have your people pair up with soldiers for the actual count in the field. They'll really get to know each other then. Have them report to the closest garrisons and I'll be sure they're set as secretaries. One guard to officially bully the lords and recalcitrant, and one hidden nightwalker to get the corrupt to talk might get all of the whole count in the end." He couldn't help the ironic grin at his tongue–in–cheek tease. Ilena and Ore laughed. Even Rei had troubles hiding his own spurt of laughter.

Ilena went sober, though. "Garen. See that they take a count of not just people. We need to know what their occupations are and how much they're producing. For the lords we need to know if they're complaining of not having enough while at the same time refusing to produce enough for them and for the region and nation. It seemed like there were some like that. They had enough resources, they just were refusing to have their people do enough work, so they could claim underproduction as their reason for underpaying their taxes."

Rei agreed. "I also saw that as we traveled. We'll sit together with some of the other ministers to put together the final list of questions to be asked. It won't just be a head count. Have you thought of solutions, other than just punishments, Ilena?" he asked.

"Yes, I have," she answered. "I suspect we could convert the census office into a training office and have the following year be a year of training the lords in how to more wisely use their land. If we open their eyes to what they could be doing in ways they haven't thought of before, perhaps that would help the whole thing shake loose better." Her eyes narrowed, "Which will then create the next test to see who needs to be replaced."

"I like it," Rei said. "We'll discuss that when we get closer to the end of the report writing on the results of the census. Any other ideas?"

Ilena shrugged. "If they won't, we can always require it regardless, knowing then what they have at their disposal. And someone else can always pick up on it and make a business out of it, I suppose, depending on what it is. I'd have to see the results, too, to come up with more."

"Okay." Rei sat back in his chair and considered Ilena and Ore for a long moment. "Are you two going to be ready?" he asked quietly.

Ilena took in a deep breath to hold herself at calm and consider the question. Ore twitched slightly and didn't answer right away either. They finally both blinked and bowed. "We will be, after our vacation," Ore promised.

"As long as it's before Sasou gets here, that's fine," Rei answered, trying for firm but gentle. That was a hard mix with these two, Garen knew. He'd already received a visit from Mina letting him know to have the soldiers on extra–sharp watch around the courtyard outside. If they ran, he was to have them arrested, returned, and placed on house arrest immediately — in an inner building of the castle with no easy escapes to the outside. He sighed to himself sadly. While everyone hoped they wouldn't, and didn't really expect them to, they also recognized that it was hard for those who'd been nightwalkers to fight their learned habits.

-o-o-o-

As soon as Garen and David were back in the garrison office, David was headed for the file cabinet and the summary kept of all the prisoners held within it. It had seen a lot of the light of day since Ilena had been announced to the court, and even before. Rei had been working with the office since he'd been working with Ilena to clean out the castle lords.

The prior general had been a little nervous about having all those lords being called to task for their corrupt ways and easily–greased palms. Since more than a few had also been greasing that general's palms, he'd had David "clean up" some of their records. David had done so, since he'd been ordered by Ilena to be obedient to his superior officer, but he'd also shoved the same "hidden" information into a separate file that had been used by the Department of Intelligence to clean said general out of the castle. Garen sighed to himself slightly and got to his other work, not complaining at David at all.

The day's work kept the room quiet except for pens on paper until David stood up from his desk. It was already past lunch time. Garen had snagged food off the cart when it had arrived, needing to pace and stretch enough to get his brain to continue to be creative. The food had helped, too. It wasn't helping that the everyday needs of the garrison were now interrupting him regularly. He raised an eyebrow at David.

David handed over the list he'd been working on. "I've sorted them by ranking, but in reverse time order, which puts the nightwalkers just before the lords." Garen gave a half–smile, understanding the need to hide that ordering. "I've also made sure to include *everyone* we've got in there, as Regent Rei specified."

Garen gave a nod and scanned through the list. It was a booklet's–worth of pages, even as a brief summary. It helped that David had also included ages incarcerated and current ages. That would help him. As he scanned those first two sets of prisoners, he kept in mind the plan he was coming up with to see if there would be sufficient matching. It wasn't all that easy. Most nightwalkers were young, whereas most of the lords who'd been imprisoned were older. He knew many would be able to impersonate older ages, so wasn't too worried, but it wouldn't do to have too great a gap in reality.

Knowing he'd get to have the list back in his hands again, he didn't take too long to reach the end of putting his own few comments to the pages, gave a nod, and handed it back to David. "Deliver it now, then eat. Go back after you've breathed and have a full belly. I suspect he'll be ready to hand it back that quickly," he smiled at David. David took it back with a brief salute and headed out the door with it.

-o-o-o-

Rei took the report from David and excused him with the firm nod of approval and thanks people in positions of responsibility with little time gave. David saluted and disappeared again, respecting that lack of time to relax they all had. He was glad to get his meal in him. He absolutely agreed with the General that the Regent wasn't likely to waste time on that issue. While Rei might have postponed it, it wasn't like anyone wanted such things hanging over their heads for long.

When he was in the Rose office again, taking the report, bound in blue this time, he wasn't surprised to see Rei's pursed lips. The brilliant blue eyes came up to look into David's. "Who put the last few pages into the jail?"

David answered privately, "The prior Regent and his father."

Rei gave a nod. "I've put what I want in there for everyone. Tell General Garen I've sent Mina to investigate. If there are changes I'll send them along immediately."

David saluted and left the room. He sighed to himself as he walked out of the Regional office building. For all Queen Kata hadn't been able to do anything about the ministers, except be present to keep them in line, she *had* taken care of the previous regent. Thus why she'd been there *as* the regent herself. Rei had been saying he'd sentenced the old regent, and was investigating those who that man had placed into prison. Even Garen and David had decided that there were more than one from that era that had been incarcerated wrongly as political prisoners because they'd opened their mouths, or were going to, to incriminate that past regent and his allies.

When he got back to the office, after getting Ilena's notes on the pages, he handed the folder over to Garen. "He's sent Sir Durand to investigate the oldest cases." Garen raised a slight eyebrow at David. David gave a small nod. They weren't the only people to use the office. "He says if there are any changes he'll send word immediately upon notice." Garen nodded and turned his attention to the folder in his hands, untying the knot.

David didn't move from in front of the desk, staying at rest attention, letting his brain rest while Garen reviewed Rei and Ilena's notes for each prisoner on the first page. Since there were a lot of prisoners, David had written on both sides of the paper. It shushed as Garen turned it over, louder than the pens scratching in the room. He made a few notes, then handed it to David.

David took it and let his eyes look at the new notes. While he could memorize it, it wasn't worth wasting his time. He dragged his chair over to the opposite side of Garen's desk, then brought his pen, ink, and paper over as well. Sitting down, he began writing the official document that would pardon or condemn every person in those pages. There wasn't any reason for this office to waste time letting this sit around either.

As they got to the final pages of the report, Garen paused and tapped his finger lightly on his desk, then sat back with a frown as he pondered. David finished his work from the set of pages in front of him, then set his pen down. He looked into Garen's brown eyes that were waiting for him. "Let the rest sit until we hear from the Regent. It's already been this long. To make sure we don't misstep it's better to wait." David had expected that. The following was what he'd hoped to hear. More quietly Garen added, "Go and talk to the ones under investigation. See if they'll talk better knowing their cases are being officially reviewed." He pushed a smaller piece of paper over to David.

David picked it up. On it Garen had written, while waiting for David to finish his writing before, "*Let's help get this over with faster. See if they'll ally with the DoI, if not the Rose Office.*"

"*Do you want her to interview them personally if they agree?*" David asked on the page.

Garen gave a nod. "*We'll have her come in secret. Let me know when you're ready for her.*"

David nodded back and Garen took the paper back. He folded it and set it aflame using the small burner on the corner of his desk. This type of secret communication was common in this office. Probably more things needing to be burned came through this office than any other. Not that it was *supposed* to be common. Usually it meant too much corruption was happening. However, since that's what they were coming from in this castle, it still wasn't unusual to keep the candles on the tables. As a matter of fact, that had become a quietly stated euphemism for "dark secret dealings are afoot", to say, "keep your candle on the table".

David was going to be very busy for a while and sleep might be in short supply. Because he'd been under the prior corruptible general, he was still the point of contact for those who thought he was still trustworthy with corruption's secrets. That had made it somewhat difficult to talk to those who wouldn't trust him in the prison. It had helped in getting clues and information for removing corruption where it had gotten a tight foothold.

-o-o-o-

Garen met Ilena and her guards outside the garrison prison late at night. Previously, Garen had sent Ilena a copy of David's final report on these prisoners, along with Mina's summary report and Rei's expected sentencing. Most of the men that Garen and David suspected weren't in the wrong had been willing to talk if the newest Director of Intelligence would come talk to them directly.

Garen led Ilena down into the far depths of the prison where the "forgotten" were housed. "The Regent's finally decided this place gets to be washed clean," he told the guards on watch in that area. "That data is so old in the files now, we've asked the DoI to come help us dig out the muck from back here," he pointed at Ilena, Marcus, and Henry with his thumb.

He got back hard expressions but relieved shoulders and backs. These soldiers would assume most of them would be offed rather quickly. They could certainly understand that it was better for another department of the castle to get their already–dirty hands dirty with that ancient history. Garen was planning on bringing those prisoners up out of the prison the same time the nightwalkers were brought out. Many of them were now old enough to actually be as old as the lords that needed replacement. He was relieved to have this as another potential help to his plan. If this worked tonight, he'd be able to present his plan in its details to Rei and Ilena at the next security meeting.

They had to carry torches down into these halls. No windows, only a few torches on the walls: enough for the guards to see what the prisoners were doing when they entered, not enough to waste precious resources on them. Very small meals, twice per day, but they did get out into the sun once per week, on their exercise rotations. Lords got windows, visitors, and no exercise rotations. No one wanted them to be broken out of the garrison, but they had to have a level of treatment "sufficient to their stations". Not that that had made any regent nice to their imprisoned lords. Many a rival was back here, too, who needed to die. Many already had.

Garen called out specific prisoners they wanted to talk to, one at a time, and took them to a private office Ilena was waiting in. He introduced the prisoner to Ilena and let her do the talking. Mostly she answered questions, getting the prisoner to relax enough into talking, then she let them talk. Garen was surprised how often she could bring up a person that the prisoner knew from that far back. Often they were happy to have her use them as personal references, or second witnesses to their actions. For a few prisoners, that clammed them up. When she couldn't pry the first one like that open, Garen asked, "Are you unhappy because they're just as corrupt and are likely to keep you in here? Or because they'll give the truth to your lies?"

"It will sound the same," that man grouched at them.

"Maybe," Ilena and Garen answered with shrugs at the same time. Garen smiled inside while waiting calmly for an answer on the outside. He let Ilena finish prying the data out of that one and the rest like him.

Some prisoners complained they no longer had a way to earn money if they were let out. Ilena offered that they could be taught whatever skill they desired. Garen thought that would be a good idea, actually. To start teaching the people who committed lesser crimes new skills while in the prisons, particularly in the cities and villages. That might help them defray some of their costs, too, if they were making things that could be sold. If they had proper skills they could use when released they might get off the streets — at least a portion of them, the ones who cared enough.

They managed to get that hallway done that night, but it would be a few more before this level of prisoner was done. They were the fewest, but it was a large prison. Having it be as full as it was really wasn't good for the castle or the region.

A week later David was telling the visiting families of the lords that their sentence had been set by the Regent. They'd be moving the imprisoned lords to a villa under heavy guard where they could receive letters but no visitors. If the wives wanted to be imprisoned with them they were to let David know by the end of their visit, at which time they were escorted right back into the prison cell. Most of the sons were arrested upon arrival and imprisoned with their fathers, same for nephews or others who were the points of contact with the lord for their corrupt allies.

By the next day those allies were also incarcerated, usually in the town or garrison they lived near. Households were informed by garrison messengers, while squadrons stood by to make arrests and capture those who were part of the greedy cycle. Householders who weren't particularly part of the cycle were told to stay put until their new homeowners showed up, and to serve them.

CHAPTER 142 Courtly Politics

Prince Rei had finally allowed he was ready to meet with the Court of Ministers. Baron Odle entered the large antechamber waiting room of the room that meeting was taking place in. Most of the assistants of the ministers were already in the meeting, having come with their ministers. It looked like he was one of the first of the department heads to arrive. The department heads were of slightly higher rank than the assistants, but weren't part of the ministry meeting with the Regent. Rather they received orders from the ministers who had purview over the various departments.

Prince Rei had attended this second meeting two or three times after he'd arrived at the castle, mostly to learn what went on in them and how the ministers related to the rest of the next level of staff. Then he'd become lost in the minutia of learning what it was to do his own work as Regent and only attended the required–for–him Court of Ministers at their weekly meeting. That had been fine. It was important for the Regent to understand how the governance of the region worked, but to focus on his own duties and work.

Odle walked slowly over to join one of his contemporaries, having been called up by his department head at nearly the same time as that one had been called up by his. They'd both moved up since then, so were still nearly equal in the court. "Do you think we'll see any of Minster Hulmer's assistants at all today?" the contemporary of Odle's asked the companion he was standing with.

The companion shook his head. "Only the ones who must be here, I suspect, if any. I've passed the office at nearly midnight and seen most still bent over their desks. They say Minister Hulmer doesn't leave until nearly two in the morning and arrives shortly after six."

"It was a harsh punishment," Odle's contemporary frowned.

"Perhaps," Odle answered in a quiet voice. The other two men turned to him, raising eyebrows at him.

"You received something similar early on," his contemporary said, to seem to be empathizing with him.

Odle shook his head. "Actually, what I received was an early warning that I've been grateful for." The two men blinked at him, completely not understanding. Odle smiled to himself, letting a very small one out to let them know he understood their confusion. "Not to say it was easy in that moment." That they could accept.

He purposely looked over towards the door they'd enter through next. "Do you think the Regent will stay for our meeting this time?"

They blinked at the door. "He might," the companion answered slowly, "if he wants to continue teaching even us what he expects from now on."

Odle gave his attention to his contemporary, wanting to know his opinion, too. He considered it, then gave a slow nod. "It's not likely he'll let anyone else teach it here at the first, now that he's decided to move. If he's a good ruler, he'll do it himself. So far he's moved in that way." Odle gave a slow nod of consideration.

The companion went to a bland scolding look. "Well, except it's all punishments so far, even from when he wasn't teaching himself."

"Oh, I don't know about that," Odle allowed the words to drawl from his mouth slowly. "*I'm* still in my position, nor was ever removed from it." They blinked at him again. He took a relaxed pose. "Nor have I been turned away unkindly when I've gone to confirm my pathway since then. Rather those who were sent to scold and teach me are quite willing to remain approachable. And they weren't wrong."

They wanted to know more. "We were mostly ignored at this level by Queen Kata, who had to deal with the worst of the Ministers. It didn't help us that she didn't remove them to teach us what she really expected, nor that she wouldn't open her mouth. She only ever outmaneuvered them, playing the same game. It's rather refreshing to have a Regent this time that's quite open about what he'll accept and not."

"It's certainly simpler to know what the boundaries are," his contemporary had to agree, "particularly when it's a Touka sitting there and they usually aren't so clear."

"Princess Ilena was quite clear, it seemed to me," the companion said dryly.

Odle smiled slightly again. "She plays the game the best I've seen, actually." He'd surprised his companions again. "Did you know? The person whom I'd been listening to was sent away in a prison carriage with a few other people from here to Ichijou for sentencing there?"

The mouths gaped open on both other men. "T–to the Throne?"

Odle nodded. "I was passing by the gate on an errand to see it with my own eyes. While I suppose I did need the lesson, and I'm sure I'd rather not have been one picked to be part of the Director of Intelligence's plan to help King Sasou in his actions here, that's what it was more than my own movements." He glanced at the door again. Because Rei had made Ilena a direct report to him, she was the only director in that meeting, nor would she stay for the upcoming meeting, typically. They all assumed that shortly she'd be a minister in her own right in that meeting.

"It was the scolding meeting we had in his office that began to open my eyes to the play," he admitted, returning his attention to his companions. "She played her part too well. It was obviously an act more than a real event for her." He blinked at his companions. "She may have really been tired, but she still was far too calm and still to be herself. She knew the outcome before we even went into the office. Her apology was real, however. She'd had to play the part from the beginning."

Odle's contemporary wrinkled his brow. "You said they've been approachable since then?"

Odle indicated that was right. "While I still prefer to speak with Lord Ore rather than with Director Ilena, because anyone is more approachable than a Touka generally, both have been calmly reasonable with me whenever I should meet them. Lord Ore always listens to what I bring to him and answers with serious intent to help me understand the truth of what's going on in the castle, or to give me his best understanding of what the Regent would expect from any of us. On the rare occasion he even has taken the question to the Regent himself and come back to tell me the answer."

Another blink of surprise came before, "He'll follow through? Have they truly forgiven you then?"

Odle gave a sober nod. "That very day. It only took humility, which isn't that hard to give." He waved a hand. "Of course, holding to the lesson is also required. I'd be receiving more scoldings or be fired if I weren't doing that much." That was expected, but he thought he ought to say it to make sure they fully understood.

He changed the focus, if not the subject. "Sir Andrew came to me yesterday, bringing two of the retrained paiges with him. I'm to see to their continuing education." He lowered his eyelids a little. "I'm sure it's the test to see if I'll continue to be obedient and wise in my position," he relaxed and shrugged slightly, "but it's also still an honor to be trusted sufficiently that they'd think I'd train them to properly be that."

The door was opening to let those out who wouldn't stay. Odle wrapped up with one final comment. "It will certainly help to have two trainees during the time I also have to help with the census and have to set one well–trained person aside to help with the financial audit. Two partial helpers will almost equal one mostly trained person." He lifted his lip slightly at his companions.

While they also found the comparison humorous and understandable, he'd left the words in their ears he'd wanted to. While he might have to figure out how to pay two new staff members, he'd been rewarded to be gifted them long enough in advance to have the worst part of the training completed — including the diverted time of the competent staff who was doing that training — before either of those events began. The Regent did reward. He'd just not been able to in visible ways until now.

The few people moving out of the meeting room had passed on by. "It looks like the Regent will be staying to teach us further today," Odle said almost happily to his companions as he straightened and moved towards the door.

He'd always been a little too confused by the machinations of the court, for all he was a competent administrator. He was fortunate that in his department competency was considered more important than how well the game was played. He was also fortunate he'd had an excellent mentor in his first department head. That man had known how to teach him to read the court faces and gestures, and even how to use them in the logical way he could comprehend and treat as a tool to get what he wanted. He was perfectly content to have Rei move in just as logical ways as he played the court, even if sometimes the comprehension was hidden until later.

It wasn't surprising to take his position and see that Ilena had been kept in the room as well. Odle was quite sure Rei used her for more than one thing at a time. The lords would all be paying closer attention to what the Regent said, since if she heard it as well they knew she'd be watching to see they toed that line. Odle was quite sure that Rei was also training Ilena to understand how the regional administration worked. She'd need that understanding if the King placed her over Tarc.

He was a little surprised to see Ore next to Ilena again. Then he smiled slightly. Ore needed even more training in that than Ilena did. It was nearly a certainty now that they were indeed going to be the ones placed over Tarc. It would be hard to not place a Princess of Touka there actually, particularly one that couldn't be married off to another nation, but had been kept close by the side of the brothers instead.

Odle thought Minister Preston didn't need to worry quite so much about his daughter going there, but that was only a guess. No one but the Regent and Director of Intelligence knew anything about the Tarc, so it wasn't a zero percent chance. Maybe they'd get some of that lesson today — if Rei was inclined to forgive Hulmer. Odle looked around the room. He didn't see Minister Hulmer at all, nor any of his late staff. Well..., maybe not then. If Rei hadn't released the punishment on Hulmer at this last meeting then he likely wasn't done punishing Preston nor Eadsley either.

While Odle's punishment by Ilena had been public by necessity of whatever plan they'd been working to, he was quite glad he'd escaped whatever punishment either she or Rei would have given him if he'd continued on the path he'd been on. It had been an honest error and they'd respected that from the beginning. It had been an interesting way to weed out those who'd been in his same position from those who should have been released from service earlier than later. Odle was quite sure few of his contemporaries would have logically analyzed it all like he had, but they'd all learn it eventually: who Rei was and what he would and wouldn't tolerate ...and that it was all for the good of the region and the nation.

-o-o-o-

"Lord Ore," Vicount Aiden kept his voice calm and quiet. He'd walked up behind Ore, not wanting his student to run away from him. Ore turned to him with his eyes already wide. Aiden smiled at him kindly. "Are you holding up okay?" he asked quietly.

Ore took in a deep breath and let it out, trying to relax even a little. "It's not a simple thing to be in these meetings," Ore admitted quietly. "They always let me hide in the office before now." His eyes darted to either side as the department staff flowed past them, the meeting having just finished. It had been a hard thing for Ore to sit through both that and the prior Court of Ministers.

Aiden had approached Ore at the end of the meeting from an angle that would allow the leaving members to see them, but they wouldn't be in the way. This post–meeting time was a time that the lower officers, officials, and staff members of the castle could mingle. Certainly casual meetings happened other times, but here it was easier for quick conversations. "I'm sure you'll be okay eventually," Aiden reassured Ore. "You're already doing well before now."

Ore blinked, then gave a reluctant nod. "Well, that's one on one. To follow all of the details of a meeting like this one is rather overwhelming as of yet."

Aiden put on a thoughtful expression then gave a slow nod. He looked at the passing persons and noticed one standing not too far off, waiting politely for the two of them. He noted it, but didn't react, turning back to Ore instead. "I don't think you need to keep track of details just yet. I think if you only come to understand the flow for now. After all, details change all the time.—"

"Lord Aiden," was called out from near them.

Aiden ignored it and continued, "— It's learning to understand what topics are important to talk about, and how to recognize when people just want to blather on about their favorite pet projects." Aiden *was* listening, for all he'd not reacted to the voice. He noted that the first man had stepped up and interrupted the second. "If you pay attention to how Regent Rei distracts those and returns them to the important things, that's the easiest to learn first, I'd think?"

Ore considered it, then agreed. "It will likely take a few rounds of practice to learn the flow, though," Ore seemed a bit depressed, but Aiden knew he could play that. Ore liked sympathy whenever he could get it.

"Ah, I'm sorry, Lord Ore, Lord Aiden," a flurry brought another person into their conversational area. "Lord Aiden, I'm sorry I haven't more time. I've been asked to finish this report post-haste." Aiden and Ore both blinked at the man. Aiden waved it off politely, saying he'd catch up with the man later. The flurry disappeared, leaving behind the feel of a fall wind–storm that had brought fallen leaves with it and taken them away with it again.

The second somewhat less impatient man stepped forward to take advantage of the interruption. When Aiden turned back to Ore, the man did push his way in. "Lord Aiden, I haven't received an answer yet to my question to you." Aiden turned back to him slightly less politely as Ore's lips also pursed just a little. The man pushed on regardless, "I was hoping to know when I might receive an answer?" At least the tone of the lesser lord was polite in understanding he was being an interruption.

"I should have it to you in a day or two at most," Aiden answered him. The man wasn't all that pleased, but only thanked Aiden and also disappeared with the final stragglers from the meeting. A few other pairings and small groupings of persons were left in the room, or were walking slowly out of it as they talked. Aiden turned back to Ore. "I'm sorry, Lord Ore," he said.

Ore waved a hand. "No, I'm sure Master would rather you handle it than him, and he's very good at escaping so he doesn't have to."

Aiden smiled a small knowing smile. "And have you already learned and practiced that yourself?"

Ore's mouth dropped open just a little, then he gave his dry teasing look. "And would I have been caught by you if I had?"

Aiden smiled a little wider. "And would I have caught you if I hadn't already practiced moving fast enough to the main person I needed to talk to right away?"

Ore's eyebrow raised, and then he had to agree. "I'd rather call someone to my office," he said dryly.

"Well," Aiden wasn't willing to let him get away with that yet, "but there are things that rightly should be done at times like this." He turned to the first man waiting on him patiently and held out his hand, inviting the man into their conversation. "Lord Ore, I'd like to introduce you a little more formally to Vicount Finlay." The man moved up and bowed to Ore. "He has several skills and qualities I think you'd find helpful."

He felt Ore stiffen a little, but he greeted Finlay well enough. Aiden had made Finlay somewhat uncomfortable suddenly as well. Aiden smiled at both of them and got them started on a conversation between the two of them. When Ore began to fidget just a little, Finlay excused himself politely and went on his way, giving Aiden a little glance of confusion on his way out.

Aiden let Ore escape then as well by taking him out of the room and into the outdoors. He stayed with Ore, knowing the knights were following behind. He'd asked Henry to take Ilena off early so that Ore wouldn't have following after her be his excuse to escape before Aiden could catch him. When Ore finally relaxed enough from seeing the blue sky and breathing the outside air, he turned a curious look on Aiden. Ore frowned at Aiden for a bit, then finally asked, "Why did you do that? What were you testing?"

Aiden blinked at him calmly. "You need someone who can stand at your side after your lessons with me are done. I was testing the ones I've been thinking of. I think Finlay would do very well, actually. You'll want to be testing him more that that, I'd think."

Ore blinked wide eyes. "I think we have enough people assisting in the office. Surely one more isn't necessary.

Aiden considered that for a while. Ore wasn't wrong that there were lots of people there to help already, but that wasn't really it. "And which one understands the lords and castle administration?"

"Isn't that Grandfather?" Ore answered with a frown.

Aiden shrugged. "I think he's household, not nobles, isn't he?"

Ore gazed into the distance, then shrugged. "Probably," he agreed, "but I think I'll test him all the same. He was the House steward for a long time."

Aiden let that go on for a while, then asked, "He's been trained to the court formalities?"

Ore almost missed a step, then slumped with a small groan. "Fine," he said so quietly Aiden almost didn't catch it. Still, it was Aiden's win and he smiled to take the point.

-o-o-o-

Count Eadsley swallowed down the bitter taste in his mouth. Regent Rei was still obstinately refusing any minister from accessing him directly without a prior interview scheduled, and he wasn't scheduling them. Postponement excuses were all anyone was getting from the Rose office staff. However, Eadsley was now desperate enough to take the only reasonably fast option available to him.

He scowled at the door in front of him, then knocked and entered. Only a small amount of his frustration was left on his face by the time he could see the petite red–head sitting at her desk towards the back of this small office: the Lotus office, office of the Assistant to the Regent over Petitioners. He walked as calmly as possible, wanting to stride in his anger, his skin crawling at having to enter it at all. He'd managed to pry an appointment out of Mizi before she'd officially opened the office, saying it was highly important and promising it would be brief. Having to humiliate himself that much had already been extremely difficult.

"Minister Eadsley," Mizi's green gaze watched him openly as he approached her desk. She hadn't bowed her head to him in polite graciousness since she'd been crowned on her wedding day. At least that prior level had been somewhat acceptable. The lack of that simple gesture was the open reminder that she'd been raised up above him. It still stuck in his craw.

Worse was that his next act was to bow slightly to her, as stiffly given in disapproval as he'd ever approached her. "Princess Mizi."

"What may I do for you?" she asked. Even the question was open, slightly cool, a commoner's casual attitude underneath it. She'd never be able to be disingenuous, nor even coat her words with the smoothness of any dark or selfish intent.

"I've come to learn if it would be at all possible to sway the mind of the Regent as regards my prior assistant, Hubert Riley. His loss to my ministry, particularly of such a sudden notice, has caused great chaos." It wasn't so great, but in this case he was trying to gain a positive answer so would need to show sufficient evidence to get it. It was beyond a mere inconvenience or Eadsley wouldn't have come at all.

Mizi sat back in her chair, still upright and paying full attention, her hands clasped lightly on the desk in front of her. "I'm sorry the Ministry of Public Works is finding such a sudden transition difficult, Minister Eadsley, but it won't be possible. As it was, the Regent had been scolded just that morning by Minister Preston for not having enough experience in his offices. Rei was glad Lord Nedlow had finally reached a point in his training of the assistants that he could call up Lord Riley to help as well, thus meeting Minister Preston's complaint as quickly as possible."

Eadsley could feel himself pale a little. He'd felt the sharp pang of anger at Preston, even if small, at her words. He tried to dismiss it as quickly as possible. Those words, and Rei's actions, had been calculated to begin to get the ministers at odds with each other. Particularly those ministers set against Mizi.

Everyone knew of Preston's punishment. Preston had been whining and wheedling every other minister in desperate attempts to discover just what nation the Regent was planning on sending his daughter to. They all knew he was desperate because the strongest evidence pointed to the backwater, unknowable Tarc. Eadsley understood and was just as glad he had no children to be sent anywhere. However, that didn't make it any easier that his own sturdiest support had been pulled out from under him.

Quietly Eadsley replied, "Wasn't that because Minister Preston was thinking of you when he said it?"

He couldn't be surprised when Mizi barely blinked. "Perhaps. However, I was placed in this position because I have the proper skills, in particular my training to research and investigation in my two years at Kouzanshi, and because I already understand sufficiently the mind of the Regent from the time I was serving him at Ichijou until now. When I answered competently to those who came and accosted me outside of appointment times as I was in training to the Regent's office, Regent Rei determined I'd answered to all of them sufficiently well. Because I've the humility to admit when I need to seek his advice, he's satisfied with having placed me here."

It didn't help Eadsley that now he wanted to strangle all of those impatient idiots for even deigning to ask an unproven, newly come young woman to intercede on their behalf. If he thought of it as them getting what they weren't expecting he could almost forgive them. No one expected her to actually have intelligent thought or words come out of that mouth until she opened it. Nor did anyone expect her to stand as a stone wall before her husband in his defense. Well..., the court hadn't before they were understood to be an item. Everyone who'd watched or participated in the struggle before they'd been married knew it with great clarity, now.

Eadsley returned to the topic at hand to be able to escape sooner, and to distract himself before he was the one who slipped. He'd only have the one upper hand: that of playing the court game better than Mizi could, because he had the lifetime of experience she didn't. He didn't let his thoughts go any further down that road. Bringing his other thorn into his thoughts wouldn't help him at all. "Could the Regent perhaps be persuaded to allow Lord Riley to return to my office for long enough to train his successor once Lord Riley is sufficiently trained to the Regent's office?"

Mizi considered the request thoughtfully, then said with slight apology, "I can bring it up to him so he knows you've requested it. It may not bear much fruit, however. I know that he's watching to see if Lord Riley will be sufficient to the weight of what's needful to be done. Regent Rei has several other potentials in mind that he may bring in if Lord Riley isn't sufficient to bear the final amount of the load.

"He mentioned to me that he hoped Lord Riley would be sufficiently competent and as useful to him as he'd seen from Lord Riley's efforts in the Ministry of Public Works. He'd like to not have to cause other ministries the same struggle yours is having, but if required, he'll have to." Slight worry creased Mizi's brow. "It's possible that he'll be concerned that if he allows Lord Riley time away from his duties here that it will add the requirement that Rei pull at least one more from a ministry to carry even that temporary burden."

Mizi sighed in slight regret. "Of course, he may have to anyway, but that's his to weigh and determine. He also understands that if the Ministry of Public Works is disturbed for too long his own burden will be increased proportionally." Green eyes rose to look into Eadsley's eyes again. "I'm sorry, but at this time that's the best I can do. Perhaps when Lord Riley has been sufficiently trained you'll see him again for that long."

Eadsley bowed an even stiffer and smaller bow than the first. The, "Thank you," barely made it past his teeth his jaw was so clenched. He turned and walked out of the office at the same pacing he'd walked into it, holding tightly to it the whole way out of the upper offices and downstairs to his own office. Only once he was behind his own closed door did he allow his rage at being completely boxed in loose.

When his need to be outwardly angry had passed, Eadsley sat in the chair behind his desk and thought very carefully of what Rei's strategy likely was, and what he could do to counter it. If he didn't warn the other ministers, or have them at least understanding the war that had come upon them because they'd thought to come between the Regent and his beloved, they'd be divided and conquered before they understood well enough to remain the watchdogs of the royals.

He ordered his secretary to call for one of the lesser assistants. Behind a closed door, he ordered that sometimes–spy to discover who all of the strongest assistants were in each ministry as quickly as possible. Eadsley would need to confirm his connections to those that were just as likely to lose their assistants as he'd had, and before one or more of those ministers came to hate him because it had been his fault vicariously their essential personnel had been stolen.

Even that was a risky move, since if those ministers found out he was sending that spy, they'd naturally assume that Eadsley was looking for one to replace Lord Riley. They wouldn't be wrong, but that wouldn't be the reason he'd give them. He'd only warn them Rei was on the warpath. Not that they needed the warning. Rei'd not let any ministry he was angry with get by unscathed already. It was more that if they were going to stay a united front to keep the upstart youths from taking over when they weren't experienced enough to yet, the ministers needed to stay united and share as much intelligence as possible to stay even that half–step in front.

Eadsley didn't ignore completely the point that one of those upstart youths was about to be titled as a minister, was already on Rei's side, and was already very strong. That would be suicide in this war. But he didn't think on it too hard or long today. He'd have a raging headache already as it was until the next morning. He didn't need to add having to be in bed with an herbed cloth to his head to his day. His ministry couldn't afford that when he was personally having to handle half of Lord Riley's load just to keep them moving forward.

-o-o-o-

Ilena put down her pen with an explosive sigh. "Ore," she called firmly, "I can't sit still any longer. We're going into town."

Ore closed his eyes and sighed. He was in the Upper office while she was downstairs, but he heard that far well enough. They were still trying to get settled into the routine again, but after a week things *were* far enough along that a break would do all of them good, he supposed. "Okay," he responded, giving an apologetic look to Grandfather.

The venerable man gave back a sympathetic grimace and waved Ore off. Grandfather had been working for Ilena for many years already. He knew she really would explode and would be able to focus better for the run and time out of doors.

Ore, Petroi, and Thayne met Ilena, Marcus, and Henry in the courtyard, coming over the balcony railing to land on the patio. Ilena didn't let them pause long. She was headed for the Cat gate, dragging them along with her as soon as toes touched pavement. Ore needed to let off steam, too, and wasn't ready to face Nijoushi in the mood he was in. He was equally as sure Nijoushi wasn't ready for Ilena in the frame of mind she was in.

As soon as they were through the Cat gate, Ore didn't let Ilena whistle for the horses. He leaped at her to capture her, growling as he did so as his warning. He made sure he "pushed" her to head out into the open rolling hills north of the castle. She leaped out of his reach, then took off running. They left their guards behind, not really caring at the moment if they kept up or not.

They chased each other around the field until Ilena finally stopped running. She closed her eyes and breathed deeply of the crisp air. Late fall snow had fallen recently. They'd stirred up the white dusting pretty good, having slipped and slid more than a few times as they'd made turns. Fingertips on the ground had helped stabilize them and return them to their footing. It was good practice, actually.

It was nice that it was a sunny day. That made it warm enough the heavy winter cloaks, hats, scarves, and gloves weren't necessary. The layers they were used to indoors were enough. That much was still warmer than most nightwalkers had to make it through the chill winters with. Besides, the run had warmed them up quite nicely.

Ilena finally opened her eyes and turned to look into Ore's watching eyes. "Are you ready?" she asked him.

"I guess," he frowned at her a little. "Why now? You don't ever go into town unless you have a reason to actually be there or I drag you along with me."

Ilena slumped. "You won't like it any more than what you're already expecting."

"Then you should go yourself?" he asked.

Ilena shivered. "Ah, no. I'd rather not. *I* don't like it either. If you'll come we can hold each other's hands and get the dirty deed done."

At that Ore raised both eyebrows. "Then we should send the boys and not go at all?"

Ilena laughed one short dry laugh. "No. That won't do this time, sadly. If I could I would have." She turned to look towards the city then took a large breath. Softly she said, "We have to review the new regalia, approve it, and bring it back if its acceptable."

Ore felt his blood go to his boots. He swallowed a suddenly dry mouth. He was even less ready for that than to be tested by all the nightwalker Heads who didn't like he was called the King of Nightwalkers by those he didn't even know. To have to see objects that he'd have to wear to show to all the world just what heights he was being made to live to would make it far more real than he wanted to have to believe just yet. It had been enough to be Consort to the Second Princess, Count Falcon's Hollow. That much he could live with comfortably. Grand Duke was far more nobility than he'd ever wanted.

He quietly moved without much thought to Ilena's side and took her hand in his, seeking comfort from the uncomfortable thoughts and feelings that had come over him. Her warm hand wrapped around his and held on tightly. "We still can't run from it, can we?" he asked, trying to not wish for it so desperately.

Ilena held on even tighter. "No, Ore," she answered quietly back, "as much as even I'm not wanting it to go that far. If we run now, we'll be hunted down as the Nightwalker King and Queen we are — by Sasou himself as traitors to the kingdom for running from our honest required work. He really doesn't have anyone else to do that work for him. If we'll only rule over the night we'll work counter to what he needs for this land to prosper and have peace." She turned to Ore and her expression was desperate and sad.

Ore stepped up to hold her in his arm, not letting go of her hand with his other hand. He could encourage her, knowing how hard she'd worked for the people of Suiran, how strongly she'd held to her role as a princess, and knowing she despised nobles as much as he did and why. It was much harder for him to apply it to himself.

He'd always run from the nobility he'd been born to, finding it only full of corruption and pain, something to reject with disdain. Running the opposite direction didn't earn one the strength to do what needed to be done when finally facing it. She and Rei had helped him turn around and accept the level he was currently at, which wasn't much different from what he'd been born to. To be placed within the top levels of nobility in the nation was different. It was hard to believe he could do it without facing everyone below him as the angry freelancer nightwalker thief.

Ore drew in a deep breath and let it out in a long whoosh. He gave one more shudder, then said, "I might be able to do at least today's chore today. ...Maybe." He gave a grimace.

"Yeah," Ilena grimaced with him. "I think I can really only do it today because I'm so needing to be out of the house. Otherwise, I'd put it off longer ...like forever and get into trouble."

Ore smiled at her. "Well, let's not have you getting into trouble." He kissed the tip of her nose and got them moving towards their guards and Nijoushi.

-o-o-o-

Grandfather sighed and collected up his papers, leaving the Upper office of Intelligence to Jefferson and Colin. He wasn't of an age to be jumping over balcony railings to the ground level below, so he walked out the main entrance to the Upper office into the inner hallway of the castle wing that had been only residential until Ilena had been sent to live there. It was still mostly residential, it was just that the whole of the Immediate Family was also the Department of Intelligence, so it was now also their workplace.

Grandfather's eyes scanned the single rooms as he walked down the stairs between the bedroom side and the suites. Rio was in the first room on the second floor, Amber in the second. The nurses had moved in quietly taking up the other two rooms on the second floor, two of them having to share one of the rooms. Jefferson, Colin, and Liam had rooms on the main floor. His room, shared with his wife Leah, was there also.

It was nice he got to at least be in a different room for sleeping than for working. It was even nicer to be able to share it with someone pleasant to be with and a friend. They'd both been single for a very long time — until this year when Ilena had finally been ushered by them to her place of belonging beside Ore and behind Rei.

He sighed again as he put his hand to the handle of the door into the Lower office. This room in particular, and the people in it, needed help sooner than later. Grandfather calmed and let his presence go ahead of him into the room.

It helped that Justinian was out with Ilena and Ore. Justinian and Liam had been called by Petroi to go with the royal couple and their guards into Nijoushi, requiring a carriage and six guards rather than four for the trip into the unsettled city. Justinian was often the most tense person in the room. His usual place in the room was sitting as close to the door Grandfather had entered as he could, on the left wall in a chair. Justinian needed to have someone close by who knew him and who he knew could keep him calmed. He never did act out. He was just afraid of being triggered. If he had a restraint somewhere in the room, he could relax.

Reynold glanced up to see Grandfather, then returned to his writing. Another desk had been added to the Lower office suite just for Reynold to write up all of his research at. It was set next after the two chairs where Justinian usually sat and before the door to their bedroom. Reynold was very lost in writing down everything he'd observed in Tarc while there for the last five years as a researcher. Even more, he wanted to get down everything from the Marluk'nak' of Chaos and Change. Because he was so lost in his work, he wasn't often one of those that needed eyes on him. However, he'd likely start asking questions of everyone soon to confirm his details.

Grandfather would make sure Reynold started with Justinian — mostly to keep Justinian busy but also because that partnership needed that little push next. It might seem odd to some that Ilena would create partnerships with wide age disparities, but for all Reynold was thirteen years older than Justinian they shared a very similar background. That meant that Reynold understood Justinian at a deep level that Justinian needed any partner to have. So far that much had been working well.

Adding the desk had filled up the left hand side of the room rather tightly, actually. After the door was the chest–high narrow wine cabinet Ore had quietly required shortly after his and Ilena's first wedding. After that was Leah's secretary's desk. She was busy with her own reports. She was perfectly capable of being the restraint everyone in the room needed, but she was as much at wit's end right now as everyone else, since she was the one who scribed for Ilena. As Ilena had just finished writing up her required report to Rei and Sasou, Leah was rather focused on getting it into the standard language of Ryokudo. The written language of Ilena was unique and needed translation.

Grandfather let a light hand of support land on Leah's shoulder but didn't leave it long. He didn't want to interrupt, just let her know he was present to help her. She relaxed under his hand and he moved on. His own goal was the desk in the center of the room close to the patio door. He also needed a surface to work on and Ilena wouldn't be using that one for several hours, nor would she mind if he did while she and Ore were in Nijoushi.

He set his papers down on the desk, confirmed the inkwell had enough ink and the pen in it, then turned for the rest of that wall to look towards the outer corner. Two pairs of eyes looked back at him. "Rio," he said quietly, "it's enough for now." Rio's brown eyes dropped and she relinquished to him, turning slightly away from Amber to focus outside the room on the courtyard and her incoming reports. It was enough that she was willing to let him take the burden she'd been trying to carry of watching both Amber and Justinian at the same time.

Grandfather looked at Amber last. Her chair was between the rocking chair near the patio that Rio sat in and Leah's desk. She'd been relaxing into her work not having the rest of the Immediate Family and staff in the Lower office, but she was quite tense again now that they were all present. She looked relieved to have him at the desk rather than Ilena, which wasn't surprising but was a little worrisome.

Amber was newly come, relatively, to the staff of the Department. She was having the hardest time adjusting to the new position. Not in the work to be done. They'd worked together closely for the first month the household had been gone on the progress around Suiran. She'd learned to take the reports, write them up, and do investigative things rather well, working hard to be quick about it to help him, Jefferson, and Colin who'd been the only ones left in Nijou during that time.

She'd done admirably well on her own for the month the household was preparing to go into Tarc and been there. He'd noticed she'd become a little unsure during the time they were waiting for the household to arrive from the border, and now she was this tense again. He called Amber over to him with a gesture. When she was standing in front of him, he asked quietly, to not interrupt the others, "Is it troublesome to have Mistress Ilena ignoring you since they arrived?"

Amber clasped her hands in front of her skirt. She took a deep breath and considered the question. "Well, it's nice to be acknowledged, but no, not really. It was so fast to be brought in before everyone left, then to have no one here, that it's okay to just observe for now. I can see she's stressed out and no one's really very present or patient when like that. She greeted me when they first arrived. I'm sure —" Amber cut off and closed her lips.

Grandfather watched her without judgment for a moment, but she chose to not finish the thought. That was good, to have the restraint, but it also meant that Amber was less than settled. That wasn't good, actually, when Ilena was what she was. "Observation will teach it to you best," he agreed, "however, if it really is more than you can deal with, please let one of us know. I've appreciated your help, and your capabilities are a good fit, but it's very difficult to work closely with Mistress Ilena."

Amber's eyes glanced towards the patio then back again. She bowed her head slightly and softly said, "I'll continue to work for it for now."

Grandfather pondered her longer. She liked Marcus a lot, and the whole of the Immediate Family understood Ilena had called her up because she could do the work but also so that Marcus could see if Amber could be a match for him. Dinners had been a little tense, even before they'd left for the progress. Amber was just as tense around Rio. It often seemed like she stood alone in a hidden place while with everyone in the office. "Why?" he asked her softly and kindly.

He watched as Amber drew in a breath, sorted through and rejected several answers, then finally said quietly, "If Mistress Ilena believes I can do it, I want to try, to see why she believes that."

Grandfather's eyebrow rose slightly on its own. Amber wasn't that deep, unless she'd been learning things from her observations. He wasn't going to get a different answer from her, by the look on her face, though. He turned from her slightly to end the conversation and return to his work and let her return to hers. "If you wish to believe that's your reason, then perhaps you might learn it, and it might bring you comfort."

When he was seated, he looked into her eyes. "You may want to add that question to the many things you're considering at this time. When you can answer it honestly to yourself, you'll know then what direction to face and how to walk." Her expression was going to either panic or distress. He added kindly, "We'll be here regardless, walking alongside you. And if you decide you want to be released, we'll do so without rancor. No one in the House of Mother is required to do a thing they won't do."

He watched Amber walk away from the corner of his eye. The look she gave to the oblivious Rio was quite poisonous. Grandfather sighed. Rio wasn't helping her partner in ways Amber could accept. There was the main problem. Ilena wasn't paying attention to what Rio *was* doing, so Rio was working in the dark to help her partner understand the Immediate Family.

CHAPTER 143 Return to Falcon's Hollow

In Kouzanshi to the far west, several weeks after the royal couples had returned home to Nijou, a spy knelt before his Head. This Head was lord in his own right, set to his position by his father, who'd been set there by his father, who'd been set there by King Sasou's grandfather. Marquis Zade Yosuko stared at his spy with cold neutrality, the nobility learned very young at his father's knee and reinforced by the hold he held over the headstrong Kouzanshi university.

King Sasou hadn't helped much at all when he'd stepped in without a by–your–leave and taken powers over the university held for the last many generations by the lords of Kouzanshi. Taking Zade's sister to be his Queen wife had been lip service to mollify Zade on the surface, but really it had been a message of warning. Sasou would hold the leash that much more tightly unless Zade somehow redeemed himself for doing what had always been done in Kouzanshi.

Zade ground his teeth yet again. It would have been proper form to have received a letter of request from the Prince, Queen, or King at any time asking that the rules of graduation be reviewed and modified. They'd already agreed to accept younger students who showed aptitude. It was the modification to the graduation requirements of a written test being replaced with options for verbal testing instead that had met resistance in the university heads.

Instead of working with Zade, King Sasou had personally stepped in and replaced the Dean and retired a large number of the oldest heads of the university. It had been without regard to understanding just why it had always been a requirement. The university of Kouzanshi was proud to say they graduated the best research minds of the known realms. To prevent any common person who couldn't even read or write from passing with a diploma meant they could preserve their reputation, which was very important to bringing in the best international students. There was little Zade could do about it now, but he definitely was having to deal with the repercussions.

Between the two older Touka siblings, Lord Yosuko's stomach held a perpetual ache he tried to ignore when he was busy with his daily requirements. He did his best to learn what he could do to remove it when he had any spare time at all. Princess Ilena in particular had been a thorn in his side for a very long time, it seemed. His spy had just confirmed that she was indeed the Queen of Night, the nightwalker Head that had taken control of half of his city to see to by the time she was seventeen. She was still only a brat, even for having been recognized with a crown on her head.

His spy looked into his eyes, and continued his report. "I also learned for you why King Sasou stepped in; although, I hadn't expected to." Zade drew in a small sharp breath and held it instinctively, his lips thinning to hold his mouth closed lest his anger burst out.

"The genius student the Dean gushes on about is also Princess Ilena. From before, when her paper was read in the Lord's Conference, the second one that she was rejected from receiving a diploma for, he's been fighting for her to receive her credentials."

Zade froze as his eyes went very wide but stopped seeing in the present. "No!" he whispered. But even as his spy nodded, the pieces all suddenly fell into place. His withheld anger and pent up frustration burst out of him in a fierce blow to the pen holder on his desk as he yelled it again, "NO!"

He turned his back on his spy and put both hands on his desk, leaning on them so as to not hit anything else as the clatter from the flying pens and case finally settled back to quiet. His arms shook and his stomach lurched and tried to leave him. The *sneak thief* that had hidden from him and bested all of his men at every turn in the city until she was Queen of it, keeping for herself illegally all the tax income she *should* have been turning over to him, was a *Touka genius*.

And not just any Touka genius. Sasou might keep the kingdom. Rei might hold it sovereign over any comers in war. *Ilena* was so broad in her understanding, knowledge, and capability — according to the Dean and others — that she wouldn't be held down. Zade trembled. He'd already been fighting that genius, that capacity to lead and rule and move in the ways of royalty, for years to no avail.

"Why didn't he say?" he whispered, but asking the question aloud made him already answer it himself. "Shicchi." The name left such a bitter taste in his mouth. That lord had been another thorn in his side that he'd been able to ignore most of the time, and had to scold often enough as it was. He thought back to all those times, but the only time Pakyo Shicchi had ever had a girl by his side in Kouzanshi had been at the Lord's Conference so long ago. Surely Sasou had seen it at that time and recognized her somehow.

Zade straightened and folded his arms, his bitter expression going to a scowl. He pressed his arms against his stomach, trying to get that to calm the pain down sufficiently enough he could think. It really was the worst case he could think of, one that made him have to understand why Sasou had stepped in without saying anything, for all that didn't make it any better. If his lips were sealed he would have just barged in to get what he wanted.

Zade wasn't feeling like forgiving regardless. Ilena still had a large debt she owed him, even if the University had finally repaid her their debt. He'd seen her name come through in the report with her newest credentials on them.

Zade's eyes turned to his secretary who flinched back at the anger he couldn't control just yet, it had been pulled to the surface so forcefully.

"Send a letter to the *Princess*." He spit it out. "Tell her the full amount of coin she owes me for all the years of hiding from me in darkness. If she's legally recognized now, and King Sasou knew from the beginning, it's time for her to pay. *All* of it. She can't play the nightwalker in Kouzanshi any longer if she wants to stay in the good graces of the lords of Ryokudo." He'd hold it over her head, even if he had to travel to Ichijou himself to gain proper redress from the Court of Lords themselves.

-o-o-o-

The front courtyard of Falcon's Hollow manor was bustling as household staff emptied the carriage that had arrived. The two inches of snow from the previous night had been cleared away from the drive. That was the proper way to greet the lord and lady of the County. Of course, *they* didn't ride in the carriage. That was for the servants.

The lord and lady of the House rode on horseback, as was appropriate for a County that now held three herds of Tarc horses, pawing through the snow to get at the grasses below. They'd actually acclimated well to the new terrain and weather. Their curly shaggy coats kept the snow off quite well, and kept them plenty warm. Grain and additional hay did have to be set out each day for them. That had taken some practice for them to find and eat, but by now things were settling down into a good routine.

The carriage had been unloaded for nearly an hour before the sound of running horse's hooves echoed around the bowl from the southwest entrance. When the sounds were heard, excitement stirred the air. As the riders rounded the last corner, the waiting household members could see it was a race and two were in the lead, neck and neck. There was a close third and three more not much farther behind. Wagers were made very quickly and calls and cheering broke out, encouraging the riders on. When the riders skidded their horses to a halt, the lady was ahead by a half–nose.

She gave a great grin to the waiting household and then to the lord. "It's Ore's curry for dinner tonight!" she called out. The household groaned. Only the three riders in the front could handle that level of spicy.

"Sounds good to me," Foster, the household marshal, said. "I haven't had that in a very long time."

"Oh, that's right, I have to make it for four when I'm here," Ore remembered with a smile. "You know I let you win, right?" he asked Ilena.

Ilena smirked at him. "I know you like to eat it too, but you didn't 'let' me win. You're far too competitive for that. I could hear you swearing at Kesheb, telling him you'd bring Usuri back out of retirement if he didn't give you more effort."

Ore rubbed the back of his head and looked away. Then suddenly he grabbed Ilena and pulled her off her horse, dropping off his as well at the same time. He tipped her back and took a large kiss. When he righted her again, he grinned. "I still get my reward, anyway, since I know you wanted it, too."

Ilena bopped him on the head, but blushed bright pink. Ore chuckled and nuzzled his cold nose into her neck by her warm ear. Keeping his arm around her waist, he turned to the household, who were all grinning and waiting. "We're home!"

"Welcome home!" was yelled out loudly by all the waiting voices. He loved the wild happy House that was his.

The general mayhem of unloading and taking horses to where they belonged filled the courtyard until it was finally quiet, only the guardian statues of the horse and falcon on either side of the main door left to watch over it. This would be the last visit of the Count to Falcon's Hollow. When they came again, he'd have a different title. There was some trepidation he wouldn't have Falcon's Hollow anymore either, his title was going to be so high, but no one said anything.

-o-o-o-

Ore sank into the couch in the office of the lord of Falcon's Hollow, pulling his wife to sit in his lap. He wrapped his arms around her waist. Ilena wrapped her arms around his neck loosely. "I want a few quiet moments with you before I have to go to the kitchen," he said to her.

They'd sent all the guards away, telling them to go and rest or do whatever they wanted. Only one day of this eight day time they were here would they have to do work: the usual work of count and steward.

"Do we need to get a proper steward?" Ore asked first. "I think you shouldn't have so much to do this coming year. It'll be hard enough with all the other things you'll have to do, and being pregnant and having a newborn."

Ilena smiled. "There's already one here. Betty's been patiently waiting. You and I can train her this week."

"Oh, is that what she's for? I do know her hand is very fine and easy to read." Betty had written down all of the household stories for the investigation against Pakyo and copied them for him. "That would be good then, to train her to it now." He frowned. "But then, why did you take it on?"

Ilena kissed his cheek. "Because I wanted more time with you, and I wanted to see you were trained properly. You know it now well enough."

"Will I know it well enough for the new title? Or does that bring additional things with it?" he asked.

"Additional things, but it's the next step," she answered.

"Count to Grand Duke is a big leap, Ilena dear," he said dryly.

She smiled in reassurance. "True, but I'll be next to you for that one, too."

"It's bigger than what you've already handled, too," he frowned at her.

90

Ilena nodded. "And we'll pull out my lesser officer from the Ministry of Finance to come be our steward for that. He's been getting the practice we don't have in handling the financials for the Region."

Ore nodded. "That's okay, then." He frowned again. "...But, pull him out? We don't have room for one more."

"Ah, well, I mean have him reassigned. I'll have him come to our office for a couple of weeks to see we get proper training and the books are started right without the oversight of the Minister of Finance. Once it's going properly, he'll go back over there and it won't be so much a problem to have the Minister breathing down his neck. If that does get to be a problem, we will have to bring him back permanently, though." Ore could live with that.

He rubbed his forehead on her shoulder, wanting the feel of her to erase the confusion while he was thinking. His brain had been going around in circles since they'd picked up the new regalia two days ago and he'd stared at it in near horror. It was excellently done, at least a second level master's work if not a third on some of the pieces.

It was the level of nobility that was the problem. Count to standing next to his master and the only Grand anything in the country was too big a jump for him. He did understand now why Sasou hadn't let Rei make him the lesser baron he'd expected at most.

"Will the crown change?" Ore asked with trepidation.

"No," Ilena reassured him. "You'll still wear my father's. That's your regalia of Consort." Ore relaxed in relief. "You do know that's your highest title, right?" she pulled back to ask him.

Ore looked up at her seriously. "Nothing makes me happier."

"Does it, Ore?" she asked him back soberly.

Ore got a suspicious niggling and he looked at her closely. "You're going to change it, aren't you?"

"Ah, ever insightful," she commented.

Ore leaned back, slipping his hands to her waist to do so. He considered her a long time. She didn't flinch or change. "All right," he finally said. "It has to be done for the Grand Duke to stick, doesn't it?" Ilena nodded. Ore reached up and ran the backs of his fingers on her cheek, then opened them and cupped her ear. "For you and for Master," he said quietly.

"Thank you, Ore," Ilena said quietly in return.

There were more things to say, but they could wait. He pulled her to him and they kissed tenderly, then again with more passion. He had kitchen duty so they couldn't play right now, but they did spend the next fifteen minutes in tender closeness, finding strength in each other for the upcoming difficult changes to their lives. This time he took her to the kitchen with him to keep him company. It was only for the talking and closeness. To let her touch the food was to ask to have it turn to poison — or charcoal.

One week after returning to the castle, Rei's blue–ribboned report went to Sasou as promised. One week later, the day after the regalia was collected and brought to the castle treasury, Ilena's report went out to Rei and Sasou. Four days after that Sasou held a letter in his hands, his eyes lingering on the accompanying folder tied with the braided black, gold, and green ribbons of his cousin and adopted sister.

Sasou sighed after reading the letter. "I don't think I've ever read such a cold letter from Ilena." He held it lightly as he looked over at Lord Barret sadly.

"You probably have," Michael disagreed. "I seem to recall the two of you had a cold battle just before you relented and let her have Ore."[†]

"Oh, that time. ...Well, yes, perhaps." He turned his frown on the current letter. "It was nice of her to send Ore down so I could see him for myself."

Michael raised an eyebrow. "I thought he came of himself?"

Sasou gave a look that said, *And when has anything happened that she has a hand in that didn't happen by her hand?* Michael kept his mouth closed. Sasou worked that way, too. "Still, it's sad. I would have thought she'd either be thrilled she could come and go freely in Tarc now, or scold me soundly for making her take the position."

"They know the test isn't over," Michael reminded him. "If you want emotionality and a pat on the back, wait until you've rewarded them for it."

Sasou put his chin in his hand. "You do take all the fun out of it, you know."

"Don't send a letter back," Michael scolded firmly. "You'll only make Regent Rei angry."

Sasou placed the letter down on the desk. He picked up the top page of the report and began reading. That made him feel better. He could see all the ways Ilena was setting up the board anew for the new situation that country found itself in. He really did love to play the boards with Ilena, but he wisely followed the advice of his closest advisor. He only wrote the notes for now as to how he'd modify her proposals to talk to her about after she was correctly in her own position to act on them.

Snow and frozen mud were flying from beneath hooves that pounded hard. Three horses were racing against each other, hot breath steaming in the daylight. Left — right — left again, circling around a post to grab a ribbon

---

[†]When Ore arrived in Ichijoutsu and Brok told Sasou about him; his first major test by Sasou being: spying on Rei and Mizi then (not) getting rid of her. Sasou was going to toss him out for not being obedient and Ilena scolded him soundly in her letters because he hadn't been there yet to see with his own eyes.

from a ring, then sight the next goal and head straight for it at a dead run again. The exhilaration of the race beat in the veins, making the rider steam as much as the horse. The race course had already been packed down with practices, then with earlier races. This was the final race, the three going specifically against each other.

These three riders in this race held their seats smoothly, taking nothing away from the run and beat of the hooves of their horses. Their weight shifted easily at the right points to add to the horses' turning radius' needs. The horses knew just when to allow for a ribbon to be reached for smoothly and when to race at full speed. The cheering and calling as they headed for the last straight–away to the finish line grew in volume as the horses approached. That goaded them on to put even more effort into their work.

The three horses were nearly all equal, but one of them was more eager with just the right amount of youth to have a slight edge of energy as well. It edged out in front at just the right moment to cross the finish line first. The watching field went wild. Ore and his newest horse had edged out Ilena and Petroi to win on the field for the first time. The other two had tied for second, only the barest part of a nose behind Ore.

They cooled their horses down, grinning at the high level of competition it had been as they pranced around inside the stable corral that had been set aside for horses to move in without harming the spectators. Ore rode close to the edge to receive congratulatory slaps of the hand.

Ilena laughed, sitting her horse easily, calling to Petroi, "He's finally good enough on his own, just lucky to have gotten a horse that wants to win as bad as him."

Petroi grinned at her. "Master Ore made Kesheb wait until Usuri had trained him well enough. They have practiced hard together."

Ilena nodded, "He's quickly become a match for us." Petroi agreed and leaned over to check how his horse was doing as far as cooling down went, patting the horse's shoulder.

Ore, finally done celebrating his win, came into the center of the corral to meet with them. He took his prize kiss from Ilena, both still on horseback, and a quiet promise of more reward to come later.

"Dance the horses!" came from the crowd and it was taken up. The Houses in Suiran had heard the stories but few had seen it yet.

Ore turned to Ilena. "Will you dance them?" Ilena hesitated. "I'd like for the Family in Suiran to see it at least once."

"Alright," Ilena agreed softly. "You two go to the rail. Have Justinian sing for me. It's hard to feel it here. I'll dance to you. It's a moving forward song and dance, almost a travel dance."

Ore and Petroi slipped off their horses and moved to the rail, calling for Justinian to meet them. Ilena put her hands on the horses left behind and they all turned together and went to the far rail, near the stable. There, she slipped off her horse and moved Reshali just a little ahead of the other two, putting her hand on Reshali's shoulder. She spoke with the horses quietly.

Ore instructed Justinian when he arrived near him. "Sing for Mother to dance the horses home. We are her home." Justinian felt the world around him as naturally as Ilena did.

Justinian's eyes went far away, then he nodded. "Give her an introduction to learn the feel of it," Petroi instructed. Justinian opened his mouth and Ore and Petroi turned to look at Ilena.

The notes soaring into the air quieted the spectators again. Ilena listened, then swayed, the horses taking up the rhythm with her. Then her feet began to move. Left–left–forward right. She moved slowly, learning the dance in her heart and body until it began to flow naturally.

The horses kept with her in pattern. When it became natural, then they kept to the pattern she'd taught them and her dance became gracefully free. The audience was mesmerized as her dance and body told of Mother's love for her Family, and her desire to be with them, Justinian's song leading her to them. The closer they came the lighter Justinian's song became and the lighter Ilena's steps, the joy of returning home becoming part of the song and dance.

As the ending of the song became obvious, Ore stepped forward and joined with Ilena's dance to show the joy of all at the return of a loved one. Justinian ended the song and Ore spun one last time with Ilena, then kissed her gently and long. When they separated, the audience burst into appreciative clapping and cheering.

Ilena bowed, then Ore and the horses, then they called to Justinian and he was made to step out for his own recognition, which made his face both flame and beam with happiness. "Thank you, Mother," Ore said in Ilena's ear.

"I love you, Father," Ilena answered in his ear. They both pounced on Justinian, Ilena embracing him with a word of gratitude and Ore with a rub to the head. With a gesture, Ilena sent the horses to the stable to be properly cared for. The four humans in the corral removed themselves from it to join in the rest and relaxation before the next events were scheduled to begin.

-o-o-o-

There were many competitions that day, before and after, set up for all of the House and Family who came to compete and show off their skills. Long and high jumping, target knife throwing and discus target as well, speed climbing, wall walking on a special wall built for it, tightrope walking between two tall trees, general gymnastics and flexibility tests, wrestling, and foot races were only some of them.

In the knife skills list the reward to the winner was to have a match against Ilena. She danced with the winner, allowing him three attempts before she took him down, just to extend her own fun. (She'd warned him in advance so he wasn't too offended by it.) Ore went against the winner of the stationary target knife throwing in a similar manner, but was a regular participant in the motion target competition, winning by a decent margin there.

When asked if they were going to participate in the hand–to–hand at all, they smiled and refused. They'd already felt what would happen if they went against each other with Ilena fully healed. They'd go for hours, just like Andrew and Mina did with sword. That wasn't useful this day of play and competition.

There was one other competition they'd participate in, starting with the other competitors but only truly competing against each other. It was called for two hours after lunch. When they arrived at the starting position they went from a loving couple back to an extremely competitive rivalry, eyes sparking and evil grins on their faces.

Petroi and Liam stepped up to them, faces stern. "You will not forget yourselves," ordered Liam.

"You will return before sundown," ordered Petroi.

"If we call for you, you will return immediately," Liam ordered.

"You will remember you are married," Petroi ended the lecture and required rules.

When both of them had sufficiently accepted their specific rules, the competition was allowed to begin. At the yell of "Rabbits, begin!" all of the first round of competitors were off. Ilena was fastest at the start, her speed her advantage, no longer hampered by the wound and surgery of her hip.

After three minutes, the countdown began again. At the yell of "Foxes, begin!" Ore and his group were off. This was a speed race of hiding, running, and tracking. Those who were the best at hiding and running were in the rabbit group. Those who were best at the tracking (and usually the running as well) were the foxes.

Ore wanted to know if he could track and find Ilena. He'd need it in the future, was his guess. Because she'd lept out first, and her stride and footprint were well known to him already, he was able to follow her easily until she was in the trees above the bowl of the Hollow.

She'd been excited for this competition. They had very rare opportunities to be up in the trees in the woods of Suiran these days. He followed her, just as happy. Running the trees was his favorite. She had a light foot and hand in the trees. He wasn't surprised. That's the way she was on the horses, too.

It only took the first three trees to understand her range and preferred perches, but he didn't let it fool him. She wouldn't hold to patterns for too long. He kept careful watch for signs she'd back–tracked and taken other routes than the initial pattern she'd set. Still, she held to the pattern longer than he expected. He paused briefly to get his total bearings and realized it was because she was getting out of range of the other competitors first.

Ore was a little surprised she wouldn't use them to hide her own tracks, then stopped where he was. No. She would. It was here she would've returned to, leading him farther out and then making him lose the trail that didn't exist. He hunted, finally finding where she went to ground.

He stayed in the tree, listening closely. His improved hearing helped with this, he found, as did his understanding of what she personally sounded like. He was able to mark and dismiss about five other competitors quickly. His mind worked on various scenarios based on only that one toe print in the skiff of snow on the ground below him. In the end, the only answer was that it had been placed on purpose where it would be easily seen. He looked at the branch just above it and in front of where it would've been.

Ilena had stayed in the trees, only going to ground to make the print and return to the next tree. Ore lept to it and carefully inspected the lower branches, then moved up to the higher ones. *Damn. She's as unafraid of tree heights as she is of being up on horses.* At these heights, longer leaps were required, and usually to smaller branches that more often broke under the greater landing forces.

He took a route one level lower, his own weight not supportable by that level. It added to his time since on occasion he had to climb up to that level to see where she would've gone to next. When her path crossed over where it had been before, he chuckled to himself. She'd watched him go under her and he'd not looked up, focused on the forward path.

From there, she'd turned and gone at a right angle away. He watched carefully for signs she'd dropped back down, then lost her in one tree. He went back a tree and checked again, finally looking up one more level. *Gods, Woman.* She'd climbed again.

He continued to go up and he was suddenly looking out over the woods. His eyes were caught by another tall tree. Instantly he knew that was where she was. He'd been moving, so she already knew he was here. She wasn't moving so he wouldn't see her.

He sat down on the branch and stretched his legs out in front of him. He put his hands behind his head while keeping a sharp watch on that tree. As soon as he moved to go back down she'd follow behind just far enough he wouldn't see her, nor where she went. By the time he made it to that tree, she'd be gone again. Not that that was bad. He'd just keep tracking her. But what he really wanted was for her to go to ground, where tracking her would be easier.

It all of a sudden occurred to him what she'd do. He grinned.

Ilena watched as Ore dropped back down into the trees again. She was very curious as to what he was going to do. He always surprised her in the end. On the other hand, she liked to tease him whenever possible. She dropped down a step behind him in levels until she reached her highest level. Then she carefully made her way by a different route than she'd come by until she could see the tree she'd come from before and Ore had just left.

She paused and carefully scanned the tree and the area. Listening, she couldn't hear anything in the near vicinity either. Ore's scent was in the air, but that was to be expected. He'd just been here. Not quite sure, but wanting to see if he'd gone to the other tree, Ilena finally made the jump into that tree at her current height.

She almost fell out of the tree when Ore appeared above her one level, grinning at her. She did cry out slightly in surprise, then slip down to grasp the branch with her hand, and drop another level. She was going to flee to the next tree but he pressed her hard until the only thing to do was go to ground.

She ran along the longest branch at the final level, feeling Ore land on it, then lept into the undergrowth and ran. Her speed was slowed somewhat in the undergrowth of the forest, but was still faster than most nightwalkers' speed. She took the rabbit's approach at first. Dodging left then right then right, then left then right, doing the random quick forward motions rabbits used to escape their predators.

As soon as she had a straight shot, she was off. She couldn't hear Ore chasing after her, but that didn't mean much. Her eyes sought a hiding place or another place to return to the trees.

Just as she reached the place where she had to turn again, Ore appeared in front of her, reaching out to grab her. She slid and went under his hand, past him, then was up and running again, headed for a branch she'd decided was hers, then right angled it at the last minute and ran up the trunk of another tree.

For another frantic ten minutes, Ilena could feel Ore on her tail ...and then she realized he'd cornered her at the rim of the bowl. She'd lost track of the internal map. She grabbed at the last branch, wheeled around it and launched into the air. She tucked up her knees and went spinning through the air.

Ilena landed over the edge of the bowl on the light snow and skied on her feet down the side of it, leaning back for balance. Carefully she worked her way just a little to her right, knowing where she was. Her speed launched her again and she was in the air over another overhang. Then she was landing and curling into a backwards somersault.

She grabbed two wooden boards and sent them sliding on down the hill, then hid just inside the cave where she could hear and somewhat see if Ore followed after her. Her plan was to leave the cave as soon as he passed by.

Ilena heard the crunch of snow and knew he was near. Just as she was about to move again, a hand reached around the wall and grabbed her arm. She jerked away and Ore moved to stand grinning in the entrance. *Damn. Trapped.* She waited but Ore didn't move.

"I think they said, 'show up before sunset', didn't they?" Ore asked. Ilena nodded once sharply. "That means there's still plenty of time."

Ilena narrowed her eyes at him. "For what?"

"We can do it again, ...or we can avail ourselves of this cave and warm each other up, 'remembering we are married'." He got a wicked look on his face and Ilena crouched down. "I think I wish the latter," he said. "And I claim you as my prize for winning this one."

"Come get me," Ilena purred. She was still the faster one in this arena.

"Oh, no," Ore said, purring right back. "I already claim the win. What I do next is just to set it in your head." Ilena's heart froze. Ore put his hand in his pocket. The smell of an orange filled the cave and Ilena's eyes went wide. Ore pulled the pricked orange slowly out of his pocket and held it up in a hand covered in a lightweight glove that had the fingertips cut off since nightwalkers didn't want to slip while climbing walls — or trees.

Ilena's breaths came faster and her eyes flicked between his face and the orange. She hadn't had an orange in a very long time. They'd only had mikans before they left and on the trip. "No fair," she whispered, her despair in the overtones.

Ore took his time peeling the orange, his eyes never leaving her face. He tossed the peels into the opposite side of the cave from where she was standing. She twitched, wanting to catch them, not willing to move to the place where he'd know to go to catch her. He reached the first fruit section and peeled it off, then broke it in half. It was a fresh, this–season orange. Ilena nearly swooned.

Ore put half of the section into his mouth, then held the other half in his fingertips for a moment. "Take your jacket off and it's yours."

Ilena knew what he was doing, but she also didn't need her jacket to run again. She took it off, not taking her eyes off him or the orange. He threw it directly at her and she caught it, but he'd unexpectedly followed directly after it and he caught her. Her look of surprise made him chuckle. "For liking unpredictability, you're very predictable, Ilena dear."

"You know me too well, Ore," she answered around the piece of orange in her mouth.

Ore lowered his lips to her cool neck and kissed it. "You'll give me my prize now, Ilena," he said low in her ear, "and I'll reward you with oranges."

"Yes, Ore," Ilena moaned in pleasure, already losing to Ore plus oranges.

When they left the cave they were both red with the cold, but warm inside and Ilena was completely satisfied, as was Ore. The rest of the household was surprised to see them return well before their curfew, but they'd only say Ore had won the competition.

The Immediate Family smelled the orange, though, and confronted Ore. He raised his hands and shook his head, saying that he'd only used it after the competition winner was decided. They weren't quite willing to believe it, knowing an orange would have bribed her mouth shut on the matter. She defended him and it had to stand since no one else had been there.

When he was asked why he'd taken it to begin with, Ore answered, "If she'd managed to stay in front of me, I wanted to make sure she came home on time. I would've led her back in with it. She came back on her own, though. I just had to trap her once she got here."

Marcus leaned over and very quietly whispered to Ilena, "You knew he had it on him to begin with, didn't you?" She gave him an innocent look, but didn't say anything.

-o-o-o-

"Your Majesty, it's good that peace with Tarc has been restored with minimal bloodshed. We're also pleased that Prince Rei was able to find your lady cousin in time to help aid that action. However, to recommend her and her Consort, also an unknown, to the position of Grand Duke and Grand Duchess of Tarc.... Isn't that a little...?"

Sasou sighed. He'd been trying for the last several months to prepare Ichijou for this, but he wasn't surprised to get pushed back. "I understand; however, I think you all know me well enough by now?" he lightly dared the minister who'd asked the question. "You remember when I took on the plight of the orphans of Ryokudo, yes?" He got nods. More than a few nobles that had rubbed shoulders with these ministers had been taken down during that action. A few of the cabinet had as well and he'd had no mercy for them.

"Director Ilena was the main source of collecting information from the underworld. She passed that test with flying colors. If you've read all," he put a slight emphasis on the word to remind his ministers he expected them to stay on their toes and not slack off, "of the reports I included as regards this issue, Minister Barret's report should confirm her and Lord Ore's capabilities sufficiently."

His sharp blue eyes pinned down the cabinet members. "Tarc is not a place to give a noble as a reward. The men of Tarc are still wild and unpredictable. The fact that Director Ilena was able to help Regent Rei win in the way they did is proof enough that she and Lord Ore are the best we have within our country to see to their continuing in peaceful relations with us at all."

He shifted slightly to take a faintly more forceful position. "Indeed, as Director Ilena's report states, from their point of view this is a year of testing, to see if they'll even be willing to remain peaceful. It's my preference to keep those whom they've already accepted in front of them.

"It's because we must also face Brulak and the other nations around us with firm resolve that I find it necessary to instate them immediately to the new posts of Grand Duke and Grand Duchess. Selicia watches us closely since Tarc interfered with them. They wish to know if they'll now be able to relax and have their own peace."

He was getting about the reaction he expected. They understood (he'd included all this in his own summary to them), but they weren't comfortable regardless. He shifted into a conciliatory pose. "I do understand that it's hard for you to accept it as it stands when you haven't had the opportunity to see for yourselves. Perhaps an interim solution might be acceptable?"

He got accepting or thoughtful expressions to that. "In order for them to be effective in Suiran and Tarc, I can instate them as interim Grand Duke and Grand Duchess. Once the weather's clear again for traveling and it can be fit into their schedules, they can come here for you to review their qualifications in person and a more formal investiture can occur at that time."

He paused and waited to see what they thought about that option. It was sometimes hard to be a good king. It was often so much easier to just order people around and expect them to accept anything the king desired. That led to discontent, resentment, and eventually insurrection. It was far better to accept that the lords who helped the king run the kingdom were in their places for very good reason (because they were), and that their advice and good will was both appreciated and considered.

Still, keeping the kingdom in peaceful growth was his responsibility in the end. Thus, when his board demanded an action had to take place, they needed to be able to bow to that requirement. This was as far as he was willing to bend for them on this issue. Brulak was already grumbling at him, and not in ways that were friendly at all.

Rei and Ilena had swooped in and taken Tarc suddenly when Brulak had been trying to worm its way into taking Tarc by strategy, the same as the Lord of Tarc had taken Selicia. As a matter of fact, Sasou was fairly certain that it had been a worm of Brulak that had convinced the Lord of Tarc to even try from the beginning. It wasn't a thing any man of Tarc should have considered: to work by silent strategy. The Tarc as a rule were face forward and blunt in their actions.

It couldn't be proven, however, even with the spies of Brulak Ilena had found and cleaned out of Tarc. It could only be said that — like even himself — the nations around Tarc had wanted to make sure it wouldn't suddenly become violent. He did wish he'd been able to have that sort of evidence. He was relieved Ilena had left the few remaining ones there and was watching them closely. He'd likely need that evidence within the year.

"Well, certainly to keep our neighbors calmed, they've surely proven themselves capable enough to be considered interim," one of the more moderate ministers allowed.

"It's also our way to see what they'll do there, to see if they have the capacity to stay there," another one agreed — one who didn't want to have anything to do with Tarc. By preference that minister would have rather had Tarc not be under Ryokudo at all. He most likely preferred Ilena's plan that Tarc might eventually some day become its own nation again.

Sasou would be using that minister to press that exact desire as often as he needed to, but for now, he needed everyone to agree to the opposite. He merely gave a nod of agreement to the statement of testing. It wasn't too much longer before the rest gave in. It wasn't like there were any of his own ministers that wanted to add Tarc to their plates, and Ilena *was* a princess, so it was only right to use her in that sort of position.

Sasou hadn't been willing to let Ilena come to Ichijou for the court and cabinet to test until they agreed to this much. He didn't need his cabinet making him put aside Aryana to marry Ilena any more than Rei did the Suiran cabinet. While everyone knew of Queen Mother Kata's hatred of the current ruling family of Selicia, that wouldn't stop them from wanting a perceived alliance between the two nations. It wouldn't really be one. Selicia would take Sasou marrying Ilena as a first step towards potential war between the nations. Quite the opposite of what the nation needed.

Sasou sighed to himself and relaxed a bit as he walked away from the cabinet meeting. Ilena wouldn't be happy, and Ore might run away instead of be willing to stand in front of the kingdom ministers and court, but really, they did need to be known at this level, too. It was time to bring them home, even if for only a brief time.

-o-o-o-

The campfires were going. The food cooking on them was making the bowl of Falcon's Hollow aromatic. Those not in the hiding and tracking competition had already set up the head tables on the stand from the summer Family gathering, in the same location of the amphitheater as before. A large bonfire was started just before sundown where the heat would get to those tables. The conversations and laughter of the crowd at the tables and picnic blankets set up around the bonfire and before the stand filled the bowl with sound.

While there was a little daylight they began the closing of the competition and beginning of the feast by announcing all the winners of the various competitions. Master stonemason Robert's statuettes of the lioness with a paw resting on three roses were handed out as the prizes to the first place winners of each competition, with the nicer ones going to the larger, more difficult competitions.

The winning "rabbit" and "fox" each got one of those, as did the winners of the knife and hand–to–hand lists. The final one went to the winner of the Tarc horse race. Ore had already received his rewards, except for the moving knife throwing competition. He received one of the statuettes from that, then discovered when he looked at it closely that Ilena had made sure they gifted him her favorite one. He scolded her, but she shushed him. If it was his, it was still hers. Their own competitions were announced, for all everyone already knew Ore had won them both, then attention was turned to Ore.

Ore rose. "Dearest Family." His voice rang over the bowl from his experience now with singing in Tarc and with the amphitheater effect of the location they were sitting in. "Welcome once again to Falcon's Hollow. Congratulations to the winners. Thank you for coming and having fun with us.

"The rules are the same. We are Family, let's keep it that way. Clean up before you leave so we'll want you to come back. We're considering keeping this a yearly activity, although timing may change. We'll think about it." There was commentary around the bowl for the season picked this time, for and against with groans and cheers.

Ore's hand, resting on the table in front of him, clenched into a fist and he swallowed. "Life will be different next time. We'll have to keep this event quiet from this time on." He paused. "Our stations won't allow for us to participate, otherwise. Please...," his voice went quieter, "let us keep this little bit of fun in our lives, or we'll forget who we are."

There was a collective pause, then from the bowl rang, "For Father! For Mother!"

Ore swallowed again, trying to swallow the tears of gratitude and despair that rose up in the back of his throat. When he was under control he said, "Thank you." He took one more breath, then punched his fist in the air and yelled, "Let's eat!" It was answered in kind from all the attendees and he sat for the food to be served to the head table. Ilena took his hand and squeezed it. He lifted her hand and kissed the back of it. She leaned over and softly, slowly rubbed his head until he finally sighed and they could turn to eating.

This time, because Ilena wasn't confined to her chair, she and Ore walked through the crowd together after dinner, stopping to talk to the groups as they went, laughing and reminiscing. They both took care to not stay overly long at any one grouping of people, wanting to make themselves as available as possible given the time they had. The sun was rising when they were finally reaching the main house again, dawn lightening the sky.

They had Liam with them already and slowly the others rejoined them. Petroi and Thayne were first, striding slowly together. A sleepy Justinian came behind them, dragging a sleep–deprived Reynold after him, complaining that he still had questions he wanted to ask people until Justinian laid a finger to his lips and told him it was time to be quiet and follow Mother and Father. Ore and Ilena smiled at them but their eyes were in agreement with Justinian's words.

Finally Marcus, Henry, and Rio slipped in, content with their contacts reacquainted with good drink. Rio hadn't allowed Amber to not come, saying she needed the practice of being with the Immediate Family during relaxed times, but she'd also given up shortly after midnight and tucked a very exhausted Amber into bed then returned to finish having fun with her friends.

"We're just missing Grandfather and Grandmother," Marcus commented quietly.

"Yes," Ilena said softly. "It's good to let them retire. It will be a quiet morning for them. I suspect that will be the best gift for them this night, or rather morning."

Ore put his arm around Ilena's shoulders. "Don't miss them too soon. Mrs. Leah will scold you for it, you know."

Ilena smiled. "True. Let's set some time aside for them tomorrow — I mean today — when we manage to get out of bed again. I haven't been able to sit quietly with them for a while."

Ore kissed the side of her head. "Okay."

They retired to their respective rooms to collapse for the night just as downstairs Grandfather and Leah began to stir for the beginning of their day — which was a quiet affair indeed until the rest of the Children awoke in the afternoon again.

As Ilena snuggled into bed with Ore, she sighed. "I love my Family."

Ore kissed her then slid down and pulled the covers over him, to cover even his ears. He cuddled into her warmth very closely. "Me, too." He kissed her chest. "Especially this member of it."

"Mmmm, Ore," Ilena was melting into him, "thank you. Thank you for being Father, for being my Partner. Thank you for being King and Consort." She bent her head down to get a kiss from him and give it back in return. "And thank you for being willing to be my family. No other dream could bring me more happiness."

As she slipped down to join him nearly completely under the covers, she whispered, "I love you so much, Ore. Thank you for loving me." She held him tightly as he slowly began to cry tears that turned into sobs of grief and loss. Her words may have rewarded him, but the cost to him of the loss of his ability to enjoy freely everything they'd enjoyed at this event was more than he could bear silently.

-o-o-o-

"Good morning," Leah teased Ore and Ilena as they entered the sitting room where a fire had been set to dancing cheerily in the fireplace. Grandfather and Leah were sitting in chairs near the fireplace, blankets wrapped over their laps and around their legs. They were holding warm drinks in their hands. The smell of wood smoke mixed with apple and spices drifted throughout the room. Ore and Ilena were bringing their own warm drinks with them from downstairs, having been told where to go find the older couple.

Ilena grinned at Leah. "You've finally relaxed. That's nice." It wasn't often Leah's tease came out. Ilena set her mug on a side table and selected a lap blanket from the pile waiting for room occupants to need them and sank into her selected chair to wrap up in the blanket. Ore imitated her, taking the seat on the other side of the table so they could share the place for their drinks when they weren't warming their hands and after the mugs were empty.

The four sat in silence for a bit as the younger couple settled into their own relaxing. It had indeed been a very lazy morning and was well past lunch now. Ore and Ilena had quickly eaten their share of the cold sandwiches and cheese left out in the kitchen by the chef. Bill had known everyone would be lazy so had set something out people could eat when they meandered into the kitchen looking to finally fill empty bellies. The warmed cider had been left simmering in a large pot over one of the kitchen cook fires and mugs had been put in easy reach with the ladle close by. It was good even he got to be lazy this day.

Ore moved his mug to his off hand, set his hand on the table and motioned for Ilena's hand. Ilena took his hand, and sighed happily. "It's so nice to get to be quiet and snuggle in today," she said.

"Mm," Ore agreed around a sip of his cider.

"A rare treat indeed," Grandfather agreed, his deep voice slow in the speaking. He looked like he'd sleep for three weeks if he could, he'd become so relaxed. Tokumade hadn't really been a place to relax, then Ilena had been near death's door, then they'd been busy in the castle, plus the progress and Tarc conflict. This was probably the first time all of them had had to just sit still and do nothing for many years.

When Ilena started getting restless because she didn't sit still very well, even during vacation times, Grandfather cleared his throat to get her attention. Ore and Leah both relaxed again, neither one really wanting to have to do the work to be her restraint just yet. "Mistress Ilena," Grandfather started, deliberately setting his mug down on the table next to him and carefully choosing his words in the process, "there's trouble between the girls that needs attending to."

Ilena froze slightly, her eyes widening. "Oh?" she asked.

"Amber relaxed into the work of the Department rather well after the progress began," he wanted to make sure she understood that there were good things as well. "Since you've all been back at the castle, however, it's become rather apparent to me that Amber and Rio do not get along."

Ilena kept her attention on Grandfather, but around the edge of her mug as she took another sip of the warm cider. He watched her calmly, waiting for her to be done."I think it's time you stepped in, or we might be training a traitor rather than an assistant."

"Hmm," Ilena looked into the fire for a moment, her lips pressing together as she considered his words. "I have noticed that most of Rio and Amber's interactions and training happen when I'm not in the wing. I suspect Amber waits until I'm not there to complain about me, or about whatever may be the problem?"

"Likely," Grandfather agreed.

"Yes," Leah said definitively. She was usually there and invisible to the two young women. The eyes of the other three turned to her. She took her time to gather her own thoughts and they waited patiently. She took a breath to relax from having pursed her own lips. "I think they've had conversations at night. A few mornings Amber has almost not come into the room, nor sat in her chair. It's become a punishment for her to have Rio be the one training her. However," Leah's lips pursed again, "Rio hasn't been wrong in her assessment of where Amber is and what she needs to be focusing on. Nor is Marcus wrong to step back and let Rio help her get there, if it's even possible."

Leah looked up at the painting over the fireplace mantle. It was of the Inner Sea and the coast from the vantage point of being on the water, as if a prior owner of the manor had wanted to be reminded of something other than cold winters and grey skies when in this room. Ore and Ilena had left it there, liking it well enough.

Her faded blue eyes eventually turned to look at Ilena. "It would be good for you to talk to Amber directly. I agree with Grandfather on that. She needs to know that you'll still face her and let her face you, particularly since she won't speak to you herself yet."

Ilena gave a little thoughtful nod. She considered the warning for a moment, then turned to Ore. "Can I ask you to be the one to take Rio out of the room while I talk to Amber?" Ilena gave Ore a small smile. "After all, you've shown you know how to do things like that very well. I was quite the difficult subject."

Ore gave her a slightly withering look. "Oh, yes," Ilena said, as she turned to her mug again, "I'm *still* a difficult subject." Ore rolled his eyes, then hid behind his own mug, but they all knew that's what he'd been thinking.

After a bit of sipping and sitting, Ore was the one who became restless. As all the eyes turned to look at him, he looked away from the rest of them, then cleared his throat. With a sigh he turned to Grandfather. "I really hate to bring up work, but I've remembered it and the thought won't leave me alone until I deal with it." Ilena wrinkled up her nose in equal distaste, completely understanding. Leah and Grandfather both gave off the air of the servant who expected him to just say it and get it over with, since it was a requirement to not let it go undone if it was "work" — and they all knew how easy it was for Ore to forget things for so long it became dangerous for the rest of them.

With that requirement hanging over him, Ore swallowed and asked, "Grandfather, do you know enough of the court protocols to stand as my Voice in the court, and teach me what I lack?"

The room froze just a little that he'd be bringing that sort of topic up. Ilena turned big eyes towards him. Grandfather thawed and frowned into the mug he was holding between his hands in front of him. He lifted it to sip from it, to give himself more time and to let Ore settle from having to ask it. "Who brought that up?" Grandfather finally asked.

"Lord Aiden," Ore admitted.

"Do you know who Lord Aiden has in mind?" Grandfather asked Ore. Ore gave a sharp nod. "They already have the court training or he wouldn't have offered a name," Grandfather mused. He gave a wry grimace, "It's more than enough to be your secretary."

Ore paused glumly, then the twinkle was back in his eyes as he addressed Grandfather one last time on the topic. "I'm glad to have you in the role of letter writer. I'm very ...very ...very bad at those. You can write them all."

Grandfather sighed slightly into his mug again, but he didn't say it. The Shicchis were even worse letter writers than the Toukas. The Toukas at least dictated what they wanted to have on the paper, for all the secretaries had to rewrite them heavily. Shicchis only said, "Write a letter."

-o-o-o-

Rei lifted the brief letter from his brother. He nodded, unsurprised by its message. "The investment court will be interim. They'll be here in eight days most likely. Maybe less since he'll likely use four horses per carriage in case they get caught by the heavy snows, and he'll want to move as fast as possible for having to come twice in only a few months."

"It's good we've already been getting ready for it, then," Mina said, lifting her head from her desk. Dane was looking at her, a little worried. "We should be ready by then, if Ilena and Ore are back in time to confirm the security arrangements one last time." Rei glared at her just a little. Mina waved her hand. "Yes, we know she sent a detailed note to General Garen and yes, we have a copy. I just want to get it firmly into her head so she doesn't forget it in all the other things going on."

Rei gave a satisfied nod to that. *Rei to Ore and Ilena. You have one additional day. I expect you back after that. There will be just barely time for you to be prepared, so don't delay.*

He received an answer back about fifteen minutes later. *Ilena to Master Rei. We have to stop in Nijoushi for a meeting of Falcon Studios regarding international trade with Tarc the morning after the last day. We'll be back that afternoon.*

Rei to Ilena. That's fine, he answered. She'd be focused if it was work with coin attached, and return properly. Rei's eyes lifted to Dane, who'd only been allowed the vacation for the one day of the competition event since Mina needed him as her trainee and assistant for preparing for the investiture. "You've been handling confirming the details of clothing and such?"

"Yes, Rei," Dane answered politely. "I've been working with Falcon Studios. They'll see that everything they didn't get before they left is brought back with them after that meeting."

Rei gave a nod and returned to the work on his desk. He had to get it caught up enough that it could sit again during the upcoming multi–day break. He was counting on his brother coming for the minimal amount of time again, but wouldn't be surprised if that was at least three days. Maybe four if Sasou wanted to sit and talk more seriously about Tarc with Ilena before leaving. Ilena had already intimated she wanted to commandeer more of Sasou's time, too.

Rei considered that for a moment, then sent, *Rei to Sasou. Plan on staying longer than you want to. We have things to talk about with you, Ilena and I. At least one full day of meetings, if not two, after the investiture itself.* It would be better for his brother to be prepared for it than surprised last minute.

He sighed a little, then returned to the paper in front of him. It was time to learn to properly negotiate with Sasou to his face as the near–equal he'd been made to be. That wasn't going to be too easy. His old habits of facing Sasou as minimally as possible were going to be hard to overwrite. He should practice in his head between now and then.

-o-o-o-

Ore, Ilena, and the rest of the Immediate Family enjoyed the quiet restfulness of that day and the next one, visiting with the members of the household. When Ore and Ilena finally could face sitting to work on the Falcon's Hollow books, Betty sat with them for her training to become steward.

When the books were settled and Ilena satisfied with the financials, Ore sat back from leaning over to see it at the desk the three were crowded around. He'd taken the opposite side so had been reading it mostly upside down so that Betty could more plainly see what Ilena was doing. As Betty leaned back as well, nodding her head in satisfaction that she understood, she brushed the lightly grey–streaked brown hair from her face. Ore smiled at her. "I'm sure we'll continue to give lots of direction, but rely on you when we aren't here." Betty hid a small smile.

"I'll be relieved to have one less thing for Ilena to have to do, too," he admitted. "It won't let me rest, but it isn't a burden to do this much," he shared a smile with Betty. "It surprises me that I do love being Lord Falcon's Hollow, since I ran so hard from Tokumade. It makes all the difference to feel like we're all family."

"Indeed," Betty agreed. "It's good to see you smile when you're here, and have Mistress Ilena relax. We'll help her do more of that from now on."

"Good," Ore approved. "I guess we'll call for Foster next and just get it all done at once." He used the code to send the request out.

Ilena came out from behind the desk and Ore moved his chair back into its place in the sitting area of the room. They sat on the couch together while Betty took a side chair. They conversed pleasantly until Foster arrived. He brought with him the map of the county he'd made so they could review the land–use plan. He set it out on the low table near the couch so that Ore and Ilena could see it properly, then sat across from them.

This was Betty's first time to hear the full land–use plan, which would now also be her responsibility to oversee. Foster would continue to help do the majority of the work. The review at the beginning helped her get caught up in activity to what she'd seen in payments from the county book.

Foster summarized how the peat sales were going. The loggers had cleared the majority of the stream bed and the lake area with the peat diggers following behind them. Marciel and Crowe wagons were going out every week or so with the peat. Foster had received a request through Ryan, who apparently had talked to the castle head stablehand. They wanted to know if they could purchase peat as a bedding in the stalls.

Ilena got rather excited at the telling of that bit of news. "If you can work it out by calculation then I'd say yes. Then I won't have to figure out how to get a profit out of peat sent to Ichijou. The delivery fee's quite high for that distance. Did Ryan let him have some to experiment with to see if it worked well enough for the stables?"

Foster shook his head. "He only passed on that he'd spoken to the stables and that they were interested. I thought I'd talk to you first and let you negotiate that." He gave a knowing smile to Ilena.

Ore was also intrigued. "Peat does hold liquids well while staying dry, but the other half might cake up the hooves more when stepped in and mixed with the peat." He frowned, putting a hand to his chin. "I can't see a mix of peat and straw changing that. It might mean more work for the stable boys, both in cleaning out the stalls more frequently and in keeping the hooves cleaned out so disease doesn't set in." The others frowned as they considered that issue and discussed it for a bit.

Foster eventually shook his head and brought up his other concern. "It may only be this year and next we can provide peat to anyone, though. This year we've got the new lake plus the horse pasture to take it from. Next year it's the lake for the village and the grain field. After that, we can take some from all over the county, but Mister Ryan has said that he prefers the fines. The county isn't large enough to have the top layer broken down into those fines by the time we work our way back around again."

Ilena glanced at Ore. "Even if we take up all of what we can in the next couple of years, there's plenty enough throughout most of Suiran that a rotation would allow the peat to properly build up in each holding. I'll talk to him about the potential to buy from other holdings in future years, once we have an agreement."

Ore gave her a sidelong look. "As in, you'll buy it off those holdings and skim off the top?"

Ilena smiled happily at him. "That's a good idea. Thank you, Ore." He left it there. If he'd helped her gain more for the county than she'd been planning on he could be content. If she was being sarcastic, he didn't want to be that upset today.

The topic turned to the building of the lakes. Foster frowned as he admitted that they were having troubles with keeping the water contained by the peat. When they hit mud deeper down that held it sufficiently well. Ilena asked some detailed questions, then shook her own head. It would take more research to be able to solve that issue. It was almost discouraging to have that problem since it could mean they wouldn't be able to have the lakes at all.

Since one use of the lakes was to have an ice making business, the topic turned there next. Foster had found a trio of experienced ice cutters who had agreed to head that work and train the locals in how to cut and store ice. They hoped they'd be able to make use of them. Ilena gave Foster some questions to ask them as professionals of the trade when it came to lake shapes and sizes. Perhaps they'd have some clues that would help them make the lakes.

"Will the horse pasture be cleared enough for planting the grain in the spring?" Ilena asked, moving to the next topic. That would be the only year of growing grain there as the loggers would clear the grain field after the pasture was cleared.

Foster answered in the affirmative. "There are several farming families in the county that will come plow and plant it. They've asked if they can have backs from the house during the general planting, and perhaps the harvesting, since we've taken so many for the wood and peat. I figure for how big you want that particular field it wouldn't hurt for us to reciprocate."

He turned to Betty. "You and I'll talk about that need from the household when we get snowed in and bored in the house." He winked and Betty nodded with a smile. It always helped to have topics of conversation that were useful when the deep snows finally snowed them in enough that shopping trips and deliveries were made from the second floor and by sleigh.

"Speaking of winter activities," Ilena turned to Betty, "how go the reading and writing lessons for the children?"

"Very well," Betty answered. "Like all children some would rather not have the lessons, but with the teen boys working hard with the herds the younger ones have the example and don't complain as much."

"As we're working on an heir," Ilena said, glancing at Ore, "we need to be preparing one to follow him — or her. In particular, we need someone who can understand the horses and the Tarc to help him when he's called up to serve over Tarc in our stead. Do you have a preference of swordsmanship training, Ore?" she asked.

Ore rubbed his head as he sat back to consider the question. "Given the ranking we're going to be in the end, we should hold to Touka preferences, I think. Kishi Knight's School won't get any complaints, and sword will be required, but anything learned is helpful, of course."

Ilena gave a nod of acceptance and turned back to Foster. "Begin immediately to train all the boys beyond what they already know on a daily schedule. Have Roald help with that, particularly with hand–to–hand combat. If we have more children than the one, we'll want to know if any of them have an aptitude so we could use them. If any of the girls want to join in, don't turn them away. You already know that the more there are who can protect themselves and the manor the better." Foster agreed.

Ilena looked between Foster and Betty. "In particular, focus on Edward. He has the best skill–set already to be the one called up to follow the heir to Tarc. As I've already promised, I'll see to him being properly trained in understanding the Tarc and their horses. You'll see that he gets the education and the training to stand as an aide and guard. He'll need to be able to help with the books and write reports. If it won't work in the end, we'll train someone from Kishi Knight's School to understand Tarc and set Edward to either be next head horseman or manservant to the heir." She looked to Ore for approval of that order of things. Ore gave it some thought, then gave the nod to formalize the order.

Ilena rose to her feet and walked to the side cabinet against the wall. She picked up a book and brought it back to Betty. "This is the Tarc Law. We need a copy for the house. Have Edward practice his reading and writing with that job. Even if it isn't a perfect hand as long as it's legible that's fine.

If Thom wants to copy him copying it, that would be a good task to distract him with as well."

The book was in Betty's hands so Ilena returned to the couch. "The laws are long for a four–year–old to write. Have Edward read the law to him, then have Thom write the summary of what he thinks it means. When they're done with the writing part, have Thom explain to Edward why he thought of that meaning for the Law. After they've discussed it together, they're to go to Novare and tell him what they thought of. He'll take the lessons from there. He already knows he's the only usuri in the household. He'll do what we need him to do. I'll test them each time I come.

"Let them work to Edward's speed. There's no need to be in a hurry. Often single Laws are discussed for months so that the children learn them properly. We'll come around to them again and again as Thom grows up, since his understanding will also grow with him. Edward will learn to be a proper Kir'nah that way, too."

She frowned at Foster. "He's not to steal a horse until he's properly had his own the right way, though. If he does, bring him back to severe punishment." She relaxed slightly, "Although, I don't expect him to yet anyway." Foster was giving Ilena a funny curious look. "I do expect everyone to be practicing that. The children all know the story from our first official visit.

"The seven–year–olds of Tarc steal a horse — usually their own companion — and head out into the wilds to prove they can survive on their own with the horse for a minimum of three days. If they're caught before then they're punished with increasing punishments. If they stay out the three days or more without being found and make it back into the encampment without discovery they're rewarded with their Kir'nah: the marker acknowledging they're ready to begin to learn to be adults.

"Because there's also the concern for the next few years Tarc will decide they don't really want us over them, there's also the concern they'll try to come down and steal the herds back. If they don't like us they won't like their breed of horses left with us. Have regular trainings with all the household, and all the Family and House in the county as well. They're to learn to track, encircle, and trap anyone who steals a Tarc horse. If a large clan sends many to do the task, fighting will be required. Only send the strongest and most trained to do that part. It's a difficult thing."

"It did help to have the nightwalker skills against them, though," Ore added. "They don't expect the thrown weapon, and think anything small is only for service, not a weapon. They also don't understand the woods, ravines, and roads. They only have the grass plain. They'll likely be slowed down quite a lot by our terrain unless they've been here to see it and have some sense of how to work in it."

Foster raised an eyebrow at Ore. "You're in agreement with Mistress Ilena? You think they'll come here?"

Ore shook his head. "The Tarc are nearly unfathomable, save if you consider nightwalkers. If you own something a nightwalker wants very badly, they'll come to get it. It's likely to be the same for the Tarc. In this case, it's far better to be safe than sorry, I think. Besides, any Tarc that does come down to Suiran without a very good reason is going to be in trouble for at least two more generations, I suspect."

"Well..., that's true enough, I suppose," Foster had to reluctantly agree.

"Train them to hunt for you," Ilena suggested to Foster with a wicked smile. "Go anywhere in the county you want to go, being rabbit, deer, and squirrel. Then train them to hide from you."

Foster laughed at Ilena. "I think I might have to do it the other way around. While they'll not be able to hide from me, they might want to understand that before they wander the woods lost for weeks trying to find me."

Ore's eyes opened wide. "Oh. Is that why you didn't participate in the Fox and Rabbit competition?"

"Yes," Ilena and Foster both nodded. "He's overqualified. We may as well have just handed the award to him, like our competitions," Ilena said.

Foster went a little sheepish. "I started really practicing it when Mistress Ilena found me the first time after my first wife died. I still don't know how she found me when she was up in the trees the whole time, by Thayne's word. I wanted to push her and see if she still could if I got better at hiding my tracks. I already could track that well having to hunt down the animals of the forest for the yearly count."

Ore pointed to his nose and Foster sighed. It surely had to be that. Ilena's sense of smell was just too good.

Before Ore and Ilena left for Nijou, Ilena looked into the library to find Edward at one of the long study tables. He already was working hard on the Tarc Law, his brow furrowed as his hand carefully copied the letters out of the book. He was very interested in being able to be in Tarc itself, so had promised to work very hard.

Young Thom was following his example and was sitting seriously next to Edward for his own little studies. It was cute to see the small lad sitting next to the taller one, swinging his feet under his chair while he held his tongue at the corner of his lips and focused on holding his pen to the paper.

Ilena rewarded them both with rubs of the heads and kisses on their foreheads as she said her goodbyes to them, promising to tell them more stories of Tarc when she and Ore returned the next time. Two pairs of eyes sparkled at her as she left the library quite content. It was nice to have others loving Tarc like she did.

CHAPTER 144 Return to Ore's Tree

The morning the household saw their lord and lady off was as rowdy as they'd been welcomed. The carriage with the servants was sent directly on to the castle. Stopping first in town, Ilena, Ore, and their guards went directly to Crafter's Row where Ilena had called for a meeting of all heads of the Falcon Studios crafters and merchants.

They met in Mister Balar's offices, which had a meeting room that fit them all. Mister Raine Marciel, ally and trader extraordinaire, was invited to attend as well. The atmosphere in the room was one of great excitement. This was the beginning of the promises Ilena had made to them all as far as Tarc went. She'd be opening up the market to the country that had been closed for seven generations.

Her presentation lasted several hours and included a summary of what Mizi had learned from Nal'fa and Mir'nah in Tarc about the tradition of their annual Marluk'nak' market and Ilena's analysis of how it was a modified version of the markets of Ryokudo and Selicia. From that general analysis, the group worked out a plan for how to help the Tarc people begin to modify their trade system back to what the rest of the world expected to see.

Ilena did warn them that this might be the only year they could trade with Tarc. There was the possibility that after a year of living the changed law the clans would refuse to allow them further entrance into Tarc and by force of arms keep them out. It was something she hoped didn't happen since within a few short years after that there would likely be a real war between Tarc and Ryokudo.

Even with that warning, all of the artisans were excited. Raine was the most excited of all. Ilena took the opportunity to further negotiate with him on carrying more of the Falcon Studios' products to other countries as well. Everyone listened to that negotiation, adding to it in support of their individual businesses.

After the business meeting, Ilena and Ore stopped by the two fighting lists under construction in town being built within the boundaries of the territory held by the House of the Queen of Night. They were greeted heartily by those nightwalkers who'd been in town and those who'd arrived recently from Tarc and were excited to both be home in the hidden alleys and to be building the lists. The lists were very popular in Kouzanshi and the nightwalkers of Nijoushi had been jealous for a while now that they didn't have the same sort of entertainment available.

The nightwalker Houses in the city were already well established, particularly the Queen of Night's. She'd been careful to always own a section that was poor for being out of the way and too close to places that were unpleasant for normal folk to want to spend much time near. Noxious workplaces had always been a necessity to any city and people. Tanning and other similar crafting processes often brought with them loud sounds, smells, and chemicals people generally stayed away from. Nightwalkers focused on competing wouldn't care once they were in the lists. The smell and sounds of many sweating bodies all packed together would overwhelm any such things from the outside.

"Will you and Mister Ore christen the lists when they're done?" Landras asked as he was walking with them during the tour.

"Maybe," Ilena answered. She looked around at the rubble and rock that was being broken up and pulled out of the ground, then sighed. "I'm sure I'd rather that than having to begin it all with fights of dominance instead."

Landras went sober, then also looked around. He moved their whole group to where it was quieter and gave significant looks to the guards. They moved out to encircle Ore, Ilena, and Landras, giving them privacy to speak. Landras spoke very quietly. "The Kouzanshi Lieutenants told us what it was like there when we told them you'd started building the lists here. We figure for now it's best to keep it low key until the construction is closer to done, and you two have the time to settle the city as a whole."

He pursed his lips, then said, "Watch yourselves when you walk outside House grounds. The Heads of the other Houses are hunting for Mister Ore, wanting to settle their claims. A few too many Heads have been offed by their Houses now and the rest that haven't been good enough to their people are getting jumpy."

Ore frowned. It hadn't even been *his* claim, but the claim of the House for him: to name him King. That sort of title challenged all other nightwalker Heads. It wasn't even the correct title as far as he was concerned, for all Ilena had told him he could have all of Suiran if he wanted. He was the King in the House of the Queen of Night, her match and mate. That wasn't quite the same.

"That many want to transfer, even with that name going around?" he queried Landras. Landras nodded soberly. Ore scowled a little. "Find out if they want to transfer because someone decided to name me that, or if it's for other reasons." He glared at both Landras and Ilena. "If at all possible, get the *right* name sent around. I've reluctantly taken King in the House of the Queen of Night. Only Ilena said it might be possible to take more than that, and I'm not inclined to."

Landras blinked at Ore solemnly, and with an expression that almost spoke to sympathy, but he only bowed and accepted the order. It didn't make Ore feel any better. He knew already that once a name had been said, if enough believed it they'd act on it regardless. He was going to have to be a lot more vigilant from now on than he cared to be usually. Even in the underworld his carefree days were slipping from his grasp, to become only history.

Ilena had been pondering while Ore had been seething. "Landras, it's better to get that pushed through faster than to let it fester. When those who come feeling out the members of our House walk away, they're to be left with an increase in desire to topple their Heads all the faster if that's what they want to be doing. They should be pushed to more firmly and openly support their Head if it isn't.

"If they won't commit yet because Ore hasn't, then be firm about letting them know we're not letting anyone in yet. Give as the excuse that we don't want to make their Heads even more angry with us at this time, when it wasn't our claim to begin with. Ore's order will help support it. The nightwalkers will have to make him take it over his reluctance and the Heads will have to accept it at that point — or he'll get to escape like he wants to."

She paused, then added pointedly, "And make sure they understand that if they're asking to join the House of the King of Nightwalkers, they aren't asking to join the House of the Queen of Night. Make them openly state that distinction of preference as well. It'll help protect the members of our House that have to move out to the other territories to train and hold the peace. We already know how to be a House within a House without conflict."

"Yes, Missus Ilena," Landras answered.

Once they were on their way to the castle, Ore complained at Ilena. "You'll push it even further and make them state it more loudly, instead of calm them down?"

Ilena sighed and looked sorrowful. "I'm sorry but yes. The House will be decimated if we don't control the flow, from all the Houses that'll come attack directly to hold their places. It isn't a given that the individual nightwalkers will be sufficient to make you take the title as your own. Nor do you have to accept it quietly. We just have to make sure the city doesn't erupt from the underside and become something we can't handle."

Ore pouted and was grouchy for the rest of that day, finally having to flee to his tree in Rei's office grounds to not snap at anyone. He sat in his favorite branch and stared up at the blue sky for a long time, not able to look towards the castle nor the city, for both had risen up to traitorously chain him before he was ready.

-o-o-o-

Mizi walked into the Rose office from talking with her secretary, Leanna, as Adjunct over claimants. They'd be opening up the Lotus office again for petitioners after the investiture and related meetings, now that Rei felt he'd sufficiently scolded his ministers. It would be good to get the research done before then for the long list of claimants waiting to be heard.

Her eyes scanned the wide room as they always did when she first entered, to see what the current state of things was. Usually everyone was heads down, hard at work at their desks, particularly right now as they were trying to get caught up from being gone for the last three months. It was relieving that the stacks of work were finally balanced to the completed side.

Instead of complete industry, Andrew and Mina were standing with hands resting on their hilts, staring out of the double doors of the balcony closest to Rei's desk. Rei was still in his desk chair, but he was also looking out the tall windows next to the door, up towards the city wall. Mizi's brow furrowed and she stepped closer to them all, wondering what was going on. That was usually not a very good sign. "Is it Ore?" she asked quietly when she was close enough to Rei.

Rei glanced at her and gave a small nod, returning his attention to the outdoors past the open beautifully woven heavy golden curtains. "Ilena says it's just he's overwhelmed and fighting the lead again. It seems the city nightwalkers are set on believing the rumor that he's claimed Nightwalker King of all Suiran. It's made him grumpy since he doesn't want it."

Mizi blinked, thought about that, then asked, "Is it only about that? A rumor?"

"Well, no," Rei sighed and sat back in his chair to look at her a little sadly. "They picked up the regalia before. It's that, too. While Ore was willing to be obedient for my sake on that, adding this was too much."

"Oh," Mizi said in a quiet whisper. She could understand that. Becoming the First Princess of Ryokudo had been like that for her. She'd run from it for five years before she'd taken herself to task (at Ilena's scolding) and settled to it. Focused on feeling those feelings, she moved to stand between Andrew and Mina where she could see Ore, her hand curled closed over her heart, protecting it yet again from that pain and fear she'd felt then. It was such a large thing to go from one who was common born to having the eyes and expectations of an entire nation on one's shoulders and back.

She knew that Ore loved both Ilena and Rei. The love kept him present there, in the tree instead of gone running from it all. Mizi looked at Ore in the tree, feeling that feeling of needing to be free while at the same time feeling the draw that pulled one to stand by the one they loved.

She finally took a deep breath, clenched her hand a bit, and gave a small nod. Turning back to the Rose office, she told her guards to stay there, caught up her cloak, and walked out. Her feet took her down the hall, then down the stairs, and out into the courtyard until she was standing under Ore's tree.

His head turned at the sound of her footsteps below him, but he didn't look at her until she'd called him softly. He seemed a little surprised to see it was her, but then it was usually Rei that went to see what was troubling Ore and to help him fix it. She'd done it once before, when he'd hid from her because he'd failed to keep her protected. This was a little different. She didn't think he'd hide from her this time.

When Ore had recovered from his surprise, he dropped down the branches until he was on one knee in front of her, an arm resting on his raised knee and his head bowed to her. "Mistress?"

Her breath caught a little and her heart squeezed a little beneath her curled hand, which hadn't left it's position of comfort since she'd been in the office. He'd not been so abbreviated for some time, not since he'd fought being Ilena's partner, she thought. She'd since learned that he was like that when he was trying hard to keep himself restrained. She'd perhaps seen worse times than now, but it still wasn't good.

"Ore," she said, hesitating a little, not quite sure how to say to him what she wanted to say. He waited as patiently as always, but his smile to help her relax didn't come. Mizi drew in a deep breath. "It is hard, Ore. I didn't want it either for a long time." Ore froze slightly, then looked up into her face, the surprise evident this time. "You remember. Ilena had to scold me severely before I'd do it. It was frightening at the time to be told that I was already almost too late, that my goal was going to slip from my grasp." She gave a sad, small smile. "Only that gave me the strength to face it myself."

Mizi drew in another deep breath. "I know it's not quite the same for you. You've already received the gift before being made to pay the price. I'm sure that makes it even more difficult, actually." She smiled at him sadly. "While I don't want to be selfish, I'm afraid I am in this case. I don't want you to go and leave me here alone. I've become too used to leaning on you, finding the strength to continue to walk forward in this difficult position because you can smile for me and tease Rei and love Ilena."

Her hand over her heart reached out for him, pleading with him to stay. His eyes watched her hand and his hand came up slowly until his fingertips just barely caught hers. It wasn't a promise, but a wonderment to him it seemed. Ore swallowed and his eyes sought hers again. She blinked the tears from her vision.

He looked away quickly, then drew in a breath and spoke quietly, a bit haltingly. "It was hard, to learn to stay, but for your sake I couldn't leave. I learned it as quickly as I could so that I could watch over you properly. Already you were in danger from before, even from me. I knew if I didn't learn it as fast as I could, then I'd already be too late." He drew in a breath, then looked back up into her face. "It was easy to be yoked to you, who'd already fought so hard to stand in the place you'd chosen." He looked down again in sorrow. "You already know it's been hard for me to not be walking with you." He shivered.

Mizi tightened her fingertips against his so he paid attention to her again. "You still do, Ore," she said quietly. "Our stations and roles have changed, and the way we walk together has changed, but you still walk with me as long as you're here and we're working on our goals together." She could see that he was still conflicted. She furrowed her brow a little, then asked, "What is your goal, Ore? Was it always only to protect me and my path?"

Ore looked away, into the distance of his thoughts for a bit, then he settled a little. "No," he said softly. "You helped me move forward on my path towards my goal, because I knew if I could protect you I could protect that which I was moving towards." He blinked. "When I finally understood that was my proper path, I was able to settle to it." He drew in a long, but sad breath.

Mizi gave a nod of understanding. "Learning to love Ilena was that goal, wasn't it?"

Ore glanced up at her, then gave a nod. "Each step has been helped because of learning who she is and coming to love each part of her."

"What's different this time?" Mizi asked softly. Ore was silent for a long time, then he only shook his head. Mizi considered him, and her own emotions that were so similar. "Is it because this time you have to stand forward instead of stand behind as the protecting shadow? This time you know you'll be in the gaze of everyone who looks upon you to see you and not just those around you?"

Ore's breath caught a little and he shivered again, his free hand clenching into a fist. Mizi held his fingers more tightly and nodded at him a knowing nod. Her lips pursed a little and he stared at her. "That was what I had to face that day that Ilena scolded me. I knew that from that time on I'd be in the gaze of everyone who looked on me. Whether to judge or to fawn, to hate or to adore. It was very hard, Ore. It's not a thing I was born to want, desire, or even act on, let alone believe could be possible."

She drew in a breath. "Standing in front of the lords without all of you here to help me was so very difficult. I felt so alone and exposed, and none of them looked on me kindly at all. But I knew it needed to be done regardless, so did it anyway. Just like standing with all of you on the wall for all of the people to see is part of this, so is that. I must learn it in order to stand in the place I wish to stand: at the side of Rei."

She held his hand now, tightly as if to keep him there with her. He kindly returned it, trying to comfort her now that he was here again with her. "Don't lose sight of your goal, Ore. It hasn't changed, for all the difficulty that it's become. We who watch you know that you can do this, too." She gave him another sad, teary smile, hoping. "If the weak and frightened me can do this, how much better can the strong Ore who's stood as my protector and support for so long do it?"

Ore was on his feet and his arms were wrapped very gently around Mizi's shoulders. "You are not weak, Mistress. You are very strong also," he scolded kindly. He released her and put his hands on her shoulders to study her face as her tears fell. She wiped at them and he smiled a small smile for her. "Well, I will also consider Mistress as I work it out, then," he promised her.

Mizi sighed to herself in some small relief. He'd moved beyond wanting to flee completely. Ore was always firm that he'd make his own decisions and took his time to do it right, but that promise was probably enough. He'd relaxed enough, anyway. "I'd appreciate it, for all it's very selfish of me," she said to him.

He released her shoulders and put his hand lightly on top of her head for a moment, then he was gone, back up into the tree again. He settled with a sigh. She looked up at him for a while longer, then turned and headed back for the stairs to respect his need to think without further pressure.

A motion caught her attention before she'd gone very far. She looked up to the balcony of the Rose office to see Rei looking at her. Rei motioned with his head towards the tree. She turned and looked for Ore again to see he was watching after her. She paused, then turned back. "Would you like company, Ore, while you think?" she asked.

He blushed and looked away, but then gave a nod. "Knowing Mistress understands is helpful," he said quietly.

Mizi pulled the hood of her heavy wool cloak closer over her head and the long length of it more tightly around her legs. It was thick enough to prevent the light snow under the tree from melting into her. As she settled to sit under the tree, she remembered that Rei had told her that it helped Ore to have others present when he had to think. It helped remind him of his duties so he could release his own internal restraints enough to work out the things he needed to work on. She sighed lightly and clasped her gloved hands loosely in her lap. She looked up into the blue sky herself, glad it was a sunny day.

Motion from the balcony caught her attention again briefly. Rei was turning away to return back into the office. He paused to glance at her once again and saw her looking. He gave her a soft smile then returned to his work. Two of her own guards were also now watching over her from there. It was the looks of approval on Andrew and Mina's faces that helped her settle the most to her task. She'd managed to do her duty to Ore and the rest of them properly enough.

She was a little surprised when about twenty minutes later two gardeners showed up with a garden bench. They set it up under the tree looking away from the office and towards the garden view. They bowed to her when they were done installing it and silently moved on to their other chores. She smiled at them, then rose to her feet and dusted off to move to the bench. Ore settled a little better himself. Mizi smiled. Rei was a very conscientious husband. He was kind to think of her sitting in the snow. He likely never sat when outside with Ore, he had to sit so much when inside his office.

Ore escorted Mizi back into the Rose office. He'd have done it as a matter of course before, being her guard. This time though, he had to admit to the change in their relationship. They were in–laws and royals now. He was going to find it hard to learn this new balance.

He rather instinctively wanted to offer her his elbow in the formal escort now that he was playing a noble part. At the same time, they were going to have to work hard to not look like a trysting adulterous couple. That would be very bad all around. The whole time he'd been her guard before the weddings there'd already been plenty of rumors that they had a romantic interest in each other, for all it had never been that. Ore worked hard to find the middle ground of walking *with* Mizi as an equal companion while staying relaxed to keep her from worrying.

When Mizi was at her desk placed next to Rei's, the location surprising Ore since he'd not been in the Rose office since before that change had been made, Ore moved on to stand in front of Rei's desk. He put his hand to his chest and gave a formal bow. "Master, we've returned from Falcon's Hollow; although, you've already heard it after asking about my health." He scolded Rei slightly with his look for wasting his attention on Ore. Rei ignored it like usual. Ore sighed to himself. He supposed there was now more real reason for Rei to care about the state of a nightwalker thief.

"I'm sure I'll be fine after I've become lost in the swamp of work after the investiture. Until then you'll all keep me distracted, I'm sure." Ore kept it dry. He'd already made himself give up the bitter before leaving the tree — for Mizi's sake and Rei's as well to some degree.

Rei had finally put his pen down to give Ore his full attention. "You'll not run then?" he asked mildly, but with the depth of unspoken words he usually wove around such simple words.

Ore shook his head. "I'll stay put. It's important, and true that no one else can do it: rule Tarc and keep sane," he teased. Rei's lips turned up. "I must be ready for Grand Duke over them if the nightwalkers are as equally anxious to call me their lord." Ore wrinkled his nose. "They hate nobles as much as I do, so that's a rather amazing accomplishment." That came out a little more bitter but Ore hadn't committed to that one yet.

He frowned seriously at Rei. "For all that's what they say they want, only a portion will really be willing to put me there — which is a relief. We've told the Lieutenants to pass the word I'm not willing to accept the title. Ilena's told them to use my reluctance to test the nightwalkers. If they'll topple their own Houses to prove to me how serious they are then they'll have done clean–up we don't have to. I'm hoping for most it's a passing interest and they come to their senses instead."

He sighed. "One small House has already come, though. Ilena and Thayne are working on that one for now. It just adds a small territory to territory her House already holds. I can't complain much about that one. That Head needed to go." Ore waved his hand lightly in dismissal.

Changing the topic, Ore said, "Our vacation was quite pleasant. Ilena is still determined to assume the land grants. I recommend you force her to tell you early this time so we can cancel unnecessary construction projects." Rei grimaced like Ore expected him to. "The household was happy to have us visit for so long.

"Novare has been fit in quite well and enjoys being usuri, not just herdsman. He scolds like any proper usuri should so the Family feels already well welcomed into Tarc." He rolled his eyes. "Why they want to be I have no idea, except to drain him dry of how to beat the Tarc if it should ever be necessary. Ilena still hasn't told them to move on her messenger business." Rei gave a nod that he'd added that note to his board.

"That said, she did have a long meeting with Falcon Studios and Raine Marciel. The plan to open Tarc as a market and to help them learn how coin works has been set and agreed to. Mister Marciel is very much looking forward to the next Marluk'nak' market."

Rei's eyebrow went up. "She'll not have him enter earlier?"

Ore shook his head. "The clans will distrust and not welcome him before their own expected market. Too many spies have tried to enter Tarc that way." He went dry again, "You remember that was her own story when she went as a youth the first time. It apparently was common then for the various nations to try to break into that market in that manner. ...Except Suiran and Ryokudo. Queen Mother forbade it." Rei understood and sat back in his chair, looking to see if there was more in Ore's report. Ore ran through the last week and some days in his memory then relaxed and waited on Rei.

"You'll be in lessons with Aiden from now?" Rei asked first.

"So we discussed before," Ore agreed, "if he can be spared?"

Rei nodded but his eyes were looking into the space of his board. "We'll let him get to where it can be fit into his schedule. A few before the investiture to get your face seen again would be good, but I think full lessons can wait until after it's over." Ore was okay with that.

"How much time and effort are you going to need to put into watching over Ilena between now and then?" was Rei's next question.

Ore hesitated. "We still need to go over our schedule. I'm fairly certain she plans on keeping at least herself busy. I haven't heard anything other than the normal for myself, and what was decided at the Security meeting."

Rei blinked at Ore. "You'll be a bit freer than expected, then?"

Ore wrinkled his brow some. "I don't know, actually. Can I get back to you on that one?"

"Sure," Rei gave Ore a rather piercing look, but let it be. "Well, I'm just wondering how much I can drag you into here and how much I can make you run around for me. Let me know when you know."

"Yes, Master," Ore bowed to him slightly.

Rei gave him a slightly annoyed look. "And will you still be calling me that after the investiture?" They'd already been brothers–in–law for four months. Likely he was thinking that to still be called that when they were family was irritating. To have Ore still doing that when they'd be nearly equals in power in the nation might be even more uncomfortable for Rei.

Ore raised an eyebrow at him, then smacked his lips a few times. "Hmm." He let the other name he was considering roll around in his head a few times, then said in a muse, "I'm not so sure you really want to be called Little Brother."

Rei's mouth dropped open. Mina's snort of laughter earned her a glare from Rei. Ore smiled his teasing grin at Rei. "We'll see what comes out then, shall we? I'll try to not talk to you until it's something nice, though."

"Thanks," Rei answered dryly. He waved at Ore, dismissing him and the thought of names he didn't want to be called.

-o-o-o-

Ore strolled back to the wing where his wife and her household waited. He supposed it was *his* household, too, but the household at Falcon's Hollow seemed more his own household. She'd set that one up too, but he'd gotten to bring them all to it, learning who they were, and coming to love them in the process. He smiled as he reminisced on those runs. It had been a fun job each time. Ilena knew how to play with him in ways he truly enjoyed.

At the same time he had to do the drudgery with her, too. He sighed. He didn't really want to think about that any more. It was why he was walking back on the ground and as late as he could from the Rose office. He'd pestered them as long as he could before Rei wanted to throw him out, but Rei had understood, giving him a testing look then nod as Ore had thrown a grateful look over his shoulder on the way out.

Ore looked around the snowy courtyard he was passing through. Somehow he wasn't surprised to see eyes looking at him. He was without guards — a first for months — and was a well-known figure in the castle. ...Not that he'd had to have guards until Ilena had made him have them. Well, okay, he'd wanted Thayne by then.

Today he'd not been able to put up with anyone following him, and they'd left him alone. He looked at the roofs around him as he was far enough from the buildings he'd been walking through. He didn't see anything, but he was quite sure that his two were still keeping their eyes on him. Nightwalkers knew how to do that rather well without being seen and Ilena had trained her guards to be better than most.

Ore stood still for a moment, wondering if the feeling of wanting to flee from them, play chase with them, would rise enough to act on or not. He balanced on his toes a little, looking at the roofs. He didn't want to go up, not really. He spun in a circle as if in his knife dance, taking his focus from the roofs to the buildings around him. That was what he really wanted to do: dance his knife dance. He took himself to a near garden that had privacy bushes around it. He didn't need the lords and staff of the castle to pass along the gossip he danced with himself in public areas.

Ore didn't need his hand knives to practice the dance, but he slipped one into each hand anyway. It helped him to forget the world around him if he held them in his hands and focused on that feeling as he practiced. The movements of slice, parry, dodge, stretch, leap, and duck flowed through his muscles, making the blood flow into them and warmed them. He decided in that moment that he'd be doing this every day, maybe about this time of day, after he'd been sitting too long and needed to get irritating emotions out of his body and into the aether where they belonged.

Deep breaths in and out of his lungs added to the motion and helped to bring clarity to his mind along with the focus the dance took. The breaths also helped to ground him in the reality of the space and time he was in. The sum was a strength that reminded him he was capable. He'd honed and strengthened his body for many years now, with a lot of focus on it during the years he'd followed Mizi.

His knives were slipped back into their sheaths and he was doing consecutive backflips from one side of the garden to the other along the long length of it. A smooth ducking turn and he was doing cartwheel side flips back the direction he'd come. The return down the length was a series of punches and kicks from his preferred martial art.

Ore ran through his martial art rehearsal, moving back down the garden slowly, as if chasing a shadow opponent. He kept his breathing deep and smooth, not letting the rehearsal fight his own body. He could do it at top speeds, but that wasn't today. Slower rehearsals like this one perfected the attacks and blocks at the higher speeds. Each punch ended forcefully, each block was held rock solid, all of them imagined in his mind to cement the desire with the action.

When the martial art rehearsal was completed, Ore paused to breathe, then he was on the ground and the count of push–ups began. Those were followed by planks, one–handed and two handed. Sit–ups were next, followed by another pause to breathe. Then it was handstands, held firmly until he desired to slowly return to an upright position. Half he returned to in the forward direction. The other half were done as back bends, with his feet hitting the ground before he brought his hands up. That had taken him a long time to perfect, his core muscles needing to be greatly strengthened before it would work.

His knife dance was a nice easy stretching beginning, but once his work–out was done his muscles required the final full stretching. He went down to the ground in splits, then turned to stretch even more in both directions. He drew both legs in front of him and folded over them until his forehead was on his legs. He breathed slowly for three full breaths in and out, then rose again. The stretching continued until he could just stand still and breathe through his nose, relaxing.

"Okay," he said mildly, his eyes still closed, "you can come out."

"Well, that was rather impressive," Thayne's warm voice said. "I never would've thought you had the flexibility for those splits at all, for all I've seen you fight before."

Ore gave him a teasing look over his shoulder. "I guess that's why you decided to come out of hiding, then? I'm impressive enough to drag you out?" He sighed, looking at the garden in front of him again. "I'll be remembering to do that more frequently now. It's been too long that I've taken the time. Too many things were unsteady."

"Not that we could notice," Petroi said dryly, a step behind Thayne, his arm resting casually on his sword hilt for a place to put it, not to be a restraint. "We will remind you, though, if you want?"

Ore gave a nod. "Particularly on the tensest days. This time of day works best."

"Got it," Thayne said.

Ore twitched and they held still. They'd only shifted a half–step closer, but that was as far as Ore could take this day, even with the work–out. They backed off that half–step and he breathed easy again. "Hmm," he mused. "I'd have thought it would've been enough, to at least have companions again, but I guess not just yet. Maybe after it's all over — the hard part." They didn't pressure him and he turned for the garden exit on the side closer to their building. They stayed at the distance of fellow pedestrians and that worked fine.

When they reached the aide's wing that had been converted into their household and department wing, Ore had to pause and take a deeper breath. He swallowed, then continued forward. One of the soldiers guarding the interior entrance to the wing opened a door for him and that helped. He wasn't sure he could've made himself go through it otherwise. He gave both soldiers on the doors nods and wished them a good evening by name. They gave him brief bows back. That was new, to get bows instead of nods of greeting, but it was another thing he had to expect, for all it made him a little sad.

Once he and his two guards were in the open central hallway, he sighed and complained a little. When he reached the lower suite doors, he glared just a little at the two usual soldiers there. "So, Hue and Sailte, I'm going to give you an order as Count and eventual Grand Duke." They straightened a little extra to receive his words. "You're to *not* bow to me when I remember you're here and greet you. You two are to remember that you've been watching over Ilena since she was a wounded witness under protective custody and I was the poor sap who had to guard her all night." He scowled at them until they agreed they'd obey and treat him casually at his own door.

Then he motioned and made Hue open the door for him. He still couldn't make himself enter the room on his own. With another breath for fortitude, he walked into the main room of the suite. He closed his eyes. "Half of you need to eat upstairs, and that's not going to be far enough away for me." The room got rather quiet. "Liam, Leah, and Grandfather: you're to take the evening off. Go eat in town or somewhere we aren't. Forget we exist until tomorrow morning."

"Thank you, Master Ore," Grandfather's voice came quietly from upstairs. Liam bowed and headed out the door Ore had just come through. Leah finished writing her last note then followed him.

"Reynold and Justinian, go with Marcus and Henry to the young lord's cafeteria, or sit with the paiges and Justinian's old friends. Come back very late." He turned his head and listened for the upstairs. "Have Colin and Jefferson left yet?"

"Yes," Grandfather's voice came from the hallway behind Ore this time.

Ore sighed. "I'm sorry to the nurses. This time it's me that can't handle having you come here. Please feel free to comfort yourselves at wherever you want to eat tonight." He heard the even softer thanks from them, since they were likely in their rooms already. They actually weren't there all the time. That would be very boring. Ilena had them doing things out some and sometimes they had their own chores to do.

When that many were gone, Ore felt the room to see what more he would need to stay put in it. Petroi and Thayne were still standing behind him, working hard to not put any pressure on him. Amber was stiff and trembling, wondering if she was going to be released. Rio was the opposite, worried they would be, wanting to ask to not be, he could tell. He sighed. "We'll have the girls on serving duty tonight, I think, and Petroi and Thayne on guard duty since I know no one wants to have *all* the guards gone. I've finally just gotten to the point before coming here that they can stay." He got silent approval from the two men, relief from Rio and resignation from Amber.

Then he could open his eyes and look at Ilena. She smiled at him. "I take it you'd like to have just Ilena tonight, then?"

"Yes, please," Ore slumped just a little, "or I'll have to send you out, too."

"Oh, no, not that," she teased him. She patted the seat next to her. "Shall I serve the wine tonight?"

He tilted his head, then shook it. "Thayne can do that tonight." Thayne was immediately headed for the wine cabinet. "Port tonight, please," Ore requested. Thayne indicated he'd heard and Ore moved to sit on the couch with Ilena. Petroi opened the door for the girls so they could go get plates fixed up from the dinner cart that was just arriving through the main doors of the wing.

Ilena motioned Ore should turn on the couch, so he turned his back to her. Her hands were on his shoulders and then she was massaging them and the center of his back between them with her thumbs. Ore was surprised at first, it being the first time she'd ever done it. His muscles responded with relief, though, so he relaxed and let her work on him.

"I think you'll put him to sleep before he eats, Mistress Ilena," Thayne teased from closer to Ore than he'd expected. "It's on the table, Master Ore," he continued. "You missed even that sound."

Ore groaned. "I'm glad you still don't attack at those times. I'm pretty sure for all I'm relaxed now, I'd have killed you and then opened my eyes."

"Yes, I'm quite sure," Thayne agreed dryly as a second light clunk sounded on the table. Ilena's drink was now on the table as well. "However, I figured you'd rather I interrupted than have you attack the girls who are ready to give you your plates. They don't know to be noisy enough first, nor can Rio who learned silence was required."

"Ah, no, we don't want that at all," Ore agreed, his eyes finally opening. It was with some regret that he turned away from Ilena's warm ministrations. "I think it's time to eat anyway, before I just skip it altogether." He sighed at his wife who smiled at him. "I still can't touch or be touched that long without wanting to just steal you away."

Ilena's eyes went wide. "Ah, then shall I undo some of that? I'm sure we'd rather eat than wake up in the middle of the night hungry." She waved her hands at him as if to blow some of the warmth away and wake him up a little.

Ore laughed at her, then caught one of those hands in his to kiss the back of it. He let it go to lift his plate. It would be good to have food in him before the port, he rather thought. He looked at the girls who were arriving with their plates. "Sit on the other couch," he invited. "It's still good to have friends and family to eat with, for all I sent most of them away." He glanced at Thayne and Petroi and tipped his head at one of the end seats. They understood and took the two "head" seats, sighing as they could finally also relax for a bit.

CHAPTER 145 Partnership Purposes

Even though Ore had found it hard to return to the castle and have everyone present this evening of returning from Falcon's Hollow, the conversation was relaxed through the dinner. It had helped him to have Mizi sit with him as he thought through their similar situations. He'd been able to recommit to his path forward of love for his wife, honor for his liege, and care for his mistress. Physically working out the stress followed by a warm meal finished helping him to relax again. There were still things that he was working hard to not think about since they made his stomach churn, but he could finally set them in the back of his mind.

Ore had to laugh when Thayne managed to tease a blush and laugh out of Rio. He raised his glass to Thayne and drank to his skills. That had been a hard thing to win. Such things Ore appreciated. He'd enjoyed getting under Mina's hard outer shell the first time. Today's laugh had been a little easier to get for having the practice now. It was good to hear Rio's laugh as well, even if it had been Thayne to do it and not him.

Ore leaned back, his dinner plate empty now, to enjoy his drink and the company. When Ilena put down her dishes and picked up her cup he slipped his fingers through hers on the close hand. She settled back against the couch to lean on him a little bit. It was nice to cuddle. Thayne collected up his, Ilena's, and Rio's dishes. Petroi took Ore's, Amber's, and his own and they bowed themselves away from the table to take the dishes out to the food cart. They'd head for their room to get ready for bed after dropping them off.

Ore let his gaze linger on Amber, remembering Grandfather's warning to Ilena at Falcon's Hollow. Her cup left her lips and it took a bit for her to notice he was watching her. She blushed a little when she did. Rio shifted and Ore gave her his polite attention. "Master Ore, if it would be okay, this would be a good time for Amber to tell you what she didn't tell you before." Rio turned to Amber. Amber's fists tightened in her lap, then she took a deep breath and reached towards her pocket.

Amber paused, then left what was in her pocket alone. Her hands came to clasp together in her lap. Her eyes gazed at them, then she gave a shudder and looked back up into Ore's eyes. "I'm sorry, Master Ore," she said quietly. "When you asked for my story when Mistress Ilena first called for me to come, ...," Amber drew in a breath, held it briefly, then continued, "...it didn't really happen that way."

Quietly Amber told the right story, of how she'd killed her best friend in a pique of frustration. It had been unplanned, and surprising, but it had still been done. Amber shivered. "I can't see blood anymore. It takes me back to that fear and shock. I want to vomit all over again, and sometimes I faint and don't revive for hours as my mind runs from what I did." She turned her head away to hide from her past even now. "I still react suddenly like that sometimes, but if I know it, I turn and run away first. I don't ever want to do anything like that again." The last was said sadly and very quietly. Her hands were tightly clenched again now, as if she'd cut her palms with her fingernails if she could, save for not wanting to see the blood.

Amber drew in a shuddering breath, trying to straighten again and yet wanting to curl into herself and hide. "Rio won't let me run from it anymore. She's said I have to tell it to you properly, so I have, but I didn't want to." She frowned, trying to not let tears fall.

Ore considered Amber and her story for a moment, then he rose to his feet and walked over to her. He sat on the edge of the couch next to her and gently took one of her clenched hands in his. He softly pet the hand until he could get it to open and relax even a little. Then he repeated it for the other hand. They finally relaxed enough to rest open on her lap. He took them both in his hands to hold them. "Amber, these hands can do much more than surprise you. They've only killed once. There's still much kindness and usefulness in them." He put them together palm to palm and held them in one hand as he brushed his other hand over the top of her head. She looked up from their hands to his eyes.

"It's hard to run from your past. Harder still to turn around and walk back through it so you can let it go. Take a deep breath. Here you're safe and we're safe from you. Here you can relax and not worry." He was letting his hand holding hers tell her that she couldn't harm him, that his hands wouldn't let her harm anyone she worked with. His petting hand was telling her that she wouldn't be harmed either. Her expression said that she was defeated, that she'd really told the truth this time, and that she didn't like what she was.

Ore continued to pet her and hold her hands until she slumped. Then he pulled her head to his shoulder. "You can love yourself again, Amber. We'll help you learn to trust yourself again, if you want to learn it." She finally sighed and relented completely. He lightly kissed the top of her head to reward her, but he didn't let her hands go until she was done with being comforted and she was ready to sit up again. Then he patted her top hand with his free hand and rose to his feet. He let her hands go last, slowly letting them slip back to her lap. They stayed put so he left her side to return to Ilena and his place at her side.

-o-o-o-

"Ore, perhaps you could take Rio out to the second courtyard and speak with her for a bit. I think Amber could use the opportunity to speak to me privately," Ilena requested.

Ore agreed and chose to not sit down. He waited for Rio to rise to her feet. He walked casually with Rio to the patio door and through it, closing it behind them against the cold late–autumn evening. Ilena inspected Amber without putting undue pressure on her until they'd had time to move into the second courtyard that held the Cat gate. Amber sat with a stiff spine, clasping one hand inside the other in her lap. Her eyes shifted between the patio door and Ilena's knees.

"It seems to me," Ilena started out, "that you've found yourself in a difficult place to be, unexpectedly. I'm certain being told you had to be honest in that way was more than you bargained for at the very least." Amber agreed with that statement. "Will you tell me what's been most difficult so I can perhaps help you?" Ilena offered.

Amber took in a deep breath that made her shoulders rise. "Rio's been stubborn and unkind to me frequently. I'd wish to not have to be her partner. It wasn't clear to me at the beginning that would be the case and it was a difficult thing to understand. The others weren't very kind in how they told it to me, either. I was expecting to come to a place where understanding and warmth were given, like you've given to others. It's only been cold and lonely." It was perhaps a good sign that she'd been willing to jump right in and be open, continuing the honest communication to some degree.

At Amber's pause, Ilena asked in questioning sympathy, "It's been cold and lonely?"

"Yes," Amber answered firmly. "If I'm not being scolded by Rio, I'm being ignored. When I try to talk to my old friends outside the office when there's a moment, they also shut me down quickly and leave me without letting me say anything. It's as if they think I'm not allowed to say anything now that I might know important secret things."

"You can't say anything?" Ilena asked.

Amber scowled slightly. "It's not like I'd ever tell any department secrets. I know how important that is to the Region. I'd just like to talk to anyone who'd be friendly to me. I can't find anyone at all like that any more ...it seems." She tacked on the latter as if to admit that she didn't know everything, but it was obvious from her perspective that there wasn't anyone to talk to at all.

"That does sound very lonely," Ilena sympathized. "What would you hope could be done to fix that?"

Amber frowned and considered the question. "I wish that at least some of the people here could accept me for who I am rather than distrust me and want to change me all the time."

"Want to change you?" Ilena asked curiously, tipping her head sideways and frowning a little in confusion to indicate she'd like to understand better.

"Yes," Amber said in great frustration, finally letting go of her restraints enough to relax and let some of it out. "Rio keeps pushing me to make me admit to things I find private and often unnecessary, all because *she* must have me face things the way she does — as crazy as that viewpoint is at times — rather than accept that I may have a different way of seeing the world that isn't necessarily wrong. It's just different. Can't we all just get along?" Amber was going now so Ilena relaxed and let her vent while paying attention to how she said her words, not just what they were.

Amber finally wound down, "...And Marcus won't even talk to me until Rio and I are 'partners'. I can't even begin to be friends with her. How will that ever happen, then? I thought it was important to get to know him more, but he won't let me." Amber pouted and her eyes glistened with unshed tears.

"That does sound sad," Ilena agreed, "however, I'm afraid I can't change what he chooses to do. I could talk to him, though, and see what he's thinking, if that would be something you'd want me to do?"

Amber frowned as she considered the offer. She looked away, then said, "I suppose it would help to understand why he thought it was so important, but I don't know that I want to trouble you."

Ilena considered that, then offered, "Well, I could talk to him to see, and then let him know it would be good if he'd talk to you about it himself so you could understand better?" Amber agreed better with that solution.

When it seemed Amber had said her most important frustrations, Ilena shifted a little. "I do have some things I could tell you that might help you to understand them all just a little better, if you'd like to hear it? Maybe that would help you to be able to approach them with a little more confidence?"

Ilena waited until Amber agreed she'd be willing to listen. She sat back and interlaced her fingers together. "Amber. What do you think Rio needs most?" It was asked with interest in hearing Amber's answer.

Amber's expression went cool and closed, a look unusual on her face. "Honesty." It was said shortly and just as cool as her look.

Ilena gave a thoughtful nod. "Given Rio's past as a doll of the Doll House, and that she watched me go through the results of the fight against it, I think that would be a fair assessment of something she'd consider important." Amber's clasped hands tightened together a little. Amber hadn't been part of that, and had been brought into the Family after that time. She'd likely heard stories of it, though.

Ilena paused a little longer then asked, "Did you know that was the event that made me set the rule that traitors to the House and Family die? Rio watched what I went through, what emotions made me decide on that action. She didn't want to die. I'd already saved her from the death that was coming for her within several weeks because she'd gotten too old to stay a doll and wasn't purchased by anyone else."

Amber swallowed, rather dryly it appeared. Ilena thought it was more because of the threat contained within all of that than because of any empathy for Rio. She continued, "Do you think that perhaps Rio wants honesty from you not just because *she* wants to be faced honestly, but because she wishes to save you from *my* reaction to dishonesty?" Amber paled quite a lot. "It is, after all, a responsibility she feels most keenly since I've told her she must be your partner — which means she must see you stay alive just as much as you must see she stays alive."

Ilena put her hands in a more relaxed position. "As a matter of fact, that became even more important to me at that same time, so she'd also be considering that a most important thing to want." Amber blinked and looked slightly confused, so Ilena cleared that up for her a little more, blinking back a slow and solemn blink. "If I hadn't set Second at Petroi's back, he would've been dead. She did die, breaking him and breaking my heart the same. If I hadn't set the Messenger of Kouzanshi together with Thayne, Thayne would've died, instead of just having his arm nearly severed. The Messenger did die, breaking Thayne and grieving me greatly.

"I'd sent Marcus to observe the fighting in Kouzanshi so he was there when the Messenger died, unable to save him either. Henry was in Nijoushi witnessing the death of Second. I sent Marcus back to help Thayne recover and Henry to help Petroi because I couldn't go myself. They learned then how important having a partner was. They also learned just how important it was to me as they had to watch my grief and bear it with me because they'd been the messengers to bring me the news."

She watched Amber as closely as before, going a little slowly to make sure the message was impactful enough. After a brief pause, she added, "Rio watched me go through that grief, through the fear of possibly also losing Petroi and Thayne. She knows how much it will affect me to lose either one of you. She understands just how important it is to me that people I allow that close to me take care of each other for their sake and for mine." Amber was restless now, having to hear things about Rio that made her more understandable, and thus made Amber more uncomfortable.

Ilena leaned forward just a little and relaxed even more. "Well, I hope you'll consider it a little more realistically now. After all, I'd far rather know early that you can't do it and don't want to care enough. Letting you go before I love you that much is much better all around." Sincerely she added, "I do appreciate you were willing to step in and help with the department work while we were gone. Having even one more mind and set of hands to help Grandfather was a great relief."

Ilena released Amber to go. Amber stood rather woodenly, curtsied the same, then left for her room across the hall. Ilena sighed to herself and was quickly lost in musing. She still wasn't sure Amber was the best fit for the department, for all her work within it was impeccable. The results of this test would be interesting.

-o-o-o-

Justinian was frozen with his hand on his bedroom door handle. He and Reynold had slipped into the suite silently and as ghost–like as possible, which was a lot in his case. Doing that when others were in motion was best since their added motion wouldn't be out of place. However, he'd been caught by Ilena's words and Amber's words.

The words from Amber might've been what she was feeling, but Justinian was quite certain they were nearly–false words. Words that said things others wanted to hear, or that came close to expressing what the speaker wanted to say but were this side of a lie to prevent offense from being given.

He'd seen Amber a few times with people outside the suite and it was true they'd not liked being with her. Their expressions had been that of those who didn't trust her. He was rather certain that hadn't been the case before they'd all left on the progress, so he'd been wondering what had happened. Amber hadn't specifically said this time, nor had Rio confided in Justinian anything before now, so he'd still have to wonder for now, he supposed.

Ilena's answer to Amber as to why Rio and the Twins were the way they were had been what had frozen Justinian. He was still trying to wrap his brain around those words. "Justinian?" Reynold called quietly from inside the bedroom. Concern was in his voice. "Is it okay?" He was standing next to his bed, having paused to see where Justinian was.

Justinian jolted just a little, then finished closing the door quietly behind him. He didn't look at Reynold as he walked to his bed, the closest one to the door so he could escape if he needed to. Once he was sitting cross–legged on his bed, he gave a nod. It was hard to be in a room with another person, but he'd been practicing at the clothing department before now, and trying hard through the progress and Tarc generally. Some nights were difficult still, which was why Reynold was concerned. He understood. Justinian appreciated that.

Now that Justinian was settled sufficiently, Reynold sat on the edge of his bed on the opposite side from Justinian's bed to pull off his boots. He set them in the place he kept them then waited for Justinian to settle a little more and nod before removing his jacket.

He carefully placed his jacket on its hanger and hung it in the wardrobe on his side of the room. He was kind to not leave things lying around since then Justinian would instinctively clean them up. He was also kind to not make sudden moves, like throwing clothing over chairs, which would make Justinian startle too much. It had taken them several weeks of being in the same room together for them to reach even this level of being able to be roommates.

"I'm sorry it's still hard for me to have a partner," Justinian said miserably, the fingers of each hand pressing together tightly.

Reynold was silent and still for a moment, then he shrugged. "You aren't a bad person to learn to be a partner to, Justinian," he said gently. "I know you're still working on trusting yourself as well as me. If knowing why

Mistress Ilena wants us to be partners can help you with that, then that's good. I appreciate that you work hard to take care of yourself so you can be careful with me."

Justinian looked up at him in surprise. "You – you can tell?"

Reynold smiled. "Yes. I hope you can reach the point soon that you can relax. Any little thing I can do to help with that is okay. You probably won't need to have them for the whole time we're partners, but I'll help you until then."

Justinian slumped and tears sprang into his eyes. "Thank you," he whispered. "I really do want to trust you, and me. I'm trying hard to get there."

"I know," Reynold whispered back. He watched Justinian for a moment longer then sat on his bed where he could lean against the wall. He reached for the book on his side table where it was lying next to the oil lamp warmly lighting his part of the room. He'd read it from now until Justinian left to help Ore prepare for bed. Then he'd finish changing to his nightgown and lie down to sleep. Even if it was a pretend sleep (which it wasn't often given how much work Reynold was doing to get caught up on his writing), it helped Justinian to not be afraid to go to bed himself.

Justinian picked up his favorite prize from the competition he'd won in the Fox Clan tents from the small collection of trinkets on his side table to slowly worry it between his fingers, and leaned back against the wall at the head of his bed. His ears listened to hear for Ore to return to the suite and head for his and Ilena's room. He also listened today to the faint sounds of Petroi and Thayne, now up in the suite above where they were keeping an ear on Ilena and eyes on Ore outside.

He found he was also listening for Henry and Marcus to return to their bedroom above his and Reynold's. He wanted to ask them for the story, to understand better from their point of view how important the partnerships were. They knew, and now he knew just why and how deeply they understood.

He was surprised when Reynold set his book into his lap and said quietly, "Mistress Ilena is really a very practiced manipulator and negotiator."

"Oh?" Justinian asked. Reynold was thinking back to that same conversation, it sounded like.

"Yes. She opened Miss Amber up more quickly than anyone else has, discovered a main problem, although perhaps not the only one, and addressed it in a way to make Miss Amber see the others with more clear eyes even though she doesn't want to. I could ponder that conversation for several days." Reynold looked over at Justinian, a bit of a dry look on his face. "Miss Amber needed it, of course. She still has a long way to go, even longer than you and I. Miss Rio's been patient with her."

Justinian considered that. "I think Amber was just made to be afraid."

Reynold's lip twitched up a little. "Well, she was, and she was supposed to miss most of the rest of it, but it will all worm its way into her now that her ears have heard it in the way Mistress Ilena put it. It really is fascinating to watch Mistress Ilena work." Justinian had to wryly agree with that. They were both seeing new things all the time.

-o-o-o-

Amber's hand was on the door handle to her room before she woke up from her stunned state. The reminder that Ilena killed traitors even from the Family had been the start of that state. Amber hadn't really considered that concept; although, perhaps she'd known at some point it was like that. She shivered and quickly let herself into her room, closing the door and leaning on it, trying to breathe.

The words that kept rebounding around her mind, though, were: "...before I love you that much...." Mother loved everyone, equally, right? She could already hear in her mind, though, Rio's scornful voice. Nothing was that simple. Amber's own color to what she believed Ilena was like had already gotten her into enough trouble as it was. She took a deep breath. It was obvious enough that Ilena loved no one more than Ore. Ilena loved Rei and Mizi more than anyone other than him. Probably King Sasou, too. If she loved them. Sometimes it was hard to tell if she was just protecting them, or if she really did love them.

Amber's eyes scanned her room but only saw that no one was waiting within it. She was still mostly trying to wrap her brain around that surprising end to her interview. She pulled the desk chair out and sat down in it heavily. She'd sleep, she was so tired from the day like all days in the department now, but she already knew her mind wouldn't let her. It would just continue to circle around and around if she didn't settle first. Breathing deeply helped keep it working to some degree, so she focused on that for a bit, letting Ilena's words settle a little more.

The most painful words Amber didn't want to think about, but she knew Rio would make those the ones she had to face, so she swallowed, then allowed her inner ears to hear them again: "if you don't want to care enough." Amber's face screwed up and tears threatened. She was angry they did. *Of course she wanted to care enough*, her heart wanted to scream. She'd already been working very hard, trying to understand, not killing Rio even though it was so hard to not scream at her in utter frustration.

Amber put her elbows up on her desk to hold her head in both hands. The tears wanted to come because she actually *did* want to care enough. However, she also knew that she hadn't cared about anything but herself and what she could get for herself in personal glory to lord over the other young women and men who cared about Mother. It frustrated her that she was so junior that none of the others in the office cared one way or the other as far as that was concerned. It had become rather painful that the people she thought she'd be able to lord it over for being asked to come serve in the Department of Intelligence just refused to talk to her at all any more. They turned and walked away from her if they saw her walking through the hallways or even in town now. Or they stiffly greeted her and cut her off early to make their excuses to escape.

One of the older paiges had finally said to her coldly, "You aren't a good example of the Immediate Family, are you? Do you mean to keep bringing the whole of them down into the gutter with you? I hope you aren't allowed to talk to the lords." He'd turned his back on her and left her there, shivering as the coldness of his words literally made her legs get goosebumps and her heart feel the loneliest it had since Marcus had told her he wouldn't talk to her again until she and Rio had finished learning how to be partners.

It made her jealous that Justinian was already beloved by both Ore and Ilena, and most of the Immediate Family as well. She'd taken to watching him closely to figure out why he was so quickly when she wasn't. He seemed to be very child–like: innocent, not quite put together. He was very serious about being strictly obedient, and he had a lot of fear both of himself and the world around him generally; although, he was able to relax around both Ilena and Ore.

Many of those things would make one want to protect him, she supposed, but she was still confused as to why they loved him like they did. He definitely was honest all the time, and maybe it was that? He still struggled with being a partner, but Reynold was quite patient with him in that regard. It was good that was the paring and not her. She did relate that much with him and often wished Rio was patient, too.

Her brain scolded her again. Rio was actually patient in her way. She'd never once yelled at Amber, not even for the many times Amber had stubbornly refused to write the truth of her story. Amber took in a deep breath and let it out. It was terribly difficult to think that Rio actually had positive motives to what she was doing, but she said she did. If Rio was afraid of having Amber die, she'd work hard, for sure.

Amber slipped down to rest her head on folded arms. She was so tired. Tired of fighting Rio, tired from all the hard work, tired of trying to figure out just what was expected of her that wasn't what she'd expected at all. Even Ore and Ilena's response to the truth had been unexpected, for all it was nearly exactly what Rio had said it would be. It only added to Amber's confusion. Slowly she slipped into sleep there at her desk, her brain not able to continue to work that hard that night.

-o-o-o-

Ore walked casually with his hands in his pants pockets through the courtyard to the next one as Rio bundled up more closely in her cloak, snatched up off the back of her rocking chair. He'd noticed she used it as a blanket indoors when the shawl from Lady Seraphina wasn't quite warm enough for her. "Are you also enjoying having warmer things this winter, like the Twins are?" he smiled at her.

Rio looked up in a little surprise, then gave a small grateful smile. "Yes," she answered. "For me, though, it's a little better that I get to have more clothes in my wardrobe than one simple dress. I was able to be in the warm house, where they had to be outside most of the time."

Ore gave a thoughtful nod. He let the conversation lag for about a half–circuit of the courtyard, then commented, "Rio, it seems to me that Amber wasn't happy to have to tell me her true story." He looked from the corner of his eye to see her expression sour just a little bit as a frown furrowed her brow for just a moment. He gave her a few seconds to settle, then asked, "Do you know what her goal is? What does she strive for?"

Rio looked away from him as she pondered the questions. She sighed a little, then shrugged. "I haven't asked her directly, I guess." She watched the path her feet were taking as they now were starting to press down even more snow in the path they'd already walked. "From watching her, she does want to be accepted and liked. She'd like to be able to have fun relaxing and being with people, but she likes the focus to be on her more than to consider others." Her brow wrinkled again, perhaps in confusion this time. "Except that she doesn't like it, because then she'll lie or twist the truth to deflect people from who she really is."

"Well, isn't that normal when a person has a past they don't want others to know about?" Ore asked gently.

Rio glanced at him, then looked away again. "I guess," she answered hesitantly.

Ore considered her, then decided to be a little hard. "That was me all the time," he said flippantly with a slightly callous tone to it. Rio's head snapped up to stare at him in shock. He stared back at her openly. "I was hiding, remember? If Pakyo found me, I was dead. I had to lie to stay alive — all the time." Rio blinked.

Ore lifted his head to look up at the dark cloud–filled sky, the dancing torch light in the courtyard almost hiding it, save for the faint reflecting glow from the many torches in Nijoushi. "I hid even more closely to me those things that were most important. I never told anyone about Ilena, save once by reference to Master when he came to me in secret because he wanted to let me out of the prison so badly." He scowled slightly. "And that was enough for him to research out who I was. It was that simple to do if I did ever speak. So I didn't."

Rio blinked a few more times, then gazed at the space between her and the ground again. Softly Ore added, "Even still, there are many things I don't talk about that are precious to me. My memories only to hold close to me, to not be tainted by others." He looked away from her as some of them rose to the surface of his mind.

He waited until they faded again, then looked down at his boots and kicked at the snow, making a few bits fly off. "Some things, like the past I was running from and had to turn to face, like what you were trying to do for Amber, do need to be brought out. They do need to be properly faced and walked back through to be settled and placed where they can be at rest instead of constant thorns." They both sighed about the same time. Ore hadn't liked his any more than Amber had, and both had been forced.

"Still, Rio," he said softly, "there are kinder ways to do it." She looked away and gave a small nod that she'd heard him, even if she didn't have that way known inside her. He tried to give her what he knew, "It's easiest if you know what *their* goals are first. Then you can encourage them through encouraging and supporting them on their way to that goal."

He shrugged and relaxed on purpose to get her to relax a little, "Ilena's the easiest example to use for that. I knew we'd be fighting for forever if I didn't know what her goals were and use that pathway. She will only ever be moved by moving herself." He gave a wry glace to Rio. She wrinkled up her nose in a grimace. She understood, having lived with Grandfather and Leah trying to work with Ilena.

He pondered for the next few slow steps of their circling meander, then added, "Actually, I know she does it, too, but perhaps more on the street. If you didn't leave the house, you probably didn't get to see that example as much. When she picks up a nightwalker, and they choose to follow her, it's because she's encouraged them to see that life might be worth living." Dryly he said, "For a lot of people on the streets, they give up on life and just exist, even though inside they're wishing to live the happy lives of those not on the street. To see there might be a dawn in the middle of their midnight can change them rather dramatically."

He drew in a breath and almost ordered her, "Rio, please try that method with Amber from now on. Even if you stumble in the learning of it, gently guiding her to her own goal will teach her more because she'll *want* to be helped. She'll do the hard work of helping herself get where she really wants to be."

Rio pulled her cloak closer to herself and took her time, but eventually she quietly agreed she'd try it. "It's hard, though," she whispered. "I don't like her. She's the exact type of girl I've never gotten along with and don't care to. All they can do is pretend like they're perfect and won't talk to anyone else with common respect and decency. It's all about them and the lies they've made up about themselves because they don't want to look at who they really are. I'm trying to help her learn that she doesn't have to hate that. That we'll accept her for who she honestly is."

"And does she want that? Is that her goal?" Ore asked.

Rio shook her head. "It doesn't seem to be, but she has dropped the mask for me a few times...., *sigh*, ...when I've pushed her hard enough she's had to." Ore just gave her a look that said he knew full well she knew that was the wrong way to go about it. Her slump agreed with him.

She pondered in the silence he allowed to go on. Her own mind would need to walk its pathways to figuring out how to approach Amber from now on. When she started to shiver a little more from the cold, he called in the code to Ilena to ask if she was done. She said she was, so they moved to slowly walk back to the door. On the way, Rio said, "Thank you, Master Ore. I'll ask her what her goals are and try to help better."

Ore gave a simple, satisfied nod. "We're here to help if you get stuck," he offered. She gave back a nod of gratitude as he opened the door. They slipped inside quickly to keep as much of the cold out as possible.

His soft, contented smile answered Ilena's curious look as he slipped down on the couch next to her to be held by her again to warm back up. Rio settled down in her rocking chair still wrapped up in her cloak to keep the extra warmth in until she warmed back up. The simple kiss Ore gave Ilena wrapped up his own feelings for that night. He was so glad to have her by his side, his ally and his partner rather than his adversary.

-o-o-o-

Rio paused outside her bedroom door. She'd waited to come to bed until after she'd thawed out from being an icicle, but then had been falling asleep in her chair. Sometimes she did fall asleep in it until Leah woke her up and sent her to bed. That was on the very busy days. Today had been one of those, actually. She was wondering if Amber had made it to her bed for that very reason.

They all had to work so hard that it was important to sleep well in their beds at night. Even the boys talked about how important that was, for all they'd learned to sleep on the floors and streets before. Henry often said he was glad they had real beds now. "If we had to work this hard and then have the hard floors, we'd never make it," he'd say with great feeling. Rio knew they'd worked hard even so when on the streets, so it must be bad.

She took a deep breath and moved to Amber's door. She tapped on it. There wasn't an answer. She didn't want to wake Amber up if she really was in bed, but she knew it scared Amber that she could pick the lock and walk in any time she wanted to. She saved it for the important times. Still, she shouldn't leave Amber in an uncomfortable position to have an even worse day tomorrow.

With a little shiver she reached for the door handle. Like Justinian was having troubles being in the same room with Reynold, for all they had separate beds, she also was so glad she and Amber didn't have to share a room. Their dislike for each other would have them fighting all the time at night. Then there was Rio's past that was just like Justinian's. She was always very grateful every night that Ilena and Ore understood and had never asked her to share.

Quietly Rio picked the lock then slowly opened the door to poke only her head in. She sighed sadly to see Amber asleep in her chair at the desk, draped over it. That wasn't good at all. She hesitated. She'd promised to be more gentle. It would be easiest and quietest to walk in and shake Amber's shoulder, but she'd jump and be so scared. Rio knew *she* would be, too, actually, if for a different reason.

Rio closed the door very quietly, paused, relocked it, and thought hard about what she'd want. Taking a deep breath, knowing she'd disturb a lot of people in the wing, she raised her hand and knocked several times very loudly. "Amber!" she called as loudly as she dared. "Amber! Wake up." She did try to make her tone kinder, rather than ordering, but she wasn't sure she made it to that. It was hard enough to be loud. She'd always been taught that if she was loud she was going to be punished. She knew she wouldn't be here, but she still cringed inside.

Rio was very relieved when she heard stirring on the other side of the door. "Amber," she called again. Slow steps shuffled to the door. She knew Amber likely didn't want to answer the door, but maybe she'd feel somewhat rewarded that Rio hadn't just walked in, and reward Rio for the same.

The lock eventually did turn and the door open. "What?" Amber asked, not as testily as she could have.

Rio gave her a sympathetic look. "It's hard to have a reasonable work day when you've not slept properly in bed. I just wanted to make sure you made it there." Amber blinked at her both with sleepiness and in some surprise. Rio shifted. "Ah..., are you awake enough to get there? Or do you need some help?"

Amber glanced back at her bed, then down at her clothing. Rio frowned at her slightly. "Enough to undress properly? Sleeping in your clothing isn't helpful either." She couldn't help the slight scold. She looked a little closer at the dress, then said specifically what she could help with and not be pushed over her own boundaries: "I could help you with the lacing and get the dress over your head at least, and put in the effort to get the boots off. I know that's the hardest when you're tired."

That much and Amber would be down to her shift and socks. Even if she fell asleep in those, it wouldn't be as bad. Rio had learned to be that specifically open with Ilena as Ilena had trained Rio to be her maid and help her dress and undress. Rio was relieved that Ore took care of the undressing of Ilena now more often than not. Undressing others had always led to far worse things before Ilena had rescued her.

Amber waffled, then was tired enough to let Rio in. Rio didn't close the door behind her, but she did push it far enough that people couldn't peek in on them. She could breathe a little better knowing it wasn't locked. That was why she'd learned to pick locks very early. She'd been living behind locked doors her whole life, until then. Walking the hall between Ilena's room and the kitchen at Tokumade had been freedom for her. Being able to walk around this whole hall, and even sometimes out in the castle grounds was having the whole world opened up to her, to the point of being overwhelming sometimes.

By the time she was done being grateful for that, Amber's dress was off and she was plopping down on the end of her bed. She handed Rio one of her feet and Rio undid the boot lacings. It was just as hard to pull off the boot as it usually was, but it was soon enough on the floor and the second foot was up. When that boot was off, Amber sighed in relief. She didn't move from her slump on the bed.

Rio paused, then lightly put her hand on Amber's head. "Thank you for your hard work today. I'm proud of you." She removed her hand before Amber could be irritated any more than briefly. The blue eyes came up to look at her in some surprise. Rio hesitated, then said, "Tomorrow, when we're ready for a rest, I'd like to hear more about what you want to say." Amber blinked at her, not sure if she was still sleeping and hearing things or not, Rio supposed.

Rio turned for the door. "Good night. Sleep well." The door was closed quietly behind her, locked already since Rio had turned the lock on the way. She silently moved to her door and opened it. She never worried Amber was going to come into her room. The lock was on Amber's door and she always locked it. Rio would likely never have to have her door locked ever again, and didn't intend to. She'd have the lock removed altogether if Ilena wouldn't frown on that.

She sighed as she got herself ready for bed. She was quite ready for her own soft bed. She was also glad she'd learned to sleep in one with Leah in the double room before she'd been here on her own. Rooms she was the only one in, with soft beds, were also rooms to be afraid of before. Working hard meant she was grateful and asleep very quickly, instead of worried for sleepless hours on end. Little by little she was learning she also could heal and be okay.

-0-0-0-

Marcus and Henry were back in their room rather late. Ore and Ilena were already tucking themselves into bed. It had been a long day of standing guard during the long meeting in town, then watching the pair at the lists. That had been after the final work that had to be done at Falcon's Hollow. For all they thought their day had been perhaps easier than Petroi and Thayne's, they weren't going to turn down an opportunity to have one more evening of vacation time before the vacation was officially over.

They'd enjoyed their meal with their friends and compatriots at the servant's dining room. As usual, they'd directed the conversations and made everyone laugh, while at the same time learning the little bits of important information they knew Ilena wanted to know. They'd been startled upon returning to hear Rio's voice. The knocking on Amber's door was unusual for Rio, or for her to speak out enough to be heard.

Marcus leaned back against the wall as he sat on his bed. His boots and jacket were off, but he wasn't ready to get any colder than that at the moment. The fire had been kindly stoked by probably Thayne before they'd gotten back, but it was still cold outside and he needed warming up before finishing his bedtime routine. It was nice Rio had paused to consider Amber this time. Given the girls had been kept, it was possible Ilena and Ore had talked to the two of them, which they definitely needed by this time. He was about to do what Henry had done before and step in.

His eyes flew open as the door to the bedroom opened. He and Henry were rather shocked to see it was Justinian who slipped into the room, pushing the door closed just enough their voices wouldn't carry far out of the room. He stayed right by the door, though, not coming any closer, his hands clasping behind him. He had a bit of a frown on his face. "I'm sorry to intrude," he said softly, bowing to them, then returning to his internal concern.

Marcus relaxed a little. "What's up, Justinian? It's a little unusual for you to willingly come visit." Justinian's head snapped up as did an eyebrow of surprise. Marcus kept to a casual, relaxed, and friendly look. He thought Justinian would need to relax a bit before he could get his question or concern out, so he continued on, "You do a good job of relaxing when you're concentrating on important things. I'd think if you stopped worrying so much you'd relax more."

Justinian blinked, his brain having to derail and consider what Marcus had said. When his look went to confusion and trying to puzzle that out, Marcus said in a sort of muse, "I think if you could think of it as always trying to focus on things that matter, instead of focusing on your worry, those things that worry you will take care of themselves, and you'll finally be able to just be. We all do like to see the relaxed you that does know how to be happy." He smiled.

Marcus was also talking to help Henry have the time to finish getting settled on his bed without worrying Justinian, and the time to finish calming down from the sudden startling so he didn't yell at or kill Justinian. Night-walkers didn't do well when startled. Justinian was not someone to yell at if he'd needed to come talk. Thus, Marcus was distracting Justinian from noticing that Henry was trying very hard to bite his tongue and calm back down. Justinian was silent enough he'd surprise the two of them every time if they didn't already know where he was.

"Well," Justinian said slowly, "it is true that when I have something to think about the worries have to wait. When I'm at loose ends all there is are the worries."

Marcus nodded helpfully. "Yes. If you can make it so that even if you're at loose ends you aren't really, then the worries don't have to intrude."

"Or, to put it another way," Henry could finally join in, "when you feel the worries coming on, if you choose to think of something better you could retrain your brain. If a concern that has purpose comes along, it's okay to think about those, but just sitting and worrying isn't usually helpful."

Justinian nodded thoughtfully. They waited patiently for him to get it worked out and back to his original thoughts. When he looked close, Marcus really had to ask, doing so very quietly, "Did Master Ore and Mistress Ilena talk to Amber and Rio? Do you know?"

Justinian nodded earnestly. "Yes. That's actually what's brought me." His brow furrowed with the look he'd entered the room with, then his eyes looked back up at Marcus. "Except, you'd want to know first, I guess. Master Ore and Rio were sent outside to talk, so I don't know what was said there. Mistress Ilena talked to Amber." Justinian blinked and his eyes were wide. "Reynold was impressed with how Mistress Ilena talked to Amber. He thinks it was good for her. I thought she just left afraid."

Marcus frowned. He wasn't sure he wanted it left at that. "What made her afraid?"

"Mistress Ilena reminded her that traitors to the Family also die," Justinian said softly and soberly. "Maybe she didn't know before?" his head tilted in querying thought. Marcus couldn't know the answer to that question. "But Mistress Ilena actually told her a lot more than that. That's what I wanted to come ask you two about." He took a deep breath, as if trying to screw up his courage. Marcus tried not to worry. Justinian had troubles just asking for an orange to be passed down the table at dinner.

"Mistress Ilena tried to teach Amber why she has that rule, and why she has the rule of partners." Justinian's eyes came up to look between Marcus and Henry. "It sounded like it was a very painful thing, to free me and the others from the Doll House. I'm sorry." Marcus blinked in some surprise as Henry stiffened with the same.

"Mistress Ilena taught me when she first tested Reynold and me at the fight at the end of being in Tarc that we're supposed to protect each other, but I didn't really understand until she tried to explain it to Amber." His brow furrowed again. "Actually, I still don't quite understand. I know the two of you do, just from watching you. You're very good partners. But after hearing that you've watched the reason why, I'm sure you understand what I'm trying to." Justinian shifted uncomfortably.

Marcus let Henry do the talking. "I wanted Marcus as my partner when he was seven and I was eight. I'd already struggled to stay alive on the streets for two summers and one winter. I didn't want another winter inside being beaten and having anything that might be enough food to eat stolen from me." Justinian eyes went wide. "We've had since then to learn how to support each other."

"I'm Family from the beginning, Justinian," Marcus looked the slightly younger man in the eyes. "That made our pairing very odd, and quite hard at the beginning to be honest. Once I finally understood that the path I was on because of Henry was better than where I'd been going, I could work with him instead of against him. I think you're already doing that, for all it's hard for you to have a partner. You're willing to try. I had to get there first. It's probably harder for Reynold to want a partner, he's so much older and used to doing his own thing."

Justinian shook his head, then paused, then answered. "Maybe, but he's willing to help me learn it. At least the learning to trust myself with a partner part. And I think our partnership will be different, since we won't be guards often."

"It'll be different anyway, because both of you are different," Henry dismissed that slightly.

Marcus nodded. "I'm the one that needs the touch for comfort." He tipped his head towards Henry. "Henry doesn't really like it most of the time. He's learned to give me what touch he can stand to give, and it's enough. Becoming partners is about learning things like that. What do you need to feel safe, comforted, or needed? What does your partner need for those things? The list is longer than that, but I think you can get the picture from those since they're the beginning.

"It definitely doesn't come all at once. It takes time to learn those things that are most important to you, the things you can let go of because something is important to your partner. You don't have to do it all at once. Little by little is just fine. You're moving forward already. Let how fast or slow it happens be a worry you let go of." Marcus paused to inspect Justinian for a bit. They hadn't found the specific thing he was worrying at tonight. "Just because you didn't chose to have a partnership doesn't mean there isn't a reason somewhere inside yourself to have one. You're already trying hard. Why?"

Justinian paused and looked as if a light had come on for him. Marcus nodded. That was what Justinian was trying to reach, what he was trying to understand. Still, Marcus had one more thing to add to all of that, something he was wishing for himself when it came to Amber. It was important to it all, he thought.

"Justinian," he called softly and Justinian paid him attention again, "in all of that, add in one more thing." Justinian gave a small nod. "Partners have a shared goal that keeps them moving forward together. Henry wanted to follow Mistress Ilena. That was the only thing that helped him do the thing that was hard for him. He didn't want to learn to be Family. It was as hard for him as for me to learn to be a nightwalker. As soon as I understood that Mistress Ilena had both the House *and* the Family, I was able to relax and feel part of the whole, to feel like our partnership had a reason to be. We could *both* follow Mistress Ilena and not lose our individual integrity.

"Most likely the reason Sir Petroi and Thayne are working hard together is because they both want to follow Master Ore and protect Mistress Ilena in doing that together. While you consider what your reason is, also talk to Reynold to learn what your joint goal is. Why's he even willing to be patient with you, to accept the partnership at all? If they're the same reason, it's much easier to help each other reach it." Henry nodded sober agreement to that teaching.

Justinian relaxed and slumped a little. "Okay," he said softly. "I'll think about those things instead of the other worries when I'm at loose ends."

Marcus smiled. "You do that. It's probably a much better thing anyway."

"Probably," Justinian smiled back shyly. He disappeared out the door again.

Marcus' smile stayed as he returned to his bed–time routine. Henry glanced at him and asked quietly, "Feeling better?"

"Yeah," Marcus whispered back. He always felt better when he'd been able to help someone move forward in positive ways. Justinian was even better for that. He really wanted to be part of the rest of them and was good for Ilena. Just knowing the girls had been talked to helped, too. He'd learn in the next few days if it had helped, but having that one change in Rio this night was a good sign it had.

CHAPTER 146 Interim Investiture

Rei, Mizi, Ilena, and Ore met King Sasou and Queen Aryana at the Royal entrance to Nijou Castle. Ilena was in a court dress for once, properly dressed for her station. She and General Garen had set up security around the driveway and door as they'd been taught the last time Sasou had come to the castle. Ilena specifically chose to have all the guards of the Suiran royals be the guards who lined the path from the royal carriage to the entrance.

King Sasou noted it, looking at each of the guards from the corners of his eyes as he walked. When he reached the end of the row, he paused and turned to one on the end. "I've not tested this one," he commented.

Ilena stepped forward slightly. "Rather, King Sasou, you have tested this one the longest."

Sasou held himself very firmly, but his expression and tone went frosty. "What have you done, Director Ilena?"

"Has this one not been always obedient to the King, the Queen before him, and the King before her? Has he not been faithful in his service to me and honorable in my House, even to the saving of my life?" Ilena spoke formally.

Sasou turned his frosty look on her. "Yet to allow him in the presence of the King?"

"O King," Ilena bowed her head and curtsied, holding the pose as she spoke, "has he not paid the judgment laid on him without fail and without complaint, even though it was the punishment of his fathers' that he carried, and not for a sin of his own? What greater loyalty can there be?"

Sasou stared at Ilena. "How do you know that it was not for his own sins as well?"

Ilena paused, rose from her curtsy and looked at Sasou significantly, standing nearly eye–to–eye. "Have these eyes not seen all things from their youth?" Sasou hesitated, remembering. Ilena's warmly golden eyes didn't look away from his own piercing blue eyes. "When a judgment is paid, is it not right to leave the error and the judgment behind so that one may move forward again? Did not the King allow for this one to leave it behind by erasing his name and giving him one that would allow it?" Ilena's eyes softened slightly and her tone went compassionate. "Can the King who has done it not live according to his own word?"

Sasou took in a sharp breath. She was asking much of him... but..., she was right. They'd both known, when Liam had watched over them when they were young, that he hadn't done the works of his fathers. He finally turned back to Liam. "Your mistress has sued for your life, yet again. I'll expect to see your gratitude for her words in your actions."

Liam bowed. "Always, Your Majesty." His quiet voice pierced Sasou. It was the first time he'd ever heard it for himself. He continued to look at the man with a testing gaze, then turned on his heel and continued his progress into the castle.

"What do you want, Ilena?" he asked quietly.

"May I meet with you when you are sufficiently settled?" she asked.

Neither looked at the other, but after a pause Sasou nodded. Ilena stepped back from following just at his heel and Rei moved up to properly host his brother, who was introspective and perhaps just a little troubled.

-o-o-o-

In the rarely–used Office of the King in Nijou there was a private meeting beginning. It was a small office, in comparison to the office in Ichijou, but it was sufficient. This was a formal meeting and Sasou wanted the setting to be correct for it.

The walls were curtained in pale gold tapestries embroidered with gold threads to make the room both warmer and quieter. The chair in the room was more an armed and cushioned throne of the same colors and there wasn't a desk in the room. That was in his quarters since if he *had* to work while he was at Nijou, he wanted to be in the more comfortable building that was his.

Sasou looked at his cousin and adopted sister, choosing to do so with the cool distanced expression he used as his shield between himself and the rest of the outside world. Even she needed to understand her place if she was going to come to the King with requests of him. She'd come dressed in the day's court dress and with a matronly lady–in–waiting, both so unlike her that it was a statement from the beginning that she understood and had come properly armored.

She met him with the properly respectful face of a petitioner. Still, having already received the lead–in to this visit, he steeled himself for a battle. "Princess Ilena," he acknowledged her calmly, allowing her to speak. He'd made her wait for his initial review of her, but chose not to rudely try her patience. She was worthy of respect for already having shown him the same.

Ilena curtsied exactly appropriately, reminding him sharply of herself as a five–year–old princess at Ichijou. "King Sasou. Thank you for granting me audience so soon after your arrival from your journey." She paid him the respect of his time by not wasting it with random pleasantries: "If you're set on lifting me up to sit over Tarc, I would speak with you on the matters of my household that only you can see to before then."

Sasou rested his chin on his hand and considered her. It wasn't unexpected, and her lead–in had been the perfect indicator of her intentions. *How much is she going to make me pay for putting her in that place?* "Indeed, I intend to make you Grand Duchess of Tarc. ...Say on."

There was a brief pause that spoke volumes in the court game. "Please recognize my husband as the last remaining heir to the kings of Suiran and allow him to be my Lord Prince, rather than Consort." Sasou raised an eyebrow. "I shall request it of the King at this investing court." Sasou nodded once. She'd answered his questions and properly seen to the protection of her husband — in *both* courts.

Ilena curtsied, a 'thank you' for his allowance. Her pause let him know that she was going to continue on. "Because of the high stations into which both of us will be placed, please allow for the titling with court titles of our household, so they may be able to properly support us and so that their faithful efforts may be rewarded."

"Tell me who you'd have raised up to which positions." He wasn't going to allow her a blanket approval. It won her a point when she didn't flinch, but smoothly acknowledged his point and right.

"I would have those closest to us raised up only. Will you hear the entire list now?"

"I would." Sasou was able to finally enjoy a face–to–face verbal fencing interaction with Ilena after many years of only playing the court game via letter. This time was much better than the scolding lunch he'd had to endure the last time he'd visited. This time she was making requests of him, so she stayed humble, if firm.

He wasn't surprised this meeting was so that she could make specific requests for advancement for her household members. He understood that she'd need for them to have royal recognition as nobles for them to work for a princess effectively in the courts of Ryokudo. He was surprised that she asked for those not surnamed as of yet to be added to Ore's family, the House of Melick.

Ilena had asked for everyone he knew on her list save the one final one he was sure he didn't want her to bring up. She paused once again, and her demeanor changed subtly. Sasou braced himself, going calmer and deeper. "If the House of Prince Melick is noble, then those in it are also noble. Please grant to his elder brother also a title: that of court count."

Sasou grit his teeth. "...You'd raise Liam as high as Petroi?"

"I would," she answered calmly.

Sasou tried to consider it rationally. She'd claimed Liam since she'd been here to claim him, Rei, and Ore. Given the titles of everyone else from that time, it wasn't out of line. He knew what she'd written about his service in Tarc as well. He understood what she'd meant by Liam having saved her life. However, that wouldn't be sufficient to the lords.

It would be hard enough to prove Liam's worth given he...no. Liam had served him and his father and mother faithfully. She'd already given him the reasons for that appointment in her earlier lead–in argument. "I should think a viscounty would be sufficient?" he raised an eyebrow, trying to find a more palatable resolution.

"Surely nobility is the King's to grant; however, Liam Melick has served longer and with greater faithfulness than even Thayne, who's to be raised to that level."

Sasou sighed to himself. She'd really tried her best to box him in from the beginning. He really didn't want to give up, though. "I could have someone else made grand duke and grand duchess?"

"Such *bloodthirsty* words. Will you choose to fail when Rei and I have already succeeded?"

Sasou stared at her, then shook his head, finally conceding with a small wry smile. "Formidable indeed. It's been a pleasant exchange."

Ilena continued to maintain her politeness to his face, but the tension in her back faded. "Thank you for your consideration of me and my household. I'll allow you to rest from your travels." He nodded as she curtsied and turned to leave.

"Ah, Ilena." She turned back, an eyebrow raised. "Please set aside some time to play a game of chess with me when you come this next summer... for my first child's birth celebration."

The slow, bright smile that came to Ilena's face was reward enough. "I'd be happy to, Sasou. Congratulations. When is the expected birth date?"

"Spring Three." Sasou was inordinately pleased. "Are you and Ore considering it also?"

Ilena turned back to him. "Yes, for all it will be difficult. We're hoping to complete it before another year is out. Rei is keeping Mizi on a leash for at least two years. Mina and I will both be taking care of it."

Sasou considered that news briefly. "A Marciel is acceptable as well. I wish you luck. It won't be easy training my little brother to understand."

"I hope it will be sufficient that he'll have compassion on his wife when it's her turn," Ilena answered.

Sasou's expression went compassionate and briefly a little sad. "Ilena..., do take proper care of yourself as well."

Ilena's eyes widened with slight surprise, then she smiled softly. "I will. Ore does a very good job of helping me do just that."

Sasou tipped his head. "Have you determined what kind of tree your sapling is?"

"Mm," Ilena nodded once. "A wild cherry. And yours?"

"She still could either become a willow or a silver maple."

Ilena pierced him with her scolding eyes. "I hope for your sake it's the latter, Sasou. A willow won't have sufficient strength to stand next to you."

"Yes, ma'am. I'll count on your support, then," Sasou gave her a small mocking bow.

Ilena narrowed her eyes at him, then sighed lightly. "Mistress Mizi and I will continue to do our best, but don't forget the timing of saplings. Your child will also be moving at that speed and will need your proper involvement." She paused, opened her mouth, then closed it again, waiting on him to excuse her.

It was perhaps childish to ask it but Sasou had one more question burning in his breast and this was a rare opportunity to ask it to her directly. "Ilena, now that I've given you everything you required of me, when shall I receive my reward?"

She answered him soberly, "It will come, ...in the timing of kings." She curtsied and left the room with her lady–in–waiting following her silently.

Sasou looked after them, wondering what Ilena was seeing on her board, or on his, that she understood already that he might not yet. "You'll see to it?" he asked the invisible person behind him.

"Yes, Your Majesty." His secretary and the scribes would be busy getting the awards put together before the court.

-o-o-o-

"...this treaty to maintain the peace between the lands and peoples of Tarc and Ryokudo is hereby signed on the sixteenth day of Autumn Two, year five hundred forty–five. Zerak' of the Storm Clan, First Prince of Tarc; Prota of the Fox Clan, Second Prince of Tarc; Rei Touka, Regent of Suiran, First Prince of Ryokudo."

The Voice of the King rolled the scroll officially making Tarc a vassal state of Ryokudo and handed it to Rei, who formally presented it to Sasou. The assembled full court clapped in approval, all of them relieved to have the matter settled 'peacefully'.

The lords and even many ladies of the court were in attendance, all dressed in bright colors of office and formality. The stiff fabrics and chains of office made for an underlying susurration of sound accented by quiet clinks. The smell of many warm bodies also underlay the sensations of the room, although it wasn't to unpleasant levels. Occasional coughs or the clearing of throats sounded, muffled as much as they could be. These sensations of being in a room filled with hundreds of bodies wasn't unfamiliar.

Sasou was sitting centrally on the raised dais on the main throne carved with the arms of Ryokudo and draped in pale gold cloths. He was dressed in a pale gold jacket and pants, both with brilliant gold trim that were the formal colors of the king of Ryokudo. The gold crown on his head was inset with sparkling diamonds of both pale yellow and brilliant clear that caught the lights in the room. His pin of office of the King set on the perfectly folded ascot sparkled in a lesser reflection to the crown.

Rei settled back down on the lesser throne that had been set next to Sasou, his part of the proceedings done. He was also in his typical formal colors of the pale gold with the brilliant blue trim that drew the eyes of both brothers out. That coloring was complemented by the darker blue and gold cloths draping his throne of the Regent of Suiran.

His gold crown of the Regent had alternating clear and blue stones set on it: diamond and sapphire. His pin of office of the Regent matched with the blue background behind the gold mountain. His pin of the First Prince of Ryokudo vied for attention at his left shoulder where it sat proudly proclaiming his heritage and pointing to his brother as well.

Other thrones were set up on the dais. To Rei's right was the throne of his wife. Mizi's golden red hair was rather startling among all the pale gold and blue. It went well with the blue dress she was wearing, piped in pale gold. She sat quietly and properly, enjoying the pomp and circumstance — as long as she wasn't thinking about herself.

Aryana sat to Sasou's left, properly and patiently as the Queen should. She really was very good at that. Her curled golden tresses and blue eyes were both a darker shade of Sasou's own and her dress was made to match. Together they studiously always made an impact on the viewer.

Kata, on the final throne to the left had begged to be let off, but Sasou wasn't terribly inclined to let her. He agreed with Ilena that she needed to get out of her rooms and see the light of day and her people more. Since she didn't have to do anything other than sit, he'd merely told her to simply enjoy the entertainment for once. She'd left him rather stiff, but he didn't particularly care. Rei needed to be dragging her out more himself. It would be interesting to see at what point he'd learn enough courage from Ilena to actually do just that.

When the room had settled sufficiently, the Voice called Ilena before the King. Ilena, dressed in her newest formal dress from Lady Seraphina in the royal pale gold with green accents just barely whispered over it, curtsied before the Throne. Her crown with the delicate pearls was tightly held down to her black hair and her pin of the Second Princess of Ryokudo was centered at the top front of her bodice. Her hair had been curled painstakingly by Rio and hung loose down her back to accentuate it's length.

She knelt on one knee in front of the thrones. Her clear, unafraid voice carried without shouting. "King Sasou, I beg a boon. My husband, Ore Melick, formerly Kase Shicchi, is the last remaining of the line of the Kings of Waldstaat. Will you please acknowledge his blood and lineage and grant him his proper place by my side as Prince?"

Sasou rose and nodded slightly to his Voice. His Voice called Ore forward. He was dressed to match Ilena and wore his crown she'd put on him as Consort. He bowed and knelt next to his wife.

Sasou took from the pillow in the hands of the waiting master of ceremonies the medallion of the Second Prince that Rei had worn for so long. The chain settled heavily on Ore's shoulders, to remind him yet again that such high offices were burdens to be borne with care and consideration. The medallion would be Rei's again within a year if Sasou's heir was a son, but such was the way of things.

As Sasou placed it over Ore's head, he said, "From this day forth, you, Ore Melick, shall be known as a Prince of Suiran, and all your heirs after you. Because you are married to a Touka, your personal title shall be Prince of Ryokudo, but your children after you will not bear the right to royalty of Ryokudo, but only of Suiran, and they will be subject to the Regent of Suiran as well as the King of Ryokudo."

Sasou glanced at Ilena and was relieved when she was pleased enough with the statement. He already knew she wanted to remove her children as heirs of any land, but he'd wanted to keep them available to use as necessary. It was the best compromise he'd been able to come up with.

He stepped back and nodded again to his Voice. A grant of supporter (a walking stallion) and a further grant of land was read off for Ore's raising to Prince and for his service to the crown in his efforts towards the peaceful negotiations between Ryokudo and Tarc.

Another scroll was unrolled. They waited patiently as the land of Tarc was named a Grand Duchy of Ryokudo. Another scroll named Ilena and Ore as Interim Grand Duchess and Grand Duke of Tarc as of the first day of Pre–Cold Solstice, year 545.

They properly swore fealty to the King and Crown of Ryokudo and to the Regent of Suiran. Rei placed the new regalia on each of them of the horse of the rising sun, giving Ore double medallions and rings for this day. Sasou tried not to notice the tears in Ilena's eyes. He chose to believe it was because she was relieved to finally have the land she loved be hers, rather than what he suspected Ore's was — which was the pain of being yoked to a station too high and difficult to carry. Sasou understood both the pain and the love all too well, carrying his own station with both for so long already.

He and Rei sat and Sasou's Voice read off yet another scroll that granted Ilena a supporter: a lioness rampant in recognition of her father. For her service in keeping track of Tarc for him she should at least have the minimal reward her husband had received — thus the supporter today as well.

For the Toukas it was a long court, this second formal high court in half a year. So much ceremony they usually bypassed as much as possible, but they all behaved properly, it being their requirement and their joy to serve their country. For the remaining part, Ilena and Ore returned to the thrones to the right of Mizi. At seven thrones, they barely all fit on the dais, even for it being the largest throne room — yet again.

Leah Undel Thorin received a supporter and the gratitude of the family of Touka for her constant care over Ilena. Randolph Thorin finally received his due, with all of his service to Tokumade and his prior accomplishments being read for the court. The former steward was made a court marquis to match his wife and was granted an award of arms and access to a small holding (freed up by the imprisonment of the corrupt lords). Sasou was sure the couple would appreciate being able to escape as their alternative to full retirement.

Petroi Somas was granted a court earlship and a mantle over an award of arms as recognition for his service to protect Ilena since her youth. Sasou took the opportunity to quietly express his own personal gratitude to Petroi. The quiet look of proud gratitude on Petroi's face was well worth the reward. Because of the level of the award Liam Melick was next and half the Toukas had to steel themselves for it. His humility at receiving the court county and Ilena's tearful gratitude was sufficient for Sasou.

The following court county award was much easier to award. Andrew's surprised look when Sasou also granted him a mantle with his award of arms, and a small holding set between Castle Nijou and Yosai made it all the more rewarding. So much so that Sasou had to give Andrew a teasing look. It kept Andrew from doing more than slightly tear up. He'd surely sit with his wife and weep afterwards, though. Just as surely he'd make her countess when the son of Earl Durand was born, which Sasou had heard should be in Spring Two of the following year. At least they were all hoping it was a son.

A viscounty for Thayne was next, then rather quickly baron for Henry, for Marcus, and baroness for Rio with all four of them being surnamed Melick for their service to the Second Princess of Ryokudo. Ilena hadn't asked for Thayne to be surnamed, but Sasou knew better and just went ahead and did it. Thayne wouldn't ever live at Wexford again, having been claimed by Ilena, so he may as well be recognized as the family he was.

Sasou had almost chosen to not award Ryan, which had been suggested by Ilena, but then had decided that since he was Head of the Nijou Department of Medicine, he really should be titled to at least baron. That was done last, to a very surprised and shy Ryan who had to be prodded up by his neighbors in the audience. Sasou smiled for him to help him feel more at ease. He was indeed a rather fun person to tease.

Sasou's work was finally done and he relaxed a bit. Andrew traded places with Sasou's Voice and read off the new Suiran appointments, starting with Ilena as Minister of Intelligence. That office gave her a second medallion to wear for this court. Somehow it looked like she was bearing up well enough under all the weight of the metal on her head and shoulders but Sasou thought there was just a bit of a shadow on her face. Then he changed his mind. It was a set look of firm resolve mixed with suffocation. He hoped she'd last the rest of the court. It was apparently too long for even her.

Ore was read in as Assistant Minister of Intelligence, calming the lords who were still paranoid about Ilena's fierceness to them early on. All of the ministers relaxed when Mitchel Barkley was read in as Associate Minister of Intelligence. Minister of Finance Hulmer seemed resigned when his capable but low enough level assistant was taken from him to be Steward of the Grand Duchy of Tarc.

Although they weren't present, Prince Prota of Tarc was read in as joint Steward of the Grand Duchy of Tarc and Prince Zerak' of Tarc was read in as Grand Marshal of the Grand Duchy of Tarc. Sasou found it interesting that Ilena had found ways to give them both Tarcian and Ryokudo equivalencies. If those two ever did come to Nijou, the court would know how to face them at least.

-o-o-o-

Finally, the court was adjourned to the relief of all of the royalty, the succeeding obligatory meeting with the court lords completed. They walked out and convened in a quiet enclosed garden, just the extended family group. Kata even attended, just to watch them all interact for once Sasou supposed since he'd expected her to still be angry with him and leave as soon as she could escape. She chose to keep to the background for the most part, though. Only Mizi seemed to have received some level of excitement and energy from the whole proceedings.

Sasou sighed as he sank into a chair languidly. He gratefully accepted a glass of light white wine from his personal server. He sipped at it lightly until everyone had a drink in hand. Then he lifted his glass. "To the new Grand Duke and Grand Duchess. May they be able to keep the wild men of Tarc tamed for many years to come."

Glasses were raised around in response to the toast and they drank to the hope that it wouldn't all come crashing down around their ears in one year. "Why didn't you bring at least Zerak' here this time?" he asked Ilena.

Ilena sighed as she leaned back against the table near Sasou that held the wine bottles as if she was still only in pants. "They needed to get their clans in order. I hope to bring them both next year, if all is stable. Otherwise it will be two years.

"Although..., well, no, we'll be too busy. I could bring them next summer sometime, but we also need the year to be settled here. We'll see if everything is calm, then invite them. Too soon and they may learn things we don't want them to know too early."

Sasou nodded. "If you need to show them just how vast Ryokudo is, in three years bring them down to visit me. I'd be happy to let them watch a display of the soldiers of Ryokudo with me."

"Thank you, King Sasou," Ilena answered seriously.

Sasou frowned at her slightly for using the title, then let it go, reaching for Aryana's hand and holding her fingers loosely. "Little Brother," he called Rei. Rei turned to look at him, an eyebrow raised in slight irritation at the casualness of Sasou's tone.

"I wanted to let you know you'll hopefully not be First Prince much longer. Spring Three, I should think..., right around your birthday. We'll hope to give you back what we gave Ore today. Have Ilena's master crafters make Ore a Third Prince medallion and regalia that can be used as the Prince of Suiran regalia when he's done with the title. We'll reserve the Third Prince of Ryokudo medallion and regalia in Ichijou for now."

Rei bowed his head slightly. "Congratulations, Elder Brother. Will we dispense with the formalities and just exchange things around again at the birth celebration?"

"While I'd like to say that this really is all I can stomach for quite some time I'm afraid I can't." The other Toukas all blinked at him, except Mizi who look puzzled. They didn't enlighten her.

Rei paused, then gave an understanding nod. "I was thinking we'd come to Ichijou in Summer's Heat. We have a visit to make to Yamanzar and it needs to be mostly from Pre–Hot Solstice to Summer's Heat to fit our schedules here. Would that work for you?"

Sasou raised an eyebrow. Rei was planning that far ahead already. It might be self–preservation. "That should be fine. When you know your schedule for sure, let my office know."

"Of course," Rei said with polite formality.

"I'll come in time on my own," Kata said from her place. When Sasou glanced her way she added mildly, "Assuming you won't let me stay quietly away?" Kata got stern looks from both Rei and Ilena. Sasou tipped his head towards them, letting that answer his mother. He looked back at Rei and pursed his lips slightly, twirling the stem of his glass between his fingers and thumb.

"Sasou," Ilena said quietly. He looked up at her quickly. She was looking at him with calm sympathy. He sighed. When he'd calmed she continued. "Lord Barret says you're headed for a vacation after this. I hope you're able to relax sufficiently there. ...Please do."

Sasou looked at Aryana and lightly pressed her fingers in his, then nodded without looking back at Ilena. He could see Ilena take another sip of her wine from the corner of his eye, then set her cup down on the table behind her as she stood. "Master Rei, do you already have entertainment prepared for our brother, who'll likely get himself into trouble this afternoon without it?"

"Ah...," Rei was a bit lost. "I was thinking rest?"

Ilena sighed. "I think Sasou's sat quite long enough. Might I suggest that the King be offered the opportunity to view some of the things of Tarc that we can show him here?" She turned to Ore. "Specifically the race. You and the Sons could show him how it's done. It would be interesting to know if it can be taught to the horses of Ryokudo, or if they'd have to learn it on the horses of Tarc in order to truly enjoy it.

"The Twins can go with Ore and First and Second. The more there are to race the better, I think, and they need the practice. Next year they need to be able to be the best of the Kir'nah in the race, or they won't be able to hold on to their titles of Seconds." Both young men sighed unhappily.

Sasou was having difficulty holding down his inner child who was suddenly getting a wish he'd never thought he might. It was enough internal excitement to make him somewhat ignore the uncertain frown on Michael's face. He noted the concern enough to promise himself he'd be careful enough to not die during the lesson.

"Mizi, Ilena, I was hoping to have time to visit with you while we were here as well," Aryana requested.

"We could meet this afternoon," Mizi offered.

Aryana nodded. "That would certainly be acceptable."

"Ah! Sasou, did you bring the books on the history of Tarc?" Rei suddenly asked.

"Mmm," Sasou nodded. "I've got three. They're in my rooms. Shall we take time to meet this afternoon?"

"Yes, please. There are things I'd like to discuss with you as well." Rei swirled his glass lightly, thinking.

Sasou raised an eyebrow and sat up, leaning forward on his elbow a bit. "You'd willingly stay in the same room alone with me for longer than five minutes?"

Rei startled back to the present. A slow chagrined smile came over his face. "Yes."

Sasou leaned back, just as startled as Rei. "Well, I think my younger brother has learned some strength these last three months."

Rei's expression turned wry. "I must say it's more likely in the last month; although, the growth had been fairly steady up until then since Ilena came. The trial by fire was quite effective.

"Dealing with you, whom I've known my whole life, is an easier thing, I think, than having to deal with a culture of people I've never seen before, have to negotiate with and step carefully around for only a week, and come back home with my head still attached and all of my family alive as well. Really, it was quite terrifying. I'll be happy to spend a few hours closeted with you. At least I know you want me alive so you don't have to do what I'm doing."

Sasou laughed. "Thank you, Rei. I think that more than anything tells me you've definitely passed your test." He rose. "Shall we all go get these beastly costumes off and meet in Ilena's office for lunch? I'll bring the books and we can take them upstairs and make her staff completely frustrated with us for not allowing them to get their work done for the day.

"There's a bear statue I'd like to visit, and it's a good place to hide. I can already feel the lords of the castle trying to crawl into my sleeves." He shuddered lightly. "I had enough of that yesterday. The ladies can have the downstairs to visit once lunch is done. Then when we can't sit any longer we can go learn a new way to ride." His gaze fell on his mother. "We'll expect to see you there as well, Mother." He left no room for argument. She wrinkled up her nose at him but then sighed slightly and dipped in an abbreviated curtsy to him. He ignored the slight given in her frustration.

He helped Aryana rise from her chair next to his, set his glass down on the table, smiled slightly at Ilena who bowed her head, giving her permission for lunch to be in her quarters, and left for his rooms. He would've kept the conversation going but Ilena was showing signs of the medallions being too heavy and he wanted her to be able to shed them sooner than later. She was already carrying the weight without needing the additional physical weight to remind her.

He did pause by Ore to whisper, "Keep your crown on until I leave. I'll forget otherwise." He was slightly surprised when Ore's expression stayed polite and calm. He might have heard a very quiet sigh about the time he reached the exit to the garden, though.

-o-o-o-

After lunch in the Lower office, which was a bit tight, mostly unplanned, and therefore very relaxed, the ladies sat and conversed over tea. Ilena made Mina stay downstairs with them. Mina wasn't too thrilled to sit at either place ...at least until she learned what topic the conversation was going to be turned to. Ilena also made Kata stay with a polite invitation followed by a stare that didn't allow for a "no" to be said. When Kata gave in, Ilena allowed, "I'm sure you don't have to stay for the whole afternoon." Kata settled back down in her seat slightly less reluctantly.

"Aryana," Ilena led right off casually, "Mistress Mizi was saying on the way back from Tarc that she's been properly considering that her next responsibility to Master Rei and Suiran is to be available to produce an heir." Mina and Mizi both had eyes pop out of their heads at such a straightforward statement to the queen, and in front of the queen mother. "Since you're already well into your own state of the same — congratulations again — will you please advise her, and the rest of us, as to what it will mean for our positions, activities, and capabilities?" Mina noted that Kata immediately went from resigned to having her interest piqued.

Mizi looked relieved and extremely interested, adding her own request for the same. Ilena sat back and let Aryana carry the conversation from that point, also listening and learning carefully. Mina occasionally commented based on what she'd been seeing from her new step–mother going through the same.

It was going to be very important for all of them to be able to carry that additional burden along with all the other high offices and burdens they were already carrying. None of them had any other way to learn it than this. None of the three of them had a living mother to tell them how pregnancy would fit into real life at their level.

Aryana seemed pleased that they were all carefully considering this aspect of their roles and was careful to stress that the most difficult complication was the diminishing physical capability as the body of necessity had to care for the developing child. She also explained the changes that would come after the children were born. In the end, though, they allowed for Leah and Aryana's head nurse, who'd come with her, to teach them all in greater detail. Even Aryana's mother had died while she was young and she had to admit she was feeling just a little the same as they all were.

At that point Kata began to join in with stories of her own experiences. Ilena kept her from getting too sharp with occasional glaring looks and pointed questions. When Kata found the balance of teaching out of serious concern for what the young royals were going to be going through, then Ilena settled. Mina could also relax slightly at that point.

When the topic of conversation finally turned to the questions Aryana had, Ilena excused Kata, thanking her for her help and advice. The others were also honestly grateful as well. Mina thought Kata left perhaps a little more happily than she normally might have. She seemed to have enjoyed remembering the stories of the infant sons she'd carried and birthed. Their wives had certainly enjoyed several of the stores that should have made the sons blush, if they were listening in on the conversation.

Thereafter, Mina noticed that Ilena remained fairly quiet, allowing Mizi to carry the bulk of the teaching time, adding only where she was needed. Mina watched Ilena for a while, then listened a little closer to what was happening above, in the Upper office. She smiled secretly to herself. Ilena was just as much interested in that conversation.

As far as Mina was concerned, she herself was now ready to escape either one. Of necessity, she had to fall into her role of bored guard to have the patience to sit still and not scream.

-o-o-o-

She wasn't the only one. Ore paced silently with his lithe cat–like pace to the other side of the room again. Sasou had been watching him for a while, while he was answering Rei's questions when they came. This time, he decided to give himself a little entertainment to break up his own boredom. "Needing freedom already, Ore?" he asked.

Ore turned and raised an eyebrow. "No, not particularly, King Brother."

"Why is it the panther paces, then?" Sasou slightly raised an eyebrow back. He'd been surprised Ore had been obedient and was still wearing his crown.

Ore paused, a bit surprised, then looked extremely unsure how to answer the question. After a pause, during which Rei raised his head from the book he was reviewing to look at Ore blandly, he sighed. "King Brother, you understand that Ilena has taught all of her network, and therefore all of us, how to hear extremely well so we can use her coded language, yes?" Sasou nodded. "She asks if we may assign a translator to Queen Sister so Mistress and her can continue to teach Queen Sister across the distances between here and Ichijou."

Sasou paused, a bit taken aback. "You mean... she asked just now?"

Ore nodded. "I've been pacing to hear their conversation below a little better at times. She's also listening to both conversations at the same time."

Sasou put a calm face on but was intrigued. "So, what are they talking about below?"

"Mistress is currently teaching Queen Sister on the topic she wishes to be taught, but ...earlier they were discussing what it will mean for all of the ladies to become pregnant, since your wife now has some experience with it, but none of the others do. Queen Mother was allowed to leave after she told her own stories about the same."

Sasou sat back amazed, then pleased. He had to award points to all of them for using their opportunities to their fullest, and an extra one to Ilena for figuring out how to keep Kata present and involved. He finally answered the first question, "I wouldn't be opposed to it, nor to my heir being exposed to it as well. All information that can be gathered as quickly as possible is of great benefit to the board of kings. I personally don't choose to learn it because my mind is now too full of my board to set aside space to learn a new language at my age."

Rei looked at him, confused, "You mean it doesn't bother you? I didn't exactly have a choice in learning it since it's at the level of the boards."

Sasou gave him a bit of a condescending smile. "It doesn't ring through my castle like it does yours. This is the beehive containing the queen bee. My place is merely a small garden the bees come to visit."

Rei nodded his understanding and went back to his reading. Sasou raised an eyebrow. "It doesn't bother you?"

Rei shook his head. "It took a long time, but I've learned to put it in the background." He looked up briefly. "I had to learn that even more at the garrison before we went into Tarc. Ilena had to have reports coming in all the time from Tarc in addition to the regular reports, and I needed them as well, so now they're a calm stream underneath the board instead of a high sea the board is tossed around on." He went back to his book.

Sasou shook his head, internally. Rei was so calm with it that even answering an external question barely disturbed him and his board. It was another new strength for him. "Hmm..., Rei, can you hear through the floor as well, or is it just the code?"

"Both," he said absently.

"Good," Sasou said, keeping his face very carefully pleasantly neutral. It took a bit, but Rei's head rose slowly and his glare finally arrived to Sasou's view. Sasou was studiously not–looking at it. "Remember it, will you?" he asked lightly, referencing the ladies' conversation.

"Of course," Rei said sourly, paused to settle himself again, and returned to his own work.

Sasou rose and paced to stand next to Ore, looking out the balcony windows with him. "This is a very nice view," he commented pleasantly as Ore glanced at him. Ore returned to looking out the window and nodded. "Just how many conversations are going on right now?"

Ore considered that. "Mostly just the two. The occasional usual report comes in, but they're easy to file or deal with."

"How is Mizi holding up. She's newest come to it, isn't she?" Sasou tipped his head to hear if she'd answer herself, and she did.

I can follow two to three now, King Sasou, so today isn't too difficult; although, I must spend most of my attention on your lady wife, being the hostess and instructor today. Ilena at this point is more interested in what your topic is upstairs, but must of necessity stay here to assist me.

"Ooh, she can speak it," Sasou said. "I thought you were only learning to listen?"

There was a pause, then, *I'm not sure how you found out any of that, but I needed to speak with Rei and Ore in Tarc also. And..., I'm sure you understand by now that I really don't like being left out.*

"That was very candid."

Rei snorted. "When hasn't she been ...other than when she's still thinking of a proper answer to a question?"

"Mmm..., true," Sasou mused. He paced to stand next to Rei and look down at the passage he was reading. "Have you found it yet?"

"Is this really the oldest of the three books?" Rei asked, sounding disappointed.

"Yes, I'm afraid so. I sent them looking deeply in the stacks and in the historical records until they were covered in dust and cobwebs and the cabinets were cleaned because of it. It did seem to me also that it was very similar in construct to how we'd set laws for those who were having difficulty understanding the basics of living decently together."

"Did you have them look in Kouzanshi?" Rei asked Sasou.

"Well," Sasou mused, "perhaps not as much as they could have. I was thinking it would be more likely here or at the main castle, since that's where we keep the oldest records."

Rei nodded, still thinking. "We'll look there during the spring requirement, then."

I'll have my people look now, if you want, Master Rei, Ilena offered.

"Sure," he answered.

A new voice sounded, now in the code since they'd been speaking at the level of the code but in Ryokudan for Sasou. He raised an eyebrow at Ore. "Rio," he said shortly. Sasou's eyebrow went back down. It stood to reason the assistant would send the request. Ilena and Mizi likely looked to Aryana like they were completely engaged in her conversation only.

Sasou moved to lean against the desk in the room, facing Rei in the chair he'd taken. "I do think it's a good start," he commented on the books he'd brought. "There are a few things that can be used from them to at least make a few points. The words of their own heritage will likely be more convincing to them."

Rei nodded. "I'm in agreement. They're very suspicious of outside influences." Rei looked over at Reynold and said to Sasou, "We found three others in the Marluk'nak'. The more modern words are begun to be translated."

Sasou asked Reynold, "Could you translate it?"

Reynold shook his head. "I'm not a linguist."

The Dean is, Ilena commented. *And he owes Master Rei a favor.* Sasou smiled a point giving smile at Rei who looked rather proud of himself. *Also, his specialty is dead languages. The desert nomads north of Selicia don't use written language either — although they have written accounting — and that was what he was researching when I was at the university the first time, he said.*

Now there were even broader smiles in the Upper Office. Sasou nodded, thought, then frowned. "Ilena, wouldn't you be good enough to do the translation?"

There was silence, upstairs and down. Sasou felt his eyebrow hit heights they hadn't in a long time. Rei sighed and stood, walking to the desk to set the book he was holding on top of the other two.

That put him very close to Sasou. Surprisingly, Rei was nearly Sasou's tall height now. "She can't read, Sasou," he said quietly, "not without great difficulty. Do you know her first two papers were in linguistics? She has the skill, most certainly, but they were for her coded language and for Ryan's written one.

"That's the only one that sits still for her. The rest dance on the page. She was tutored enough she can work out words with difficulty and with even greater difficulty get letters written on a page, but only Leah can sometimes decipher them. If she's sending them to the Dean, she can't read them either."

The sadness from Rei and the others in the room settled on Sasou. He looked around and blinked in utter surprise. "It's why she's only just been given her diploma and professorship," Ore said just as quietly, "and why Mister Shiotsu fought so hard for her."

Sasou would've sat down hard in a chair, except he was already leaning on the desk. His heart felt constricted and it was just a little difficult to breathe. He remembered Shiotsu pointing her out to him at a conference at the university before he was made king, after Shiotsu had read a medical paper that had been brilliant and extremely useful to the people of Ryokudo.

Everyone at the conference had assumed it was Shiotsu's latest research. Then he'd dropped the news on everyone that it had been completely researched by a fourteen year old. The room had exploded. Sasou had gone straight to Shiotsu and asked who'd written it. Shiotsu had turned him and pointed to a girl in a corner, next to a man he hated for his evil works. A man he couldn't touch.

That had been his first clue Ilena had returned to Ryokudo alive. Her eyes had been dead, but he'd been sure it was her. He'd had Michael feel her out once everyone had returned to their homes. As soon as they'd worked out a relationship, she'd moved to begin to show Sasou her board without giving away who she was. That was sufficient. Only Toukas and kings had boards.

Sasou had been allied with Shiotsu since that conference. Both the paper and the man she stood beside were enough, but Shiotsu had never said she hadn't written it. Sasou shook his head at himself. Of course she'd written it. He'd been the pen, but it had been her words, the same as Sasou's reports were written by his secretary, but the words came from his mouth.

He took a deep breath. "Kick Shiotsu in the shin the next time you see him for not telling me when he should have," Sasou said. He lifted his head so the lump in the back of his throat went down instead of out his eyes. "I would've fought for you harder, and sooner." He might still have left her at Tokumade, but he would've seen she'd been properly recognized at the least.

It's fine, Sasou, Ilena said. *Already I wasn't trusting the university. I didn't research the medical one for the diploma. I researched it to help the household of Tokumade. I had to have it done before the end of the conference since when it was over I had to leave the university to return to Tokumade.*

"She had her diploma with the oral language, King Brother," Ore said quietly, "they just didn't know how to give it to a twelve year old without heritage."

Sasou groaned. "*Without heritage?* Ore...," he rolled his eyes at the man. Ore only looked back solemnly. Sasou sighed. "I did wonder why Shiotsu insisted that particular clause be added to the changes to the university charter, but to be told that the Princess has no *heritage* is a bit beyond my capacity at the moment."

He held up a hand. "I know, that was then, but this is now." He put his hand back down and just breathed for a minute. "Which one did you get the diploma for?"

"Medicine," Rei answered. "Shiotsu, Mizi, and Tiana tested her for it. Her linguistics professor died shortly after she returned for the medical research, so wasn't available to test her. They tested her to professor directly after, and had her test her student of statistical strategy immediately thereafter. I've called him to come here as soon as the paper's published."

Sasou blinked. "That's the favor he owes you?"

Rei nodded. "I made her sit still for the testing so they wouldn't lose him."

"*Him?* What about *her*?" The room smiled. It was as much a difference as the room being sad. Sasou looked around again.

"She was still going and acting as a professor without it being formal," Thayne explained. "That's why they tested her for it. They hadn't lost her."

Please stop. Aryana doesn't understand why I'm blushing, came from below them.

"Then tell her I've called for you," ordered Sasou, folding his arms.

They stood in silence until Ilena arrived, coming in through the door this time. Sasou's eyes watched her until she arrived in front of him. He'd never seen Ilena so timid before and he could feel everyone's protectiveness go up eight notches, twenty from Ore — although he didn't move.

Sasou's heart hurt again. This was the damage done that Shiotsu had been so angry about. Quietly, tenderly, he said, "Thank you, Ilena, for not giving up, for being true to your heart and goals. I'm already indebted to you more than I can repay, although I've tried to, and now I learn the debt is even larger." He stood and bowed to her. "Thank you. Thank you for loving Ryokudo and Suiran."

When he rose he suddenly had her arms wrapped around his chest and her head hiding on him. He felt her body shake with tears. Recovering from his initial surprise, he held her comfortingly. He was glad that for her he counted as both king and big brother. He could perhaps help her heal.

Between that surprising news and the excitement of getting to "play" by learning the Tarc horse race, Sasou completely forgot to complain at Ilena about having to stay for more meetings. He decided later that night that perhaps the activities that afternoon would tide him over the extra few days before his vacation could begin. Besides, he hadn't teased Ore yet about earning the title of Suiran King of Nightwalkers.

CHAPTER 147 Launching the Ministry of Intelligence

Rio watched the last of those going to participate in the late afternoon Tarc horse racing lessons for King Sasou walk out of the courtyard and into the hills north of Nijou castle. Queen Aryana had excused herself back to the King and Queen's quarters to get in an afternoon nap, pointing out that it was really a necessity when pregnant to underscore the after–lunch lesson. Rio had paid just as much attention to the lessons as the mistresses had. She'd also need to know how to take care of her own. They'd already lived through Ilena having regular afternoon naps while in her convalescence after her surgeries, so supposed they'd already had experience with that much.

Rio gave a bit of a sigh at finally getting a little break of her own that afternoon from all of the stress of the interim investiture just before lunch. Getting to be dressed up for once had been somewhat exciting. Having to kneel before the king himself in front of the large court had been faint–worthy. She was glad she hadn't. It would take a while before she felt anything like a baroness, but she was grateful for the consideration from Ilena and the king, particularly in that she was now related by surname and adoption to her closest friends. It made her blush to think she was a younger sister to Ore, though. Returning to comfortable maid status for lunch had been rather relieving.

She turned to look at the corner chair in the room. "I think that was a very good example of what Mistress Mizi is." Her stern gaze was on Amber, who was sitting quietly with her hands folded in her lap. Rio had told her firmly she was only there to observe for the afternoon and not to move or speak. "What did you learn?"

Amber's thumb nervously rubbed on her hand. She finally answered, "You're sure Princess Mizi isn't just listening and being attentive to get into the Queen's good graces?" She was very puzzled.

"No," Rio shook her head. "It was all because of her love for the country that she's adopted and that has adopted her. It was all genuine. None of it was drama or affected. She has no need to get into the Queen's graces. She's where she wants to be and is content, save with her own growth that she can see she still needs." Rio let Amber work on that for a while, moving to clean up the tea.

When she was done putting things away, she turned to Amber again. "We'll see about having you shadow Mistress Mizi now that we're all back again and the investiture's behind us. Likely you could learn some good things from her." Rio paused, then sat down in the chair next to Amber's, clasping her hands lightly in her lap. Taking a deep breath to face things that were hard for her, she asked, "Other than that lesson I promised you before we left on the royal progress, what things do you wish to learn, Amber? What are your goals?" Amber stared at Rio in shock.

Amber opened her mouth, a petulant look on her face, then she stopped. Her mouth closed and her look became a bit more penetrating and real. That seemed like forward progress. A bit crossly, Amber finally answered, "I'd say you don't care to hear it, except for some odd reason you actually might."

Rio was a little scolded. "I'd like to understand it, Amber," she said quietly. "I'm not good at listening, but I'll try."

Amber sat back and considered Rio, her lips pursing a little. Her hands were still wrapped one around the other, but were a bit more relaxed than they had been. "Mistress Ilena says you were a doll in the Doll House that she rescued."

Rio nodded. "I was. I was terrified the day she purchased me and took me straight to Tokumade. I thought she was the Doll Maker's sister and I was going to have to live in his House." Amber blinked and actually looked a little sympathetic. "Even worse, she took me right to her room and told me I was to stay there. It wasn't until she ordered me to make my own bed in the corner on the floor that I thought it might be somewhat different from what I'd lived up until then." Her hands tightened together a little at the remembered fear.

For the first time Rio and Amber sat and just talked. Amber was willing to talk more now that Rio was willing to answer her questions without being upset. Rio didn't mind since that was part of becoming partners: learning to understand each other.

As Rio wrapped up telling Amber about her past, she said, "It helps to have people who care around me, who want to help me feel safe and reach my goals." She smiled at Amber. "If possible, we want to be that for you, too. Tell me what your goals are. If I can, I'll help you reach them."

Amber sat and gazed at Rio soberly. Finally she said, a bit hesitantly as if she was trying to learn those things for herself for the first time, "I think I'd like to understand what it is to be a real friend. I never did believe I could be once I'd killed the one friend I'd had. I suspect I wasn't even really her friend, not knowing how to be one from the beginning. I've spent all my life trying to please others, trying to understand what they wanted out of me so they'd smile and want me around."

Her face went to a bitter look. "Not like it's *ever* given me any of that. The court game is all it gives me, and I hate that. The court game is people saying things they don't mean, promising things they'll never give. That isn't being wanted. That's being used, which I hate."

Rio nodded in understanding. "You appreciated that Mistress Ilena and maybe Marcus wanted you, then, at the beginning." Amber glared blackly at Rio but agreed. "And thus why you're so angry now."

"Obviously," Amber answered dryly.

"I'm sorry we can't accept you as the false you, so it's easier for you. We'd much rather accept you as the real you so that you can believe in yourself. And in this case, that you really have earned real friendships for yourself. If you continue to give us the false court face, how can we return anything else to you?" Rio's look pierced Amber. Amber looked down at her hands, not having an answer.

Rio considered what Amber had said, then added, "Everything you did to try to please us was what you used to please the court as well, even if it was the court of servants or common–folk. Did you really want those kinds of friends from the beginning?"

It looked like Amber was struggling with having eaten worms. Finally she managed to say as truthfully as she could, "It always worked before I came. Not only did it not work here, it stopped working everywhere else it had worked before. You all ruined me."

"*We* did?" Rio lifted an eyebrow. "We weren't even here. I think most people would say you earn your own reputation for yourself."

Amber scowled openly at Rio. "Not like I need you to tell me."

"That's good then, if you can see it yourself," Rio backed down. "I'll help you with learning the better ways if you're willing to let me. I had to learn how to get along with people at all. I might not know all the tricks and court methods, but I can help you understand when you've used one that doesn't help and what you can do instead that does work."

Amber bit her lip and looked away. "That might be hard, to want to learn from you." She caved in on herself, though.

"I understand you're angry with me right now," Rio said gently. "That's okay. I don't mind that. But I do think perhaps I've taught you that you can trust me to do what I say I'm going to do, and that I won't be hurt by what you do." Amber slightly glared at Rio from the corner of her eye. "That's the better place to start from. Friendships and partnerships are built from trust, not from liking, even though that's a good place to be, too."

Amber slumped, then took in a deep breath. "Will I learn that from watching Princess Mizi, too?"

Rio smiled. "Yes, but only after you've learned for yourself why the court game of taking without giving doesn't work and being truly yourself does. You can't see with the right eyes yet. Learning those things for yourself will help your eyes open to how Mistress Mizi is a very good example of friendship and partnership, and even more, an excellent example of personal integrity."

Rio thought it would be very hard lessons for Amber, but now that she'd said she wanted it — if it was truth — then she'd learn it better than if Rio had tried to force the lessons on her. She appreciated that Ore had reminded her that part was important.

She'd remembered as she'd pondered on it that there had come a time when Ilena had asked her what her goals were, and they'd worked on them. Then she'd remembered that Ilena always asked each member of the Family not only what dreams they had, but what they wanted to do with their lives. Both things pointed the direction the person wanted to move themselves in. Ilena helped them get there. Rio would do her best to follow in her footsteps as she learned and practiced what it meant to have and train a partner. Maybe someday they might even be able to say they were friends.

-o-o-o-

The day after the interim investment Sasou swept into the Lotus Office, his usual all–business stride making the distance to the desk at the back short. Rei, Ilena, and Ore (because Sasou was determined to make him immediately step into the position of Grand Duke) were already waiting for him, for all he'd not given them much time to arrive.

"Isn't this Mizi's domain now?" he teased as he set his folder on the desk. They watched him a bit bemused as he seemed to be walking right back out, only to turn around and walk right back to the desk. The turn back towards the door settled them to understanding and they stopped watching him. It was a bit difficult to watch someone pace, even if they did want to be polite.

That was enough settling of the younger set he could start spilling his thoughts. "Ilena, the folder is mostly for you. It's my notes from when I received your report. We'll discuss that in more detail in a bit. When you two come to Ichijou for your testing by the lords there you'll have quite a bit to learn about what they care about versus what you think I care about."

He paused long enough for his eyes to get his point across to Ilena and Ore, then he was pacing again. "I've had Barret and Aryana write up what they think might help you for that. I might have some time to coach you a little at the beginning, but when they really start testing you they'll be watching to see I keep my nose out of it." He gave her a sympathetic glance at the last. He'd help her more than that if he could, and likely he'd send either one of those two to do it if it became necessary.

"Do you know Lord Finlay?" she asked. Sasou furrowed his brow, going through the list of Suiran lords in his head. He did remember the lesser lord after a bit of working on it and said so. "Will the lords of Ichijou find him an acceptable tutor?"

Sasou blinked at her, a little surprised she'd thought of it, but Rei's small smug look gave him the answer. He confirmed the point to Rei with a lift of his eyebrow and got back a small nod. "If you bring him with you for them to remember him, it should be at least points in your favor," Sasou answered Ilena.

Sasou paused and raised an eyebrow at Ore. "And you'll be seeing to the proper settling of the nightwalkers in the meantime?"

Ore blinked in surprise, sitting stiffly upright in the most respectful pose he'd ever put on before Sasou. He really was afraid of Sasou's response to Ore being titled the same in the underworld. Well, that was good, then. "With Ilena's help, yes," Ore answered honestly.

"See you do live up to the title, then," Sasou answered, returning to his pacing to let the pressure off of Ore just a little bit, for all his words didn't. "If you can't keep them under control you're not fit for it, are you?"

Ore paused, then slumped slightly. "And you really are the top Head of the nightwalkers of Ichijoutsu."

"Of course," Sasou answered mildly. "And all of Ryokudo," he added. Sasou considered those two topics for the next pass and a half of pacing, then moved on. They knew what needed doing and would do their best.

On the return pass he was speaking on the next item on the list in his mind. "Regent, I'm not sure it's wise to have the financial audit this year." He stopped his pacing in front of Rei, giving him the respect of facing him more directly. "With Aryana due mid–spring it will be very difficult for her to give it the focus it should rightly have. She's the only one that fits your needs. If it were postponed even one year she'd be recovered and could properly do the work."

Rei's brow was furrowed in his unhappy look that boded a coming argument. Sasou waited for it patiently. In the past Rei would have taken days, or at least summarized his argument very briefly. Sasou was interested in seeing what the new strength Rei had learned would be.

After only about a half–minute, Rei shook his head. "I understand it would be difficult, but I'm having the same sort of timing problem myself." His blue eyes rose to look into Sasou's. It wasn't an obstinate look. It was a commanding and firm one. Sasou approved. "There's still discontent in the lords who are trying to do their best. A lot need to have the graft dug up and put on the dung pile. I think there are more than a few who have old projects draining funds from them that even they don't realize is unnecessary. They'd use those funds for the things they complain there isn't enough funds for now."

Rei glanced at Ilena and continued, "Taking away the corruptible staff hasn't helped them either. They need trained competent people as replace-ments." He sighed a little. "I think they're worried that we'll all have to cut back even more when the census results come in. That doesn't help anyone's stress level. I'm hoping if we can open up funds from within the departments during the same time, or before," his look came back on Sasou again, but Sasou couldn't promise anything right now, "they'll be able to relax a little better." Rei shook his head. "I really don't think I can wait a year at all."

Sasou was sufficiently impressed with Rei's handling of himself and the topic. "Aryana's currently meeting with the ministers, directors, and department heads, letting them know the standard rules for an independent audit. We've brought the auditors with us since making them travel any later into the season is ridiculous."

Ilena shifted and raised an eyebrow. Sasou gave her a small nod. "I'd like to request one more meeting, Your Majesty," she said rather simply for her. Sasou tried hard not to sigh at her. He'd rather she talked about it right now while she had him. More meetings wasn't on his list of preferred activities, and he wanted his vacation sooner than later. He almost didn't catch her relaxed pose in time. He barely had a half of a heartbeat to tense before the words fell from her lips. "I'd like to request a National Security Council meeting to be held tomorrow morning. I'll be inviting Queen Aunt and her Ministry as well."

The sneak attack had him off balance. "You do like to surprise people a little too much, Ilena dear," he frowned at her. Such a large and important topic really should have had more preparation time than a single afternoon. But then, she'd probably done it to keep him out of trouble. Now that she'd come to Nijou, Sasou certainly wasn't allowed to be bored or lack work when he came.

She gave the polite nod of apology, but that was never very reassuring with her. Sasou blinked a slower blink at her as he considered her request. "All right," he agreed quietly. "To what level?"

"Top secret," Ilena answered. "I'll send the agenda to Michael and Mitchel." Both brothers glared at her as she gave a short order in her secret language.

Sasou asked cynically, "Well, shall I assume it was handed to him just now?" Ilena indicated he'd guessed right as she held out a message folder to him, bound with her green, gold, and black cord. He took it, assuming it to be part of the "top secret" agenda as she'd handed it directly to him.

Rei gave him a dry, slightly frustrated look. "She won't tell me anything about what's next until we have the meeting, except to drop all kinds of hints. Please be there. I'm tired of being the only one still not knowing." He turned his frustrated look on Ilena. "I *hope* this is the last thing I have to be blind on?"

Ilena gave him a real apologetic look. "Yes, Master Rei. And really it's because Sasou's been keeping me in the dark other than guesses, and Queen Aunt even more so." Her tawny eyes turned to Sasou. "With Sasou here, she can't keep her mouth shut any more." Sasou sighed but agreed. His mother wouldn't even tell *him* everything she did and knew. It was well past time she did. In Kata's case, Ilena's sneak attack last–minute request might be the better choice.

-o-o-o-

Carl Stern sighed as he sat back in his hard wooden chair at his desk. His hand ran through the wisps that remained of the hair on the top of his head. He wasn't too pleased to be balding early. The winters made for particularly cold unpleasant reminders of the same. He had that and the round face of his mother's brother and her short stature to remind him of them, rest their souls. Not his favorite reminders, but it was what he had, nonetheless.

He was glad that a high court in the castle and a visit by the King meant that he got a bit of a vacation. Vacations in the castle for him meant he could get his desk cleared off a bit again, uninterrupted. Not that he didn't appreciate his senior's trust. To have the Queen Mother's Minister of Intelligence trust him enough with clandestine intelligence gathering outside the castle was an honor. To have been trained almost at Mitchel's feet was as well, for all it kept him excessively busy.

Carl closed his eyes and relaxed, his hands folded in front of him. He wondered just what would happen now that Mitchel had been called up by the Second Princess. It wasn't an unexpected move. It showed that she understood how to play the court games and keep the lords soothed. Carl wasn't sure she'd let Mitchel into her own networks very deeply, though. At least not at first.

Surely over time she expected the two disparate information networks to combine. Kata would eventually want to truly retire and Ilena would reach an age of experience to handle all of the weight of intelligence gathering for the Region. Surely they'd expect to see some attrition of agents. Kata had already let go of, or changed the focus of, most of her agents by now anyway.

Carl sighed, not sure which direction he'd go in the end. He'd continue to follow Mitchel's orders, of course. He just wasn't sure now how secure his own position was. At thirty he had a lot of useful life still to go with the experience he'd gained and not a lot of capacity to change careers at this point. But he really didn't know the Second Princess at all, other than what he'd observed when he'd been in the castle between assignments.

"Come," he called at the knock at his door. It wasn't usual to receive visitors at this time of evening — except one that he'd expect by now. He was sitting up respectfully by the time Mitchel had stepped through the door. "Congratulations?" he wasn't sure how Mitchel felt about his new assignment.

Mitchel gave him a bit of a nod, but his face didn't say much. Carl blinked as, rather than close the door behind him, Mitchel was followed into the office by three other men, the final one closing the door behind him. Carl took his time looking over the three newcomers, his face going to court neutral as he did.

Carl really hadn't expected to ever see Ilena's guards in his office. He wasn't sure he wanted to see them there. His perspective of Henry and

Marcus was that they were both too lackadaisical in their work and too dangerous underneath it all. They knew too much, while at the same time acted like they couldn't care. It wasn't a mix he was comfortable with.

The third guard Carl knew almost nothing about, only that he was come new and recent. His calm face was almost like Mitchel's, if slightly softer maybe. It made one want to trust the person who wore it. Carl wasn't the kind to immediately distrust such a face — he trusted Mitchel after all — but he still wondered.

"Welcome," Carl said neutrally, himself also one who hid behind calm politeness. "Can I help you?"

"Henry ...Melick." Henry raised his hand to introduce himself. The pause before the surname meant it must be new.

"Marcus Melick." Marcus also raised his hand, and equally almost stumbled over the surname. "And this is Count Liam Melick," he introduced the third and newest who gave a slight nod. The slight glare out of the corner of his eye thrown at Marcus said he'd not appreciated the title being openly stated. Perhaps Liam was as relaxed as the rest of that office seemed to be, then.

Carl had to pause a moment to internalize that they were all related now. He'd not been at the court, but could infer that's where it had happened. It seemed an odd thing that Ilena would want everyone in her staff to be in the same family. Maybe Mitchel could explain it to him later.

"Carl Stern," Carl decided he probably ought to introduce himself as well, just in case. It wasn't lost on him that Mitchel was keeping quiet, for all he'd been called up to a higher position than the two who'd spoken.

Henry let Marcus keep talking, but Carl had noticed he was the most personable of the two. "Princess Ilena tasked us with looking for people to help out in the Ministry, knowing that we were going to become extra busy once we also had to add in the Grand Duchy to everything else we were already doing."

Ah. Carl took a hidden slow breath and set himself as best he could, trying to stay calm. He was sure he wasn't ready for this so suddenly. For all he'd just been wondering about it, he still hadn't made a decision yet.

"We've been watching you, and like what you do. She's approved having you brought in to help. Her first order is that the three of us will be trained by Lord Barkley and you'll join in to become Liam's partner."

And like that it was done. Carl had kind of forgotten that when a royal ordered something, it was done regardless. He sighed. He'd either learn loyalty on the job, or he'd ask to be released once he had enough proof and evidence he couldn't carry through properly. He placed his hands flat on his desk and pushed himself up to his feet. "I guess it's good I had the time today to clean off my desk, then."

He looked at Marcus and Henry quizzically. "Do I need to put in an order to have my office moved?"

Marcus shook his head as Henry said, "No. You can keep it here for now. Things are going to rearrange for the Ministry over the next several months and there really isn't room where we're at right now. We figure it will take a few months to be able to run together smoothly anyway, so no need to make it harder than it needs to be."

Carl was a bit relieved at that ...until Mitchel opened his mouth. "You'll need to put in a move order for your quarters, however." Carl couldn't help that his mouth fell open a bit as he stared at Mitchel. Mitchel had kept him out of the castle on purpose until now.

Henry raised his hand. "Actually, that's what we're here to take you out for and why we all came along. So we can get to know each other a little better, and so we can help you move. Mistress Ilena will have you move into the Ministry as an administrator once we're in place. In the meantime, she wants you moved in town to where we can all keep a watch over you. You currently live in a district she's not in control of."

Marcus crunched up his face. "While we know you don't particularly care, we've promised to help keep you safe now, too, so we care. The new room's being opened up now. You'll like the board mistress. She's everyone's grandmother, makes the best dumplings, and will take out anyone who comes and threatens her boarders. You can keep your current face to the city just fine. We just need you to come unlock your door and tell your current boarding house manager we aren't stealing your things."

Carl had to chuckle a little. "And if you two show up to help me move, the whole city will know I've been claimed by the Queen of Night."

"Well, yes," Marcus put on a sad face, but Carl knew he was playing it. "But then, she's never been very subtle about who she chooses. She likes to let everyone know who they'll have to answer to, even for minor administrators." He gave a teasing look to Mitchel. "It's actually the Associate we'll be testing. *He* has to stay hidden or *he'll* give it away." Mitchel sighed a long–suffering sigh.

Henry took it up. "We'll be heading out ahead with him to see what he can do and show up next to you at some random time to see if he can stay hidden. You'll leave out the gate with Liam, who's also a new administrator no one knows, but your senior having been called up first. He'll be the obvious moving help so the city can get used to seeing the two of you together — on occasion."

Carl gave a nod. He understood. They'd appear to be colleagues who got together on their rare days off so it wouldn't be unusual to be seen together.

"And are you going to tell him ahead of time, or let him be surprised?" Mitchel grumbled at the Twins.

They gave him wide eyes, then teasing grins. "We'll let you decide, eh?" Marcus said lightly. "He probably doesn't even know himself." Mitchel shook his head.

Carl's brow furrowed as he looked at Mitchel. He thought of Ilena, and what Marcus had just said. "You have an apartment in town instead of here?" he asked, very surprised by the concept. Kata kept a tight fist on her people, what few she had left. As far as everyone in the city knew, Mitchel lived in the castle.

Mitchel's face went a bit ruddy. "The excuse is that I need to have my ear to the ground as well, but it became necessary when she locked herself up. The rumors around the court were terrible."

Carl gaped at Mitchel. "And you haven't had the courage to tell her? You gave *her* the excuse."

Mitchel looked away, completely embarrassed. "I don't think I know a man alive, save one, who's willing to be tied to a Touka female, and he's as crazy as she is."

Three in the room had to laugh. (Liam merely smiled.) If Mitchel even worried that Kata would take the rumors to heart and follow through, he would've acted to stop that at the door immediately for sure.

"And it's probably just as embarrassing that the Queen of Night made you live in her quarter when you did it," Carl said knowingly.

Mitchel sighed and waved a hand at Marcus and Henry. "Well, yes, but that was the lesser evil of the two. My face is known, as they said, so it's nice to know Princess Ilena protects me when I'm sleeping."

Carl nodded, knowingly. "I get that. So we'll at least be able to discuss work to some small degree at the breakfast table — if we can stand it." Mitchel gave a grimace of a look back that Carl agreed with. Talking about work would amount to complaints of the level of work that was being required, but it would still be enough excuse if they did need to talk.

Liam finally spoke, surprising Carl with his soft voice full of kindness. "I suspect Mistress Ilena would also put me there to be closer to you, but she still needs me close to her at this time. I was given the last room they had available in the wing.

"Regardless, I'm quite sure there won't be an apartment open up for me until Mistress Ilena is ready to let me stray that far away." His own look went very wry. "I'll hope it's sooner than later, but I've been warned winter may be very difficult for her. Prince Rei's rather concerned. He's not quite sure what a claustrophobic Mistress Ilena will do having to be locked up in the castle. He says Master Ore's harder to manage over Suiran winters than he thought." Liam sighed. "I'm sure I'll be working extra hard and hoping for release myself come spring."

Marcus patted Liam on the shoulder sympathetically. "Wise of Master Rei to warn you ahead of time. We'll let the ma'am know you'll be ready by spring, then." Liam gave a nod of thanks.

Henry opened the door to Carl's office and they got moving out into the evening early winter air, being bundled up against it by the time they exited the building. "I so love having warm cloaks, boots, and mittens, not just a hat," Marcus sighed happily. Henry gave Marcus a rub of the head, making Marcus' hat shift off an ear. Marcus pulled it back over his ear to cover it again. "So, Carl, you know about the House of the Queen of Night. Do you know about Mother's Family?"

Carl thought about that, then shook his head. "I know she calls all of you that, those she has in the office."

Henry nodded. "We're Immediate Family. Family's more general. It's the top–side network. The boarding house is actually run by one of the Family, not one of the House. It's in the House's territory so that it's protected both during the day and the night." Carl blinked, then decided to just absorb it as new information. There was going to be a lot of learning for a while.

-o-o-o-

It was a nice enough night, for a Suiran early winter. The wind was little swirls and eddies instead of blasting wind, and the skiff of snow falling was made up of tiny flakes that were light. It wouldn't add a whole lot to the total on the ground — a good thing since they still needed to have the King escape before the heavy deep snows fell in earnest.

Liam and Carl turned away from the other three who headed for the Suiran Ministry of Intelligence's wing to exit from the Cat gate. Liam didn't say much until they were close to the Crane gate. "You'll be helping me with the census requirement in the Lower office, once we can figure out how to fit another desk in."

The guards opened the gate to let them out. It clanged closed behind them and the jangle of the keys in the lock were as always. Sounds like those, common and regular, were soothing. Many people lost them in the background of life eventually, but Carl had learned to always hear them. Changes in sounds meant changes in patterns that were important to pay attention to.

Liam took up again once they were headed the direction Carl always walked every night — when he'd been on the castle grounds anyway. "Come there in the morning and we'll have a meeting to discuss how we're going to move forward. Likely I'll want us to meet every morning even briefly, since we won't be able to talk during the day, particularly as the weather gets worse."

Carl nodded, then frowned. "How extensive is the census requirement going to be for the Ministry? *Everyone?*"

Liam smiled. "No. We got the census for Tarc completed when we were there and I wrote up the report while everyone else was working on the reports for the war effort. We do have Prince Ore's holding, though, particularly now that it's been expanded beyond what it was originally listed as. That'll be the work in the main for us next."

He clasped his hands behind his back and looked up at the pale grey sky above them. The lights of the city reflected off the low clouds making the evening lighter than it might've been during the rest of the year. It was like having a blanket over them. The feeling was comforting for now. By the end of the winter it would've been too much grey and the mood in the city would be as depressed as the weather.

"We'll be plenty busy after that's done, even still. I took the liberty of having the household of Falcon's Hollow get started on hunting down everyone living in those boundaries that they hadn't already found. Mistress Ilena asked the Marshal to get a census started about four months ago, but I want them to make sure we've got proper numbers with the new boundaries."

Liam looked back at Carl. "I brought back with me Foster's most recent report and we'll add as we get more information. It shouldn't take too much longer before we can get that report written, I'd think. That much already being done means I'll be able to focus on training you to what little you'll need to know."

Carl tried to word his question in a way it could be asked in public on the street, taking his time since they had a ways to walk. It was after the dinner hour by enough that the streets weren't terribly busy, but there were enough citizens still headed home that it was best to be careful. "How's the Regent going to handle those in the larger cities who live in the alleys or hide from the eyes of law–abiding citizens?"

Liam's eyes smiled. "He hasn't said yet. I presume his census takers will have to do their best."

Carl blinked at Liam. "She doesn't want to know?"

Liam chuckled quietly, but didn't say anything. Carl guessed he should know. If she admitted to owning them, she'd have to pay for them, since the census was taken to know how to — in effect — tax the lords who claimed the people. "I wonder if he'll let her get away with that?" he mused in a murmur. Liam didn't have an answer for that either, but that wasn't surprising.

After they'd walked probably another ten blocks, Liam sighed. "You'll see those numbers eventually, I shouldn't be surprised. We'll need them when it comes to the next requirement. She's still trying to figure out how to handle that part."

Carl waited calmly, liking that Liam was comfortable with long silences. In their line of work it helped make anyone tailing them get bored and wander off between comments and regular citizens not hear a full conversation to spread rumors with. "Next part?" he raised an eyebrow.

It wasn't until Carl was unlocking his own boarding house room door to let Liam in that Liam answered. "What's she supposed to say about how the Ministry supports itself, when it's never been paid for by any other royal than her until now?"

Carl went into a little bit of shock. It took a bit to get moving again. "Ah...yeah. I guess that would be a hard thing to explain, wouldn't it?" Then his brow wrinkled. "It hasn't been a Ministry until now. Would she have to say prior to now, or only from here forward?"

Liam turned to him with wide eyes. Gently he put both hands on Carl's shoulders and leaned in to give him a soft kiss on the forehead, being about four inches taller than Carl. "Thank you."

Carl was in a lot of shock now and could only blink back. Liam turned away to pull off his gloves and stuff them into his hat. "That's from her. Sorry, but it was so to the point that she wanted to reward you right away."

Carl shook himself, then pulled off his own coat, stuffing his hat and gloves into one sleeve. As he hung it over the peg just inside the door he said, dryly, "She rewards with kisses, huh?"

He got a rub of the top of his head as Liam's coat went over his on the peg. "Yes, and rubs of the head. But you saw Henry do that to Marcus."

Liam was moving for the window as Carl turned to stare after him. "That's all," Liam said calmly as he unlatched the window and opened it.

Carl watched as Marcus and then Henry slipped in through the window. He leaned back against the wall and folded his arms, watching them as Liam closed the window again, relatching it. "You forgot she'll do hugs if that's preferred," Marcus added as his hat, gloves, and coat came off as well.

"Mm, I did. Sorry. She doesn't prefer it, so I'd forgotten," Liam said, softly apologetic.

Carl raised an eyebrow, staying where he was. Henry answered it. "Hugs aren't a reward for her. Those she uses to stay put when she wants to run away."

Carl gave a nod. "I'm beginning to understand just what Lord Barkley meant by 'crazy'."

He got a full house of grins. "Take your time," Liam suggested. "Where can we start?"

"With providing boxes?" Carl suggested mildly. He laughed at their startled looks. He made up some tea to warm them all up while they figured out how to get a real start to packing up an apartment. It appeared that none of them had ever moved a house before. He wasn't very surprised as far as

Marcus and Henry went. He was a little surprised as far as Liam went, but it was another thing to add to what he was learning about the man he'd been paired up with.

He wondered what Liam preferred as his reward, but decided to not ask just yet. He might get to learn it by observing how Ilena interacted with Liam in the office later. Likely the most he'd personally be able to tolerate would be a rub of the head, on the rare occasion it was actually warranted. "I'd prefer a cash bonus," he said over his shoulder at Liam when he thought of it.

Liam chuckled. "I think all of us would. She isn't *that* wealthy, and she's had to run the department from her own pocket. Cutting costs was a big thing from the beginning."

Carl nodded. He might be able to train her to it, now that she finally had a stipend from the Crown. It was the *normal* reward for work well done. Perhaps she could begin to learn "usual and customary" now that she was in that place.

He sighed to himself. It was going to be hard to be the first and perhaps only sane, normal person brought into that Ministry. Well..., he hoped Mitchel would also fit the same category. And perhaps he wasn't being kind. There might be another one or two there he didn't know yet. He hadn't spent any time in the office before, after all, only watched what they did on the outside.

-0-0-0-

Mitchel was sure he wasn't ready to be tested by Ilena's people, any more than Carl had been prepared for their sudden visit and moving announcement. That wasn't really fair, though. He'd at least had warning and a proper handing–over from one Queen to the other. It was probably more that he hadn't quite expected to have the youngest be his testers and trainers. That was a bit hard to take. Somehow he'd not quite come out of the mindset that he was the one testing and going to train Ilena. He'd been focusing on that person instead and was having to rearrange his expectations a bit tonight.

Still, he decided to ask it anyway. "Why you two instead of Ilena and Ore?" He knew the royal couple wouldn't mind if he used the informal. It was a test of if these two cared.

Henry gave him a testing glance. Marcus answered the question, "Mistress Ilena only likes to test others when she can have fun. Not only is she too stressed to have fun right now, Petroi won't let her out of the house without six guards on her until the city's settled. She can only handle half that and less when stressed." His eyes glanced at Henry, a slight expression of concern on his face. "We also need to run tonight."

Ah. Henry was a bit too stressed out as well, and was one of those people in the office who didn't do well in castles. He'd be the one to watch, then.

Marcus was in control enough to stay in character. Henry would let the little clues slip, like the look at the question.

"Our chore today," Henry picked it up while they were still on the quiet road and not to the city yet, "is to test the Houses in Traveler's Row." Two sets of eyes turned onto Mitchel. "How about you take us first to the one you like least?"

Mitchel shoved his hands into his pockets as he let his shoulders rise and then fall as he relaxed into the role he was supposed to play tonight. He let out a long quiet breath as he looked up into his thoughts and at the clouds above them. He'd be tested on his local knowledge first, and of course on the immediate actions that were going on. Likely his knowledge of far places would be tested by Ilena herself as she had questions on them.

"Just to view an example or two of their standard behaviors? Or do you want to see full–House actions?" He thought he ought to narrow it down a bit first.

"Mm, behaviors is sufficient, if you tell us actions later or on the way in," Henry answered.

Mitchel almost blurted out that Petroi knew all these answers, but caught it in time. They'd be confirming Mitchel's answers with Petroi to see how much more or less he knew than the House of the Queen of Night already did. He had to wipe the scowl off his face before it got out, too. He'd retired from clandestine activities on purpose. He really was too impatient for them. Hiding in the Queen Mother's suite helped him as he was also far too impatient for minor, middling, and a few self–important high lords.

It wasn't hard to name his least favorite House and list off a few of his least favorite actions they'd taken in the city and around it. They'd managed to put more than a few of the higher level people in it into custody, but it had been hard to remove altogether.

Henry nodded at the end of his telling. "We're making sure that one's cleaned out. It turns out the little lordlings still talking to their fathers in prison were helping that House and a couple of others move forward. General Garen's taken care of that side of the Houses, so they've lost their patronage. It shouldn't be too hard now. It'd still help to know their boundaries, though. We'll wander there first and see if their tune has changed since the lords were removed." That suited Mitchel fine enough.

The second question to Mitchel when they were done watching that House was which House needed training the most. That surprised him and it took a while to figure out what they meant by that. The answer came to him rather quickly when he considered it that way. He grimly took them to the inns that catered to the rough transient workers.

They watched as he pointed to the men entering the back alley of one of them from inside. "It's not the ladies?" Henry asked quietly in some surprise.

"Oh, it's them, too," Mitchel said, "but that's an expected example so harder to see. This makes it obvious."

They had to agree as they watched coin trading hands with both drugs and stronger drink than the establishment was willing to serve (or they'd have more broken tables and chairs than they did). "Where are they taking that one?" Marcus asked, pointing. Mitchel was beginning to learn Henry had the street smarts and Marcus the better eyes. He'd been wondering if they'd catch on to that.

"To places more depraved than you want to know. Think Doll House, but he's the toy."

Two pairs of eyes stared at him briefly. "*He's* the toy?"

Mitchel nodded soberly. "That means he gets his highs from being beaten and played with. Why there are men like that in the world, I have no idea." The Twins couldn't really understand it either.

Henry frowned. "And if we get rid of that, it'll just come back up or run rampant and even more dangerous, won't it?"

Mitchel shrugged, "Maybe." He watched as they silently sang. That was good, that they were sending someone to observe more closely, not just randomly hack off fingers that might be necessary, even if warped. Mitchel walked the boundary of that House with them, then led them to the next one they wanted to know about.

That was the expected one: which House did he think might should stay around and keep the rest of that area in check. He actually had two potentials. Marcus and Henry watched both of them for a while, then asked where the head safe houses were for them. In both cases they left him in hiding and entered those houses to observe in person the people that mattered for themselves. They didn't stay long at either place.

Somehow they managed to arrive at Carl's place at nearly the same time as Carl and Liam did. Mitchel was a bit surprised, since they'd been doing so much. As he waited outside the boarding house he reviewed the evening so far. Henry and Marcus were actually very succinct, didn't waste time or movements, and delegated with great efficiency. They had a good sense of judgment of people given how short a time they'd been in the safe houses. Or they'd only needed to see the faces to put knowledge they already had into place.

In the final review of that part of his testing, he had to admit that they hadn't wasted his time, either. They'd known what they needed to know and hadn't wasted their time on random whim, and he'd been glad to have his opinions on those specific things asked for. For being young, those two had quite a lot of experience in the information–gathering field. And they cared. He wasn't sure just how much they cared yet, but it had been obvious they did. That was good enough for a start, he supposed.

When a wagon showed up outside the boarding house, Mitchel inserted himself into the small group of helpers and helped move Carl's few personal belongings. He made the wagon owner let him drive it, saying he knew where they were going — since he did. He helped move Carl's things into his new room (so he knew where it was), then excused himself to his own room as "just another person helping out" who also happened to live there.

He was relieved to be left alone to actually sleep at that point. He'd kind of thought they'd drag him out again. He learned they wouldn't when Carl stopped by his room to thank him "one more time for helping out" and let him know in their own code that they were both released for the night. He wished Carl a good night and settled in, grateful they could sleep without worry.

CHAPTER 148 Ryokudo Security Meeting

The following morning saw all of the royals of Ryokudo together again. This time they were in a reasonably sized meeting room in the depths of the castle. The attendees had been specifically chosen and invited by Ilena as Minister of Intelligence.

Sasou and Aryana were present along with Michael Barret, the Kingdom Minister of Intelligence. He'd brought one assistant with him. Queen Kata was there, sitting soberly with Mitchel and Carl. Rei and Mizi were both there with Andrew and Mina. Tanner had been allowed to come in with Mizi, but her guards had been asked to stand on the doors to the hallway the room was in to prevent anyone from entering it.

In the main that arrangement was because all of Ore and Ilena's guards were in the room as well. It was already well known that Ilena didn't trust the soldiers quite so much to have them on the doors when sensitive information was going to be talked about. Grandfather, Leah, and Rio were also present.

General Garen was also in the room, with Corporal Tellius, adding in the castle security to the three Ministries of Intelligence. The final count was of all the people Ilena trusted most with security issues, plus the royalty.

When everyone was present and seated, or standing as their station made them feel comfortable with, Ilena stood at the front of the room. She looked soberly at them, particularly Sasou and Kata. Addressing Sasou specifically, she said, "I've set up the security to be trustworthy as best I know how. Mizi has opened the door for there to be a mouse within, which she'll need to correct. I believe he can be of use, however, so have let him remain." Sasou blinked at her but didn't comment.

She continued, "I've asked Prince Airn's aide to be prepared to address us as well, when we've reached that point in the discussion." Sir Erlic Yetherly was sitting outside the room, across the hallway on a bench. Ilena had sent for him to be fetched from the place the Second Prince of Altherly had reached on his journey to Nijou and would return him when this conference was over.

Ilena took a slow breath, her preliminaries over. "We have two issues facing us, which are perhaps one but we'll of necessity have to face them separately to some degree.

"Firstly, those who know that Prince Airn is in the country know that his father made sure he was. We've already taken care of letting King Roland know we've found him and are willing to tutor him. The true reason he's here is because of a secret agreement between King Roland and Sasou that we protect Prince Airn while King Roland focuses on the war Gael has begun to bring against him. Even now he's formally asking Sasou for reinforcements so that he doesn't fall and our east border become the next target of that far nation." As a few wide eyes glanced at Sasou, he tipped his head to acknowledge the statements were true.

"As we promised Airn, we'll keep him here in Nijou with us for training and protection. If necessary, however, he'll be sent to Ichijou. Openly for Sasou to add in his brand of training as well. Politically, it will send a stronger message to Gael if they're staying belligerent and getting too close to Ryokudo."

She looked soberly at mostly her people, Rei included. "When the Lord of Tarc began to do things against me that were confusing, I began to look into things more deeply. When Tarc Seconds were sent after my top agents, to remove them contrary to the understanding of Tarc, that was a sufficient clue to me. Just as my uncle was the hand behind Pakyo, just as the Lord of Tarc was behind King Sandras and the death of my family, and just as the Lord of Tarc was behind my uncle, Brulac has always been behind them all. This is the second issue we'll be addressing."

It didn't take long for Rei to glance at his mother and brother with knowing eyes. He, as the bright strategist he was, was already fitting all the pieces together. She'd not let him know before because she knew Tarc alone was stressful enough, following on the heels of Pakyo Shicchi. Rei was brilliant enough to catch up quickly and move as fast as necessary.

Soberly Ilena pronounced, "From the beginning, when King Uncle was murdered, the King of Brulac has been moving." She looked compassionately at Kata. "Queen Aunt set her Intelligence network to finding out how it had been done and discovered Brulac was the most likely hand behind it. It had been done like the others, though, so she's had to move carefully and slowly to find the evidence.

"When the Polovs of Selicia fell, it was hard to believe it could have been the same hand, I'm sure, but Sasou has understood for some time. My evidence to him against the Lord of Tarc allowed his agents there to finally learn what he needed to know to find the link back to Brulac.

"The reason the two issues are one is that the action against Altherly is also in part pushed by a secret alliance between Gael and Brulac. The agreement is that together the two nations will take down Altherly and Ryokudo. They'll let Brulac have Ryokudo so that they can finally have access to the waterways of the Inner Sea.

"Gael already has access to the water and will distract Sasou in the south, if they can free up their navy from the war against Altherly, or get him to send naval assistance to Altherly. We've gone through the test — and really it was training — against Tarc, in order for us to be able to protect this corner, where Brulac will send it's main forces through when Rei has left it to go and be Sasou's answer of aid to Altherly." Rei and Mizi both paled. Andrew and Mina did, too, if not as badly. Ilena ignored it. They needed to firm up quickly.

Ilena's eyes went hard and her face cold. "Brulac is terrified of me, particularly now. They expected Tarc to fall completely, or kill us all. I've allowed the spy to watch what I can do personally, and he's already warned them. They most likely expect me to come against them myself, and will thus plan their protections accordingly."

Ilena addressed Kata. "I've opened up the hole for you to work in, to gain your revenge. They'll keep their eyes on me for as long as they think they know where I am, and will hunt for me desperately as soon as they lose sight of me.

"They're more afraid because we now have an alliance with Tarc. They fear the Tarc as much as we did, and don't want to fight against them. As long as the Princes can keep the spies out — and they will because all of the clans will — they'll remain nervous. Using the Tarc with the soldiers on the corner border will be effective, but also expected. They're likely even now adding in how to deal with that into their plans."

Once more she spoke to Sasou. "Because of the spy, they'll also expect me to send Ore into Brulac, and will be watching for him. They already know that if he's captured and injured or killed what that will do to me. You'll need to modify your expectations to account for that one fact that we can't change." He blinked at her.

"Given that overview," Ilena turned back to everyone in general, "we'll hear first from Queen Aunt and her people what they've already done in Brulac and what they anticipate seeing happen there. Sasou and his people will follow with the current political state of events both with Brulac and with Altherly and what he expects to see going forward. I'll then detail the plan I've seen and begun to set into motion."

Her eyes finally pinned Rei. "And then Rei will synthesize it into a workable plan with our input and approval. When Flandras arrives from Kouzanshi we few will sit with him and have him run the calculations of the possible permutations to confirm the final expected casualties so we're sure we haven't strayed into something worse than we're hoping for." Ilena bowed slightly to Kata and sat down.

-o-o-o-

Kata rose to her feet. There was no tease in her today. "Because I was here to watch Rei and Ilena, my agents are already in place in Brulac and my House here is cleaned and ready for us to move. Mitchel's now in place to work with Ilena directly, so I can move against the enemy of my husband and nation."

She bowed slightly to Ilena. "Thank you for understanding my wish, and being the distraction." Ilena tipped her head in acknowledgment, but both Rei and Sasou got slightly worried looks on their faces. Kata continued,

"We've set up the stage for me to personally be the hand that removes the King who removed our King."

"They won't let you near him either!" Sasou protested.

Ilena and Kata both gave slight hard smiles. "No," Kata agreed quietly, "and they'll watch all my household I bring with me that they feel they can't trust. But even still, the King of Brulac has always desired me from the beginning. Didn't he send me a proposal of marriage when he'd killed my husband, after my father had rejected him to be the same? He's always underestimated women. That will be his undoing, even in the end."

"But you'd still have to be sacrificed in that case," Rei protested. "I already don't like that plan."

Kata smiled gently at her sons. "And what use do you really have of me, but to continue to be a weight on you? I've lived for this time of revenge. We'll explain what we've set up, and you can see how it fits into what must be done.

"If I can come home again alive, we'll all relax and I'll enjoy grandchildren. If it's impossible, then it was sufficient. Ending a war before it can ravage my nation is still my requirement." Her firm, calm statement shut their mouths, for all they were unhappy still.

-o-o-o-

Ilena's household served plates for lunch from carts delivered while Lord Yetherly had spoken. The carts had been sent for when he'd been called in to tell the Ryokudo royals what King Roland was hoping for in sending his second son from Altherly. They didn't want to make assumptions that caused more troubles for them down the road. Lord Yetherly had been humble and somewhat apologetic, as well as grateful that they hadn't done Prince Airn harm nor sent him back home without understanding the situation first. Sasou had made sure Lord Yetherly understood what he was willing to do and not do before excusing him. Clear communication in this international case was rather critical.

Sasou put his utensil down and sighed a little. He stretched his legs out in front of him and folded his arms as he finished putting the details of Prince Airn into his already–formed plans. He nodded a distracted thanks to Mina for removing his empty plate from in front of him. His turn was next. Lunch had allowed him to get his thoughts in a useful order. A glance at Michael as he rose to his feet let his MoI know he'd be talking today, too.

Sasou faced his family. "To be clear, yes, I am planning on helping King Roland. To what extent and when we join in is still unclear, with the final goal being helping for the least amount of time possible with the least amount of resources. We're already going to have to conserve with Brulac breathing down our necks. That direction can't suffer because of what goes earlier into Altherly." He pierced Rei with his blue eyes. "And let me also be clear that I *don't* want to send you."

Sasou shifted slightly as he shifted focus slightly. "Where I *do* want to send you is Yamanzar. I think you've already told me you want to visit there?" Rei gave a nod. "I'll tell you the details and give you the seal to sign an agreeable treaty when you stop by at Ichijou, but I want you to negotiate with King Rayis. If we can have his help to defend our sea border along with Altherly's sea border, then that's fewer of my resources that have to be on the water and more that can be sent up here."

Sasou hesitated, then added, "My sources have told me that one of the reasons Gael is moving is because they finally have a navy sufficient to move on the sea. Warning King Rayis of that — which his own spies should already have corroborated — should make him agree. If Gael and Brulac take both Altherly and us, they'll feel sufficiently strong to move against Yamanzar next."

Rei understood that reasoning. "And do you want me to bring up that Princess Alia's older sister is betrothed to the Crown Prince of Altherly, so there's also that tie that could be called upon?"

Sasou was always proud of Rei, but it came strongly to the front at that very apropos question. "Yes. I think that would be quite appropriate. ...As long as it doesn't make that wedding fall through instead."

"Of course not," Rei promised more soberly than was necessary. It had been at least half a tease, mixed in with the warning.

"As for Brulac," Sasou turned to the most concerning of the topics, "I do wish the Inner Sea would spill over it's bounds just enough to flood them so they can have the water they wish for." His great frustration really couldn't be contained any longer.

Just because the nations that surrounded the Inner Sea were able to more easily do business with each other because of the waterways didn't mean that Brulac wasn't getting trade and goods from other nations. There were even a few nations the rest of them couldn't get to easily because Brulac taxed them too much when they merely wished to pass through to those nations. They'd get *more* revenue if they'd relax that one thing and have better financial policies generally. But the royal family there was both greedy and spent more frivolously than most and the graft in the nation as a whole was horrible for it. "Truly, if any nation needs to be cleaned out from the inside, it's that one."

His eyes pinned Ilena this time and she gave a firm nod. "I'll discuss that during my turn," she promised. Sasou relaxed just a little, pleased he'd been right and she'd already been thinking along the lines of their own lessons learned from that same corrupt king.

"I'm pleased you moved quickly in Tarc, surprising King Gastonne and upsetting his table even a little. I'd like to use that to our benefit and move more quickly rather than less, continuing to keep him off balance.

"The King of Brulac is not to be underestimated. He's been working for this time for generations already. Because Rei moved faster against Tarc than he'd planned for, we have a brief window within which to work, but he'll also move quickly to make up for that difference in his plans. We must not be slow to use what small advantage we do have." He paused in a bit of surprise. Rei was already shaking his head. He raised an eyebrow at his brother.

Rei answered, "With the northeast corner and border currently under greater watch generally by our military because of needing to keep an eye on the Tarc, they won't move yet. They'll wait the same amount of time we would, wanting to make sure our forces in this corner are small enough again to surprise and overwhelm.

"Even if they surged through to the castle to hold us in siege while they move the greater forces into the nation, they'll want to keep those initial casualties at a minimum. Plus, if they wait until you've committed even more troops into a hard–pressed Altherly they'll have even fewer to fight here. I *can* see them wanting to move while the Tarc are still weakened by our movements there, but unless we send soldiers very soon from here to Altherly, they won't move."

Sasou shrugged. "That would be okay. He doesn't know yet if I'll move to defend Altherly early to completely prevent Gael from coming near us, or if I'll wait until Altherly is nearly defeated and then defend my border. If we do the former in order to pull him out on our timing, I'm willing." Rei frowned, still unhappy with that, but he didn't complain further. Sasou also let it go.

It would take Rei some time to fully assimilate all the wants and wishes and boil them down into a workable plan. Sasou himself was still unhappy with his mother's wishes and plans, so he knew it wasn't going to be easy. With a wave of his hand he called Michael up to talk about what the Kingdom Ministry of Intelligence knew.

-o-o-o-

The meeting had come around to Ilena again. "From the time the Seconds of Tarc directly attacked my Seconds, to remove them from me, I've seen the hand of someone other than the Lord of Tarc acting against me personally. It was never his desire to see me weakened. That was confirmed when he sent two spies that died to a very minimal dose of the Little Death earlier this year. He would have been *very* angry to learn it would kill me, so would have sent me the warning. I suspect that was when he killed the spy from Brulac that had been whispering in his ear, as we didn't find one in the Saddle Clan encampment nor on the field from there after the Hunt.

"The Little Death was never in Tarc, for all some of his men were couriers of it at the beginning before Brulac built the facilities to manufacture it in Selicia and Suiran. Queen Aunt was able to stop the influx of Little Death into the country from Brulac, but two facilities had already been put into production. I worked with her agents to get Ivy into one of them. That worked to our benefit in more ways than one. Ryan was able to create the antidote to the third and final poisonous herb before we left to enter Tarc."

Ilena motioned to Marcus and he passed out sheets of paper with neat handwriting on them. "This is Ryan's antidote. While none of the rest of you have had the Little Death given to you, as far as you know, you should make sure that you have this in hand, and a copy at the Ichijou infirmary."

She motioned to Henry. He pulled out a small vial and unstoppered it, then carefully passed it to Sasou with a bow. "This is the poison," Ilena informed them. "Please learn it by scent. As you know, the Little Death in tincture form doesn't have a smell unless you're me. We're fortunate the poison does have sufficient scent for you to learn it today."

Sasou had sniffed the vial already. He held on to it while he 'tasted' the scent on his tongue and lips. When he'd learned it sufficiently, he passed the vial to his mother, who learned it and passed it to Rei. He passed it to Mizi, who wondered who to pass it to, since she'd already learned the scent when she'd been working with Ryan on the antidote.

Henry took it back and took it to Aryana to smell, but he didn't let it go. When she nodded that she'd learned it, Henry put the stopper loosely into the vial and handed it to Michael. From him it was passed around the room from person to person, being stoppered between each person.

Ilena continued as soon as Michael had the vial. "I believe that Brulac is as afraid of the Tarc as they are of me and have already poisoned them as a back–up to any plan that might include the Tarc fighting against Brulac. That's a harder direction for them to defend themselves from because they've had the poison and would be given the hidden Little Death to destroy them.

"Any plan to include them as mounted soldiers in our forces sent to Altherly or against Brulac should also include that those forces be given the antidote to the poison before they leave this area, or there was no point to having sent them to begin with." Ilena pursed her lips and waited for Sasou to nod his agreement and approval.

Ilena turned to Mitchel with a slightly confused expression, glancing also at Michael as she spoke. "Neither of you has commented on something I've seen. Is there a reason you believe it's not feasible?" She got two raised eyebrows of confusion back as they silently asked her for more information. She frowned slightly. "Is there a hand moving behind Gastonne, wanting to topple him and take his place? One who would keep important information from him, ...like how to become an emperor instead of just a king?"

The room went very still. Ilena's eyes flicked between Kata, Mitchel, Sasou, and Michael, reading them quickly. Tension was in all four of them. Michael opened his mouth first, but Sasou beat him with words. "It's a possibility." He glanced at Michael.

Michael said what he'd been going to say, "There's no evidence within Brulac that our spies can ferret out. Only external movements point to it as a hypothesis."

Mitchel agreed with a sharp nod of his head. "It's not even a hypothesis on our end. Only an unprovable postulate, and not where we've been focused."

Ilena frowned at all of them. "Everything I can see points to it being nearly fact." Even the reports and data that had already been said in this meeting had pointed to what she'd seen. She pierced Mitchel with her gaze that demanded truth and answers. "Did the Brulac Ministry of Intelligence change heads any time in my lifetime?"

Mitchel's gaze went distant and he tried to remember. "Yes," he answered slowly. "Roughly the time of the coup in Selicia. That was before we focused so strongly on Brulac ourselves."

Ilena shook her head, suddenly a little impatient. "Go back and research that. How was the prior one removed from office?" The other four she was focused on were now a little impatient with her. She blew out a silent breath and drew in another one. "Do none of you think in generations?" she scolded, particularly Sasou. He was offended, but she didn't relent. "Why would an ancient king want a queen with no power unless he was being led around by the nose with an old dead dream, and himself mostly insane enough to believe it still worth his time and attention, while allowing his nation to decay as badly as it has?"

Her hands were on her hips now and both Sasou and Kata had stiffened at that. "If that king's Minister of Intelligence wants his throne, how hard would that be, to spread dissent among his people and between the lords?" Sasou actually shivered and now Rei was stiff, his eyes wide. "If an ambitious young apprentice of an old willy Minister had designs on that throne, how hard would it be to assassinate or incriminate his superior and be put into his place instead, particularly when the king is already that unstable mentally and easily manipulatable?" Now Mitchel and Michael flinched and Ore stiffened.

Ilena's lips pursed and she drew in a long breath through her nose. She glared at Rei. "Tell me. How hard is it to believe that every repeated pattern up until now has been a learned one from a superior's hand, and that younger hand is still wanting that goal? Particularly when they found me and kept that information silent from the one they were *supposed* to be reporting to?"

"But," Mitchel protested now. "We can't know —"

Ilena's glare fell on him sharply and Kata flinched a little as that glare was that close to her as well. "If one as prideful as that wants that much power and is willing to attempt to topple Selicia, Tarc, Ryokudo, *and* his own nation and king, and then has the one key in their hand to own them all regardless, I don't think he would have told anyone at all. *I* am the clue there is another hand behind Gastonne, seeking for the title of Emperor." She folded her arms and let them stew in that for a while.

"Well," Sasou said almost timidly for him, "it is true that is the thought path that led me to the same hypothesis. But again, we can't tell."

"But," Michael was quick to jump in to defend his liege from any more scolding from Ilena, "likely if we look back those few years, we very well might find the data to prove or disprove it." He gave an almost pleading look for help to Mitchel.

Mitchel drew in a deep breath, then gave a nod. "It's a thing I can request and get information on fairly easily. It may take two months given the travel time to get the request in and the data out."

"See that you do." Ilena and Rei both said it at the same time, and both just as coldly as the other. All four under the focus of Ilena paled.

Ilena took a few breaths to calm down, then continued her portion, moving on to how her people would help Kata and Sasou's people topple Brulac from within, finishing what that minister had started. To her it was only turning the tables on the man who'd done it to her own nation. It was nice of him to have already done the hard work for them (with the help of Kata and Mitchel).

Her report continued for over an hour before they took a brief break and she turned it over to Rei.

-o-o-o-

Rei faced his family and their closest supports. He was still trying to wrap his heart around the news that they weren't done with war. They'd only reached the severe face of it, everything being preparation and leading up to this time. It helped to know that all of his elders had already prepared for this time, and were now ready to face it openly.

"Let me add a few of my own things to the picture so I can know if or how they fit," he started with. "When I visited with Queen Aryana's brother, Lord Yusoku, while in Kouzanshi, a few things came out of that conversation."

Rei turned to Sasou. "The conversation started as cordial as normal; however, after he realized that I wouldn't be presenting the Second Princess, nor her Consort, it seemed Lord Yusoku became somewhat irritated. He expressed it as an irritation later about the underworld of the city.

"I reassured him that I'd look into it — and did since I followed Ilena all over the worst parts of town," smiles tugged at lips in the room, including

Sasou's, "and even made a move to begin to clean up one of the more desolate parts of town. Is there a way this is related to what's going on with Altherly?"

"He's willing to help support the effort to support Altherly," Sasou reassured Rei. "He'll be sending medical supplies, medics, and what little food the city can spare. We'll also send our worst casualties there for recovery once field triage is complete. Lord Yosuko will be quite busy keeping the logistics of that part of the effort in hand. It's just underneath, he'll likely try to see if he can get the wasp in his own beehive ejected. Ilena will have to decide how much she wants to continue to hold on to a place that isn't hers to begin with."

Ilena sighed slightly. She'd given up her close watch over Yosai to Lord Durand when they'd started to move openly against Tarc there, but she hadn't been willing to give up Kouzanshi to its proper lord yet.

"So far, you've sided with her," Sasou pointed out to Rei.

Rei froze slightly, then closed his eyes. "I see," he answered. He'd not had full understanding at the first, but he'd rather known that. He'd wanted to learn just how far Ilena's reach was in Kouzanshi. He hadn't thought too hard about it since they'd left Kouzanshi with his focus on Tarc, but he needed to decide where he'd stand when it came to Kouzanshi before they moved into Altherly to help them.

This wasn't the time to decide that specific point. He set it to the side and moved on to his next point that had come up. However, when he opened his eyes Sasou was holding up a message folder, bound in Ilena's tri–colored cord. "You'll be wanting to add this to that information, but Ilena and I will handle the details." Rei held out his hand to accept the folder.

Nothing more was said on the topic, so he continued, "The other landed lords in that area are just as stubborn as any lord of Suiran. I think they'll help the required amount, but it'll be easier to win them over by requesting another minimal amount of help to actually go into Altherly to hold their western border, and leave the main part of their allotment to hold our own if Altherly falls.

"Not that they wouldn't understand the wisdom of not letting them even get to our border, but because their natural caution will have them wanting to defend their own lands. When we get to the details of how many we need to take with us into Altherly, if we need more numbers than the minimum can gain us, there are a few lords who'd be quite willing to send extras into Altherly ...if they're made to come at the head of their men. They'll hate dying with fewer protections more."

Rei went on to his next point that had woken up in him while they'd been eating lunch. He looked soberly into Sasou's piercing blue eyes. "Protect your Queen well. We'll fall if she falls." Sasou's spine went stiff and Aryana froze in sudden fear. Rei didn't move on until Sasou understood and had put it onto his board. It was even more important now that Ilena's point had been made.

Coolly he said, "I think I'll just go with the assumption Ilena's 'hypothesis' is the right way to think about Brulac. Only if the evidence from the pending research disproves it without doubt will it be worth considering any other possibilities. Even I see it as obvious as she's explained it." He shrugged a little. "Of course, you've all left my training in this up to her, so I would see it as similarly as she does."

He glared at the same four she'd been glaring at. "You'll also *all* tell me *everything* from this point on as relates to what's going on in Brulac." He glared mostly at his mother. When she began to go from stiff to an uncaring attitude that didn't promise it he snapped, "Or you can do it all on your own and die for all I care." Sharp breaths were drawn in and Kata was staring at him with very wide eyes. "That's what you want, right? Then why bother to bring me in at all, since you can do that just fine without me. I'm sure I have enough to do being a Regent so young no one wants to listen to me."

Sasou moved at that and Rei's scowl was on him as well. Sasou drew in a breath and held it instead of speaking for a few heartbeats so he mostly calmly and very firmly was able to say, "We'll do it, Rei." Sasou glared at their mother until she caved and bowed her head to the both of them. Rei relaxed slightly but he was still glaring at Sasou. He'd pursed his lips, trying to keep the rest in.

Sasou drew in a slow breath. "I'm sorry we've put you in a hard place to be, Rei," he apologized. "I'm grateful you're willing to try your best regardless. I know it's also hard that I'm not easily available to answer questions and help when you need it. But I am willing to do what I can." He paused, then drew in another breath with a bit of a wince. "Ask me on the wind and I'll have Michael answer the same. It's the best I can do."

Rei blinked in surprise that his brother would be willing to be interruptable. It helped him calm down, though. It was likely the only answer that would. Ilena was still working hard to train him to recognize when he needed help and open his mouth when he did, but with that promise he'd work harder to do so. "I'll count on that, then," he said in a deadly quiet tone, not letting Sasou get out of it. Sasou winced again slightly but gave a promise nod.

Rei took his turn to breathe back to some level of calm, but he couldn't and wouldn't let go of the firm requirement that he was holding over them. "If you really want my help with this, then we're going to go with Ilena's plan. I've already seen how they work. From the summaries Michael and Mitchel gave, it sounds like King Gastonne can be overthrown by mid–summer, roughly. She and I will sit and go over details and ask questions over the next few weeks to months, since we shouldn't move until we do have that last piece of data in hand. It wouldn't be prudent to move if different data comes back. I want to have the time to decide if that's true, anyway, since it might be irrelevant and her solution the only proper answer regardless." He scanned the group and didn't get any dissent.

"I'd like to make Altherly wait." His eyes stopped on Sasou. "This next year is already going to be a very busy year for us." He paused again to purse his lips slightly. "And I'll ignore it altogether if you won't keep me informed."

Sasou immediately shook his head. "We'll be passing everything we get to Ilena. And I'd appreciate having your very capable brain working on the details to make sure we don't have any holes in the plan."

He paused, his eyes going unfocused as he looked internally at his board. He actually launched into openly revealing all of the pathways he'd already walked in his attempt to decide when and how to face both Altherly and Gael. It was true that it was a complex puzzle to decide just when to begin to help. How long to sit it out meant the possibility of not having to worry at all if Altherly won early, or missing the important moment of giving needed aid and having to defend their own borders. Rei soaked all the information in rather automatically, it being similar to his war and strategy lessons. However, it was incomplete because it was current rather than historic data.

When Sasou was done, Rei finished settling it all on his board then gave a nod. "I'll work on that around the edges. We'll discuss it when we come down in the summer unless the final sum says we need to move sooner than that." Sasou gave Rei a withering look but Rei didn't care. His brain worked at the speed it did and was needed for other things as well. "I'm sure I'll be asking enough questions you won't wonder if I've forgotten," he scolded Sasou. Sasou slumped a little at the reminder he'd promised to be interruptable but he accepted the answer, having at least received the promise of support in thinking about it.

-o-o-o-

Sasou pulled Ilena away to talk to her privately after the meeting was over. Quietly he asked, "Why did Rei snap?" He was genuinely concerned. He had to ask because he wasn't there to see things in person. And deeper down, he was afraid to ask Ore. If Rei had snapped Ore already would be angry as well, for his master's sake. Ilena pursed her lips at him and he was reminded that she'd scolded them all first. Maybe it hadn't been a good idea to ask her, but she'd openly tell him truths. And, he needed to know how well Ilena understood Rei by now.

"Because you and Queen Mother neglected him too much while at the same time making him take on tasks larger than he was prepared for without the training you weren't giving him. Learning everything by being thrown into difficult situations isn't the best way to be taught. It's what you know because you didn't have any other option, but it's not what he needs. He's been bottling up that frustration for his whole life, Sasou."

Her lips pursed again. "And since that isn't *my* preferred way of teaching, when you both make me do it as well it makes me angry too. Giving him as much data as possible, answering the brief questions as they come to him, helps him to fill in the gaps without making him feel abandoned and like a child who has to carry the whole world. Tarc was very hard for him, for all he did it and did it well. Telling him to do it again with limited information again is what made him refuse this time. You remember our meeting yesterday morning. He's done with being kept in the dark."

Sasou blinked as he put that data into his understanding of the world. He sighed. "Well, I'm sorry it's been that way." He'd already promised to correct it properly, it sounded like. That was rather relieving. He really did need to rely on Rei quite a lot.

He really looked at Ilena for a bit, then bowed his head to her. "Thank you for taking on the teaching we couldn't do. Please feel free to use your preferred method. I'm sure we'd rather not continue to make him angry." He received a scowl for his trouble but she eventually blew out a sigh and gave a nod she'd continue in that role.

He thought he might be able to escape at that point, but she shifted then returned the sharp look. Even more quietly she said, "And you'd best figure out how to repair what you're beginning to damage with Ore while you're at it. He's not been dealing well with the levels of responsibility you're making him take on as well."

Sasou blinked as his heart beat harder. "Which ones?" As she opened her mouth he raised a hand to stop her. "I know he doesn't like being pushed up to the heights he's had to go, but I don't understand why he didn't already know it was going to be required once he understood who and what you are."

That made Ilena's mouth close and her brow furrow a little. She turned to look across the hallway to the far end of it. The others were respecting Sasou's silent request for privacy, but Ore was watching them. She looked Ore in the eye and motioned with her finger for him to join them. He moved immediately. Sasou stiffened inside and set himself for another round of diplomatic battle. Their last visit's scolding was rather tame compared to today. He'd rather fix it early and now than have things fall apart later, so he'd bear with it today.

Ore's gaze on Sasou was as suspicious as it ever was, and as judgmental. The anger was there, beneath the surface, but perhaps it was for his own sake this time. "Ask him, Sasou," Ilena said.

Ore blinked and Sasou prepared himself. "Ilena says you're angry with me, specifically for the levels of responsibility you've been given." He waited briefly and got sharp silent agreement. "Why weren't you preparing for that once you understood what she was? You already knew I knew from before. Why wouldn't I use her and therefore you?"

Ore's mouth dropped open briefly. He closed it and rubbed his hand over his head. He scowled but took a while to answer. Finally he let out a breath and said, "Because it was too hard to believe that you'd trust me that much."

Sasou thought about that answer, then replied, "After you and Rei both demanded her, that became nearly irrelevant. I need Rei and I need her. If she was to be yours, then you became mine by default. Of course I'd watch you and see if you could stand next to her." He shrugged. "I suppose we can all be relieved you *can*. But it seems odd to me that you'd choose to be angry at me about it." He looked Ore directly in the eyes, almost daring him, and he saw it. The flash of understanding that if Ore *couldn't* have stood next to Ilena at all of the levels he'd been planning on using her for, Ore would have been removed from the boards completely for demanding to have her.

Ore stood rock hard still and Sasou watched him closely. Anyone would instinctively react to that realization with anger. He wanted to know what would be next. Ore relaxed rather suddenly. Wryly he said, "Well, I guess if I'm still alive and Second Prince and Grand Duke and Suiran Nightwalker King, all from just being me, then I can only be upset with myself for not properly thinking about it from the beginning." He hadn't quite forgiven Sasou, though. His pupils weren't relaxing from the black almonds they'd become. Quietly he added, confirming Sasou's expectation, "But it will stop here. Even she can't do more than this when Minister of Intelligence is more than enough."

Sasou bowed slightly mockingly at him. "I have no intention of adding anything further." He went back to serious, though. "And I'd take back the duchy if I could. None of us want Tarc, but it wasn't ours to refuse once it was pushed on us from outside." Ore did understand that much.

Sasou sighed and looked away from them. "I'd also take away Queen of Night. If I could have saved her out of Selicia, I would have." He looked back at them to see them both looking at him in surprise. He smiled sadly at them. "I'm grateful, regardless. The kindness and blessing that's been to the people of Suiran has been more than we can repay." It was enough to see the blush on Ilena's ears and Ore's expression relax. Even he understood that and loved his wife for it.

Sasou sighed to himself and turned away from them. "Keep Rei walking forward. And keep him alive for me. Thank you for doing so until now." He didn't look back, but he did keep his ears on them. They followed him far enough behind to not make his back twitch which was sufficient. They'd forgiven him enough he'd not die today.

-o-o-o-

Ilena took some vacation time after the meeting. She needed to come down off of the high tension and heavy thoughts. "Ryan?" she called as she entered the medical offices.

"Ilena?" he called back and walked through to his office from within the herb repository. His face lit up in a smile. "Hello! It's good you've stopped by. I've got some hopeful news for you."

"Oh?" Ilena lit up at that. "I'd love some good news about now. This has all been so busy and hard." They hugged briefly and Ryan invited her to sit with him.

Ryan folded his fingers together. "I've done enough research on the plant Mizi sent me from Tarc to learn that it won't kill you at what should be normal doses. I don't know the long–term results, yet, since it hasn't been that long since I received it to experiment with it, so I don't want to let you take it yet, but it's a promising start."

"That's wonderful, Ryan!" Ilena clapped her hands together. "I'll wait, but I'll be very glad if it's one Ore and I can use without worry." She paused, then added, "Ah, but we're working on an heir now, so you have the time." With a slump she said, "Now if there was a way to guarantee I could get pregnant in the time I have. We're expecting the same difficulties my mother, aunt, and Touka grandmothers have had — on top of the missing months."

Ryan gave a thoughtful nod. "I can probably help there, as well. There are a few hard–to–find herbs that help one become pregnant. But, there are sometimes cases of multiple births then. Would that be a deterrent?" he asked clinically.

"No," Ilena answered, "since I'd expect it to be hard regardless, and having them sooner isn't all bad." She went humble, remembering her lessons, "I'll confirm with Ore, though." With good news to bolster her a little she turned to the bad news.

"Please begin not only to increase your assistants, but your stock. War comes. I'll be letting you know details as we learn them, but now is the soonest I could tell you with certainty it will be happening.

"Sasou has announced he'll be agreeing to support Altherly. Gael is threatening to invade them and they've asked for our help. We'll need to send medical supplies with whatever men we're required to send over there. I wanted to let you know as soon as possible so there's time to stockpile it. Mizi might be able to help with that project as well."

Ryan had stiffened. Now he slumped and sighed slightly. "That's not good, but we can do that. Do you know how long we have to increase the supplies?" He looked a question at her.

Ilena shrugged. "As I said, I'll let you know details as I learn them. Numbers of men to send hasn't been decided yet, either." That wasn't what he wanted to hear since it would be difficult to know just how fast to stockpile just how much, but this early that's all she had. "Did you enjoy your visit with your family?" she asked him, turning the conversation to gentle topics for her own sake of needing to wind down.

Ryan perked up. "Yes. It was good to see them again after so long. They were very grateful they could be allowed to watch the court to see me granted peerage." He blushed and said more quietly, "I'm grateful for the trust of King Sasou." Ilena smiled softly, happy to see him happy.

When she'd relaxed enough to have the pressure of needing to get back to work rise up too far again, Ilena rose to her feet. "I need to get back to desk work now. Thank you for good news, too, at this time. I'll come visit again and help out when things get too stressful at the office."

"Please do," he smiled a very happy smile at her. She impulsively gave him a hug, then really did have to hurry back to her office.

-o-o-o-

Rei and Mizi saw Sasou and Aryana off from the royal gate of Nijou. Sasou pulled Rei aside to where they could speak privately before the carriage arrived. "Is there anything else I can answer before we go?" Sasou asked. Rei gave him the court neutral face for a while, then shook his head. "You'll continue with the census and audit?"

Rei nodded curtly. "I can't let that go. You know why."

Sasou did and couldn't complain. "For all Brulac says three years before they move, Gael really wants to move now. It's hard to tell which is the feint."

Rei considered it. "Go ahead and announce you'll support Altherly. If they're still in negotiations with Brulac it will make Gael back off a little and give Altherly breathing space. If they don't care then we'll know something."

Sasou gave him a nod and looked at his brother. Rei had grown nearly as tall as Sasou was, a tall height for Ryokudo. The broad shoulders from the back would make anyone think he was already well into his twenties. In the end, he might have to admit Rei would be more handsome, if not ever more beautiful. It would be enough. His lips quirked up a little and he reached out and pulled his brother into his arms. "I don't think I'll get away with giving you big brother hugs much longer. You're going to surpass me, soon."

Rei shuddered but it was with a muffled laugh. "Maybe," he admitted, holding Sasou gently and briefly back, a first for him.

Sasou let him go and teased, "I see Ilena is rubbing off on you."

Rei smiled. "Well, yes, rather a lot, actually. But it's likely possible because of Ore's years of hard work before then." Sasou could only agree. Deep down he was grateful they were good parents for Rei.

The sound of the coming carriage came to their ears. "Take care, Sasou," Rei said solemnly. "Even if you don't want my job, I really don't want yours."

Sasou gave him a slight smile. "Well, I do know that. But let's not let it go to Ore, shall we?" He winked at Rei. "He just scolded me he won't take anything more."

Rei chuckled. "Then don't die or he'll have to take this seat, too, so I can take yours." He paused and let his eyes go wide. "Oh, wait. You mean so I don't drop Queen in Ilena's lap and make him take your spot."

Sasou teasingly nodded a sober nod. "Yes. That. He'll come into the afterworld and kill me twice more for doing it, too. ...By the way," he glanced at Rei out of the corner of his eye, "your lady assistants, Mina and Ilena, will become pregnant also this coming year. You might like to include that in your calculations." Rei's jaw dropped. Sasou's eyes twinkled in his tease. "They're both determined to bear the sons that will become your son's guards."

Rei could only put his hand to his head in disbelief. It took a bit before he'd recovered enough to decide it was probably not a bad idea. "Fine," he sighed. "If it doesn't fit, I'll be scolding them both off the idea, though," he grimaced at his brother.

Sasou hesitated and then shook his head. "Like I'm late, so are they. You can afford to wait, but they can't. I don't recommend interfering on this one." Rei rolled his eyes and sighed. Then Sasou was tucking Aryana's hand into his elbow to walk her to the carriage. He was very much looking forward to his own vacation at his personal home, which he only got to see once a year or less. It would finally be even slightly restful now that he had Rei and Ilena working with him on the hardest of his current tasks.

-o-o-o-

Ilena called for a staff meeting to get her staff going on their next tasks. She discovered in the middle of their meeting that Michael had slipped in and joined them.

Ilena paused, looking at the Kingdom Minister of Intelligence and main aide and guard of the King in surprise with her mouth open in the middle of a sentence. She blinked, then finished her thought. When she paused to allow him time to have his say, he only looked at her innocently. So, she continued on until the meeting was done and everyone broke for their tasks.

"They don't need you to get to where they're going?" Ilena asked him.

"I get to stay and have my vacation with you," he smiled.

No one bought it, least of all Ore, who folded his arms and stayed close to Ilena. "Really, to have both of you. Don't you think it's a bit much? I think I'll put you to work," he said with a bit of a scowl.

Both Michael and Mitchel smiled predatory smiles at him. "Of course you will. We're here to train *you*." Ore's shoulders slumped. Ilena listened to the lessons with half her ear as she got to work on the things that had been languishing on her desk from what felt like forever ago.

CHAPTER 149 Getting Back to Work

Rei reached out and took Mizi's hand in his, making her pause in her morning preparations for the day. "What is it, Mizi?" he asked.

While she loved that she didn't have to fret for sometimes weeks before she could talk to him again, to have him ask it of her made it rather obvious that she was an open book to the people she loved. Particularly since she wasn't used to being asked that question the very next day after a worry cropped up to furrow her brow. She squeezed his hand and let it go so she could finish getting dressed while she thought of how to answer to it.

The national security meeting had been hard to sit through. So much of it had been worrisome that she'd taken a lot of time to work through it all. Most of it she'd finally been able to set aside by setting the responsibility back on the shoulders that were already carrying it. But this was her's to carry, her blame, her burden.

Rei was kind and patiently let her get her words together; although, he somewhat impatiently sat down to eat without her. He was getting faster in the morning, with all the busy he was under. Not that she ever was slow, he'd just sped up. "I'm sorry, Rei," she said the words that most wanted to be said first, sitting down next to him. She raised her eyes to look into his. "I'm sorry I let in a spy without knowing."

Rei gave her a thoughtful nod as he considered the toast in his hand and took a bite of it. She paused a little longer, then turned to her own plate. He'd be done before her at this rate. She wouldn't eat much, though. Worries made her not very hungry. "It's really not that uncommon," he finally answered her, wiping his buttery fingers on his napkin before reaching for his glass. "Some are very good at hiding themselves. We hope we choose right, and we're sad when we haven't." She felt he was very much speaking from experience.

"In this case, it's okay because Ilena's already on top of things and needs to know more." He glanced at her. "You remember when we got back from fighting Earl Shicchi and you told me her answer to why she lets some of the vermin stay in the castle?"

Mizi reflected back then gave a nod. "Because she can control what they hear and say, and because it's often harder to have to fight them constantly." She shuddered. "Still, for all she said it yesterday, that it would be better to have them stay in their place, I can't help but have shivers in my back now, all the time."

"I'm sure," Rei was sympathetic, "but you still must do your part."

"I will," she promised again. Because she'd let a spy in, she had to pay the price and bear with it, allowing Ilena's ministry to use him until he became either too much a threat or useless. She was pretty sure Ilena knew exactly who the spy was, but they weren't telling Mizi. She was certain it wasn't Delia or Tanner, since they were already Ilena's. She really didn't want it to be any of the others. She liked them all so much.

Rei rose to his feet, the rest of his small breakfast of eggs and ham already eaten, and leaned over to kiss her. "I trust Ilena and the rest to keep you safe, or I'd have argued it. Just don't let any of them be alone with you. Always keep two or more with you. And don't forget your knife and defensive lessons."

"Of course, Rei," she smiled up at him. "I think I'm going to finally be happily so busy as to not be able to worry about much at all." Rei chuckled at her and left for the Rose office.

She herself had a meeting in her quarters next with Brianna. Well, Tanner was next, so she followed Rei out to sit in her chair in the outer sitting room. Tanner was waiting as usual in a chair off to the side for her to be ready for their scheduling meeting. Rei and she had summarized their schedules while in the bath, since it was so short for them today: get their regular daily lives back in their heads again now that the interim investiture was finally over. That meant a lot of work for them both, but neither knew what it really was, particularly with the new things out of the national security meeting. It was her meeting with Tanner that would help her sort most of it out, and then the meeting with Brianna that should settle the rest.

"Tanner," Mizi began a little hesitantly.

Tanner raised his hand to forestall her. "Mistress Mizi, may I make a suggestion?"

"Sure," Mizi's brow furrowed a little.

"Miss Rio is looking for an opportunity for Miss Amber to learn more about that and other issues. Would it help you to have one more of Mistress Ilena's by your side? In particular she could go with you to the teas and such for your lessons with Lady Brianna. If you needed to relax from that 'prickling between your shoulders', you could send the guards, or even a subset of them, to the Rose Office to help there during those times."

Mizi's lip twitched, "And let Rei's back prickle instead." Tanner's lip twitched a little. He hadn't meant it himself, but he did see the humor in it now that Mizi had said it. "Ah, well," Mizi sighed, "I'll think about it. If it would help Ilena's office then I'd be willing generally anyway. I think I'd like it known sooner than later." She gazed off into the distance for a bit, trying to come to terms with her unhappy requirement yet again.

When she returned, she asked Tanner what was on the schedule generally, not just for that specific day. Tanner looked into his own mind for the list. For all Mizi made him write down some things for her sake, he still preferred to use memorization over writing. "Adjunct to the Regent duties, which are set by timing, somewhat flexible if a particular issue is difficult and needs extra research. Help Lord Ryan with the intern and assistant applications and testing."

Mizi nodded to herself. Yes, that was going to be the newest big requirement on her plate. She should meet with Ryan fairly soon on that one.

"Then there's your lessons with Lady Brianna on learning how the court ladies interact." Mizi gave a nod. That was the next meeting's agenda. "Dance practice, defensive martial arts lessons, knife lessons and practice, and Mistress Ilena has required that you continue to practice horseback riding at least once per week." Mizi tried not to have her nose wrinkle up at that one. It wasn't that she disagreed she needed it. It was just one more thing to add to those small things that seemed superfluous in the face of the important big things.

"Ah, yes," Tanner added, "and unlearning how to hear the whispers in the castle." Now Tanner's teasing glint was in his expression.

Mizi blushed. She'd complained that morning to Rei at just how busy the Intelligence network was around the castle. It wasn't really loud but now that she could hear at that level it certainly wasn't quiet any more. Rei had sympathized and suggested she learn the voices that were important to her and focus more on them when she heard them. The rest would become background noise eventually, he'd reassured her. "And those who are talking directly to you will be loudest because the person closest to you is always loudest." She did already know that.

"Well, I think I'd like to make sure I can pick Ore, Ilena, and Ryan out of the noise for sure," she said. "And I already know your voice and the other four. I honestly haven't heard Delia much, but I think I could learn it fairly quickly."

Rei had admitted that learning to hear Ore and Ilena was good, but not useful except in rare cases. They talked a lot, he'd told her, and usually it wasn't things they'd need to hear. "But sometimes I come out of working completely alert, my ears having caught something from or about Ore or Ilena and it's completely germane to what I need to know. So it's good to know." He'd shrugged and smiled. "And if I'm not listening for their voices specifically, I miss when they're going to come surprise me with a visit. So I've learned to key to that, too, so I can get to a pausing point in my work." Mizi had laughed at that one. That was what she wanted to be able to do as well.

"I heard Ilena a lot at the garrison and on the way north, so I know her voice. I'd like to make sure I know Ore's; although, we did work on that while there for the Marluk'nak' of Chaos and Change. I don't think I've ever heard Ryan speak the language while in front of him to know it was him." Tanner was adding it to the list, Mizi could tell.

"Ah, and there's one more thing to add," Mizi suddenly remembered. Tanner was already nodding. He'd been in the security meeting. "How do I make sure they're passing the reports of Prince Airn's progress on to me?"

"That order was passed on late yesterday during the Ministry's general meeting," Tanner answered her. "All of those who are watching him, or who have reports about him will address them directly to you so that those in the castle keeping track of where you are will know to pass them on."

"Okay," Mizi was satisfied with that. With so much already on Rei's plate he'd delegated that small but important detail to her. It would be a small thing to add to her schedule so it was something she was happy to help with.

She reviewed the list one more time, particularly the shorter seemingly non–essential ones. Some weren't really non–essential. She really did need to learn to defend herself and practicing both ways every day would help her learn them faster and be better at it. "When does Ilena's household practice?" She was sure they still did. Then she remembered that Ore would practice while watching over her but sitting around bored otherwise. She didn't think he did that anymore. They weren't ever bored anymore, nor hardly sitting around.

"Some do it first thing in the morning to get the body awake and the blood flowing. Some do it as a relaxation in the evening as they prepare to go to bed. The rest make Master Ore and Mistress Ilena do it if they've gotten too focused on work and are making the rest irritable. That settles them back down and work can get done again." Tanner paused in thought. "I've heard that they've scheduled in time for their partner hand–to–hand practices now, too. I'm not sure when, but I suspect in the evening."

Mizi nodded. Each fit it in where it fit their schedule and needs best. That's rather what she thought, but it helped to have heard it said that way. "Well, my classes are when my classes are, but —"

Tanner was shaking his head. "You're the First Princess. You decide when the instructor will show up and where."

Mizi's mouth gaped open. She ruefully closed it. "I suppose that's rather necessary, given how busy royals are."

Tanner nodded firmly. "Most royals rise early enough to practice before they must do their other work, either just before or just after breakfast."

Mizi's eyes widened. "When does Rei practice?"

"In the past, Lord Andrew and Miss Mina would drag him out of bed before dawn and he'd practice, then come back here to bathe and eat. Rutherford says he was usually sleeping through all of it until he set his fork down on the table, yawned, and woke up." Tanner smiled.

Mizi laughed. She did still love hearing the stories of the younger Rei. "But I've never seen him practice since we got married?" she asked.

Rutherford appeared to her eyes in his usual chair on the far wall because he shook his head. "He hasn't had time, and has wanted to enjoy his new wife." His expression also sparkled.

Mizi blushed lightly but shook her head back. "That won't do, and I'm sure Mina must be biting her tongue bloody not chastening him for it." She pondered for a bit, then gave a nod. "We'll both do it together. It'll be hard for a little while, but with war on the horizon we'll both need to have the practicing in. I'll talk to him about it tonight. Tanner, keep that as part of the list, that we'll be doing the defensive practicing in the morning somewhere near where Rei practices so we can go and come back together. I think it'll be easier knowing we're working together even if differently. That did help on our progress around Suiran."

Thinking about that a little more, she added slowly, "Maybe you should have the instructors both come for my first session and watch me, then they can discuss what the specific schedule should be. I don't know if it should be both the martial art and the knife in the same morning or not." She sighed. "And maybe one day of the week we can both skip that practicing and can ride together at that time. I don't really enjoy riding unless I'm with others. It's a practical need, but that's all for me. I'll ask Rei that also and see if he'll come keep me company for it."

It was dancing that was the most unnecessary now. She'd learned most of them fairly well. She just didn't want to forget them, nor lose her callouses now that she'd earned them so painfully with great effort. She pondered for a while, then decided that one might be a question for Brianna.

She was fortunate that Brianna was announced just then. She welcomed Brianna in and waited for her to get settled. "I've just been talking to Tanner about the general schedule, Brianna," Mizi said respectfully, still wanting to remember that manners from royalty was a gift to others, particularly when she wanted kindness in return. "Can you give me a summary of where we are and what's next so we can fit it in?"

Brianna folded her hands in her dark grey skirt, still keeping to the less–formal mourning clothing since the death of her husband. Maria and Delia had confided to Mizi in her bedroom as she was getting ready one morning that they thought she did it to keep potential late–in–life suitors away. Having such attention was rather common, particularly if the lady would bring even more wealth or status to the lord. It seemed Lady Brianna was of both categories. Mizi could understand her not wanting to deal with any of that at this point in her life. Surely a full year of mourning wasn't asking for too much anyway; although, Mizi didn't know if Brianna had loved her husband that much.

"I think you're ready to begin practicing what you've been learning from me. We could begin by attending the open lunches. I thought we could also select two from the list that would be good beginning practices for teas over the next two weeks, but I've heard you'd rather practice harder than that, so it could be two teas this week," she gave Mizi a small smile.

Mizi smiled back. "Well, getting back into things, I'm not sure if I can do lunches and two teas in *this* week, but two teas next week I think would be doable. I've been thinking more about Ilena's comment that in order to get to know the Queen Mother better invitations to tea might be the better way. I know not many people know her well, but do you think it would be okay to invite her to one this week, specifically letting her know that I'd like to observe how she interacts at teas, letting her know obscurely that I want to act correctly at them without embarrassing her or the royal family?"

"I think she'd be both very annoyed and pleased you'd asked. She really does hate teas generally, just like she hates being public at all. However, she does have a vested interest in seeing that you don't fall flat on your face in Ichijou. Even you will be tested there, if not so hard as Ore and Ilena." Mizi felt her face fall. She'd already been observed there, but now she really was Rei's princess. Now they'd watch every little detailed thing she said and did.

"Well, all the better reason, then." Mizi pursed her lips. That meant keeping lunches open for a while. If no invitations came, if she was missing Rei and the others, she'd go to the Rose office for lunch on those days. She wasn't preventing herself from that. "Let's go to a few lunches and watch the ladies on the easier list. We can choose who to have a tea with this week after I've seen them again."

"Very well," Brianna agreed, her own point–giving expression of approval coming on her face.

Mizi had Tanner add the open ladies' lunches to her schedule for the rest of the week and into the next, starting the next day. She'd use today's lunch at the Rose Office to explain what she was doing, since Rei was expecting her to be there.

-o-o-o-

After meeting with Brianna, Mizi was off to her morning meeting with Ilena. For the second time Ilena's staff requested that Amber be allowed to shadow Mizi at the young ladies' luncheons. Mizi had agreed, but after being reminded who Amber was she wasn't so sure she wanted Amber following her at the same functions she was already going to have to deal with the same sort of young lady at. Then again, that might make her the perfect companion. Amber would get along with the other young women just fine, would enjoy the lunches (which Mizi already didn't), and she'd be yet another learning and testing example from both Brianna and Ilena's perspectives. Mizi swallowed and tried to let it go. It wasn't until tomorrow and later.

Arriving in the infirmary helped Mizi's stomach some. Being greeted by a Ryan happy to see her was even better. After greeting each other, Mizi immediately turned to her usual group of followers and waved them off with both hands. "Get. Go. Have a break. Eat. Something."

Her guards looked at her with wide eyes while Brianna smiled a small smile. "I'm going to relax for a bit with Ryan. I can't do that with all of you here, too. Just leave Tanner standing around bored. You can hear him if he calls for you, and he can defend me easily enough here if it takes you more than two minutes to get back. Go!" She flapped her hands at them again.

It wasn't very characteristic of her to address her guards this way, but Mizi was actually rather desperate for even this little break with a friend. Brian, Kirk, Sam, and Leon all bowed to her and wandered out of the medical wing. She knew Sam and Leon would stay the closest. Sam was rather particular about fulfilling his duty, but he also knew how to stay far enough out of her irritability range. If they stayed, Brian and Kirk would wander farther since they also liked to have occasional free time to breathe away from their responsibilities.

"Will you need me again today?" Brianna asked Mizi. Mizi shook her head. "Then I'll go help in the Rose office," Brianna informed Mizi. That suited Mizi fine. Brianna also didn't like to be bored and Mizi didn't want her to have to be. Brianna curtsied and followed the young men out.

"Would you like to come into my office?" Ryan offered, "Or perhaps a greenhouse? We could chat while doing simple weeding."

"Oh, yes, that would be wonderful!" Mizi hadn't been in a greenhouse with her hands in the soft loamy dirt for more days than she wanted to count. That would help her relax even more. She did check with Tanner, though, not sure if that would be safe enough. He gave her a smile and nod, so she happily followed Ryan out the side door to the greenhouses, followed by the silent secretary–guard she knew she could trust. The itching between her shoulder blades relaxed finally, down to a slight tickle.

"How are you doing Ryan?" Mizi asked Ryan on the walk over to the greenhouse that was next on Ryan's list for maintenance.

Ryan's expression went a little shy. "I'm keeping busy. It's still hard to remember dinner, but I'm getting a little better with it." They'd reached the greenhouse door. Ryan held the door open for Mizi and changed the subject. "Are you free to help with the internship testing now?"

Mizi was happy to say, "Yes. That can be top of my list now. I'll be happy to be back here helping you. Lunches are busy for a while, and a few teas. And my Adjunct duties in the late afternoons." She sighed having to bring up that list. "So mornings at this time and — when I can squeeze it in — after lunch for a little bit." That last would probably be either impossible to squeeze in, or absolutely critical to helping her calm back down.

"Okay. I'll make sure that I have the candidates come in the mornings for interviews and the training," Ryan accepted that easily as he led them to the first bed to care for. They were both lost in pulling the little weeds out and thinning out the too–small or unhealthy plantings rather quickly. Still, Ryan didn't get as lost as he would've if he was writing things down. "Would you be willing to research what test we should give the candidates when their training time is done?" he asked. "I did that last time, and it's your turn to learn how to pick a test. I'll review what you think it should be before we agree to use it."

"Okay," Mizi agreed. Ryan had chosen her test. She'd thought at first Parmenia had. That had been a funny one, actually, but a good one generally.

Ryan's dark eyes lifted from the herb bed in front of them to look into hers for a brief moment. "Ilena stopped by. She asked that we begin to overstock supplies to be used when King Sasou orders men into Altherly. She said you maybe could help with that, too? It would help me a lot, and I'll sign any requisitions you need signed."

Mizi considered that. "I might go talk to the garrison medical officers. Then we can know what they'd use most in their work. I know roughly what was used up most when we were in Tarc."

She looked up in a bit of surprise, "Oh, that was helpful that I went. I helped in the infirmary tent there. While it wasn't a war in the full sense of the word, they did fight. Some of the wounds were rather severe, since the Tarc are so vicious. I'd want to confirm with them what I learned there and see if there'd be more of that kind of need and wounds. We're already short on bandaging in comparison to what the medical soldiers take with them."

She pondered on that issue while her hands continued to work with the herbs. "Maybe I can ask Ilena to have her weavers focus on that a little bit on the side. ...I wonder if they'd donate it?"

Ryan blinked at Mizi and smiled. "You're already thinking hard about this."

"Well, yes," Mizi agreed. Her cheeks warmed as her eyes fell to the herbs in front of her. "It was hard to fall asleep last night after that meeting in the morning. I wandered the castle all afternoon while everyone else was busy, getting all the stuff from it settled in my brain."

She wrinkled her nose at Ryan. He patted her arm, understanding. It was nice to be doing something useful and relaxing while with a friend. It had been a while and Mizi was sure she needed it.

"We've just finished the fall inventory," Ryan said, returning to the plants in front of him. "It's good timing to visit the garrison medic and confirm his own inventory. You could go on the requisition trip, if it fit into your schedule?"

Mizi wasn't surprised she'd missed yet another inventory, but it was a little sad. "I'll consider it." She wasn't sure how to fit in yet another trip away from the castle, but it could be useful. "I can go talk to the medical officer after lunch."

Tanner reminded her quietly she needed to learn Ryan's voice, so they spent some time talking pleasantly in Ilena's secret whisper–sung language while they worked. It was good to lose herself in the work of tending to the tender plants of the greenhouse nestled in their loamy beds.

-o-o-o-

When Mizi and her contingent left the Lower Ministry of Intelligence office, people stopped working and turned to frown at Ilena. "If you know about the stress levels being too high, then let's fix it!" Marcus said first, referencing a comment Ilena had let slip to Mizi. "I'm about to turn into three pieces of a stick trying to keep you and Henry propped up. It's why I was sleeping on my feet last night. The numbers won't stay together for me and Henry can't handle them on his own."

Ilena blinked at Marcus. Marcus was almost never the one to scold, and certainly not first nor seriously. He'd just done all three ...with the accountant–seneschal of the Grand Duchy present. Lord Hayward was nodding quite firmly in agreement, though. He was getting rather frustrated with having to be Marcus' remedial math teacher.

Ilena gave a nod. "Okay. That's why I said it. I wanted to know just how deep that had become. I've been feeling it but just because I can feel that it's time to fix things doesn't mean I have any idea of how soon it needs to be done. Scold more and sooner." Marcus blushed but Henry just agreed.

"Everyone, please," Ilena added. "It's a problem we all need to fix together." She got sighs from the upper floor, since they didn't want the interruption, but they also agreed and came downstairs: three down the stairs, the rest over the balcony taking the time to stretch in the fresh air while they waited for the more sedate, slower three to arrive.

It was, as usual now, a crowded room when they arrived. Ilena wasn't going to pay for more furniture, so those that didn't already have chairs on this level leaned against walls and lounged on couches while she sat in her desk chair this time. Ore decided to perch on her desk where he could be close to her but watch everyone with her.

"Since Marcus is the one breaking, and from propping up Henry more than normal, we'll have Henry start," Ilena said.

The look Henry gave to Ilena was one of wild complete overwhelmed astonishment. "Whyever did you give to two *wanted nightwalkers* the job of keeping track of royal super–important financial documents, when we've learned a lot of things for you until now, but never numbers? I'm having walking nightmares that we'll screw up even a few minor things and they'll throw us in jail, behead Ore, and disown you."

Marcus nodded, "Yup, he is, and nothing I say talks him out of it. He's about to hate me for not being able to keep the addition and subtraction right, for all I've memorized the simple things already. The action of adding and subtracting scrambles the numbers in my head. I'd rather not have him hate me for a thing that isn't going to happen in the first place, but I'd also like to not screw things up."

Ilena pondered on that. "Well, I want you over the audit, but you don't have to do the books. What I really want you for is to chase after people who're giving us fishy numbers that might need thumping, or have shown to them the evidence of why we know they're keeping money back they're not supposed to be, or to teach them what we expect out of them. You already know how to do that." They agreed but Lord Hayward shifted uncomfortably. Ilena raised an eyebrow at him.

"The Ministry books really should be kept by someone who's already trained. I'm afraid they already aren't going to be acceptable to the Ministry of Finance and during the audit it would be considered more problematic than unconventional. However, I shouldn't be doing both the Ministry and the Duchy books, for the same audit reason. If I'm doing both it could be seen that I'm hiding money from one in the other."

Ilena gave a thoughtful nod. "That makes sense." Her eyes roved over the grouping until they settled on Grandfather. "You did the manor books and have an impeccable record. Will you do the Ministry books and let the Twins do the rest? You can tell them where things seem off and they can do the investigation and correction."

"For now, Master Ore isn't using me very heavily as his secretary, so spending the extra time right now to get them set up and going would be good timing. If it becomes too great a burden later, I can call up an assistant to help," Grandfather agreed.

"Thank you, Grandfather," Ilena said. Marcus and Henry echoed her and Lord Hayward relaxed.

"Who's next?" Ilena asked, her eyes scanning the group again.

Carl raised his hand. "I can understand needing to get me up to speed in understanding how the Ministry works; however, you haven't actually spoken to me yourself yet, to explain what my specific duties are and will be. It helps to know those so I know where I'm headed for and what I should spend time on or not waste time on. ...And just how much I really do need to learn. I'd like to know the boundaries of my tasks. And one other thing after that's answered."

Ilena blinked at him and answered, "You're in training right now for Agent, and potentially Captain level work later, so you can communicate with my people and so you learn how I like to be communicated with. Then you'll train Liam in how you work and communicate with Uncle Mitchel's people. The two of you will be the points of contact of this office with his network, continuing the work you've already done for him.

"At the moment you'd be reporting to Petroi and Thayne. Depending on where I settle Mitchel, it may be to him — which I know his people would prefer — and then he'll report to Ore. While I want to know what they're willing to tell Mitchel, I don't really want to replace him. That's hard to change loyalties like that, and they have important things to tell us. They're used to telling them to you. They don't even need to know Liam's mine if that's easier on you.

"I've put Liam over the census because I've not got anyone else to do it. You're helping him with that because you're his partner now. It's also a good smokescreen since why would two of the lowest of the ministry be frightening or doing some of the most important work of what we do? You already understand that part, though." Carl did. She raised an eyebrow at him, asking if she'd answered to that part enough.

"Does the request to interrupt more often and sooner apply to everyone?" Carl asked.

"Yes, when it's something important I haven't addressed yet and is related to work," Ilena specified, particularly for his case. He wasn't allowed to actually scold yet, and he'd phrased it in a way to say he understood that much.

"Liam's explained to me that you reward with intimate physical rewards. I'd like to request the usual and customary bonuses or increases of pay." He got smiles around the room for that one.

Ilena smiled also, "There are several reasons why. I'm sure he's explained that early on, as a nightwalker with no pay myself, there wasn't anything to pay with except that. However, that's not all I pay with. The typical pay is a gifting of a dream: minor, middling, or major depending on the level of effort, difficulty, or life–threat involved. I'd like to know yours, so be thinking of them."

Her smile dropped to almost severe soberness. "I never pay with bonus coin, nor does any Touka, for all it happens within the castle departments. To pay in coin is to teach a people to offer and accept bribes. They're no different from each other. I will, however, grant pay increases as level of effort increases, etc., now that I can. That's working for an honest wage and offering one in return." That caught the interest of more than one person in the room, since they were getting their first wages ever to begin with now that she had the budget of a ministry of the Region. "That won't happen, however, until after the audit. Even I don't know how much we really cost and how much we'll be granted in the end when Master Rei changes it for everyone."

She could see that Carl wasn't quite satisfied and wanted to argue it. "Pay increases are negotiable if you feel you aren't getting enough. Have the patience to see if dream gifting works sufficiently for you. If not, we can discuss it in private: the merits and demerits of bonuses. I also love a great debate." Carl gave a nod of sufficient satisfaction to that.

Mitchel raised his hand next. "I'm a little confused as to why you have Marcus and Henry training me first."

Ilena could see the Twins slump a little. Even they felt that was a little too much, for all they'd been obedient to it so far and hadn't complained about it on their turn. "They're my best agents, Mitchel," she answered simply. "They trained themselves to it very hard for my benefit. And Henry trained both Marcus and Thayne, so he's also my best trainer. They understand very quickly what you need to learn to understand both the House and Family to the level I need you to know it, so won't waste anyone's time doing it.

"When they're satisfied you can get around in my networks sufficiently, you'll shadow then work with Petroi and Thayne on the actual work and details, since they're my outside heads. Henry and Marcus are actually my inside heads, but the city comes under that hat, too. Since we're all learning way too much right at the moment, we'll focus on training you and Carl. When things lighten up a little, then you can train me how to use your network, and Ore the same. He's over all outside information, so does need some level of training from you, but it's a different set of skills than I'll need to learn.

"In the meantime, we're trying desperately to fit in learning from you how to be a Ministry at all. So I hope you're not feeling left out of the training circle." Mitchel raised an eyebrow then waved a hand of negation.

He seemed satisfied with that, so Ilena moved on. Ore raised his hand. "Go ahead," Ilena said since she was behind him.

"Lord Aiden has suggested that Lord Finlay become my Voice. I don't want it. We're already full to bursting and with almost too many new people all at once. I don't think we need one more person around who shouldn't be hearing the secrets we keep, either. I'd like it to be Grandfather, since he's already going to be in that position for me as secretary."

Ore was staring at Grandfather. "Now that I know your true name," it had been said during the interim investiture court, "I can with confidence say that you'll be enough. Ichijou already knows you, and with respect. I propose that you shadow Lord Finlay when I'm required to be out in my lord–ing lessons. If he can learn from you what more you need to know, or to brush up on, then he can teach you while he's teaching me."

Ilena sat back and interlocked her fingers together, watching Grandfather and Ore. Ore had learned something about Grandfather, either while at

Ichijou himself or from the network. Grandfather finally bowed his head. "Very well."

Ore wasn't done. "I've been scolded it's time for the Suiran Nightwalker King to take to the streets. That needs to be added into the already full schedule, cutting into couple's time." He sighed and she watched his fingers curl up.

She put her hand over those unhappy fingers. "I'll come with you," she said. "I'd like to enjoy running the roofs with you there and back." He interlaced his fingers in hers and she let him keep them.

"That also means I'll be becoming a more active participant in those meetings." Petroi and Thayne both gave nods. They'd be glad to have him added in since they also felt he should be already. He'd been begging off because of all of his other training and meetings — and of course because he hadn't wanted to take that role. Their load for handling the nightwalker reconfiguration of the city was higher because of it. If Ore would step in now, then their stress would reduce even that little bit.

That made her think of one of the things on her plate she really should also delegate. It would answer to some of the other things going on. It looked like Ore was done. She looked around the room but didn't get any other people speaking up. "I'd like to delegate one thing on my plate," she said. "I'd like to make sure the prison wardens are rightly treating my men. I warned Garen I would and it's becoming an itch that needs scratched. They'll not be happy it's not me who's come, but it'd be an excellent test when Marcus and Henry think Mitchel's ready for it."

She got some rather large eyes from most of them, particularly the prior nightwalkers. "You know they won't trust him," Henry complained. Petroi was quite in agreement.

"No, the point is they're to learn to," she replied back. "And he's to figure out how to get my network to trust him. Henry and Marcus can help, but they're not to go in." That got even more consternated looks. She looked directly into Mitchel's eyes. "You're to take Liam and Carl in with you. They need to learn who you three are, and what to me now, since they'll be reporting to you three.

"You need to figure out how to get them even slightly integrated with your people so that if they have a pressing need they can communicate across the lines. I want to stay as far away as possible from being the one Brulac can point to after they cross the border; although, I'll keep in touch with them. When you get back, I want to know they've understood, are still willing to do the job, and that the soldiers are taking proper care of them, not abusing them or letting them heal slowly. Based on Rei's comments, they absolutely must be healed before spring."

Unlike the upset nightwalkers, Mitchel merely stared her in the eyes, then bowed. She decided then and there he'd been pining for a really difficult assignment, wishing he had any evidence she really did know what she was doing in taking him in hand. Since she'd just given that to him, he'd be content for a while. When it looked like everyone was now settled and mostly relaxed, as far as they could get at this point, she shooed them all back to work, feeling her own shoulders relax as well. That was much better.

-o-o-o-

A message came in from the Family network: *Tarc on a horse with two pack horses arriving in Kouzanshi. Do we keep him out?*

Justinian leaped up from his chair next to Reynold's desk and was running out the door. Reynold followed him a bit belatedly, being rather surprised. He was in the inner hallway in time to see Justinian turn from the top of the stairs to head for the Upper office doorway. He hurried to follow. While he heard Justinian's words, he didn't see him leaning over the balcony railing, hands white he was holding on to it so tightly, an intense expression on his face, until Reynold made it through that door himself.

The Tarc entering Kouzanshi: It's the Regent's Advisor. Allow him to pass. He's to go directly to the Dean with some very important books for translation. Don't let those get stolen. They're irreplaceable treasures. Justinian paused to take a breath. *He's to help the Dean with the translations and then write the missing history, by order of the Regent. He needs to be back here at the castle in the fall.*

Justinian went quiet, listening intently to his message disappear into the distance, then listening just as intently for the return message to come. It took a while. Reynold looked around the room just a little timidly. They didn't come upstairs much. Everyone was giving Justinian rather bemused looks, watching him like Reynold was. Reynold belatedly realized that what Justinian had just done was not only unusual, it was out of turn for his given responsibilities.

However, it *was* Justinian who answered most of the questions that came from Falcon's Hollow about Tarc and how to handle Novare, the Tarc herdsman. It had seemed simpler to let Justinian handle those questions, with Reynold's help, since between the two of them they usually knew the answer, and it wasn't that important on the scale of things handled by this office. Two junior members of it could handle that much to help out.

Reynold observed as the other men in the room continued to receive the reports they were receiving, but also continued to observe Justinian. And maybe they were making sure Justinian was okay and wasn't going to go toppling over the edge of the railing. They weren't feeling threatened, nor were they interested in punishing him for interrupting, it seemed.

Justinian's answer came back and he relaxed in relief. He breathed a few breaths, then returned back into the room. He nodded to the usual occupants of the room in apology for interrupting on his way back through the room and barely saw Reynold, who opened the door for him so they could leave. Reynold just trailed after him as they returned to the Lower office. Even there he didn't get scolded or any comments. Ilena was watching for them with keen interest, though. She often did that when Justinian moved or spoke. When they sat back in their usual places, Ilena watched them until they were settled, then went back to her work.

Reynold really did wonder at how they all treated Justinian with patience and silent observation. It had been interesting to have the little whole–office meeting just now. It had been very similar to the meeting before the "horse–pile" while in Tarc, when Ilena had needed to settle everyone's higher level of stress there, too. No fault–finding, direct answers, no anger or frustration from Ilena where he'd seen many heads over departments find such meetings irritating interruptions at best. But then she'd said before it started that even she needed things settled by then to be doing her own work better. So she understood how helpful and needed even those brief interruptions were — and she knew how to keep them brief and focused. That helped, too.

Reynold couldn't settle, though. He finally rose to his feet silently and walked back out of the door. Justinian watched him, fidgeting. At the last second he hopped up and followed Reynold out of the room. Reynold didn't comment, just walked up the stairs and back up to the Upper office.

"Excuse me," he said softly. He'd learned fast that everyone talked very quietly in these offices. It was rather obvious it was necessary when verbal reports were being received so those weren't interrupted (at least as much as possible). It had taken a long time for him to understand it was also because people sometimes didn't want Ilena to be interrupted specifically. That was one of those things that had needed confirmation through asking. This was another one. He chose to observe how the men in the room reacted to him, and how it was different or the same as towards Justinian.

He let his question be to the room at large. "Why is it okay for Justinian to say anything he wishes to someone outside the office?" He'd learned that everyone had patience for researcher's questions, and understood that's what they were. Most people would be offended by the questions he asked. He'd never learned to ask them politely. He'd learned the court face from his adoptive father, but had been told to never talk to anyone unless he had to, so lessons in conversation had been in short supply.

Some of the men in the room blinked and smiled softly at Justinian who'd come in as Reynold's shadow. A few pursed lips and thought of how they'd answer that question. Ore answered it first, as was proper. "We're listening, too. If it's contradictory, we'd correct him and have him fix his error. We're also learning where he'd like to insert himself. We're rather used to it being with things of Tarc, since he really is the Naluk's son, in the end."

"Because he is passionate, where he inserts himself is obvious. How he inserts himself is intriguing — and not usually wrong," Petroi said. "To let him speak when in those moments is to allow him to practice his strengths."

Reynold nodded slowly. That did fit with what he'd been observing. "Thank you," he bowed and excused himself.

Justinian caught the back of his sleeve as they reached the landing to the stairs. Reynold paused and looked back at him with an eyebrow raised. Justinian was looking at the double doors that led from the landing out into the small resting garden. "Um..., can we...?"

Reynold gave a nod and turned for the doors. Justinian didn't let go. Reynold sighed to himself. Justinian did forget sometimes what he'd done. It was almost funny how the young man could be so afraid of human contact, even humanity at large, and yet once he'd latched on he couldn't let go. As if he was so starved for connection he'd relaxed back into his mental fog to finally have the contact.

It did happen a little more often for Reynold because Justinian still held on to the person he wanted to talk to, making sure he didn't get away from him before the words were said. That brought up the old irritation from Tarc, but Reynold was still working hard to stay patient with it. Justinian would either learn it eventually — that he wouldn't run away — or Reynold himself would get used to it and forget it was happening when it did. Either would be okay. It was just right now it was irritating.

Reynold let Justinian lead them to the bench in the garden. He hoped the conversation would be short. They were wearing their jackets but they'd get cold fast in the early winter weather. Reynold sat down. Justinian let go at that point, hesitated, then sat gingerly on the bench so he could look at Reynold's face. Reynold waited for Justinian to get his words together. "Um..., why..., or rather, are you trying to understand me, too?" Justinian frowned. It hadn't come out the way he wanted it to.

"Yes," Reynold didn't bother letting him think longer on it. He'd get around to answering Justinian's question faster if he just start talking. "Most people who'd interrupted like that, without permission to speak, would've been punished and likely fired if that wasn't their job or responsibility. The Immediate Family treats you differently than they treat almost anyone else. I've been trying to understand why."

"Oh." Justinian's hands clasped together in his lap as he blinked and tried to place that sort of thing. He did finally blush now that it had been pointed out to him. "I didn't — before. I only did what I knew I was supposed to do." He looked towards the center of the garden. It was mostly woody shrubbery now that winter was upon them. His face fell a little.

"I don't think you need to worry about it," Reynold said. "They said it. If they'd wanted to scold you I'd given them a second chance to, even. They still didn't."

"That's true," Justinian reluctantly agreed. It looked like he was thinking about the answers Reynold had been given because he relaxed again. Then he looked at Reynold in puzzlement. "You think it's okay with them that I want to help in those ways?"

Reynold shrugged. "They said it: that they want to see what your strengths are and see that where you have them you practice them. I presume once they're content with understanding that much they'll begin to mold you into the place they want to put you."

Justinian nodded in a musing fashion, then turned bright focused eyes onto Reynold. "I want to know that, too. What do you want to become in the Immediate Family? What do you want our partnership to be like? Can we have a common goal?"

Reynold leaned back and rubbed his head and thought about that. He'd been waiting for Justinian to bring it up again, ever since his visit up to Henry and Marcus. That had been interesting. He really did learn the most about Justinian when he listened to him talk to other people. "Have you decided for yourself yet? What your goal might be?" he asked instead of answering right away.

Justinian tilted his head. "I've been thinking about it, but I thought if I heard what yours was that might help me decide, too. I like being in the Immediate Family. I'm comfortable with these people. They're like me and want to protect me and help me learn my strengths. They're trying to be safe people for me, like you are, and they're willing to teach me things I want to learn. Even if we weren't partners, though, they've told me I won't be sent away, so I think that's not part of it: *our* goal, the reason to become partners."

Reynold gave a nod of agreement to that. "That would be a reason why you'd work hard at being obedient to becoming a partner, but not a goal or reason to stay in the partnership."

"Right," Justinian agreed.

Reynold rubbed his thumb on the back of his other hand. "I obviously can't say no to royalty. That's harder than to a master. So I'm here because of that. I'm staying almost more because of my insatiable curiosity. The Immediate Family became my research project in Tarc, when they were so different from anything I'd ever experienced, yet all of my background could tell they were so much more than most."

He took his turn to look up into the air. "I'd like to shadow Regent Rei and Princess Mizi a little more, too. They're also very different from what anyone would expect of royalty — or at least anyone with my background and expectations." He smiled a small smile at Justinian. "Just those two research topics would keep me here for more than a few years; although, I suspect I'd eventually want to turn to other topics. But, that also isn't a goal for a partnership. I do like that everyone here, including you, understand my researcher's mind and odd penchants. That makes things a little easier and more comfortable." Justinian smiled a small smile back.

They sat in silence for a bit, musing on the question. Reynold wasn't sure that he had an answer yet. Sometimes such things took years to arrive to. He knew Justinian was more impatient than that, though. He was needing to get it settled in his head so he could not have it as a worry. That made Reynold have a thought. He leaned forward and put his elbows on his knees to look at Justinian earnestly.

"Justinian, I'm not sure I'd like to be anyone else's partner, at least of what's available."

"Not even Colin? You're like he is," Justinian protested.

Reynold shook his head. "Colin isn't a researcher, and has already been Family for a long time. I'd be out of place with him. You're quiet and let me focus on my work, and are patient with my questions, which is enough. We're both beginning together, trying to understand what the Immediate Family is, who the people in it are. I don't have to feel awkward alone and wish I was anywhere but here." He looked into Justinian's eyes, trying to covey sincerity.

"I'm grateful that you love the Tarc as much as I do. I think when I've gotten my research written up and submitted that we could work together to help them with Tarc. I was told before I went there I'd be using the knowledge I'd learn of that people. And Mistress Ilena said it that one day: that she'd use me to help protect them from the minds here that don't understand them. I think that much would be sufficient for us to have as a common goal: that we'd be working to help them protect the Tarc, and help the Tarc as much as we and they can."

Justinian's face lit up and he sat up straight in excitement. "Yeah, that would be good, to do that. I can't face the lords like you could, but if we can also help with the reports from there, or something like that, I can do that."

"Right," Reynold gave a nod. "And I've noticed that you see things most others don't. When you walk the castle?"

Justinian gave a rather enthusiastic several nods. "Like Amber isn't as honest as Rio wants her to be yet. No one in the castle ever liked her, really. I'm hoping she'll learn from Rio so she can learn to be happy."

Reynold blinked. That had taken a turn he'd not expected, but it answered what he'd been suspecting. "Right, so if you took regular trips around the castle, specifically to try to hear things about Tarc — which probably won't come up often, but it would be really important if it did — then you could help with that, too."

Justinian went into his thoughtful mode again, but with the sparkle in his eyes that said he was imagining just how helpful that would be, and how he could go about doing it. Reynold sat back up in relief. It was the one thing he'd thought of, and it had helped Justinian get settled on the question. It might not be anything large, but none of them needed that, Reynold thought. Just enough to have a reason to care.

CHAPTER 150 Regional MoI Begins to Move in Nijoushi

Kata sat in her office and mused on her youngest son's words. She'd been very surprised by his anger in the kingdom security meeting. While she was somewhat sad to understand where it came from, she couldn't be sorry. Life had been so hard for all of them after she'd lost her sister and husband in one harsh blow. Retribution upon Brulac had been her whole focus, her whole goal in life since.

She rose to her feet to pace a little, restless now. To stand alone at the head of a nation was difficult at best, nearly impossible when there were no props to help her stand at all. Her staff had been those pillars for her, holding her up. Mitchel in particular as he'd seen immediately what she'd seen: it hadn't been death by accident, nor poor health. His handling immediately of the Brulac spy network, to strengthen and increase it, and get information into her ears quickly and frequently had helped her the most to continue to walk forward each day.

Having Michael be immediately obedient to every warning Mitchel sent him had saved Sasou. That had also helped Kata to relax even slightly. As long as her heir was growing stronger each day and her ability to understand Brulac until she could tear it down, she could push away the pain, sorrow, and extreme loneliness. She still mourned and ached. It was hard to finally have the time of retribution at hand.

She held still, stopping her pacing, her hand clenching at her side as she raised her head to look at a sky she almost never saw. She wanted to both exult in her fierce anger and to weep all the harder again as this time they'd arrived at brought it all up again: those same sharp and deep emotions from then that hadn't reduced even until now. Her hand clenched to hold the tears back. Tears for then. Tears for a quiet and loving future she'd turned her back on years ago.

She *did* regret not being able to be Rei's mother in the way any child needed. She hadn't had a choice and had tried her best with what she'd been given, knowing that would be a lifelong regret she couldn't afford to feel. She *did* want to hold her grandchildren. To hear their voices calling in the yard and hallway and dining room.

It was hard to have Rei tell her she didn't have her choice available as an option any more and have Sasou support him. It made her resolve slip just a little, her iron will that bound her emotions away weaken. She knew they acted out of love for her, but it no longer was kind given how long death — hers and Gastonne's — had been her plan. She fought the tears until they were bound again and she could breathe around the knot in her chest again.

When she could, she returned to her desk and sat down to return to her work. Losing herself in her work — the work of tearing down Brulac — was all there was that comforted her and let her rest. It would take a while to become comfortable with the new restraints on her, however. It would be hard to learn how to live with living again.

-o-o-o-

Rei had just arrived back in the Rose office after meeting with the auditors from Ichijou. Even his offices would be audited, so he'd also needed to know what the regulations around that were. He'd also wanted to let them know why he'd asked for it and what he expected. He'd explained that, because he'd just removed the most corrupt of the court, the new officers needed to know what their predecessors had left behind. Because he was newly come to the Seat, he needed to know what his own predecessors had left him. He didn't expect it to look pretty. He expected it to increase all their workloads once the report was completed as they corrected the graft.

Rei leaned back against the royal–blue cushioned back of his seat in the Rose office and looked at the ceiling. Somehow he was surprised. He'd thought they'd painted it blue like the walls during the renovation, but it was actually white. That was good. He could relax into the more difficult thought juggling he was going to do next. He was lost for quite some time, getting all of the facts and desired requirements from the national security meeting lined up in his head.

When he had the short list of things to get started as soon as possible, he rose to his feet. "Andrew, Mina," he called to them quietly. They finished writing their word, set down their pens, and rose to follow him out the door.

-o-o-o-

When Rei entered Garen's office after giving a single knock, he scanned the room. Two desks were empty. Word had likely been sent on ahead that he was coming, then. The two still in the room were on the "could hear secrets" list. Rei didn't waste Garen's time.

"Several things, please, Garen," he waited long enough for Garen's nod. He asked first for one of the secret details that Garen could handle for him. David immediately rose to his feet, fetched a folder from a cabinet and sat down to write. Rei approved that he was one of those aides who completed tasks immediately rather than added them to long lists and got to them whenever he could fit them in.

Rei leaned back against an unoccupied desk and crossed his feet in front of him and changed topics. "I've been thinking a little more about the gathering of garrison heads and assistants. I think it would be okay to call it war games or training, as a reaction to suddenly being presented with Tarc, and as a response to having Sasou visit this time. We'll put it out that he's warned me that Altherly has asked him to send military support. It could be still seen as a training, as well as a testing to see who we'd send out as heads of whatever support we send." The war practices were done on a fairly regular basis in lower Ryokudo, but irregularly in Suiran. That did need to change.

"I definitely still want it to be understood as a conference as well. We'll tell the commanders what's really coming up as best we can then, so they can begin to be prepared." Rei tapped a finger on the desk he was leaning on. "That should be about the time of the annual castle garrison review and exhibition, actually. I was thinking that we could combine it all?"

Garen's eyebrow rose as he sat back to think about that. "You'll be okay with having the lords from all over rubbing shoulders with their garrison commanders like that? When you may have secrets to tell the latter you don't want the former to know?"

"Well, yes," Rei answered. "While Ilena and I talked to all the commanders during the progress, and Ore knows them all pretty well, I want to see with our own eyes just how well the commanders are getting along with their lords." He wrinkled up his nose a little. "Sometimes the greased palms occur, you know. It's been long enough since the last time that was cleaned up I'd like to make sure it's still cleaned up." His look was significant. "And those who are genuinely working together..., I might not mind letting some gossip out now."

"Ah," Garen agreed with that. They both knew that the loyal garrison commanders would keep their mouths shut until they were on their way home. Then they'd quietly let the lords over their part of the Region know what to watch out for in the coming months. Those lords that were trustworthy would immediately begin to prepare their people and lands for war.

"I think if we can let some of the gossip out there, the lords will generally be more helpful for the census as well," Rei continued. "If they're honest in the number of persons they have under them, then they'll not have to pay so much in personnel than they want to. And they'll finish a little faster so that if war does come earlier than later they'll have the supplies and reassurance of the throne they won't be over–taxed."

Garen understood. "That's rather soon then," he said, "for the conference."

"True, but I think we can be ready. Do you?" he did want Garen's confirmation since his office would have the most work to prepare for it.

Garen glanced at David, but gave a nod. "It'll be my first review and exhibition to be over, but there are still enough here who've helped with that I should be okay." He shrugged, "It's also helpful that I can have the excuse that since I'm new the whole thing gets to have changes I want to make to it." He smiled a little.

Rei smiled back. "I like that idea."

"All right, we'll work to that schedule," Garen said.

Rei stood up on his feet. "Thank you," he said. Garen and David both rose and bowed him out, with David actually following him out to immediately complete Rei's initial request. Rei smiled his approval. David gave him a short bow and disappeared.

Rei sighed, then turned for the royal practice list. "I'm still needing exercise. Shall we?" He received silent approval from both of his friends. Any sword practice he got in was only good in their eyes. He was quite sure they'd work him hard, too. He might have to go back to his suite and nap later, actually, but that wouldn't be all bad either. A hard work–out followed by lunch and a restful sleep often made his brain work better.

-o-o-o-

Garen walked into the Lower office of the Ministry of Intelligence, having been granted entrance by Private Hue who stood guard on that door. He was even now still shuffling his papers, reviewing his notes, reconsidering his plans. He came to a halt behind the chair at the close end of the low table. He flipped through the final pages in his hand, then closed the sheaf of notes and looked up. His eyes scanned for the differences in the room.

The main one was that Mitchel and another man were in the room for the first time, sitting on the couch opposite Ilena and Ore. Garen's eyebrow rose. He hadn't expected that Carl Stern would be invited to the Regional security meetings. He decided to not think too hard about it and took his seat. He always brought David with him, and Rei had at least one or two of his come as well. If Mitchel had been assigned enough work to do to also need an assistant, who was he to comment?

Garen had barely made it in time. Hue opened the door one more time and Rei walked in with Andrew and Mina. There was a slight hesitation from Rei as he also noticed the newest attendees. He kept going, saving his comment until he was at his chair opposite Garen. "And their role in this is?" he asked, looking rather sharply at Ilena, still not sitting down just yet.

"Mostly to keep us updated as to the newest things out of Brulac," Ilena answered. "Carl is Mitchel's head point of contact for his spies there."

Rei gave a satisfied nod and sat down. They were five days into the last month of the year. There were things to finish before then, lots of things to be getting ready for in the coming year. The hard thing they were all trying not to face was that the winter season had begun. From here on out the cold darkness of the days would creep into their bodies and souls until they were shadow people who struggled to not pull blades or fists on each other.

Rei looked around at the people around the table. "Now that the interim investiture is over and we can get back to normalcy to some degree, I'd like to see a few things change." That made people get wary.

The brilliant blue eyes looked at Garen. "Mizi and I talked last night. We both need to be returning to regular self–defense practices. The two of us will arrive before breakfast for those practices on the royal list. We'll come eat with the soldiers for breakfast after that on a regular basis. She's going to be spending mornings in the medical building next door, and I like the soldiers to know I'm generally approachable."

Rei's attention turned to Ilena and Ore. "I need you to find and keep a balance of peace and understanding between your Houses and the soldiers. We've already discussed this from Garen's point of view, but I'm in agreement with him. I don't need the garrison to stay on guard against you and your guards when all of you need to be working in partnership." He pursed his lips at Ilena until she acknowledged his desire. "I'd like to see you two over there doing something similar to what Mizi and I'll be doing. You don't have to come to our practices, but you do need to come up with something."

Ore shifted and Rei let him answer. "I've been thinking about it since we had that discussion." Ore glanced briefly at Andrew. "The main reason the past king ordered only practices on the protected list was as a protection against assassins, or against practice weapons that got away, right?"

Rei and Andrew both let Ore know he understood. Ore turned to Petroi, standing on the wall. "Throw your knife at me or Ilena." While eyes got very wide from the guests, Petroi's hand had thrown the knife without him blinking or telegraphing he was even going to move.

Heads turned from looking unconsciously at Petroi to looking at the pair on the couch. Garen almost spurted a laugh to let his tension out. Ilena was holding the tip of the blade between two fingers and Ore was holding it just above the hilt. It wasn't really possible to tell which of them it had been thrown at, but that wasn't a detail to worry about now.

Ore took the blade gently from Ilena and tossed it back to Petroi, then turned back to Rei. "I think we could practice on the field generally and be okay. We're already adding in our couple's practice in the evenings. We could do it there and keep it then, or move it to the morning. We just don't like to wake up earlier so the second is harder, but not impossible."

Garen raised his hand to be acknowledged. "Evening is fine. We have the most cross–over of soldiers coming from duty and headed out for it then. The field generally is quieter then, so even fewer assassins and wild practice weapons," he looked balefully at the nightwalker pair for putting on a dramatic display for them. "That means they'll come sit in the stands or just stand around and watch, but that will do nicely." He was content to hear a solution that fit with his preferred answer.

"Fine," Rei agreed, content as well with getting an agreed–upon answer. Andrew frowned, but didn't complain any more than that. Mina stayed bland, as was her habit, but Garen thought he knew how to read her enough now to see faint approval from her.

"As to the other side of that," Garen decided to keep going since it was related and top of his list this morning, "Master Rei came to me yesterday and suggested we combine the conference with the annual castle garrison review and exhibition." The annual garrison review was simple enough. It was just another garrison review by the Regent. It was the exhibition that made it more than that.

The exhibitions were held bi–yearly at the nation's castles. The fall exhibition happened at Ichijou, the spring one in Nijou. All of the hopeful graduates of Kishi Knight's School were there with their instructors to be reviewed by not only the castle garrisons as officer candidates but by the lords to be called up as aides to heirs generally.

It was held in the spring in Nijou because winters were so bad in Suiran that the soldiers of the castle needed to get the claustrophobia worked out of their systems in order to have less in–fighting. The graduates usually didn't appreciate that they got to be the beating dummies for the shut–in soldiers, but often the better students held out for it for that reason. Lots of graduates wanted the prestige of being selected by the King (especially as good a fighter as Sasou), but there were those who worked just as hard at being very strong so as to be able to stand against Nijou.

A goodly number of those graduates had ended up as the commanders of the northern garrisons, actually, so having both that event and the war game conference at once would be a reunion time for them. Garen was one of those who'd held out for the spring exhibition and stayed in the north so it would come as no surprise he'd chosen to host it that way.

"I was relieved to be allowed to call it a war game. I think with the news you all spread on the progress that war was coming from Tarc it'd be a natural thing to have the gossip say that the castle has 'woken up' and decided that regular war games again would be a good thing for Suiran. I've already not felt good in my belly about that being so irregular as to be almost a forgotten thing here."

Garen wrinkled his nose to express his distaste and continued. "Master Rei has also suggested we use it as the opportunity to spread the rumors of war coming from Altherly so that the landed lords can be planning that into their planting in the spring, and maybe be the push for them to help get the census done early." He glanced at Rei who gave a nod that he'd indeed said those things.

"I've got a team as of yesterday working on the annual castle garrison review and exhibition. They're men who've planned for it before and who are quite willing to handle it while letting me learn from them what's involved in that and how it's been done in the past. I'll change it next year once I do understand."

He sat back in his chair and pursed his lips. "I'm handling the conference and war game part of it. Mostly because I've already had lots of ideas from before in worrying about the lack of them." He tapped the stack of papers in his lap with a finger. "I'd like to go over the detailed outline with all of you when we're done with the summaries here at the beginning."

Rei gave him a firm nod. It had been put on the meeting's schedule. "Where do things stand on cleaning out the prison?" Rei asked Garen, letting him continue.

Garen picked up his stack of notes and tapped them on his lap. He gave the current summary. They were ready to let people go, now that they'd received the official documents of pardon.

Ilena raised her hand and turned to Garen when Rei gave her the nod. "Mitchel will come confirm for me that everything is truly in place, as far as my people go." Her piercing look moved to Mitchel. Her Associate Minister bowed his head to her. Garen blinked, a little confused.

Mitchel turned to Garen. "I'd like to test them without soldiers present. I think to have both a prior MoI *and* castle soldiers staring them down and they'll shut down hard."

Garen mused on that, then said neutrally, "I'll let the guards know."

-o-o-o-

Ore, Ilena, Petroi, Thayne, Henry, and Marcus arrived in the Upper office of the Ministry of Intelligence shortly after the completion of the day's regional security meeting. Colin, Jefferson, and Grandfather were already there, working on their day's work. Ore rubbed the top of his head and sighed. Sometimes it was odd to not have the Tarc markers jangle around his ears when he did that. He was sure it would happen again, but it was okay to not have to wear them in Suiran where it would only be weird.

He'd been avoiding looking at the several large sheets of paper nailed to the wall. It was in total an enlarged map of Nijoushi. He'd heard threats that it would be joined by a large map of all of Suiran, and maybe one of Kouzanshi too. He'd rather the maps stayed the smaller (although still big) maps that fit into the map cabinets. He understood why this one, though.

Not only were all the streets drawn on this map, but every alley, the outline of every building, and the city walls and gates. Often what a building was used for was written inside its rectangle. There'd been discussion when it first went up as to if they were going to draw on it, but Ilena had nixed that and gotten out her (mostly–untouched now) needleworking basket. Pins with colored embroidery threads wound around them decorated the map.

The most definitive areas were those claimed by Ilena and the House of the Queen of Night. Those boundaries were firm for now. They'd used her green to outline those areas: Crafter's Row with the section of inns and restaurants closest to the castle on the northeast side, and one that included some of the more noisome businesses in town to the southwest, usually referred to as "Stinktown". Really her boundary included only a portion that. The rest was the most run–down housing that was near it.

The rest of the areas were bounded by red, yellow, blue, orange, and brown embroidery threads that were moved daily, if not more frequently. The orange and brown areas had been changing and shrinking the most. They were the most contested areas and the areas run by the smallest Houses which were almost completely gone now. The larger Nijoushi Houses with their three week head start had taken over those same smaller Houses early to increase their own territory before Ilena got too strong. Barter of small Houses had become a fad for a while. A few Heads of Houses had retired fairly wealthy, for nightwalkers.

The Lieutenants and Petroi had been busy negotiating with the remaining lesser Houses as to when they'd submit to the House of the Queen of Night. Thayne was doing a lion's share of the mental work on that since he'd already done this process of subsuming all the other Houses in Kouzanshi. Those smaller Houses that wanted to be under Ore instead had been persistently sending messengers to Ilena's Lieutenants. The timing was getting a bit late in those nightwalkers' minds.

"So we're down to the solos and freelancers in the brown zones now?" Ilena asked Petroi.

"Yes," Petroi answered. He pointed to the orange zones. "It would be good to get those areas settled now, so that both sets are firm and we can focus on the others."

They all turned to look at Ore. He sighed a bit to himself. They were filled with nightwalkers who wanted *him* as their head. Those who declared loyalty to the Suiran Nightwalker King. His hand clenched just a little as he straightened up and took on that mantle he didn't want. "We'll go tonight, but only to the safe houses we've already set up. I want to get my rules out and let them spread them around. Let's let them sort themselves one more time before we make it any more official than that."

"Okay," Ilena agreed. She made sure he was okay enough with that much, then pointed to the large red zone that took up most of the central eastern part of Nijoushi. "I want to visit with Flynn, too, at some point. He seems to be keeping his section fairly stable." The others agreed. She pointed to the multiple medium–sized yellow zones in the north. "It'll be interesting what comes of this. I think we won't have much to do there. Raine's already handling it for us." She gave a small smile. He'd sent her a message asking if she'd be okay if he and the other businessmen picked the Head who came out on top there. She couldn't refuse her favorite caravan trader.

The smile faded as they focused on the blue thread snaking around the west and south sides of the city. Thayne shook his head. "That's still a roiling pot. We may have to step in and make it happen the way we want."
224

Both Marcus and Henry agreed. The alliances there were very tenuous and most of the Houses unworthy of becoming a top head House of the city.

"The information Henry and Marcus brought us from Mitchel helps, though," Ilena said. "Let's discuss it one more time so we know what final pieces of information we need to make that part settle." That took them a while, but it was good to have concrete things to do to keep moving forward on getting the city settled.

-o-o-o-

Flynn's next meeting was three and a half weeks after the request to take in the ladies of the Rose Flame. The first lady to walk into his safe house was dressed in the nicely crafted dress and shoes of the upper servants of the lords and ladies of the castle and city. She so didn't fit in the environment of the house full of nightwalkers that every eye watched her walk up to the dais. She was quite calm for someone of the day streets, though, so Flynn guessed fairly quickly at who she was.

Her hair was up on her head to be out of the way. It was decorated with a beautifully crafted comb and hairpiece of enameled flowers and delicate gold chains. It wasn't quite as opulent as the one the Head of the House of the Rose Flame had worn, but it would have been gifted by her. When she gave just the barest dip of a curtsy, Flynn tipped his head in a bare bit of a bow to her.

"I am Miss Peony. I've come as requested," she declared herself. "I also come ahead of the others so that I may let you and yours know who they are. There are some who won't enter unless we receive the promise beforehand that they won't be molested while they're in your house and territory."

Flynn looked out over his nightwalkers. "Spread the word. The ladies who come to negotiate are not to be touched while they walk the streets of our House, nor while in this building." Those in the room bowed and five left it to spread the word on the street. Those waiting to enter would hear the word and be willing to come now.

In the end there were five present. One had come covered in a long cloak, the hood pulled far over her head. She stood in a slightly hunched pose, balanced on the balls of her feet as if to run at the slightest loud noise. Once she'd introduced herself, Flynn understood. Just loud enough to be heard by his nightwalkers in the room, he ordered, "No one is to say outside these walls who has come today." That one relaxed just a little. She'd come from a House that would beat its own ladies.

"Thank you for being willing to come," he said directly to her. He looked at the rest after to let them know it was gratitude for all of them. "I propose that you all move your Houses into my district, but remain separate Houses from each other." He looked at the ma'am he'd called for. "You'd sit as a

Lieutenant at my side to teach me what's proper to be done to run them as businesses, and will pass my orders on to the others."

The ladies considered that for a while. It took a bit of negotiating since some of them would lose clientele to move their location. His House's territory was central enough he was finally able to get them to agree to move at least to the outside edge closest to where they were currently located. People would always travel far enough to get what they wanted, when it was what these ladies offered. It helped that he promised to try to negotiate for at least buildings outside his territory once things settled down better. It had worked so far for the House of the Rose Flame, he just didn't have the same kind of alliances in the other territories.

For now, in two cases they'd have to temporarily suspend operations altogether and move the ladies into buildings he had available. In one, they refused to move until the nightwalkers of the Gold Lion freed the ladies from their terrible House Head, then they'd move quickly and also have suspended operations until he had not only a building available, but also a trained ma'am that would obey him and be kinder to the ladies.

When the ladies had left, Flynn and his House planned that House battle. It'd be better to get it done sooner than later; although, too early and the ladies would starve. Such things were hard to time when the whole city was still unsure of when the Queen of Night would make her moves. That didn't help his stomach, but forward movement finally was good.

-o-o-o-

The nightwalkers who'd once been under the House of the Rose Flame and were now considered under Ore, if still in the same building as before, had grown in number to nearly twice as many as before. Some good portion of that increase was in people from the House of the Queen of Night, happy to have a place to spread out to. Some smaller number were from other Houses, having left their prior ones to change allegiances. The slightly more crowded atmosphere was offset by the fact that everyone that stayed in the house was helping buy it.

There'd been some level of suspicion to have those of the House of the Queen of Night move in with the nightwalkers who wanted to be in the House of the Nightwalker King. That had been finally put to rest in the main. Some had said that the House of the Queen was the House of the King just as much, and since they were married even more so. Some had only shrugged, not really caring much. It had been decided that perhaps those who were still strictly loyal to the Queen of Night had stayed in her territory. These perhaps were already the King's to begin with and had moved over to be more comfortable.

The head of this house, Aron, was out currently. It was the time of evening when day–working nightwalkers were coming back into the house and those who worked the night beat were waking up and getting ready to go out. That busy time was when business usually got done if any was going to — thus why Aron was out doing that business. A few new people came into the room over that time and settled down in random places. Those were people to talk to, to determine if they were newcomers, spies, or testing the House to see if they might change allegiance. That was also a common occurrence right now as the whole city was unsettled and changing. A few more of those who might've left to their jobs stuck around to talk and test.

Aron walked into that setting, his eyes automatically scanning the room to place everyone. He knew the faces of all of those he'd specifically brought with him. They were the ones he'd captained in Tarc. They'd turned into a good team while there, protecting the Nightwalker King together. He'd asked those who would to come with him to help him keep the peace, plus gain more lucrative work outside the normal boundaries of the Queen of Night's territory. Most had come.

The faces of those who'd moved from the House of the Rose Flame to the House of the Nightwalker King were also now known to Aron. Most of those were still in the room, which actually wasn't quite normal. It was the persons who were new to the room that told him why, though. He counted eight that must've come in separately to be seated so casually with the regulars. From his perspective, standing where most were sitting, and coming in late, he could only sigh. *All* of them were in brown jackets and pants. It made it rather obvious when they'd come in their uniforms, just because they liked them.

Aron scanned the room one more time, then headed purposely to one who had on a cap and wide scarf obscuring most of his face. His little grouping was quite relaxed and having fun. Aron grabbed the back of that one's jacket and lifted him to his feet. "Excuse me. This one and I need to have a little chat in the back," he said firmly. He was a little surprised to get a humble response, but then the King knew how to role play quite well.

Aron "escorted" his "prisoner" into the back room where secret meetings were held out of earshot of those out in the main room. Closing the door firmly behind him, he put his hands on his hips and scowled. "Have you all learned sufficiently what you wanted to learn? And are you going to stick around and admit to them you're here, or just slip out and move along?"

Ore blinked at him and the corners of his eyes crinkled up in a smile. "You'll not let me just slip out, I'd think?" he answered.

"No, I'd not," Aron growled at him. "It's far past time you came out to let them know you care."

Ore waved a hand. "I know. That's why I'm here," he reassured Aron. "And yes, you know we'd want to test them back before just showing up. It looks like this house is pretty firmly for the King?"

Aron gave a sharp nod. "It'd be best if the Queen sat quietly and not let on she's here," he agreed, pursed lipped.

Ore sighed. "Well, that's fine. It's my test by her anyway."

Aron was still scowling. "That's not going to fly here, if she's still obviously pulling the strings."

Ore raised an eyebrow at him. "She wants to see what I'll do just as much as anyone else. We all know none of them would be here if they thought I'd caved to her that much. I've only married her, you know."

Aron paused and was made to remember their time in Tarc again. He raised a hand in acceptance. "Fine. Are you ready now?"

Ore shook his head and passed on orders first.

-o-o-o-

The door in the back of the room opening again had people's attention. Those who were ready to go to work wanted to know what the negotiations of the early evening had brought. Two others rose to their feet from separate parts of the room. They walked up to stand in front of the dais of the head by the time Aron and the person he'd taken with him arrived at the back of it. They stepped up onto it and walked towards the front.

It was then that the nightwalkers in the room connected the two other newcomers to the one with Aron. Those who'd run with them in Tarc sighed at all three of them. The house head let the other one go first. "Hey." A hand was raised in relaxed greeting, then used to remove the hat and pull down the scarf from the face. The whole room went still in sudden anticipation. The smile was hard to not smile back at. "I hear y'all think I'm a reason to band together."

There was general noisy agreement in the room. They were quite happy to have Ore finally show up. Ore waved a hand at them and they quieted. "Well, I guess that's all well and good, but you also already all know that I've never been a Head before, and ran as a freelancer. Since that's what I am, I'll expect all of you to just keep doing your best like you already do.

"I do have a few rules, since Houses should," he glared at them just a little in a scold. "Don't make me a House Head then besmirch my name. I believe in being honorable. If you want to follow me, you also have to be at least that much, or willing to let the rest of the world believe you are.

"I *am* married to the Queen of Night, regardless of if you will or won't follow her. Don't make me have to fight her, and don't fight with her House. We both have the same opinions on all the same things. You know what her House allows and doesn't. This House will be the same. We'll ally with them most likely on a regular basis. You won't have to participate if you don't want to. If we have a need to act, we might ask them to ally with us. You'll respect those alliances when they happen. You're free to take on your own jobs outside of those."

He was being rather firm with them, but Ore hadn't said anything that was out of line with expectations yet. Many had relaxed to hear he'd let them take jobs outside the House. The House of the Queen of Night already worked like that, but many others didn't, making any who swore allegiance to them only work on their own House jobs and projects.

Ore waved his hand at Aron. "I picked him. I do expect you to keep answering to him. Order makes the world move smoothly. You all have enough to worry about just getting enough to live. Let him do his job, do yours, and most likely things will work out just fine. If you get bored, go get a job outside Nijoushi. A change of scenery always helps that. No need to fight the House. Walking out is fine. Just let us know so we don't think you've decided to be traitor."

Ore paused to decide if that was all of the rules he cared to announce that night. So far everyone liked what they'd heard. "I'll be out and about, here and there, since I do have other duties to see to," he shrugged. "Aron and I communicate regularly, so if there's anything that needs my attention here, he'll let me know. If you need more hand–holding than that, then I suggest you reconsider what House you settle in. As I said, I expect the members of my House to be mostly self–sufficient, since most nightwalkers are.

"Ah," he looked around the room a little more closely, then added, "I'd like it if we became a House that worked hard to help those who are young. I know they're the competition, but they're also all where we once were. All of us were desperate for anyone to lend a helping hand in any way so we didn't have to die alone on the street." He rubbed his head in thought, making his black hair unkempt. It wasn't as short as he'd kept it before, so it didn't stand up on end.

"Let me work out the numbers, since we still need to pay for all the safe houses, but," he dropped his hand and raised an eyebrow at the room slightly, "how about if we offer a small discount on the tax for each adult of the House that takes on one apprentice, two at most, from the young who need the helping hand to get on their feet?" Since the young would also have to pay the tax, it wasn't all that bad a deal for either side, even if it did mean a few more mouths to have to feed on the territory. That would have to be worked out and one raised his hand to ask.

Ore understood. "Actually, we're on our way to go finish out that negotiation." He grinned. "We wanted to stop in and see you when most of you were here, first." The nightwalkers appreciated the love. "We'll let you know." He shrugged, "Of course there's going to be a lot of changes this winter overall, so we'll revisit it again, most likely. It's the headaches of starting up something new ...which isn't new for me at all lately," he gave a grimace.

They understood. He'd been given a lot of new high hats to wear. It was one of those things that made some who might not have known him from before flock to him and some run. A noble of his stature would protect them, but those who hated nobility of any kind would stay as far away as possible ...even if he was a nice guy.

-o-o-o-

The first Flynn knew anything was different about this night was when a young man walked up to the front corner of the dais to whisper in his assistant's ear. That particular assistant was rather jaded by now and little perturbed him, so the sudden tension in him and the faint sheen of sweat on his brow had Flynn's curious attention.

The young man moved off as the assistant climbed on the dais to walk to Flynn to whisper in his ear. He almost didn't hear the words at first. He blinked, tried to focus a little better, and asked, "What? Say that again?"

The assistant swallowed, cleared his throat just a little, and spoke a little slower the second time. "The Queen of Night requests you visit with her in your council room — immediately."

Flynn blinked again. "*Mine?*" He said it quietly. This was definitely a thing to be whispered in this room. He got a nod. "*Now?*" Again another nod. Flynn slowly turned around to look behind him, putting a hand on the wood platform for balance in case he needed to be kicking to defend himself next.

Not directly behind him, since that's where his guards were, were two men in brown. One was the young man who'd whispered to his assistant. The other was a man closer to Flynn's own age. Behind them were the guards on the wall as they should be, but there were two new ones on the door into the back secure part of the house. They were also in the same style brown jacket and pants.

Flynn rose to his feet, only slightly hanging on to his scowl, his look punishing his guards. As he reached the first two in brown, the older one said in a naturally quiet voice, "No need to punish anyone. You're the one who said you wanted to negotiate. For them to kill would've been disobedience."

Flynn paused and blinked at the man, the scowl going more to a curious expression. Somehow he felt like he should recognize the voice if not the man. His face was one to barely notice and pass on ...which could be dangerous in this world, actually. "And if they won't protect me who can I trust to do it?"

"We aren't here to protect her," the man smiled as he turned to fall in behind Flynn. "We're here to protect you and your House." It was said so simply and honestly that Flynn's eyes flew open in surprise. The attitude of the others from her House was that it was simple truth to them as well. He was still in a bit of shock as her man on the door opened it for him and let him through, closing the door behind him and the two who were still with him.

"And how do you do that?" he asked crossly as he headed down the hall for the small room he used for secret meetings.

"By being present to remind her that she'll be sad if she kills anyone without a good reason to," the young man answered just a little sadly himself. He paused briefly, then added, "But Master Ore will kill to protect *her* so she doesn't have to worry about that any more."

Flynn sighed to himself. So. He'd have to watch the Consort more than the Queen of Night, according to these. He decided to not relax when it came to the Queen of Night. Just because these said it didn't mean it was true, nor safe.

His conference room was guarded by the Queen of Night's Messenger and his partner: somehow not surprising. He had a few seconds before entering the room to sigh that he was going to have to move safe houses after he searched it yet again to see how they might've gotten in. That was supposed to be extremely difficult to impossible.

Flynn took in the Queen of Night and her Consort, and then that his own two guards had actually followed him and been allowed to enter the room as well. So had her two who'd called him out, although they stayed to the side. It was at least a little relieving to know that the Messenger and his partner had stayed outside the door.

"I'll only come this once," Ilena said in what seemed to be a promise. "Having seen how you run your House, I'm willing to negotiate with you."

Flynn raised an eyebrow at her. "And you get to choose that? Who'll live because you like how they work?"

Ilena blinked at him, then gave a small almost cynical smile. "I certainly don't get to choose how any man or woman will live and interact with those around them. I do get to choose who *I* will ally with. If the others can survive on their own, that's up to them."

He scolded her. "You know that's not how it works in the underworld. Particularly when you're moving in to take over the whole of the city."

Ilena shook her head at him. "Even still, the nightwalkers themselves have moved before even I would've. Aren't we all now moving according to *their* desires?" Flynn gave her an even more scolding look. She shrugged slightly. "We weren't the ones to make them decide to follow the Suiran Nightwalker King. He set that up a long time ago without even being aware he had. They were only waiting for anyone to make it official. *My* purpose was only to have him become King of the House. He didn't take that at the beginning, and I suppose it should've been left alone at Consort, but our House wouldn't let it. Even in that thing the nightwalkers have been running with it on their own."

Flynn had to process that in several different ways. One: it was interesting the background of where that had come from. Two: it didn't address the actual issue. It was a side issue meant to distract. He narrowed his eyes at her. "The two are unrelated. You *did* send the message directly to the Heads you were going to make your place this winter, with a threat included even: to negotiate or die."

"Well..., yes, that's true that it would've been interpreted that way." She waved a hand at the cushions on the floor. "Sit and I'll explain what needs to happen and why."

When the discussion was over (discussion because Flynn interrupted with questions, salient points to make sure she hadn't left them out, and dry comments to rein her back in when she got intense), Flynn sat in silence and mused, fitting it into the overall picture he'd seen while pondering and waiting on her before now. When he looked back at her again, feeling rather solemn, she asked, "Why did you decide to negotiate with all the prostitute Houses? It's not your usual."

Flynn shook his head. "You already said it. Consolidation for protection was obvious. It was equally obvious the Rose Flame would fall from within and remove the buffer between the two of us. That left me with little choice, actually. We all know you wouldn't take them in. The lady Lieutenant of the Rose Flame can tutor me as my Lieutenant and it'll be sufficient. The rest of what I do is keep wild people just tame enough, like all Heads do. The only question that can't be answered without you is how to divide that strip so our Houses don't fight over it."

Ilena was in agreement that needed resolution. She leaned forward on a raised knee and made her offer. "Because the ladies only need the residence but the nightwalkers need the streets, and that's who's come to our House, let me have the territory. They already have a working relationship. Those who have the experience are willing to continue. Let it be an alliance of peace in the streets of that zone for now. When we're closer to the final round of consolidation, then let's discuss with all the Heads that remain the full drawing of lines. We'll have to then anyway, to keep the full peace."

Flynn pondered on that, then frowned. "Except those nightwalkers follow the Nightwalker King, not the Queen of Night. Will they obey such an agreement made today?"

Ilena glanced up at Ore. "Is he not my husband? Tonight he set the requirement of peace between the Houses." She looked back at Flynn. "Besides, we know how to not tread in ways we shouldn't. He and we will teach them the same, eventually."

That satisfied Flynn for the moment. Such things took time and alliances weren't solid things in the nightwalker world. Ilena had a question of her own: "Will you negotiate with the street ladies? So far you've only approached the Houses."

Flynn pursed his lips a little and asked back, "What would you do with them? See if the chaos will clean them off the street for you? I'll not take them in here or they will die. The Houses have already rejected them, or them the Houses."

Ilena shook her head. "If you'll not take them, I will." Flynn sat upright and blinked at her in surprise. Ilena gave a soft smile, not a usual expression on the face of a nightwalker Head. Softly she answered him, "*That* is who I take into my House: those who need the most."

"You'll give charity to the poorest and expect to have the House live?" he asked, not understanding.

Ilena's smile didn't change. "They're only the poorest in hope, Flynn. Even those who won't move beyond the deepest slums still crave hope. I can give them that much: a place to rest where perhaps others might steal from you, but they won't kill you and the guards won't take more than you can afford to give. Those in that place also know what you know. That death might come tonight or tomorrow, but for some reason the body and the soul won't die, so there's only waiting for it, moving through time until then."

She took a breath and looked solemnly at his face. "Many are the ones who can move beyond that when they're offered a word of hope, a hand to hold as they try to move one step forward, encouragement to take even the next step beyond that. In my House is that. In my House are those who've moved from there to a life they can live without wishing for death that night or the next morning.

"I may have to purchase safe houses in other Head's districts, or work out an agreement with all of them that will allow those to enter their zones...," Ilena looked off into the distance a bit, then sighed. "I'd rather train all of you how to help your own street nightwalkers so I didn't have to do all the hard work myself, but many don't want to, and often don't have what it takes to actually do it well." She looked back at Flynn with her small sad smile. "It's my gift. I will give it while I breathe."

He sighed at her, slumping down on his hand, his elbow on his knee. Flynn considered her for a while, and that particular issue. He hadn't considered it very hard before, but it had crossed his mind. Often the street nightwalkers — who were different from the freelancers because of that lack of hope and caring — were more trouble than they were worth. Many of them couldn't understand even basic societal necessities. They were the most uncaring of the assassins, the most debased drunks, the most despondent prostitutes. Those who only earned coin to become oblivious to the world around them.

"They don't all come into your safe houses," he accused softly.

"No," she agreed softly. "I still watch over them."

Flynn considered it a little more. "Teach me what you do for those who'd come into the safe house. If you can teach me that, you can teach the others that. One step will have then been ours to do, and do rightfully in our own territories."

Ilena taught Flynn most seriously, making sure he understood. He sat for the lesson just as seriously. He wasn't surprised that she sent out others of her House that understood to bring them in. She surely didn't have any more time than any other human on the planet. Delegation was essential for Heads — and royalty — and she was now both. It did surprise him a little that she purchased separate safe houses for the street nightwalkers. It made sense when she explained that it was to allow for them to feel comfortable about moving in. They were then told there were no boundaries to moving up if they wanted to, into the other safe houses of the House. That allowed them to grow comfortable with being members of the House and the idea that they might could make life better for themselves if they kept working at it.

Flynn understood with much greater clarity once she and her House were gone from him. Ilena was beloved by the nightwalkers because she was both "them" and royalty. For the first time those who ruled this nation had not only watched and cleaned up the "low lifes", but one had come down to dwell with them and she'd brought compassion with her. He was quite sure that was a blessing that would be unique in this generation. Such things never happened in the cycles of nations.

Flynn sighed and let that weight go. It wasn't his to carry, but it was now his to help her carry it by carrying his portion of it. The others who'd end up at her negotiation table might not understand it, but he did. And he cared enough to take it as a serious and solemn responsibility. For a first negotiation, she'd somehow gotten lucky in that as well.

He settled down into his place on the dais again, his guards rather relived actually. He gave a calm nod to his assistant so he could stop sweating. Then he had to fish for the part that the House cared about so he could give the announcement. "The streets of the Rose Flame belong to the Queen of Night and the nightwalkers of the Suiran Nightwalker King. The ladies and their house are mine. Truce will be held to in that zone. The nightwalkers have agreed to continue to help bring in business to our purses as the return payment."

There was some stirring in the room as they'd been hoping to have more space themselves. Flynn shook his head at them. "As the chaos the Queen of Night brings with her settles, there'll be a final negotiation to make the boundaries firm." That settled them sufficiently for now. They all knew the chaos was still ongoing. No future was certain. They could wait.

CHAPTER 151 Young Ladies of the Court

"A Miss Opal Preston has arrived, as ordered by the Regent." The whole of both offices of the Ministry of Intelligence froze at the announcement from Hue, who stood in the opened doorway of the Lower office. When Ilena's eyes were glued to him, he bowed and moved out of the way, letting the daughter of Marquis Preston into the office.

The young lady entered a bit uncertainly, looking very much like she really didn't wish to be there at all. It was a mutual feeling for those who knew she'd been the first of the princess candidates to fail Rei's testing. She'd caved to her father's pressure and used unacceptable and dramatic means to win Rei into accepting her. She knew she was here as a punishment and wasn't liking it at all. But then, she expected to be sent to Tarc. She was there to learn a new language that only the Ministry of Intelligence could teach her.

Petroi closed his eyes as his mistress laid down the sentencing, and relieved the suspense the poor young lady and her father had been under since they'd all arrived back from Tarc. "You'll be working with Petroi to learn Selician. Please go to the Upper office, just above this one. He'll have to work you into his schedule." It was he who was going to have to bear this burden because the only other person in the castle that knew Selician was Ilena herself. She already didn't have any more time in her day.

The other men in the Upper office were giving him sympathetic looks (or irritated ones since it would take up more of his time he didn't have to give away). He appreciated the former and completely agreed with the latter. It might be the lady's punishment, but it wasn't right to take out his irritation on her. She had no choice in the matter, and if Rei had decided it was time to enforce it, then it was time. He sighed and rose to his feet to answer the timid knock at the door. "Miss Preston, please, let's meet in the inner hallway. There are no other offices in the building in which to meet and not interrupt the work of others."

He ignored her surprise at being so directly addressed, before any introductions to the office itself. He walked before her until they were back down in the open hallway of the wing on the main floor. He pulled out a chair for her to sit on from the several set against the wall, then sat on one near her. She was certainly beautiful enough, with light brown hair curled — likely by her maid — and light brown eyes to match. She'd kept her figure nicely, even with the depression after the failed interview with the First Prince. Perhaps she'd eaten even less with the worry since the punishment had been named. He suspected she was also air–headed, but that would come out in the testing and training.

"Miss Preston, it would be best if you could come in the mornings," he started with.

"Ah, well, mornings." Opal paused as if disappointed but trying to not show it much. "I suppose I might be able to fit it in ...somewhere." She scanned the hall as if trying to find some place in it rather than in her schedule. "You know, there's dance lessons and comportment, history, and of course the hour before lunch is reserved for meeting with my maid." He let her peter out after a few more lame excuses for why she couldn't open up even forty–five minutes in her mornings. He suspected it would've been the same answers for an afternoon request.

"Well, I think you could come right after breakfast for less than an hour, then," he stated it as if it was a final decision and order. She protested weakly and nonverbally, but then slumped in resignation.

"I would like to test you just a little to see how much work you will have to do. I am sure the shorter your lessons each day can be, the more you would like to have the time for your other activities?" he raised an eyebrow at her, trying to stem the next thing she would drag her feet on. She'd not learn the language at all, pretending to not understand, just to put off the next portion of the punishment as long as possible. (That was going to be: being sent to a far away country where the First Prince wouldn't have to see her face nor remember her terrible behavior in front of him. Petroi thought it a proper and fitting punishment, actually.)

He carefully spoke through the Selician alphabet, which included the basic sounds of their language. Then he had her repeat it after him. That was pulling the teeth of a feral cat. Miss Preston did indeed feign indolence, incompetence, and then a headache when Petroi continued to press her to say the sounds at least partially right.

"All right," he finally said, drawing on the patience he'd learned following after an even more willful princess that this one would never rise up to touch. "Let's have you learn one short sentence." *Do I have to?* was in her eyes, but he'd said it as if they were almost done, so she sighed and pretended to listen intently. He got her to say the few words sufficiently well, then rose to his feet.

Miss Preston jumped up to her feet and nearly fled right then, only stopping just in time to look at him with wide eyes. "Ah, when should I come?"

"Don't," he said as kindly as he could. "I will be sending a language instructor to your rooms. You will work with them until they are satisfied you can survive in Selicia just enough to ask for food and a room. I am not sure if that was Regent Rei's intent, or if he meant to send you to the home of a lord of Selicia. You aren't sufficiently competent enough for the latter, so we will make sure you can at least do the former."

The blood ran away from the young lady's face. He excused her and she lifted her skirts and fled the hall. Perhaps she'd now properly learn her lessons, but Petroi wasn't about to be the teacher. He knew people in town that could do it, had the time, and were very firm–handed about it.

When he arrived back in the Upper office, Thayne asked him, curious, "What were you teaching her? Mistress Ilena had to leave the office and go out into the courtyard to laugh so hard she cried."

Petroi raised an eyebrow at Thayne. "I am incompetent." The entire Upper office dissolved into laughs. Petroi turned to Ore. "Do you think she will choose to work harder now, Master Ore? Now that she knows we don't know if she is to be sent to become a brothel woman or a lady wife?"

Ore choked on his laugh and couldn't answer. He finally waved a hand in front of his face and caught his breath. "I'd think anyone would, Petroi. That was rather scary, actually."

"Good then," Petroi said most evilly and with great coolness to his tone. The room's occupants shivered and got back to work. He sent out a request on the Family line to Nijoushi for his Selician language instructor to meet him in the morning at the gate to the castle. She'd be plenty severe with Miss Preston, making sure she learned properly how to speak as one who was coming from a castle should speak. He was quite glad to wash his hands of that chore.

-o-o-o-

Amber's fingers were interlacing again but she didn't see them as she stared down at them. She really couldn't believe she'd just witnessed such a putting down by the most gentle man in the whole Immediate Family. Nor that everyone had laughed about it so hard. Wasn't being sent to another nation, never to see your family again, a hard thing? Surely Opal was afraid to be sent away like that. While the threat might have conveyed what Petroi had wanted her to understand, didn't it only make it all worse, all the more fearful? Even Amber wanted to cry inside for Opal, a little.

The big ball of confusion, hurt, and sympathetic understanding she could have for Opal finally got so big Amber rose to her feet, one hand clenching at her side. Even if she wasn't the innocent Justinian, or even Reynold to be a researcher, so far everyone had been willing to answer the questions of those in training. They might not like her, but they might be willing to answer her's, too. This one very much needed answering to.

When Rio looked up at her in concern, Amber only glanced at her, pursed lips holding back her emotions. She wasn't going to hold back this time out of fear. She wasn't too surprised when Rio followed her. She ignored her as best she could. The walk out the door and up the stairs to the Upper office door was almost long enough for her to lose her nerve, but the ball of emotions that tightened her chest was big enough to help her push open the door and look into the room.

She'd of course gotten everyone's attention. She scanned the room until her eyes locked onto Petroi's amber eyes. "Why? Why were you so mean? Why was that okay? Isn't she only afraid?" Eyes went wide on the men in the room, but she studiously ignored them to the best of her ability. It helped that Ore relaxed slightly. He already knew she was trying to learn and was struggling.

Petroi shifted to sit a little more comfortably as he faced Amber and her question. "You are probably right. She is probably afraid. Master Rei has held the suspense long enough both she and her father have been afraid for a while. Selicia is kinder than Tarc, but it is still different and far away.

"I was what you call 'mean' because I was irritated by her purposeful slothfulness. If she had humbly come and diligently worked to be obedient to her lawful liege, we would have been done much more quickly and I likely would have accepted her as my own student. Instead from the beginning she fought her order, fought being here, and fought me. I have no time for that, nor any patience for those who won't obey their liege. It is better for her to be taught by someone else who can help her without becoming angry."

Amber's brow furrowed as she tried to understand. "Can she tell Master Rei she won't go, that it's too far from her family?"

"She may protest, but no, she can't disobey," Petroi answered softly. "She already has passed the tests of having the qualifications of being a princess save for her unfortunate weakness of being too obedient to her father and being of a weak will." He only gave her one second for her lips to pucker before he explained that. "She can't choose on her own to stand for what she knows is the right thing to do. She couldn't choose to actually *be* a princess. She could only pretend in the end, for all she knows the right things to say and knows what motions to perform."

Amber's eyes slowly widened. He seemed to be saying what Rio had been trying to explain to Amber. They didn't like it when people could only pretend. Her brow furrowed again and she suddenly turned to Rio, standing behind her in the hallway. "But to pretend what she wanted to be to get it isn't okay?" Amber waved her hand irritably. That wasn't what she meant. "Then what should she have been being if that was her goal?"

Rio raised an eyebrow slightly. "Herself."

Amber glared back at Petroi. He agreed with Rio. "If she couldn't be a princess by being herself, then at least she would have received what she would be happy with. Now she has put herself into an unhappy corner by her own decisions and actions."

Amber felt that in her gut and thought about it hard. It really was what she'd done, too. Put herself into an unhappy place when she'd thought she'd be happy there. Was she miserable here because she'd pretended to be something she wasn't, or because she'd not understood what the reality of things were? "Why isn't it because she just didn't understand?" Amber really wanted it to be just that.

That question made Petroi ponder a little longer. Rio answered it first, softly and as if trying to put the words together, "She didn't understand, but it's because she didn't really understand herself either." Rio drew in a breath to try and explain further as Amber looked impatiently at her, not wanting that answer already. "She saw the world from the point of view she *wanted* to see it from, not the reality of it. Thus she couldn't understand that what she was asking for was something she wouldn't want."

"People who won't see reality for what it is, who won't take into consideration other's expectations, perspectives, or their reality, miss the things that will make them unhappy until they have to actually live what they thought they wanted to live and those realities come to face them painfully," Petroi added. "Master Rei — and all Toukas — know that most people see them not from the reality of where they stand, but from the fanciful delusions the people have in their heads of what their lives must be. They use that to keep them off balance, so that they can accomplish the things they want in ways surprising to those who won't learn the reality of who they are.

"When Miss Preston finally faced Master Rei alone, she interacted with him from her clouded perspective of who he was, from the fanciful delusion of what it must be like to walk with him. He could face her politely, but he couldn't accept her as his princess. He needs one who will face him as who he is and who will face him as they are."

Amber sighed to herself. That was exactly her position, but still.... "So why is it okay to be mean to someone like that?"

She got a raised eyebrow. "In my case," Petroi said, "it is as I said. I have no patience for such behavior when it stems from slothfulness and disobedience. If in something I have said and done she can learn a lesson to lead her away from those two, to help open her eyes to the path she *should* be walking, then I will do it."

Rio's hand fell lightly on Amber's arm. Amber looked into her eyes, but Rio was trying. "Amber, what that means is that when facing Petroi, watch that you're not displaying either of those traits. *He* can't abide them. Here you aren't either one. You work hard and do what you're supposed to do."

Amber came full stop and blinked, her mouth open. Rio was saying Petroi wouldn't be mean to Amber herself if she continued to do her work and obey Ilena in performing her tasks. She already knew Rio was mean when Amber wouldn't be honest, so that was Rio's equivalent. She closed her mouth and finally gave a little nod. "Thank you," she bowed to Petroi and the room and let them get back to work. She'd ponder on that much for the next while. Maybe she'd go find Opal, too, to ask her about how she was feeling about this, and if she was struggling with the same problem Amber was. Maybe at least they could commiserate somewhat.

It wasn't too much later that Amber was scheduled to meet with Mizi's entourage at the young ladies' luncheon. She'd been trying to process what she'd learned but had gotten the beginnings of a headache so had stopped so she wouldn't be unpleasant company at the lunch. Her eyes looked everywhere as they always did when she walked the castle campus. There were people out on errands but none that stopped her or that she knew well enough to stop herself.

It was upon arriving at the luncheon that she realized that maybe she'd come a little too blithely. Her fingers twisted in her skirt. It was a skirt now of nice construction, but in the brown of the Ministry of Intelligence. Being in a Ministry was certainly many steps up from sweeping the floor, but to compare it to the bright colors at the lunch made it very drab again. She nervously tugged on her shawl which at least was a nice color and of fine construction. She'd managed to figure out how to have it match with other accenting pieces to the Ministry uniform. It wasn't quite enough now that she was here to compare it to what the other young ladies and their servants were wearing.

Amber stayed at the outside edge of the grouping, hoping Mizi would arrive sooner than later. She'd imagined eating with this group for a long time, practically since she'd started working at the castle. Now that she was here, she realized she really had no idea how to even begin to talk to them. She'd practiced with the other castle servants what she'd thought was the right way to go about it, but now they wouldn't talk to her at all. Amber bit her lower lip, suddenly even more insecure. She decided to listen to the conversations around her while she waited. Maybe she could learn by observation.

She'd almost relaxed, finding most of the conversations comfortingly familiar to what she knew, when the movement of a larger group of people neared the garden. The red hair of the shorter woman at the front let Amber feel a little relief. However, when Mizi and her lady attendants were close enough to really see, Amber shivered and slumped a little more. Even they were dressed in colorful and beautiful dresses (except the matron who was in at least the genteel grey, far better than drab brown). She definitely wouldn't blend in at all today.

She curtsied to Mizi when she arrived close enough. "Mistress Mizi. Thank you for letting me j– observe today," she said quietly and politely. At Mizi's brief sharp look and nod, then her turning to face the luncheon, Amber slipped to the back of the grouping of four ladies, in front of the guards, her hands clenching together in front of her skirt. She had to take a long deep breath for the courage to walk with them into that luncheon.

It was hard to pay attention to everything, and even more to Mizi. Mizi was certainly polite. She answered to the ladies who'd talk to her. Most were just as coolly polite to her in return. Amber paid closer attention when Mizi managed to draw one of the young ladies into actual conversation. The young lady was quite willing to talk about herself, but when the topic turned to Mizi, the conversation petered out. Amber wasn't sure if it was because Mizi seemed reluctant to talk about herself, or if it was because the other young lady didn't really care to hear anything once the question of, "What's it like to be married to the First Prince?" didn't get a very exciting answer.

Amber hadn't found it an exciting answer either, but she couldn't help but make it a point in the favor of the lesson she'd had earlier that morning. It had been a truthful and realistic answer, she was sure. Just as sure, she knew Mizi would always give those kind. Petroi had said that Rei wouldn't have and hadn't picked a princess that would lie and always give flighty flashy answers to questions. She could see from that example why Rio would like Mizi and want Amber to learn from her.

A time or two Mizi paused and quietly asked the matron of the group a question about how to handle approaching the other young ladies a little differently. Amber listened closely to the answers to those questions. She liked how Brianna spoke calmly and with kind encouragement.

Then came a moment that Mizi had just finished talking to a young lady and another one walked up rather brashly. Amber saw Mizi's spine stiffen as she turned to face the newest young lady to approach her. The young lady gave a proper, if brief, curtsy. Then without preamble she said, "Miss Preston went to the Ministry of Intelligence this morning as ordered to by the Regent and was there told she'd be going to Selicia. Even if they'll assign her to learn the language, surely she won't be going as a banishment to fend for herself as a washerwoman?! Why would the Regent be so cruel to one even you picked as a top contender for your position?"

Many were the breaths drawn into lungs rather sharply. Eyes turned to Amber even and she cowered slightly, her drab brown clothing marking her like the words had. She tried to draw in a breath and stand up straight and not show her fear and uncertainty. Mizi blinked and pondered the accusation. "While I was aware Regent Rei was intending to send Miss Preston to Selicia, I'm sure he wouldn't send her away without something she can do with her skills and talents to help others with and to be a strength for her while she's there. Regent Rei isn't one who wastes good talent." Mizi said the last with certainty.

Amber didn't know what skills or talents Rei and Mizi had seen in Opal since they'd not come up in the brief visit and Petroi had only complained about her, but she rather suspected that Mizi wasn't wrong. She *had* watched Rei enough now at the meetings in the office. He was practical and didn't waste people, even if he hadn't liked Opal enough to choose her as his wife. He was also mean, though, when he was angry with people, so there might be a germ of truth to him not caring if Opal lived or died in Selicia.

The eyes of the ranting young woman defending her friend turned onto Amber and Amber froze under that attention, completely not prepared for it. "Miss Preston says the language is impossible to learn and the man she had to deal with in the Ministry unbending and cruel. Why would such a person be assigned to teach a delicate young lady?"

Amber swallowed and glanced at Mizi. Mizi blinked at Amber, then allowed her to answer to the accusation. Mizi hadn't been there, so wasn't really the person to answer to it. Amber took a breath. "I'm sure Miss Preston is very afraid to be sent away to a country she doesn't know anything about, but Lord Petroi was very patient with her in trying to help her understand how to say the things he was testing her with, to see how much work she'd have to do. He says that the person he'll send to teach her will be able to be even more patient with her." Amber struggled. She really wanted to not offend this friend of Opal. Amber really did want to talk to her, but wouldn't be able to if she couldn't say the right words now.

Thus it was an utter surprise to her when the young lady scowled at her for her words. "Well, *I* think the Regent should rethink his plan and send *some*one *else*!" Her eyes glittered at Mizi again. "...Instead of being willing to bow to *your* whim to get rid of a competitor now that you're in the place you wanted to be and don't want to see her face anymore." She tossed her curled hair behind her and flounced a little. "*I've* even heard that he's going to get rid of the other two as well, sending them away so *you* don't have to deal with them as possible continuing thorns in your side."

Amber was frozen. Mizi was becoming colder and colder as were the rest of her entourage, save for Brianna who was trying to become large enough to hold Mizi either in comfort or from acting in anger. Amber really couldn't believe the absolute rudeness of the fight being held in the public forum of the luncheon. With a start she realized she'd also held such open scoldings of other maids she'd wanted to put in their place. Her face turned red in embarrassment for her behavior of the past. Looked at from the outside it had been rather atrocious.

"Miss Contina," Mizi's voice was hard and cold, "while I understand you wish to defend your friend and don't want to see her leave, *I* have nothing to do with this. As I said, Regent Rei doesn't waste talent. Because he had the opportunity to interview all four of us when he was looking for a bride, he learned what talents we all had. He's seen fit in his own mind to find uses for them so they don't waste away here, unappreciated for anything other than their beauty and comportment. She may request a different assignment, but the rest of us don't decide what he will and won't do."

Amber had been hearing similar scattered gossip from the ladies before Mizi had arrived. Many had said that they thought Opal had brought it on herself, but they'd be just as happy to believe Opal's friend. Even more coldly Mizi added, with narrowed eyes even, "And if you think that the

Regent has married any one of us only to go play in the bed of any woman he wants, then you are so sadly mistaken that perhaps you should be sent with her to also learn your lessons in what it is to be a proper lord and lady. I'm sure she'd appreciate having a friend by her side as her lady–in–waiting."

Miss Contina pulled back so sharply in fear that she nearly jumped backwards. "Wh–why would you say such a thing?"

"Because you've thought so low of your liege, as to insinuate he'd do such a thing," Mizi said with quiet cold firmness.

"I never!" Miss Contina protested. "It's *you*...!"

She wasn't allowed to finish as more than one person in Mizi's group stepped forward threateningly. "It's time to leave, Miss Contina," Brianna said firmly. "You've already damaged your reputation enough." Her cold eyes bored into the young lady until she turned and fled, tears already beginning to drip from her eyes.

Amber stared after her in some amazement. She again could sympathize with another young lady. *But at the same time,* ...she turned and looked at Mizi who was holding still in her attempt to calm down. *At the same time...,* she could understand Mizi's anger. Mizi, who understood the true Prince Rei, had been deeply offended by the insinuations against her husband. She *hadn't* flinched or complained about the dirt thrown at herself, and yet her answer to protect her husband had brushed that dirt away as if it had never existed. *Why? Why was protecting someone else, rather than herself, the right answer?*

Amber stood quietly with the group as Brianna talked Mizi back to calm and taught her how to excuse herself from the luncheon and still stay the princess she was. She watched as Mizi followed the instructions exactly and did indeed leave on the higher ground. She silently stayed with the group, listening to Mizi's lesson from Brianna that discussed what had happened.

It would have been better, in the end, for Mizi to not give such a threat openly. Rei was likely to like it and send them both, thus there would be truth to the rumor Miss Contina had left behind. But, Brianna said, it wasn't likely to be a rumor that couldn't be overcome. And it would give the young ladies as a whole pause in the future to think harder about what they said and the accusations they threw at Mizi.

When it looked like the lesson was mostly done, and they were nearly at the Old Regent's building, Amber timidly inserted herself. "Um, Mistress Mizi?"

Mizi looked over at her in surprise, likely having forgotten she was with them, or surprised she'd continued to walk with them. "Yes?"

"I appreciate being allowed to learn things with you. May I ask a couple of questions to understand better?" She thought in this case asking would be better than just showing up to ask like in the Ministry.

"I guess," Mizi actually brought the group to a halt in the lawn near the building. Amber was suddenly the center of attention and she thought she didn't like this center of attention so much as the fawning one she didn't get to have anymore. This was hard: to be judged instead of adored.

Amber swallowed, remembered Rio's scolding face for courage, and asked her first question. "Why are you trying to talk to the young women when you don't like them?"

Mizi looked a little surprised, then answered, "Because I think it's important to know how to get along at least a little with everyone in the castle when it's my home and they need to live here, too."

That had been put in a funny way. Amber had to think about that: what it meant for the castle to be "Mizi's home" but the rest of them just "lived here". The answer was probably the first part, though, that getting along when they all had to live together regardless was important to Mizi. Amber guessed she could understand that.

She asked her second question. "Why did you only protect Regent Rei in every answer you gave to Miss Contina?"

Mizi considered the answer to that question, then asked, "Why did you defend Petroi?"

Amber gaped briefly, then shrugged. "We'd had that lesson before I came here. I thought he was very mean, actually. Miss Preston had only sounded afraid to me. She *doesn't* want to go and leave this place she knows. They explained to me that he's only mean to those who are lazy and disobedient, and he sees her as both. He's assigned someone else to teach her so he doesn't have to be impatient with her every time she comes for lessons. I wasn't trying to offend Miss Contina. I wanted to be able to go and talk to Miss Preston, to understand if I'd understood her rightly." She turned a confused frown to Brianna. "Why did what I say offend Miss Contina?"

"You didn't support Miss Contina because you said, in effect, that it wasn't Master Rei that was at fault. And you openly said what the real feelings of Miss Preston were, not protecting her either."

"Oh," Amber's face fell. She really hadn't said the right thing then.

"Soo..., you were protecting both Rei and Petroi, then, even if you didn't agree with them?" Mizi asked Amber.

"I – I guess so. I didn't know that's what I was doing, though," Amber said. "I was trying to be understanding and reassure them." Her brow furrowed again. "But, I don't understand why in protecting Master Rei, you weren't damaged by the things she said about you."

Mizi shrugged. "I don't care what they say about me. It isn't necessary to defend myself beyond the little I did. And when I included myself with the other candidates then it isn't me that anything can stick to. Then it becomes 'us' and that included her friend." Her green eyes glittered. "I *always* defend Rei. No one else does it, nor can they do it in the situations I find myself in. If there's a problem he needs to fix, I take it to him and let him know and he fixes it or he corrects my misunderstanding. That's one of my responsibilities."

Amber stared at Mizi, her mind not quite getting it. "I think," Brianna said quietly after watching them for a bit, "that if you continue to watch, you'll be able to understand better over time." Amber could only agree. That part would take time, but it seemed to be a powerful thing to understand if she could. Mizi was the strongest when she did that.

Amber gave a little start as she realized that this whole conversation had been like the ones in the Ministry: honest, open, and very real. She slumped then curtsied to Mizi. "Thank you for allowing me to observe, and for answering my questions. If you'll excuse me?" She waited for Mizi to dismiss her, then headed back to the Ministry at a bit of a trot. She felt late to be getting back; although, she wasn't sure she really was. She'd been thinking of going to look for Opal after the luncheon, but now she thought she shouldn't. They wouldn't want to see her after all that.

-o-o-o-

Mizi walked into the Rose office after changing out of her lunch dress at the Old Regent's building. Rei looked up to smile at her. She smiled back, walked to his chair, and leaned down to give him a kiss. "How'd it go?" he asked her, sitting back in his chair.

Mizi sighed, then leaned back against his desk to rest a bit. "I'm worn out," she admitted. "It didn't go as well as it could have for a first luncheon." She wrinkled her nose. "I was accosted towards the end of it. We managed to survive it, but it was just a bit too much for trying to ease back into being social." Rei was kindly sympathetic.

She frowned at him a little, remembering the basis of the tirade. "Miss Contina showed up to defend Miss Preston." Rei's eyebrow rose a little. "She said Miss Preston had gone to Ilena's this morning and it ...hadn't gone well. When she blamed the person assigned to teach her from there, she dragged Amber into it." Mizi hadn't really wanted to be reminded then, or anytime, Amber had been with them. "I let Amber answer to it, since she'd been there and I hadn't.

"Surprisingly, Amber answered fairly well for herself and Petroi, although Miss Contina was displeased." Mizi gave a bland face to say she didn't personally care about Miss Contina's displeasure. Rei gave a slight smile back. "Apparently Miss Preston doesn't want to go, she's 'afraid' according to Amber, and Petroi was impatient with her lack of caring and obedience. He's going to assign someone he knows to teach her so he doesn't cut into her every lesson." Mizi frowned a bit at that, too, but Rei seemed to be fine with that assignment being delegated. Mizi's problem wasn't the delegation. It was that Petroi had been unkind. It seemed out of character for him. She *could* understand being impatient with people who wouldn't do the work that was theirs to do.

"Miss Contina claimed that it was me that was behind your assignment, demanding that I not have to see her face again. I set her straight, letting her know that if you were sending Miss Preston away, you had a work for her to do that was hers to do. If Miss Preston has the courage, she may come request a different assignment."

Rei blinked at Mizi. "But I am sending her away to not have to see her face again. I don't want to deal with having the reminders of that awful week. That's me, though, not you."

Mizi blinked back at Rei in surprise. "But surely you have a thing for her to do?"

Rei relaxed his arm on his chair. "The letter I've already sent to Selicia says it's ostensibly to see if the king can find her acceptable as a wife to one of his sons. I'll be surprised to hear she can be one for a higher lord. At best, I'd expect them to place her next to a lesser lord ...or send her home for her father to try his best. I'd send him away, too, if I could."

Mizi was gaping at Rei. "Rei!" she protested and scolded in one breath. "Surely a prince should have more concern for his subjects?"

Rei raised his eyebrow at her rather high for him. "Mizi, they were both extremely disrespectful, bordering on sedition. A consequence must be levied, as we've already discussed before, or they'll continue to think they can control the person whom they're supposed to be supporting."

Mizi furrowed her brow, then said, "At least find something she can do to be of help to either them or us. To banish her from all she knows will be totally unkind otherwise, particularly when it was her father that put her up to it."

Rei gave a nod. "I know. I'll be officially sending her as an assistant ambassador along with the new official ambassador I'm calling up — assuming she can learn her language lessons. It's time to cautiously re–open relations with Selicia and she'll be part of that beginning."

"Then I think it'd be wise to let her know sooner than later that's what you want for her to do," Mizi said dryly as she shifted to stand on her feet and turn for her desk. "She's already so frightened, not knowing what's going to happen to her, that she's not likely to learn anything at all by the time it's time to go, according to the words of the girls I talked to. Maybe if she knew what strength you wanted from her, she'd give it to you in a timely fashion."

Rei swallowed just slightly. It was as harsh a scold as she ever gave him. She was satisfied when a note went from him through paige out the door of the Rose office. He might be upset, but he should still be honest and kind when he should be.

Amber blinked at the persons standing in front of her, scolding her intensely. She'd come out of the Ministry offices to run an errand for Leah. She certainly hadn't been expecting to be waylaid by a pair of young ladies of the castle; although,.... As she thought about it she slumped. Of course they couldn't accost Mizi. It was always simpler to scold and blame the person lower than you. She knew. She'd done that plenty of times, too. She wasn't liking it, and it was quite unfair since she was only ancillarily related to the whole issue.

She decided to try her new lesson, for all she didn't know why it worked, nor if she could even pull it off. "I'm sure it's hard to be told you still have to leave your home, but surely you knew you'd have to go somewhere when you at least got married, and not necessarily remain here at the castle? Isn't it an honor to be asked by the Regent to go to a nation we're trying to form peaceful relations with again, to represent him and your country?" That at least got them to be quiet, for all their looks were rather poisonous.

"While I know that the Regent and his wife talk to each other regularly, I'm not so sure it was her that said anything at all. And if she did, I'm not sure she was wrong to think that maybe you'd be better off having a friend at your side while there?" She narrowed her eyes at the looks they wouldn't give each other. "And if you weren't really friends to begin with, and can't stand to be alone together in Selicia or even on the road there, then you've made your beds, haven't you?" That last came out because she'd been wanting to scold someone else with them for once, rather than herself. It was still bitter in her mouth all the same.

She took a deep breath, then reaching even further, said, "I do sympathize with you both, very much. I'd also be very afraid. I'd be sad I'd even thought to follow my father's order," she looked Opal in the eyes, trying to convey her sincerity. "I wanted to come talk to you, to let you know, and to hear from you myself if that was why you were being lazy with Lord Petroi. If the Regent has let you know that you're being called up to serve as an ambassador, isn't that at least somewhat better than having to worry about if you'll be abandoned there? Or is there something else, some other reason you were that way with him?"

"Lazy!?" Opal was incensed. "I wasn't being lazy! It really was hard."

Amber looked at her soberly. Suddenly she understood *exactly* what Rio felt when Amber was being obstinate about facing the reality in front of her. "I see," she answered quietly after a bit. "Thank you for answering my question. Good luck to the both of you." She turned and went on her way to finish running her errand.

Surprisingly, she'd learned that defending others instead of herself actually worked. And, she'd learned why the Ministry wanted her to learn honesty with herself and others, and why facing reality as it really was was much preferable. Both of those young ladies would suffer because neither of them would see the world as it truly was and learn that they'd get what they wanted by simply being obedient and working hard — the very things Petroi cherished most.

She sighed to herself but her shoulders relaxed in a way they hadn't for a long time. She still had a long way to go to learn what it was to be a friend, but it was nice to finally have the lesson most important to Rio, Marcus, and Ilena learned. And they hadn't even been the ones to really teach it to her in the end. Having her own mistakes so glaringly shoved back into her face had, she thought quite wryly.

-o-o-o-

That evening Rei and Mizi had a somewhat intimate semi–formal dinner they were attending. Rei had instigated it, actually. He was holding it for a sub–set of departments. The various heads of the departments were set near him on both sides of their long head table with their staff arrayed around the tables beyond them. Wives and adult children had been invited to attend as well, so it was a bit lively.

Rei was certain that the rumors had started during the before–dinner conversations, and he was getting plenty of curious looks from the room during dinner. The rumors were actually going to be mostly correct this time. It was extremely rare to invite the children, adult or not.

Mizi had worked with most of the young lords in the library when she'd been studying to become Rei's princess. Before coming Rei had asked her to name the ones she thought had been studious and good potentials for raising up to positions in the castle. He'd also asked her if she knew of any of the young ladies that could be called up the same. She hadn't been too sure there, but there had been a few names she could tell him. By the time dinner was over Rei had already mentioned those names to the department heads sitting around him as potentials to help with the increase of duties, or to fill empty places.

As they began walking around the room after dinner, Rei wasn't so casual as normal. He had people to actually talk to. He started with department staff members he'd received complaints and questions from, answering them directly. He kept those conversations short and to the point, then moved on.

When he'd completed that list, he moved on to the young lords and ladies, having Mizi introduce him to them. Those who'd helped her he was more open with, trying to understand them a little better. Those who had some level of competence and respect he openly told about positions available in the departments. That surprised the few young ladies he encouraged to fill such positions. It had surprised the department heads, too, but he was going to continue to encourage that for a long time.

His final set of people to talk to finally came up on his list and his feet were relieved. He hadn't had to stand and talk to people for this long for a while. He went to one of the department heads who was the father of one of the two remaining daughters that he'd interviewed during the princess candidate testing and asked him to collect his wife and daughter. Then he went to collect the son he'd selected for her.

That was enough to get that son's parents walking their direction so that they all met up at the same place and time. The murmurs in the room said that the guests had indeed wondered if that was the main reason for this meal. It was, but the other things had been on Rei's list of important things to do as well, so it was good to get it done all at the same time.

Rei introduced the young man to the young lady and let them know that their parents had already agreed to the alliance. That didn't shock the two as much as it could have, so he knew the parents had warned them. "Please take the time to get to know one another. When I return from Yamanzar and Ichijou in the fall, if everyone is still amenable to the agreement, I'll see it completed for you," he said. At their bows and curtsies, he moved on to repeat the whole process for the other princess–candidate.

It would be odd for the alliances to not be completed, with the Regent making the request to begin with. However, he wouldn't force it if the couple couldn't stand to be together. He knew the caliber of the young ladies, and he knew he wanted the alliance, but he surely couldn't know if the personalities would clash or be sufficient. All parents arranging marriages for their young adults had to go through this same process for the same reason.

While they were where people could still hear them, he let Mizi ask her question. "Rei, if they're of princess caliber, then why not marriages to ministers' sons, or to landed lords' sons?"

Rei nodded a thoughtful nod of understanding. "Because while the ministers do an important job for the kingdom, it's the lower departments and staff that are essential. A minister is actually easier to replace than the person that you replace him with. It's because they understand in detail a specific task that no one else has learned.

"If a young lady has proven she can be an excellent example of comport-ment, then why shouldn't we want her to remain here in the castle to be that example? Why marry them off to someplace they'll be forgotten save the few full lord's courts we have? The only better I could have done was to marry them into Ichijou, and I'd far rather keep them here." He gave Mizi a small smile and then excused them from the dinner. It had gone well from his perspective. The gossip would tell him if he'd gone about it wrongly, or if it would take a few more like that for him to get the castle trained to how he rewarded.

-0-0-0-

Baron Odle stood with his wife and son, watching the Regent work the room after the dinner. His son had become an apprentice at the castle two months ago, so was newly come to all of this political dancing. He wasn't quite ready to leave his parents' sides to visit with the other young lords and even less the young ladies. Odle had watched the Regent even at the dining table. The number of times he'd brought amazement or surprise to the faces of the department heads around him had tickled Odle. He'd been glad to be among those closest to Rei and Mizi as one of the department heads so that he could see those looks.

He was feeling very smug now, though. He could tell he'd understood it first: that the prince rewarded with praise, time and attention, and with small helping hands — or larger ones in the case of the princess candidates. His contemporary he'd talked with at the meeting almost a month ago now had come up to him while the prince had been introducing the young couples and had asked openly if Odle thought that's what Rei was doing. He'd very directly said, "Yes." The other heads were going to be mulling that one over for a while.

He turned to his son now and said, "Watch Prince Rei when you can. He will be the best example of royalty you'll ever see in your lifetime. I hope you have such a blessing in your whole life. I'm glad to finally have it in mine." He held out his elbow for his wife's hand and turned to take the three of them away from the dining hall.

"What was he doing?" his son asked as they walked the passage to their suite. Odle recounted it clearly and in detail from the beginning so his son could understand and learn from it.

When he was done, his wife said, "The Regent was kind to talk to our son, also." That had been at the dining table.

Odle agreed. "But," he put his more stern eye on his son, "you need to understand that wasn't a reward. That was him testing you, trying to feel out what sort of person you are. He'll be watching to see how you grow while you're learning here. If he could someday reward you in even one of those ways, it would be good." With another look he added, "And if he can't, and comes to scold you instead, be sure you're obedient and learn from the scolding, then mend your ways. He isn't the kind to judge unfairly. He's the kind to warn and straighten you before you stray too far from proper judgment and reason. He'll listen to your defense as well, as long as you're honest."

His son nodded thoughtfully and he let it rest. His son would watch Rei as much as Rei would watch him and the rest of them. Someday his son would understand. In the meantime, Odle was very content. He'd been intrigued by one of the young ladies Rei had mentioned and had gone to talk to her after the meal. While she'd need training since she certainly hadn't ever considered working for a department of the Region before, she'd seemed as competent as Rei had said he thought she was. Maybe he'd snatch her up before any of the others did and call her up tomorrow even.

-o-o-o-

One week after the formalities of the interim investiture, Mizi was sitting in Ilena's office at her normal time to visit in the morning. Mizi was both excited and quite nervous. So nervous, in fact, that her hand clenched over her heart was shivering. Ilena decided to focus on the nervousness first, to perhaps abate it just a little, if possible.

"It's this afternoon's tea with the Queen Mother," Mizi admitted. "I still don't know how to face her, and I don't want to offend her at all."

Ilena took the hand on Mizi's lap between both of her hands and warmed it up a bit. Mizi was so stressed out about it her hands were very cold. "She really can be faced as you face Rei, me, or even Sasou. She is stern, and likes to put on a face of cold disinterest, but she's as human as the rest of us. The only thing she doesn't like as far as a topic of conversation is the past. Don't bring up her husband, my mother, or anything of that sort and you'll be fine," Ilena smiled.

"Would you come with me?" Mizi blurted out.

Ilena hesitated. "It would actually be more stressful for her if I did. If she could focus on just training you in the things you've asked from her, I think she'd enjoy getting to know the wife of her youngest son." Ilena considered it a little longer. "Perhaps if you thought of it as if you were in Tarc again. You faced the wives of Prota and Zerak' admirably, and even the whole of the market.

"You can come back here and talk to me about the visit and I'll let you know if you did slip anywhere, but I suspect you won't." Ilena smiled at Mizi again. "Remember that I promised you'd be the one even all the Toukas couldn't reject as Rei's princess. You've already passed her tests. Now is when you can show her who you are. You always do that with gentle strength and grace. I have great confidence in you."

Mizi considered Ilena's words, then drew in a deep breath and let it out, working hard to let the anxiety out with it. "Tell me, what's exciting you today?" Ilena thought changing the topic at this point would be helpful.

Mizi's eyes sparkled and she took her hand back to clasp both hands together in her lap. "I think I've found the thing I can do to help the Region, both in the field I know and in perhaps starting a business." Her look went a little unsure. "That's what I want to ask you about today. I don't really know anything about businesses in Ryokudo. I ran a small remedy shop in Yamanzar, but this is a lot bigger than that. Can you help me with it even a little?" Her look was so earnestly pleading Ilena couldn't say no — at least not yet.

Ilena tipped her head to indicate she was listening. Mizi took in a deep breath and said earnestly, "I'd like to open a general hospital, putting it east of the castle. It shouldn't be here in the castle, or even in the city, because a full hospital might have cases of contagious illnesses, like the plague that hit Kouzanshi. We can test for both the hospital and the Department of Medicine at the same time, taking into consideration the wishes of the candidates, and do the testing and training here while the facility is being built or readied. In particular there are some students at the Kouzanshi Medical Department I worked with that I think would be excellent candidates — for both projects."

Mizi bit her lip a little, then admitted, "I don't know how to turn that into a business that brings in enough income to all the surgeons and medics and also be able to pay its share of taxes. And I don't know where it could go, or who'd be willing to let it be on their land."

Ilena nodded slowly as she thought about the details of such an idea. "It's not a bad plan, actually," she praised Mizi. She blinked as the pieces fell into their places; although, it was by no means a complete plan to setting it up. "I think I'd like to handle it like we did the princess training," she said for a start. Mizi nodded that she'd be willing. "There are specific initial steps that you as the sponsor need to do to get it to a point you can present it to others." Her eyes pinned Mizi. "First off, if you haven't talked to Rei about the details yet, don't."

Mizi blinked a little in surprise. "Well, I've only told him things around the edges: thoughts Ryan and I were having, that sort of thing. I thought if you couldn't help me set it up as a business, or point to someone that could help me with that part, then I'd talk to him in more detail."

"It's okay to tell him the general things you're thinking of, but don't tell him any details — yet." She looked significantly at Mizi. "Right now you're in the exploration phase. There isn't any way he can help you until you have a firm plan in place he can approve or modify and approve. Nor should you try to 'sell him on it early'. Signs of favoritism to a spouse are common in a corrupt society. We're trying to prevent that for as long as possible, and fix it up from the previous years. Let it be an announced business proposition when it legitimately can be shown to be such." Mizi could understand that argument.

Ilena launched into the early details of getting funding for such a large project. Mizi wasn't happy to hear the Court of Ministers would need to vote on such a large project, but Ilena thought this might be a better way to be before them than while trying to sit in Rei's seat. It was a thing Mizi was passionate about that would show them yet again that she could work hard with her own strength.

Ilena finished out the assignment, "When you have a location picked out, if not actually in hand, and a general idea of how much the annual costs would be — calculated by the knowledge you have of tax percentages, costs of materials, and expected pay of the employees — come back and I'll teach you where to go to ask for loans. You need those first two items to sell the idea to those people." She folded her hands in her lap and watched Mizi, then thought of a question. "Would you be going to Kouzanshi yourself? If so, when were you thinking of going? That will impact how much time for research you have."

Mizi paused, then drew in a breath. "That's true. I'll consider that in the planning, too. I can do that much in not too long a time, I think. Maybe a couple of days. When I have the answer I'll bring it to you." She rose to her feet. "Thank you, Ilena."

Ilena smiled. "Good luck," she said. "You'll do just fine." She left it open to be applied to both issues in Mizi's mind this day. Some days she wondered just what would be coming out of Mizi's mouth when she came to visit, but she had yet to be disappointed. Mizi was still continuing to move forward earnestly with her own strength in everything she did. She was hard working and hated to be still, for all she could now that things were quiet for her and she'd reached her place.

-o-o-o-

Ore extricated himself from yet another middling lord of the castle. At least he'd graduated up to that level, from the minor lords. He held himself from running away, jumping up to the roof, or even just ranting. Instead he listened to Lord Finlay quietly teaching Grandfather behind him. It wasn't related to that interaction he'd just had, they were just doing two things interchangeably. Aiden dragged Ore (well, escorted him) to a lord and Ore practiced his lessons, then Finlay taught Grandfather what it was to be a Voice of a royal while they walked to the next one.

He was about done being helped by Aiden. This was the last morning for that. After today, it would be Finlay and Grandfather who'd escort Ore, and Ore who'd have to pick which lord he wanted to face. When it came time to face the higher lords of the castle, Finlay would train him. Ore hoped that was a short set of lessons. There were fewer of the high lords, and he'd already had to face most of them already. Ore had already finished the lessons on how to approach and disengage from the lords. The current lesson set was a study in how to let them come to him and still keep them at a safe arm's distance from him.

The numbers of middle lords who thought they could worm their way into his good graces was already rather staggering, for all Ilena's play earlier that year had been to scold them almost mercilessly. He'd had to be reminded that he'd played the good officer then, sympathizing with them and helping to distract her from her tirades. Of course they'd think he was approachable beyond what he'd expect. Some gave him disappointed looks for having gone "too cool" since his formal wedding, so he was trying to learn to temper it to some sort of middle ground.

Ore's attention was caught by the movement of a rather large grouping of persons. His eyes caught the red in the middle front of the group and his eyebrow raised. Mizi was headed towards the medical wing or garrison. She often went that way after her morning meeting with Ilena. The look on her face was determined, but also the one she wore when thinking very hard about things.

He smiled a little sadly. He wished yet again he could still be by her side like her guards were, but they were both working hard on the same things and for the same reason. It helped him that she and Rei had begun coming occasionally to the Lower office for dinners, now that her lunches were full. Rei had decided he was done with sitting in his office longer than he reasonably should, so had told them all that dinners would most certainly *not* be in the Rose office.

Ore considered interrupting Mizi, but she looked very focused on her thinking. It probably wasn't the best time. He smiled to himself and merely watched as she and her flock continued on out of his sight through another courtyard. It was good that he could even see her in passing. He wanted to stick his hands in his pockets, but he'd already been scolded for doing that early on by Aiden. Apparently lords and royals weren't allowed to be relaxed.

Ore wrinkled his nose and then did it anyway. When Aiden turned scolding eyes on him, Ore only glared back balefully. "Just because I'm learning how to face Ichijou doesn't mean Nijou needs to think that's who I'll be from now on. Sometimes they all have to learn who I am also." Aiden rolled his eyes and let Ore be. Ore smiled to himself, rewarding himself a point. He didn't think anyone else other than him made Aiden roll his eyes. It was his way of giving in without having to say it, and Ore always had the best reasons (or excuses) that Aiden couldn't scold him for.

"But, Lord Ore," Finlay complained anyway, "I thought the point was to learn how to be the Second Prince?" Finlay had finally been with them long enough to be comfortable complaining at Ore and with the slightly less formal address.

Ore looked at Finlay just as balefully as he had at Aiden. "I'm already the Second Prince, from being just me. Even King Brother has to put up with that and hasn't complained — much. I'm learning how to make Ichijou accept that King Brother wants me to be the Grand Duke of Tarc."

Aiden gave Ore wide eyes. "Is that what it is?" Ore thought Aiden was teasing him, having learned enough of the nuances now from observing Aiden as he taught him the finer points of the court game and face.

Ore waved a negligent royal hand at Aiden, "Of course it is. Master Rei might've told you something else, but it's really King Brother's order that I not stumble there and shame him into having to call on someone else to take the new troublesome stepchild." Ore grinned negligently at Aiden, who was
254

pursed lipped. "Really, I think it'll be more fun to pass around the gossip of just *how* difficult that stepchild is. Even if I do stumble, by the time we leave they'll be just as glad to leave it in our laps, incapable as we may be." Aiden grumbled at Ore, but Ore only smiled the distant smile of high lords that said nothing and stuck his hand back into his pocket. He'd won again.

Ore glanced at Finlay. He was frowning, either in concern or confusion. "What do you think Finlay? Would any of the lords here want to take care of Tarc, or would they become so confused and impatient that they'd merely beat them with a stick then tell the Toukas to just leave them alone to their own chaos?"

Finlay blinked and thought through the lords he knew. Finally he shook his head. "No. Everyone's quite happy to not have to deal with that." He looked a bland look at Ore, "And just as happy to have the two most unruly royals have to do it."

Ore gave a nod as he kicked at the ground in front of him, enjoying having his hands in his pockets considering it was chilly this day. "And thus it is. At the moment I'm allowing them all to remember I am that unruly royal. It's been getting too stifling to have them look at me with eyes that wonder if I was playing that part and the stuffy lord is who I really am. It really is quite the reverse, and I'd far rather play the stuffy lord only when absolutely necessary.

"They should be able to relax now, no? They've learned I can play the part well enough to survive Ichijou, but I haven't fooled *them* at all, have I?" He grinned at Finlay and Aiden and they both slumped, having completely lost the match. He walked a little proudly after that for a while, until they reached the next lord who chose to be subjected to the noble Ore.

-o-o-o-

As they left that lord, Ore looked around again, wondering if he could end the lesson a little early. He was sure it was getting colder the longer the day went on. Winter days did that as the fall was left behind. He looked up at the clouded sky then frowned. "Stay here a bit," he told the three men with him, then ran towards the pillar of the closest sidewalk overhang. He was up it and hefted over the lip and on top of the overhang fairly quickly. He moved up to the building rooftop to look west and frowned even more. Darker clouds were coming up more quickly than the fainter breeze down below said they should be.

Ore to the castle. Winter storm coming in. Should be here in .... He paused to calculate it one more time. *About twenty minutes. Inform the castle staff immediately.* Ore squinted at the dark grey clouds above and to the west of Nijoushi again. It was kind of hard to tell where the dividing line was, for all the clouds in the far west were obviously darker. He also couldn't tell how far the storm extended. *Ore to North road children. How far does the storm extend to the west? How long will we be under it?*

That answer would take a while to get back to him so he headed back down to rejoin his companions. As he did so, his ears caught the sound of a familiar voice passing his message on from not too far away in the castle. He arrived with his men and began moving them in the direction of that voice. "First winter storm is on its way," he informed them. They gave stoic responses, but the undercurrent of anxious resignation all Suiran residents held about winter storms was in them. "I think we're done." He excused Finlay and Aiden so they could get back to their offices before it arrived around them.

Ore's response to winter storms was a little different. His instinctive reaction was more of a panic one. Like he'd become the cornered horse with no way out, not even to fight. He managed to hold that down for now. It wasn't actually snowing yet. He breathed deep breaths instead until he got that under control enough. This still wasn't Tokumade, and he still loved the people in this castle, the same as they loved him. It was still hard to overcome the training of youth. Ichijou had been simpler for this one reason. It never became snowed in unless it was an unusually cold winter in Ryokudo.

He was a little relieved to distract himself when he reached his goal. He kept himself and Grandfather out of sight in the shadows where he could just see and hear Amber and the person she was talking to. It looked like she was trying to finish the conversation so they could be out of the snows when it hit. It was good she was trying to learn, but the conversation was obviously not going the way she wanted it to.

When Amber was on her way back to the Intelligence offices, Ore and Grandfather casually joined her along the way. "You're working hard," Ore praised Amber, surprising her just a little. "It's still hard though, isn't it?"

Amber's face wrinkled up a bit and she looked away. "Why doesn't either one work?" she finally asked, looking down and kicking her foot forward in frustration. "When I'm normal, they scold me. When I'm honest they look at me like I'm from the moon then scowl and leave." Her face twisted in some internal agony, she begged Ore, "Why?"

Ore considered the question and the person for a bit, clasping his hands behind his back as they meandered towards the office. "Sometimes, if they've already formed an opinion of you, they'll not take the honesty well. But like you call the first part normal, you already understand that they don't want the bald honesty. That's why Ilena has few friends. She can't be anything but that."

"But!" Amber protested, then paused, then continued, "Even Mistress Mizi's like that, and they don't —"

Ore was already wagging his head at her. "Even Mistress doesn't have many friends. Only those who also can hear truth and be grateful."

Amber hung her head and agreed. "Then why do they want that? Isn't it better to have friends?"

Ore tipped his head in thought as they passed through a corridor between buildings, his attention on their surroundings since this was a location they could be jumped. They weren't so he went back to thinking. "I think that balance is what Mistress is trying to learn. She wants to understand how to be friendly enough, even if they can't like her honesty that she loves.

"I'm sure she'd rather they faced her with honesty, and perhaps they'll eventually learn how to do that enough they can also keep the balance of peace in the castle so they can all smile at each other in passing." Ore was feeling quite a bit of sympathy for Mizi. He'd worked hard to learn how to be friendly to all, but he'd also spent all of that time lying to the world about who he was: rather the reverse of what Mizi did. Ilena didn't lie per say, but she also often skirted around the direct or whole truth.

"If you're being honest when you're trying to win friends, it only works with those who also love honesty, and who can be forgiving if you slip and are rude about it. If you spend all your time lying, you forget who you are and in the end no one can trust you. There's a balance." Ore looked at Amber. She was paying careful attention. Grandfather opened the door to the building their wing was in and they were glad to get out of the cold wind that had picked up on their walk. The snow would be next.

"While I never told anyone the truth about who I was, or my past, I also didn't lie when it was important to be honest. I played parts that were lies, but they were parts. They weren't who I was. If I'd finished a job, I told the truth about it. If I couldn't finish a job, I told that truth, too. If I couldn't do something, I didn't lie and say I could. If I don't like someone, I don't have to lie to get in their good graces. I can be just polite enough, keep the conversation short, and move on. If possible I don't go hunting for them to spend time with them. That's also a lie: that I want to be with them. I don't want to be so I don't."

The guards on the wing let them through the door and they began to shed their scarves and other warm outer clothing. "Was that answer enough to think about it more?" Ore asked Amber.

"I think so," she answered as Hue opened the Lower office door for them. Grandfather bowed and took himself up the stairs for the Upper office at Ore's nod of gratitude to him for yet another agonizing morning of effort (from Ore's perspective — he rather thought it amused Grandfather to follow him around).

Satisfied with that answer, Ore walked into the office and straight to Ilena. As she sat back from her work at her desk, he immediately wrapped his arms around her. "Storm's here," he murmured into her hair and shivered a little. The clumps of flakes were already falling thickly outside the glass doors behind her.

Ilena wrapped her arms around him and hummed at him. "It's good to be cooled off by you. I was getting too warm." He chuckled at her, then stuck his still–cold nose into her neck. She shivered and clucked at him but let him warm it up before he moved again. It was good to have his warm protecting arms with him finally so the child inside him didn't have to be so overly worried and afraid any more.

CHAPTER 152 Amber Comes to Understand

The trip from the Lower office of Intelligence to Mizi's tea with the Queen Mother was an awful slog through not only five inches of snow (*already!*) but through nearly–blinding snowfall. Sadly the world didn't stop for storms unless one couldn't even open the door. Since this was the first heavy snowfall of the season, that wasn't now. Amber grumbled to herself a little. Every time after the first lunch with Mizi, she'd remembered most carefully to change out of her uniform into her nicer clothing. At least then she hadn't been glared at just because of where she worked.

It had still been hard to be present at them. Knowing how hard it was for her, she eventually could only have a grudging respect that Mizi kept going, kept trying to understand the ladies of the court and castle. While Amber felt like she was still learning very slowly, if at all, this tea she wasn't going to miss. It would likely be the only opportunity she'd ever have to attend a tea with Kata present. She was sure there were stars in her eyes to get to go, so slog through the snow storm was what she was going to do. If only she could brag about it to anyone.

Even today's attempt to talk to any of the people she'd been able to talk to before had been abysmal. She would've thought honesty to one of those would've been appreciated, but Ore's comment that once a person had learned your patterns you might be out of luck had struck a chord with her. She was quite sure that's what she'd done: burn bridges already and she was too late to make them into friends. Maybe she could learn that lesson later, but how to repair friendships was advanced lessons she was quite sure.

Upon arrival at the Queen Mother's building, the guards directed Amber where to go. She stood outside that door, shifting from foot to foot until Mizi and her entourage arrived (unless another invited lady appeared: then she stood politely and calmly until they'd entered the room). This time Mizi gave Amber a piercing look, the green eyes standing out suddenly to Amber in their judgment. Amber swallowed and curtsied humbly. "Delia, is she sufficient?"

Delia's experienced eyes said she'd already decided. She curtsied slightly, "Almost Your Highness." Delia stepped up and Amber had to endure the humiliation of having the Princess' hairdresser fuss over her and fix up details. She was a bit shocked at that feeling. Normally she wouldn't have truly acknowledged it, and it would have certainly been a boast after the fact: "I was even seen to by the very hairdresser of the princess," that sort of thing.

Amber swallowed again and tried for humble, also recognizing that on some level she was, or should be, grateful. She wouldn't walk into the tea at less than she should to humiliate herself without knowing it. She wouldn't humiliate or shame Mizi, either. Amber wasn't sure if that was important to

Mizi or not, but normally she could only assume it was. Maybe that would be a question for Rio or Ilena after she got back, or to Mizi herself if there was time. Mizi didn't always have time to answer her questions.

She followed in her usual place behind Delia and Maria as they entered the tea room. It was decorated as beautifully as Amber could have imagined. She did wish she'd get to taste the food and the tea, but the ladies–in–waiting and guards didn't get to. They were only there to see to the needs of the ladies who'd been invited.

There were three other ladies present with their entourages, plus Kata and her ladies–in–waiting and two guards. At least Amber assumed they were hers. None of the other ladies had brought guards, just the ladies–in–waiting. They were also all older ladies of Kata's generation. Amber recognized Mizi's slight hesitation. Amber wasn't sure she'd practiced with the older ladies yet. Still with a breath, Mizi curtsied to Kata and joined the rest at the table.

As usual, Brianna stayed close by Mizi, standing nearly behind her but just off to the side where Mizi could see her if she turned her head. The rest of them stood back the proper distance, finishing out the surrounding persons and filling in. They rather stood out since Mizi's group was the largest of those brought with.

Kata's eyes were on them even. Amber fought hard to not blush in embarrassment. "Princess Mizi, is it so necessary to bring *everyone*?" Kata asked in light complaint.

Mizi bowed her head in apology. "I'm sorry, Queen Mother. While I'm in lessons, yes it is, as they are as well. Once we've passed all of the tests related to me being head female in the castle, then I'm sure we'll all be relieved for at least some of them to have time to waste in idleness instead of standing around in boredom." Amber almost choked, but as Kata's eyes pinned Mizi so that the rest looked as well, there was a sparkle of humor on Mizi's face.

"I'm grateful you were willing to have me come for lessons from you directly," Mizi continued on politely, "and that the rest of you would have the patience to willingly also come to a training tea." She neatly included the rest of the ladies in attendance, while at the same time establishing exactly where they were all starting from in this tea. She received tips of the head from the other ladies. Most were reserving judgment generally Amber could tell. Maybe they would anyway if they understood Mizi was considering herself still in training.

The rest of the tea was as much a training as any of the luncheons had been. Amber paid close attention to the questions Mizi asked and the answers she received. There was a lot less of the pandering vapid statements that vied for position that occurred when the young ladies met. These ladies already had their positions set by their marriages long before. Instead, there were slightly more of the stinging barbs. Even Kata used them more frequently than Amber would have thought. She found Mizi's responses to them interesting. Most of the time they were well phrased to turn the person who said it, and even the topic, but on occasion her answers seemed too childlike in this grouping of mature ladies.

When she received looks from the ladies that were closed and proud at answers like that, Mizi drew in a breath, then directly asked how she should have been, or for the person who'd just spoken to rephrase their comment or question. When she had the additional information, then she had a more adult answer. If she didn't, then she thanked that person for the clarification then let it lie. Amber knew she'd ask Brianna about those, and the ones that still troubled her she'd take to Ilena the next morning. Her own lessons had continued at those times as well. She was sure Brianna was giving Mizi better answers than Ilena was, since even Ilena deferred to Brianna most of the time when those questions came up.

There was one other difference at this tea that Amber noticed after she could relax enough to not only focus on the tea table. In this room, the other servants didn't talk to each other. They paid attention to their charge. After a bit, though, Amber began to notice that they were still communicating with each other. It was through glances to each other and sometimes motions, rather than vocally. Sneers to each other when Mizi stumbled. Looks of humor behind hands held over mouths when Mizi had said something she'd meant to be humorous, but the looks said they disapproved and they were teasing her. The more she watched the angrier Amber became and she had to purse her lips tightly together.

She glanced at Delia and Maria. They were standing straight to support Mizi, but she thought they were also being stern to some degree, as if giving off disapproval. The guards behind her were doing the same. Amber wanted to scowl when a few eyes glanced their way, and she suddenly wished she *was* in her department uniform. Trying to stay true to Ilena and the Ministry of Intelligence, instead of scowling she gave back a bland raised eyebrow (as best she was able). Maybe if they'd already heard where she worked, or if she could let it be known directly after, then maybe they'd stop being so rude.

-o-o-o-

When the tea was over and Mizi had thanked the hostess and excused herself, they all relaxed a little bit to be out of the tea room. Brianna turned her head and said over her shoulder, "Miss Amber, please come with us to the Regent's quarters."

"Yes, ma'am," Amber answered, surprised at the invitation. "I'm sure Mistress Ilena won't need me for a while yet." She heard a soft intake of breath from the entourage that had followed them out of the tea room. Served them right, to make awful assumptions from the beginning.

When they'd braved the storm (still ongoing) and arrived at the Old Regent's building, they paused in the large entryway and turned to stand in mostly a circle. Amber suddenly hoped she wasn't in trouble, since the attention came on her rather quickly. "Miss Amber, please tell us what you observed," Brianna asked.

Amber's eyes went wide and she drew in a breath. Then careful to be honest but trying not to be mean, she explained what she'd seen. She cringed just a little to have to be honest when she explained the times Mizi had been too childish and that had been not only the other's opinions but hers as well. To balance it, she also honestly said when she was impressed with Mizi's responses. Amber also had to express her frustration at the other servants, so included that as impassively as possible, probably not making it to that since she'd always had difficulty with being anything other than dramatic in her speech.

When she was done, Brianna asked, "And what questions did you have come out of all of that?"

Amber blinked to be allowed to ask them. "Mistress Mizi, why did you have Miss Delia confirm my appearance? It seems to me that usually doesn't matter to you."

Mizi shook her head. "It does because I've learned it matters to the court. In this case it was particularly important because I was so nervous to face Queen Mother Kata. Everything needed to be right before we went in so that I could calm down all the exterior details and focus on the lessons."

"Ooh," Amber could understand that. "But you never look nervous at these, even when you first arrive."

Mizi smiled wryly. "Well, if I don't look it then I've practiced the court face enough. I guess that's relieving on some level. I'm nervous every time. I'm hopeful that sometime I'll have enough lessons under my belt to be relaxed at them, like I am now at the lord's teas."

Amber blinked. "And what was that thought?" Brianna asked.

Amber turned to her and mostly blurted out, "That's very brave. How can any lady be relaxed at the *lord's* teas?"

Brianna smiled a small smile, then turned to Mizi. "I've asked Amber to explain what she saw from her point of view both to show you that she also has been learning, and to show you what the point of view of every other young lady of the court *actually* is. I think you wouldn't have defended Mizi at the tea to the other servants before you began following her?" Brianna asked Amber directly, her eyes telling her yet again to not lie.

Amber bowed her head and clasped her hands together. "No, probably not. I'm not sure I would've been as sophisticated as the servants today, though. I would've been more like the younger servants of the young ladies who are also still learning how to follow them."

"Sophisticated?" Mizi asked. "After you complained about them so strenuously?"

Brianna smiled again. "Thus the two minds she's still in as she learns. Yes. Those servants are tutored enough to know when you've stumbled in the game and they answer to the points you're earning or losing. I'd say from Amber's description you won none in this round. You'll have to decide if that's important to you, though. You did well enough in the rest of your lesson."

Mizi considered what both Amber and Brianna had said, then shook her head. "For now I won't worry about earning points. Ilena has said that for advanced lessons if I care to learn it I can, but I already know that Rei and King Sasou don't care if I do." She gave a self–scolding look. "If anything it's what endears me to the King: that I don't think of it and don't care." She shook her head at herself and them. "It would give them great delight if I were to suddenly understand it and use it in front of them. Then they'd be sad and scold me to be myself again. Even Ilena and Ore would do that."

"Well, of course *they* would," Kirk muttered under his breath in the background.

Mizi looked at her guards with wide eyes. "And you'd approve?" Neither Brian nor Kirk could look at her directly.

Brian finally said, "It's not our place to make you something you shouldn't be for Regent Rei, but yes, it would relieve us greatly if you could put the rest of the court into their places properly."

Mizi's brow furrowed. "Is that what the game is for? I still don't really understand it."

Amber answered without thinking. "Yes, that's what it's for. Everyone in the castle has a placement in the hierarchy. They hold on to it by playing the game, or lose their places by losing the game too much. You aren't even placed. You stand next to Master Rei which gives you position, but in the hierarchy of the castle you don't exist." She blushed furiously when she got scolding looks from Delia and Maria.

That turned into a detailed lesson for Mizi from her staff in how the court game was used and how people were set into the hierarchy of the castle by it. That there were sub–categories within it based on the level of caste one was in: servant, staff, young lady or lord, and established lady or lord. Each person vied for visibility to or attention from others in the castle in order to gain a desired position within the hierarchy of their sub–category, but the placement wasn't made firm until a person was called up and set into their place permanently. *Who* a person was called up by made a great difference in how they were viewed by the others in the castle, whether favorably or with disdain, but it didn't affect the level of placement in the hierarchy like the position did.

When the lesson was completed, Mizi asked, confused, "How I'm treated is how you are, regardless of the game?"

Brianna nodded. "Thus why Amber, and the rest, are upset that you're still not seen with eyes that understand why you're outside the hierarchy altogether."

Amber blinked in surprise, but then so did Mizi. "Why would I be outside it?"

Brianna answered, "Because you refuse to play the game. It's not because you don't know how to, which is how they're seeing it. Those who refuse to play the game aren't actually in it to be caring about their placement in it. That's why Rei, Ilena, and King Sasou don't care if you do play it. They'd like to see you earn a few points, to put the rest to shame, but if you do, then you step into it instead of remaining outside of it."

Brianna paused, then pointed out, "Ore plays with it. He stands outside the game, then pokes at everyone, proving he knows how to play it best and teasing them that he won't take it seriously. Aiden quite complains about it to me when we have time alone to chat." She smiled a small contented smile. Amber thought Brianna quite liked Ore's approach to the game, then.

"Ilena abuses it and uses it. She also plays it best, but she manipulates it and doesn't care either. Rather than it being a tease, it makes those who do play it angry. I think the only one she plays it seriously with is King Sasou, but they're playing their own game: the hierarchy of royals. That's limited in number to only four in the country right now. Rei won't play it either, and Queen Mother Kata won't come out to be faced so that makes it only two to play." Mizi nodded, understanding that.

"Because neither Ore nor Ilena will play it, no one in their office does either. That confuses the court. They don't know how to place any of their people, so the whole of the Ministry of Intelligence is outside of it." Brianna's eyes turned to Amber again. "Thus one of your difficulties. You're still trying to insert yourself into their hierarchy — and they don't have one."

Amber felt her mouth drop open. "Then..., what am I to do?" she asked plaintively, still not understanding how to fit herself in at all.

"It's in their partnerships. If you settle to your partnership, understand those duties, and act accordingly, the rest will accept you. Because that's what *they* judge by." Amber closed her mouth. That still wasn't what she really wanted to hear, but since it was all she'd been hearing since she'd been called up she could only be resigned to hearing it again.

"How did you learn that, Brianna?" Sam asked.

Brianna gave him a long–suffering look. "By showing up randomly according to my order from Master Rei to observe them and trying to overcome many headaches as they completely turned my understanding of how humans work at all upside down every time." Amber covered a sudden laugh behind her hand. Brianna understood.

Kirk relaxed. "Oh, we guards have it made then. We're already in our partnerships and getting along just fine."

"Indeed," Brianna agreed with his tease.

"I'm glad I'm partnered with Delia," Maria agreed strongly. She shivered. "I was so low in the young lady's subcategory that I was also one who really was outside it. I couldn't break in at all. To understand that Mistress Mizi didn't care helped me relax so much. I don't care where I am even now, but if Lady Ilena's office can accept me because Delia helps me, then I can relax there now, too."

Amber frowned. "Why does that matter? They're outside the game." Eyes like the eyes in the Intelligence offices looked at Amber and she looked back between them, confused. It was Mizi's almost–cool expression that almost told Amber what she was missing. She finally settled on looking at Brianna, wishing for an answer she could understand.

Brianna tried, speaking slowly to fit her thoughts into words. "Because there *is* a hierarchy of the royals that the rest don't understand, and that's what the households of the royals care about." Brianna drew in a breath, still trying to find the right words. "King Sasou and Rei respect their mother so what she says holds the most weight, but isn't law. Her staff is respected but that is all.

"Sasou is King. His word is law and carries great weight. His staff is obeyed. Rei is Regent. His word is law to those royals under him, the same for his wife for they are equal. Their staff has freedom to act in their name, but they can't command any staff of any other royal, only make requests.

"Ilena is Second Princess *and* the Minister of Intelligence. She's feared even by the royal brothers, for any word of hers that goes into the ears of either of them is believed and acted on, even if it were to be to tear the other brother down. Ore balances that with his face of friendliness, but their staff are walked around carefully.

"Ilena's household staff is equal to Rei's because both Rei and Mizi have placed her and Ore where they are, which is at the top of their *staff*, not just a placement in the rankings of royalty. Thus Ilena's staff have the freedom to act in Ilena and Ore's names, and they also have the freedom to act in Rei's name because by extension they're also his staff.

"That imbalance makes it hard for Rei and Mizi's staff, because for all we're part of the higher household, we're lesser by a slight margin than Ilena's household. The only thing that prevents that from becoming danger-ous is the fact that Ilena's household doesn't command Rei's household, and won't unless it's related to the safety of Rei and Mizi. Then everyone in our household will act immediately to obey, as that's our sworn duty from the beginning. Thus we're allies in that respect.

"Our household — other than Maria," Brianna gave the young lady a kind look, "— does play the court game because we always have. With both households playing it differently, it was confusing. They're relieved to understand it now. Now we know how to act to keep the balance of the households, rather than walk in worry or fear." Amber could understand, but it seemed the lesson wasn't quite finished because Brianna's eyes turned to Mizi.

Amber looked at Mizi. She was still looking rather coldly and sternly at Amber, as if she hadn't listened to that long explanation at all. Then she remembered: when Mizi faced Ilena she always did so as the lesser of the two, even if she did have times she was more firm. She fished for her question, her mouth opening before she had the words to fill the space. Finally she asked, "Where have you placed yourself?" Knowing they were all outside, and Mizi hadn't even known about any of the game until recently, was Mizi still outside the royal game? Brianna had said Mizi was equal with Rei, but that wasn't how Mizi positioned herself to the outside very often.

"I watch and test them all," Mizi answered, then seemed to be surprised herself at that answer. Then she firmed up. "I was warned early that Ilena would put me here, but that she'd always test me in this place. I respect her and need to learn from her, but she'll answer to me before I answer to her." That was said with such certainty Amber had to bow internally to it, which told her where she fit into that hierarchy.

"Ore was given to me when he first came. He's always supported me in the same way Ilena has, and I've always been his mistress. When he oversteps his bounds, I firmly let him know. When Rei stops being the prince he should be, I also hold him accountable," Mizi continued. "I'm obedient to him because he's Regent and my husband." Amber sighed to herself. That did put Mizi equal to Rei, then, with both of them over her own master and mistress.

Mizi sighed. "I'm still afraid of King Sasou, for all I'll stand up to him and speak my mind. It's helped to watch Ilena interact with him since she really does treat him like an older brother. I like Queen Aryana, but she's still learning her position. While it helped to have the tea with Queen Mother Kata, she's unfathomable to me so far, so she's scary too. I can't meet her expectations without knowing what they are. I hope to continue to learn them over the next few visits we'll have."

"*Ah*," Amber sighed. It was no wonder the rest understood Mizi was outside the court game of hierarchy. She actually was already in the royal hierarchy, not in the noble hierarchy. Amber had a suspicion. "Have you told Lord Aiden that Master Ore is in the royal hierarchy instead of noble, like Mistress Mizi is?" she asked Brianna.

Brianna smiled a point–giving smile that crinkled the outsides of her eyes. "Is that what you learned from that?"

Amber nodded resignedly. "I'm not too surprised to see Master Ore that way, but Mistress Mizi is not just outside the game, but already within the royal one." She studied Mizi again. "Probably from when Master Rei and King Sasou met her and accepted her." She nodded, to herself mostly. The rumors about the red–haired commoner from Yamanzar had abounded in things that would point to that, long before they'd gotten married. "So yes, no one is looking at her with the right eyes. It's no wonder Rio wanted me to watch her longer." Amber felt a lot better for having had things finally put to rights in her model of the world she lived in. She curtsied to Brianna. "Thank you."

-o-o-o-

Brianna headed for her room after the review of the Queen Mother's tea. Mizi had excused all of her staff, wanting to rest. Brianna wanted to rest as well. It really was tiring to teach Mizi, surprisingly. Mizi was very determined to learn as much as possible, so dug into the details deeply. The only saving mercy was that because she didn't know what she didn't know, most lessons could end earlier than she knew to carry them on to. That was also helpful for Brianna to have the flexibility to teach what she felt was important in the moment. Today it had seemed important to add into Mizi's lesson the point that Mizi's point of view was the odd one in the castle. Brianna still wasn't sure she'd quite gotten that point across, for all she'd tried to weave it into the lesson even after Amber had been excused.

Brianna had been visiting the Lower office of Intelligence enough now to have discovered Amber's trouble. Likely no one else in that office would understand it, except maybe Reynold who was too distracted with his re-search to talk to Amber about it. She'd seen the greater burden lifted from Amber's shoulders that afternoon. Maybe that would help the Lower office generally, now.

Brianna wasn't sure that was part of her job description, but given how tightly intertwined the two households were, for all they were separated at the moment by space, it might be that it was. Certainly the slowly–rising walls of the new Regent's living quarters being built made her stomach tighten in panic. If the two households weren't ready for living that closely together before that building was done, things could go very wrong.

"Lady Brianna," the male voice was quietly polite. Brianna hadn't quite made it through her bedroom door, although her hand was on the handle. She turned to look at Sam, relieved it was him. "May I have just a few more moments of your time? I'm sorry to prevent you from resting for a little longer."

Brianna had the right to refuse, as she'd been placed at the top of the household staff. Sam was technically the next one in the hierarchy, or perhaps the equivalent. Together they made up the equivalent of the senechal–marshal pairing of a noble manor home. (Andrew and Mina were above the two of them, but they were kept too busy to supervise the household rightly.) She gave a nod to Sam, allowing the interruption, but she allowed enough of her tiredness to show so that he'd do his best to keep it short.

"Has it been hard, then, to sit in the office with Lady Ilena's household?" Sam asked kindly.

"Well, yes, actually," Brianna answered. She was practicing being more openly honest within the household, since that was what Rei and Mizi preferred. "I really had a very hard time the first time Aiden and I went. We were exposed to all of Ilena's oddness in the one visit, since she didn't have the patience nor time to be slow about it. Liam apologized for her for that, and has done his best to translate for me, but he's not castle trained either. I've really had to work hard to puzzle them out on my own mostly." She smiled a rueful smile.

Sam smiled back in sympathy. "I suspect you've had to be immersed in that far deeper than the rest of us." She could only agree. "I'm curious about one thing you won't likely talk to Mistress Mizi about directly, if you'll answer it?" Brianna allowed him to ask on. "Why is Mistress Mizi willing to fit into Lady Ilena's oddness? We already know she has great patience for it generally, but have you been able to understand it better than we can tell, from your observations there?"

Brianna let go of her door handle and clasped her hands together in front of her waist to rest her arms and think on that issue. "I've been there a few times when she has been, although not often. It's actually answered better by watching Mizi generally. I think it's because Ilena and Ore give her a feeling of normalcy, not just one of security or family. She's not castle born and bred, but common. Their wildness and having come from common childhoods on some level lets her not feel alone and lost here. She'd be very lonely without them to give her that connection and relief from the stress the nobles place on her."

"*Ah*," Sam sighed. "Yes. I can see that." His eyes went distant as he remembered the past, for he confided in Brianna, "I was assigned by King Sasou to follow her at a distance once he knew she'd come to Ichijou at the invitation of Prince Rei. While she was very industrious, and interacted well with those who she had contact with, it did seem as if she stood apart and could have felt very lonely.

"There she wasn't the only commoner in the Medical department, but she was the only person not of our nation, and very young for what she was working to attain. They only accept the very best interns at Ichijou. It was a hard training and test. King Sasou was suitably impressed with her ability to be accepted there on her own strength.

"I can't say I was surprised to be sent to continue to follow her here in Nijou. Perhaps I was surprised to be given permission to show her my face and then to be assigned as an open guard." He smiled at the reminiscence.

"Well, thank you for answering my question. I think the young lords will be able to understand that answer acceptably," Sam gave a wry smile to Brianna that she gave back. They all knew the young lords were having the hardest time with Ilena, and Mizi's patience with and love for her.

"I'm hoping my own explanation today helped them as well," Brianna admitted. "Poor Amber quite needed it."

"Indeed," Sam agreed dryly with both sentiments. "I'm sure it helped me even." Brianna chuckled. Sam bowed and she let herself into her room. She really was glad Sam was there to help her stay calm and to help with keeping the young men in line. It did always help to have both a head female and a head male for that reason.

King Sasou was surely wise to have placed someone where he was needed most by the young royal couple. Rei was quite oblivious to what happened directly under him even if he did keep the whole of the Region in his sights. He also would need his own training eventually. It could wait until she'd learned to understand all those under him first. Then she'd know what was actually important for him to be taught, and who'd teach it best. That might not be her, she suspected. It was more likely she'd need to educate Andrew and Mina first, then let them do it.

Brianna's maid loosened the ties on her bodice for her and she lay down in bed. She sent her maid for ice for her head again. Both Princesses did that to her. She almost regretted saying yes to both of them, except that she really did appreciate she was protected now from being the top pick of the castle for second wife of the higher lords. She hoped she could survive this beginning learning phase she had to also go through. She was asleep before that thought finished running through her mind.

-o-o-o-

Brian rose up from his bed where he'd been lying with his eyes open for a while, his hands behind his head. He tightened down the laces on his boots, having only loosened them rather than removing them for their rest time. "Alright!" he faced Kirk. Kirk looked back at him, a bit bemused. Brian didn't often behave so abrupt. "I think it's high time someone around here took specific matters into hand, and I'm going to do it. Come along."

Kirk almost laughed at him. Instead he shrugged and pulled out their winter gear. It was likely still snowing. "What's brought this on?" he asked.

Brian scowled just a little. "We stood on our feet for the whole excruciating tea. We were brought back here and made to stand for another same length of time for the lesson when Lady Brianna was obviously already weary. Hearing from Sam how exhausted she was by the time she went to

269

bed and having her send *yet again* for headache meds and tea...," he growled just a little. "There's a simple answer to the whole mess, but our money–wise leadership will never even think of it."

It looked like he was holding back a whole lot of other unkind expletives and complaints. Kirk appreciated the restraint. He knew Brian was often frustrated with Mizi's obliviousness to court niceties and common courtesies.

Once they were out of the Old Regent's building Kirk put his hand on Brian's shoulder and squeezed it. "Will you want a practice session on the list once your chore's completed?" he asked. That had been the best solution to Brian's frustration when it was brought up.

Brian glanced at him. "Probably, since I won't want to go back until the solution's completed. I think it should take about that long if I impress upon them the importance of a request from the 'royal household'." While he was teasing because of that afternoon's lesson, Kirk knew that Brian was quite proud to be a member of said household.

Kirk kept Brian entertained with low–stress topics of conversation, letting him complain about everyone else he was allowed to complain about so he could at least get the need to complain out. Brian led them to the Châtelaine's office. It was late enough the châtelaine himself wasn't present, but there was still staff at the front desk.

"I'm sorry for a last minute of the day request," Brian said kindly but firmly, "but the Old Regent's building is in desperate need of some immediate guest seating." He waved his hand in mild mock irritation, masking the deeper irritation that was actually present. "I'm afraid that there isn't any office in the building at all. All there is, is the large front entry and the landing at the top of the stairs to the second story.

"They need comfortable seating in the main entry, not right in front of the wind path of the door to the outside, for a group to sit and converse pleasantly. Likely for a minimum of fifteen people. Side tables to place drinks on would be a pleasant addition.

"For the stair landing, at a minimum four chairs, two to each side of the hall doorway, with a small table between the chairs that could hold pleasing floral arrangements or small decorations to brighten that space. Right now it's *very* dead, dull, and dreadful." He wrinkled his nose. "Furniture tonight, but perhaps the decorators could fit it into their schedules first thing tomorrow. No need to pull them away from their dinners, but certainly for future visits it would be good to not have that space quite so sterile."

Kirk stayed the silent support. Brian was handling it quite well, without claiming powers he didn't have. They probably could have, but in this case Kirk would also have been this cautious. Mizi would be rather aghast, thinking it would be very expensive. Rei would find it more irritating than useful because he still would rather not be in the building at all, and he liked plain and simple himself. Still, because Mizi kept "holding court" in that room, treating it as an office, it should properly be made such. He really couldn't disagree at all. Even his feet would thank Brian into the future. Mizi was the only one of them that got to sit at all and it really did just escape her when her brain was so full of things of greater import to her.

"Certainly, Sirs." It was the only answer the poor clerk could give. They were recognized now by everyone in the castle, even if they weren't wearing the uniform all the time. Kirk would be glad when they could have their next vacation and he could wear something with color in it. It would be hard to be in black all winter. Maybe he could get away with minor accessories of red to match Mizi's main color. Even blue or gold would be nice. He sighed to himself.

"Ah, and...," Brian paused in the act of turning away from the desk. The clerk hadn't moved. It was the expected next step of an order to remember last minute one of the important details. "...please use furniture that's already lying around the castle in some wasted space or storage room, but is in good repair. No need to spend even more money on a building that's already being replaced." He dramatically rolled his eyes and sighed in despair over the state of the ancient ruin that no one would be sad to see go.

"Understood," the clerk was hiding his own laughter about said building. It had been completely abandoned until Rei had taken over as Regent. The gossip around the castle had been very vibrant about that decision for the first month or so he'd been there. Even having him move into the King's wing would've made more sense to any of them. Ilena's opinion of that building upon first looking at it was the opinion of everyone from many years back: tear it down. They were all glad she'd had at least that level of reasoning within her, and the clout to make it stick with Rei.

Kirk knew the ulterior motive behind that last order though. When they were away from the building he smirked at Brian. "Even still you don't want to be scolded that severely if either of them protest heavily."

"Well..., no," Brian agreed. "It will definitely help to mollify any dissension. But I'm not wrong with that reason either." He looked side–long at Kirk.

Kirk laughed. "No. Not at all." He teased further as they headed for the garrison, "However, you might just have consigned us all to having to have that same furniture in the new building."

Brian punched Kirk in the arm. "Never! I might not be able to stand in the presence of Lady Ilena, but I can trust her on one thing."

"That is?" Kirk carried it on like the partner he was.

Brian finally grinned. "That she'll still make the Regent and his wife pay out the nose for her own overly ornate artisans' works to be the only works in *that* building. She'll be just as happy as the rest of us to have the old worn out furniture be burned down with the old worn out ancient monstrosity."

Kirk laughed with Brian. "You're probably right. You're probably right," he agreed. "The businesswoman will be just as firm on that issue as the claustrophobic child will be on the other." Brian nodded quite wisely, pleased with finally getting something he wanted and that Brianna needed: proper comforts of home in the home they had to live in here in this place.

-o-o-o-

Thayne thought it perhaps a good sign that the whole of both the Upper and Lower offices relaxed when the guards opened the door to their wing and let someone in. That person's footsteps were familiar now, faster than most and light. Amber was back. That was confirmed when the door to the Lower office was opened without being knocked on and Hue's kind voice welcomed Amber back. Justinian's lighter voice echoed the welcome as the door was closed behind Amber. It was also a good sign that Rio didn't ignore Amber but did wait until the current report she was receiving finished. It had taken a long time for this place to reach this point of beginning to accept Amber might be family to them, too.

"Welcome back, Amber," Rio's voice was the careful neutral she made it when talking to Amber. It was almost light and friendly, but Rio still couldn't force herself to actually be friendly to Amber. That was okay. She was still at least patient and trying. "How did it go?"

There was a pause, then Amber's voice coming from closer to Rio, slightly muffled at the first, as if she were still in the process of removing muffler, hat, gloves, and cloak. Pretty much everyone listened when Amber gave Rio her reports. Somehow Amber still seemed to find it simple to forget they could all hear her, but they did pretend for each other like they couldn't to be polite. Thayne figured that was why Ilena kept her mouth closed and let Rio do the teaching. Ilena wasn't clueless. She was observing. If she interjected herself then Amber would be reminded they could all hear and she'd stop being as open as she'd learned to be.

Thayne observed as well, like the rest of them. Like Petroi, he was an older brother, watching to see that the tenor of the whole didn't become out of balance. They'd been surprised to have Amber come confront Petroi after Miss Preston had left, but upon hearing her arguments Thayne had to agree with her. He'd given Petroi a silent scolding himself after Amber had left the Upper office. In response, Petroi had silently apologized to all of the Upper office for not watching himself more closely.

Since then, the training sessions with Mizi had been helping Amber quite a bit. In the past Amber would boast of herself, so sometimes it was hard to tell if her reports were including that habit still, but some of them more recently had seemed more honest and real. This report started out that way, and in a somewhat surprising way: Amber's voice was humble and serious. Thayne raised an eyebrow. He wasn't the only one in the room to take notice of the difference. Something had changed in a major way for Amber this day.

She was surprisingly honest even about her reactions to herself. It felt like she was telling more details than she would have in the past, as if before she'd leave out things. Her anger at her observations of the behavior of the servants of the ladies present at the tea was honest. So was her report of how Mizi had behaved, and even how Kata had and that she'd been surprised that Kata had been the thorniest of the ladies present, giving Amber a surprisingly sour first introduction to the Queen Mother.

When Rio pressed her for the details of what Kata had said, then pointed out that Amber herself had used those tactics, Amber didn't protest, didn't fight back. Instead she paused, then quietly said, "I know. I've seen it now all week. Those things I used to do and say, the pride I held while I was doing them. I've learned more this week by being the person on the other side of me than I've learned any other day except today." Everyone in the Upper office sat back in their chairs at that declaration, giving up the pretense they were doing anything other than listening.

After another pause, Amber said, "After the tea, Lady Brianna asked me to continue with them to the Old Regent's building. In order to punish the other servants, I said that Mistress Ilena wouldn't need me for a while and I'd go. At least one party heard it and was concerned. Maybe they'll have learned their lesson about making assumptions. It was the one time I'd wished I'd worn my uniform. Except that after, Mistress Mizi explained that she was able to relax better because I'd come dressed more appropriately for a tea."

At her pause Rio interjected. "You were mean because you were angry about incorrect assumptions?"

There was another pause, then a surprised Amber said, "Ah! I – I guess that was the same wasn't it?" She pondered on that for a bit. Thayne assumed they were talking about her point from earlier that Petroi had been mean because he'd been upset at another person's behavior and not considered their point of view.

Rio asked, "Is that one of the things I should watch out for, or is it something new you've discovered and need to learn about first?"

"I – I think it's new," Amber wasn't sure. "But..., no, but maybe that's what made me angry with my friend. She'd just assumed I'd done something to her that made her angry, but she didn't come ask me if it was true first. She just got angrier and angrier the more I tried to defend myself...!" There was a sudden shocked pause, then Amber was excited.

"That's it! That's the defense I was trying to understand. Mistress Mizi always defends Master Rei. If ever she's attacked, she'll give one dismissive defense of herself, but the rest is always defending someone else. The attacks become pointless when she does that. It even worked when I tried it to try and understand it better. When I tried to defend myself to my friend it didn't work at all, nor has it ever. But that's why it's been important to me to learn it, just like I guess incorrect assumptions anger me." She was back to musing at the end, putting her new insights about herself into place inside of her.

Rio gave her time to assimilate them, then said, "Then I'll remember it, to come and ask you before I make assumptions. If you want help remembering to defend others as the best defense for yourself, I'll help when I'm in a position to." Thayne glanced at Marcus. It looked like he was taking mental notes as well. That was good. It meant he hadn't completely written Amber off as a potential. Amber had been trying very hard lately. Perhaps it would still be possible.

Amber was very sober with her next statements. "Actually, Rio, that's the important lesson I learned today. Lady Brianna had me tell Mistress Mizi everything I'd observed and how I saw it. And she had me ask all my questions. I think she's using me to try and help Mistress Mizi understand how the young ladies of the castle think and see. Some of the things I said made Mistress Mizi confused, some a little angry although I was trying to be kind while being honest enough to explain it. Lady Brianna never scolded me, only said at the end that she'd asked me to tell it from my point of view so that Mistress Mizi could see that I've been learning from her, and to show her what the point of view of every other young lady of the court actually is. ...I'm not sure I'm really that, but I do know that the way I know how to communicate is a lot closer to them than to anything else.

"But that's not what I needed to hear. The lesson Lady Brianna gave us all next is what I needed to hear. I've been so confused by this office, and even by Mistress Mizi for all I'm enjoying learning from her. Lady Brianna taught Mistress Mizi what the court game is for. We talked about the different branches of the hierarchies, that Mistress Mizi isn't even on the lady's branch, that Miss Delia was at the top of the female higher staff branch and is now *the* top of that branch because Mistress Mizi called her up, but all of Mistress Mizi's staff are held in the same contempt she is because they follow her. She was surprised to learn that how she's seen is how everyone in her household is seen."

There was another pause, then a sigh. "Oh. That's why I'm.... Well, that explains that part." She wasn't going to openly say that new epiphany, but they all sort of got it anyway. She would care that Ilena was avoided thus so was she. The rest of them considered that 'freedom'.

"But Rio, what really made the difference is that Lady Brianna finally was able to explain for me why I've been so confused. I've been trying to fit this office into the castle hierarchy, and it isn't possible. She says that all of the royal households are outside the castle hierarchy as most of us think of them. They're in the *royal* hierarchy. Everyone — even me — keeps thinking they're in the *noble* hierarchy." Thayne heard Ilena begin to hum. It was felt more than heard at that level. She'd been pleased by that observation and point. "Especially Mistress Mizi and Master Ore. *Everyone* thinks they're in the noble hierarchy because they weren't born royalty." Now Ore was pleased as his eyes lit up as if with the game itself. Thayne sent him a scolding look that was twin to the one Petroi was giving Ore.

"Lady Brianna was able to set us all at ease by explaining that because the Immediate Family is outside the castle game, rather than playing it, is why we've all been confused. She explained to me that it's the partnerships that are important and why. I know you've all been trying to teach that to me, but because she said it in this way, I was finally able to understand." Amber was back to sober from excited. "I think I can do it. It will still take a long time to really learn it, I think, but now that I understand it this way, I think I can do it."

Rio was silent for a moment, then quietly she answered, "I'm glad you've found a way to think about it that helps you, Amber. Please keep asking me questions when you're not sure. And maybe Lady Brianna can help translate when you and I can't find the common understanding."

"Mm!" Amber agreed firmly. "I will. I think she's willing to help, too. She was very kind today." There was enough quiet after that to signal that the two young women were getting back to work, so the Upper office did as well.

Thayne glanced at Marcus again. He was looking a bit confused, but shook his head at himself and focused again on his work. He and Henry had moved back upstairs to work on their part because there was more room, it was quieter, and Henry's cursing under his breath and Marcus' agonizing pulling at his hair disturbed this room less than it did Ilena. They were still having troubles with the work they'd been assigned. Petroi and Grandfather were also closer at hand to help them over the worst parts.

A throat was cleared down below. The noise caught ears but they didn't stop working. "Miss Amber," it was Reynold, "would you be willing to come tell me in more detail what you learned from Lady Brianna?" he asked. "I've also been trying to understand from my background. It sounds like she's seen things very similar to what I've worked out, but I'd like the confirmation, if you have time?"

"Sure," Amber answered. She hadn't started her reports coming in yet and they could wait that long. This office also needed him to understand. Ilena had already let the rest of them know that he was allowed to interrupt as long as it was only for brief enough times and direct simple answers were given so that the interruption didn't turn into three–day–long expositions and grilling sessions.

There was the pause that said they'd moved over to Reynold's desk so he could take notes if he needed to and they'd be out of the way of direct interference. Ilena would clear her throat if they got too loud or annoying, so the rest ignored it and focused on their work. While the details of how the castle hierarchy worked weren't important to them, some of the conclusions of either Brianna or Reynold were funny to the rest of them.

-o-o-o-

It wasn't too long after that conversation got started that the door to the courtyard below opened and closed, then a head appeared at the balcony railing. Rio was through their door as quickly as she could be, bringing in a cold swirl of snowflakes and wind with her. She impatiently brushed the snow off her shoulders and headed for Henry and Marcus. The two of them rose to meet her. Henry lightly brushed the snow on top of her head off before it could melt into her hair.

Ore quietly shifted from being at his desk to being closer to the inner door. Thayne thought it was interesting he wanted to listen to the odd lecture as well, but couldn't be surprised. Ore liked playing the court game as a tease, and he'd been sucked in when Amber had admitted Brianna had seen through Ore to understanding that.

"What is it?" Henry asked Rio softly.

Rio puffed out a sigh and spoke even more softly, "I guess I'm glad she's finally understood, but why do they care so much? The court game is just vanity and cat–fights. How can it even be a researchable topic that someone can get a diploma in?" (Reynold had begun their discussion by telling Amber that he'd gotten his diploma in that exact topic.) *Ah.* Rio had come to complain. Thayne listened with a quarter of his brain.

"I don't think you have to think exactly the same to have a partner," Marcus teased Rio. "If we did, Henry and I wouldn't have even lasted our first week. As it was I would've left in the first six months if we didn't have to stay together for me to live. A common goal isn't common backgrounds, nor even common beliefs."

Henry blinked at Rio and asked seriously, "Have you decided on a common goal yet, Rio? Have you and Amber talked about that yet?"

Rio shook her head, still impatient and wanting to complain more, not think reasonably about it. "I asked her what she wanted to learn, which she said was how to make friends, and she seems to be learning that fairly well. Like she's taking her lessons from Mistress Mizi and using them, she's been doing the same from my help. But we didn't talk about what we'd both want to do together."

Thayne raised his head and looked at the three. That was actually rather dangerous at this point. They should be getting to that agreement fairly soon at least. Henry was frowning at Rio and Marcus was looking concerned.

"Rio, do *you* even know what goal you could have together to make the partnership work?"

Rio looked away, then down and blushed a little. She scuffed her toe on the floor. "No," she finally whispered. "I don't want it either. Being with Mistress Ilena and serving her are the only things we have in common or care to care about together." This time even Petroi looked up to stare at Rio.

"That could be enough," Thayne whispered back at Rio. She turned to look at him. She still wasn't happy. "It's the wanting it that counts, though, if it is." He was quite serious. That's why he and Petroi were partners. Perhaps it wasn't so urgent for Rio because she'd always been accepted by Ilena as she was. For all Leah had been Rio's partner, it hadn't been a partnership in the same way. Leah had been a teacher and protector of Rio. Justinian had been a student of Rio, and temporary. If Rio was going to have a real and permanent partner, the desire to stand in her place had to be a stronger motivator than that.

Rio shook her head. "I'll talk to her about it," she obviously didn't want to have that pushed on her at the moment. "But I don't understand why she's so excited to understand it from the point of view of the game. She told me she hates the court game because she feels like it's just use and abuse."

Marcus tipped his head, then said, "Did she say she hates to play the game, or she hates what happens to her when she does?"

Rio frowned. "I guess the latter."

Marcus nodded. "She may hate that, but I think playing it is all she does know. It's familiar to her. She's struggling to understand the world from our point of view, or even any other point of view than the court game. As soon as it was explained from that point of view, she understood. While that's going to be hard for you when it comes to communicating and explaining things, I don't think you'll be able to completely wean her of that. Everyone has different ways of seeing the world. Once we understand as close as we can, we can communicate as best we can. It's not always perfect, nor easy, but it is more possible."

Rio blew out a frustrated breath of air. "Go and ponder on it longer, Rio," Henry said softly. "Come up with reasons why you do want it, why it could be important to you. What you'd like to see happen is good to consider, but often we don't get the perfect answer. What can you set aside? What can you compromise on? What are the absolutes — really the absolutes that you can't give up? Then talk to her again. Try to find that common goal."

When Rio left the room, she didn't go back to the Lower office and stay. Instead she went just long enough to dress for the weather, then she left the wing altogether. They knew she'd go talk to Ryan. There wasn't any other place she was willing to go in the whole castle, and she was too afraid to leave the castle grounds. Thayne caught Henry's scowl and Marcus' hand on his shoulder to help him calm down. That was the reverse of what Thayne would've expected. Thayne's brow furrowed as he went back to his work. Henry was struggling with something related to Rio.

-o-o-o-

Ilena stopped by Reynold's desk. "It sounds like you've been taking a lot of notes about us." She was bright and friendly in her tone of voice. Justinian watched her from his seat near Reynold. It didn't seem like she was upset, but sometimes she was and only started there.

"Well, yes," Reynold shifted, uncomfortable to have that noticed and called out.

"I'd like to make it official." That surprised both men. "We need a duchy historian. Please compile the story of the creation of the Grand Duchy from the start and keep it updated. It's a lifetime appointment: Chronicler of Tarc."

Reynold bowed. "I'd be honored, Mistress Ilena."

Justinian was proud of Reynold for being given that office, but his brow furrowed just a little. When Ilena had moved on to her next task — which was heading up to the Upper office to talk to Ore about something else which she did when she needed to stretch her legs — Justinian quietly asked Reynold, "Will that stick if they aren't made the actual Grand Duke and Grand Duchess?"

Reynold shrugged. "It's very unlikely they won't be. If she's said it now, she likely thinks she'll forget to later when it is official. I'd like to keep it regardless, so even I'll worry about that when and if it happens."

"Oh. Okay," Justinian could understand that. All Reynold had to really do was organize what he'd already been learning and write it up in history order ...after he was done with the research paper. But that was almost done. Reynold had had him review it recently. Justinian hadn't followed it very well, but what few things had stood out to him had seemed truthful. It was on Ilena's desk now. Petroi had just finished reviewing it last night and put it there this morning.

Justinian pondered on what it would be like, the history Reynold would write, while also returning to listening to the office as a whole. After a bit his mind turned again to Amber and Rio. He agreed with Marcus and Henry..., and Thayne. It wasn't very good that Rio was less ready than Amber to be partnered at this point. He'd actually been a little surprised Rio had admitted she wasn't. By the way they'd been interacting, he'd thought Rio was only waiting on Amber to be ready. He did understand how hard it was to come up with a reason to partner, though. He was still glad Reynold had had an answer he agreed with. While Justinian's reasons hadn't been solid enough to put into words when they'd talked, Reynold's answer had solidified most of it into a core that said very loudly, "yes, that's it."

Justinian wondered if the fact the girls didn't have to share a room was making it harder for them, too. He'd already instinctively understood that he and Reynold would share space, in Tarc and when they'd gotten home. Amber and Rio hadn't even yet. Maybe that would help them if they did? He wasn't quite sure why Ilena, nor Ore for that matter, hadn't made them. Then he shivered. He understood why *he* wouldn't want to, and was still having troubles with it. Maybe one of them had a similar trouble.

Rio had also been a doll of the Doll House. Maybe she was just as afraid to be in a bedroom with someone else. Then he remembered when he'd gotten a glimpse into one of those rooms and he wrapped his arms around himself. Oh, yes. Rio would be very afraid. They were single bed rooms, and while not as fancy, were very much like the rooms bad things happened in. Justinian shivered, very glad he and Reynold shared a two–bed room that was long and more like the barracks–like room he'd shared with the other man–servants–in–training.

It wasn't likely there was a place in this wing that the girls *could* be in the same room. He knew that two of the nurses were sharing a room, but they probably either already knew each other from before or had a different arrangement. He shivered again, wishing they could already move into the new Regent's building, for all it was only a foundation and partial walls. That would make many things easier for them, or so he felt. This place was nice and useful, but it really wasn't working as a place to live anymore.

"Are you okay?" Reynold whisper–asked Justinian.

Justinian gave him a wide–eyed silent response, then shook his head. Reynold shifted his chair to face Justinian a little better. "What do you need?" he asked. He'd had to help Justinian before, to get him out of the fears his own thoughts brought to him.

"Ah, ... ah." It was hard to decide. "I guess ...a hug, but I'm afraid."

Reynold moved to sit in the chair next to Justinian and gently wrapped his arms around him from the side. That helped, that it wasn't a full–on hug. The gentle pats on his head helped more until Justinian could relax enough to rest his head on Reynold's shoulder and breathe better. "Okay," he said when he'd breathed a few times. "Thank you. I'm sorry."

"May I ask what it was this time?" Reynold asked, releasing his hold on Justinian.

Justinian shook his head at himself. "I got lost in the bedrooms across the hall wondering why Rio and Amber didn't have to share one." He shivered again and Reynold patted his head a few more times. "I answered that one for myself very well," he was a bit bitter in his smile at his foolish tendency he sometimes wished he knew how to stop doing. He took another deep breath and said, "You can go back. Sorry to interrupt, but thank you."

Reynold nodded, moved back to the desk, and picked his pen back up. Then he turned back to Justinian. "You were worrying about their partnership?" Justinian nodded. Reynold smiled. "That was kind of you." He was lost again in his work.

Justinian sighed a bit to himself. Maybe it was kindness, and maybe it was a lack of understanding. It always started with wondering things, after all. He tried to think of the important things rather than the worries, practicing again what Marcus and Henry had suggested ...not that Rio and Amber weren't important, it was just the worries weren't.

Still, when Rio entered the Lower office again from outside, still frowning and looking upset, as if her time away hadn't helped her at all, Justinian was on his feet. When her warm things were put away, he was slipping his hand barely into hers, to take her fingertips with his thumb and first two fingers. He looked earnestly into her questioning eyes. "Please, come talk to me for a minute." Rio followed with him as he led her out of the office and up the stairs to two chairs near the doorway out into the garden. That was as far as they could go with snow falling today.

When they were sitting, Justinian put his partially fisted hands on his knees and took in a deep breath. "Rio. I can tell it's hard. It was hard for me, too. I only knew that I wanted to be part of the Immediate Family so badly that I did want a partner. Even then I didn't want it at the same time." He looked away from her, then drew in a breath and looked back to continue. "When Mistress Ilena told me to trust her, that she hadn't given me a partner amiss, I could only disbelieve and believe her at the same time. Disbelieve because I'd already learned to trust no one. Believe because I so desperately wanted to have her be the one to make that decision so I didn't have to, but could have what I wanted so badly." His eyebrows turned down at the outside in reaction to the distress he'd felt at that time returning again.

"It very much did help to hear Reynold's story, to have him tell me himself why he might be a safe partner to have. I don't think it's quite the same in your case. You've already talked to Amber about some of those things. But..., is there something I can do to help you? I thought maybe if you heard what Reynold and I decided, maybe? It's not very big or fancy, but it helped me finally decide it could really work for us: finding the common goal. I'd not been able to really settle at all until then, even for all my wishing."

Rio looked at Justinian sadly, then finally sighed. "I guess it can't hurt, and I know it'll help you if I've heard you out," she allowed.

Justinian appreciated that she was willing to let him help with the little he could do, even though she wasn't wanting to have to think kindly of Amber at the moment. He understood that, too. "Reynold agreed with me that my reason for being willing to have a partner was a reason to be obedient, but wasn't a reason to stick with a partner or a common goal that would help us have a path to walk together. It's the same reason you have to be obedient: because you want to please Mistress Ilena and be a member of the Immediate Family in the same way the other partners are. Even she and Master Ore are partners with common goals." Rio's eyes widened a little, in surprise he thought.

"But what that goal could be wouldn't come to me with my own thinking. Like Marcus and Henry taught me, it really did have to be the both of us thinking about it and then talking about it. I had it in here," he put his hand on his chest, "but I couldn't get it to be words, just concepts and feelings, some few wishes and thoughts. Reynold put it into the words I couldn't." He looked up and smiled at Rio, putting his hand back down on his knee. "He and I both love Tarc very much, the people and the land. He remembered that Mistress Ilena had promised him he'd protect Tarc from here. Our common goal is that we'll help her continue to protect Tarc and to help the Tarc all we can from here or when we're there."

Rio was staring at Justinian's face. He knew he was showing his excitement and happiness at having that as his goal, but he wanted her to see that: to see that having a common goal was a good thing. "Reynold and I have a lot of work still to do to be able to actually be the kind of partners the rest are for each other, but Marcus and Henry say that comes over time. Thayne and Petroi agree, that even they still have things they learn about each other on a regular basis and have to discuss and compromise on. I still see Master Ore and Mistress Ilena be surprised by each other, too.

"So I've been worrying about that part less — or at least practicing worrying less about it. When those things come up, or while we're practicing one, that's enough. One at a time is a lot better than worrying about all of them all at once when you don't even know what they all really are. Instead I'm able to focus more on the other things I'm trying to learn about being in the household and the Ministry, my other goals."

He paused and gauged Rio. Her demeanor had changed, but he thought she wasn't quite ready to be thinking seriously about it. "Rio..., why weren't you already ready for Amber to say she was ready? It seemed as if you were, anyway."

Rio looked down at her hands clasped together in her lap. "I think... I was hoping she'd give up so I wouldn't have to worry about it. It was lazy and wrong of me, I suppose. ...I still wish she would. I don't want to have anything in common with her."

Justinian laughed a little, covering it with his hand. "She wants the same. I'm not sure you can have a partnership built on the shared goal of not having anything in common, though." He looked at her soberly as she smiled at the joke. "But now that she's seriously said she can try, it isn't good to still believe that. Not when you've been acting as if you were also trying. That wouldn't be being honest, which we all know now is what makes you angry."

Rio looked away, down the length of the long main hall. "No, I know," she said quietly.

Justinian nodded. "Even you said it to her, that partnerships were built first on trust, not on liking someone. If you're not working on learning to trust her, too, then you need to work on that first, maybe. But I think that can maybe come after the goal, too. I have a very long walk to learn to trust not only Reynold but me, too.

"I have learned to trust that he's willing to help me. When I learned that, it was enough for me to be ready to discuss our common goal. I'm not sure he trusts me very far yet either, but I finally learned to use my words so that I didn't surprise him and so that he knew what to do to help me, so he's learned to trust that much, I think. Surely there's a starting level of trust you two can reach so you can reach the common goal."

Rio sat back. "Well, I think that was what I needed to hear, actually. But," her brow furrowed, "when did you hear that? I thought you'd gone out for the race lesson the time I told her that."

Justinian blushed. "Well, I did go out, but I wanted so badly to understand partnerships then that I waited and listened. I'm sorry."

Rio stared at him. "You can hear through exterior walls?"

"Glass isn't very good at making voices quiet," he corrected her.

"Oh, that's true," she agreed. He was relieved she wasn't terribly angry he'd listened in on their conversation. He'd gone to race after the conversation had ended, so she'd not known since he'd come back in with the rest when that was done.

It looked like she was properly thinking about her and Amber now, so he rose to his feet. "I hope some of all that helps you." He smiled at her. "You can do it. If I can, probably anyone can."

Rio laughed. "Well, you might think that, but even I've seen some that don't work out in the end. Sometimes a potential pairing really doesn't have a goal to work towards together, save for a temporary one so that the partnership ends at the end of the job." She shrugged then rose to her feet as well. "We'll see once she and I have had the time to get to that conversation." Justinian paused to take that in, then had to agree that perhaps there'd be those endings as well.

He was glad she was able to walk back into the Lower office more relaxed. He returned Ilena's smile of gratitude with his own smile of happiness that he'd been able to be of help. He was even happier when on her way past him the next time she had to move from her desk she passed by close enough to give him a happy head rub. He sighed happily after her. Maybe Rio and Amber would become partners, and maybe even friends, but at least he'd been able to make Ilena happy another day. And a head rub was a treat to treasure for a while, too. That and Reynold's new position.

Ore's head lifted to hear the somewhat surprising request: *Ryan to Ore and Ilena. Please come and meet with me this morning, if it can fit into your schedules.*

Ilena was also keenly interested in receiving that notice this breakfast. She looked into Ore's eyes brightly. He gave a nod. He could fit it into the morning since it wouldn't likely take long. *Ore and Ilena to Ryan. We'll be along shortly,* Ilena answered for them.

Being close to done with breakfast by the time the request came they were soon bundled up and holding hands for the walk from their building to Ryan's. Ilena leaned close to Ore and held his hand tightly. "I think it might be the get–pregnant herb has arrived," she confided to him.

"Ah," his heart fell just a little. He was past ready to have children of his own, and was looking forward to that part. The timing was a bit bad for the rest of life's requirements. It was going to be a hard year to have his wife pregnant and giving birth. So many things were already on Rei's schedule and Ilena's plate, and with possible war on the horizon things were suddenly a little too unsteady to face this simply. He wasn't too interested in having his own children parentless if they ran into the worst of the difficulties they didn't want.

Ilena was looking at his face, a bit concerned at how long he'd been quiet. He gave her what smile he could. She hesitated as they were passed by another small group of castle residents, accepting the brief bows with nods of greeting. "When Ryan told me about the herb, he did give me one warning that he'll likely talk to us in more depth about when we get there." She blinked at him a bit soberly. "He says there's a possibility of having more than one child in each birthing it's used for. We'd need to consider if that would be a problem for us, to have more than one."

Ore blinked, not sure how to take that thought. "It might be hard with just one this year. More... *haaa*, I don't know." He frowned slightly.

"But it could take over half a year to even get pregnant, or more, other-wise," Ilena pointed out.

Ore agreed, but..., "Well, let's see what the little Mister says in the details." It was a hard thing to think about in just the little time they had on the remaining part of the walk. It was still hard when they had the herb in hand and were on the walk back. He gave a rather bland look to Ilena. "Well, this time I guess I'll let you just do as you will."

At Ilena's expression his brow twitched and he pulled her to him, to hold her firmly, one hand on her back. She looked into his eyes and relented as he scolded, "But if there are complications, you will live. We'll have any others using the normal and natural methods, and only when I say so and life's calm enough to have the pregnancies and birthings also normal and natural."

"Yes, Ore," she agreed. He kissed her soundly until he was satisfied she'd remember it. It was hard to have her go through something like this when he'd already almost lost her thrice. Multiple births wasn't something to take lightly with her, now that he'd made Ryan explain in full detail what that would mean. It was just as common to lose the mother to normal term pregnancies as to lose at least one of the children to too early a birthing.

He sat and complained at Leah once they were back until she'd reassured him sufficiently that she and the other nurses would watch Ilena closely, particularly for the last several months of the pregnancy. It helped to hear that there were also herbs that could make the birthing happen earlier if it looked like carrying the children to full term would be detrimental to the health of the mother. He made Leah promise to have them on hand within a month.

CHAPTER 153 Chaos in Nijoushi

The House of the Sage Seraph was getting proud on the streets, particularly in the northern section of Nijoushi. Somehow the Head was coming into high levels of coin. They'd bought up all the little Houses that ran in the merchant alleyways. A lot of those Heads were now retired and sitting pretty themselves, quite content with their new lot in life. Those Houses that had only a small headway in the market district were pulling out of it, not wanting confrontation in an area they didn't have enough presence in. There were three other larger Houses in that district that weren't so interested in giving way. It was one of the lucrative areas, after all — particularly when they knew how to lean heavily on the businesses in the area.

Those four Houses weren't the only ones with territory in the market district. The House of the Queen of Night owned one entire street district of it and she as of yet hadn't pulled out of any of her large holdings. The three who were unhappy with how proud the House of the Sage Seraph was getting really wanted to know if there'd already been a deal made between those two. There was no word on the streets at all on that, though. As far as anyone knew the Queen of Night wasn't negotiating with anyone yet. There were only a few unconfirmed rumors she'd talked to the Red Lion.

With such a state running in the merchant streets, it was no surprise when the House of the Sage Seraph attacked their closest neighbor without warning. The news the next morning was a surprise: a portion of those that had run with the Sage Seraph had been merchant–employed guards. The other two Houses shivered at that news. The merchants themselves were speaking up and had made the decision to support the Sage Seraph.

The next House down, in panic, tried to lean harder on the merchants in its territory. They got attacked two nights later, and this time the merchant guards were slightly in the majority. The merchants were done being leaned on, having to pay too much hidden taxes, done with losing customers to the merchants of the Houses of the Queen of Night and the Sage Seraph because their prices were just that small amount lower. Not to mention they were ever so done with the threats. With one large House staying out of it, another one being willing to be helpful and reasonable, the merchants weren't afraid anymore. The final House Head caved, but asked if he could stay as a Lieutenant, particularly since they were on opposite sides of the market district.

After some negotiation and investigation, the Sage Seraph said yes, then had him and his first Lieutenant assassinated and put his own second Lieutenant in as the new Lieutenant over that side of the district. There was one final cleaning up of the nightwalkers of the three Houses after that, removing those who wouldn't be obedient to the Sage Seraph and his refusal to upset the merchants. He did business with the merchants, respecting them for being businessmen and women. He didn't fleece them or terrorize them. His people would do the same or move out.

One week from the Sage Seraph having his House move the whole of the market district was his, save for the Queen of Night's section. He tapped his finger on his knee, considering the moves he'd saved for last. She'd still not moved in the city. Her top operatives had been seen keeping watch over what was happening. His contact with Raine Marciel had told him that Raine would make sure she didn't move until this point in time. What happened next was anyone's guess or move, he supposed.

The Sage Seraph didn't want to move unwisely against the Queen of Night, but he wasn't thrilled to have a piece of his district in her hands. Not that he couldn't share that smaller section now that he held four times what he'd held before.

He did wonder if she'd be willing to pay him for leaving her section alone, but it wasn't likely when she was already prideful enough to stay out of the positioning for this long when she'd been the one to threaten them all from the beginning. And like children they'd fallen in line and moved to her whim. Which made him curious as to why she'd done it.

He closed his eyes and considered the map of the whole of the city. His section was consolidated. The Red Lion had been moving as well and seemed to have solidified his boundaries sufficiently. The Queen of Night still had her sections sprinkled around the city and to some degree that was coalescing as well; although, that was mostly because of the nightwalkers flocking to the banner of the Suiran Nightwalker King. The latter had consolidated enough since he'd finally come out and answered to the claim. Both Houses would fight together more likely than not.

He pondered it longer, then called up a house messenger. "Go to the Red Lion. Tell him I've sent you directly to answer for me: Has the Queen of Night talked to him? Is it wisdom to hold and wait until she comes out?" The messenger disappeared.

The messenger returned after a few hours. "Yes. To both questions. He was quite sober. I think he's allied to her on his own."

"Thanks." The Sage Seraph tossed the messenger the usual pay and pondered on that. Speaking to those in the room as a whole, he asked, "Anyone here been in Kouzanshi?" He waved up to the dais the two who raised their hands. "Tell me what the Queen of Night was like during the take–over there."

While they could only tell him what it had been like since then and the stories they'd heard on the street about that time, in the end sum he could only nod to himself. The Queen of Night was royal on the streets, not just in the castle. This was now the time to sit back, wait, and watch. At the next full–house time of day he gave his order: "Leave the Queen of Night's boundaries alone. More time will show us what she's thinking."

-o-o-o-

Rei sat in his place in the Lower office for the second Regional security meeting of the third week of the last month of the year. His eye landed on Ilena. Her posture was straight–spine, hands clasped loosely in her lap. The mantle of the Queen of Night and the businesswoman were on her. That might be good news actually. He raised an eyebrow at her, inviting her to go first.

"The city's ready for us to get involved," she informed him, confirming his slight hope. "There's only one final district that can't tame itself on its own. Mitchel," she tipped her head at the man on the other side of the table from her, "has confirmed our own opinions of that district and the Houses that hold it. It will of necessity have to be battle to clean it up, I'm afraid. I'd expect that to take three to five nights, given that it's not a single section of the city but interwoven throughout."

Her golden eyes fell on Ore, sitting next to her as usual. "The Suiran Nightwalker King and I are in negotiations as to if some of them will be owned by him or if we'll help the closest top Houses take them." Ilena's gaze came back to Rei. "I'd like Ore to take most of them. They're outside the natural boundaries of the other larger Houses. We'll of necessity have to place our own preferred House over the final district that's large enough to have one Head over it. I'm willing to take a few of the minor areas based on negotiations with that person.

"Once this battle's completed, Nijoushi will be run by four Heads. You should expect to see messengers from the other three in a few years as they become comfortable and begin to see that it's only reasonable to have some level of relations with the real Head of the city. I'm sure you'll do just fine with them, but because Sasou has sadly left that training in my lap as well, instead of teaching you as he ought to have since his hands are already so full, come and ask me questions if you're not sure you're dealing with them in a way to protect yourself right.

"It's quite a bit better to have a proper city council over the nightwalkers just as it is over the daywalkers, but to deal with them is just slightly different. If you make them enemies you'll have the worst nightmare living at your feet. If you're over–friendly they'll eat you alive just as surely but more silently and sweetly. As I said, I think you already have the right balance and know how to handle it, but please remember to not leave things to chance and forget important holes when I'm right here."

Rei tipped his head at her to say he'd heard her warning and would obey it. He knew how to deal with her and Ore in the main now, for all she certainly hadn't tested him to the worst degree she could and likely would. He wouldn't be surprised if she trained him if he remembered to get the training, and she'd let it be the test itself if he didn't. The future him really didn't need that ulcer. He made a firm mental note to not forget.

"Do we have your permission to choose the fourth Head and form the Big Four of Nijoushi?"

Well, Rei knew enough to not just say yes to that. He made her tell him the details of who were the options and why they'd chosen that particular Head. Then he was happy to give permission, for all Andrew rolled his eyes and sighed.

-o-o-o-

That night the Queen of Night, Suiran Nightwalker King, two Messengers, and the Queen's Guards went into town together. They didn't go in hiding nor did they go noisily. They were noticed enough that the quiet word ran through the streets that they'd arrived in town to talk to their people. The House of the Sage Seraph went on alert. They'd only just gotten settled, but had kind of thought that group might be seen about now. The unsettled parts of the city stirred, unsettled but still also not cohesive yet. Would she move against them this time?

"Landras," Ilena said soberly and quietly, "I know you're both still struggling with not having Danel replaced yet. Please be patient. Please continue to find people that have the capacity to take care of everyone to be over the other safe houses."

"We're to the point the House needs to move," she told them. They sat up and paid attention. The whole of the House had been waiting for the order to act to come. She detailed the plan that had been worked out in the Ministry offices before they'd come.

"But," Barakka frowned, "that gives you the south territory in the end. That's the poor district. Will there be enough?"

Ilena shook her head at him. "I've learned how to deal with that in Kouzanshi. It'll be enough as long as we have the lists, Crafter's Row, and I have the daywalker businesses." She named the captains she'd chosen to put over the safe houses in the south district of Kouzanshi and her Lieutenants settled. The captains were also some she'd trained in Tokumade, called in from other places she'd had them until now. They'd be new faces to Nijoushi, ...not that anyone in those districts knew the faces of the House of the Queen of Night anyway.

"And the west side?" Landras asked soberly.

All of the Immediate Family on the stand shook their heads. "That's where we'll focus second," Ilena said, "once we have the weak south side consolidated. Both Houses will move against it, and I'm going to go talk to the other two to see if they'll ally with us to get it properly cleaned up. The city residents won't go over there, but the visitors to the city don't know any better. That's not good for a city's reputation outside of it. It's past time that got cleaned up by even the Regent."

She gave them a significant look that made them think she'd also be making the city guard fight in that one to properly help them. Even the guards had almost given up over there, only patrolling during daylight hours from dawn to just after dark, and in groups of three or more.

Given that outline, they worked out the details of timing and numbers, then the Queen and King and their guards were gone again. Landras and Barakka put the word out that the House had orders and nightwalkers flocked to the safe house.

-o-o-o-

The rest of the order–giving was to be done with Ore and Ilena separated. The nightwalkers who gave allegiance to the Suiran Nightwalker King but not to the Queen of Night had grown to a rather large number, to be about the size of one of the previous medium to medium–large Houses. Aron had been hard pressed to call up more safe house captains himself, but had somehow been keeping up. Ore would be going there next to give orders to his House while Ilena continued on to her other territories in the southwest part of Nijoushi. They gave each other kisses on the last roof before they needed to separate. "Stay safe," Ore ordered Ilena. He knew how dangerous the south side was.

Ilena smiled at him. "You've seen where my Kouzanshi houses are, Ore, but I will. You, too." She gave him a warm hug to tide him over until they were together again. She knew he didn't really like to be out in the cold snowy city, for all the city was better than the castle. He held her tightly for a while, then let her slip out of his arms. They leaped for the next roof in opposite directions and were soon out of sight of each other. Ilena wasn't worried for him with most of the city actually neutral to kindly towards him at the moment and with Petroi and Thayne at his back.

Ilena was probably the most pleased of all of them to be in the open, stretching her muscles with the run, leap, and pull of being up on the roofs of the city. She'd been sitting at her desk entirely too much the last three weeks. The couples practice had kept her muscles from atrophying too much and let her have a physical outlet, but nothing was like a full stretching run being in the city was.

Here in Nijoushi there was room to sprawl. Not that humanity liked to very much when they had to walk or use horse and wagon. There were walls around the city, but wherever there was room on the outside of them the city boundaries had expanded. The buildings closest to the castle were side by side in some places so that more businesses or staff housing could be closer to the castle and it's money and needs. The houses and businesses in the nicer parts of town were spaced so that there was more privacy between them, were only three stories at the most, and regularly the streets and alleys were so wide that they couldn't be jumped.

Where the lords of the castle lived, if it was in town, there were wide lawns around their houses, protected by fences and sometimes even guard dogs with a few guards and household staff. That district was in the northeast corner of the city and extended beyond the old city boundaries north of North road for those lords and upper level administrators who wanted even more space and distance from the press of the people of the city. Businesses continued on in the north after the lord's manors where merchants who wanted access to that clientele but also had caravans in and out regularly had built up around the access gate to North Road.

That led to the west side and the inns and places that catered to visitors to the city. There were two Castle Road gates on that side of the city wall to allow said visitors to enter the city, along with other wagon trade traffic. The inns were no more than four stories tall since tired people didn't really want to walk up long flights of stairs to get to their rooms for sleeping in. There were more street vendors for food and other goods in that area as well. The south side had always been the manufacturing businesses inside and outside the wall and warehousing outside the wall.

Going in towards the city from that outer ring was more housing as the people who served the castle or the Nijoushi businesses had built up over time. Those houses followed the wealth as well: well–to–do staff on the north, getting–by staff or employees on the west and east. On the south side, as the old city had expanded towards the south wall and people houses had begun to get mixed into the businesses, they'd had to put houses right up next to each other, often with narrow alleys between two rows of them. The original roads had stayed broad, however. It being for manufacturing and the "unclean" businesses, the houses there were lived in by the poorest who did their best to get by, still needed but not paid enough to do more than live.

The night city as a whole had a glow that rose up from the streets so you could see people on roofs when they were moving either between houses, or if you dropped low enough, to see their silhouette against that glow. It was rather the opposite effect when walking on the streets. Then the lamps lit by the night city guards cast a glow downward on the streets to light the footsteps of the citizens who were walking to or from work and dinner during this time. They were fewer than those who made the city teem during the day, but it was currently still a comfortable level compared to the full depth of night when very few would be on the streets.

When Ilena got to the first broad street, she and the Twins slipped down to the alley before it, then walked two houses beyond it before going back up again. Here, Ilena followed Marcus and Henry. They'd traveled it before. She hadn't so much, and they knew where they could go safely. She'd been running ahead to get her exercise before now.

"How's the leg?" Henry asked Ilena, now that they were together and could converse quietly in the night.

"Fine," Ilena answered. "It's not as hard here to keep one's balance. The ups and downs are a little more invigorating because they're more frequent, but that's just a good warming–up." She breathed a bit, then wrinkled her nose inside the scarf that covered it. "Rather, the problem is actually we're not high enough in altitude. There weren't roofs to run on the earldom property so I only got this much exercise in the trees and in Kouzanshi. It's surprising that even the short fall from Tokumade to here makes a difference in how hard the air is to breathe."

"Well, that's true, but if you're going to go to Ichijou and even Yamanzar, perhaps you'd best get used to even heavier wet blankets lying on top of you. Or stay off the roofs there," Henry gave her a very scolding look that said she'd better be seriously considering the second option. She wasn't going to promise so she didn't say anything.

They slid to a halt to let another nightwalker three houses down and going perpendicular to them pass on through. They crouched down low until he was gone into the distance. Marcus quietly explained the layout of the area they were in and where they were going to Ilena. She listened intently as they continued on. The noises on the streets and in the houses would tell her the tenor and mood of the area.

A few more broad streets down and she suddenly slid to a halt and turned their path. The Twins heard it much later than she did. They tried to cut her off, but she was down to the ground before they could. By the time they reached her there was one man dead on the street, one man weeping. Ilena was pulling his cut and torn clothing around him as best she could, holding it to keep the man from freezing where the bare flesh had been exposed. She tossed her head at the dead man.

Together Marcus and Henry had his clothing off of him, now that he didn't need it. Ilena talked to the man with her quietly the whole time they put the clothing on him. She refused to let them take the cut clothing off of him. He was already raving and panicked at having her touch him as it was, even though it was to keep his clothing on him. Once they had him warm again, Ilena managed to get him to say where he was staying. Henry led them, keeping watch ahead of them. Marcus watched their rear. Ilena let the man go when his eyes caught sight of the familiar place of home. He nearly ran to the door and it slammed shut behind him. "Not the first time for that one," Marcus said wryly.

Ilena shook her head. "No." She shivered and looked up at the houses around her. They were up on the roof before they spoke again. "This whole area will begin to see assassinations like that from now on, all night tonight and until we're ready to really move. I want the message ingrained in them. No more." Her brow was furrowed under the edge of her warm hat. They continued to head for the safe house, leaving her alone until she was ready to talk. "Marcus, Henry, send it to Ore. I want his House involved in this part from now also."

Marcus sent it while on the run. He chose to tell the whole story so Ore understood why the order had been sent. Still, they got back from Ore, *Why? It's too pervasive isn't it?*

Ilena considered the question and herself. *Maybe, but nothing really is when there's enough manpower to prevent it. You know that from your own war and have understood it from Sasou's and mine. I want every nightwalker caught in the act dead because I want the person under it all to have to put up their head, to show where they are. We might be able to take the territory but if we haven't got the right Head of that House and they just stay the mouse in hiding we'll have an even harder time in the end. It's already a cancerous disease that needs eradicating. I don't need that spreading outside of Nijoushi.*

Yes, My Lady, Ore answered to the Queen of Night as the Queen's Knight. She shivered again. She'd probably have to send said Knight against this one directly. He wouldn't be an easy vermin to remove. The next order she sent to her Lieutenants told them to postpone at least three days. That long to put out the message of the assassinated might be long enough to get the awful rat to show their head, or to attempt to move out of the city in fear. Either way, she wasn't going to let this go.

"But," Marcus protested, "we already know who it is. Mitchel said."

Ilena pursed her lips, then shook her head. "We'll come out and keep participating in this until I know which scent is his or hers. I want confirmation that he really has the right person. Some like this never come out of hiding: the poisonous snake that no one sees." They grumbled at her, but she only looked at them with the cold eyes of the Queen of Night.

Her head whipped around as she scented the air. Both of them went on full alert. Six dead men later, all three were panting. "Weelll. You diiid come to talk to the rabble toniiight, tooo," the sibilant voice came from two house–roofs away. Ilena hissed back, but not a vocalization that one could hear. It was at the level of her own language.

Marcus and Henry had already called in the same way for the House members closest to them to come to their defense. They didn't move from their defensive stances, watching towards their thirds of the full circle. None of them were going to admit that the person was right, either. They'd not come in castle clothing. Petroi had made them wear the nightwalker's shabby as their disguise today.

There was a sucking, slurping sound, as if the speaker was sucking on his own tongue. The three froze and Ilena's head turned. They were already as low as they could get and nothing could be seen from that direction.

Whomever it was wasn't moving. Ilena's ears heard the next sound — a firm puff of air — and she was grabbing both Henry and Marcus and pulling them sideways. As soon as the darts had struck the roof, she was gone from that roof.

Marcus and Henry made enough noise and moved enough to sound like one of them had been struck and slipped. Holding still while three meant they'd likely defend themselves sufficiently. However, just two and they needed to keep moving. They moved to the other side of the roof, Marcus popping up one more time so it looked like all three of them had gone to the far side. Of course they had to clear that side of the few who'd already moved to trap them. Then they were moving again, staying below the peaks of the roofs so that the blow darts couldn't get to them.

Ilena went to the side of where that sound had come from, but it was her goal. Either that person or someone next to them had sent the darts: both sounds had come from the same place. She was on the same row of houses as her target by the time Marcus and Henry were over the peak of the house they'd started on. She was on the roof of the house the sounds had come from by the time Marcus and Henry had moved two more houses over. The heavy breathing of a man who was very afraid had been coming clearer and clearer. That man was toppling over from her first blow. The man next to him was very focused on where Marcus and Henry would appear next. He put his mouth to the blow gun again.

She snatched the long tube at the same time as that man died. She didn't need it to clatter on the roof and give her away. Instead, she threw it so that it clattered around the place the Twins would appear next, if closer to her. She knew what poison it was from the first set blown at them, but it was confirmed by the smell on the pipe and the person who held it. She'd let Ryan know it was in town so he had enough antidote in stock for it.

The scent on the first dead man on the roof was one she didn't like at all, nor was she in a hurry to touch him again. Not only did that one like to live in filth, he liked things she'd killed the Doll Maker for. She sat as far away from his body as she could, waiting patiently. For something to do, she counted the thuds on the roofs as they traced a pathway around from where she and the Twins had been cornered, passed her, then continued on.

"Hey, ah, boss," a very quiet voice said nearby in a place the Twins hadn't made it to yet, "we've lost them and lost contact with everyone on their path." Ilena tried to quietly replicate the slurping sound and a soft grunt of frustration. She got into position to attack again. She was only guessing after all. There was a soft carrying whistle off in the distance. Since it was one of hers, she didn't worry overly much. A similar sound came from closer in from several positions. She smiled. Footfalls were coming her way from the place the words had come from. She waited until they reached her side of the roof, then gave the same soft whistle.

The man spun around and his face met her foot. He kept spinning until he was face down on the roof. He slid a bit from the forces still acting on his body. She was still dropping. The silent man on the other side of the roof had moved at her whistle. He backed up rapidly as she turned towards him next. She didn't like his smell either. It was similar to the already–dead potential Head with blood intermixed with it. It had been a while since she'd fought a practiced assassin with serious intent. She began to hum, knowing it would carry here better than her voice would. It drew very fast feet, actually.

That made the assassin panic as soon as he could hear them. She kept him distracted and as far from the edges of the house as she could, only letting him get close to the edge that would put him closest to those feet. The thud of a thrown knife in the back of his neck was rather satisfying. He'd not gotten away. She made sure.

She was surprised to be wrapped in arms next. "Ore?" she whispered at him. She'd not expected him to come himself.

"And on the first day, too," he complained at her and the situation generally.

Ilena shrugged, then rubbed her hand over the top of his head and down the back of it. "Thank you for coming to rescue me," she said, teasing him but not in her tone. He needed to hear those words and not be mocked. He still wasn't comfortable with her getting into fights without him or he wouldn't have come himself. Before he could consider what she'd mean by those words other than gratitude, she'd grabbed his hand and pulled him over to the pair she'd taken out. *I need identification on these two.*

Henry and Marcus appeared. *The rest are taken care of and the area is secured by Children,* Henry said as he dropped down near her and Ore. Marcus was sparking a small reed light. When it was lit he held it over one of the men. Ilena let Ore get nearer to the bodies, but refused to get any closer herself. Henry and Marcus stared at the face, then lit the other one briefly. The reed light went back over the first man. *That's your poisonous snake,* Henry finally looked up at Ilena and said.

Ilena nodded, not quite believing him. *Toss him over the edge. Have him taken to Uncle. He's to present me the proofs of that claim. Toss the other one as well. The dart isn't one of our standard weapons. I want to know if he's from out–country.*

She pointed to the one Ore had taken out. *And that one. The smells on those two masked his smell and he was silent enough I wasn't sure he was there at all. I want to know if we know what assassin House he's from or if he's solo owned by this House. Once the morgue has the bodies cleaned up I want to visit them one more time. There are too many smells mixed up.* She frowned at the assassin. *And why he didn't attack me when the other two hit the roof,* she whispered. *He waited until he heard my whistle response.*

Marcus carried the reed light over to that man and looked at him as well. He frowned and motioned Henry over. *We'll have to clean them both up, but I think they're twins,* was Marcus' final summary of that.

Hm. Then that one might be the Head and this one the decoy, Ilena said with distaste. *That one liked blood, in addition to the other sick things this House does.*

She turned to Ore. *You may choose to come with us or go back. That was the only House I was even remotely worried about, and they were kind to come themselves. The order will still stand to eradicate it fully, however. I'm rather sure that wasn't everyone since not all of them fight. Most are interested in self–pleasure of the worst sort.* She got nods.

Ore waffled, then finally let her go on her own. They didn't want to be out that late tonight. They had this set of chores to get done then they wanted to be home in their own warm bed. However, half of the Children stuck with her and the other half followed after Ore. Ilena didn't complain. They followed far enough away Ilena would still be the trap if another Head tried to save his skin early.

-o-o-o-

Ore was still grumbling to himself on the run back towards the first safe house of his House that he needed to visit. He couldn't decide if he was jealous Ilena had gotten to have her fight first and without him, or if he was frustrated that he couldn't be in two places at once. He knew her back wasn't bare, but he really didn't like not being the one standing to protect it. He took an extra deep breath on the next intake of air just before leaping across the gap of an alley.

His back between his shoulder blades tingled as he hit the next rooftop. He didn't stop moving. Maybe someone had thrown a weapon up from the alley floor and maybe he was still feeling the aftereffects of his minor participation in Ilena's battle. He was still on high alert from that, he was sure. Regardless, one kept moving if one was being targeted. He did weave his pathway some after that, though. He didn't need to become the next target right at this moment. Too many people were relying on him for that.

Master Ore! hissed at him from his left rather urgently. He turned that way until he'd reached Thayne, three housetops over. He slid to a halt and took in the scene in the alley below them. Two blades had left his hand and thudded in the back of the man below him. They dropped to lie down on the roof and watched just over the edge of the roof.

The woman had held still for that long, not sure what had happened to make the man stop moving so suddenly. Then she was jerking out from under his arms that were becoming heavy on her as the dead weight shifted him down. She stared at the man for a second, then with a sob she was running down the street, holding her torn clothing to her chest, red with the blood that had been drawn either because of carelessness or sick entertainment. Ore was sure he didn't care to know which.

Ore frowned. *It's another trap, another set–up,* he muttered, frustrated. It could be for him or for Ilena, it really didn't matter. He sang just a little louder, *Where's the trap set at? I'd like to not waste my time this time.* Then he had another thought. *Actually, are there more than one, all around the territory?* That would take a while to answer.

Petroi was still far enough away from this location, though. *Eldest: go around this one and to the safe house. Get them up on the roofs. If they're going to try to take us out tonight, we can thank them properly for gathering up for us. See messengers are sent to the other territories. Get them all up on the roofs. Tell them we dance tonight.*

He frowned in thought a little longer. *Ilena, they've come out to meet us tonight. Shall we grant them their wish? Or make them wait on us?*

He waited until he heard back, *It will be a grand pain to go around them all and it's rather convenient to just meet them. It will add time to the expected schedule of when we get home, though.*

And shorten the schedule for the week. One or two nights out instead of most of the week isn't all bad, he countered. When she agreed Ore sang the long–distance code loud enough to be heard over most of this section of the city, using the method they'd used in Tarc to unnerve their enemies. *Ore to the House of the Queen of Night. They come to us tonight, hoping to take us out before we take them out. Come out and play. House of Mother, collect up the House of Father and bring them with you. They've set traps to draw us, knowing the debauchery we hate most. Trip the traps and dance tonight. Come and dance with the King and Queen, Children.* By the end of the call Ore's voice was quite firm.

He could tell when a nightwalker that had been in Tarc picked up the message. It was just as loud and eerie as his call had been. Eerie because it wasn't a language men of Ryokudo would think of as a language. Ilena always used sounds ears were either used to hearing as common background noises, or that were so strange the ear would turn away from hearing them, the brain not wishing to acknowledge them as a sound at all. Combining them into the patterns of speech twisted the hearer's brain. *Let the song of the disturbed be heard by those that should be disturbed. They've called for us to dance. Let's dance.*

Thayne had Ore's arm in his hand and was pulling him away from the place they were hiding. That had been long and loud enough for them to be pinpointed and attacked. Ore didn't fight it. They separated a little again as they went. The message reached the central safe houses first because they were the closest. Ore knew the south House nightwalkers had met Ilena because her own voice carried over the city, then.

No mercy to those who follow the path of the worst debauchery. We take them out from now until they're purged. The Queen will own the south and all will know it. The King's territories have been decided. Come dance and they'll be yours. When you reach an ambush, call aloud so that others can come and join in your dance until we've wearied them enough to meet the sun and moon in the clouds.

That got a lot of new voices very shortly afterwards. It was rare that the underworld battles were death battles. The whole of both Houses had just been told they could go all–out. That was a level of excitement and focus for all of them that they'd dance strongly to. It would take a while for the hot blood of the nightwalkers to calm down, but Ore suspected there'd be enough fighting this night they wouldn't stay hot–blooded into future nights.

The safe houses of the House of the Queen of Night in the east finally heard the news as well. From the northeast came the stronger deep voice of Barakka. *And shall we come dance as well?*

Yes, Ore ordered, *Both Houses. Keep the silence until you reach the closest of the King's safe houses. I can't reach them. See they're up on the roofs dancing with us. I'll give my orders after the fact.* That was irritating, that he couldn't talk to them, but he knew why Ilena didn't want to let his House know the secret languages. Actually, every established House had some form of secret language or other, sometimes hand signs, sometimes vocal. He didn't expect his House to ever be long–term established it was such a loose network of nightwalkers who just wanted to be independent while having some level of brotherhood. He sighed, yet again wondering why they'd wanted to push it on him. Idiots.

Thayne caught Ore's attention quietly and he went into the crouching run of the hunter. Thayne was paused on a roof one house over and one up from Ore when he got over the peak of the house he was on. They'd managed to work their way around to the back–side of the ambush waiting for him from the trap he'd tripped. He leaped over and up to be with Thayne. He picked his favorite sounds from an earlier form of Ilena's language and they undulated around that area. It definitely called the men on the closest roofs over to them. They approached cautiously, not sure why the strange sounds were going around the city recently.

Ore was pleased to hear several responses from not very far away, then he was fighting, a knife in both of his hands. It was different to hear Thayne kill instead of knock people out. Bones crunched and it only took one or two hits with his fists before they weren't moving any more. The first hit usually made it impossible for the opponent to flee, the second one was the killing blow. It was rather impressive that both hits from both fists were equally heavy. Thayne wasn't one of those with a weak off–hand. Ore decided he'd really rather not be on the other side of an angry Thayne (since it would take Thayne being very angry with Ore to actually hit him hard like that).

Ore's own knives were farther out from his palm than he usually had them. As he'd told Ilena before, he typically kept them held in the palms of his hands with just the tip or so held past his fingertips. That was a marking depth. When they were held so that half of the blade or more was past his fingertips they killed or heavily damaged his opponents. A slash across the eyes to blind, then a thrust through the throat. A deep slice under an ear. The small knives weren't enough to kill with an attack to the torso, but it was enough to maim an ankle tendon, knee cap, or elbow tendon. That wounding was enough to get in an attack that did kill.

The fighting was messier than that, of course. Opponents moved, dodged, made their own attacks that had to be dodged. Occasionally Ore and Thayne would fall back to rest back–to–back and take stock of how many enemies there were immediately around them. Their ears then would hear the fighting of the others that had come to Ore's call. None of them had the capacity to focus on the fighting, breathe, and make noise. It was the nightwalker habit to fight silent anyway. It was enough they'd come and were helping. However, when on the third pause there were still more numbers of opponents than Ore liked, he called again. *If there are more that can come, we're fighting rather a lot over here.*

That was all he had time for, but as the others fighting with him had their times to rest, they also called for more, to lead them to that place. Two pauses for Ore and Thayne later and Ore was pleased to hear more groupings around them. He wiped the sweat away from his eyes yet again to see that the number of opponents was now dropped to better odds. They were about to enter the fray again when three of those facing Ore fell as if in slow motion, but one after the other. His eyes continued to follow the circle around them until all of the five or six were no longer standing around them.

Instead, a grinning Ilena was on Thayne's side, down in a splayed crouch. *My turn,* she teased in a quieter whisper since she wasn't egging on her people nor the enemy. She killed with her hands or feet, leaving no blood behind.

Was that the last, then? Ore asked. For all Thayne was looking at Ilena, he hadn't relaxed much at all to release his fighting spirit. Ore could still feel his tensed muscles at his back. The air from both of their lungs rasped as they breathed deeply to recover.

Ilena pulled in to a more relaxed crouch and tossed her head. *Yeah. Sorry to be late. I had to get through one of my own ambushes to get here. That was fun, to meet them coming the opposite direction than they were expecting. The Children were glad to be called up and run with me. I think for both Houses the promise of finally getting their territories officially did it.* She frowned and sighed. *We'll still have to go visit them, though. They'll need to know the official boundaries to protect until the rest of the city understands.*

Ore agreed that having to go visit all the safe houses at this point would make for a late night. He tipped his head as he thought about it. When the last of the fighting noises in their area was done he called to the Children in the area, *We need a count of those still fighting, those places that still need cleaning out, and zones that are clear. Start from the most north.* He named the street they'd decided would be the north boundary for now.

They listened as the words came to them from the north, then passed them and continued on to the south past the wall and beyond. The northeast had been cleared by the nightwalkers that had come from Crafter's Row. The areas around the current territories held by the House of the Suiran Nightwalker King were clear as well. The areas most troubled still were the far south and some of the southeast and southwest. *Move to the south. Help finish battles nearly done, but let's focus on getting the last bit of the south clean,* he ordered.

Ore took up Ilena's hand and pulled her to run with him as he led Thayne and those with him towards the south. Just to her, he said, *We'll have it as a joint meeting on the roofs when the fighting's done. They'll all be there anyway.* She gave him a nod of agreement.

-o-o-o-

The next morning there was a bit of an outcry over the excessive numbers of corpses found in Nijoushi's southern half. The western and southern guard stations had to call in help from the northern and eastern ones, and even request help from the castle garrison. That was how Rei ended up finding out about it. He called Ilena and Ore to him first.

"I thought you were going to do that over time and more quietly?" he scowled at them rather fiercely.

Ore rubbed the hairs on the back of his head. "Sorry, Master. We were going to, but the Heads between here and the safe houses we were trying to get to decided they'd take us out first. It was just simpler and less time consuming to meet them immediately since they'd come out on their own."

"Why is this the first time I've heard of this many deaths?" he demanded to know.

Ilena wouldn't look into his eyes. "Well, like we said yesterday morning, the south district has been quite troublesome for a while. Most of the time it only takes wounding. This time it took more than that. We're sorry to leave a mess behind."

"It's a big enough mess the guard stations have requested help from the garrison and the city folk are quite upset!"

Ore raised an eyebrow. "Even if it's only seedy folk that needed to be removed?" Rei pursed his lips at him, holding back.

Ilena was a little more keen–eyed. "Then shall we help investigate and settle the city for you?"

Rei scowled at her even more. "Not only 'shall you', I expect it to be settled by tomorrow. Don't come back until it is. Then you'll explain yourselves to the city council."

They both bowed perfunctorily and left immediately. Immediate obedience was the best answer when Rei was that upset. Ore looked at Ilena a little sadly. "Master hasn't been that upset in some time. We'll be very busy."

Ilena shook her head. "It's best if we do help. We can spread the fame of the Ministry of Intelligence through the city now. Let's stop by the office first. Let Garen know we're on our way to the garrison to collect the men he can spare to the clean–up effort. ...And as many wagons as the castle can spare to cart away the dead."

Ore sent the message. He was pretty sure Ilena had a plan in her head to clean it up and settle everyone down by the time they'd made it home last night. That was her strength, after all.

Ilena collected up Mitchel, Grandfather, Leah, Rio, and surprisingly the three nurses and Justinian from their office. Then they were heading for the garrison and Garen's office. "We're here to help with cleaning up the mess in Nijoushi," got them into Garen's office rather quickly. Ilena explained to Garen exactly what had happened the night before.

"...So, we're sorry to cause a fuss, but we're here to help clean up the mess the city guards couldn't contain to begin with." She frowned a stern scolding glare at Garen, placing the blame of the state of the city guards directly on him. "I want to be the one in charge with Ore. We'll be directing traffic and investigations. The guards and soldiers will be doing the footwork, with the help of our staff," she indicated the ones arrayed behind them.

Garen unpursed his lips enough to say, "Fine. Meet the wagons at the gate and go with them. The wagons can cart you and the soldiers that I can afford to send into the city."

"Thank you," Ilena said. On the way from Garen's office to the garrison gate, she sent orders to the Family in the city. Specifically she called for water bearers and body carriers. She sent orders to the House to stand by to help take bodies off of roofs so they could be carted out of the city properly. Leaving them to rot on top of buildings would only bring disease and even nastier smells to that part of town.

Then she turned to Mitchel. "Call in all of yours as well. I want them identifying people. They're to help wash the bodies if more hands are needed for that and to make positive identifications to the guards who'll be writing down the who and what of the investigation. The goal is to be able to remove the majority of the wanteds and frequent arrests off the rolls of the guard stations in those sections of town. Your people know as much as mine or more. Those not dead yet need to also be dead by tomorrow. That can happen quietly in the prisons tonight and the bodies dumped before dawn with the rest."

Mitchel now pursed his lips at her. "That's worse than cold, you know."

She only glared at him. Ore snatched up her hand and held it tightly just before her mouth opened. She managed to only say, "You know..., I'm still only cleaning up after *you*."

Mitchel turned red and snapped his mouth closed. Ore gave them both looks that told them to cool down before opening their mouths again. Ilena knew that Mitchel hadn't been able to move even if he had kept tabs on things. Mitchel knew that it all had needed doing for all the method had been a bit different than they'd planned on before the night had happened. "One can only do what's presented in the moment," Ore said quietly. "No plan goes perfectly. What happened was sufficient."

They relented enough but stayed silent until the soldiers and wagons were gathered. Ilena's group took up one whole wagon, and they took the one in the front. Their black cloaks with the golden badge of the Regent stood out compared to all the white ones with the Ryokudo badges in all the other wagons. Seeing not only the soldiers coming to help but castle staff as well would settle the citizens.

Ilena stood up on the wagon seat and faced the other wagons. Her voice carried as usual. "Let me tell you truths about what happened last night." Ore and Mitchel both gave her disbelieving looks as she told them in summary what had happened that night. That she and Ore had gone into the city on Rei's orders to begin to settle the nightwalkers of the city, who'd been in a state of unrest for the last month or so. They'd been attacked on their way to the southern part of the city and had called out their Houses to defend them.

Ilena shook her head sadly. "You know who and what I am. I guess because they knew I'd gone into town they thought they'd take me out for good, to remove whatever influence they believed I'd be on the city underworld. I don't know the numbers. I only know that it took all of my House and the help of others to finally get Ore and I free of that part of town."

She waved a hand at Mitchel. "Minister Mitchel has been watching the city for as long as he's lived next to it, and probably longer. I've called in his people to help us as well. You'll partner up with either a city guard who knows the residents of that part of town well, or with one of Mitchel's people. Our goal is to confirm all the dead are rabble that should've died. If we've been able to clean up the city the same as we did the lords, traitorous, and prisoners, then we might be able to all rest easy for a little while." She ignored the reactions to that statement. Not all of them were bad, but most were suspicious.

She finished her general orders then sat down next to the wagon driver. Ore sat on the other side of him. Mitchel chose to stand behind them, holding on to the back of the seat for balance as they got moving. Ilena gave her orders to her staff on the way to the city. *Grandfather, you know the city now almost as well as Petroi. You'll direct the House and Family that come to help, being our point of contact with them on the southeast side. Petroi, you'll take the southwest side. Thayne take the central south. Stand on the wall so we can hear your voice clearly on both sides of the wall. Make sure the guard captains of those areas know you, know your face, and get regular reports from and to you. The city guards need to know what we can and will do for them.* She got three positive responses.

Leah, you and the nurses will pair up. I want two of each of you at the same washing stations Rio and Justinian are at. Keep your eyes on them and let the guards there know you're staff of the Ministry of Intelligence. You're to be our contacts with the Family helping at the washing stations. They can send you questions and you can ask questions as well. If we need to split you up into individual locations we will, so be listening for order changes. Again she received quiet obedient answers.

Justinian and Rio, you're bait. I don't really expect the nightwalkers to show up and do anything except watch today, but on the off–chance some of the non–combatants really are stupid I'd like to take out as many as will give themselves to us. Let them drag you out of sight, kill them, and drag them back to add to the piles. Help with the washing or with the carrying, but let yourselves be on the edge of the work and catchable.

They both shivered. Rio protested with some pleading, *But Mistress Ilena! You'll return us to our traumas and set Justinian back that much?*

Not to mention set the sleeping assassin loose? Thayne even shuddered a little as he added to the protestations. Justinian's eyes got even wider and his hands clenched tightly closed.

Ilena turned around in her seat. The look she gave them all was un-yielding stone neutrality. Her whole being exuded extreme disapproval. Rio and Justinian both caved in on themselves and humbly looked down, very unhappy. Ilena kept the silent punishment going until they all understood that she expected her Ministry staff and Immediate Family to always be able to act as supports in the field, not just as weights in the office. When the pair were sufficiently humbled she spoke to the nurses, teaching them how to take care of Justinian and Rio.

When the nurses indicated they understood she continued, *Justinian will only be able to handle two on his own acceptably. Be sure you tell us when he's reached that number. Rio should be able to handle four to five. Again, let us know when she's reached four.*

When she'd received nods, she moved her attention to her own guards. *Henry and Marcus, you'll be my runners as usual, but when you're not on orders: Henry you'll be hidden guard for Rio, Marcus you'll be hidden guard for Justinian. See you prevent them from slipping away into too much panic if they can't get themselves back to the nurses in time.* They gave her sober responses.

Ilena gave one more stern look to the young broken pair and they gave her small nods of obedience. *I'm relying on you to help me clean this city of the filth that's unacceptable in a society of peace,* she said to them a little more gently. *Every one we remove from the street is three more people who don't have to be traumatized this week. You can do this. I have faith in you.* After a bit, their backs relaxed. Having the altruistic reason to continue forward helped them both.

Ilena turned back around and sat royally in her seat. They'd arrive in the city soon and from that point would be on display to the citizens of it. It was important to show them the strength and conviction of the Toukas.

When enough time had passed for emotions generally to calm down, but before they reached the central guard station to talk to the city sub–general, Mitchel asked Ilena, *But what will you do about those who seek out the pain when they no longer have a source?*

Ilena gave a nod of understanding that was also their responsibility. *I've set Rei and his office to considering that. He also needs to be able to take care of his people properly. I've given him some suggestions based on my own experience in Kouzanshi. Most of them are just like the nightwalkers. They need a source of hope to counter the despair that drives them to seek the external pain to counter the internal pain that's killing them just as surely. He learned things in Ichijou that will help, too.*

Her eyes looked into the eyes of the citizens of the city as they watched the wagon train move through the city. Most people were curious but enough were relieved to see them that she was sure the word of the many deaths had passed through the gossip chains.

Ore's eyes watched the shadows. Whenever eyes looked at them with anger or threats, handsigns from him sent day and night Children chasing after them. They'd keep all the nightwalkers of the city in hiding this day. Today they'd entered as the Second Prince and Second Princess, Heads of the Ministry of Intelligence. It was good to remind them all of that last title.

They'd seen just how many nightwalkers had come out against them and then to their call. The city was already too full. Having cleaned out the worst would help with the pressure on the city and the nightwalkers generally. "Why were there so many last night, so many nightwalkers in the city generally?" Ore asked Mitchel. He hadn't thought it so full when he'd been running in the north before heading south to Ichijoutsu.

Mitchel shook his head. "It's mostly the same reason as the others. Too much corruption in the castle brought coin out of it and into the city. More coin was more that could be bought. Because we couldn't move against the corruption in the castle it became difficult to move against it in the city. Coin bought the guards, too." He gave a sidelong look at Ilena. "Removing the flow of coin out of the castle has caused even more strife in the underworld as the other sources became fought over even more."

"Which is why I couldn't postpone the restructuring of the nightwalkers," Ilena agreed. "As to the corruption in the city guard, I do hope General Garen has properly instructed this set in what to be watching for to gain the evidence he needs to finish that final cleaning job. I really don't want to have to step in and make him let me take that one, too." The hands of the man driving their cart clenched ever so slightly more on the reins he was holding.

Ilena turned and stared at him obviously. He began to sweat, but didn't say anything. She eventually turned away from him, but they knew he was going to watch what he did for a while, expecting them to be watching as well. He hadn't given them enough clues to say he should be in prison, but because he'd reacted at all it put him under suspicion.

On the off–chance it had been a reaction of distrust of Ilena or the Ministry, Ore said casually, "I think removing the greedy grasping hands from the playing field altogether only opens up space for the rest who are hard working to breathe in relief, myself. Then there's enough honest coin for everyone." Ilena nodded a single nod of agreement. The driver seemed to relax slightly. It was okay for them to appear cold–hearted for the sake of righteous prosperity in the city and Region.

Having cleaned up both ends of corruption in Nijou and Nijoushi after this week (assuming Garen would clean out the guards after today), they could finally get rid of the corrupt lower staff of the castle. They hadn't moved against them yet, other than obvious spies from other nations. Until now Ilena, Garen, and Mitchel had been using them to follow trails from inside the castle to outside of it. If the driver passed on what he'd heard as gossip in the castle, enough of that level of people would perhaps begin to move out of the castle on their own. They were hoping those that actually had places to hide would lead the Ministry to the final outside sources they hadn't been able to find yet.

CHAPTER 154 Treasured Bait

The streets of southern Nijoushi were filled with a fear that filled Justinian. (Well, he'd already been filled with fear since Ilena had told him what his job was going to be.) What regular citizens needed to be out on the street were quick about it. They did seem a little relieved to see that people marked from the castle and city guards were present in the streets finally.

The chaos in the open area they were setting up the collection and cleaning station in was helping Justinian feel a little more secure. No one would come do bad things where there were a lot of people. He helped with the setting up to keep himself busy and not thinking. He was near where the city guard lieutenant over this station was talking to some of the others when he overheard, "We need to get some depositions from the regular citizens who live here, to get their witness of what happened last night."

Justinian's eyes snapped to the lieutenant. That man's eyes were roving over the group as a whole. Justinian swallowed and walked up. "I can help with that, if you've got a guard that can help me. I haven't got writing things, though." He actually preferred that job himself. He could talk to people who were scared and trying. If he could help them feel a little calmer or safer because the Ministry of Intelligence was helping, that would help him feel the same.

All the same, just before he was collected up by his assigned partner, he went to the nurses. He stood shivering in front of them. "Ah," he hunted for how to say it. The smaller of the two nurses motioned to him, making the offer but letting him take the initiative. He swallowed, then was wrapping his arms around her and burying his head in her shoulder. The warm arms around him and caring comfort were what he needed most. As tears burned the back of his throat he swallowed again.

"It'll be okay," the nurse whispered to him. The other nurse patted him on the head, then moved away again before it could be overwhelming. "We'll hear you if you call, and Marcus will come. If he can't, we will. We're also Mother's children. We'll defend you."

"Can you defend yourselves from me if I get lost?" he asked.

The nurse pondered on that. "Not if you're assassin grade," she admitted. "But if you can hear our voices and bring yourself back to the point you can obey us, then we can help you regain yourself. Has Mistress Ilena taught you what to do?"

Regretfully Justinian belatedly remembered he was supposed to have been working on those skills. He'd used a modification of them to get through the first month or so with Reynold at the castle, but he'd not really been practicing them for what they were meant for. "Yes," he answered. "I'll practice them while I'm working so that I'll hopefully stay at least there, or can get back there and remember you."

He pulled away and looked at the two of them earnestly. "I actually still have some little control, but I'm not gentle until I'm not so afraid. If you can, order me and reassure me that it's safe." He frowned a little. Thayne wasn't here this time. He'd have to have more self–control this time, to believe them regardless of how afraid he was. "I'll do my best."

"So will we," the older one promised. Justinian took in a deep breath and gave them a nod. He was collected up soon after that.

"We'll just walk the street about two or three blocks and see who's home. If they'll talk to us we ask questions and listen to their stories. I'll write it down. Then we'll come back on the other side of the street and continue on down the other direction the same," the guard with him instructed when Justinian asked him what they'd specifically be doing.

"Okay," Justinian said bravely. "I can ask the questions. I've gotten really good at getting people to talk with my practice in Tarc."

The guard with him blinked, then smiled slightly. "I can believe that. If those people will talk to a Ryokudan anyone here should quite easily."

Justinian giggled just a little. "Maybe. I think Ryokudans are harder, though."

"Well, we'll see," the guard allowed.

"Ah, but will you knock?" Justinian asked, not sure he had that much courage. The houses here were so run down that they were more imposing than the people, as if the broken shutters and sagging eaves were frowning at them, telling them they weren't wanted anywhere near the door into those homes. The broken windows were like blinded eyes that would cry if they worked properly, but instead could only warn away any reasoning and sane human from trying to learn what secrets lay behind them. He was glad the guard agreed to do that part.

At the first house when they knocked, the door opened a crack. Surely the noise in the square had made the person curious. The guard got a look full of suspicion, then the tired eyes in the worn face looked at Justinian and stopped to stare at him. "Hello," Justinian said respectfully. "We'd like to ask you about what you heard last night. We're trying to understand what happened in the area. We'll listen to what you have to say."

The mouth opened, then closed. The person swallowed, then glanced at the guard and he tried again. His voice was very quiet and a bit raspy, but Justinian listened very respectfully as the person talked about hearing strange noises a couple of hours after dinner time, like "demons calling to each other", that came and went. He'd cowered in his bed and been startled a time or two by thumps on his roof. He complained that it had been hard to fall asleep even after the night was quiet. Only because he was so tired from his shift at work had he finally been able to sleep at all.

The guard asked, with a raised eyebrow, "And you're home now?"

The man scowled a little at the guard. "Ah'm on second shift. Ah'm up earlier than Ah'd like to be because of all that ruckus." He pointed at the square. "Ah'll be leavin' in a few hours to the job."

"We're sorry for the noise and to wake you, sir," Justinian said. "That's the city guard and castle soldiers collecting the dead to remove them to the grave. We didn't think it would be a good idea to just leave them around to cause diseases and troubles."

"At least they can do *somethin'* right," the man muttered to himself in complaint. "Next time come take care of it *before* it becomes this much a problem. Ah'd like to not die on my next walk home from work."

Justinian frowned just a little. "Where do you work?"

"Down at the tannery," the man frowned back.

Justinian looked around, then said, "If you're second shift, why were you home hiding in bed two hours after dinner? Isn't dinner time your lunch time? Aren't you still at the tannery until midnight?"

The man stared at Justinian, then nearly slammed the door in their faces. Justinian's toe was in the way. He was glad he was wearing a boot. The man growled through the bare gap of the door. "Ah's heard it while on break, and Ah cowered after Ah got home. Happy?" He glared at Justinian's toe, then finished slamming the door shut when Justinian moved his foot.

Justinian thoughtfully turned away from the door and passed the guard who was writing the last part down. Justinian paused between that house and the next, still thinking. When the guard reached him, Justinian looked up at him and said quietly, "Put a note next to that one. I think he's a spy for one of the nightwalker Houses that didn't participate but wants to know what's going on."

The guard gaped at him, then said as he obediently went to add that note, "Next time ask for a name first."

"Oh. Do we need to know that?" Justinian asked.

"Yes. If we need to come back and ask more questions," the guard said as his pen wiggled on the page.

"Okay. I'll try to get that, but most of them won't talk if you ask them for that."

An eyebrow was raised at him. "If they're legitimate, they do."

Justinian thought about that, his head tilted to the side. "Well, I guess they might," he agreed, "unless they have something different to hide. I won't promise I'll press them for a name, since the information's more important to have, I think." He turned towards the next house. "He would've given us a false name, anyway, unless he knew the name of the person who actually lives there — but no one does."

"How do you know that?" the guard asked him. Justinian thought it was more a testing question than because he already had a formed opinion on the matter.

"He knows we might come back on a later day, and he doesn't know what time the actual owner would be there and he doesn't care. If he was impersonating a real person who did live there, they'd be at work right now, not waiting to go to second shift." *Or dead*, Justinian added to himself, but he was quite certain that man hadn't killed anyone recently, and that he wasn't Ilena's.

Justinian wasn't surprised that only one in four houses or more had anyone come to the door. A portion of those would talk to him through the door but not open it. Some cracked the door open, curious as to who they were talking to. Some of the first he could get to open the door by promising they were there to make sure that part of town was going to be safer now. Those he was glad he could help be a little less afraid. There were two houses that he was afraid of and he made the guard mark them special, but he didn't really say anything about them to the guard.

Instead he called to Ilena, *I'm working with a guard to get depositions. I'm having him mark the houses that I'm quite sure non–combatants of the House you want to get rid of live in.*

There was the typical pause. Lots of reports and notifications were going around on the air generally. Then he heard above him, *Justinian, which ones? I'll mark them for the House to check tonight.* Justinian pointed to the two they'd passed so far so Marcus would know. *Okay. I'll ask for the report when I'm here.*

Is it something I can do? Justinian asked. *I know you're busy.* Marcus had been called away a lot and had been answering a lot of questions from both Ore and Ilena.

No. It's got to be marked up here on the roofs, Marcus chuckled a little. *Besides, we don't need the guard wondering what you're doing and learning how we mark houses.*

Oh, I guess that's true. But he's going to wonder why every now and again I'm pointing around, Justinian pointed out.

Just stand and look at them directly for one second each. That's sufficient, Marcus responded.

Justinian nodded and hoped this door would be answered. The last four hadn't been. He was glad they were headed back for the square. To not get knocks answered was more unnerving than to get grumpy people to talk to. He wasn't sure why, but it was. Maybe because it made this part of town feel even more dead and hateful of people generally.

-o-o-o-

Justinian was nervous about being jumped, even by the guard he was with, but the work kept him just busy enough to not panic in the time they worked their part of the streets in that area. He and the nurses weren't surprised when the older one and he were called on the air to go to another station farther out to the southeast from their current one. They'd all started closer to the central part of the city and they'd work out from there.

For all they got moved, the guard Justinian had been working with did not. That was his station generally. When they got to the next station, bodies had been piling up already for a while. Family was taking care of them, but Justinian was told he was trained enough now in getting depositions he'd be working that job in this area now. He gave a rather terrified look to the nurse, but she smiled and gave him the encouragement he needed yet again.

After the second house to not have anyone home, Marcus whispered to Justinian from above. *Justinian, this guard is one of the suspects. Watch him. If he goes for you, don't let him touch you, then scold him. He'll likely deny. Let him, but let it also be part of your evidence against him. If he argues with you, argue back once, then let him win. We've set up a trap for him but it won't hold him if he's been paid enough. You can't kill him, but you can knock him out and complain very loudly on his third attempt. Keep it all as public as possible. I'll show up and help you drag him back. Keep your eyes on me until you're calm again. And remember your lessons.*

Justinian's fists clenched. He drew in a deep breath like Ilena had taught him, then gave a small nod and went back to the same sort–of–relaxed he'd been before. It helped to know that others were going to be involved, that he wasn't alone. And someone who claimed to protect the citizens but was willing to be bribed to hurt them shouldn't be in such a position of trust.

That thinking helped him when the first attempt came to grab him and pull him a direction he didn't want to go. He slipped out of reach enough times for him to know it was obvious. Then he turned and glared at the guard. "Really, you don't want to do that. I'm not yours, nor whomever paid you's. Don't touch me. Do your job as a guard of the city properly."

"I am," the guard protested. "I only wanted to get your attention."

"You don't have to touch me to do that," Justinian answered coldly. "My ears work just fine." The guard fumbled the apology, but Justinian ignored that.

The guard was coldly silent after that, only participating as he was required to. Justinian figured he was fuming and trying to find a different way to capture him. When they'd reached the end of their required number of blocks to the east of the cleaning station, Justinian turned to cross the street. "Where are you going?" the guard asked sharply.

"This side is done," Justinian answered. "It's time to go back."

"No, we're required to do another two block's worth of houses, then go back," the guard argued.

Justinian stared at him, then took a breath and argued stiffly with him until the guard got a little too angry. Justinian backed down from the argument but narrowed his eyes and said, "Fine. But again, don't touch me. You won't like the consequences."

"Why would I touch you when we're on a job?" the guard asked, frustrated. Justinian only turned and walked to the next house.

They were nearing the end of that block when a young man hurried up to them. "Mister Justinian, you've been called back to the washing site," he gestured back the way the two had come from.

"Why?" the guard immediately said, very suspiciously. "Who are you?"

The man blinked at the guard, gave his name, then answered, "I don't know, I've just been sent to fetch him."

The guard pushed out his chest self–importantly and growled at the messenger, "Tell them we're not done with the depositions. We'll be back soon enough. It's not safe enough to be out here just one of us, and I'm not going to waste the time to go back with him, then both of us come out this far again. They can wait." He waved his hand impatiently at the messenger, to send him back. Justinian protested, too, but the guard pulled on his city guard status and insisted, enough the messenger had to relent and leave without Justinian.

Justinian glared at the guard and said, "If I get in trouble, I'll tell them your name and they can discuss it with you."

The guard glared back and dismissed the threat. Justinian wasn't sure why the guard was so insistent. Surely his black cloak should give away he worked for the castle, not the garrison. Was it not understood that he was part of the Ministry of Intelligence? Had that information not been shared with the lower level guards? It felt more like that was it than that the man knew and wanted him anyway, ...except for this newest insistence.

After everything else going the way Marcus had told him it would, it wasn't surprising when at the next alley entryway there were sudden hands at his back, pushing him into the alley. Because they'd both come to solidly pound on him with the push, there wasn't any getting away from them. Justinian stumbled into the alley, managing somehow to not fall down.

Even still, his hand went down on the ground and with a flip forward his foot was meeting the top of the head of the person leaning forward to grab him with two hands. As he ended up back up on his feet, he was suddenly very worried. He was quite sure he'd broken the neck of that one. He couldn't stop moving, though, since the guard was coming into the alley behind him and he'd been told to keep the whole thing as public as possible.

His next kick hit the guard in the arm, hooking it just enough to spin him back around. When he'd spun just enough, Justinian's shoulder shoved him back out of the alley and helped the spin to put the guard on the ground. As his fear–reaction brain calculated for the next action, the smells on the man behind him finally reached his reasoning brain and reassured him that the man had indeed been someone to kill.

He spun to put his body out of the center of the alleyway, so that anyone coming from that direction would have to exit it and come around the corner a bit. He was relieved to see it was still empty save for a shadow presence far enough back and unmoving as of yet. And that seemed to be the back of the person as well, now that the alley was clear.

"What are you doing?" Justinian's clear voice was hard and cold and not quiet, although he didn't shout, since he never shouted. "Why would you send me into the arms of someone who wishes to kill me? There isn't anyone else here who would've done it." His foot came down on the elbow of the guard who was moving now to stand back up. The crack made the guard cry out and collapse back on the ground. "I told you. Don't touch me. I'm not yours to touch, nor anyone's to take."

The guard was rolling on the ground, holding his broken arm. The eyes that looked up at him were confused and the pain made the guard's eyes water. Feet landing on the street let Justinian believe that Marcus was finally coming, but he made sure of the guard then looked.

Marcus was indeed running up to them. "What happened here?" he called out. The hand he put on the guard was grabbed, but Marcus instead of being pulled anywhere broke a finger of the guard. The guard gasped and immediately let go, his eyes going in surprise to Marcus' eyes, and then to his cloak, and then sword. The guard groaned.

"Let him come, Justinian," Marcus looked up into Justinan's eyes and held them. Justinian heard hesitant footsteps in the alley. He backed up to be out of the way and out of grabbing distance and nodded.

The person who'd been at the end of the alley came out and stood next to the guard, close enough to see his face. "Yup, this is one of them who paid us, and took the gold from the noble," that person said.

Before the guard could do more than have the thought of killing the witness, Justinian was back by his side, pinning him down. "I *will* kill you with the next blow," Justinian said very quietly. "Decide right now if you're going to relent or if death is preferable. Marcus won't be able to hold me back for longer than one second, maybe two." He was glad the witness had jumped back as soon as he'd realized that Justinian had moved that close to him. That was healthier for all of them.

The guard relented in extreme surprise and fear. "Back off, Justinian," Marcus said immediately. "I'll hold him."

Justinian obeyed immediately, but he still warned the guard one more time. "Don't move at all. Not even to run away. I've been released and that will be just as dangerous as anything else you could do. Just breathe quietly until Marcus decides what we're doing next." He got obedience and pointed into the alley. "That one is dead, Marcus. He reeks, though, so I think that was okay."

"Yes, if he reeks. Mistress Ilena says that about them, too." Justinian could understand. Marcus frowned at the guard. "How they could've afforded to hire someone to take you, though...." His fist clenched tighter around the guard's neck. Then he looked up at Justinian. "Can you smell it on the air, or only on the body?"

The question surprised Justinian. "I don't know?"

Marcus gave a nod, then whistled. Justinian moved back a little more, but not so the guard was outside his range. Two more men showed up behind Marcus. "I'm changing the plan a bit. Guard him here. They might come and finish the job. Take them out and add them to the pile if they do. I need to focus on Justinian a bit and do a little more investigation."

-o-o-o-

When the guard was under guard, Marcus moved to face Justinian at a distance Justinian found acceptable. "You okay? Under control just enough?" he asked.

Justinian nodded. "Do I calm down now?"

"Can you hold it a little longer, actually?" Marcus asked. "You're doing very well this time."

"Maybe," Justinian answered.

Marcus gave a nod. "I want to send you hunting. That heightened level often lets the senses be more sensitive. I want to know where that one came from, as far as you can track his path," he pointed to the dead man in the alley. "It's new for you, so if nothing comes of it, that's fine. I'll be following along with you. Just let me know when you lose the trail, or find a source."

Justinian looked at the alley, not really wanting to go into it, but when Marcus moved out of the way, he did anyway. The smell of the days he wanted to forget rose up into his nose again. He really didn't want to be there smelling that. "Go!" The order from Marcus spurred him to leap forward and run down the alley. He focused on the smell that was fainter now that he wasn't by the body.

He paused at the exit to the next street, crossed it, and moved directly forward into the alley in front of him. That instinct was right. The scent was held in very well by the walls. Out in the street the air moved too much. He tried to not let go of the fighting instinct he was holding. Having the scent spur him quickly through the alleyways helped.

The first alleyway directly in front of him to not hold the scent made him pause. He went back to the exit of the alley he'd come from and checked to either side. One corner that faced the street held a stronger scent of it, as if the man had been leaning against the wall. He turned that direction, which was to his right as he'd first exited the alley, stepped onto the street and looked around. Slowly he walked down his side of the street passing the steps that let up to the doors. Here, like all the places of these streets so far he'd walked, the houses were nearly pressed up against each other, or really did share walls.

Most of the doors he passed by, but in one place between steps he moved to be closer to the walls. He moved his head to get any scent at all. It seemed to be there, but very faint. He crouched down and it became stronger. Perhaps the man had crouched there to rest or hide. He moved away and back to the passage in front of the steps. Two houses down and he frowned. Something had changed, but in the past he was following.

Justinian moved backwards until the scent caught his attention again. He took one step forward, then on a whim one wide step left. Justinian zigged and zagged a bit as he crossed the street at an angle until he was about four houses farther down the street but on the opposite side. He paused and let his fighting sense check the area for him. He moved again, but this time it was more to hide that Marcus had come down from the roofs and was crossing the street at quite some distance from him. This street was quite wide, so he supposed Marcus wouldn't be able to jump that distance unless he could fly.

Another five houses down was another alley. Justinian decided to pass by it first by a few steps. He didn't like that there were doors in the alley farther down beyond the next street. He remembered what it was like to go to Ilena's safe houses with Ore and the others. There would be guards at about this level, or maybe the next street. That might be dangerous for whomever the guard was.

He paused just past the first set of stairs. *Marcus, stop at this alley but go to the other side. I'm going to go around the block. I think it's the next block down, where the doors in the alley are, but I want to confirm on the other side without going through this one. I might lose where this is by going around the block. If you're here I'll know where it is.* He got a positive response and went back to walking.

He was hit with a sudden whiff of the scent he didn't want to smell, and jumped into the middle of the street. *What is it?* Marcus was worried for him.

Mark this one. It's one to burn down. He hated that house with a passion.

Okay. We will. It's okay. We'll take care of it now that we know. You can keep going for now. Marcus was soothing in his tone, promising it.

Justinian took a bit to calm down because he had no interest in taking a deep breath to do it while standing in this place. When he could move again, he didn't get quite so close to the houses. He had Marcus' companion that was still following him up on the roofs mark another two houses in that half of the block on that side. He rounded the corner cautiously at the next cross–street. When he only saw normal people walking, and not very many since this was working time, he continued forward. There were only normal houses along this shorter side, then he was turning the corner again.

He blinked and paused, his eyes staring at a person who was sitting on the steps of the first house on the other side. That person had their elbows on their knees as if they were tired, and the head hung down too, until the head lifted enough to look at him. He blinked at those eyes, then moved on. *That's the guard,* he said, marking him too. He liked that he could mark and move on, instead of have to kill while in this state.

He almost relaxed too much, almost lost the scent he was following. It helped that the first house for him to mark on this street wasn't too much farther down, and was the most run–down scary–mean looking house. He gave it wide berth. *Mark,* he said. He tried to put his attention back on the street and what he was doing when the whole of the street seemed to widen then narrow. The houses looked like they were rising up to swallow him up. He dropped into a crouch and put his arms over his head to prevent them from eating him if he could.

Just–ii–nian! he was called to. He knew that voice. The people he loved called him that way. He took three deep breaths, trying to remember why he was hiding. *Just–ii–nian! You're almost back to me. Come. You can do it.* Then there were words but they weren't directed at him. They were almost too quiet to hear from where he was. He took one more breath and looked up towards where the words had come from.

The houses still wobbled in his sight, but he could make out a figure on the roof of one down by an alleyway. *Marcus, what was I doing?* he asked plaintively.

Following a reek you hate, to show me where the evil is. Marking the houses that have it so we can burn them down, Marcus answered and called kindly, *Come. It's enough. Come to me.*

Justinian took one more breath. Right. He had been doing that, or something like that. Trembling he tried to stand, but his body wouldn't. It really didn't want to. Instead it wanted to stay crouched like a frightened hare. He put his right fingertips on the ground. The feel of the rough stones rubbed off the old cobblestones and pulled out of the dirt between them grounded him.

His left hand clenched into a fist and he fought the old fear. Pushed against it with the will that wanted to be part of the Immediate Family. Demanded that the present was what he wanted, the past he wanted to kill, erase from him. With a burst he was suddenly running down the street, still on all fours: hands and feet. Like an animal he pushed himself until he was past the alley Marcus was standing over.

He slid to a halt at the second set of steps, slipped into the narrow space between the houses, his shoulders pressed by the outer walls of each house, and faced the continuing alleyway on the other side of the street. *It's there. The place I hate is there.* He was absolutely sure of it. The tang of blood was almost stronger than the other scents he hated. *Death plays there, taking what's left over after the others play. Kill it.*

That's the plan, but hold for now, Marcus said gently from above him. *More come. If it's the king ratsnake, don't let him escape. Mistress Ilena wants him dead over all others. But don't put your own life on the line. She'll be very unhappy if you die because he has too many little snakes protecting him. Wait if you can for the rest of us to come play, too.*

There was a pause, then Marcus asked, *What frightened you earlier? Can you control and move your body sufficiently or is there a poison in your system? One of the fights last night had a dart gun blower involved. If you've been poisoned we need to get you the antidote.*

Justinian considered that soberly. He'd not heard anything, nor felt anything. He thought he'd at least have felt it. His whole body was so tense this whole time nothing could prick the skin unnoticed surely. He licked the top of his mouth. There wasn't the taste of a poison in his saliva. He'd learned that when a poison entered the body it could be tasted, even if it had entered by another way.

He shook his head. Certainly the odd visuals he was having could be related to a poison, but..., *I don't think that's it. I think the scent became too overwhelming so close to this place.* He shivered. He didn't want to be this close either, but the scent wasn't as strong. There might be a small breeze blowing it away from him on this side.

He considered that, replaying the run in his mind, this time while looking at the houses on that side of the street and alley. *It's possible that whole half block is houses of this kind: sex and death. The guard sits at the first one to protect them all, rather than at the alley entrance where the door to the lair is.* Speaking of which, he wondered what the reaction of that guard had been to his sudden fearful reaction and run.

He didn't have to wait long to find out as the man himself appeared in the middle of the street to look at him. Justinian quivered with the effort it took to hold still. "Are you afraid to come here?" the man asked softly. Justinian could only blink at him. That would be both a correct and incorrect assumption. "You know what happens here, don't you?" he was still being soft, as if trying to comfort Justinian in some sick way. "Do you want it again?"

Justinian shook his head without looking away from the man. He never wanted anything like it anymore in his life. However, it looked like the man had expected that answer. "Well, that's okay. The drive comes anyway. The urge to feel like life is real again." He held out his hand in offer to help Justinian overcome his reluctance to enter that kind of world again. Justinian backed into the space even farther.

The man, emboldened, came closer and talked to him more, but Justinian wasn't listening anymore. He was watching, calculating. The man crouched down to be closer to the level of Justinian. Before he could think Justinian was completely refusing, Justinian moved just a little. The man held out his hand again to encourage Justinian. Justinian let out a sigh and the man relaxed completely and smiled.

He died with that smile on his face, Justinian's hand at his throat snapping his neck as he flew at him and slammed him to the ground sideways so hard the head bounced and snapped a second time. He quickly shoved the body into the very narrow space between houses where he'd been hiding, then crouched in front of it again, to keep the body hidden.

They'd been between steps. Only someone watching from directly across the street would've seen it. He watched those locations closely for any movement in the broken windows, listened for any slight sound that anyone else would be coming to look for the man, look for him.

-o-o-o-

Really, he's quite frightening, a voice Justinian didn't recognize said from the roof of the building he was watching. His eyes snapped up to look for the source.

Well, yes. But we're quite proud of the King's Assassin. He's learning his lessons very well, and does such a good job at everything he does. Justinian settled down to hear Marcus still above him. If there was Family now with them then they might get this resolved soon enough.

Really, can we just burn it down? he asked plaintively. *That's very big, and the smell won't let me go in. Burning it will remove the snake and the smell, right?*

Well, that's not all that bad an idea, another voice said, shocking Justinian so badly he nearly jumped up to the top of the roof. He did jump but tried to not move very much from his hiding place. He was supposed to stay alive, after all.

Mother?! You've left your post? He felt very bad about that.

No, Justinian, she said soothingly, *it's okay. I've left Ore and Mitchel in charge. The guards are more comfortable with that anyway. This needs addressing and they agree. While it might or might not be where the snake himself lies hidden away, it definitely needs to be gouged out so the leg can heal. A burning cauterizes to remove the infection and would save us from the dangers entering the safe house of another city House brings. We've already surrounded the block.*

You'll have to be very patient, though, Justinian. When the burning's done and cooled enough, in about six hours, I'll want you to go in and sift through what's left of the room the door in the alley leads to. We need to know if the Head was in there or escaped. That will be the hardest since the smoke will taint the smell. We'll also lose any clients we might've been able to save and heal that are already in there.

Justinian shook his head. *It's daylight. The innocent ones are working to earn the pay to enter. Those who are trapped want release. They aren't allowed out.* His head shifted from side to side as if he were a trapped or confused animal himself, but it was because he was uncertain. *Is it safe to enter the street, to come out?*

There was quiet for a moment, then a soft, *Yes*, from Marcus.

Justinian crept out of his place and slowly moved to where he could look down the alley. It was empty still. He ignored it then since the House was watching it. Instead he closed his eyes and used his ears and to some degree his nose. Slowly he rose to his feet then walked just as slowly down the street, his head turned towards the buildings he'd barely been able to pass before. Quietly he reported as he walked, *This one is sleeping, waiting. ...This one also. ...This one...,* he paused and frowned, then turned his head so his right ear was facing the door and upper windows better. He could just make out soft intermittent sobs. He knew those intimately.

This one sleeps, but one who's like me cries in his sleep. Top floor, a back room. He was listening so closely he heard the footsteps of the nightwalker walking towards the back of that house. He moved on. At each place he reported what was in the house, how it felt, what he heard. Then he turned back around and did the same for the houses on his side of the street he'd already marked. He reached the central alley and continued on, turned and went back to the center again.

Good boy, Justinian, Ilena purred. *We'll watch this side. Go around and do the street on the other side. Watch from there for anyone to escape that shouldn't.*

Justinian took a deep breath of the fresher air, then ran down the cleaner side. He checked the cross–street and it was clear. Both houses in the center of the street on his side he marked and reported on, then he was on the next street over. His wide eyes took it in. It was even worse. He put his hands over his ears. *They all cry. All the houses cry.*

The houses cry or the people in them do, Justinian? Ilena asked.

Justinian paused, then took his hands down from his ears. *The houses.* They shouted at him, their dilapidated state crying out their distress to his eyes and mind. He took a breath. It wasn't the houses he needed to care about. He closed his eyes again and walked slowly down the street. Pointing to his right, he named the grief there. Pointing to his left, he named that grief. Then he moved to the next pair. A few pairings the left–hand house was empty. Almost all were sleeping. However, the closer he reached the alleyway the more he trembled and the more he slowed until his feet stopped.

Softly came encouraging words from his Mother. *It's too much weight to bear all at once. Just the left–hand ones first. One at a time until the next street is reached. One is one more saved, one more punished.* He could do that. He gave a nod and shifted in his dance steps until he was nearer the steps on the left side. Then he did continue on one house at a time. He didn't point this time, only named the grief.

His head turned about halfway down the second half of the block to face the right side of the street. *They've seen me, been watching me.*

Mmm. And you've been being odd in their eyes, so they're curious and only watching for now. Give them reason to continue to believe you're innocently mad. Continue on. They won't move until you come back, and then it'll be to see if they can tempt you in. Justinian agreed with Ilena so turned his head away again, not having opened his eyes even then, knowing that if he made eye contact with them they'd become afraid and act to hurt him.

Still, it had perturbed his state just enough that his feet danced a little now. Smaller than the dance itself, his steps followed the sword dance's dance of grief, the solo grieving for comrades. He refused to think of his feet or it would disturb him even more. Instead he returned to his reporting of what the grief was.

With a sigh for being done with that much, he stopped at the end of the street. He crossed to pass along the side–streetfront of the worst block. The houses in the middle were the worst, but all of them were bad. He took a breath and returned to the last bit he still needed to do. He stepped a few steps into the street, then sat down crosslegged in the middle of the road to rest his legs, ears, and mind, letting his head bow in tiredness. While people occasionally had passed on the side streets, none had come here and no wagons or horses had been in this neighborhood at all, so he was safe enough where he sat.

The grief of this section to his left now was too much, too heavy. He was nearly done. It could be burned and released soon. He just needed to finish. But before that he needed to rest. He drew in a breath as if preparing to sleep. To his ears came a song, a lullaby in the language and voice of his Mother. He rested in it until he was humming with her, a cadence to sing the song of the contented child. When he'd rested just enough, his body wanted to dance with it and he swayed to the song, letting his feet rest from their dance.

He came out of the song and dance as a new sound began to reach his ears. He stopped moving, then stopped humming and his eyes popped open. Mother's song ended softly, not leaving him sharply, letting him know she was still present. The man standing on the road about three house–lengths away was almost as slight as Justinian. And almost as pretty. Justinian tipped his head in curiosity and watched him. He was older, Justinian saw as he moved to step a few steps closer. "What are you?" the man asked, very curious about Justinian, too.

Justinian thought about the right answer to that question. The pause made the man walk enough steps forward to be two house–lengths away. "The Treasure," he finally answered the question, rewarding the new man. That had been his first title in the House and it was appropriate in so many ways. He knew how much Ore, Ilena, and all the Immediate Family treasured him. He was so grateful they'd taken him in and taught him that he could be treasured in that way.

He felt his face go soft with that gratitude and rose to his feet. He looked calmly at the man who'd paused to watch him. He was also so grateful that he'd been able to walk with them in Tarc the first time they'd all been there. He'd learned to treasure truth and wisdom while they'd been there, to even become that wisdom some.

This one he faced had neither in him. In fact he was the exact opposite. Justinian wasn't even sure he'd be able to touch him, he felt too much the antithesis of all that existed, as if he'd just be smoke, air, and ash. He was one who'd already been burned from existence. That was actually rather sad. Justinian's face fell to sorrow and the man moved another three–quarter's of a house closer.

Justinian rewarded him again, holding out his hand in invitation this time. This one was as skittish as he was and would be difficult to surprise. Like the skittish colt. Like the herdsmen, Justinian remained calm and quiet inside and out, inviting only, saying nothing, even when the man asked, "Will you come with me?"

When that wasn't enough to get the man to take his hand, Justinian answered him, "Do you dance?"

That lit the man's eyes up. Even more quietly than Justinian had asked, the man asked, "Do you sing?"

"I dance to the wind and the song that can't be heard," Justinian answered.

"*Ah.* That is beautiful," the man sighed. Then he answered, "I sing the song of life." Justinian highly doubted that because his words and being were still the opposite of everything that was truth. Still it was the right thing to say in that case because he really meant he sung the song of death. This close and Justinian knew who this was.

His hand was taken lightly in a cool hand. He allowed it, allowed the man to be fooled by softness. He was led down the street towards the alleyway. When they reached the center of the road where they were going to turn into it, Justinian paused, as if slightly uncertain. When the man turned to him again to reassure him, his answer was already leaving his lips, his arm moving to wrap around the neck of the man who was already dead. "I am the consequence of your actions," was whispered into the ear that never heard the end of the sentence. He held the man in his arms, then let him down to the ground, not really able to hold up his dead weight very gracefully.

Mother. That was him. You don't have to worry about him anymore. His head turned to face the building. *However, we'll have to worry about the rest of them very soon.* He stood there sorrowfully as first one, then about seven men poured out from the alleyway to face him with absolute shock on their faces. They stared between him and the body at his feet. "Was he your Head?" Justinian asked. "Would you make me your Head now?"

Finally one swallowed and said, "Well, he *was*, yes. But we'd not take you or any stranger as Head. How did you do that?"

"What are you?" one in the back asked that was looking very much like he was seeing a ghost.

Justinian spread his arms wide in a careless shrug. "I am the Treasure. Anyone who touches the Treasure dies, ...by order of the King and Queen." He smiled just as carelessly at them as the street was suddenly filling with nightwalkers from the Houses of both nightwalker royals.

He stood in the street, the fighting swirling around him. No one touched him, not even those of the Houses of the Suiran Nightwalker King and Queen of Night. When the flames finally licked up to crackle as it ate the angriest houses in the block, Justinian smiled. He'd finally earned his place as King's Assassin, the beautiful face that walked directly behind the Nightwalker King because only he'd be trusted in that place.

-o-o-o-

Rio sighed tiredly as she took the dinner dishes from the hands passing them to her. The long day in Nijoushi cleaning up the mess made by Ilena and Ore and their nightwalkers had really done her in. Amber glanced at her and sneaked in to take an extra set. Rio tried to give her a smile of gratitude. She was sure it was quite small. She was too tired to even do that much.

She managed to get the dishes out to the waiting cart in the middle open hallway. Once there, she didn't want to go back into the Lower office. She paused and raised her head up to look at the ceiling far above her. That was better than having it be open. The distance between walls in this hallway was about the size of the smaller roadways of south Nijoushi. A ceiling said it wasn't; that she was indoors. She took a deep breath in and closed her eyes as she sighed it out.

The light hand on her arm startled her, but she didn't jump or shake it off. "Is everything okay?" Amber asked quietly.

"Not really," Rio answered softly. "I've not worked physically that much in a long time. But there was a lot of emotional stress, too, and that didn't help." She was trying with Amber. Trying to trust her a little bit, that maybe she might care now about people other than herself, that she might have been telling the truth that she wanted to learn to care about Rio. She opened her eyes and looked at Amber.

Amber actually did look a little sympathetic to Rio's weariness. "What do you need?" Amber finally asked. Rio was surprised she'd thought to ask that one. Maybe she'd heard the men upstairs say it enough to each other, or Reynold ask Justinian enough times.

Rio looked at her bedroom door. "I need to sleep. I need to not be shut up in a small room just yet." She slumped and whispered, "I need to believe I'm still safe."

Amber considered those answers then took her hand and led her away from the door of the Lower office and towards the stairs. "You are still safe," Amber said firmly as she walked with her. "Pretend we're both young girls. We're in a large hall; you aren't locked in anywhere. Only people who protect you are in this building."

Rio had to smile. It was humorous to think of themselves as young girls, but she thought she understood why Amber had said it. Because they were of similar ages, and because Rio had told her that it had only been when she'd been with the other children that she'd felt even remotely safe. It was certainly what she needed: to be reminded only her protectors lived in this place, only they were surrounding her.

She sighed and closed her eyes again and let Amber lead her up the stairs. Her feet stumbled just a little on them, her legs too tired to lift them up high enough to walk up them. After the first time Amber went just a little slower and that helped. So did grasping hold of the stair railing.

When they got to the upper landing, Amber paused. "It looks like you need sleep more than staying out of your room." She had a smile in her voice.

Rio opened her eyes and nodded. "Probably." But her grasp on Amber's hand tightened.

Amber looked a little surprised at that, then she held back more tightly in return. "I'm right here. It's okay."

Rio looked at Amber in amazement. "Where does that come from? When were you ever like that?"

Amber blushed a little and looked away, then looked down and scuffed her toe. "My mother ...she was like that to me after ...after that time. When I was too afraid to do pretty much anything."

Rio went soft. She pressed the hand holding hers again. "Thank you. I never knew my mother. I'm glad your mother loved you."

Amber nodded without looking up. "For as long as she was alive, I was fortunate to have that support. ...She died not quite a year after it happened, but she tried her best for as long as she could."

Rio took Amber in a soft hug and held her until Amber shifted. "You really will make me cry," Amber scolded a little more firmly, not wanting that at the moment apparently. "Come on." She tugged on Rio's hand.

Rio let Amber lead her to her room. Amber stopped outside it, looking at Rio. It took Rio's tired brain a while to figure out why, then she laughed a tired laugh and opened the door. "I don't even lock it when I'm out. There's guards on the outer doors. That's good enough for me."

Amber blinked wide eyes at her, then nodded in understanding. "Okay. We'll leave the door wide open for now, okay?" Rio relaxed just a little and agreed. Amber gently led Rio into the room and sat her down on the end of the bed. Rio decided that was okay since she was used to it being her bed now. Amber walked over to the window and opened it up. The air was cold as it blew in the window, through the room, and out the open door. Rio sniffed in the air, glad to have it as a reminder she wasn't shut up in a small room she couldn't get out of.

Amber walked back. "Let's see, it's boots and lacings, right?" she teased a little.

Rio gave her a wry smile. "Yes. Boots for sure." She shivered. "Lacings will be harder, but I think I can manage that if you don't also help with taking the dress off." She shuddered again, then wrapped her arms around herself and shook her head. "Not yet," she managed to get it out as a whisper, although she choked on it.

Amber's brow furrowed and she sat down on the bed near Rio but without touching her. "What happened? Why's it harder again?"

Rio looked away, wanting to take her turn to cry, too. "Mistress Ilena had Justinian and I.... We were bait today."

Amber's eyes went wide, then she was holding Rio's arm again, more tightly this time. "That sounds awful. Why would she do that? She knows how hard that is for both of you."

Rio nodded. "She does. We're the best bait, though, for nightwalkers. Justinian's was more of a test and learning experience for him, to help him learn what he could do. He passed it with a lot of pride, actually." She smiled sadly at her knees. She was proud of him, too.

"And you?" Amber prodded her.

Rio shook her head. "It was okay at the beginning. We were all fairly close to each other and no one was going to do anything in a crowd. Leah and one of the nurses were with me then, and Henry had been assigned to watch over me when he wasn't running errands." She took a breath. "We moved twice that morning to new areas to collect the bodies into the wagons. I didn't mind doing the washing. I couldn't carry bodies for long, so washing was what I was doing, but I had to do it at the edges, to be able to be bait to begin with."

She lifted her eyes rather miserably to Amber's. "I'm not good bait. Those who can do that have courage, have some reason to hate so that it's getting revenge. I can't do that. I don't know if Mistress Ilena expects me to be able to or what. All I could do was become more and more afraid."

She shivered again. "When it got really bad, I'd go back to the nurse, since I was allowed to do that. She'd help talk me down until I could go back to work. When he was there after those episodes, Henry would let me know he was still watching over me. Those things helped." She took a breath, trying to have those reminders help her now.

In a small voice, Rio said, "It was after lunch and we'd moved to a seedier part of the south side —" she gave a sidelong glance to Amber, "— *all* of which is seedy, so that's saying something." Amber wrinkled up her nose in understanding. "I was called to come help with a body that still needed to be brought. I went, and was pulled into an alley and dragged away. I panicked and couldn't remember any of my lessons for that whole alley. My brain just shut down. It took stumbling on the cobblestones to come back to my senses." She shivered.

"I almost wished I had your snap reaction. I would've already been back on the street I was supposed to be on. It wasn't until we were in the next alley that I had the capacity to resist even. When he turned back to scold me, or whatever, I killed him." She shivered again and swallowed the bile that wanted to rise. "I'd rather not have had to, honestly. Dragging his body back to the main street all by myself was rather difficult. Henry didn't get back from his errand until I was already on the main street and resting from the first pull."

Rio looked at Amber sadly. "He was very apologetic and helped me get the body to the station, then stayed with me until I was able to calm down enough to try again." Rio drew in a breath and straightened her spine. "I was told I had to put up with at least four of those today. I was relieved it was only two. The third one Henry took down before he could touch me. I did have to help him take the body back, though." She closed her eyes, weary again. A soft hand came on her head and pet it gently.

Rio squeezed Amber's hand where it was still on her other arm, needing that one more touch of warmth. It was okay because she'd initiated it. "I learned that I don't like to kill. This isn't necessarily the first time for me, but for some reason, this time...."

"It is different, in the heat of the moment versus in cold awareness," Amber said.

Rio looked at Amber with wide eyes. Then she gave up. "Yes. I'm sorry." Amber just patted her on the shoulder.

After sitting for a bit longer, Rio realized she was going to really fall asleep very soon, for all the cold wind passing her was keeping her somewhat awake. "Thank you. Let's do the boots now." Amber rose and helped with unlacing and pulling them off. Rio shivered now that her warm feet were cold. Her hand reached out and took Amber's hand. "Please, close the window. The open air was good, but cold is not." Amber squeezed her hand back, then released it and went to the window and closed it. Then she stoked up the fire again. It would take a while to rewarm the room but that much crackling and popping and dancing light was enough for now.

"Okay, I'd wait for the lacings, but I'm so tired I *will* fall asleep before it's done if we don't do it now." Amber smiled and Rio rose to her feet. They had that done in not too much longer.

"Rio," Amber hesitated, then said, "I'll go back over to finish clean–up over there, but if you need anyone tonight, just call me. I hope I won't be sleeping too soundly to hear you." She smiled and teased again, "I suspect *you'll* sleep even more soundly, though, for a long time."

"Probably," Rio agreed. "I will call you, though, and ...if I could come to your bed, that's better than if you come to mine."

"Really?" Amber asked. She hesitated.

"I won't stay long. I'll just hold your hand long enough to stop shivering in fear," Rio promised. "That's how Leah and I do it. And I sit on the bed. Lying down is too much for me."

"Okay," Amber said, still a little unsure. "We can try it."

"Thank you," Rio said, relieved. She waited until Amber was out of the room before she finished undressing just enough she could fall into her bed and sleep. She was glad the fireplace was near the bed so was already warming it up. She almost got up to lock the door this night for the first time in a long time, but she was asleep before she could actually move to do it.

-o-o-o-

Justinian took in a deep breath and looked Reynold in the eyes. "Guess what happened today?" They were getting ready for bed, or were about to anyway. Justinian wanted to tell him before then. Reynold had heard some of the story once they'd gotten back but this was Justinian's news to tell him specifically. The hard part was that the words he was most proud of he wasn't allowed to say. He'd said them to Ore, though, and then whispered them to himself a few times. That had helped him some. Now he had to make it through this obediently.

Ilena had very specifically told Justinian that he wasn't allowed to tell Reynold he'd killed. She'd praised him for doing it, and doing it well, but he could understand that it would make Reynold very afraid of him again, probably worse then ever before. "Reynold is only of the light, of the Family. There's a reason the Family helped with the washing but only the House helped with the rest." She'd given him a look that said he needed to understand the difference. He'd considered it very carefully, then agreed.[‡]

Reynold might've been damaged by his time with the Doll House, but he'd not been broken the same. Not the same way the nightwalkers were. The difference really summed up to that too: death and murder. He knew Ore wouldn't go killing just because, but Ore was capable of being cold and of killing regardless. It was the same with Ilena. Because Justinian had killed, and was as cold in doing it, he was different from Reynold in that way. Reynold would never be able to do that unless something broke him even more or he was in desperate times. That would be very sad. He didn't want that to have to happen to Reynold. If he could live the rest of his life peacefully happy, that would be very good. If it was just the two of them, he'd do the killing for Reynold.

That had made him pause in surprise. Even back in Tarc, Ilena had done that: had Justinian be the one to be the protector, to fight to protect Reynold. That had made him relax a lot and settled in him the same way his win against the awful house Head had. He could do that: protect Reynold like he'd protect Ore. That had been one of his questions to Ilena after the battle was over and she'd said to never tell anyone he'd killed people. "Why did you have me learn to kill? Why did Marcus want me to learn to hunt?"

Ilena had ruffled his hair kindly, but he knew she was mostly the Queen of Night in the city generally. The Minister of Intelligence was almost as dangerous as the Queen of Night, and was who Ilena was today to the city. The Minister of Intelligence was cold, not kind. It was the Queen of Night who killed. That was the only differentiation between the two. It was that the Queen of Night had accepted him as one of her children, too, today.

"To kill because you'll be called on many times to kill for my sake and Ore's sake, to keep him alive. We'll hope it won't be as often as it could be, but you already know from your own training in your martial art to begin with." Justinian did understand that. The manservants had been told at the beginning of that training they'd use it to protect the lord that called them up. He was in a position next to a person who'd likely have the worst assassins sent after him. If he could stay better than them, Ore would stay alive even if Thayne and Petroi didn't.

"Marcus caught on to a skill you might have, similar to my own. Hunters are a little more than assassins, more dangerous. People can't hide from hunters. Assassins have to learn the patterns of their targets, know where

---

[‡]Editor's note: This chapter was added by a different hand than Baron Reynold Tennyson's. Likely Justinian added it after the fact, keeping to his requirement. He was so proud of it being a major part of his own history in the Immediate Family, it's not likely he wanted it lost.

they'll be when, or gain their trust and confidence. Hunters don't have to. They only have to be put on the scent when it's recent.

"Never tell anyone you're a hunter. We'll keep it secret too. You'll be hunted down mercilessly and killed by a pack you won't be able to defend yourself from. Or they'll use distance weapons on you while you're encircled. Humans don't like to be hunted. They always remove something that hunts them so they can survive. Practice the skill but call it tracking. That distinction will keep you alive."

She'd leaned back and looked at him sharply. "*You* are actually even more than that. You have an intuition, a 'knowing' that isn't wrong. That skill you should also keep close to you and take care of. We always enjoy seeing it come to show us things." Justinian had flushed at that.

She'd patted him on the head one more time as she prepared to return to her important duties. "Be proud of what you've done today, but then let the pride go. It'll get you killed, too. Humble practicing even if you think you're good enough will keep you alive." The golden piercing look had come on him. "There's always someone better than you, time wins against your body eventually, but never forget to practice first your control. Pride will make you slip there first. You'll be the most sad to have that happen."

Justinian had bowed to her and let her go. Watching her climb quickly to the roof of the closest house that was still whole, he did agree with her. He'd be sad to let the control slip the most at home. Then he'd make them all sad, and perhaps even angry. He didn't want that, now that he felt like he'd passed his test to fully enter the Immediate Family. *When will you let me test against you?* he asked after her.

He got back a purry chuckle. *When you can attack and* not *kill.* Oh. That made sense. He'd probably get the same answer from the rest of them; although, Ore had tested him once already. But that was a good reason to practice control very hard.

"What happened?" Reynold asked to bring Justinian back again.

Justinian smiled a small triumphant smile. "I passed my test to get into the Immediate Family. I'm finally in the place I've been working to get to. I still have a lot to learn, but it feels good to have that confidence now. I'm not so afraid now. I was able to control my fear and my actions in a very stressful situation. The others helped me to stay aware, but mostly it was just me." He thrust out his chest in his pride and smiled very big at Reynold.

Reynold gave Justinian his soft proud smile. "That's wonderful. I'm very glad for you."

Justinian gave a nod of thanks. "Mistress Ilena told me that I could be happy, but that I shouldn't stay overly prideful, that I should still work hard on my practice of restraint and control. ...And perhaps there are still things that will startle me so I really should." He could also see himself forgetting the strength he'd learned that day just because life in the offices was the same all the time. He'd already been forgetting to practice his skills to overcome his panic responses because he didn't have them when in the office anymore. He'd work hard to remember both: his practicing and his new strength.

Continuing to Reynold, Justinian said, "I don't know for sure yet, but I think it was enough to help me with us, too." He shifted just a little. "I'd like to try slowly to make sure, but I think we can relax a little."

Reynold wasn't too sure about that so suddenly and his eyes narrowed a little, but after studying Justinian for a bit, he finally nodded. "If you think you want to try, but I do want it to be slowly. And I'm going to tell you before you do something if you start to slip."

"Okay," Justinian agreed heartily with that. He did want to know before-hand. "I'll talk to you, too. I can do that, and even then I could. I just forgot I could at the beginning until I remembered this time." He'd not remembered to open his mouth the first few times in the office together, getting him into trouble with Reynold then, even though Ilena had scolded him and told him to practice that, too.

Reynold's eyebrow rose. "It was that difficult this time?" He was frowning in concern.

Justinian shook his head soberly, his eyes still looking into Reynold's. "It was much harder this time." He took a deep breath, "But it was okay. I only lost who I was very briefly once. Marcus talked to me and I came back very quickly. I never panicked, although I did become dangerous. I was able to control that, though, too. That's why I think I can try to be braver now."

Reynold sat on the edge of his bed. "Well, that's good, then. I'm sure, however, that you're confused as to where and how to start. So how about I start to get ready for bed and you start to get ready for bed at the same time. When you start feeling uncomfortable, let me know and we'll pause for you to figure out what you can do next."

"Okay," Justinian agreed. That would be a good first step.

CHAPTER 155 Nijoushi City Council

"The Houses of the Queen of Night and the Suiran Nightwalker King have remained active throughout the day, Sage Seraph," the messenger reported that evening. "They continue to hunt without mercy even into this night." The Sage Seraph was *not* happy to hear that news. "However, it's now restricted in the main to the House of the Grey Snake and those few who won't bow their heads to any House nor live lawfully."

The Sage Seraph sat back at that news to ponder yet again. Most of the freelancers of the city had joined with the House of the Suiran Nightwalker King at this point. He suspected it was more for their own personal protection during this chaos than because they'd stay loyal. Just because a respected freelancer had said that his House would have freelancer rules didn't mean freelancers really *wanted* a House. Although, with winter setting in it wouldn't be a bad trade for them to have houses to keep them warm for one winter. They'd probably stay until the spring thaws warmed up Suiran just enough they could stand to sleep outside again. He hadn't required them to stay, after all.

"Is she moving to take all of the south and the west as well?" he asked the messenger.

The messenger shook his head. "We could assume it, but no word's been said. They were the most contested and unsettled areas, though. Word has it that they moved as Minister and Assistant Minister of Intelligence because the tourism trade was beginning to suffer the ill effects of the actions of the nightwalkers in the west, and because of the spread of the sickness the Grey Snake was feeding. That it was simpler to just remove them both at the same time."

"That was the word they spread themselves, then?" the Sage Seraph asked dryly.

The messenger indicated he'd understood rightly. "The word from the nightwalkers of their Houses, though," the messenger frowned. "It's hard to know if it's truth, but they say the Heads were headed to the safe houses with messages only. It was the fear of the other Heads in those areas that made them move. Apparently all of them set ambushes to catch the Heads on their way through, in case they were coming to visit. They may have wanted to win against the Heads before the Houses were called up. Apparently that made the Heads call for them anyway. Most of the House members who would answer me were irritated because the Heads were. 'The war would've come later if they'd left well enough alone,' was the most common complaint at the end of the conversations."

The Sage Seraph almost had to laugh. "I can see it. The hope that catching the few would prevent the full from coming out. The irritation that they'd asked for it outside the planned timing. And the whole of the two

Houses answering to the call when they've been sitting and waiting so long their legs can't stand to do anything but run." He frowned, "But why the kill order that night, then?"

"Some said because of the irritation. Some said because of the Grey Snake House extermination order. They couldn't know who was which last night, so it was everyone who'd come out just to make sure. ...They did kill any of that House they found today, and hunted them specifically, even burning down a few city blocks when they found the nest."

The Sage Seraph's eyes went wide at that. "Even to burning?" he asked. The messenger nodded soberly. That had been the large cloud of smoke that day, then. The city'd seen it and wondered at it, but most citizens had then said, "At least it's down *there*," and shrugged it off. Those that had been concerned it might move beyond that part of town and take the whole of the city had rushed to the guards that were out in great force because of the many murders the night before. They'd been told that it was contained and being watched closely by a large portion of volunteers with water bearers standing by. His messenger had already told him that was because of the washing of the bodies of the dead.

He shook his head. The Minister of Intelligence knew what she was doing surely. At least she knew what words to have people say to the public. Only the underworld would know the full story of that night and day. "That's cleaned up a lot of the worst and opened up a lot of space," he murmured. Of course, that was poor space. There wasn't much for pickings there in the south.

The west, though. He rubbed his jaw as he thought hard about that direction. It was on his border after all. He wondered how much of it he could take and still hold. It was already new to be holding as much as he was. If he could wiggle Crafters Row from the Queen of Night it would be enough and he'd wish to not have the more.

There was the knock on the door of a nightwalker messenger. The Sage Seraph waved his hand at the door guard. The messenger was let in and walked up to the dais. The clothing was just a little different, like pieces of other places had been added to the typical Suiran clothing. The man bowed just slightly and the Sage Seraph tipped his head. "I've been sent by the Queen of Night." That got every ear in the room listening. "She's asked that I take over the west and Travelers Row. Can you hold off on moving in that area until she's settled the south?"

"Who are you?" The Sage Seraph was having a hard time believing that a potential House Head would walk into another House Head's safe house. That was considered life–ending. He couldn't prevent his face from showing his extreme puzzlement.

"Raine Marciel's younger brother. He's been having me run his product for him for a while now, but I'm tired of the traveling and ready to settle down. I've been in enough run–down and up–scale hostels and inns that I already can see the need to straighten out that row."

That hadn't helped. "Well, okay, so that puts you on the city council, but why a nightwalker House Head?"

The man grinned a nightwalker's smile with no humor in it save the humor all nightwalkers found in the ironies of life. "Because he made me run with the wagon trains in order to get me off the street and stop ruining the family name. Or rather his own reputation." There were snorts of laughter all over the room at that. "I'm the black sheep in the family, obviously, so I think I'll go with that name, just to hold it over his head." That got full out laughs.

"I don't recommend it," the Sage Seraph said dryly, pointing out the laughter as the case in point. "Sheep are who we fleece."

"Well, that's true," the man agreed. His clothing was a little easier to understand now. He'd added in his favorite pieces from other cultures he'd liked — or stolen so were badges of capability. Since the Sage Seraph worked with the merchants, he'd already recognized a few of them that were on the rarer side.

"Why you? Why not one of the Heads that are already there?" the Sage Seraph asked.

The man shook his head a little regretfully. "She had her day and nightwalkers out looking all day. There are none she's willing to set in that place. The few who didn't come out against them last night — and thus survived — are small fry without the capacity to hold any loyalty, nor lead that many." Before the Sage Seraph could protest, the man held up a hand to forestall him. "I've led caravans, but not large groups of people, so I've already argued with her I'm not the best pick either, but she won't listen. It's 'do it', so I'm here.

"I've walked the western streets on my way here and they're so disorganized now I suspect it won't be hard to call them to any banner. Particularly mine since I can promise them safety from her blade and that's what they're most desperate to have at the moment."

The Sage Seraph snapped his mouth closed at that and frowned in thought. That was actually wisdom on her part. While the nightwalkers were most afraid of her, to send in someone with that promise would flock them to this man. He'd have to eventually win their trust to become a long–term House Head, but for now it would hold the west part of the city stable. And the Sage Seraph did owe Raine — another point to her wisdom since anyone else he didn't know wouldn't have that point in their favor.

"All right. Truce for now. Good luck holding on to them ...if you care to," he gave the ironic smile back. "Want to pick some other name now so we know how to call you when I pass the truce order out?"

The man chuckled. "Well, how about the Black Ram?"

"That's better," the Sage Seraph agreed. "Let him pass unharmed," he told the room as the Black Ram turned and left it. He did motion to the door guard to not let that man into the safe house again, though. From this point on they were rivals and almost–enemies.

-o-o-o-

The knock of a messenger came on the door to the safe house of Flynn, the Gold Lion. He sighed, but motioned for the door guard to check who it was. There was a bit of a pause that was longer than normal, then the door guard let two in. One looked like he'd come running up. The other was looking bemusedly at that one. The Gold Lion raised his eyebrow at them as they walked up. The fanciful one pointed at the runner and said, "I just came from where he's just come from. He decided he'd rather not wait until I was done."

"Okay?" Flynn was sure he didn't need this on top of everything else this day. He already felt like the beleaguered housewife trying to keep the children and panicked animals corralled and comforted while the wild storms raged around them. Then he recognized the messenger from the week before. He slumped. "Oh gods. It's about *her* yet again, isn't it?"

"Well, yes," the man said as the messenger slumped and nodded in sympathy.

"I think we might be near the end of the wondering and chaos, though," the messenger said. "Hear him out first, then I'll give you the witness and the message."

Well, if it was for that, he could do that. Flynn listened with as much confusion and astonishment as the Sage Seraph had. At the end of the Black Ram's short commentary and request, and the witness from the messenger that the Black Ram had already been to the Sage Seraph with the same message, the Gold Lion dropped his head into his hand, resting his elbow on his knee. "Gods man. Don't walk into the safe house of a Head as a Head. Don't you know how dangerous that is? It'll be the third time I've had to move in two weeks."

"Ah, sorry," the Black Ram said sufficiently contritely. "It's not like I have any messengers to send. And you don't have to move." Flynn sat up crossly at that and the Black Ram hurriedly said, "No really. She means to have truce next. And," he furrowed his brow, "I think she means to have a council as well."

"As in group of people or meeting?" Flynn said crossly, "And yes I do, because when you *do* have messengers and a House, assuming you can do that, I don't need you and yours sneaking in here —"

A hand was held up at that. "I don't want it," the Black Ram said completely sober. "I don't want war, I don't want your side of town, I don't want your seat nor your head. I already wouldn't take the job either except she's not wrong. I'll be more hard pressed to not just hand over my seat to the first reasonable person to even look like a Lieutenant in that part of town — if one exists. It's better I come myself to protect you than send a messenger that might sell you out."

Flynn stared at him, then slumped just a little. That was actually reasonable, and he sounded very sure of himself. That would give him a month or so to find a new place instead of two days. That might be do–able. The Black Ram frowned at him and scolded, "In Ichijoutsu the Head of the Rose Garden lives in the most posh of her ladies' houses. Everyone knows it and no one goes there to kill her unless they're very clueless or very angry with her."

Flynn's mouth dropped open. He was certainly very tired by now. "Okay," he scowled and waved his hand impatiently. "I get it. What kind of council?"

"I don't know, it was a word dropped as a clue, but not in context," the Black Ram answered. That wasn't so helpful. The woman would wiggle her way out of everything and anything she could unless she was pinned down. He already knew from their one conversation.

He was relieved she'd found a way to clean out the south side and somewhat the west side of the people even she didn't want to deal with, but he was quite sure he'd rather she'd used a different method. His people had been shivering in the safe houses since they'd rolled into town that morning. Half were too scared to peep. The other half wanted to fight them tonight, the panic making them want to move in dangerous ways. He'd been sitting on them all day already. He looked tiredly at the messenger. "Did you give *any* good news to the Sage Seraph today? I could really use some about now."

When the messenger was done with his summary of what he'd told the Sage Seraph just before then, Flynn was feeling better. The city would do a lot better, especially the south side of his boundaries. The ladies who'd come from there were the most afraid. The news that the Grey Snake was gone for good would help them immensely. He frowned as he put the puzzle pieces together, given what he knew of the Queen of Night. "She'll take the south, then," he whispered and nodded. It wasn't surprising she'd just take the side that needed her most.

The other two men narrowed their eyes at him. "You're sure?" the messenger pressed him.

Flynn nodded. "She's the reason I had to move before. She showed up in my council room before I even knew she was in the house at all," both of those men shuddered. "Yeah. Anyway, we had a long meeting because I made her spill everything she was willing to tell at all. ...Mouth of a weasel, that one.... She knows how to take care of the poorest of the nightwalkers from her time in Kouzanshi. She can have it. I've got enough headaches learning how to have the brothels under me."

"How likely is she to give up Crafter's Row to the Sage Seraph?" the messenger tried to feel after the Gold Lion's opinion.

Flynn shook his head. "Not likely at all. She owns that as the Princess, not as the Head of her House."

"Oh, yeah. I get that." They all slumped. "Well, the Sage Seraph wants to know if you'll also hold to truce until the Queen of Night shows up to talk again. We don't expect that to be tonight. She's got to come back into the city again tomorrow during the day to help with the final paperwork, and maybe the next day as well, from what I heard," the messenger said. He pointed with his thumb at the Black Ram, "And he has to get a House under him before he can even think of meeting with her, so...."

Flynn agreed and shooed them out. He was going to go to bed as soon as his own House meeting was done. That much information should calm everyone down enough he wouldn't be interrupted for enough hours to get solid sleep in.

-o-o-o-

Ilena sighed, sat up, and stretched her back out. Hunching over a desk was never her favorite pastime. She turned her head left, then right to get the kink out of her neck, then rose to her feet to pace to the glass doors. They were closed to keep out the worst of the cold, but she kept the curtains pulled back so she didn't feel quite so claustrophobic. It was good to have a glass wall in the long room instead of a closed in small office to work in.

Rio had moved her rocking chair closer to the fireplace so the cold that did seep through the glass wasn't seeping into her bones so much. The fire kept her wrapped in warmth instead. Ilena smiled at the image. It almost made Rio seem like an old woman. Leah had already been working that way for years. Ilena didn't mind that much cool air but her desk was farther from those windows than Rio's chair had been during the summer.

She let her mind continue to relax for now. The report on her desk was as complete as she could get it. The witnesses were already in the castle. She'd already dressed for her part. After today, she could go back to using her days on the things of the Duchy and her businesses. Those had been set aside to handle the fall–out of the nightwalker work. (She'd not stopped working on Ministry work. That couldn't stop or important things would fall through dangerous holes.) The one minor break they'd had during all the preparations over the last several days was a birthday dinner for Grandfather, to thank him for all his hard work for Ilena until this time.

Ilena clasped her hands behind her back and looked up the tree in the courtyard. "Justinian, my scarf, hat, and finger gloves, please," she requested. He was happy to be used that way during the day, being rather bored still in the main, and she didn't want to move. Her body was still trying to relax. She let him fuss over her until she was wrapped up more warmly, then she rubbed his head and smiled at him. "Thank you, Justinian."

He gave her a bright smile back, bowed, and headed back for his chair. Ilena waited until he was past the level of the fireplace before she opened the door and slipped out quickly to keep as much cold air out as possible. She stretched to reach her toes, then touched the ground and held it for a bit until her legs stopped complaining and relaxed. A few other stretches warmed up the muscles. Enough laps around the courtyard, crunching through the snow's ice crust here and there, got the blood flowing and warmed her up nicely. Then she was climbing up the tree.

Somehow, she'd forgotten she hadn't been up in it yet. Life had been very busy since arriving back in Nijou. The strain of the pull of climbing was nice. It was a similar yet different pull as climbing the buildings. It smelled a lot nicer, too. Each tree sap had a different smell. A few were unpleasant, but this one was nice.

As she passed the top of the wall, she could see why Ore always stopped just high enough to see out. The branches got too small for him higher than that. She smiled and went the one branch higher, settled into it, then looked out at the view she'd been wanting to see for as long as she'd been in this wing. She'd seen it from the rooftop of the wing, but she'd always been jealous she couldn't get into the tree to see it. In the west were the outside edges of Nijoushi, mostly not visible from this angle. The multiple manor grounds to the north of the city were visible, but from this distance one didn't really notice the homes, just the hilly knees of the mountains.

Really being able to see that rise to the mountains and the mountains themselves was quite grand. Only the tops showed over the walls of the castle when one was walking on the ground. Seeing them this way made one really understand just how close those mountains were to swallowing them up. She leaned her head back against the tree trunk and just took in that view for a long time.

The tree shook for a bit before her hand was caught up in another warm finger–gloved hand and her fingertips kissed. Ore's warm breath on her fingers dampened them slightly and reminded them they were in the cold air. They didn't at all mind that he held on to them to warm them up again. "Lost?" he teased her as it took a bit for her to look down into his golden eyes.

"Mesmerized," she agreed. She pressed his fingers holding hers.

"Well, I'd sit and stay with you," she could tell he'd really prefer to do that, "but I've come to fetch you down with just a little exercise myself before we have to be shut up with lords." She blinked at him, but he tugged on her just a little. "Ah, I really don't recommend continuing to look at the rest of it. You'll not only not come down, you'll run away."

334

She furrowed her brow in confusion, then she remembered the forest that was the eastern part of that view and laughed with him. "Yes, I'd very much like to run the trees today, too, but maybe that can be our reward for getting through the council meeting."

Ore's eyes lit up at that and he kissed her fingers again, then tugged one more time. She gave a nod that she'd come and he let go to head on down ahead of her, so she could have the room to climb down as well. Ilena glanced at the hills and mountains one more time as she let herself down. The wall hid the view soon enough. Ore's hug and kiss at the base of the tree helped. His slight shivering made her keep that short so she could tug him back into the Lower office to warm him back up.

Ilena picked her packet of papers up off her desk. It was two sets of the proceedings of the meeting they were headed for. One was written in Ryan's language so she could follow along. The other was in Ryokudan, translated by Leah, to give to Andrew. Rei had already been given the summary the day before so that he knew what to expect. Ilena looked up into her thoughts and sighed. It was time to get ready internally now.

She closed her eyes and took back on herself the Princess and cool logical Steward. It would be important to be calm and non–confrontational, conciliatory and empathetic, while being sure and confident. She could do it. It wasn't even the worst of the ways she had to be in the castle.

She looked back down at her people in the room, quickly reviewing their readiness. She gave a nod. "Let's go," she said. Marcus opened the door and the muffled and cloaked group poured out through it to head towards the council chamber that was the medium–sized throne room.

-o-o-o-

The city council regularly met with Rei, at least once per month. This meeting was a special meeting requested by the city council to hear what had happened in the south part of the city and why. They'd allowed for Ilena to have another couple of days to get the witnesses pulled together and the report written. It helped that she'd been at the Lord's Court and helped Rei when he'd put that together. Just as Rei had had to explain to the court and landed lords why it was okay that he'd gone against Pakyo, she needed to explain the same to the city council. She didn't have to admit she'd been one of the ones actually involved.

Ilena stood on the dais, waiting for Rei to arrive. Henry and Marcus were standing at guard's rest attention just in front of the dais in front of her where they could guard her but not block Rei's vision too much, nor stand directly in front of him. Ore, with Petroi and Thayne, was standing to the side of the dais where he could be called on when necessary. They were all dressed in their Ministry uniforms: the formal ones that were more spiffy than the casual ones, and thus took a little longer to get just right while they were dressing. And also, therefore, were just a little less comfortable. Her badge of office was a bit heavy on her jacket, a trinket she didn't wear often so found noticeable.

The rest of the attendees were already present. The city council members stood closest to the throne, as they were the ones meeting with the Regent. There were only nine, compared to the over–one–hundred lords that came to the larger court meetings. Some of them had brought staff with them. The rest of this room wasn't quite filled, but the meeting was rather well attended this time. Some were lords who lived in the city that wanted to hear what had happened with their own ears. Some were concerned citizens with a little more position, like business persons with a larger vested interest in the city as a whole. Ilena made sure Raine was present. She'd specifically invited him.

Some of those that were concerned citizens weren't of the sort of background the rest would expect to be in that room at all. Ilena had expressly sent invitations to the three other Heads that they come, or at least send witnesses to the meeting. Mostly that was so she wouldn't have to repeat herself and present her defense three more times. If they heard it in this meeting, she could be all done. They'd post the summary in the city on the notification boards so everyone could know and not worry, but that was a minor task that would also be completed later this day.

She heard Rei and his guards enter the office behind her where she'd left the papers for Andrew. She gave him time to read through it, then straightened up a little, her cue to her own people who got that little bit more formal themselves. Andrew was very soon up on the dais on the other side of the throne from her. "Regent Rei Touka," Andrew announced and the very person appeared on the dais and sat in his throne, upright but in relaxed control. Mina wasn't far behind him, stopping in her usual position at his right elbow.

"This city council meeting is convened. Please state your concerns," Andrew addressed the city council members.

The head of it stepped forward slightly and bowed to Rei. "The unrest in the city has come to a head recently, with a surprising number of deaths resulting from it. Can this be explained? Has anything been done about it other than the cleaning up of the bodies? Will our people continue to live in fear? Will travelers not come to visit any longer from the rumors?" He stepped back. The faces of the council members ranged from firmly set to slight worry.

Rei motioned towards Ilena. "The Ministry of Intelligence was tasked with working with the castle and city garrisons to determine the cause and if there should continue to be concern," Andrew said. "Hear the words of the Minister of Intelligence." He stepped back to let Ilena have the floor.

Ilena drew in a breath, tried to remember she was louder in this room than she'd been before so she wouldn't inadvertently shout at people, and began the report of her investigation. She had to start back at the "beginning" of the unrest, carefully not lying but also not admitting her own fault as being the cause of it. Instead she blamed it on the other reason that had been truth: that the imprisonment of the corrupt lords removed the source of wealth for a large number of nightwalkers.

She gave the count of the dead nightwalkers in comparison to the numbers of hard working people in that district as proof of those large numbers, but applied it to the rest of the city as well. Protecting the Gold Lion and the Sage Seraph, she explained that the merchants of the north and east parts of the city had used their own guards and spent their own money to see that the unrest in those parts of the city had moved out of the zones where income to the city and safety of the people were the most necessary.

That had pushed those nightwalkers into the south and west parts of the city, making too many in those zones for them to live peaceably with each other. She shook her head sadly. "Even before then, there had been a worse corruption in those sections of the city." She waved her hand behind her to direct the attention of the attendees to three witnesses that were being brought to the stand while she continued. "We discovered it as we began our investigations into the general unrest. What began as a small group of sick men was turning into a deep and awful disease." She let the first witness explain what had happened to him there.

The expressions on the faces of the city council, and even many of the others in the room, turned to some horror. It always started with disbelief, but the witnesses of the second and third were the same. It had to be believed sufficiently with three. Ilena took back over. "In trying to understand if this needed to be rooted out or contained, our investigations uncovered that it had been prevalent long enough to already be a threat to the external industry of Nijoushi." She looked over the heads of the city council members. "Mister Marciel, will you please tell them what you told me about how our fine city is being rumored about outside of it?"

The council members turned to look at him. Raine cleared his throat and bowed briefly. "My caravan drivers have recently been returning with the disturbing news that travelers who've stayed at the inns on the west side of Nijoushi are telling people outside of the city that it's no longer a safe place to come and stay overnight, and some have heard that even coming to eat a meal is untrustworthy." He bowed again.

"Thank you, Mister Marciel," Ilena said soberly. "This corruption had been seeping into the western part of the city as they looked for victims and potential customers from visitors, who bring in valuable outside income." The council members were paying attention to her again. "With even more nightwalkers in both of those zones, neither the rumors nor the evil canker was being helped.

"What we were able to determine from our investigations after the fact was that those nightwalkers who preferred to make a more reasonable living — like runners, messengers, horsemen, escorts, shoppers, and the like — decided that they wouldn't put up with the corruption interrupting their more legitimate businesses any longer. The decrease of out–of–town visitors was also hurting them. Therefore, they determined to also push the undesirables out of the west side, putting a rather large number of them in the south."

She sighed sadly and waved her hand slightly. "Because there was already tension in the underworld from the conflicts in the north and east, the conflict this time turned violent. The pressure of too many people in one quarter of the city engulfed it. Because the deep corruption of the expanding House had been the main cause of the western part of the city moving, that House was turned against and removed.

"We investigated that one most particularly and made further arrests in order to clean it out completely. Such dark and debased behavior and actions cannot be allowed to continue to besmirch the reputation of the capital city of Suiran. We and the city guard have committed to continue to watch for it and take it out until it's completely rooted from Nijoushi. I've also requested that my informants across Suiran watch for it to rear it's ugly head anywhere outside of Nijoushi. I'm sure we don't need a repeat of the Doll House in this awful adult form." There were shudders that she was relieved to see. They did remember it well enough, then.

"We're also watching the nightwalkers generally, to make sure that there's a better level of them in the city now. With the majority of the most undesirable ones having been removed by the fight that night, we're hopeful that those who remain are those who work legitimately and that the total numbers aren't as unreasonable as they were before. If there continues to be problems in areas, please let the city guard know. We'll help them either make arrests and banishments as needed, or attempt to help settle disputes." She stepped back slightly to indicate she was done.

Andrew stepped forward. "Out of the investigations have come two issues that need to be addressed. The first is the very poor state of the south part of Nijoushi generally, as has been discussed before in these meetings. The other is the sad state that those involved in paying that House were willing customers. While we can't understand at all why some persons would feel the need to be so physically abused that they'd pay for it with what limited income they have, surely they need to be helped." Council members were nodding that they were in agreement.

"We'll be authorizing for clinics to be put in the southern and south-western parts of Nijoushi to study this issue and help those who need help recovering from such warped desires," Andrew said. "Please put together the proposal and cost estimates for each individual clinic for presenting at the next regularly scheduled meeting." The entire council bowed their obedience to that request. They were content to have Rei already be proactive on the issue, rather than having to whine at him.

"As for the state of the southern part of the city, it's been proposed by the Ministry of Intelligence that a revitalization plan be proposed to the Throne by the construction companies of the city, including cost estimates, to be reviewed by the Regent's representative for feasibility and cost effectiveness. It's expected that with sections of the city repaired progressively in order, eventually a full revitalization of Nijoushi can be accomplished. Once the proposals have been reviewed, a summary report will be presented to the city council for final agreement and approval."

Ilena blinked a little. Justinian had recommended that idea to Rei at one of the Regional Security meetings during the clean–up phase. She was sure she'd be that "representative" and would be in front of this body again. Somehow she'd not taken into account that this body would have already been complaining to Rei about the state of the south side of Nijoushi. At least they'd not tread where the council had already made plans. She did have to wonder just what they'd been suggesting for it to not already be addressed. She probably wouldn't ask, though. The answer would just irritate her most likely. It was the council's job to think of those answers themselves. She sighed. Rei likely had the same amount of hard work to get this council to do anything that he had with the other ministers and department heads.

"Have the questions of the council members and the issues brought to the Regent today been sufficiently addressed?" Andrew asked them.

There was some thinking, then one glanced at Ilena. He stepped forward and bowed. "There are rumors that the Ministry of Intelligence was involved in or even instigated the bloody nightwalker war. Can those be addressed?"

Rei nodded at Ilena. She looked the questioner in the eye and said, "We were participant in the investigations of the unrest and the results of the battle, as directed by Regent Rei." When she said no more than that, the man bowed and stepped back.

-o-o-o-

The Sage Seraph turned and left the council chamber of the royal castle of Nijou. It had been an interesting visit, to see for himself how the Queen of Night worked. Very poised and confident, for sure. Calm in front of daywalkers. She wasn't going to incriminate herself, of course, so that could be used against her if he should decide he needed blackmail material. That might be very dangerous, though, given her position in that room. Minister of Intelligence was quite high and powerful. It would take a lot of real and proper evidence for anyone to believe him over her.

Not that it really mattered in the end that she'd instigated the fighting. Cleaning up that mess had been someone's responsibility eventually. Having her take it on was something he and the other Heads could find relieving.

She'd defended it well enough to keep the council calm and thus the citizens of the city — without there being a manhunt against innocent nightwalkers. He also appreciated she'd protected him by not specifically calling out that the nightwalkers of the north (or east) had participated in those efforts. Those who needed to know he'd been involved already knew and that was enough.

He had to laugh to himself at the payment she'd required of Raine. He was quite sure there were no such rumors going around anywhere in the rest of Suiran or abroad. Not to say it wouldn't have happened eventually with the House of the Grey Snake causing problems. That was another distasteful action that she was welcome to have handled. Honestly, so far he had few complaints about what she'd done to the nightwalker half of the city. Of course, he'd risen to the top so was far less likely to than those that had been squashed.

She'd even taken that poor step–child of the worst part of town, leaving the rest to the rest of them. Likely she'd been the initiator of the revitalization project, though. She was smart enough to understand that no sheep or only a few very poor sheep meant very unhappy nightwalkers. Unhappy nightwalkers were hard to handle. Or they moved to more lucrative places. The Sage Seraph shivered a little. He wasn't going to welcome them back to his zones. He'd finally cleaned them out and was happy with the numbers and how they were working.

When he arrived at his safe house he stopped by where his First Lieutenant was resting until his shift started in the late afternoon. He kicked him (gently) awake. "Raine should be arriving at his place soon. Go ask him a question for me." Smithson sat up and tried to wake up enough to remember the words he'd hear next. When he looked ready, the Sage Seraph said, "Ask him, 'Is it true that the rumors outside the city are so bad?' I expect him to say he was paid to lie, but I'd like to know if we need to be helping repair that image. It will hurt our business, too."

Smithson gave a nod and rose to his feet. The Sage Seraph kept him just a bit more. "I don't know if he knows the answer, but ask him if he knows if the revitalization plan is for the whole of the city or just the south. You can go back to sleep when you get back with those answers." He got a bob of the head, then continued on to his place at the back of the room. He stepped up on the dais and moved to sit. He stopped and stood upright again and stared at the man who'd stepped up to face him.

"Didn't I just see you?" he finally asked.

The young man with the wild hair and dressed in brown gave a jaunty salute. "Just got done with posting the summary notices here in this part of town and thought I'd do my other order before moving on."

The Sage Seraph glanced at the door. He'd not heard any knocking this whole time. The young man continued to smile a teasing smile at him and shook his head. "I just followed you in and they thought I was with you."

The Sage Seraph sighed, then decided not to sit down. This was one of the Queen of Night's guards after all. Even in that room he'd been. "So, what's the message?" he asked dryly.

"Please be sure to be at the first meeting of the Big Four — of which you are one — to be held tonight at Raine's place an hour and a half after dinner meal–time. He's agreed to be the neutral meeting place this time."

The Sage Seraph gave a dry laugh. "She's made him pay even more with that. I thought that was light payment." That got a twinkle of the eye out of the Queen's Guard. "I can't just send an envoy?"

The Queen's Guard got sober and he shook his head. "Nope, not for this one, and probably not for any of them unless you've been seriously injured. You'd like to have someone else making the top level decisions for the nightwalkers of your district?"

The Sage Seraph closed his mouth after a moment's thought. "No, not really." He furrowed his brow as he tried to work that one out. "She'll ...make it a council?"

"Yes," he was answered rather directly. At the Sage Seraph's pause, the Guard hesitated, then said, "I understand that's how it works in Ichijoutsu. She'll see it happen here." The Sage Seraph blinked at him and the Guard offered him more, but he rather thought the whole of them might just be more talkative than most. "She'll explain why it's important to be so at that meeting. Plus it's to set the boundaries more firmly."

"Ah," the Sage Seraph would definitely want to be there in person then. "Safety is guaranteed, then, I take it?"

"Yes," he was reassured firmly. Then the twinkle was back. "Of course, you have to promise the rest of them that same courtesy."

"*Pft,*" the Sage Seraph couldn't help the laugh. He waved a hand at the Guard. "Of course. And I'll assume you'll allow me the same courtesy today and into the future?"

The Guard gave a secret grin. "We've already been doing that for quite some time."

The Sage Seraph sent a kick at him that didn't connect because the Guard had danced away. "Stop teasing people just because you can," he scolded at the Guard's back.

On his way out the door the Guard answered back, "What's the fun in that?"

The Sage Seraph sighed at the closing door and sat down cross–legged to slump into a relaxed pose. At least they hadn't called him back into his conference room without him knowing they were there. He shook his head. That would've shocked him as much as it had shocked the Gold Lion. He would far rather it never happened. Then he was grumbling at himself. He could've asked that one about the revitalization plans. At least he'd have the opportunity to ask at the meeting that night.

-o-o-o-

Henry fumed slightly to himself. The Gold Lion had been easy to get to, talk to, and leave. Flynn was already resigned to Ilena and her ways and would show up for the meeting. Finding Raine's brother, on the other hand, was proving difficult. He'd finally called Marcus to come help him. Marcus saw small signs and indicators better than he did. It didn't help any of them that the new "Black Ram" still didn't have any safe houses, barely had real followers yet, and wasn't settled.

He'd had a few more days than they'd thought he'd have, so his name was known now in the streets. By what Henry was hearing this day, he'd been winning nightwalkers over to him by telling them he'd protect them from the Queen of Night. A few of the nightwalkers who were more into the business side of things had been complementary of the Black Ram's ability to understand the market of the district. They'd mused on the effectiveness of some of the ideas he had about how things could go better. That was good news, as far as Henry was concerned. The man knew how to sell ideas, and had some decent ones.

So far Henry had been following the trail of information from those who knew about the Black Ram. That was the hardest way to go about finding him, though. He was sort of hoping that if he kept asking questions about the man, he'd come answer them for himself. Marcus got to him first, then followed after him a bit of a distance to watch and listen to the crowd. When Henry got to his fourth person, Marcus interrupted. "Hey, what time of day did he talk to you?" Henry blinked. He hadn't thought of that. When it was after dinner two days before, Henry slumped.

When they'd released themselves from that conversation, they moved to walking back along that street, asking at the inns if there was a sleeping client. They were looking for a friend, but he'd had a long night and might not have woken up in time to meet with them. He'd only given them the street name and restaurant to meet them at, not what place he'd be sleeping.

Eventually that found payment. They sighed in mock irritation and were led up the stairs to a back room. The innkeeper knocked on the door. "I'm sorry sir," he called. "You've visitors." The Twins were listening for footsteps. For some nightwalkers they'd be headed for the window and escape. It took a while and another knock and call before they heard movement in the room.

The door opened and a disheveled thin man opened the door, scratching his head. He stared at them, then closed the door. "I'm not talking to you two again."

"You don't have to talk to us," Henry answered through the door. "You just have to hear our message then we'll be going."

"Thank you," Marcus said in aside to the innkeeper. "You can go. We won't do anything to him. Promise. It really is just a message of words we're ordered to deliver." The innkeeper gave them a suspicious look, but Marcus was very good at putting on the innocent believable face so he gave in and left them. Besides, they were both dressed in official castle clothing.

Henry was somewhat relieved the Black Ram hadn't run and escaped out the window yet. He opened the door and walked in. Marcus followed him, but stayed at the door, closing it behind him. Henry was a little surprised the Black Ram had just lain back down on the bed again. Henry pondered him, then said, "You know, you don't have to stay up all night to talk to them. Start at an hour before dinner and stop an hour before the middle of the night. You'll gather up enough that way just sitting around you. That's the range most Heads give out orders so they're used to that."

The Black Ram cracked an irritated eye at him. "You do it, then."

Henry shook his head. "Can't. I get you're not thrilled, but you can do it for long enough to get the area settled enough. Then if someone you're willing to have be your successor shows up, go ahead and retire. I suspect Mistress Ilena's not wrong, though. It'll grow on you and you'll prefer that income to the other you've had so far."

"Shut up and let me sleep," he was grouched at.

Henry shrugged to himself. "Show up at Raine's place tonight an hour–and–a–half after the dinner hour. It's the meeting to set the boundaries. If you want to have the least amount possible, be there to complain at the rest, or they'll give you the lion's share so they don't have to deal with this place."

He got both eyes open and glaring at him. "Like I want to show up there and let *him* know what I've been pushed to become. He already doesn't want his name sullied as much as I have."

Henry stepped up to the Black Ram, patted him on the head, and pulled his blanket up even farther to tuck him into the bed more tightly. Softly he said, "He already knows. You think his best customer wants to fall out of his good graces? He's decided he's okay with you here if it cleans up the place and keeps it calm and his other customers happy."

The Black Ram gaped at him, then started laughing. "You mean she's bullied him into accepting it and found reasons for him to give in."

"Maybe," Henry shrugged. "Either way, be there."

"I get it," he was grouched at again. "Go away so I can get enough sleep to answer to that."

Henry patted his shoulder and took himself and Marcus out. They could answer to that now that they'd answered to the other order. The Black Ram was the only one who'd not sent a representative to the city council meeting, but he'd gotten enough of the summary when they'd called him up. He really didn't care about the details anyway ...except that the city was cleaned up enough it could be made safe in his district if he did the final work on it.

"I really don't envy him," Marcus said in a muse on their way.

"Nor do I," agreed Henry. Marcus had voiced the very thought in Henry's head. He'd be hard to deal with in the meetings generally for a while until he did settle. Still, his grumpiness was understandable. They spent the next little while being his salesmen in that district, hitting some of the harder to reach places as they headed towards the south side to post the city council meeting summary there.

CHAPTER 156 Inception of the Big Four

Raine wasn't quite sure how he'd gotten himself this deep into the nightwalker world. He did have to admit that because he'd stepped in as far as the merchant district went, perhaps he'd asked for it without fully understanding. It probably didn't help that he kept turning a blind eye to what Ilena really was, since he'd far rather see her as a princess before anything else. Being the favorite of royalty always had nice perks. He'd enjoyed the few so far and was looking forward to what was coming up. However, he supposed he should've remembered that there were prices to pay that sometimes were more than one wanted to really get into. ...Especially when that princess was also a nightwalker House Head.

He sighed at himself. Given he'd done both of those to himself, it was true he couldn't really complain too heavily when the door to his office opened and his younger brother stood framed by the opening. "I'm surprised you were willing to sell me out." Russel had said it dryly, but he was irritated all the same.

Raine's lip quirked up slightly at the irony he understood quite well. "Like I had any more choice than you? I'd already dug my grave before she told me she'd called you up. While I greatly enjoy negotiating with her when she's in the mood, even I can't say no to her when she's being the royal she is."

Russel slumped, then rubbed his hand over his eyes. His other hand held his gloves shoved into his hat, both off now that he was indoors. "It's a complete mess over there. No one turns me down, though." He snorted a dry laugh. "No one wants to stick their head up right now, and with all the other Heads gone, no one's gonna." He waved his free hand. "Not that it guarantees loyalty. I'll still have a lot of hard work to get that far."

"Well, at least that much is good for you," Raine leaned back and put his fingertips together. "A good use of all that energy you need to put to good uses."

Russel scowled at him, then ignored the comment. "Where'm I supposed to go?"

"You're a bit early, but it's upstairs in the common room of the guest floor. I've got no customers up there tonight, so it's open." Russel gave a tired nod. He'd been in this building plenty. Raine's brow furrowed as he considered his younger brother. "Have you got staff? ...Lieutenants yet, to help you?"

"Of course not!" Russel was irritated by that, too. "It's only me right now. It's going to take at least half a year to learn who everyone is and who can be trusted. Not to mention for anyone with a brain to decide they want to help take all that on."

Raine shook his head at Russel. "You've got contacts all over now. Pick a few and send messengers to call them in." He let his eyelids droop. "I'd probably prefer you not tap my caravan guards, but I assume you know enough of them now, too." Most of them were in town, actually. They'd be out drinking for the time of the meeting and arrive to sleep the drink off after the Heads left.

Russel tipped his head in curiosity. "Why would you offer to help?"

Raine raised an eyebrow back. "Because even I'm affected by that zone. I'd like to see it calmed down and straightened up faster than slower."

"Then you should take it!" Russel scowled.

"Nope," Raine answered back. "Already too busy with the small empire I'm building. You didn't have anything better to do and like that kind of life."

"Yeah," Russel teased meanly, "you like being a nightwalker while looking like a daywalker on the front. At least I'm honest."

Raine blinked at him calmly. "Which is why Princess Ilena trusts you with the job. She'll make me pay every time. You she'll train and protect." He let Russel gape at him for a moment, then waved him out of the office. "Go get settled. There's drink in the cabinet in the kitchenette, but don't be angry drunk when they all get here or she *will* make you pay for that. And keep the grumpiness down several notches as well." He pierced Russel with his look. "She *is* the Second Princess of Ryokudo. Remember that. She's as sharp as King Sasou and he's the top Head of the nightwalkers. She's top in Suiran because he's given it to her. Watch your mouth."

That got some gaping, too, but he ignored it and went back to his musings and strategic planning as the door finally closed behind Russel. To stay the top merchant of Suiran meant he had to work hard on staying ahead of everyone else. The information Ilena paid him with was more valuable than the coin, every time. He was glad she'd let him know which of the nightwalker Heads in his district was worth it way back years ago. That relationship gained had been very profitable. He was looking forward to it continuing into the future.

He was a bit surprised when that very face, that he hadn't seen personally in quite some time, was suddenly in his doorway, his office door open again. For some reason they wouldn't actually cross the threshold. Maybe it was to respect his own "safe house"? "I just wanted to stop by on my way up to tease you." The grin on that face was indeed a teasing one.

Raine sighed at the Sage Seraph. "Yeah, go on," he said in resignation.

"She's made you pay up rather quickly, but I still haven't seen enough to say she's considered it done and equal. I wonder what's next for you?" Really he didn't need to lord it that much.

Raine pursed his lips, slightly irritated. If he didn't have the interruptions he might be able to figure it out since that's where his thoughts were trying to take him. "While she was able to get an early start on taking bites out of my hide for helping *you*, I've been wondering when she'll start in on you. You got even more out of it than I did."

He received his satisfaction as the Sage Seraph's face went a little pale. "I think having to learn how to manage a whole quarter of the city is enough for now." It was said a bit weakly. Even he didn't believe that was going to be enough payment to the Queen of Night.

Raine gave a sage nod. "I think you'll get to learn the start of it tonight. She's not slow, even if sometimes the payment date gets postponed."

"I'm expecting so," the Sage Seraph agreed. He drew in a breath. "Anyone else here yet?"

"Yes. My brother. Go make sure he sticks to wine and only one and a half glasses. If he makes her mad, he'll pay instead of get the help he needs; and we all need the latter." That wasn't quite fair since he was the one that had told his brother where it was, but the one glass would help him relax just a little. It was the "too much" that would be bad.

"Got'cha," the Sage Seraph gave a little wave and shut the door.

Raine waited for it, just sitting and looking at the door. Sure enough, it opened again about one minute later. The man with the long wild red hair was a new face to Raine, but he was obvious given that much and the timing. "Gold Lion, I take it?" he got a curt nod. "Nice to meet you. Up the stairs to the first open room. You won't be bothered except by her once she gets here. Feel free to sit on my brother until then if he gets rowdy. He just needs to get out the irritation at how hard it's going to be for him for the next while."

Flynn relaxed just slightly and gave an understanding nod. The door closed again. This time Raine took in a deep breath and purposely relaxed. He still didn't move from looking at his door. His right shoulder kept wanting to twitch as his back told him that Ilena was going to appear from behind him, not in the doorway like normal people. He knew better, but still, his back wouldn't believe his mind.

This time, the doorway was full of two people and even more were behind them. It was nice they felt they could relax and not come in uniforms this time, he supposed. The smile on Ilena's face said she was happy to greet him. The slightly more sober look on Ore's always relaxed, genial face said that it really wasn't a casual visit for them. "Thanks for hosting, Raine," Ilena said. He received the gratitude with a nod of acceptance.

"We'll stop back by when it's done and let you know the summary." That meant she didn't have quite enough information to drop the next payment due bill on his desk just yet. He shivered just ever so slightly. "The guards are set around the place with truce between them all on pain of death by my hand, although I'm sure that threat wasn't necessary." Petroi shifted so he and Thayne had glared hard on arrival, then.

"The rest came in alone. Are you sure all of them are necessary?" he cautioned as he tipped his head at the guards behind her.

Ilena only grinned at him. "You know I need my horse pile, Raine. They'll fade into the background." He sighed at her as Marcus gave a small shrug at him. They knew the rest would feel threatened, at least at first, but she wasn't ever concerned one way or the other.

He let his brow furrow in concern for her well–being. "You know, you *can* die. Please be careful."

Ilena went a bit more sober. "I'm human, yes, but I work very hard to make sure that doesn't happen." Well, at least she had some level of self–preservation. The point had made Ore's hand clench, though. He still worried, then. Likely the guards obeyed her on this issue because they understood Ore, then.

Raine gave a "satisfied" nod and leaned back in his chair. "They're all upstairs waiting on you. The guards will get back when they're drunk enough. Don't take too long." He could at least father her that way tonight, plus make the point she was wasting time standing in his doorway. Even she was doing it, but she wasn't there to talk to him really, so maybe it was that.

Ilena went casual and Raine's stomach tightened. "Oh, you're coming with us," she waved him up out of his chair. Since she'd just contradicted herself he had to wonder if she'd had a new thought, but he never believed it when this happened.

"I'm not a nightwalker Head," he protested, letting his eyes go wide in concern.

"That's okay. Just this time," she promised. He groaned inside. That's what she'd said when she'd told him to be at the city council meeting. Since he commonly went to those as a concerned citizen and invested merchant, his face hadn't been a surprise there. Having his face at this meeting tonight would mean he'd be given even more work he didn't want. He dragged himself to his feet and obediently followed after her people, keeping his expression neutral. If the other Heads teased him too much, he might force their worry to become truth and become a head over them himself. Not that he wanted it, as he'd told his brother.

"Flynn, Brendan, Russel, good to see you tonight." Ilena nodded at each one. Of course she'd call them by their real names. They'd all turned to stare at her in some shock. But then, she'd interrupted Flynn having an arm wrestling match with Russel while Brendan refereed.

The three other Heads watched with suspicious eyes as Ore and Ilena's guards bowed to them and moved off to stand at the top level of the stairs on the part of Petroi and Thayne and on the nearest wall on the part of Marcus and Henry. Once those four were settled, the suspicious eyes came on Raine. He held up a hand to say it hadn't been him. The suspicious eyes turned to Ilena. She ignored them and sat, motioning to Ore to sit with the rest of them. Raine being ignored and not seated answered the Heads sufficiently for Brendan and Russel to give him teasing looks. He took his turn to ignore something and stood as if an aide behind Ilena.

As he'd warned, Ilena wasn't slow at all. As soon as she had everyone's attention she began with the opening they all sort of expected now, from the messengers that had been going around. She wanted them to run the underworld as a loose committee, each in charge of their district, but meeting on a regular basis or when necessary to make sure things were going smoothly in the city. If any city–wide crises or needs among the nightwalker half of it came up, they'd convene to take care of it.

Ilena leaned back and put her fingertips together. "I also want a guarantee from all of you that you'll help police the nightwalkers to some degree." That got dark looks directed her way. She looked back at them from under her brows. "You know I already own Kouzanshi, but let me tell you one of the reasons why. I need to keep it policed to keep spies against Ryokudo out of it. Gael's been sending spies into Ryokudo and Kouzanshi is the easiest place for them to mix in and infiltrate. There aren't any other large cities on that side of the country." She had all of their attention now.

"My House has been trying to keep Brulac and Tarc out of Nijoushi, but with as many nightwalkers as were in the city just before now it was impossible. They're expecting us to crack down on their spies in the city now that I've moved in it, so now's the time to accommodate their expectations. I've already taken care of the Tarc spies they were sending in, so that part shouldn't be so hard. Anyone from out of the country should be treated with suspicion, but Brulac spies should be discouraged, removed, or fed conflicting information and sent on their way."

Brendan put his elbow on the table and his chin in his hand. "You have lots of motives for moving in the city," the Sage Seraph accused. Ilena shrugged, agreeing without comment. It wasn't any different for Brendan after all.

Once again Raine was getting looks, a very direct one from Brendan. Raine gave a resigned nod. "The reason the rumors about the decay in Nijoushi are as high as they are is because Brulac merchants have been spreading them more viciously than most would have."

"Rumors like that really aren't good business," Brendan said, a slight scowl on his brow. Raine could only agree with him, but the merchants would find that the most painful.

Ilena agreed and returned to the main point of this part of the meeting. "I need to know if you find the council of four acceptable, and the purposes reasonable."

Ore got looked at. He shook his head. "I'll be a neutral party if there's a tie that needs to be broken, and I'm here for the boundary line drawing, but I'm not willing to add that hat to my titles when I don't want Suiran Nightwalker King to begin with."

Russel gave him an appraising understanding look. "Why'd you take it, then? Her, too?" he pointed at Ilena.

Ore shook his head. "King Sasou's requirement." Russel gaped at Ore and Raine gave Russel an "I told you so" look. The other two Heads looked away. They'd not fight Ore either now. They didn't want that Head over them, for all he watched all of them.

Flynn finally shrugged. "They're fine with me. It'll be easier to complain at each other than try to hold a quarter of the city up alone."

Brendan cleared his throat, then agreed. "Who knows if we'll want to kill each other or not once we actually get into the thick of things, but at least for now it's better to be united that much."

Russel sighed at them all. "Not like I can say one way or the other. If we agree to the council, I'll at least be able to come and get advice and complain at someone. I'm sure I'll have the hardest time with figuring out who to throw out or not, since they'll all come spend the night in my district."

"True," Ilena agreed. "It's if they stay longer than they should, and who they talk to and about what. I'd think that if your House knew they had that information job, they'd be a little more content?"

Russel stopped with his mouth open again. Then he glared at Ilena. "Who's paying?"

Ilena shrugged. "Anyone who comes asking. People who buy information know they have to pay for it." She stared him down, until he slumped and looked away.

"Good, then." Ilena waved at Marcus. He approached the table, pulling a folded paper out of his jacket. He unfolded it and laid it on the table, then stepped back to his place. The others leaned forward to take a look at it. Ilena turned it. "North," she pointed to that side of the map of Nijoushi. Raine realized that the map had been waxed, as if for use in the weather. Ilena pulled out a wax pencil and pointed to the lines already drawn on it. "These are roughly the current boundaries."

Brendan held out his hand for the wax pencil and Ilena handed it over. He very definitively drew in the lines he wanted as his boundary. (He left her part in, not calling it out separately — a sign he wanted it if she'd give it up.) Flynn was quick to take it second and draw in his lines. He looked at Russel. Russel waved his hands at Flynn, "What the heck boundaries do I know yet? Less is better than more," and the wax pencil was handed back to Ilena.

Ilena darkened the lines around her district, including the contested streets on Flynn's side. She very definitively marked what she wanted on

Russel's side. Russel leaned forward and looked at what was left for him and sighed. Ore took pity on him. "If it helps, here's where my House already is," he pointed to a few smaller circled sections that took up some of the open space.

Russel continued to look through it then frowned. "All right. Tell me what the rest of the smaller circles are."

Brendan immediately pointed to the long narrow strip cutting through his section. "The Princess already owns this section. I want it for my House because it's awkward to have it cutting through my section like that, more than anything."

"And it's lucrative," Ore added dryly. Brendan didn't answer that.

Ilena shook her head. "Not letting it go. Not until the revitalization of the south is done. Then if they'll move you can have it."

Brendan said dryly, "I'm not sure I want my wealthiest to be stolen down there."

Russel's eyes widened as he tried to get it, then his eyes snapped to Raine, and back to Ilena. "Oohhh. *That* strip. Yeah, that'd be hard to have move out and replace." Brendan nodded.

Ilena shrugged. "It's not now, and I haven't talked to them yet since we don't have a revitalization plan to convince them with yet. It's just an idea in the works for now. Mister Balar is, in particular, fond of his custom–built place."

"Which brings up one of my questions," Brendan frowned at her. "Is that plan going to be good for the whole city, or just the south?"

"Whole city," she answered. "It'll start in the south, though, since half of those buildings are empty and all of them need to be torn down. It's a good place to begin since we won't have to kick people out of houses they like. Still, we'd like to see the whole city properly updated and repaired." Brendan was satisfied with that.

Raine realized why Ilena was so good at what she did. She didn't act like royalty, nor make the rest treat her as such. She worked with them as any equal businessperson. It was much easier to negotiate and feel heard when the interactions were done that way. It was how he'd been sucked in, too. It made it harder to remember that behind that negotiator face and voice was a Touka mind. They all kept trying to remember, but facing a House Head was one thing. Facing a Touka was another. She'd stay the wealthiest for as long as she kept her little empire, which would be for as long as she wanted to.

Ilena had moved on to negotiate for the contested strip with Flynn. She didn't give it up until he agreed to help her pay for a safe house for Ore's people in the next set of streets over on her territory, since she was going to have to give the current one up to his House. Then she rubbed her head and turned to Ore and negotiated the size of that space. He finally agreed to her taking one of his sections on the southwest side in exchange for just a little more space in the zone between Flynn's House and Ilena's. (Plus her paying half of the cost on the safe house.)

When she turned to Russel, he made her pause by getting in a question first. "Why'd you ask Flynn to help you pay for the safe house? Don't you already own enough? Or have enough to just buy it outright?"

"Of course not," Ilena answered, an eyebrow rising at Russel. "The taxes go to Sasou and Master Rei for use on things the nation and region need. I'm only a princess. Nothing comes to me; although, the taxes help pay for my housing, food, and regalia. Anything else I want is funded by what I bring in with my own two hands, like everyone else."

Russel narrowed his eyes at her, then said, "Thus why you've practiced to be a very good merchant and negotiator."

Ilena gave him a modest nod that none of them believed. Then she was negotiating in earnest with Russel for territory in the city. She wanted a rather large chunk of the southwest, actually, eating up into the current territory of the west. That wasn't very much to Russel's liking, for all he'd already said he didn't want lots of territory. Even Raine had to agree, though, that it wasn't looking "fair".

Eventually Ilena scratched her head, then turned to Ore and negotiated with him again, pulling him in to give up some of his central western territories to Russel in exchange for gaining more of the central south from her. The three of them ended up arguing over individual streets and sometimes even blocks until there was a rather odd zig–zaggy line from the west–southwest wall heading at a northeasterly direction in average until it closed in on the center without quite eating it completely up. On the return to the northwest, heading towards Brendan's territory, it went to the south of Ore's central northwest territory where it bordered Brendan's territory, then met up with Brendan's southwest border to finish out at a rough northwest location on the wall again.

By the time they were done, the other three were both bored and very entertained that Ilena had suckered Russel even further into becoming the Head of the west side by giving him a reason to fight for it. Ore's locations were mostly central, almost a circle with bulbous off–shoots, but off center towards the east and south. Flynn frowned at that and looked soberly at Ore. "Is that enough for all the nightwalkers who want to follow you? Not the freelancers. They'll go wherever they want."

Ore shrugged. "If they don't like it they can move again. I expect them to anyway once the final winners of all this are announced. I've already told them what I look for in members of my House, and honestly it isn't that they sit and squat in one place all the time. Eventually those kinds will get bored and move on, likely to Ilena's or Russel's, I'd guess. I've even pushed them to move out of the city altogether. There's more to living life than just this one city that won't have enough coin for all the remaining nightwalkers as it is for at least another year. The revitalization has to have already been making a difference before everyone has heavy pockets."

There were concerned frowns at that. "True enough," Flynn agreed. His eyes turned to Ilena. "Then, what've you told those in your section to make it so they don't come flooding into ours?"

Ilena nodded. "I've already told them if they don't like what I have to offer to go west." Russel was outraged, but she continued, "I'll be giving them other options to consider, like Ore did his. That's a lot of construction help they could be if they help with the revitalization, which will also get them places to live, then people to farm the sooner it's done. There are a few other things I'll offer; although, by no means will they be happy to hear they've got nearly nothing to farm for now. I can't guarantee they won't come for a while.

"They're all used to winter being lean so I think they won't strenuously complain until the usual time work is supposed to pick up and it doesn't. It's one of the reasons I wanted more of the west where there are people and places. It's my responsibility to see they have at least some income until we can bring more in." That settled Russel a little bit, to know that he'd already given up some of the space they would have come into anyway. Raine, knowing Ilena well enough by now, thought that might be one of the lesser reasons she'd wanted the space. The other reasons wouldn't come out until later.

Flynn raised his hand for a turn, then folded his arms and put on a bland expression. "Now that the boundaries are decided, I need to negotiate for space for the brothel houses. Some of the ladies have moved into my territory only on condition they get to move back to where they were before." He scowled at the looks of interest and disinterest he was getting. "They stay *my* ladies is also part of that agreement." The other four drew in deep breaths and another round of intense negotiations began. Raine found that extremely entertaining, even though his feet were beginning to hurt from standing this long. He was glad he wasn't one of the Princess' guards.

With that done, no other person spoke up. Ilena folded the map back up, the wax pencil already back in her jacket. "We'll get copies of this made, particularly several for the west side and south side so those nightwalkers can understand without having fisticuffs at the difficult–to–remember border." Russel moved to scowl and complain. She cut him off. "We'll post it on the west side. Just get out the word that you've negotiated the boundaries for them and can guarantee they're firm. That should give you one more boost. Look for a safe house next. Ask them where their favorite was and have them show it to you. If you don't like it you can have them show you all of them. They're already paid for until the end of the month at least, so you've got a little time to try them on.

"Make sure they tell you which ones they want to keep and which ones they'll not pay for anymore." Ilena raised an eyebrow at the other two. "What rates are you charging for similar locations?" Grudgingly they let that out. Ilena stated her's and they were at minimum half as much. When they all glared at her, she shrugged. "It *is* the poorest district." She directed her attention back to Russel. "Find something close and don't believe them when they tell you what it was unless it's close to one of the others we've told you. They might be liking what they're hearing, but they can't actually join up with you until you give them a place to. Once you have that place, they'll do the marketing for you."

Russel sighed and nodded. "Thanks. I'll miss sleeping in the inns with mattresses." The rest raised eyebrows at him. "What?"

"You think we all sleep on the floor?" Brendan snorted at him. "The whole point of being the Head is you get the largest cut so you can retire the wealthiest and happiest. Who needs to live in squalor when that's the goal?"

Flynn nodded. "Just don't be fast and obvious about it. They all understand building up little by little and hoarding. Stay on top and they'll know better than to steal it."

Ore leaned back and put his hands behind his head. "And you don't see the top Heads living in small basement cellars, either." The rest blinked at him. "None of the nightwalker council of Ichijoutsu live in them. They live in the places they work best in, owning the whole building openly." His lips twitched ever so slightly. "King Brother, Master, Ilena, and I are all in the castle." He almost got jumped for that one.

Russel had lit up though. Raine was sure he'd be buying a whole inn as soon as he could get a loan for it, complete with kitchen. It was the only reason he'd made a bad nightwalker. He kept showing up at Raine's to eat real food and sleep in the customer's rooms. Raine had only been making him pay properly for it by working for him.

Ilena rose, bringing the rest of them up. "We'll be in touch. I think we should rotate which district we meet in. Mostly to keep everyone else confused. Flynn, we'll be in your zone next. Pick a place that can properly be neutral and protect us. We'll just continue on around the circle after that. We should have a lot of safe places to meet in my zone, if very uncomfortably cold and full of holes." She gave a wry look to them.

"Not the castle again? Really?" Brendan put on a disappointed look. "I hear they have such good food, though."

"You'll really tempt fate that much?" she asked back. "I don't have to arrest you, but I can't prevent it from happening if General Garen decides to crash the party." They shuddered and declined.

Russel pulled his hat on and his gloves, bowed ever so slightly to Ilena and Ore, and took himself out first. He had a lot of work to do still that night. Flynn waved a hand at Ilena and said to Brendan, "Sit down with her sometime and pick her brain on how to help your street nightwalkers. She's got good ideas. I've managed to get half into the safe houses and another half of the ones still outside are waffling, considering the benefits. The rest will freeze this winter, the usual to do so." Ilena was pleased with that report. Flynn waved at them all and followed down the stairs after Russel.

Brendan shook his head at Ilena. "I'll wait until after things finish settling down. We're both too busy right now. But I would like to know it if it has those kinds of results."

"Sure," Ilena answered. They returned Brendan's goodnight and waited for him to walk down the stairs.

Ilena took her turn to lead the rest for the stairs and down to Raine's office, closing the door behind her this time, Ore staying with her. Raine stood next to his desk to be more respectful than just sitting down. "Raine, talk Brendan into letting you host every time it's in his district. He and I are going to fight out more of the details we didn't get into today. He knows I've got Family establishments here in this district, and in the West. He's not going to be content to ignore them anymore. This is the only place up here I'll trust for a while." She paused, then mused as if to herself, "We'll probably have to remind him that Mother doesn't negotiate with those who bully, threaten, or bribe."

Raine swallowed and gave a nod. That was the next payment he'd be paying her. "Also, make sure you have a contact whom Flynn knows, and a regular contact with Russel. I'll be passing messages to all three through you. I don't need so many faces in those Houses seeing my Favorites all the time to know who to torture me with merely by refusing to let them back out the door." And that was another one. "I'll be sure to let you know if more things come up." And that was the warning she still didn't feel the payment was made in full even then. He didn't think she'd take it too much further and become egregious, but she wanted the hole left open like any good negotiator and businesswoman.

As they walked out the door again to finally leave him in peace for the rest of his evening, Ore paused, letting the rest of his group walk on without him. He used the door to somewhat cover the conversation and said to Raine, "Two crates was just right. Three would've been too many. I think yearly mikan anniversary presents is an order to add to that list."

"Ah!" Raine did protest at that. "I don't think you'll be ending that any time soon. That's a lot of years of costs. Five years."

Ore shook his head and narrowed his eyes. "I think you'll be getting plenty enough profit from being the one to come out on top, having only the one Head to pay off instead of the four. The comparatively small percentage of that profit to pay for the crates won't hurt you at all." He gave the night-walker's grin of both ironic humor and threat, "And remind you who let you have that ease of restrictions."

Raine waited until Ore was gone before slumping in defeat. Ore really was the worst nightwalker Head there was. He actually knew how to be one and enjoyed doing it. The city as a whole looked the wrong direction for Ilena being so public and vocal. Sasou wasn't wrong to let Ore take Suiran Nightwalker King. They'd be about the same and Suiran wouldn't understand it at all, thinking Ore just walked in Ilena's shadow.

-o-o-o-

The night after the first meeting of the Big Four was yet another in–town one for Ilena. She took Liam and Carl with her, Marcus, and Henry this time. While Carl knew why, he wasn't thrilled to be going. He glared a bit at Ilena. "So, what's going to make it worth my while to expose my connection to you to all my contacts?"

Ilena glanced at him mildly and considered her answer to the question. "Carl, why do you work for the Ministry of Intelligence? Generally, not necessarily my office specifically."

Carl blinked. "Because it's a job and I get paid to do it."

"So not necessarily any noble and high reason, then?" Ilena asked mildly.

Carl shrugged. "Not really, no. People need money to live and take care of themselves. I do too." He really hadn't liked it at all to learn that she wouldn't give coin bonuses and wasn't sure what to do about that when he'd rather relied on them for the few extras he'd needed before.

"Hmm," Ilena nodded to herself. "So, then..., if Brulac paid you more than Ryokudo, you'd already be a double agent, then?"

Carl froze inside. Suddenly, instead of walking with a person who was younger, junior, and had less experience than he did, he was walking with his superior. He slumped inside — not outside as that would likely be very bad. He did sigh audibly, though. "If you put it like that, how'm I supposed to answer? Am I already incriminated, for being normal?"

"Ah. That's what it is," Ilena murmured to herself. She glanced at him. "You know, I've never in my life been allowed to be 'normal'. No royal is. No one trusts a royal that's just a 'normal' person. No royal lives to young adulthood if they're 'normal'. Please try to reframe your expectations to meet that viewpoint. I realize I'm still odd from there, but perhaps that can be a proper beginning rather than the one you've come into the office with."

Carl drew in a long breath through his nose, trying yet again for some level of patience and to get his brain to be a little less scrambled. In a very short amount of time she'd rather dramatically turned it from pay to traitorship to a lesson in how to face the office and her specifically. That last one was so different from the first two it was a bit like slipping on ice and trying to find any sort of footing.

She at least let him try to gain some level of stability before she continued. "I realize that normal people need to work to earn money to support themselves. However, that means that normal people can be purchased on any whim, save they have some sort of stern internal moral compass. Ore can't be bought, for all he was one of the poorest for years. His internal moral compass is what makes him what he is." Carl got the example.

"How strong is your moral compass, really, Carl?" Ilena turned to look at him directly, her expression sober. "I'm willing to negotiate rewards for exceptional effort, but no Touka will bend on this issue, at least in this generation. If money is really your only motivator, I think we need to know earlier than later."

Carl was decidedly uncomfortable. He wasn't sure how to answer her at this point in time. He'd have to have some rather deep thinking time to be able to. "I don't need an answer right away," she allowed, seeing his discomfort. "I do have a position for you still if money is your answer. You're valuable and I'd not waste your efforts for Mitchel." She looked away from him to let him relax just a little.

"I've hijacked you and made you come with me. You don't have to give away anything when you talk to them, and you can be as grumpy as you want that I hijacked you for the job. Or fawning or whatever fits the character you've shown them. They need the reassurance I'm not showing up to randomly kill. I need the reassurance I shouldn't be doing the same. Once I've learned them in this visit we'll all be able to peacefully co–exist, in the main, since the only interactions after tonight that I'll have with them will be to visit occasionally and to scold when necessary."

Carl sighed and tried to get himself into the right frame of mind to play that part. She'd made him skittish, of all things. It was one of the signs that not only was Ilena odd and difficult, she was also dangerous. He just might have to admit she was a House Head for a reason. He'd always been glad he'd not had to have many direct dealings with them.

"Go collect them up and have them meet me on the roofs," Ilena ordered quietly. She gave Carl the street names of where she'd meet them. When he'd promised it she took Liam with her and let Carl go on alone to do his duty. That helped him, but then made him wonder if he'd have been better off keeping his mouth closed at the beginning of all that. He slumped, his hands in his pockets balling into fists as he tried hard to not pull his hat down even farther over his ears and forehead. He couldn't hide from Ilena anymore at all.

He shivered. He couldn't wear a castle–issued cloak in town so he only had the jacket and three layers of shirts underneath that. (Which was still more than most of the nightwalkers had.) He tried to tell himself the shiver was only from the cold, but he couldn't lie to himself that well. He still tried to ignore the other voice. Mitchel was dangerous, but never had been towards Carl. Carl had learned a sternness he needed in front of the nightwalkers of the city to protect himself, but Ilena was different. Her kind of dangerous really wasn't something Carl wanted to call up and direct towards himself. Brushing against it just that much was more than he wanted.

He'd arrived home to Nijoushi with Liam after the fighting had happened on the streets. Mitchel had met him at breakfast so they could walk into work together the next morning so he could bring Carl up to date before they got to the office. Carl had been quite dismayed to learn that he might have almost no contacts left anywhere in the south or even west sides of the city. Mitchel had strongly encouraged him to go visit the prisons and then walk the city streets after the Ministry meeting that morning. If he hadn't protected what contacts still did live, he might have not had any to talk to tonight.

He shivered again. Those contacts he'd pulled out of prison, vouching for them, had been supremely grateful and had disappeared into the streets, giving him a few fearful glances back over their shoulders as if needing the reassurance from him that they'd still be alive by the next morning. He understood that feeling a little better tonight.

He used that understanding to empathize with his contacts as he passed around the Queen of Night's order. Every nightwalker in the south district was to be up on the roofs tonight. He told his contacts to tell everyone else they could in the area. He openly shivered and glanced over his shoulder in fear when they asked him why he'd been sent to tell them. "I think one of her ears learned I'd been actively protecting others on the street." He rubbed his hands together nervously as he said, "I couldn't just let it go, and it's something she would have noticed."

He shook his head sadly and in some worry as the contact he was talking to could only allow that she'd do that for sure. The rumors of the Queen of Night had always been that way. He knew a lot of the rumors were wildly outlandish and way off the mark, but he knew many of them held truth as well. There was no reason to disabuse anyone of those.

Carl wasn't sure how Ilena would know if or when all the nightwalkers of the south of Nijoushi were present in the place she'd called for them to come to, but when he'd found all of the contacts he could find, he was there, too, to listen with them. It wasn't right away that anything happened, but he hadn't expected that. Word was still being sent out and people were still coming in.

He was rather surprised to hear on the wind, "The Queen of Night has arrived. Give heed to her words," in Liam's voice.

"Who are you?" was asked back.

"Her Voice," was the reply. Carl blinked. He'd not known Liam had been picked for that position. It had never come up in the office, nor had he thought to ask.

He'd told his contacts to not test the Queen when she arrived, nor her people, but the scuffle that occurred next said that warning hadn't been believed by everyone the call had gone out to. He was nearly as surprised as the rest when those who'd done the testing were allowed to pull back without dying. For all he'd been told by Ore she was the most lenient of Heads in the city, he hadn't believed it any more than these around him did. He had, however, already been seeing some level of relaxing in the southern nightwalkers as those of her House talked to them openly about what being under her was really like.

He suspected these hadn't carried the testing on as far as they would have normally for the first time a Head showed up to take power. They'd already had the example of what she and her House did these past six days. It was likely done more because it wouldn't sit right with those to not do it. They'd always wonder if they should have, if her House and she really did have enough understanding and strength.

Liam continued once everyone was settled again. He started by listing the current street boundaries of the House of the Queen of Night now that things had become the newest way of being. There were hisses of unhappiness that cut through the chill air. "That leaves nearly nothing but the poorest for us," came the complaint. "They already have nothing we can have."

"Not even those of us who're willing to work to earn it," another agreed with frustration.

"True. For now, it's that way," Liam agreed with Ilena's words. "At the Head conference held last night, the Queen of Night argued for as much of the west as the Black Ram would give her. It was the best she could do at this time. However, the Queen of Night has already brokered an agreement with the Regent." Carl nodded. These would need to understand that first. Even that much had their interest. She had that kind of clout so was a better Head than most to follow in that regard.

"He's agreed to consider revitalizing this part of town with reconstruction so that those with sufficient income will come into it again. The Queen of Night promises to keep the reconstruction to a reasonable enough level that the current residents don't get angry and the House's cost to own safe houses isn't outrageous to impossible, but allow it to become a place daywalkers are willing to move to. Business will be wooed to come as well to meet the needs of both the daywalkers and the nightwalkers who wish to earn honest wages."

"Tha's all well an' good, but tha's years!" complained an older voice.

"Are you willing to work now to see it happen?" asked Liam. Carl heard Ilena in that tease and temptation. Silence was returned, but that was better than more complaints. Liam therefore kept going. "If reconstruction is going to happen the whole quarter over, the construction companies are going to need arms and backs to tear down the old buildings and build the new ones. Hire on. There's already some construction going on that could use some help on the southwest side. It can't handle all of you working on it at once but it's something to do until then."

Carl had to smother a laugh at the next suggestion. It was such a sales pitch. "The census needs people to walk the streets of the city getting a count of the people who live here. Hire on." He blinked in surprise at the next suggestion and there were comments of surprise from the nightwalkers. "The city guard just lost a lot of traitors to the prisons. Offer to hire on." At the surprise, Liam added, "You already know what to look for, the places to find, and how to protect yourselves. If you're sufficiently loyal enough to peace and the crown, you're already qualified."

Carl put his hand to his forehead and shook his head. He wasn't sure that would work at all, but maybe there'd be a few who really would rather work than steal or extort who might try it as an option. It was quiet for a while, then one asked, "What more will you do for this district? Will it just be a residential area, along with the noxious businesses?"

"No," Liam said softly, a smile in his voice that Carl recognized. It was the soft smile of Ilena when she was called Mother that her people carried. "Eventually this will become the entertainment district for nightwalkers. We here in the city and those who'll come from the rest of the nation and internationals. Those will fill the inns and eat at the restaurants to add to the income of the city as a whole."

There were a few intakes of breath from the nightwalkers who traveled the North Road. "You'll bring the lists here?"

"They're already begun," Liam answered definitively. Those nightwalkers got excited and murmurs went around as they explained to the rest what the lists were. Carl blinked, then slumped against the wall he was standing by. That was Ilena's ulterior motive to owning the south. Her main nightwalker businesses were already in the works there and she wanted to protect them.

He couldn't fault that part at all. Even he'd heard how much they earned, how much the nightwalkers who heard about them from the few that had visited them yearned to have them here also. These would settle now, in the main. It might be tight for a month or so, but that wasn't new in the winter. People who didn't leave houses couldn't be fleeced and only unattended houses were safe to steal from. Only runners really made money in the winter.

Liam continued, "We'd like to change the perspective of the south side of town to get people to move in as the renovations are starting to take place. The Queen of Night hopes to build a merchant strip for the crafters to sell their stuff, closer to the west side and the money that will come with visitors to the city. Start spreading the word that the south side will now be called Crafter's Mall."

Liam concluded the orders from the Queen of Night, "Stay in the safe houses you're already in. If they're in good enough repair, the Queen of Night will purchase them. If they need fixing up, they'll be moved once enough houses have been repaired she can get one. Established members of the House will move to them to collect the tax that will help with those purchases." He listed what that tax was. Carl shook his head. It was such a small amount that he was sure it would take even ten years to earn enough to buy any house at all. It was small enough to keep the nightwalkers on the roofs and in the streets from complaining too strenuously, though.

The street meeting was wrapped up shortly after that and Carl headed for his apartment. On the way he stopped at a small restaurant that sold hot drinks to warm people up and only had that. He'd had dinner at the castle. He just needed to warm up and not go directly to his place after being surrounded by an entire quarter of the city's nightwalkers. He wasn't too surprised when Liam walked in, feigned surprise to see him there, and sat down with him to "just chat".

"That's not a job I'd expect you to have in a million years," Carl said dryly to Liam.

"I was gifted it in Tarc," Liam gave a bit of a reminiscent smile. Carl wasn't sure if Liam was being facetious or not. Since this wasn't the place to ask to that detail, he let it go.

There was companionable silence between them for a bit, then Carl chuckled, "The sales pitches were almost too much. The guard job seemed quite impossible."

Liam shrugged. "Maybe, maybe not. It was one of the suggestions put forth by the team when they discussed the options. Maybe it will get people thinking about what they can really do, instead of assuming they're stuck where they are when they'd rather not be. Those who don't care to move on and help themselves won't, of course."

Carl agreed with a wise nod. Liam let the silence go for a while, then said, "I was glad the testing was short and she'd ordered me to let them go when they backed off." He looked up from the mug his hands were wrapped around to look into Carl's eyes. "I don't want to kill anyone. I never have and don't want to even begin."

Carl sat up straight in surprise and blinked at him. "You work for *her* and can say that?"

Liam gave a solemn nod. "She's trusted me from the beginning to not do that. I wish to never betray that trust." He looked back down at his hands and drink. "If she ordered me to, or was threatened and couldn't protect herself, I would anyway, but I think she means to protect me from that if she can. She understands that's my wish, I think."

Carl sighed a bit as he sat back and gazed at Liam. He finally swallowed the last of his drink and rose to his feet. "Well, it's not really my thing either, but if it comes to it, I'll do it for you."

Liam looked up in surprise, then smiled a bit. "Thanks." He finished his drink and rose to walk out with Carl. They walked together in their comfortable silence as long as their paths coincided, then they wished each other a good night and Carl watched Liam walk off. He shook his head and sighed as he entered the boarding house. Ilena was dangerous, and a House Head, but she also touched people in soft ways.

-o-o-o-

Thayne put his hand on Ore's shoulder. He knew Ore didn't want to be going into the city yet again, but this was the last time he'd have to do it for a while, they hoped. When Ore sighed and shrugged Thayne's hand off, Thayne fell back and followed him in silence. Petroi moved to keep pace two houses over and one up.

They'd already passed the message of gathering to the nightwalkers of the various sections of town that were now the Suiran Nightwalker King's. They were headed for that meeting place now. The section Ore had been given in the central part of town was the largest, and the southern part of that the quietest with the most roofs to be on. None of them were particularly convenient for outdoor House meetings, but it would be good enough.

It was good Ilena had taken the time to make them have a break after the city council meeting to run the trees before coming into town for the nightwalker council. That had helped both of them a lot (and the guards, too, who'd also needed that restful break of just being in the trees). Still, that had been yesterday and only a few hours. *Master Ore,* Thayne whisper–sung while they were still far enough from the meeting place, *shall we stay in town a bit to drink after this is done and all's well?* He knew Ore's pattern before the weddings had been to spend some evening every week or so out drinking (or riding his horse). He'd not even had time for that sort of relaxing in some time. Perhaps that would be reward enough to get the current job done.

Ore paused on the next roof and looked up at the clouded sky, reflecting back the pale light of the city lights. *That would be good.* He said it softly and his shoulders relaxed a little. Thane nodded to himself. That was it. Ore couldn't drown his sorrows in drink like most could, but he'd still learned to use it that way. Perhaps doing that tonight would help Ore settle the final residuals so he could carry all his hats calmly. Thayne suspected the horse rides were for when he had anger he needed to get out, rather than irritation at being yoked. He planned to test that the next time that rose up.

"The Suiran Nightwalker King has arrived. Give him heed," Petroi's voice said in the cutting quiet way of the nightwalker. Ore and Thayne settled down four houses away as if just other nightwalkers having come to listen. Ore had told him to tack on the location limiter every time, saying Sasou was the Nightwalker King, really. Ore only had followers and clout in Suiran. "But if you will test him, you will only test me. Killing the one you claim as your Head by all coming at once is stupid."

Both Thayne and Ore raised eyebrows at that. Thayne hadn't been quite as smart as Petroi to figure out that they'd *all* want to come, to see if Ore could really hold on to a title that high. They still watched closely to make sure that Petroi stayed alive. He did fine since he'd already been the equivalent of a House Head in the city for Ilena, and enough had given heed to his warning that he wasn't overwhelmed. Thayne was able to relax in relief after the testing was over.

"The boundaries of the five remaining Houses of Nijoushi have been decided and will be posted on the notification boards," Petroi began with. "The House of the Suiran Nightwalker King is not a House to need boundaries, nor walls; however, space has been granted by the other Houses for safe houses for those who wish to have them, and street boundaries for those who find freedom difficult so that competition can be only within the House inside those boundaries." Petroi listed off all the street boundaries, which was difficult because each separate area had to be described exactly.

There was a little muttering in the listening crowd. Petroi answered, "Once again the Suiran Nightwalker King wishes it to be said: you know how to live. Living is not only within walls, nor even only within one city. Nijoushi will continue to be poor for another year or so, until the revitalization that is planned has been able to take hold. If there isn't enough for you here, find work at other desks in Suiran until there is enough again. Or help rebuild Nijoushi when the revitalization begins."

Petroi again said the things Ore had said in the safe house he'd been to, letting all of the nightwalkers here know those things: how much it would cost to stay at the safe houses, requesting the older House members to take on apprentices of the youngest of the nightwalkers for a discounted rate and what that was, and listing off the rules to not fight with the House of the Queen of Night, to respect alliances made but they weren't required to participate, and to let the safe house captains know if they were leaving the House so they'd know it was an amicable parting. None would be forced to stay.

And finally, "The House of the Suiran Nightwalker King is an honorable House. If you can't live honorably under his banner, you will be asked to leave and find a more suited House for yourself. If an order comes down, you will be expected to obey it, but none will live your life for you, to order even your sleeping and waking. You picked a freelancer. If you can't be happy with him still being a freelancer, move on. If that is why you picked him, have fun — but don't cause complaints to rise up to his ears or he will get to have fun hunting you for it."

There was silence for a while as the word was absorbed, then a few asked questions. Ore answered a few of them instead of letting Petroi do it, which made Petroi a little upset, but Thayne knew why he'd done it. Some of the nightwalkers out where they were had become unsettled by the end of Petroi's announcement. Independent nightwalkers didn't really like not being faced by the person they wanted to be facing. Knowing Ore was actually there and hadn't complained at anything Petroi had said let them know they were actually Ore's words and helped them calm down.

In particular they had to give a more detailed accounting for the section moved from Gold Lion's district to outside of it and next to Ilena's, and the section lost to the southwest. Locations of the new safe houses for those areas were given, and again an allowance that if they wanted to stay in the current location, they could join the Houses that now owned those territories.

When the nightwalkers were satisfied and had faded away into the darkness again, Ore led Thayne and Petroi to one of the places he wanted to drink that night. They confirmed that he kept it within his House boundaries. Until the city settled fully they wouldn't allow him to wander into other Houses' territories. Because there was truce between all Heads currently, he'd be okay about anywhere, but all of the nightwalkers still needed to learn about the truce first.

They let him drink until he was near falling asleep, keeping the conversation light and completely unrelated to anything about work, his high titles, and even Ilena (unless he needed to bring her up). That meant Thayne got to hear a few more stories about Petroi's childhood in the youth barracks of Selicia. Those seemed to be Ore's favorite stories to hear. Thayne told a few of the funny ones from when he was trying to go from back–country woodcutter's son to nightwalker. It was good to have Ore laugh at him and tell one of his own. It was obvious he'd always had a soft spot for the unfortunate young that had little choice but to eek out a living on the street.

Back at the castle, Thayne rubbed Ore's head. Petroi patted his shoulder a few times. He'd done well that night. Ore was content to be tucked into bed next to his wife and fall asleep quickly. As they walked up the stairs to their room, Thayne put his arm around Petroi's shoulders. "I think that was a good thing to learn tonight."

"What was?" Petroi asked as he opened their bedroom door.

Thayne teased, "That the nightwalkers don't like you as much as they do Master Ore," Petroi glared at him, "...and that he misses being able to drink outside of the castle to relax."

364

Petroi nodded at that. "It was a good night," he agreed softly.

-o-o-o-

The next morning maps of Nijoushi showed up on the city notification boards. No commentary or reason was given, but the city was divided into four districts: one outlined in red on the east side, one outlined in blue on the north side, one outlined in a golden brown on the west side, and one outlined in green on the south side. A few odd zones were outlined in grey, including a central southeast zone, and there was one section outlined with a dashed green line within the blue zone. Eventually those general areas were titled, from the east and counterclockwise: the Northern Gardens, Market Street, Traveler's Row, and (because of the hard work of the nightwalkers of the south to spread the name) Crafter's Mall. Mostly they were named after the main business of that quarter, so caught on fairly quickly.

Only the nightwalkers knew what the map was truly for. As the news spread of the revitalization plans most daywalkers assumed the map was related to it. The maps also came in handy when city residents needed to show visitors to the city where to go to find a particular business or street. When they'd get too worn and fall off someone would invariably go to the closest city guard station and request that it be replaced properly. They'd send the request to the castle, and a new one would show up.

Nijoushi's nightwalker population began to settle down with each district working hard to learn how to take care of itself. Complaints went up to Heads who worked hard to find solutions. It wasn't quite so hard to find a day's coin, as far as competition went, but it was still hard for a while to find anyone to pay it. People had to be a little creative.

Surprisingly the Queen of Night's district didn't rise up in revolt and stayed rather quiet except for the few that moved into the Black Ram's district. Ilena's people kept a close watch there to help Russel until he could get his feet under him and know who his people were. Petroi finally just assigned him a Lieutenant who already knew that part of the city and could help train him and the other two people Russel had called up from his own contacts to help him.

CHAPTER 157 Ministry Vacation at Falcon Studios

Ilena woke up stretching and sighing at the temperature of their room. It was almost too hot. She wasn't going to be able to just get out of bed. "Justinian," she complained at him, "I know Ore likes it warm, but I can't move when it's this hot. Let it be cool enough to wake me up."

He was suddenly leaning over them both, fanning them, but with a bit of his teasing sparkle to his expression. "But Mistress Ilena, Master Ore was just complaining yesterday that the bathroom wouldn't warm up sufficiently when it was kept that cool in here."

Ilena rolled her eyes at both men. "How about I order a cast iron stove for the bathroom, then?"

Ore's eyes were open and very interested at that comment. "I'll take it as the compromise," he said. "Even I'm having troubles moving this morning." He smiled at Justinian, "Although I'm definitely enjoying not waking up to a cold morning. Did it actually work?"

Justinian looked up as he thought about that, then shrugged. "I'll go see." He stopped fanning them, so they got out from under the covers before they warmed up too much again. His voice came from inside the bathroom, "It's warmer than it was yesterday." He poked his head back out to say, "It might be too warm, too, since the water was also warm." They had to agree as they walked in and saw the walls were covered with water dripping down them slowly.

"That's almost hard to breathe," Ilena said lightly.

"Like the sea coast," Ore agreed. "Shall we pretend we're in the far south seas?"

Ilena laughed as Justinian smiled with them. He patted the towels he'd set out for them. "What are you doing today? The usual office work?"

"Not today, I think," Ilena mused. That got Ore's attention. "Clothing for going into town. Then we might go out on the horses so we can run for a while."

"Why back to town again?" Ore asked, beginning to wash since Justinian had rather automatically doused him with a bucket of water, not having anything else to do right at that moment. He'd moved on to the bedroom right after that, though, to set out the clothes. They'd been in Ichijou a lot in the last two weeks dealing with the nightwalkers there.

Ilena gave Ore a bit of a cynical look. "We can't go back to Master Rei until I've talked to Mister Balar and we've made sure to at least some degree that everyone is settling back down. If we can walk through town as us and not be jumped, we might be finally done." She was done getting her hair wet but filled the bucket one more time and doused Ore to rinse him off. She sat down on the wash stool and he lathered up her hair.

"Mm," Ore said after a bit. "It is a bit hard to breathe, isn't it?" The high humidity was becoming a bit of a problem for him.

"Yes," Ilena agreed, "but Justinian stirred the fireplace a bit ago, so it should be cooling off soon." Her eyes took in the walls. "I'd expect to see that going to ice to let us know it's time to be moving on."

Ore laughed. "The rest of the room will already be too cool for me well before then." He took his turn to douse her (three times) to rinse her hair, and her since she'd washed the rest of her while he'd worked on the lower two–thirds of her hair. With a look at the bathtub, then each other, they chose to reach for the towels next and skip the bath. They'd already sweat enough just in the air of the room.

"Hmm," Ore mused as they had to move out into the bedroom to get the air to dry them off the last bit. "Maybe not put a stove in there. I've heard from Mistress that they're very warm. I'll ask if they have one in their bath room and how cold it is if not, before we decide that's necessary."

"Okay," Ilena agreed.

They were dressed fairly quickly in clothes that Ore had to pause to admire. They were new to him. "When did we get these?" he asked.

Ilena ran her hand down the front of the green jacket she was wearing over a gold shirt. Both had a very feminine flair to them and were well tailored. "The castle tailors have been working hard to catch up to Lady Seraphina, I'm given to understand." She opened the doors to their wardrobe and it was nearly full to bursting, trying to fit the clothing for two people in it that had somehow arrived in it.

"I don't even see any of the things I used to have in there," Ore said, peering around her.

"Oh, the costume's gone, but your jackets are still here," she pointed to them. "And it looks like someone defended your garrison cloak so you can keep using it as a disguise, but yes, the rest have been replaced."

Ore looked at her side. "I see the first two dresses are still here, and most of what you picked out early on, but they're almost hidden by the rest." He pointed to the opposite far end from where his things were.

Ilena nodded and ignored the dresses yet again. There still wasn't a reason nor place to wear them, as far as she was concerned. They'd only come with her because Mina and Mizi had put them in her lap at the tailor's office. She'd worn one of them once because Ore had told her she had to for their date night. She stepped back and looked at the space of the room, then asked him, "Shall we go ahead and ask for the second wardrobe, or is only having one a good excuse to not get even more clothes?"

"The latter, I'm sure, Mistress Ilena," Rio answered dryly. "If they want to sew you even more clothing you won't wear, they can bring the wardrobe with them when they come. I'm sure I'm glad the court formals and regalia are kept elsewhere."

"True enough," Ilena mused and sat in the chair Rio had moved into the room from the wall.

Ore sat on the bed to stare into the closet a little moodily. He then ran his hand down his jacket front. "I guess it's comfortable enough, and understated enough I won't complain strenuously." He tipped his head, then finally got up and went to the mirror next to the bathroom doorway and looked more critically at his newest outfit. "It even looks good. I guess it will do for a Second or Third Prince."

Ilena snorted at him and he mock–scowled at her. "It's funny to see the vain Ore come out," she teased him. He couldn't do anything about it because Justinian had finally caught up to him to brush his longer hair. Ore hadn't seen it in a while, not having bothered to look in a mirror since before the progress around Suiran.

"It still dries too fast," Justinian complained with a frown. He finally disappeared into the bathroom and came back with the bucket almost half–full. He dipped the brush into the water and got Ore's hair all wet again, then brushed it. Ore protested when it went to curling, but Justinian was focused and ignored him. Ore gave up and watched in the mirror what Justinian was doing.

When Justinian was done, Ore could only stare at the him in the mirror. He finally turned with wide eyes to look at Ilena, showing her what was done. She blinked and couldn't say anything. Finally she said, "Justinian, did you like hairdressing best?"

Justinian blinked back at her, then took in Ore as a whole, then blushed and bowed. "I'm terribly sorry, Master Ore." He headed for him with the brush again.

Ore held up his hand, forestalling him. "It's actually not bad, just very different. Having the longer hair lets you do more with it?"

Justinian nodded a bit miserably. "That's why it's popular for the young lords of the castle to have hair that long or a little longer."

Ore turned and looked at it again, then said, "Try one more time, but use one of the ones you learned for the older lords. I actually prefer that level of sophistication. While it might distress you, I'm not really a young lord at heart."

Justinian timidly approached Ore with the brush again. He looked at Ore's hair a bit distantly as if picking a hairstyle from the list in his mind. Then he drew in a breath and began over again. When he was done that time, he frowned. "You shouldn't let it get any longer if you like these styles. It's already almost too long." He looked at the overall effect in the mirror from behind Ore as Ore reviewed it.

When Ore turned to face Ilena this time, she considered it, then she thoughtfully nodded. "I could get used to it, I think."

"It's well done, Justinian," Rio praised him.

"Marcus," Ilena called. He came in from the outer office. "Justinian, give him one similar to the first one."

Justinian lit up. "Can I, Lord Marcus?"

Marcus had been about to nod, but stopped and scowled at Justinian. Justinian blushed again. "Just 'Marcus', Justinian. I'm not ready to get used to that yet." As he got level with Justinian, he knuckled the manservant's head. "I hope you're not already lording me in your head. I'm not sure I've even gotten to just Marcus with you yet."

"Well," Justinian admitted as he dipped his brush into the water bucket one more time, "Sir Marcus comes easier, but I wanted to respect the gift the King gave you."

Marcus raised an eyebrow at Justinian in the mirror. "Well, that's all right. I do appreciate it as well, but since court baron seems only a name, and doesn't change who I am, I'd like to only get 'lorded' by the other lords in the castle, not by family."

That made Justinian blush in pleasure. The rest of them smiled at that reaction. When he was finally done fussing over Marcus, and Marcus had turned for the rest to inspect the hairdressing effort, Henry's voice came from behind Ilena. "Is that what the first one on Master Ore looked like?"

Justinian shook his head. "Curly hair takes a different hand and style, but they're close. The curls stay in better and can be smaller. I just thought Marcus wouldn't want it to be styled that way, so went with the calmer look."

"It's definitely calmer than his usual wild," Henry agreed, teasing Marcus. "I'd want closer to Master Ore's look, though, if anything at all."

"Would you do Thayne's similar to Marcus', Justinian?" Ilena asked.

Justinian nodded. "There's another one that would be for older men with curly hair that might work better, though."

Ilena's eyes went distant. "How would you do Petroi's?"

There wasn't an answer for a while. They realized she'd made Justinian drool and get very lost in his head. Marcus even waved a hand in front of Justinian's eyes and couldn't get him back out. They all laughed and that pulled him back. He went sheepish. "That would be difficult to decide, and would very much depend on the place he was wearing it. These can be worn mostly any time of day and place."

"Ah, yes, location does matter, doesn't it?" The way she said it made them all put piercing looks on Ilena.

"Just what are you thinking, dear?" Ore put his hands on his hips, accusing her in his stance.

She waved a hand at him, and thus all of them. "Ichijou." That got mixed sighs and growls. Justinian got excited, then shivered and held his brush in front of himself with both hands as if to ward off an enemy. Ilena gave Ore a look and motioned at Justinian.

Ore put his hand on Justinian's head and pet it a little. "You've got time before we get there, but these are already very nice. She's not wrong that we'll *all* have to be presented rightly there. If you're not sure, then you and Rio can go get lessons a few times between now and then until you think you've got some styles that will work. You can practice on us, too, but if it's too fancy, I'll make you take it back out before I *actually* leave the offices," he ended with a dry threat.

That got Justinian to calm down and breathe again. He bowed to them, "Yes Master Ore, Mistress Ilena." His eyes went to Rio and she nodded at him, promising they'd go when he was ready to go. Then he turned to Ore. "You'll go in that, or should I fix it back?" he asked.

"I'll wear it this way today," Ore allowed. "No one will recognize me, and it will be ruined by the hat I'm sure, but thank you." He rubbed Justinian's head and the young man relaxed again.

Rio had put Ilena's up in a nice look for her, not leaving it the simple braid either, but gathering enough of it up that it wouldn't go to a wild snarly mess while they were out or on the horses. Ore collected Ilena's hand up in his elbow to lead the group out to the common room. "Keep yours for now, too, Marcus," Ilena said. "It's nice to see it looking tailored rather than mopish."

Marcus whined at her for the awful tease, but let it go, saying to Henry, "But it does look nice. I wonder if I could learn to do it myself? It didn't look easy, but it also didn't seem supremely difficult."

"I could teach you, maybe?" Justinian offered.

"Sure," Marcus said.

Ilena tapped Ore with her hip and tipped her head ever so slightly at Amber. Ore's lip twitched up. Amber was quite taken by the slight change in look. She was definitely one who liked modern fashion, and on Marcus even more. Marcus caught Amber looking and blushed slightly. Amber looked away, embarrassed, her hands clasping in front of her skirt. Then she said, "It does look nice, Marcus."

"Thank you," he answered, then they were sitting to the table to eat from the plates Amber and Leah had made for them all. Thayne gave open appraising looks to the hair styles of Ore and Marcus, likely trying to imagine what he might be given when it was his turn to be dressed up for Ichijou. Petroi was studiously ignoring the fact that Justinian was staring at him, vaporiously lost in the thoughts of what hairstyles he'd put into Petroi's hair if only he was given permission to. Reynold kept having to pull him back out of his head to get him to eat at all.

-o-o-o-

"Who wants to come with us into town?" Ilena asked the rooms at large after breakfast. "It's been a while for everyone to have a bit of vacation. We can fit one in today, if we still take the reports this late afternoon. I was thinking it would be fun if we all just went together as friends, for all I do have to get some work done."

"Isn't that how you usually do it?" Rio teased a bit. "I seem to remember that's what I got to do the last time you gave me a vacation: go into town with Amber and shop while doing work, for all I was in Tarc at the time." There were laughs at that reminder, although Amber sunk into herself, a little uncomfortable with that particular reminder. "Will we go to Lady Seraphina's again?" Rio asked Ilena.

"Heavens no," Ilena waved her hand at Rio. "The wardrobe is already full and she'll make us all new cloaks since we can't wear the shawls openly in the streets in the winter. The castle tailors are only just now mollified. Let's not start the new clothing war just yet. Maybe in the spring," she winked at Rio who wrinkled her nose back. "We might stop in at the leathercrafter's and then go see where Robert is in his workings. I want to see how far the experimental saddles have come. Maybe there's at least one ready we can try out after we're done in town."

Ore slipped his hand into Ilena's briefly, setting his fork down to do so. "While it's fun to eat in town, do you think we could be back for lunch with Master and Mistress? Even if we have to go back out to run the horses after that?"

Ilena smiled at him. "Sure, that should work fine. The others don't have to come back with us if they want to stay in town." That earned her a dark look from Petroi, that she'd even think he'd not stay with them.

Justinian finally worked up to ask, "Even me? Or Reynold?"

"Of course!" Ilena answered. "The more the merrier." Her sparkling eyes went to Leah and Grandfather. "You two can come, too. We'll walk slowly enough for you."

Leah snorted at her for insinuating she was that old. Grandfather pondered it more seriously. He answered slowly, "Actually, it's been a long time since I've been in town, and I'd like to see what your changes have done. I have a few contacts we could go visit in the afternoon, and have just a couple's lunch?" he raised an eyebrow at his wife.

Leah blushed ever so slightly. "I'll bundle up warmly, then," she answered him. Ilena smiled a happy smile at that, content to have them relax with her in the morning.

Liam cleared his throat and Ilena paid attention to him. "Mistress Ilena, I'll invite Carl as well, if you'll allow it."

Ilena went a little wary. "Why?"

"It isn't often you're able to relax. I think if he can observe the relaxed Ilena I'll be better able to teach him some things he needs to learn. Then I think I'd like to give him the afternoon off. He also could use a bit of vacation, I think," Liam answered.

Ilena considered the request, then allowed, "It's true that would help him see some different things. If that's what you wish, it's fine."

They were mostly dressed in their cold–weather gear when Carl arrived in the office. Liam went to him, preventing him from removing his own gear. "We're going into town. Come with us, then the afternoon is holiday." Carl had already been looking at everyone curiously, but the final phrase caught his attention and he gave an accepting nod.

Mitchel walked in followed by five others. He looked at the grouping standing closer to the double doors to the outside and just kept going. "Shall we then?" he asked, not even bothering to ask where they were going. He could see he was the last to arrive, and with the nurses and Collin and Jefferson having come through the main hall with him, he just went with the flow.

Ore opened the door and everyone flowed out through it. "Dale, see that Hue stokes the fires every now and again or they'll freeze inside, not just you here outside. Or do it yourself to warm up a few times." Ore winked at Dale, who gave a wry smile and bowed. The outside guard was quite wrapped up to keep warm, and likely had on three or more layers of each set of clothing as well.

True to their nature, Marcus was the first one to throw a snowball. Henry threw one back at him. They ganged up on Thayne who didn't hesitate to fire them back. Petroi calmly picked up snow and was soon teamed up with Thayne. They were kind to keep the nurses, Leah, and Grandfather out of it, but somehow they managed to get Colin and Jefferson to join in when Amber and Rio joined Marcus and Henry's team. Since that was a lot of people running around in the general direction of Nijoushi, some snowballs did hit "innocent bystanders" who on occasion threw some back but complained so weren't included in the overall snowball fight.

When Justinian was hit, he blinked, then deliberately leaned down and picked up two handfuls of snow. He focused on packing it long enough they forgot he had. Then suddenly a snowball out of seeming nowhere hit Henry. "Yah!" he cried out. "Who was that?" Justinian was looking away, but had empty hands. "Reynold, was that Justinian?" Henry cried. Reynold gave a small nod, ratting out Justinian. "Don't let the Treasure hit you," Henry warned. "He uses ice balls."

That put Justinian and Reynold solidly in the middle of the snowball fight. When it became obvious that Justinian never missed, there was another snowball coming from an unexpected direction. It hit Justinian full on and exploded into a rain of packed snow chunks. He looked around to where it had come from then was quickly picking up snow to throw it, but not as a packed ice ball. It landed squarely on Ilena and she turned a challenged face to him. Petroi, Henry, Marcus, and Thayne all froze in fear, then backed off holding up snow–free hands. The rest of the players paused, curious.

For about five minutes there was a furious flurry of snowballs between Justinian and Ilena until one of the snowballs got snow down through Justinian's scarf to skin. His hands went up empty. "I yield," he begged.

As the others laughed, Ore tossed a snowball in one hand. "Well..., but really, it wasn't Ilena." He gave both of the last set of contenders a teasing challenging look. Ilena wasn't slow at all to throw the one in her hands at him, since he'd been the one to make Justinian throw one at her. When it looked like Ilena was going to lose to Ore, Justinian joined in as well, to make his own point that Ore shouldn't have made him think it had been Ilena. He'd had to take a lot of direct hits in his fight with her.

Eventually Marcus and Henry tackled Ore to get the snowball fight to stop. Ilena went to get comfort and pets from Petroi, moping that Ore was better than her at it. Thayne rubbed Justinian's head and thanked him for helping Ilena. "But don't throw the ice balls at me," he requested. Justinian just smiled.

They trotted to stay warm and caught up to the older non–snowball–fight group that had kept walking to stay warm. "So, Mistress Ilena didn't join in not because of her station, but because she's that good?" Amber asked Rio from the back of the group as they arrived. Carl turned his head to listen.

"Correct," Rio answered. "I suspect the same for Master Ore. They were kind and waited until they learned who could match them so it could be fun for everyone, even them." Those who'd had those snowballs land on them glared at the better throwers, not so sure it had really been "kind", although Rio wasn't wrong.

"It's because he hates wasting his throwing knives," Ilena moaned to Mitchel, whom she was walking next to at the moment. "He has to be good enough to never miss, and to hit hard enough to kill with only one every time. I'm sure I'll need Justinian's tending when we get home," she slumped in dejection. "I managed to deflect a few, but it's hard to do that when your own hands are also full of snow you want to throw next."

Mitchel chuckled at her. "That sounds like good reasons to me." Ilena couldn't disagree.

"I'm sorry I thought it was you, Mistress Ilena," came from Justinian where he was walking with Reynold, warming up inside. They could tell because he was holding on to the back of Reynold's cloak.

"It's okay, Justinian," Ilena said. "I was about ready to join in anyway." She glared at Ore, though. Ore only grinned at her.

-o-o-o-

Their walk into town was just as casual as their snowball fight had been, the conversations being several or intertwined as they stayed relaxed. Most of them did have their awareness kick up a notch (two notches for Petroi) when they were finally on the streets since they were testing the city. Amber stayed curious, not afraid to ask her questions with everyone present now that she'd confronted the Upper office and not been scolded for it. "Why come into town like children on holiday, instead of genteel and in carriages? I always thought royalty wanted to be seen that way, as persons to be in awe of and not touchable."

Ore spurted a laugh into the back of his hand. "Even Master hates that. He'll go this way every time if he can. He loves to hold Mistress' hand as they walk through town, everyone not even knowing he's there. Mistress' hair gives it away eventually, even if she does cover it, but he still can pretend and stay relaxed." He grinned over his shoulder at Amber. "The high lords and ministers might like to put on airs like that, but royalty only does when royalty *has* to. Mostly because they have to the most when the expectations of the citizens require it."

Ore waved his hand at the people around them, passing by on their errands. Most weren't out to be casual in the cold, but a few were enjoying the daylight. "Even most of these don't know what we are, nor care. If we cared to *make* them care, that would be different."

"And no fun," Ilena added. "It's not relaxing at all to have to meet other's expectations when they're as onerous as that."

"Is it all about having fun?" Mitchel asked quietly.

Ilena stuck her tongue out at him. "I'll be eleven today if I want to be. But you know that it's always around the edges. We're here for work, too. Relax or you're ejected to your vacation early."

"Ah, that's what it is," Mitchel relented, not really wanting to be sent away before he was done mentoring them for the day.

Liam pointed over his shoulder at Ilena and said to Carl, "That's the spoiled princess, but she's having fun relaxing so we live with it."

Ilena jumped on Liam's back and attacked him playfully about the head. It didn't work as well as if she'd really been eleven. He pulled her off and tickled her. That didn't work as well as if they'd been dressed for summer. They both sighed in disappointment. Ilena took Liam's hand in hers, letting him lead her along as if she were five instead. He asked her where they were going, since she wasn't in the lead and they were now well and good into Nijoushi.

Ilena pointed to Leah and Grandfather in the front, "They know." Grandfather nodded without looking back at the large group of grown children they were trailing behind them.

Marcus had taken the opportunity to slip into Ilena's slot next to Ore and take his hand as if Marcus was also five. After a slight hesitation, Justinian let go of Reynold and slipped up to Ore's other side and shyly put his hand in Ore's free one. Ore looked at Justinian in a bit of surprise, then smiled at him and held his hand. "I think it's the first time for me to be a father in town," Ore commented. "Although you two are awfully large for young children." They laughed and the others laughed as well.

Rio dragged Amber up to the front and took hold of Leah's hand. That worked better since now it looked like a young adult granddaughter holding her grandmother's hand. Amber glanced at Grandfather, blushed, then just let Rio hold on to her hand, holding just a little more tightly to it in return.

"I'll hold your hand, Petroi," Thayne offered. He got a cold stare. "Never mind." But Petroi stopped being jealous that he couldn't hold Ilena's hand just at that moment.

Liam had to grasp hold of Carl's cloak to prevent him from wandering off very quickly in embarrassment at being in the middle of this group. "If you do that then they'll tease you forever. Just sigh and ignore it the best you can. It's temporary."

Carl rolled his eyes but decided very quickly Liam was probably right and stayed put. He did have to turn to Jefferson and Colin on his other side and ask, taking Amber's example and out of his own final full frustration, "Is this really okay, even with you? How do you manage?" He got a small tolerant smile from Colin and a shrug from Jefferson.

"I knew Mistress Ilena when she actually was eleven," Colin said. "I was one of Tokumade household she sent to Kouzanshi for safety when she could. I'd far rather see her a happy eleven than what she had to be then, even if it is fourteen years later. As Liam said, it's temporary and lets us know she's relaxed.

"The rest are odd, or are teasing, but it's also temporary with them. There were a lot of broken people she helped, and a lot who could find happiness again because of her. It's not bad to want to see them smile and be comfortable instead of so afraid."

Carl blinked, then turned a little more soberly to Jefferson. Jefferson blinked back, then uncomfortably said, "I'm also strange, if differently. It's at least comforting to know that I won't be judged just because of that. I won't participate since I can't choose to, but I'd rather walk in this group than with those who say they're normal. I'm accepted even less by those kinds, who don't understand."

"You don't seem strange. Just shy and quiet, but otherwise normal," Carl said in surprise. "And very competent, too," he tacked on.

Jefferson turned a bit red and looked away. "Thank you, but strange is easy to hide with quiet and shy, and that is mostly my strange. I don't deal well with people at all."

Ilena nodded. "Like Robert, only a little worse in the shy department. But I like Jefferson." He blushed a deeper red and couldn't speak after that for a while.

Carl went back to thinking and observing and the conversation bounced around the group again. As they reached the first corner of Crafter's Row, Ore called the little group to a halt. He took the two young men who still had hold of his hands to the center of the corner they were on and began to dance with them, turning first one then the other under his hands, then dancing with them again.

Since they were the two who liked it most, they happily danced with him. Thayne and Ilena clapped the rhythm for them. Once the rhythm was understood, Amber began to sing a simple common song that matched it. Rio joined in, then eventually Henry when Rio tugged on his hand and then continued to hold it without thinking about it so that she was in the middle of their trio.

The rest moved back to allow them room and a crowd of observers began to stop and watch the impromptu entertainment. Someone held out a coin, looked for a place to put it, then flipped it onto the ground near the dancing feet. It clinked on the ground where the snow had been walked off the road with a bit of a ring at the end as it spun a bit. Soon other coins were joining it, some plopping into snow that hadn't been walked on. Ilena was shaking her head. She was ignored since the people were watching the three dancers. The singers sang through the song twice and Ore drew the dance to an end. They bowed to the street audience's clapping and thanked them.

"Will you do another?" an old lady asked querulously.

"What song would you have us sing and dance to, Grandmother?" Ore asked kindly. She named an old favorite of the area and the three singers began again, going first this time. The clappers picked up on it and the dancers followed Ore's lead, letting go hands this time to dance in line and clap along as well. The old lady clapped along with them, pleased to get to hear her favorite song. When it was done, the old lady fished in her bag for a coin. Ore stopped her. "Please, instead can I get a hug from a beauty like you?"

The old lady blushed and laughed at him, but he held out his arms. She waved a hand at him, blushing harder, then gave in and accepted a brief hug.

"Thank you very much, dearie," she laughed at him, then hurried on her way, needing to be embarrassed and pleased away from so many people. Justinian and Marcus had picked up the coins thrown to them by the time she was gone.

Ore waved at their grouping to continue on into Crafter's Row. He ended up near Carl. "How was that any different than what we already do with each other, Carl?" he asked, his tawny eyes fixed briefly on the least comfortable member of their group. Carl's brow furrowed in a bit of confusion. "If we help others to smile in whatever way we can or know how to do, by dancing or being royals, or by gifting a song and hug and complement, how is that wrong? Most people don't have the self confidence to let their inhibitions go long enough to be so kind. If we can, then isn't it good to give that gift to those who need it, when it's an okay time for them to ask for it?"

Justinian nodded enthusiastically. "That was the best way to help the Tarc be happy and smile, too," he said brightly. "They didn't smile much ever, until I'd talk to them kindly, or sing and dance in the tents. By the end of the Marluk'nak' of Change they were all smiling more."

Ore put his hand softly on Justinian's head. "Yes," he said softly, "you have a special gift for that."

Carl gave in. "Okay. I get it. That's enough lessons for now. I'll think about all that and see if I can live with it a little better." He got smiles back, half of them near–threats that he'd better, but that didn't last long. Ilena was suddenly pulling away, dancing ahead of them to the first crafter business she wanted to visit.

"But Touka's aren't like that," Carl protested after mulling it over for a bit.

"Master is," Ore answered softly. "He just doesn't get the opportunity to be so free to show it very often." Ore's expression was rather sad and shadowed as he considered what he knew and had seen of Rei.

-o-o-o-

Their first stop was at Falcon Leatherworks. Ilena had business with the shop master, Emerson, to review the special saddles he was making her for the messenger service. Both of the first prototypes were done and ready for trial. Ilena was pleased and requested they be delivered for Marcus and Henry to test. Ore thanked Emerson for the saddles he'd made for them to use in Tarc, and mentioned that Petroi's had been damaged. Emerson was as dismayed as Petroi, who'd repaired it as best he could. Emerson offered that perhaps he could replace just the damaged part and Petroi agreed to send it back when the messenger service saddles were delivered.

Ore took the time to visit with the master cobbler, Derrik Keembler, praising the boots that had kept his feet attached to his legs. Derrik was displeased they'd been marred by the Tarc swords, but Ore only let him polish them back up. Full repairs would take too long when the floor was very cold and he'd not brought extra boots with him. He might send them later, if he remembered.

Ilena let those who'd been mostly bored pick the next place to go visit. They had fun at the hairdresser's shop, perusing the wares there. The male guards were mostly bored there this time as the young ladies looked at all the hair pieces, mirrors, and brushes. Justinian had just as good a time as the girls did, and Leah picked out a new brush to purchase for herself.

That is, it was boring until the haberdasher invited the men into the back. Marcus and Henry were particularly pleased to see the line of hats laid out on a table. These were the formal ones worn by the lords and more wealthy of town, not the warm knitted hats they were all wearing now. They immediately gravitated to that table. Ore, Grandfather, and Mitchel were drawn by the stand of canes. They were very nice and stately.

The haberdasher was very attentive to Ore and politely pressed a sale on him. Ore couldn't say no, now that Ilena had reminded them all they needed to be ready to put on the proper display to Ichijou in the summer. Because this was the newest shipment of goods from Ichijoutsu, according to the haberdasher, it would be a good time to buy something in style. Ore ordered a cane he liked, requesting it be in his quarters at Ichijou by the time he arrived there. He didn't need it up here.

Marcus and Henry had picked out hats they liked. They asked if they could wear them at Ichijou. Both Ore and Ilena debated slightly, then agreed that it wouldn't be good for them to do that there. They might set a bad impression if they were mistaken for suitors trying to woo Ilena away from Ore. Ore teased, "The only way that would be acceptable is if King Brother still thinks we have too many guards. If you were in the costume of lords you'd at least be ignored by him." They laughed at that.

When they looked back at the hats a bit despondently, Ore relented a little. "Get the hats if you like them. Then figure out where and when you can wear them here before you try in Ichijou. That's a very high level playground. I only made it for the first part by being at a very low level, ignored until Master caught me. It was good to have that level of practice first." He received wrinkled noses from the both of them as they turned back to review the hats one more time.

Ore turned for the final table to see what it held other than spectacles. He noticed Thayne had slumped, too. Ore patted his shoulder as he passed him. "Just wear the blacks and be normal. You'll pass just fine. You'll only get strange looks when I get them. They're used to me being low and now I'm higher than them. They'll spend more time trying to get used to that than caring about you and Petroi." Thayne sighed and gave a nod of thanks for the relief.

The second table held similar things for hairdressers to put on their male clients or lords as was out in the storefront for the ladies: short wrist–length gloves of masculine colors and designs, pocket handkerchiefs that were stately rather than frilly, a few hairpins to go with the current curly styles, knickknacks that Ore was sure he'd never understand the use of nor how to apply in the first place. As Ore reached that end of the table, Justinian looked up from those knickknacks and studied Ore. His eyes went between the two for a while, then he reached out and picked up two items and trotted over to the proprietor.

Ore watched him and listened to him order similar items, but more suited to the Second Prince. Ore sighed. He supposed Justinian knew what he was doing and he was sure it was again related to their trip to Ichijou. That was already becoming an expensive trip.

He went back and looked through the hats, trying them on for Ilena to tell him which ones worked on him and which didn't. When they found a style they liked, they placed an order for one of those, too. Ore *could* wear one in either castle since he'd be playing his part a lot, and he did like them. He wouldn't mind paying for the hat and cane, but he wasn't sure he wanted to pay for whatever Justinian had ordered. He couldn't say no to his manservant and hairdresser, though, so he merely sighed and moved on when the rest were ready to go.

Ilena took them to Robert's statue shop next. They were fortunate to arrive at a time that the storefront was empty of customers, since they filled it up almost completely. Justinian's eyes lit up and he looked hopefully at Ore. Ore blinked to remember that he'd promised Justinian a statue from the master that was of the third–level. That is, one that felt like what had been carved.

Ore walked Justinian over to the display case that held the small statuettes that had been carved that way. "I have to special order the lioness, but you could chose one of these instead and have it now," Ore told Justinian. Since he had other things he wanted to do, he addressed the clerk behind the counter. "I've promised one to Justinian. If he wants the lioness most, see the order is submitted." The clerk gave a nod and turned to get a statuette out of the display case Justinian wanted to look at more closely.

Ore headed into the back with Ilena, she having spent that time scanning through the current offerings in the storefront. They waited for Robert to reach a pausing point in his work. As usual, Ilena put her hand in front of his eyes to let him know she was present. Because his work was visual she let him know that way instead of by interrupting suddenly with her voice, which surprised the shy man too much.

Robert froze, then turned quickly, his eyes looking for Ore first this time. Ore smiled at Robert to set him at ease. The last time they'd come it had been Ore's first time to come. Robert likely felt he'd been too forward with

Ilena then, not knowing Ore had come at first, so wanted to make sure this time. Robert rose to his feet and bowed to them both, then immediately launched into a report.

"The King's statue was received well and payment returned. I've already given Mister Balar the amount you said to pay him. I'm not done with the most recent request from the King as I chose to finish the one to the King of Yamanzar first." He waved at the statue behind him that was taller than them by half–again of a lion on a cliff about to pounce on a gazelle below it, still only roughed out.

Robert's eyes went to Ore again. "Missus Ilena requested yours be done in time for your birthday. When is that, may I ask?"

Ore blushed just a little. "In three days. The 29th of PreDark." He wasn't sure that was enough time, with all the other work Robert had been doing.

Robert merely nodded and said, "I'll see it arrives at the castle by then." Ore scolded him to eat and sleep, too, not just work on the stone. Robert smiled and reassured Ore that he did.

Ore reached into his pocket and pulled out his lioness. "Robert, I'm terribly sorry but I've damaged the one you made for me." The raised paw and top rose had been chipped off. "A set of nasty Tarc decided to try to take my head. In the thankfully–successful attempt to preserve myself, I lost some of the stone."

Robert took the statuette with some dismay. Ore put his hand over the lioness so Robert had to look at him. Softly he said, "I don't really want a different one. I was hoping instead that you could round off the broken edges so I don't thoughtlessly cut myself while holding it. The damage is a memory of something important I was doing."

Robert drew in a deep breath then gave a nod and Ore let him inspect the damage. "It shouldn't take me too long," he answered after a bit. "If you could stop by again on your way back through?" he looked up at Ilena, who nodded. He blinked and looked back down at the statuette, not wanting to rudely get lost staring at her. "Do you want to see how the King's statue is coming? I'd like your opinion on it."

"Sure," Ilena said as Ore nodded. They'd like to keep that one under inspection for the sake of peace in the kingdom.

Robert led them farther into the workshop, past where the other stone-smiths were working, to a set of storage benches that had many unfinished works on them. Some looked like they were only waiting for the final polish before being set out for sale or delivery to the owner. He put his hand on top of the head of the upright–sitting panther they'd already seen the rough of and felt the "fur" of. It now had a rough–out of a panther curled around it, the head not worked yet.

Ilena touched the fur on the chest of the first panther then nodded her head. "That's better."

Ore reached out and touched it as well. Instead of the very soft, never–let–go–of–it feel it had had when they'd seen it before, it was slightly coarser, like that of the Ryokudo horse perhaps, and just slightly longer than that. "It's still touchable but not a feel to get lost in," Ore agreed. "It's a better balance now."

Robert was relieved. "I'll do that then." He paused, then said, "Master Ore, if I may send for you to come visit when I'm ready for the head of the second panther? I'd like to make sure I get the right look."

Ore smiled his pointed nightwalker death–smile. "I'd be happy to come then."

Robert blinked at him. "That's a good look..., but I don't know if I can replicate that on a cat."

Ore and Ilena laughed. "I'd be happy to go through all of them for you," Ore said kindly. "Maybe you can then come up with something close." That satisfied Robert.

Ore left to wander over to the other stonesmith he wanted to talk to. This time Peter was watching them. They'd apparently passed by him closely enough to get his attention. "Hi, Peter! How are you doing?" Ore asked the apprentice.

"Well," Peter answered shyly. "I've been given my first commission, if you'd like to see it?"

"Congratulations! I would." Ore was happy for Peter.

Peter waved at his workbench. Set slightly to the side was a half–wreath of delicate intertwining flowers and leaves bordering larger five–petaled flowers. "A young lord has commissioned it for his bride–to–be. Apparently the flowers are her favorites and he wants to be able to put it over her vanity mirror." That would explain having an apprentice do it. That young and he'd not have the money to pay for a full master to make it.

Even still, "It's still near–master work anyway," Ore praised Peter. "It's quite well formed. I still don't know how you can see to do that kind of fine detail. I do hope your eyes stay young for a long time." He grinned at his half–tease.

"Thank you," Peter ducked his head in slight embarrassment at the praise and tease. Then his expression went concerned. "Ah, did you have my stone with you when you had troubles with the other?"

Ore fished into the pouch at his neck and pulled it out. "Yes. They were in here, together with a crystal vial of liquid. I think the crystal is what cut into the lioness."

Peter took the tiny falcon and inspected it closely. "It must be," he finally allowed. "Even this one has some slight damage, but perhaps this stone is a little harder than the other. Master Robert has to have a softer stone to get the feel he's looking for." He looked up from the falcon. "I can't repair it properly because the details are so fine. I'm sorry, but it's one of the weaknesses of working in such detail."

"No, it's okay," Ore shook his head as he took the statuette back and put it safely back in the pouch. "If I notice them, they'll also remind me of the important work I was doing at the time, and of my gratitude I came away from that particular moment alive."

Peter was just as relieved to see him living at the moment as well. They talked until Ilena came to say hello and to collect Ore. Peter gave them a bow and they returned to the rest, who were waiting on them again. Ore could see many had small bulges in upper coat pockets.

He smiled to himself, then found Justinian. "It sounds like the master's very busy right now," Justinian said. "I've selected one from the case." Ore gave him a nod and paid the clerk for the statuette Justinian had picked out. Then they were all out in the cold day again.

-o-o-o-

"Here," Ore paused Ilena and turned his back to her, crouching down slightly. "Let me carry you a bit so you can keep at least my back warm." Ilena laughed at him but complied, allowing him to carry her piggy–back.

She wrapped her arms warmly around his neck which kept his ears, head, and neck warmer (which was what he'd really wanted). "I'm already done," she whispered in his ear. "Let's go on to Mister Balar's shall we?" That was her last stop before she and Ore could vacation for the rest of the day.

Ore was in agreement. "Okay." He headed that direction, instructing the rest, "If any of you want to stop anywhere else on the street, now's the time. Meet us at Falcon Construction when you're done shopping." Rio and Amber immediately peeled off to head for Lady Seraphina's. Ore smiled, not surprised they'd want to go there. Likely they'd been disappointed, then, when Ilena had said they wouldn't.

The Twins waffled. Ilena waved them off. "Go with the girls. It's okay. You know we can't peel Petroi and Thayne off us. That'll be sufficient." Ore gave a nod of agreement. Collin and Jefferson bowed and headed off together.

Leah and the nurses had been in conference and they turned, taking Grandfather with them, headed for one of the medic stores on the street. Ilena huffed a soft sigh that brushed Ore's cheekbone with moist warmth. "What?" he asked her.

"They're off to get stuff in case I do actually get pregnant sooner than later. I guess being prepared is better than not." Ilena slumped down a little on his shoulder.

"You don't want to be?" he asked in surprise since she'd brought it up to begin with.

"Mmm," she pondered that. "I'm not sure I want to be reminded of what it actually means. I don't want to lose my energy level when I have so much work to do. I'm trying to ignore that part."

"*Ah*," Ore sighed softly. That he understood.

They watched Mitchel, Liam, and Carl peel off from them and head for an alley. Likely they'd like to get a little work done this morning as well, while in town. Ore looked around for Justinian and Reynold next, finding them walking with the four going to the construction office. Justinian just gave him a happy smile, so Ore let them be.

Ore was settled enough then to ask, "Why didn't Queen Mother use the herb to help with pregnancy, or your own?"

Ilena shook her head. "I don't know the history of the herb. And maybe Ryan found a reference to it during his research at Kouzanshi. A lot of that research still needs to come out of there and be understood to the rest of the nation and world. Aryana has decided that will be her work — other than Master Rei's request to head the audit of Nijou. She's going to focus on getting the research done at the university into the hands of the people of the nation so we can use the research, not just have it gathering dust in the library."

Ore walked through the door Petroi was holding open for him. They entered a lobby with artistic drawings of buildings Balar had built, or could build. As Ore set Ilena down on her feet, he said, "That would definitely be a good project for her to head." Ilena agreed.

"Welcome!" Balar's booming voice came as he walked to meet them, having risen from some work he was doing at a table in an open workroom off the lobby. "How are you this fine winter's day?"

A heavy paw of a hand came out for Ore's. Ore allowed Balar to shake his hand. "We're just fine, thank you," he smiled back at the large grin on the large man's face, having to look up to see it.

"Mistress Ilena," Balar took Ilena's hand next. "You've come here instead of meeting me at the castle construction site?" He released Ilena's hand and gestured them into his office, which had a door tall and wide enough to accommodate his size.

"Yes. This is a formal and official castle visit, on behalf of the Regent," Ilena answered.

Balar raised an eyebrow at her, then sat in his custom chair at his custom desk. At least the guest chairs were normal size. It still made them feel a little like children facing a large adult, just by scale. "What can I do?" he asked, folding his hands together on the desk, making that feeling a little bit stronger.

Ilena faced him soberly. "It's a request for all the construction companies in town. He'd like to receive submissions of city renovation contracts from each one as soon as they can be drafted. He doesn't need it down to the nail detail, although we'll get there eventually. This is the feasibility study. He does need estimated costs, suggestions on how it could be done, and realistic time frames. We're thinking of it being done in sections around the entire city, starting with the south. We'd like you to pass along the request to the other construction companies, since you'll be able to explain what we want best to them, rather than by messenger or notice board.

"With the fire damage done in the south part of the city, and knowing that side of town is the least popular to live in right now, we thought it would be simpler to start there. Demolition of the houses and businesses there is fine. We also don't want to put in expensive housing or businesses there. Keeping the prices to a reasonable amount for those that don't earn as much is still fine. We'd like to be able to draw those who are hard–working and want to have safe living environments there. We'd also like to cater to the fact they need to have grocers and other living item suppliers near them, so small business buildings or districts should also be planned for. We don't see the major businesses moving there, but I do have one request contrary to that."

Ilena drew in a deep breath as she faced the one most likely to not want to move, other than maybe Lady Seraphina and the master jeweler. "I want to move Falcon Studios to the southwest, just south of the western hotel district. I'd like it to be a crafter's mall specifically. I want it to be where visitors to the city can get to it easily and buy the products coming from the masters that should be seeing international acclaim. It's all well and good to have it here by the castle, where the lords of Suiran come, but everyone is good enough now to expand their businesses beyond that, and many are beginning to do so." Her gold eyes held Balar's dark brown ones. "Can I count on you to help with that?"

Balar was sitting with a neutral face. He rubbed his thumbs together as he considered her requirements and proposal. "So, you'd like me to let all the construction companies in town know about the request for feasibility proposals?" he confirmed first. Ilena gave a nod. "For the whole town, so keeping each district roughly at the level of income it's already at, but renovate it all?" Ilena nodded again.

Balar pursed his lips as he considered a little further, then asked, "And you want me specifically to propose the crafter's mall design early so you have it to take to the committee meeting to propose it?"

"Correct," Ilena answered.

Balar tapped one thumb on top of the other one as he considered her request. Finally he said, "I've actually been considering talking to you about that generally. I'm already outgrowing this location, for all I like the building

I got to design. I won't fit in well there either, honestly. I need to be farther south, maybe even outside the city walls. The more construction I do, the larger a storage warehouse I'm needing. I've been looking to buy one down there already, but I don't like most of what's available." His expression went wry. "Mostly for the same reason. They all need updating, or tearing down and replacing."

Ilena was understanding. "I can see that. It would be a good time for you to move if the reconstruction's happening now as well. We're expecting to hire more than just you to do the construction. No one construction company can do the whole city in the amount of time we have."

That got an eyebrow up on Balar. A little on Ore's, too. He wouldn't have thought this needed to be part of the war preparations. Still, she did bring it up. "Rei's beginning to move under the direction of Sasou. Gael is bringing war drums against Altherly, and Tarc has opened the eyes of Nijou. Keeping Nijoushi as it is has become dangerous if we also should suddenly become surprised by an unruly neighbor. We need at least the south prepared. Having those derelict buildings will put the whole city to flame if they catch fire with so few people living there to help put it out.

"If the construction companies want to recommend moving the south wall farther south, that's fine. If you want to keep those businesses outside the walls, then I recommend you get suggestions included in the proposal for how to keep the people working outside the city walls safe."

Balar had frozen. He took all that in, then blew out a sad breath. "That's a sad thing to prepare for, but definitely better to be prepared than to fall as fast as we would if we weren't prepared." He pondered his thumbs for a bit. "All right. I'll write up the feasibility study request and get it sent around." His eyes rose to look into Ilena's again. "What kind of time frame are we looking at? It'll affect costs."

Ilena answered, "Hire all the southern and half the western nightwalkers as soon as you can. They're the cheapest labor you can get and they need the work. They're going to starve this winter and light it all on fire themselves otherwise." She straightened her spine and drew in another breath. Quietly she said, "Sasou wants to move no later than this coming fall. Rei and I are trying for at least the following spring, in 547. If we don't move at all, and Altherly falls, Gael will likely come no later than the following year, but we can't know for sure."

Balar's eyes were as wide as they could go. "That – that's no time at all in the construction world!"

"I know," Ilena stayed soft. "Get the demolition of the worst houses and businesses in the south done first, particularly the closest ones to the wall. If we have at least that buffer, inside and out, we might be okay if things happen early. I think if we say we've hired you to do that much while processing the studies, people won't complain and your competitors won't get too jealous.

The proposals do need to come with income solutions. The castle can't pay for every house in the city to be updated. The construction companies will have to help us bear the costs until people purchase the houses to move into them. Get their ideas on how it can be funded."

When Balar had agreed to that much, Ilena had him pull out pen and paper to take notes on and dove into the details. Apartment housing for the poorest closest to the businesses on the south side being the first to build. Exactly what she was envisioning for the small business districts. Ore sat as a support for both of them, going through his memory, drawing up the prior conversations they'd had on this topic to make sure Ilena didn't forget to mention any details.

When she was done, Balar was still frowning. "By rights, it'd take six months to come up with a proper plan of this scope. Four minimum."

Ilena shook her head. "I know, but call it the feasibility study and tell them by the end of AnteDark. Rei and I can come up with the city plan faster than you guys can. Once we get it laid out, we'll send it back for construction cost proposal. Any disagreements on the city layout can be sent back during the time we can give for that. The city council will be doing the same: arguing with us on what we've selected. Once there's been a round of that we'll send out a changed proposal that hopefully won't be too far off the initial one so that minor changes to the construction proposals are all that'll be necessary. Then we'll go from there."

Balar sighed and leaned back, twirling the pen in his fingers. "All right. I'll get this out at soon as I can get it written and copied."

"Thank you, Mister Balar." Ilena rose to her feet. "I'll let the Regent know to be expecting the studies." They were bowed out of the office.

Justinian sighed as they walked out the main door. "Mistress Ilena, is that why you allowed for my request to burn down the houses? Because you wanted to know what would happen if it were to happen in an uncontrolled event?"

"Yes, Justinian," Ilena answered softly as they looked around for the rest of their group. Some were coming but still down the street. "It only worked because I had enough water, buckets, and people already in the district."

Justinian and Reynold both pierced Ilena with sharp looks. "Meaning you were already going to burn down buildings from the beginning," Justinian accused her. She just looked at him, but she didn't deny it.

Ore had to wonder if she would have burned down the entire southern section along the wall when the Family and water had reached the point in the zones she'd wanted to have the buffer reach to. He slumped and sighed to himself a little. She'd probably decided to test it first on just the House in the more controlled location and decided that the other plan was too dangerous to attempt. There just hadn't been enough residents of the area to care and help.

CHAPTER 158 Mizi's First Lesson on Having a Household

Lady Brianna was quite relieved to have Tanner turn to Mizi and say, "Mistress Mizi, Master Ore asks if you'll come have lunch with them at the Rose Office today. They're finally done with their requirements in Nijoushi and would like to see you and Master Rei."

They were sitting in the entry to the Old Regent's building. Chairs and tables had shown up there one morning, to the relief of her feet and back. Two days later one of the cast iron stoves had appeared, installed and already filled with burning wood. The guards at the top of the stairs didn't wear their warm hats, gloves, and scarves any longer, nor did they look so stark there. The company of even just a few chairs and decorations on tables made them look like royal guards instead of prison wardens. Brianna had been relieved to have these changes, too.

Mizi was a diligent hard–working student, but she'd pressed Brianna to her limits. She'd been trying to figure out this morning how to tell Mizi that it was time to stop going to the lunches and teas for a while. The ladies of the castle needed the time away from her as much as Mizi really did need the time away from them. When Mizi turned to Brianna, the question of if she should on her face, Brianna drew in a silent breath and said, "Mistress Mizi, I really do think that would be just fine. To take the ladies in smaller doses is perhaps better at this time. You've learned quite a lot in these last weeks. Let your mind rest and it will remember what worked and didn't best on it's own."

Mizi accepted that answer and told Tanner to let Ore and Ilena know that she'd be at the Rose Office. Brianna didn't miss the slump of relief Brian and Kirk had in reaction to the reprieve. While they didn't seem to mind the standing, they were attuned to the state of mind of the court ladies and Mizi. A fight instead of a calm meal had been brewing for a few days now. It had helped Mizi some that Amber had stopped attending with them, but it hadn't been sufficient in the long run.

Mizi took that as the opportunity to rise and take up her warm gear right then. Brianna could understand not wanting to just sit until lunch. They all had things they could do at the Rose Office and not waste time. Given that was how Mizi worked generally, Brianna would be glad for the excuse of resting her mind by doing office work. Sitting next to Aiden would help her nerves as well. His was a very calming presence.

Brian kindly helped Brianna into her cloak while Kirk settled Mizi's cloak around her. "You don't want to change first?" he asked her, being the help to Brianna he'd become essential for. It helped very much that Mizi saw Kirk as an older–brother figure, and he had the capacity to fit into that position quite nicely.

Mizi looked down at the tea dress she had on and sighed at it. It took her a bit of waffling before she finally chose the right answer. "I guess I should." She looked at Brianna who curtsied to her briefly in answer. Kirk took the cloak back off of Mizi and she hurried up the staircase, at least as much of a hurry as said dress would let her go. The guards at the top of the staircase let her in and Brianna sank back down to her seat. Maria was still in the suite cleaning up from the morning rising so didn't have to be called, thankfully.

Brianna closed her eyes and rested while waiting. She'd been working on teaching Mizi which non–verbal answers meant what so that she could understand at the upper levels she needed to. That had been a moment that it had been critical. Mizi had bordered on asking again instead of telling. Brianna was about to scream for that single lack of confidence the young woman had in herself. She was going to have to ask others for advice on how to train Mizi out of it. For some reason, Justinian came to mind. Perhaps because Ore was also a very difficult person to train. (Ilena wasn't trainable at all, so asking any of her personnel was pointless.)

It didn't help that Mizi was constantly moving on other issues as well. Like the hospital she'd decided she absolutely must see constructed. Mizi had decided to turn to Aiden for help on that issue when Brianna had apologized for not knowing how to frame the type of letters Mizi wanted to send. Her husband had handled correspondence of that sort. Mizi was good at writing letters generally. Getting her detailed brain to slow down and work to the genteel pace the lords expected was the most difficult task Aiden had. Brianna had been just as relieved to not have to be called on for any other part of that issue. The afternoon naps had become quite required by this point.

She must have fallen asleep because she was surprised by Brian's light hand on her shoulder and the soft voice in her ear. "Mistress Mizi comes."

"Thank you, Brian," Brianna said softly, slightly embarrassed she'd fallen asleep; although, they might not know and just had let her rest. She rose to her feet and resettled her cloak. She pulled on her gloves and pulled the hood of her cloak over her head. Mizi had arrived by then and was having her cloak put back on her by Kirk.

Sam and Leon were already at the office. Mizi had decided a week ago that the guards understood well enough, and she'd been having the pairs alternate duties. They'd been doing this part as well, since about the time the furniture had come. When it was Sam and Leon, Sam took care of Brianna and Leon took care of Mizi. Brianna had appreciated that support as well. Having the guards help her teach Mizi without her asking had been a boon.

They arrived at the Rose office from the inner parts of the office building. Brianna remembered that Ore's group would arrive from the balcony, bringing in the cold with them. She kept her cloak around her and her gloves on, but relaxed the scarf from around her neck.

"To what do we owe the surprising visit?" Rei asked Mizi as she arrived at her desk.

"Ore and Ilena are coming to lunch," she answered. "They've asked I come be with you and them."

"Oh?" Rei's eyebrow rose. "Well, then, we'll welcome them and you."

"We'll be glad to help until they get here," Mizi said, sitting down to her desk already, and missing Rei's bemused look that turned to Brianna. She curtsied to him calmly, then also sat down without answering him, since that would be answer enough. She was only being obedient to her mistress' wishes.

The office had been in industrious near–silence for several hours when the first noises of the wild couple arriving were heard. Brianna was a little surprised to hear them all at the back patio entrance door. That was the only door that opened, too. They had some sense of propriety then, to allow the rest of them to not deal with quite so much cold air. She noted Ore stopped in front of the fireplace to warm up before continuing on up to Rei's desk. Ilena passed by it without much comment, however.

They'd left their winter gear on the back tables. For once their guards for the day were only Petroi and Thayne, not the whole household. Petroi was staying with Ore, but Thayne followed Ilena at the proper distance. Brianna had learned that was to prevent Ilena from attacking anyone she shouldn't be. She still had a hard time seeing that. Ilena was so slender that it was hard to imagine she couldn't be restrained easily by any man, but the guards had reassured Brianna when she'd tendered some disbelief in their presence. Brianna had no intention of ever seeing such unlady–like behavior, so hadn't commented beyond that.

"Nijoushi's properly settled, Master Rei," Ilena reported. "We've just come from testing it and from passing on the request for city renovation feasibility proposals. I've given the construction companies until the end of AnteDark to get them to us. Mister Balar says it would normally take six months after that to get more full proposals in, or at a minimum four months. I've given him permission to immediately begin demolition in the south, particularly around the wall since that's where we'd like to start with the apartment housing. I don't think the other construction companies can complain if it's just demolition."

Rei had sat back in his chair when Ilena had approached his desk. He pinned her with his brilliant blue look until he seemed to believe her. "I'll expect to hear relief from the city council into the future, then," he set his expectations of a calm city from then on rather firmly. Ilena gave him a nod.

"It's good to see you, Mistress," Ore had joined them now. "How've the lunches been going?"

Mizi wrinkled her nose at Ore. "Not so good. I think I have the lessons down, but I can't get what I want yet. Brianna suggested easing back to let things settle a bit more. I think I need to do that before I explode. I keep wanting to teach them what I want them to know about me. They aren't ready to understand that to even the smallest degree yet. We're still having orthogonal conversations in the main."

Ore nodded in commiseration. "That would be hard."

"People do take time to change," Ilena agreed with Brianna. "If you've learned well enough, then give them the time to continue to observe you. Maybe in a...," she turned to look at Brianna, who chose to look her directly in the eye instead of pretend to not be listening, "...year or so they might be ready to try again?"

Mizi went to absolute dejected horror. Brianna answered calmly, "At least nine months. Maybe in a year they'll be ready to listen to what she has to say to them."

Ilena nodded as if that was completely reasonable and turned back to Mizi. "That would be about right. You'll have positive relationships with them in about five years or so."

Mizi was gaping at them. Ore chuckled. "Mistress. The court is very different than the university. They change very slowly, and you're far from what they expect to see, even for all you're very good at what you do. Be patient and do what you love to do. They'll understand eventually."

Mizi eventually sighed and said, "Well, if it's enough, then I'll gladly give that a rest for now. I have plenty of other things to be doing." Brianna slumped in relief, keeping it small enough to not be noticed by the people at the front of the room. Aiden gave her a sympathetic look, however. She had the sudden urge to ask him for release from her current burden. Since that was ridiculous and this wasn't the time, she went back to her work.

"How long have you been working on this current goal, now, Mistress Mizi?" Ilena asked. Mizi told her and Ilena mused. "Mmm. Yes, I do think that was long enough given how well you learn." There was a pause, then Brianna's head came up in shock as Ilena requested, "Can I please send Brianna and Aiden on an errand? It may take a couple of hours." Aiden's head came up in equal shock.

Rei had raised an eyebrow at Aiden's time being requested. "And what would that errand be, that both need to go?" Rei asked.

Ilena shrugged. "An errand of mercy. I'm quite sure that Aiden has had quite enough of Ore for a while, and Brianna of Mistress Mizi's unstoppable pressure to learn as much as possible as fast as possible. I really am the only one with any capacity to stand in front of that. Both surely need at least a few hours of vacation time that I'm sure they've both earned in great measure."

Brianna couldn't believe the expression of great court scolding on Ilena's face as she stared down both the Regent and his wife. "Leah and Grandfather are out on vacation for lunch in town. I'd like to send Aiden and Brianna to visit with them. Perhaps the four can complain about the four of us to their heart's content and come back relaxed enough to keep going for another half–day."

Ore spurted a laugh, then couldn't hold back. "Yes, I'm quite sure Aiden's earned a respite from me. And Mistress could barely come down far enough to admit that she can't tolerate her own lessons any longer. That surely means Lady Brianna needs to sleep for four days straight."

Rei scowled just slightly. "And I haven't earned that respite myself?"

"You did have it, just these past four days, Master," Ore said innocently. "It's past time we came and bothered you again. Your smile's missing. You can't have that without us here to torture you." Rei threatened Ore. Ore only grinned and danced away somewhat.

Mizi was glancing rather guiltily at Brianna. She let the weariness show just enough to let Mizi know Ilena wasn't wrong. Mizi blushed slightly and gave a nod. "It would be okay with me," she said. "I'm sure Brianna's earned it. She's worked very hard with me."

Ore and Ilena both turned looks onto Rei. He blinked at them, then looked away and waved a hand. "If Aiden would like to escort Brianna and call it a vacation away from Ore, I won't complain."

Brianna turned a hopeful look onto Aiden. Aiden looked at her, his piles on his table, then said, "I think spending a few hours with Lady Brianna won't be near so difficult, nor take me from my work so long as 'helping' Ore did." He made a dry grimace and rose to his feet to hold out a hand to help Brianna to her feet. "Shall we, before they begin the process of making the only royals in the castle relax so far we must protest and start all over again?"

Brianna laughed a little and let him lift her to her feet. "Yes, please. I think I'll scream if Mizi has to relax that much with them, for all she needs it more than anyone in the room. Maybe she could get the ladies to smile if she'd relax enough to smile herself." She ignored Mizi's open mouth of surprise at the statement.

As they were nearly to leave the room she looked over her shoulder to the surprised young woman and added, "And I'd recommend letting your guards have their own vacations soon. That was a lot of working hard they did with you, all while silently on their feet the whole time." The look of gratitude on Brian's face was all she needed, then she was out of the office and on her way into town. The name of the restaurant the other older couple were at was in Aiden's ear by then, but Brianna couldn't really care where they went. As long as it was away and she could relax in her own way.

She'd remember it, though. If she needed someone to stop the unstoppable Mizi, Ilena was the one to turn to. If she needed someone to get the oblivious children to open their eyes, both Ilena and Ore together would do it. She should figure out a better way to have them be her allies than being at collapse's doorstep herself. It hadn't been a thing she'd understood before this day. Now that she did, she wouldn't forget it.

-o-o-o-

Mizi was frowning as she looked at her guards sitting in the back half of the room. Rei recognized the look. He let the silence of Mizi's look go on long enough that her guards looked up to see her looking at them. He let her read them until she slumped. "I'm sorry Sam, Leon, Brian, Kirk. I've been too focused on my lessons again, and not on what's right in front of me." Ilena's look was as keen as Rei's likely was. Even she tested Mizi in things like this.

Mizi hadn't even begun to consider Ore's needs until Rei had left Ore in Mizi's care when they'd found Ilena for the first time. She'd learned to read Ore well enough now, and Ilena as well, but the rest she hadn't bothered with yet. This was an important lesson for her. More important than learning to get along with the young ladies of the court.

Mizi took a breath, but before she could give anyone time off, Rei raised a hand to her. She stopped and waited for him. Rei looked at the room generally. "Which one of you requested the front lobby changes in the Old Regent's building?"

Brian's hand immediately shot up. He was definitely done with walking with Mizi for a while. Kirk's silent support meant he'd supported Brian generally, and certainly had known about it as his partner.

Sam quietly said, "I requested the warming stove. We'd been having impromptu office meetings in there, standing, for over a week nearly every day after lunch. Lady Brianna relaxed quite a bit to have it looking like a royal living space rather than a prison space."

"It wasn't kind to make her stand on her feet so long afterwards, either," Brian wasn't willing to hold back any longer. "It would have been better to have taken her up to the suite office so they could both sit, but I think Mistress Mizi wanted to hear everyone's opinions when necessary and altogether we're rather a lot for the suite office."

"And at the beginning Amber would often be with us," Kirk added. "Mistress Mizi was very uncomfortable to have Amber with us, so likely didn't want to invite her into her personal quarters. But then the habit had been established, so even when Amber wasn't present we still held the meetings in the open foyer space."

Mizi's face was going rather red. Rei returned his attention to Mizi and let her scold herself and learn this lesson. "I'm sorry everyone," she said.

"Thank you Brian and Sam for filling in where I was blind. I'll try to do better into the future. Please feel free to tell me when I'm missing things so I can learn it better."

Rei turned his own scolding look on the guards. That was the thing they should have done from the beginning. They bowed. "We're sorry also," Kirk said. "We talked about it after the stove came. We've been trying to do it since then. Today before we came was an example."

Mizi blinked and thought back to just before, then nodded. "Those reminders in that way helps, yes. But," she was back to somewhat dejected, "I think it wouldn't have really sunk in very fast that way. I suppose I needed the more direct scold just now."

Ilena patted her on the head gently. "Well, now you've had it, you can work on doing better. Listen to their gentle reminders and scolds. That's how servants do it. For them to scold like I scold isn't right. I can only get away with it because of our unique relationship ...and because I'm not nor ever was a servant. I don't know how to do that, as you already well know." Her look was very bland and somewhat a self–scold. Mizi's side–long glare at her agreed with her.

Rei made sure he had Mizi's attention, then taught her the next part of it. "Brian, how long do you need to recover?"

Brian scowled just a little as he considered it. Rei would only ask this once. Mizi would have to remember the answer. It would be different for each one. "Until the day after tomorrow, likely that afternoon."

"So, two full days?" Rei confirmed. Brian gave a sharp nod. "With or without your partner?"

Brian glanced at Kirk. "Either way, this time."

Rei understood. He turned to Mizi to make sure she did. "When he was so overwhelmed last time, he asked to go for a week without anyone. That was too long for him, but we'd not had any choice in that matter. This is a better level, but usually you should watch so that they don't need more than a half–day to one full day. A simple evening off is best." He turned to Kirk. "And you?"

Kirk shrugged. "I'm not as bad off, but I do need at least the rest of this day. And I need to ask: I'm really not doing well with only the blacks to wear. I need a bit of color every now and again. What can I do that wouldn't offend? I was thinking even a little bit of red as a symbol of Mizi, or the blue or gold of the Regent."

"A pin would be enough?" Rei asked.

Kirk mused on that. "Well, sometimes it's bad enough I need a whole shirt of color, but that would do most times. Or a small ribbon."

"A shirt wouldn't be too bad, because you'd still have the outer appearance of a guard. A pin is acceptable as might be a small ribbon, particularly in any of those three colors, but much more than that would be too much," Rei allowed. "If you're finding you need more relaxation than that, ask for the half–day off and wear all the color you need."

Kirk smiled at that answer. "That would be completely acceptable."

Rei turned to Sam, then changed his mind. Leon was so tense it was like looking at the hound waiting for the order of release. "Leon?"

"Ah..., ah...," Leon swallowed. "I think I need to be released to the practice ground at the garrison. I keep wanting to hit things, but I'm not really sure why."

Kirk snorted. "Because you *couldn't* hit all the ninnies we had to watch for the last weeks."

Leon blinked, then nodded rather enthusiastically. "Yes. That would be it. Maybe just this afternoon as well, then, and get to sleep in in the morning. I haven't done that since we were at the northeast garrison and Mistress Mizi was bored, so not working so hard." Mizi blushed again a little, but Ilena was nodding sympathetically. It wasn't like guards ever got to sleep in unless the royals were being lazy.

Rei answered, "Then take the afternoon off as well and sleep in. Come here to the office when you're ready to face your day." Leon gave a grateful bow of the head. "Sam?"

Sam sighed. "I'm more like Lady Brianna. I need to leave the castle grounds and stare at nothing for a while. Then find a place to breathe and drink without requirements until it's time to stumble home to sleep it off."

Rei gave a nod to that one, too. That was similar to Ore, but he'd learned to tell when Ore just needed the evening off. They'd help Mizi get to that point of understanding. "Now that Nijoushi is settled, I can let you go into it. I didn't need any of you coming into troubles while it was unsettled." It helped them to hear why he'd been holding back until then.

He really hadn't been just oblivious, for all he'd not been paying much more attention than Mizi since, as Ore had pointed out, he was still having his own difficulties that were demanding his focus. "Kirk, you can decide if you want the full two days Brian needs, or if you'd rather have the half day and let him be frustrated on his own for the rest of it. You know if he needs people or solitude."

"Thank you, Rei," Kirk said with relief. Rei understood he was saying it for both of them. Brian would take that half–day to reach the point the words could get out of his mouth.

Rei turned to the invisible person. "Tanner?" Mizi jumped, blinked and turned to her secretary as well. He was even more washed out than normal, truly as if a pale shadow of himself.

"I'm so sorry, Tanner," Mizi was immediately apologetic. Rei raised his eyebrow at her. She went very dejected. "He's been so helpful every morning, but I forget by the time we're out of the suite that he's with us and don't even think to talk to him, or let him rest or anything until we're talking the next morning."

"That's rather bad, Mistress," Ore said quietly in his soft scold of her. She agreed, still dejected.

They all turned questioning looks on Tanner. He slumped and nearly collapsed right there. "I'll go sleep for a while, if that's okay?" he asked.

"And take the day off tomorrow," Mizi agreed immediately. "Ah..., but please rattle off the schedule for me in the morning on my way out the door." She glanced at Ilena who gave a bare nod that she'd send a substitute hidden guardian to let Tanner have the day of vacation.

"Thank you," Tanner said quietly. He bowed and walked out the door to the office. That was pretty tired, that he didn't leave by roof or balcony in the usual manner Ilena's people traveled — even Tanner when he wasn't directly following Mizi.

Rei had been paying attention to his own, for all Ilena and Ore's insinuation was that he hadn't been. It was that Aiden had been content to lose himself back in his work again. He got more stressed out when the work got ahead of him. Thus his slight reluctance to leave at all. Going had been his point that he'd felt that working with Ore had been harder than he'd expected and a reward for that had been due. The rest had been in a rather good balance for now.

However..., Rei leaned back in his chair and looked over Andrew and Mina sitting closer to him. He got back negative responses, but they had a slight tension. "Leave early today and take the evening for yourselves. We've been working hard so it's not an imposition to close up and let even me relax for once." He leaned on his elbows on his desk and sighed out a breath. "If Ore and Ilena work on me too hard at lunch, I'll be a puddle anyway and we'll all have to take the afternoon off."

Ilena laughed at that. "We've done the same: let everyone have the afternoon off to not have to look at each other unless they want to spend the time together. It's a good thing, I think, if we can help you become that puddle."

Rei glared at her from the sides of his eyes. "Why must you become Ore when he's standing right here?" he pointed at the man himself.

Ore laughed with Ilena this time. "Because we're good for you, Master. And if you're so stressed out you'll become jelly, then perhaps there's something you need to let us help you with this afternoon. You and Mistress are welcome to come with us after lunch for a few hours, then have the rest of the evening to yourselves." He turned that teasing eye on Mizi and Rei's guards. "We'll guard them again this afternoon, with all of you on vacation. That will be a vacation for us: to get to tease them again." Rei groaned and

Mizi was right with him. Ore and Ilena didn't relent, nor did the rest of the guards who most definitely needed their vacation time.

Rei looked around his desk, then picked his pen back up. "Let me finish this one thing, then, before you really start," he said to Ore. He got teased more, but he ignored it. He'd had Ore around long enough he knew how to get work done when it needed to be.

-o-o-o-

Having Ore and Ilena join in on the office work when Mizi and Rei's guards left for their vacation day had reminded Rei of what he wanted Ore to do next. He waited to bring it up until after they were settling down from lunch, relaxing with food in their stomachs.

"We were going to ride the horses next," Ore said. "We'd love to have you both come with us. We can just ride without running for Mistress' sake, if you'd prefer."

"That'd be good," Mizi said. She'd been enjoying the riding time once per week that she and Rei had been having together. It would be good for her to show Ore and Ilena what she could do.

"Getting out of the castle would be good," Rei agreed. Getting out of the castle but *not* going into town would be good. Things hadn't settled down that well yet, he was quite sure. "Going slow enough I can talk to Ilena for at least a portion of it would be good, too." He'd been needing to pick her brain again, get her insights where he was a little fuzzy.

"I'll have your horses prepared, then," Ilena offered and immediately sent the order in her code. She even had people in the stable who could answer to her.

Ore amended the order with his own request. At Ilena's slight glare, he said, "I need to ride Fenrier. He probably thinks I've forgotten he exists and is getting extremely fat and lazy. Besides," he winked at Rei, "I have a wedding present to appreciate in front of the giver of it." Ilena relented and Rei gave Ore a small smile. He was quite sure Ore still preferred Fenrier to the Tarc horses, for all Ore appreciated them.

As Ilena and Mizi carried the plates to the cart, chatting on the way, Rei turned to Ore. "Ore, I need you to come back to the Rose office for a bit. I want to train you to your next requirement. Now that Nijoushi's settled, and Aiden's done with you, can it fit into the schedule?"

Ore sat and stared at Rei in silence for a bit, then he took in a deep breath. "I suppose. But what would it be for?"

"I need for a member of the Ministry of Intelligence and of the royal family to help me with the highest level security communications."

Ore blinked and took a moment to digest that. "Well, I do fit that requirement. I guess you want me to learn how to answer them?"

"Yes. You already have most of the training, since it'll be in the main the garrison communications and Sasou's."

Ore's mouth fell open. "You want me to ...read King Brother's messages he sends to you?"

"Yes. And answer most of them. I'll train you to which few need to come to me directly. It's okay for you to read them all, though. I've already trained you to the garrison ones, when you were working in Kouzanshi as my Messenger to them. You already have that background and can answer them because of our security meetings. I just need the summaries like you already know how to give me."

Ore closed his mouth. "Oh. Well, that won't take long to learn, then, and shouldn't be that hard."

Rei nodded in agreement and encouragement. "Will you let me have him for that reason?" Rei asked Ilena who'd arrived to stand behind Ore.

Ilena allowed for it. "It'd be good to have that connection between both offices now. His replacements are ready to step in anyway." Thayne and Petroi shifted slightly uncomfortably at the other table, but they didn't otherwise protest. Rei raised an eyebrow at Ore anyway.

"Ah, they'd rather work from here also," Ore explained. "If I come alone to let them work in the Upper office, they'll feel like they're shirking their first duty."

Rei considered that. "If you come in the mornings, they take reports in the afternoon?"

"Some still come in. Will it bother you?" Ore asked.

Rei sighed a bit to himself. "If they sit in the back, it might not be so bad. We'll have to see how much traffic there is. I've got most of it background now anyway."

"Okay," Ore agreed. "When should I start coming?"

"Tomorrow?" Rei requested. He'd wanted Ore more than a month ago. It looked like they'd have to get comfortable with that, but Ore agreed he'd come after the next day's security meeting.

Ilena retrieved Rei's cloak and settled it around his shoulders. Ore did the same for Mizi. Once they were all dressed warmly, Ore caught up Mizi's hand and made her go out onto the balcony. "Petroi, Thayne," he commanded. The two jumped down and held up their hands.

"Okay, Mistress. Sit up on the railing, then turn around and hold yourself on the branch of the tree. Let yourself down as slowly as you can. Ilena and I'll each hold one of your arms and help you go slow. There will be a drop but those two will catch you. Just relax and trust them so you drop straight down. You've been in and out of plenty of trees."

Mizi shivered slightly, then smiled. "It's been a long time, Ore." She did as he directed, though, and was dropped off the edge and down to the waiting guards. Rei tried hard to not have his heart in his throat because he knew what Ore was doing.

When Ore turned those golden eyes to his, the challenge was there. Would Rei really relax this day or not? Rei put his hand on the railing and hopped over. He wasn't quite that relaxed yet, but being obedient would get him there. "You're not going to make us go over the roofs?" he teased Ore as his brother–in–law landed next to him.

Ore arched an eyebrow at him. "Not yet. When Mistress knows how to fall to the ground herself, then we'll try it."

"Ah..., will I really have to learn it?" Mizi asked a bit nervously, her hand already curled at her heart, likely to get it to stop pounding from the new somewhat exciting exit from the Rose office.

Ilena put her hand on Mizi's head. "Of course, if you want to learn how to escape from an attacker in a city. Up is better than running forward. Forward and they follow you easily. Around a corner and up and you're lost to them."

Rei shivered just slightly. He'd learned it to escape Andrew and never been scolded for it. It hadn't occurred to him that was the reason why. He'd rather not have had it so openly said about Mizi. He held his tongue. He was the one who'd told them to train her so she could be safe in any instance.

Ore's Tarc horses were confused when he didn't mount either of them when Ilena called for Reshali. Fenrier, on the other hand, was quite excited to be out and dressed to ride in his sleeping cat regalia. He wasn't kind to Ore, either, for ignoring him for the last several months. It took a bit for Ore to get him to calm down, and still Fenrier wanted to run.

Rei looked at Mizi. She was studying that paring and Ilena and Reshali. "Why don't you two go ahead and run first. We'll do my usual practice along the way while we follow you. Then we can all be settled down and just visit and enjoy the ride."

Rei smiled a small rewarding smile. She did know these two well enough. They'd interrupted their plans to include Rei and Mizi, but they'd really needed to ride in order to run. "Will it be the first time for Fenrier to race a Tarc horse?" Rei asked them.

"Yes," Ore and Ilena said at the same time. Both were just as eager to see if Ore and Fenrier's experience would win out against Ilena–the–master–horsewoman who could make Reshali fly.

"All right," Rei said and made them get in position at the same "starting line". "Ready. Set. Mark!" He smiled at Mizi as the pair sped off. They followed after at their usual warm–up gait, their attention more on the becoming–smaller horses in front of them than on the ride.

"How long do you think they'll run for?" Rei asked Mizi, knowing his own answer.

Mizi gave him a sidelong dry look. "Until Ilena becomes bored."

Rei laughed. "Because Ore would run for three days straight," he agreed. Mizi nodded her agreement rather emphatically.

It was good to do the usual riding practice they'd worked out since setting this in their schedule. It had been good to have that on Princes Day each week. It meant Rei could relax without over–concern he was wasting time, and it meant they'd been able to have couples time outside the castle regularly. While that wasn't today, the regular practice meant that they'd relaxed by the time Ore and Ilena arrived back again.

The pairs were still somewhat distant apart when they heard other hooves come up from behind them. In some surprise, they watched as Kesheb dashed past them to reach the other pair, then turned to catch back up and race them back. The trio raced past Rei and Mizi, who turned in their saddles to watch. They weren't usually the finish line in this direction, so didn't comment on that. "He's trying very hard, isn't he?" Mizi asked.

Rei agreed. "It looks like he'll have to keep working hard, though. Not many can match Fenrier and Ore. ...Ilena's doing good to, though."

When the trio passed them again, which was the end of the race, Kesheb was a bit surprised to leave the other two in the flying snow of his hooves as they slowed down to cool down the horses. He finally re–arrived with the rest of them once Ore and Ilena had joined Mizi and Rei. Kesheb snorted at them, particularly at Fenrier, who tossed his head back in return and bared his teeth.

Ore clucked at them both, then made Fenrier hold still while letting Kesheb come up close. Ore reached down and rubbed Kesheb's head. "Keep working hard. It'll come and Fenrier will retire eventually." He motioned to send Kesheb back to the woods. Kesheb still wasn't happy and pranced off, finally returning to a run, as if to practice more on his own. Ore and Ilena both smiled after him.

"A little frustration will be good for him, but make sure he learns to breathe right or he'll die the same as Sirius's horse would for not learning to run right," Ilena admonished Ore.

"I'll let you do that," Ore answered back. "You do better at it and now he won't listen to me at all until he's proven to me he can match or better Fenrier."

Ilena sighed, but agreed. She patted Reshali's neck and shoulder. "Reshali did very well. It's hard to match Fenrier, though." Fenrier raised his head proudly and shook out his mane. Ore laughed at his horse for putting on airs again. Fenrier was very vain for a horse, oddly enough. But that matched his master.

"We're warmed up as well," Rei said to the other two. "Ore, why don't you take Mizi ahead for conversation and to give her pointers if she needs them. I need to talk to Ilena about things that will bore the both of you. Then we'll just ride comfortably until we get too cold to be out anymore."

Ore bowed from the saddle with one hand over his heart. He'd only been ordered to do his favorite thing. "Mistress, shall we?" He took the lead and Mizi followed after him to ride by his side.

"Ore's just as happy to have her riding by his side as behind him, isn't he?" Rei mused at Ilena.

"Yes. His mistress and his horse make him more comfortable than anything else," Ilena agreed. "It's a good reward for all of his hard work."

Rei agreed. He looked at her out of the corner of his eye. "He almost told me no for the first time ever, and that was a light request."

"He still would have if it hadn't been," Ilena said knowingly. "He's already told Sasou he won't take any more responsibility. I think you can expect that limit applies to you."

Rei agreed but let it go. It had been sufficient. He looked at his sister, just watching her until she turned to look into his eyes. After a bit, she smiled her soft, almost sad, understanding smile. He smiled back. "Thank you for pointing out the obvious in the meeting instead of making me discover it for myself."

Ilena shook her head. "I almost didn't. I thought they'd not mentioned it because they wanted that test: to see if you could figure it out on your own." She scowled slightly. "As I said to Sasou later, I hate doing that. So I'm glad I decided to bring it up." She shook her head. "That they wouldn't think about it because there wasn't enough 'evidence'."

Rei chuckled slightly, completely agreeing with her. "I think you're rather large evidence," he teased her, his eyes crinkling at the corners. "I can't fathom how they'd miss it." She made a face at him and he laughed.

They rode in silence for a while, until Rei remembered the other thing Sasou had said. He frowned at her slightly. "And when were you going to tell me you were working on having children?"

Ilena looked up at him with slightly wider eyes. "Sasou told you?" she guessed. He indicated that was right. She shrugged, perhaps a little embarrassed? "In my case, since I have our mothers' blood and half the chance to get pregnant, trying sooner than later makes more sense. Since it will likely take a very long time, it didn't seem useful to say anything yet."

He pouted at her. "Yet you told Sasou?"

She stared at him for a moment, then spurted a laugh. "And you'll be jealous over that?" He scowled at her laughing at him over it. "It was a response to him telling me Aryana's expecting. He asked because he was already thinking about it himself. It's only right to answer him."

400

While that made sense, he continued to pout at her a little. "Life this year's already going to be busy."

"I know," she answered, "but society continues regardless. Having children is keeping society going, and the familial goals, too. It interrupts some, but we're already late and it's already going to take a long time. Or at least an indeterminate amount of time."

Ilena's hand was warm on Rei's knee. When he looked into her tawny eyes again she said, "Rei, I'm here. I'll be here even through that." She continued to hold his eyes. She smiled her sad kind smile again. "It's only adding one more child to the many I already have, and you're one of the most important ones. You already know I'm very interruptable. Continue to do so so you can know I'm still here."

Rei sighed out a long sigh. She'd again answered a deep inner need that he'd not been able to put into words. "Thanks. I will," he answered quietly.

She reached for his hand and he gave it to her, gloved as they were. She pressed his hand. "We love you, Rei. Sasou and me. Ore and Mizi. Andrew and Mina. We won't leave your side. Lean on us."

He held her hand tightly until he could swallow the lump in the back of his throat and blink the tears in his eyes back where they belonged. It really did help to know that he wasn't carrying the region and worries alone on his singular set of very young shoulders. Ilena kindly let him hold on to her hand until he was able to finish releasing all of his tension and worries and set them aside.

Mizi and Ore didn't come back right away, but when they did they came with smiles and were lighthearted, helping Rei to finish recovering. He was grateful that by the time Ore and Ilena left them to go have a quiet couple's dinner he was indeed relaxed again and that Mizi was as well. They'd both needed it quite badly. It was a good day for it to happen.

CHAPTER 159 Working Out Interpersonal Stressors

Marcus was decidedly nervous and somewhat uncomfortable with being sent with the girls on their shopping excursion in Nijoushi. That wasn't particularly normal for him, but there were reasons today. Amber and Rio *seemed* to be getting along better recently, but it was awfully hard to tell with them. That made him nervous to be going along with them as he wasn't sure how much to insert himself. If they were still building their partnership, he should remain detached. At the same time, that wasn't him either. He liked being a participant and helping others smile. That would be a reward for Amber if they really were getting along better, too, so he was torn.

He was uncomfortable for Henry's sake. Henry was still finding being around Rio discomforting. He did it because it was an order, and because of his future requirement, but he couldn't relax in the present. Marcus had tried to help him many times, but an outing that could be seen as a date was something more difficult. He reached out and took Henry's smallest two fingers in his own first two. It was something they'd done when very young, and still did when Marcus was feeling insecure. This time it was to hold Henry down and keep him present.

Henry looked back at Marcus with a raised eyebrow. Marcus held him back a little so they didn't enter Seraphina's shop right after the girls. "Don't run, Henry," Marcus pleaded with him. "I don't know how to face Amber yet." Diverting Henry's attention from Rio made him pause to rearrange his thinking.

Henry finally sighed and calmed down just a little. "I suppose it's hard for both of us right now." Marcus nodded his complete agreement. Henry looked around at the people on the street: going around them, passing the stores, some looking into storefront windows, some going into or out of establishments, others hurrying on their errands, all of them bundled up against the cold.

After a bit of contemplation, Henry looked at Marcus again. "I suppose you could just ask Rio for a report. That would let you know where they are. She's not afraid to say it in front of Amber, I think."

Marcus shifted. "I'm not sure. Rio was finding it hard to relent on her side. If she's still struggling she won't answer honestly."

"Then Amber's there to complain," Henry pointed out. "She's been doing better with that much." There wasn't an argument to that. That much had been obvious.

"Well, I guess," Marcus said. He looked at Henry for a while, then said, "I really don't know what to do to help you, though. Except hold you down and make you do it anyway." He switched to fully holding Henry's hand and squeezing it briefly to try to pass along some comfort to him. "It really will be okay in the long run. I do wish I could take the words away, so you could be as oblivious as she is still. This stress on you isn't good."

Henry's expression went a little dark. "I wish I could take the words away also. They haven't been helpful and if it was supposed to happen it would've eventually anyway."

Marcus hesitated. That wasn't quite truth. "I think having Ryan show up to ask Mistress Ilena and Master Ore for her hand and being rejected at that time would've been harder for him, and made Rio very angry with them, for not understanding. Helping them to be distant now will allow them both to come to it on better terms. I don't know if it would've helped you or hurt you at that time, since she might've turned to you for comfort. But if Mistress Ilena had pointed to you and said, 'There's your rightful husband,' she could've thrown the knives at both you and her and run."

He let Henry think about that. Henry wouldn't meet his eyes. He really didn't want this. It was going to affect how he interacted with Rio even more soon, particularly when Rio and Amber were finally settled to their partnership and Rio could look outside of it again. Henry finally shook his head. "No, there really isn't anything that can be done about it. I'll come along, but there isn't anything I can do to make it any easier either."

Marcus pondered him a little longer, then said, "Well, then I'll do my best to carry the conversation as usual. Please do your best to not be snippy. That will confuse them." Henry sighed a long–suffering sigh at Marcus, but gave a nod he'd try.

Marcus didn't bother having any sort of conversation at Seraphina's. They merely did their own window shopping in the storefront while the girls did theirs, being sure to meet back up at the door at the end so they walked back out onto the street together. It had helped some to eavesdrop on the girl's conversation in the shop, though. It did sound like they were a bit more relaxed with each other now.

"Do you know where you'd like to have lunch?" Marcus asked, as they needed to know which direction to walk.

Amber named a couple of places she'd heard of but not been able to afford before moving up from castle maid to staff of the Ministry of Intelligence. Rio was taking her time to think of anything, but she often did that as she was typically introspective. "Henry, you and Marcus have been here a lot, right? Especially after Mistress Ilena entered the castle. Was there a place you liked that we could afford? I'd like anything you like, and anywhere warm is sounding good right now. I don't know what places are in town."

Henry blinked, then pondered the list of eating places in town. He named one Amber had selected. "It's got good food and isn't too expensive." He named one other that would be more in line with their pay, but the other wasn't bad since they weren't spending a lot of money at the moment generally. When Rio picked the one Amber wanted to go to, Marcus slumped inside with a little relief. That meant Rio was considering her partner, too. That was also a good sign.

Marcus had decided to walk next to Amber, so they were four–abreast for a little while since Henry wanted as many people as possible between himself and Rio. It made Amber blush after a bit to have Marcus there and she'd throw him shy glances, but he was testing her. It was more surprising when Rio let Amber's hand go to fall back and take the back of Henry's cloak in her hand.

Marcus looked around the neighborhood they were in. He caught Henry's attention and tipped his head at an alley. They'd left Ilena's area and were now in the Sage Seraph's district. While there wasn't a threat attached to the person watching them, they'd picked up attention. Henry's protectiveness rose above his level of discomfort. He fell back and pulled Rio's hand into his elbow to hold her closer to him, within his defensive and protective bubble.

Marcus kept going, letting Henry pick how to place Rio so she felt as comfortable as they could get her. Amber frowned and looked around for Rio. "Is it okay?" Amber asked, her expression clearing a little to see Henry holding on to Rio.

Rio shivered but nodded. "It's just bringing back my last visit to town, to see people in alleyways again." She held on tighter to Henry's arm. He patted her hand to calm her down.

Marcus smiled at Rio. "We're all here with you, and this time you're not a target. It's okay. We'll be there shortly and you can forget again while we eat."

Amber was silent, looking around them a little. After a bit she said, "Rio, shall we spend the rest of the vacation time this afternoon at the castle? Or is there somewhere in the city you feel comfortable? You seemed okay earlier with everyone."

Rio tipped her head in thought. "I think we'd both like to be out of the castle, honestly." She sighed and looked down at her walking feet. "I wish we were in Osterly. That was small enough to feel homey instead of open and wild, unsafe like here does." She drew in a breath. "Where we were before was not just having everyone there, which helped, but it was also Mistress Ilena's businesses. There weren't people in alleys there to watch us. This isn't the same."

Marcus nodded at Amber soberly. "We're all neutral now, with truce, but we'll still be watched when we're outside our Head's zones."

Amber stopped them from walking, her eyes wide. "Shall we eat some-where in one of Mistress Ilena's zones, then?"

Henry and Marcus both shrugged. Marcus hesitated, then admitted, "We're supposed to be testing them, and a lot of them recognize Henry and I now. We'll be watched, but if they do attack we'll take the word back to Mistress Ilena who'll take it to their Head. It would be strange for them to act."

Rio drew in a breath. "Well, then it's okay. I just have to fight the most recent stress."

Amber gave Rio a smile. "Let's make it a fun time, then, so you have that to balance the stress. I hope it's been fun until now?" Glimmers of her previous attitude were coming out in that, but Rio took it rather well, only giving a nod that it would be good to try.

Henry patted Rio's hand to encourage her and Marcus got them walking again. They really were very close to the restaurant. It helped to enter the warm environment and be seated to a table not far from the fireplace. Rio relaxed to be warm again, too. She was like Ore. She didn't like to be cold. Henry sat next to Rio because she wasn't going to let him go until he did. Marcus let Amber pick, and relaxed slightly when she picked to sit next to Rio rather than across from her. He took his place between Amber and Henry.

However, then he had a problem. His back twitched. He took in a breath and looked at Amber. "Can you be sure to pay attention to the room somewhat? With both my back and Henry's back facing nearly the same direction, I'm not going to be able to relax and eat politely."

Amber blinked at him, not quite understanding. Then she looked between Henry and Marcus. "You usually eat out across from each other?"

Henry nodded. "Because we grew up on the streets, we learned to watch each other's backs. That meant we ate back–to–back or facing each other. The only places we don't are in the offices."

"Oh!" Amber was surprised but seemed to understand. She frowned at Marcus. "Shall we trade places then?"

Marcus considered her soberly. "I was testing to see if you'd pick the right place. Since you passed, I'd rather we did, actually."

Amber stared at him with wide eyes. He waited since this was another test. Finally her eyes narrowed at him. "I do hate that you keep doing that. It makes me want to say no, you picked your bed, sleep in it. At the same time, I'm somehow pleased to have finally passed a test of yours. I never thought I would."

It was Marcus' turn to have wide eyes at her bald comments. Rio snickered. Amber rose to her feet and offered her chair to Marcus. He decided the blush on his own face was deserved and rose to his feet. "Thank you," he said to her as he put his hand on the back of the chair he was leaving. He waited for her to sit down and helped push in her chair as his way of apologizing. Then he sat down, able to breathe a little better for the exchange.

They placed their orders and Marcus let the girls carry the conversation for a bit, observing and recovering from the surprising answer he'd been given. It had been true to Amber's background and understanding, yet at the same time had been delivered so honestly. At this point he didn't really want to ask Rio to give a full report, since he'd almost seen enough on his own. It was when their food had been delivered and he was taking the first few bites that he knew what he could ask as his final test.

He looked between both young women, getting their attention, then soberly asked, "Have the two of you settled on a joint goal yet?"

Amber's eyes went wide and she looked at Rio. Rio drew in a deep breath. "We haven't discussed it formally yet, no. But we've only just reached the point where we could even think of it." She looked away from the rest of them, then set her fork down and put her hands in her lap.

Taking another deep breath, she admitted, "Justinian scolded me and taught me where I was still being obstinate and blind. He reminded me that trust goes both ways or a partnership doesn't work. It was time for me to work on me." She looked back at Amber slightly apologetically. "It really helped me to have you be so supportive when I got back that night. I learned then that perhaps I could trust you."

Amber relaxed a bit and then gave a nod. "You need a lot of work, but I get it." Henry rolled his eyes since that was normally fighting words when one wasn't ready for it to be teasing. Marcus merely continued to observe the two.

Rio tensed a little, but then agreed. "We all need a lot of work." Then she laughed a little. "Well, on the inside. I'm sure we don't need any more office work." The rest chuckled at that, completely agreeing. Rio looked Amber in the eye. "What Marcus is talking about is what we need to work on next. A partnership has a common goal they're trying to reach together. Justinian was excited to learn that it could be his and Reynold's love of Tarc that could be their joint goal."

Rio pointed with her head at Henry. "Their goal is to walk behind Mistress Ilena. They've earned it and are content with being there now. Sir Petroi and Thayne's goal is to walk behind Master Ore to protect him for Mistress Ilena. Now that they have it, they work even harder to be good partners for each other, so they can continue to have that as their joint goal. It doesn't have to be big. It's a reason to walk together."

Amber's brow was furrowed as she tried to understand. She glanced at Marcus. He nodded. "I also like Master Ore and Mistress Ilena's partnership. They make excellent spouses *and* partners because they both desire to protect

Master Rei and Mistress Mizi with their whole beings. It's not necessarily required for spouses but it helps, in my opinion.

"When two, or even more people have a common goal, they have a reason to support each other, to see that they don't fall, singularly or together. It was hard to choose to be a partner to Henry until I understood Mother, that she'd love me for being different than Henry. I can follow Mother. He follows the Queen. Since it's the same person and we can do what we do well together, that's our common bond."

Amber rubbed her hand on her skirt. "What..., what about if there isn't one? We're working together rather well now."

Rio understood. "It is possible to work together without being partners. That's being co–workers. Like we are with Colin and Jefferson, and they are to each other. I don't think Mistress Ilena would send either one of us away if that's where we ended up, but I think she expects us to try first. If for no other reason than for you to truly understand everyone in the Immediate Family, and to understand her: why she wants that kind of relationship around her."

Amber relaxed a little, but cautiously. "Okay. But it's the first I've heard of this part, so I have time to think about it?"

"Yes," Rio reassured her. "It's important enough that we should take the time to properly consider it. Then we'll discuss it until we reach agreement, ...or don't." Rio shrugged. "Even I don't know yet. There are lots of possibilities, but it takes understanding what we want for ourselves, what moves us forward generally. Most people don't think that hard about their lives, not often anyway."

Her sharp look at Amber said that Rio wasn't sure Amber ever thought hard about herself. Then that look suddenly went distant and she looked down at her plate. She stayed silent, then took another bite of her food. She'd remembered a counter argument to her own accusation, then. Marcus relaxed just a little bit more. Amber also stayed silent on the issue and went back to eating.

Marcus let the eating happen for a while since the food was cooling off and he'd rather eat it warm. Enough time finally passed that he could bring up a different casual topic and get the air around the table to be lighter. When both girls laughed and Henry smiled, Marcus finally relaxed for real. Things were still moving forward for now. It wasn't time for him to step in, but he could relax around Amber now. He glanced at Henry. He'd relaxed enough for now as well, getting to forget his own concerns for a little while.

Marcus sighed out a very quiet breath and worked on thinking of a thing they could do for the afternoon that would continue to help Rio stay relaxed and not worried. That would be harder, but maybe they could also go riding outside both the castle and city. Rio didn't like the openness so much, but it wouldn't remind her of her time in the city. The other zone of Ilena's wouldn't work at all. It was the same district as where Rio had been before.

-o-o-o-

Carl was quite happy to be able to walk off with Liam and Mitchel upon being released from having to be with the whole of the Ministry of Intelligence in Nijoushi. He was equally relieved to be able to just walk for a bit, not thinking much of anything.

"I'd like to get a bit of work done while we're in town as well," Mitchel requested. "When does the actual vacation time start?"

"Lunch, or afternoon, depending on if you include lunch as work time," Liam answered with a bit of a tease.

As they left Crafter's Row, Carl followed after Mitchel and Liam followed after him as they all dropped back enough to not really seem to be together. It took a little bit for Carl to come out of his daze, but nothing had caught his attention particularly before then. Mitchel's connections were normal and the persons he'd expected.

He was called out to a side street briefly to answer to one of his own contacts. He'd been seen with the full group when they'd entered Nijoushi. That didn't bode well, but the word of him coming under Ilena's eye was already known in the streets now. It wouldn't be too far a stretch for people to believe she wanted to keep an even closer eye on him. "Naw. The Ministry called me up as a minor associate since they're short–handed. Minister Touka made us all come out today 'cause we've been in too–close quarters for a while, an' her even more stressed out than the rest of us."

He waved his hand. "It's vacation time now, so I'm just wanderin' to let the stuffin' fall out of my ears." He shook his head to shake that feeling of fluff out that had been with him since Ore's lesson to him. "They're slave drivers for sure so the vacation's much appreciated."

Mitchel and Liam had waited for him he noticed as he returned to his "meander" following after Mitchel. Mitchel led them through a food street vendor section, picking up a few hot things to carry and eat "on the go". The other two did the same, but at different vendors. A short while later Carl had a good idea where Mitchel was headed. It was one of the few hiding–holes they'd meet in outside the castle. When Mitchel entered it, Carl walked on by, then around the block taking enough time to do it so that people on the street who might be watching had moved on.

He was a bit surprised to find Liam there before him. At his raised eyebrow, Liam shrugged. "Came in from the other side of the alley." Since that was smart, Carl let it go.

He sank down gratefully into the chair Mitchel waved at. They unwrapped their lunches and focused on eating. When food was down into bellies, they relaxed back to talk. "I take it you're feeling like they're not listening to you?" Mitchel said astutely. "That was a lot of teaching today, particularly for Ore to get in on it to that degree. Care to talk about it?"

Carl wasn't sure he did, but it might help him get the confusion it had created unraveled a little. Complaining to a sympathetic ear would help, too. "It was too much today," he agreed. "I'm now feeling highly confused rather than helped."

"Can you walk it back?" Mitchel asked kindly.

Carl tried starting with the final confusing point. "It's really unfathomable to me that any Touka royal has a shred of true kindness or caring in their heart. Is that what Lord Ore was trying to say, though? That during the snowball fight they actually enjoyed participating and were really being 'kind' of all things, like Miss Rio said? It was surprising enough they'd actually fight full out against Justinian of all people, but her word really doesn't stick with me at all."

Mitchel raised an eyebrow at Liam. Liam smiled his soft smile. "It's as Colin said. He summed it up best, actually. There are a lot of broken people they both helped to find smiles again. I'm one. Justinian and Reynold, Rio, Jefferson and probably Colin given he was at Tokumade under Thunder Fist. Robert the master stonesmith and his apprentice Peter, Emerson the master leatherworker and the cobbler Master Ore talked to. Everyone at Falcon's Hollow. All of Tarc.

"Mistress Ilena probably had extra motivation for the master crafters, wanting them to help her with her goals, but she'd have let them go if they'd not wanted to work with her. Master Ore would never have chosen to serve Master Rei if he didn't also know how to be kind." Liam folded his hands together on the old worn wood table they were sitting at. "What I've observed of them is that it's *because* they're the royals of Ryokudo and feel beholden to their station. Mistress Ilena and Master Rei both take their duties very seriously. If they don't care about the people of the nation, no one will."

Carl felt his jaw drop at that last sentence. Somehow, it made it all fit together, yet at the same time was almost just as outrageous as the rest of all the things said that morning.

"I think I can guess where the confusion is coming from, though," Liam continued. Carl gave him a nod. He may as well keep going. "They also require that each individual give all that they can in return. If the royals of the nation are going to do everything in their power to help the people, they need the people to do everything they can do to see that the nation continues forward in peace and prosperity. A nation doesn't thrive because of a few people at the top. Nor does it find happiness if only the people at the bottom do all the work.

"I do know the Toukas love each other as the immediate family they are. You can't have love without kindness in a single person. Mistress Ilena scolds both of the older two when they forget it, but she never has to scold Master Rei for that one, and both Mistress Mizi and Master Ore adore him. Neither one would if he wasn't also kind."

Liam's kind eyes took in Carl, who was feeling a little too full again. "You're like Amber: trying to understand a thing that's outside your experiences and expectations until now. Maybe it'll come with time and maybe it won't. Their expectations must be the highest and are. Their requirements are the most stringent, even upon themselves. But when it's the time to be kind and compassionate, they are. Even if that means holding the hand of an insecure young man who needs to know that the world can be kind."

"Do you know Princess Ilena's history, Carl?" Mitchel asked.

Carl shook his head. "I know what's in the books, the explanation that was told to the court, and the hearsay on the street, but I haven't heard it from her or someone who knows her."

"She had hard experiences when she was young that taught her to be the way she is. I think what they're trying to tell you is that you can't approach her from the normal understanding we have of Toukas, but you do have to remember she is one. Like King Sasou, she understood her grandfather's laws on good rulership by the time she was four. Those and her past drive her every decision and action. If you've not read that treatise yet, it's in the castle library. Reading that might help you some."

Liam added, "Reynold's probably the best person to ask for her history, but you can confirm things with Mrs. Leah if you want."

Carl sat and mulled that over. He wasn't sure he really wanted to know Ilena's personal history, but reading the treatise might help him if she lived by it. He narrowed his eyes. "The unwillingness to pay bonuses because they teach bribery.... Is that one of the grandfather's laws?"

Mitchel nodded. "Yes, it is."

Carl rolled his eyes. He'd definitely read it now, to see if he could come up with decent arguments. He'd already been minded to take Ilena up on her offer to enter into a good debate on the issue. If he knew where she was coming from in strength, then he'd be able to debate it better.

"Once we're all trained and in place, would *you* still pay bonuses?" Carl asked Mitchel. Mitchel had been, after all, and Carl and Liam were supposedly going to be working under Mitchel once things settled.

Mitchel hesitated and looked away. "I'm not sure," he answered slowly. "I think I'd need to ease that one in. Queen Kata, and to some degree King Sasou look the other way on that issue, although they don't pay them. They don't micromanage that. None of us know how Regent Rei, and in this case Ilena, are going to handle that. Because we're in her close gaze for now and for a bit, it wouldn't be wise, I think. Once she releases the reins she may not care." Mitchel could only shrug at Carl. Carl had to accept that answer for now.

Still.... He looked away and frowned a bit. His fist tightened on the table. "...*normal people can be purchased on any whim, save they have some sort of stern internal moral compass. ...How strong is your moral compass, really, Carl?*" Somehow, it all boiled down to that. He wasn't even sure that it was important whether or not money was what motivated him. He just needed it for paying the bills and staying alive, like everyone else on the planet.

He didn't like facing the question of if he had a moral compass or not. How strong it was didn't matter if he didn't even have one. The very question seemed to claim that he lived life without thought, just moving through thoughtless motions, each passing day melding into one long life that might or might not have meaning. He'd be just as content to not have to think that deeply about life or himself, but it was a question waiting for an answer.

He supposed he could take the easy way out and just say "yes" that he was happy to live with money as his motivator and see where Ilena would put him. Somehow that wasn't sitting very well with him either. He shifted and sighed. "Lord Mitchel, why did you hire me?" he looked into the eyes of his long–time mentor.

Mitchel rested his elbow on the table and put his chin in his hand. "*Hmm.* I'd been watching you a long time. As a teen you were bright and personable enough with a calm personality. Those are all good traits for becoming a middle agent." His eyes turned to look at Liam. "Like Liam." Carl understood that. "When you were old enough to begin learning the trade, I introduced myself to you so I could see if we could have a working relationship. That went well enough I offered you the first job. I think it's gone well since then." Mitchel gave Carl a small smile, his eyes crinkling at the corners. "Why did you accept?"

Carl leaned back, still resting his fisted hand on the table, although it relaxed slightly. "It was an easy job, the first one. I'd say that generally it all has been, for all some of the learning was a little harder and some of the people I've had to deal with are difficult. The pay helped me to live a normal life, which was sufficient enough. A little intrigue gets the blood flowing and I like knowing things." He didn't like a lot of intrigue or overly life–threatening situations, but he'd learned how to keep those minimal. It really wasn't necessary in his line of work, for all he could defend himself if it became necessary.

That hadn't answered his question very well, though. It still said that normal, easy was what he liked and wanted. "*...normal people can be purchased on any whim...*" Maybe it was that he didn't like the most. He didn't like that accusation. It wasn't "any whim" that purchased him. Carl blinked. Then..., why did he work for Mitchel? That had been rather an easy path that just showed up, but he definitely *could* sell his information to someone else that paid him more.

He'd been approached a few times since he was *supposed* to be getting information on Brulac. He'd also been ordered to be a double agent a few times. Carl frowned again. He'd not liked that feeling in his gut, when he'd taken the money handed to him by the Brulac contacts. He'd felt proud and happy to get the bonuses from Mitchel. Were those feelings from a "noble reason", a sense of nationalism? Or was it a loyalty to Mitchel himself?

Carl closed his eyes, folded his arms, and relaxed into the back of his chair. "I wasn't ready to be called up by the new Minister," he admitted to both other men. "I was only even just beginning to think about what might be next when you all walked into my office." He pursed his lips and tried to follow the feeling, the thoughts. "That night I just had to suspend everything and observe the flow. I've not really gotten past that, but Minister Ilena keeps pushing me. Every lesson is something I'm not ready for. So they throw me and I've got no purchase."

He breathed through his nose for a bit, focusing on not falling into that feeling again. He was supposed to be working on getting his footing. He'd really prefer to, actually.

"She likes to do that," Liam said quietly. Carl opened his eyes. Liam was now in a casual pose as well.

Since Liam didn't look like he was going to say more, Carl raised an eyebrow in invitation at his teacher for everything 'Ilena'. "Why?"

Mitchel smiled and answered, "Because she's a Minister of *Intelligence*. And a Touka."

"And a researcher of people generally," Liam interjected.

"She wants to know who you really are. People react instinctively as their real selves. It takes time and thought to be something else on the surface," Mitchel was in his teaching mode now. "You've learned your cover story well enough now to not be caught by the general person you interact with, and possibly to cover yourself with even Ilena when thrown off balance. But she's got the practice to see the hidden, small clues. They teach her the things she wants to know. It takes a while to learn them sometimes that way, but she's an expert at that one now."

Liam nodded his head. "The rumors she can read minds comes from that. Master Ore's still in lessons for that one, but his instincts are almost as good as her training is, so he doesn't have much longer to go. Justinian's instincts are also that good. I suspect Mistress Ilena started with good instincts, too." Mitchel nodded confirmation.

Carl sighed a bit. "So, Lord Mitchel, where I'm going with this is: she asked me point–blank if I'd only be motivated by money." He raised his eyes to look out from under his brow at Mitchel. "Of course in the same breath she accused me of being a potential traitor, and told me I don't think hard enough about life generally." He scowled and let that frustration out, then tried to let it go again. "I suppose it was kind of her to let me know almost as immediately that if that was my answer, she wasn't going to kick me out the door completely."

Carl ran his hand over his head and had to let it all out. Keeping it inside wasn't helping him come up with an answer. "I want to have that debate — any debate — with her so bad. Almost more to have the thrill of the fight against her than to have any agreement reached." He grimaced as they laughed. He would too if he was on that side.

"The office is a comfortable place to be, honestly, for all it is so *not* normal." He rolled his eyes as Mitchel rolled his eyes at Carl. "Probably more because I'm still working for *you*," he tipped his head at Mitchel. He ignored the slight blush on the man's neck as he turned his head away. Carl frowned slightly. "That's important because, as she said, the loyalty to you specifically *is* one of my motivators." Yet, somehow it seemed more than that. Carl couldn't reach it, though.

Carl sighed as he looked up at the ceiling. "The money is a motivator because I do want to live my comfortable life. I used the bonuses for the extra niceties and sometimes the needs the rest didn't cover. It's worrisome to have to wonder where that will come from. It's not like I *want* it to come from somewhere else." He snorted a little laugh at that. Mostly at himself for feeling that way.

"Ask for a raise to cover the difference," Mitchel suggested. Carl gave a nod. He'd been thinking of that as an option once the training level was done. She'd said they could after the audit, and that had been a reasonable request on her part for patience. (Thus the other reason the debate over the bonus issue would be more for the fight than anything else.)

"I'm not interested in learning a new trade at this point, but sometimes lately I have to wonder if I should work for the Ice King instead. At least then I wouldn't be so confused." Mitchel and Liam snorted laughs at that one. Carl shook his head. "I don't want to move, though I could, I suppose."

"Interested in reporting to him on what Ilena's doing?" Mitchel raised an eyebrow at him. Carl raised one back. Mitchel teased very dryly, "You'd still have to do exactly what you're doing, though."

Carl complained at Mitchel for that one. "What would be the point in that, then? All he has to do is ask her himself. She'll tell him."

"Well, actually, she would, but not everything," Mitchel agreed. "She has her secrets, too. Mostly from him and Regent Rei, actually. She trusts royalty about as far as any nightwalker does."

Carl had to backtrack and review that one. "Right. And then I'm always being reminded of what facet of her's I'm forgetting. I can't keep track of all of them. That makes it even harder to know how to face her." That was a complaint he could make for hours, actually.

Liam shook his head. "Just be yourself. She'll mold around you, like she already does. There are just a few to be wary of: the Queen of Night is the main one. That's the one that will kill you. Most people's instincts are very good and pick up on that one when it comes out, though."

Carl shivered. "Yeah. The very slight brush up I had against that one was plenty. I'd like to not have to deal with that one."

Mitchel looked curiously at Liam. "*Are* there any others than that one?"

Liam nodded soberly. "Neither of you are likely to have to worry about the other one. It's the Naluk'. She'll argue you into the ground and if you can't see the wisdom she's trying to open your eyes to, she'll kill you as soon as you've turned your back and proven you'll stay blind. I've never seen her be the Naluk' outside of Tarc, though."

Carl was wide–eyed at that statement, though. "So if I debated with her?"

Liam shook his head. "That's the Professor. If you were still adamant on your position, she'd just move you into the place you'd be happier."

Carl tried to calm down again. "Like I said. This is far too hard and complicated for me."

"Let me worry about those details," Liam said. "That's part of my job requirement. I'll warn you if you need it. It really is better for you to just be yourself."

Carl had to agree. "It's true that she never does scold me for doing that, nor anyone, I've noticed." Both Liam and Mitchel corroborated that. "I do appreciate that sincerity and respect, actually. ...But isn't that contradictory to the examples you just gave?" Now he was confused again.

"Mm," Liam pursed his lips as he thought about the comparison. "There's a difference. It's in the people themselves. If you were one of the lords who can't get their heads out of their own arses, you wouldn't be in the ministry and she wouldn't even talk to you. There's a reason she hides, you know. She'd be tearing off too many important heads the Region needs. Come watch her at the next Court of Ministers meeting. It's good practice for her in restraint."

Carl groaned. "That must be fun to watch her at."

"Actually it is," Mitchel smiled a bit. "Regent Rei has let her be his bite since the beginning of the Tarc war. She restrains herself until he gives her leave. Then she silences them with the coldest bite they've ever had, delivered as warmly as they deliver their own barbs to each other. They've eased back on how badly they ignore the Regent. I've quite enjoyed the show each time. I think they're getting tamer, so perhaps it's more boring now, but likely you'd still get to see her bite her tongue off many times during the meeting."

Carl could just see it. He wasn't sure he needed to actually see it, though. "Liam and I are getting along well." He motioned in a circle at their little grouping. "This much is comfortable. I'm sure I don't really need to hang out with everyone, though. This morning was more than I was comfortable with. Co–workers on occasion is sufficient for me." He fished for the term. "I'm sure I don't need to be a member of the Immediate Family."

Liam shook his head. "She'll not include you or Lord Mitchel any more than she has already in that. I'm sorry for this morning, though. I asked if I could invite you. She wasn't going to make you come since she's still just as uncomfortable with you as you are with her."

Carl blinked at Liam, "Why'd you do that, knowing that?"

"You've never seen her relaxed. Ever. This was a rare opportunity to." Carl was sure that was a teasing look on Liam's face. "You seem to think her working self, or herself at the lunch table is her relaxed self. It isn't. This morning was."

Carl frowned at Liam. "You mean..., those times I finally relax and think she's being 'normal' ...she isn't?"

"She's doing normal things, sure," Liam corrected slightly, "and if that's all you want to see into the future, that's fine. She can live with that, too." Liam put his chin in his hand as he rested his elbow on the table–top to muse, "I guess I might be a little more like the rest of them than I think I am. We all like the relaxed Ilena most. Probably because she's the happiest then. A royal being relaxed and happy is one of the rarest sights of all."

At that Mitchel had to smile. "And because you all know how to make her get there, you like to do that most of all: see the rarity only you can create."

Liam laughed a rolling laugh, the first Carl had ever heard out of him. "That's a truth. That's a truth," Liam wiped an eye. "Not any other royal can be made to get there. Not even Master Ore. But Mistress Ilena needs it more than they do and knows it. She has the most self–confidence of them all, being able to let all inhibition go and get there."

He gave Carl a look that made Carl roll his eyes. Really. Bringing Ore's lesson back up again to make a point like that one. "I'm not so sure that's self–confidence. Rather, I think it's her general obliviousness to social norms and niceties," Carl argued back.

"She's not oblivious to them," Liam scolded just a little. "She just finds them irrelevant."

"Or too difficult to reach," Carl rejoined.

Liam gave his small smile. "Well..., you might be right about that regardless. For all she works hard, she also prefers to be lazy — by her own admission."

Carl shook his head. That would explain it, but was another hard thing to apply to her. It might become his favorite reason to explain all the things he complained about, though. "Just because she's lazy." Mitchel chuckled and Liam smiled. Carl smiled back. "Then I think I'll take my time to answer her, just to see if she's lazy enough to decide to forget she ever asked me the question to begin with."

Liam pondered that for a time, taking the time for the slow communication they did while walking the town. Finally he said, "You know, ...she likes to play, and that's one of her kind of games. If you want to turn it into that." Carl was satisfied with that.

-o-o-o-

Petroi and Thayne traded with Marcus and Henry after dinner so the older guards could get in at least a little quiet resting time outside of the office where their greatest stressors were. The younger guards helped to keep the final part of the day lighter as Ore and Ilena walked to the garrison for their evening partner's practice. Ore was glad Ilena had decided to have it be a vacation day that morning. He was feeling much better already.

When they arrived at the garrison they casually greeted the soldiers they passed, receiving casual but respectful responses back. The only one that still had to help the soldiers relax was Ilena, since the three young men had already done that a long time ago. Still, Ore thought they were doing better now when she came. They weren't quite so wary and the respect seemed to be increasingly because they knew what her skills were, not just what her station was. Likely they'd never relax for her in the same way as for Ore or the Twins, but then she didn't relax the same either.

They picked an open list and waved Marcus and Henry to do their own partner practice on the next list over. They picked a different list each time so that they wouldn't set patterns for assassins to learn, but this pattern of practice was necessary. Ore grasped Ilena's hand and pulled her close for a quick kiss. He used that as their reminder to be kind to each other, and because he always needed to remind her he wanted to protect her. Even when they were working to learn how to fight side by side the competitive spirit they each held got a little too high. Then they'd practice stepping back to let that cool down before they continued.

When Petroi and Thayne were with them they added some sword practice to their time. Petroi in particular had been unhappy with Ilena's lack of skill with the sword now that she had one. Ore had been slightly amused that Petroi felt so strongly that anyone who carried a weapon should know how to use it, or leave it on the mantle as a decoration. In truth, Petori taught all three of them. Then they'd practice, rotating through who their partner was. Ore had decided to alternate if he practiced with his right hand or left to keep his back balanced as much as he could. Tonight would be a break from that practice.

Ore paused as he turned for his place on the list. Henry and Marcus were facing off against each other to begin with this time. That was unusual. He watched just long enough to understand it was because Henry needed to work off some tension. Ore rubbed the top of his head as he got into position for his warm–up. That seemed to be a little more of a problem of late. Because Henry hadn't spouted off to Ilena yet, Ore might need to get the Twins alone to ask what it was.

He breathed in and out two deep breaths to get focused, then began his usual warming up, starting with the stretches. He'd appreciated that Ilena had been able to easily adjust her own practice patterns to more closely match his. The first night they'd watched the other's warm up and practice. He'd had to stare at her as if she was crazy, like everyone else was. She'd laughed and waved her hand at him. He'd been relieved to hear her promise to adjust to his patterns. That was what she liked to do anyway, being somewhat random. Fitting to his practice hadn't been hard for her.

It helped that he could ignore her and just relax into the feeling of companionship. He moved from the stretches to the competitive forms that had taught his muscles to memorize his defensive and offensive movements. He moved from that into his strengthening routine. He wasn't surprised when Ilena came and sat on his back while he was doing his push-ups. She liked to do that when her routine ended early. She didn't spend as much time doing strengthening exercise as he did, so would tease him when she got bored. He didn't complain. It only helped him.

He did have to fight to not just roll over and hold on to her today, though. He wasn't quite sure he'd make it through the practice. He'd relaxed enough to just want her close. So instead, he took a deep breath and told her like he usually did that he was done. She stood up and he rose to his feet. She smiled at him, then took another look. "Ah, oh dear. ...Um, a shortened practice today, then?"

Ore smiled at her. "I think we should," he agreed. He was sitting rather tenuously between competitive and lusty. Neither of those were good for a partner's practice session. Getting the blood flowing did that to him, though. He turned away from her and breathed deeply through his nose a few times, then asked, "Ready?"

"Yes," she said softly from beside him, already in her own beginning pose.

They'd been working on trying to feel each other's styles enough they could mesh them together. Unlike Marcus and Henry, who'd learned to fight from the beginning together, Ore and Ilena were already mature fighters who couldn't unlearn what they already knew. Ilena had suggested that they take turns fighting a past opponent, replicating their own moves as they best remembered them. The other would match as best they could what they'd do to fill in holes and open sides. That was a bit difficult since they couldn't "see" what had happened in that past battle, but it gave them something to work against instead of just be random.

Ore had discovered that it helped if the person remembering the past battle gave comments along the way to describe what blow had been coming, or even if the opponent had stepped back. Then the partner had something to work with, too. Tonight it was her turn. That helped Ore to focus more on the practice than on her, since he had the more difficult task.

Ilena always used someone she'd fought against in the Kouzanshi lists. She didn't waste time outside of it. It didn't help to have a couple's practice where she just moved for the kill and it was over. Sometimes Ore made her do it anyway so he could figure out how to work with that without interfering or dying. Ore pulled from both street fights and from the occasional tournament he'd participated in.

Tonight Ore focused on breathing, Ilena's movements, and her comments, trying to see what she was seeing. He just about had down the length of her knife, where it would reach to, how far she swung it around her body. He needed that distance down so he wouldn't get accidentally injured.

The other difficulty in working with Ilena's memories was that by the end she was into her acrobatics. He had to either work opposite her (another thing that slipped them into competitive mode) as if attacking the back of the opponent, or use his own acrobatics to greater effect. Today he stuck to the latter, but she also stuck to a simpler opponent she hadn't had to use them on so much. The practice did, therefore, end a little sooner than it could have. Easier opponents went down faster. They were still working easy to middling opponents anyway at this point. Once they felt comfortable working together then they'd add in the difficult opponents.

As Ilena's knife went back into her sheath, Ore slipped his into his sleeve. They'd decided to use the live steel as another deterrent to potential assassins, but they'd not told Rei. He'd likely be unhappy they weren't using practice sticks. Not that the garrison had any the sizes of their blades.

They stood side by side, breathing down to become relaxed again. "*Ah*," Ore sighed, "to move the muscles at the end of a day like this is very good. The last of it can all melt away."

"Um hm," Ilena agreed, "but then I'm suddenly very sleepy." She laughed and Ore chuckled. It was true that now that the muscles were so very relaxed, that would be what they'd want next.

They turned to watch Marcus and Henry finish the last of their partner practice. "An early night?" Marcus asked them. They both gave a nod. Marcus looked at Henry closely. "Was it enough?" he asked.

Ore patted Ilena on the arm and walked over to that list. He motioned to Henry but Marcus shook his head. "I know you want to protect her, but he needs to fight Mistress Ilena." He turned to Ilena. "Let him."

Ilena gave an understanding nod and traded places with Ore. Henry went from working up the courage to face an opponent far above his capabilities to almost killing intent. Ore raised an eyebrow. That was pretty bad, since Ilena was actually slightly better at fighting the Twins than Ore, having already had the practice against them.

Ilena didn't bring out a blade this time. The Twins hadn't had them in their hands either, so it was a hand–to–hand bout. Ilena kept her strange and wild moves minimal, focusing on defending or dodging. She only took openings to attack that were obvious rather than forced. She did attack, or it wouldn't have been a serious respectful battle.

When Henry stepped back, breathing hard, Ilena paused. She brushed a few stray hairs out of her face and watched him. He'd relaxed some from the exertion, Ore noted. They'd also picked up a few more watchers from the soldiers than usual. They didn't often go against the Twins.

Henry drew in a long breath and bowed a stiff bow to Ilena. "If you could continue to practice with me when I'm in need of it, I'll be able to face my requirement slightly better."

Ore and Ilena were rather surprised by that comment. "It's that difficult?" Ilena asked Henry.

Henry pursed his lips. "I'd rather have remained oblivious. She's not ready. Nor am I." The last was said rather darkly, like as if he'd knife Ilena in the middle of the night if he could for having had said requirement placed on him.

"Ah," Ilena sighed and slumped just a little. "I'm sorry, Henry, to not consider you properly." She bit her lip and looked at the sky while looking inside her head, trying to find a way to explain herself. "While you're right that she's not ready to make an open commitment, she *is* ready to fall in love." Ilena frowned. "It's one of the hardest things for young adult women. To find someone they suddenly discover they're in love with and have it taken from them."

Ilena's eyes returned to Henry. "Young ladies are given to a young lord they didn't pick. Young commoners fall in love to only have it unrequited. When they fall in love with someone who returns it with the same tender emotions, a bond of trust and common comfort is formed that ties them together stronger than any other bond can. Rio very much needs that kind of marriage or she won't be able to be strong enough. She's *already* in love with you, without knowing it. You *already* return it."

Ilena shook her head at Henry's thunderous look. "I understand it's too early for both of you, and you've the wisdom to understand that putting her in that place right now will be just as damaging. I'm sorry you feel it's also damaged you, but she needs you standing in the position of already having won her. The future her needs you defending your claim now." She narrowed her eyes at Henry, studying him. "You already know that."

Henry scowled and looked away, then gave a reluctant nod. Ilena sighed. "I'll take your frustration with practices like this one when it comes. Don't let it go too long. Marcus will remind us when it's time, and we'll both listen." Henry promised it and Marcus relaxed.

It still took most of the walk back to their quarters for Henry to finally slump and relax enough. Ilena then turned and took him in her arms, for all he'd still be stiff and awkward when she did that. "You're very good for her, Henry. Thank you for always being that for her, from even when she first came to my room.

"I think she'll be ready when the next hard thing is over. Such difficulties bring people to think more deeply of the important things, to realize that what they have is precious and should be held on to more tightly. Even you'll become ready for that same reason. Even you'll learn to trust in living through it: trust that you'll live for her like you live for me and for Marcus." She held him until he nodded into her shoulder.

Ore sighed a bit as he and Ilena prepared for bed once they were home. When they were ready, he reached for her fingers and pulled her gently to him. He slipped a hand into the back of her hair at the nape of her neck and pulled her ear to his lips. "I would've had you when I was sixteen. I ached to have you with me when I was twenty–three. It already felt far too long by then. I'll hope Henry understands soon that even we young men need to have with us the one who returns our tender emotions so that we can stand stronger for it."

He kissed her gently and long, grateful that they'd not been torn apart by the circumstances of their lives for any longer than they had been. Grateful that Sasou and Rei had both understood how much they needed each other and not given them to others instead.

CHAPTER 160 Ending Ryokudo Year 545

"Princess Mizi? Excuse me." Mizi turned her head in surprise to look at the man addressing her so quietly. It had been a while since she'd been addressed by her title in the Rose office. She blinked, then blushed just slightly to realize that meant Petroi respected her generally for all she was the youngest.

"Yes, Lord Petroi?" she decided to give him the same respect back. She had to smile when he blinked in a bit of surprise to be titled back. Just like it had taken her a while to get used to her title when addressed, she knew all of Ilena's people were just as unsettled as of yet.

His small smile agreed with her. "It is time," he informed her. Her eyes flicked to Thayne, waiting patiently by the main office door.

"Thank you." She put her pen down and stretched out her back. She'd been working on not hunching over the paperwork, but one still had to do that a little just to work properly. She looked over to her personal staff and guards. Just loud enough to catch people's attention she said, "I'll be going with Petroi and Thayne now. When you're done, please enjoy a quiet evening." She got the frown from Sam, the raised eyebrows from Brian and Kirk, and the hidden relief from Leon and Brianna that she'd come to expect. Everyone relaxed to see Petroi and Thayne in the room, though.

However, it was as she thought. Not only were they not quite recovered from the stress of the last month, they weren't going to be upset to not be included with Ilena's household. Firmly Mizi kept the frown furrow off her face and turned to Rei. "I'll see you there," she said as kindly as she could.

Rei smiled back. "I'm looking forward to it." They both glanced at Andrew and Mina. Their small nods let them know they'd be present for sure. Aiden's calm face said that he'd be doing his usual of not participating beyond the work in the office. It was completely acceptable for Aiden to live his own life outside of the office. Mizi knew Tanner was the same. He'd appreciate having his evening off to sit quietly with Rutherford in their suite, once she was safely ensconced in the Lower office. He'd already agreed to be invisible for this next part.

Mizi sighed to herself as she rose and followed Petroi and Thayne out. Her mind wandered as they walked down the stairs and out into the cold. She was also looking forward to this evening of vacation, so soon after an afternoon of vacation. She'd needed the last one very badly to let go of having to deal with young ladies of the court. This one was because she was already working very hard all over again, this time on the hospital under the direction of Ilena — who was a much worse taskmistress than Brianna. With only a few words Ilena could make Mizi have to work hard enough for three people.

The most frustrating lessons so far had been in how to write letters of request to lords. Aiden had been teaching her that because he'd trained many young men of the castle to do the same. Mizi was greatly struggling with the concept that fluffy letters with almost no substance to them, that only said the briefest thing that barely related to what she wanted to be talking to the lord about, was the only acceptable way to begin to open dialogue. Aiden had reassured her that the lord would get the single message sufficiently and send a response that would let her know if they'd even be willing to begin that dialogue with her. "There isn't a point to continuing on until that much has been established," he'd said.

Mizi slumped just a little as she pulled her cloak around her more tightly to prevent the cold winter wind from blowing it and the warmth it provided away from her. It was the lesson that was pointedly showing her why Ilena had little patience for the lords at all. Mizi could only shake her head at herself, the lords, and Ilena and hope that the lessons also taught her how to get what she wanted in the end. If she could get that reward for the empty–air lessons, she might be able to survive having to do it over and over again for the rest of her life.

She was surprised to have a hand land on her right shoulder. She looked back and saw Thayne. His face went from slight concern to a smile for her. She smiled back at him. It was wry and self–deprecating she was sure. "I've learned I'm nearly as impatient as Ilena," she explained. Thayne's eyes crinkled up at the outer corners. She sighed and agreed with him. "It very much points out why I was failing with the young ladies, if they're expecting such gentle treatment as the lords do."

A light hand landed on her head and she turned the other direction to look at Petroi in surprise again. "And thus why she loves you," he said gently. "You can give Prince Rei the common–sense haven he needs in the midst of all the fluff he is forced to stand in the middle of."

Mizi had to laugh, it was so true. "And thus why you love her," she teased Petroi. "Because she won't settle to that level of laziness and keeps even you running after her."

"Indeed," Petroi answered at the same time Thayne said, "Absolutely!"

It was good to share a laugh with the two of them. Mizi sighed in a bit of loneliness. "I think I might be jealous that Ore and Ilena have such good companions as guards."

Thayne's hand patted Mizi's shoulder, then was removed. "You'll learn it with yours as they learn you," he promised.

Mizi gave a pleading look to Petroi, but he nodded just as wisely as Thayne had said it. "It is hard right now as they are still learning each other, too, but it will come. You have already had good times with them supporting you the way you need. All of you learned a lot about each other while in

Tarc. You are learning more now. It will come." He gave Mizi a teasing look of his own. "You are impatient, as you have just learned to recognize. Now that you have recognized it, add it into your equations and you will settle to it." Mizi glared at him, but had to agree. Once she'd had this evening's vacation she'd be able to do that, most likely.

Mizi was glad to enter the warmth and bustle of the kitchen and shed her cloak there. A kitchen staff member immediately handed her an apron and she put it on. She'd dressed down for the day in her preferred short dress and leggings (warm ones for winter), but any cook should properly protect their clothing from the food and grease splashes that were inevitable. "Over here, please, m'lady." She was led to one of the smaller sauce and soup stoves.

"Hi, Mistress Mizi!" Justinian's smile was as warm as the pan he was working over.

"Hi, Justinian," she greeted him kindly. "Your smile is exactly what I needed just now. Thank you." She was suddenly enveloped in a soft hug that was just as suddenly removed as Justinian rescued his falling ladle, since he'd left it behind.

"Of course," Justinian's smile didn't leave. "We'll help you smile, too, tonight."

Mizi smiled at him, although it was still small for now. "I'm looking forward to it," she said very honestly. Because she was having the opening to be honest with herself she turned to Petroi and quietly asked, "How much longer before Ilena is done with the mouse?"

Petroi sighed through his nose and gave her a compassionate look, understanding the basis of her main stress. "We still don't know, but Master Rei has asked that he be the one to decide that. He seems to be thinking of a plan that will use that means. It may be even up to a year. I am sorry."

Mizi slumped and was surprised that she was near to crying. She had Justinian's arms around her again, but this time Thayne had taken the ladle to stir the pan. Justinian's earnest gaze into Mizi's eyes held her grounded. "You can do it, Mistress Mizi. You're very strong. No one is going to hurt you. We'll make sure they're gone before it gets there, ...or that you're protected very well if it's part of the plan." He let her go and went to petting her head. "I know it's hard when you're worried, but even they don't want to hurt you for as long as they need to get information. You don't need to be afraid." Mizi could only nod. She'd ponder on that in the morning, too. Tonight was the night to set all of the worries to the side.

"So, which station is mine?" she asked, looking around. Justinian waved to the station next to his and directed Petroi to the one farther down from that one. They got Thayne involved fetching ingredients while they picked out pans and utensils. Mizi watched what Petroi did to make Ore and Ilena's favorite, making comments as to what she'd done to make it in Tarc. He and

Justinian watched her with just as much interest as she made her Yamanzar favorites. It was fun to know that their birthday dinner for Ore would be just as interesting an international mix as their group was.

They enjoyed arguing over if they'd add in the Tarc dishes they knew how to make now or not. Ilena was the only one who'd eat them, though, and Mizi had a general distaste for wasting food, so they decided not to for all it would have teased Ore quite nicely. "Maybe we can experiment later on using the Tarc base, but add in Selician spices...," Petroi mused. Justinian wasn't quite so sure since he didn't like the heat of those spices, like most Ryokudans.

Mizi considered it longer though. "That might be a fun activity for when we're in the new house in Kouzanshi and need something to do to keep our hands busy."

She liked Petroi's smile. "Let's," he agreed. "Then we can have Master Ore's help. He likes to experiment like that. He keeps telling me he wants to figure out how to add the mikan to the curry."

Mizi giggled. "Then we should."

Thayne gave an agreeing nod. "And Mistress Ilena and I will sit and critique with our noses until something *actually* edible is created." They all laughed as the cooks threatened him teasingly.

-o-o-o-

"Hello, hello! Welcome!" Ore's happy and kind voice welcomed the cooks and final guest into the Lower office. The food cart with its heavy warming cover barely hiding the steaming warm smells coming from it was taken farther into the room as cloaks, hats, gloves, (and even a few boots) came off and were hung on the pegs near the door. It wasn't as full a room as it could have been since several of the staff of the Ministry of Intelligence had also been given leave to run away from their work place. Ore would have been one of those, but when it was homemade dinner by Mizi, Petroi, and Justinian staying in was preferable. They would have been outside on the lawn if it wasn't the dead of winter. As close to the fireplace as possible was Ore's preferred seat then, so that's where they found him.

His hand was resting on a statue of a stalking cat that looked rather amazingly like a real one, if a bit larger in size. "Come feel my present from Ilena," he offered, patting the black stone cat.

Mizi and Ryan went, Mizi's group having picked Ryan up from the infirmary on the way to the Lower office of Intelligence from the kitchen. "Oh, my!" Mizi said as she touched the fur of the cat. "That is so soft!"

Ryan agreed. "That's very surprising."

Ore smiled. "Robert's third–level master works are excellent, aren't they?" They both had to agree. "I'll be having it sent to Falcon's Hollow to be put in the office there."

"Why?" Mizi asked.

Ore went a little sad. "If it stays here, I'll be too tempted to touch it all the time and ignore my work."

Ryan chuckled. "Yes, and you'd like the excuse, too."

"Yeah," Ore sighed. He reached for Ilena's hair. "I'd rather touch Ilena anyway. That's a temptation already hard enough to resist." Petroi clucked his tongue at Ore and received back a glare that said Ore knew he'd have to restrain himself tonight regardless.

Mizi was handed a plate of food, dished up by Amber. She made sure it didn't have Ore's food on it, then accepted it with thanks. She sighed at herself. Of course there'd be at least one person to make her shoulders tense up. She firmly pushed that down as far as possible, reminding herself that was the same issue she was having with her staff from the other direction so she needed to do her part, too. She went to sit next to Rei, who'd been waiting patiently for her attention and saving her a seat.

The chairs usually against the wall or at desks in the Lower office of Intelligence had been brought to join with the couches to make a larger circle. Well, really it was an oval in this room. So that much seating would fit, Ilena's desk had been moved to be closer to the glass patio doors. The heavy blue and gold brocade curtains had been pulled closed.

Reynold sat down next to Ryan with his plate and immediately engaged him in conversation, asking him questions about the early time he'd met Ore. Mizi smiled to herself. Reynold's research into the Immediately Family was still ongoing and rather strongly. She'd agreed to review his paper at the end of his research (if that ever happened). She was interested in seeing if she saw things differently.

She also hoped it would help her and Brianna to fit them all together when they moved into the new Regent's residence. The apparent chasm between the two households at the staff level was worrisome and was her next personal project: learning how to help them all live together since she was the one that wanted that.

Fingers interlacing into hers brought her out of her thoughts. She looked up into Rei's kind blue eyes. "Sorry," she said quietly. "My tired brain is having troubles letting the worries go; although, Petroi, Thayne, and Justinian were very kind and helped me relax while we cooked."

"That's good, then," he answered just as quietly. "But, still...." Mizi nodded. She knew she needed to try to be present for everyone. She'd not even been able to be present for him much of late in their own quarters, with her mind continuously distracted by all kinds of worries.

"So what's this?" Ilena was looking at Mizi straight in the eyes. Mizi wanted to shake her head at Ilena, but because Ilena could read her, the lips of disapproval were already pursing at her silence. Mizi slumped. Even

Andrew and Mina were looking at her sympathetically ...and with the looks that said she should let it out early. She just didn't know where to begin. There was so much and not all of it was really the problem in the end.

Ore tipped his head as he studied Mizi, who couldn't look up at him or Ilena. His eyes that had been watching her for years turned to Andrew and Mina. "What's she looking at but not talking about?"

They blinked at the question and talked to each other silently for a bit, like they did so well. "Her staff," Mina finally answered.

Justinian shifted and the eyes of the wild pair were immediately on him. He sighed. "She's too worried about the mouse. I tried to help her today."

Mizi shook her head. "You did help, Justinian, with that part." She wanted to reassure him of that. She knew she'd get the same answer from Ilena and Ore that he'd given her. She gave them a sad look. "I seem to have picked the wrong sort of people. They don't want to live in the same building as you and your household. Or..., at least I think that's what I'm seeing. They were very relieved — most of them — to not have to come tonight." She felt discouraged. Here was where she was most relaxed. She wanted to be able to relax with those immediately around her, too. "I don't know what to do to make that change."

There was a bit of quiet while people ate and mused on the issue. "I'll talk to Lady Brianna," Andrew said. "She may have already thought about what could be done, since she takes responsibility for things like that." He glanced at Mina.

Mina gave a sharp nod. "We'll talk to the guards during group sword practices, to see what worries and uncertainties we can help clear up."

Petroi agreed. "We can also gently insert ourselves into their lives a little more, so they can get to know us outside of responsibilities. That will also tell us who is unwilling to move that way. Those will be harder and may have to go." His eyes said many things to Mizi.

She looked into those wise amber eyes, then sighed. "Thank you. I think I'd rather know that sooner than later." If she did need to replace someone she should do that before she was even more attached, nor should she waste their time.

Ilena kindly said, "You work very hard, Mistress Mizi. That's a good thing, but please remember that friendships are built upon the gift of time. If you wish for them to be your friends..., are you remembering to take the time to visit with them and turn them into friends?"

Mizi's mouth dropped open just a little, then she sighed at herself. "Well, now that you've said it, no, I'm not." She wrinkled her nose. "It's not like I feel like I have much time for such things. But," she waved her hand, "I'll work on that, too." She sighed loudly this time. "And now I'm going to eat." She said that firmly. "Thank you everyone." She focused on her plate, not wanting to focus on all the things she was supposed to be doing. They smiled at her and returned to their own plates, and other conversations were taken up.

As the food filled her, though, Mizi's thoughts still turned back to her long list of things she was working on. She didn't want to talk to Ilena yet about the hospital project, but there was one thing that she'd been tossing around in her head that she'd not had time to bring up to Rei yet. Listening to Ore having fun made her think of it even more. She'd really been missing his comfortable presence.

He turned to her and caught her watching him. She was glad to receive his smile. "How goes the preparations for testing the new Medical department staff?" he asked her and included Ryan.

"Pretty good," Ryan answered. "We've got the initial written test outlined. We've mostly decided on the schedule and are working on writing the initial request for applicants. We want to word it rather generally for the Medical Department, but...," he looked at Mizi, uncertain since she'd told him she wasn't to talk much about the hospital yet, "if we want to have people who are qualified to run the hospital, we need to do something a little different."

That led into what Mizi had been meaning to talk about with Rei. She turned to him. "There are two professors at Kouzanshi university that could perhaps be convinced to come out and help run the hospital, but they won't necessarily come out on a letter, since they're researchers and professors comfortably in their places." Rei blinked at her but was only going to listen for now.

Mizi took in a deep breath. "I'd like to go, rather soon, to talk to them myself, and to talk to some of the people who were students with us, to explain what we're trying to do and see if they'll come for the training if I ask personally." She glanced at Ore. "And..., I'd like Ore to come with me. He knows how to pry them out without letting them say no." Ore sat up in surprise and blinked at her. Ilena frowned slightly but also let it go without comment just yet.

Rei's eyes went distant as he considered the request. He frowned. "I'm not happy with letting you go in the middle of winter when the storms are heavy and delay travel."

Mizi understood. "I know, but travel still has to happen regardless. We know how to have patience and how to clean the roads fast enough, particularly since it's only travel on North road which is cleared first. I'd also like to pause and look at the *holegn hanatake* on the way there or back, since we missed my fall requirement."

At that Rei did shake his head. "If you were to go, I'd want to know you were going straight there and back so if there is a delay I don't overly worry.

And I'd send you by carriage. Horseback in the cold is too harsh. In the heavy snow it's even worse."

"That takes almost three times as long, then," she frowned back at him. "I'd have time to look at the plantings if we went by horseback and still be back in that time."

Rei shook his head but didn't argue it any more. His final answer was, "I'll think about it." It didn't sound too promising, though. Mizi knew that he'd write the letter himself if he really didn't want her going, to make sure whomever she named came. She really didn't want that, not when she was trying so hard to have the hospital be her business. It might be enough to have said it for now, though. He'd already told her the schedule for the entire year was rather tight. It was for the intern training, too. She'd need to leave this next month, particularly if she had to take the three week trip instead of the one and a half week trip.

"I wouldn't mind going with Mistress if you decide to let her go," Ore said quietly, "however, we need to request time to go to Falcon's Hollow sometime soon for our monthly requirement there. We're already past the month we'd usually go at."

Rei blinked at Ore and took a moment to answer. "I think we need to have you in the office for another week or so first. There are things I need you to help complete before I let you go." Ore agreed humbly.

Mizi submitted silently for now. She appreciated Ore's support, glad that even still he was there for her when he could be. Tonight's gift of food to him and her time was a very small token of the great gratitude she felt that he'd accepted the position behind her those nearly six years ago now. She really needed to rest in that feeling again. She tried hard to for the rest of the time of the birthday party until she could relax enough to not worry, finding for the first time some small relief in getting drunk very quickly on small amounts of the fine birthday alcohols.

-o-o-o-

The Lower office birthday party room had thinned out. It had been a fun dinner with friends and family, a bit rowdier than normal since Ore was like that when he could really relax and he'd chosen to relax that much as his birthday present to himself. Reynold, Justinian, and Ryan had begun the exodus of sleepy people. The girls had been next, with Grandfather and Leah. Marcus had dragged Henry off shortly after that. "Go to bed soon, you six," Thayne scolded as he and Petroi headed for the door. "Even you need rest, for all we're glad Master Ore has lived yet another year longer." Ore agreed heartily with the last sentiment.

When the door clicked closed behind them, Ilena sighed and settled down more into his side. While Ore hadn't necessarily been holding back on tasting all his favorite drinks everyone had brought him, he hadn't been drinking them to the dregs either. Ilena had been the watchdog on Mizi and Rei's intake so Mina and Andrew could relax and drink, too. Not that they were drinking to excess tonight either. They still needed to see the young royals safely back to their quarters.

"It's been a wild year," Ore said softly, giving Ilena a bit of a squeeze around her shoulders. "My favorite present is having Ilena with me finally. It's been a long road to get here." She turned her head and gave him a kiss that he was happy to receive.

"It's been good to see you finally happy and mostly relaxed," Andrew agreed.

Mina blinked at Ore. "That goal was the one that got you out of the crow's nest, isn't it?"

Ore blinked back. "Yeah," he admitted, "deciding I could get there walking behind Mistress with supports like you two." He smiled at their red ears then put on a musing look. "I just never expected to end up a prince of the country. I didn't know Ilena's rank, just that I loved her. That was very surprising."

"I'll say," Andrew said dryly.

"Me, too," Rei agreed. "It seemed so far–fetched that the person Ore had said he was protecting was the lost princess. Mina brought me several names, but that was the only one that stood out to me as the one to watch for. For Ore to bring me more evidence of it...." Rei shook his head. "It was hard for me: that walk to your room, Ilena. Facing Mother first didn't really help."

Ilena answered as dryly as Andrew had spoken. "I wasn't ready to be found, either. Having that forced on me was highly irritating. There were things I still would've liked to have gotten done first. Having my plans slipped away from me doesn't make my mood any good." She sighed at the looks she was getting. "I know. I've been working on letting that go." She turned a teasing look onto Rei. "I've been enjoying getting to let things drop into Rei's lap, though." He rolled his eyes at her.

"It was a difficult beginning for me, since I didn't know," Mizi complained slightly. "Still, I'm glad you came and have helped me so much, Ilena. It's such a relief to finally be here, having my goal met, too."

Ore smiled at Mizi. "Yes. We were glad you could also reach that this year." Ilena nodded her agreement.

Rei gave Mizi's hand a light squeeze of agreement. "I'm also very glad for that goal being met. Thank you, Ilena." Ilena smiled kindly at the pair.

"Us, too," Mina agreed, her head nodding just a little too sleepily.

Ilena looked at her a little sharply, then rose to her feet. "I think you four need to be moving along. We'll have the hidden guards help watch your passage." She held out a hand for Mina's and helped her up so Andrew could rise to his feet as well. Then she gave Mina a sneak–attack hug. "Thank you, too, for all your hard work."

Mina returned the hug after her brief surprise. "My pleasure." She turned to Ore. "Happy birthday, Ore. We're glad you came, too, to help us watch over Mizi."

Ore grinned back, up on his feet now also. "Also my pleasure." He bowed to Mina and Andrew who waved the tease off and helped steer Rei and Mizi towards the door.

After the farewells, Ore took Ilena's hand in his and interlaced their fingers. He pulled her towards the door to their bedroom. "I'm also barely standing," he admitted. "Having a party is nice, but we're all working so hard now that it reaches hardly endurable by this time of night."

He leaned on her as they walked from the door to the bed. He managed to snatch a kiss before toppling over onto it. She laughed at him, then scolded him, then ignored him as she changed for bed and crawled under the covers. He'd have to wake up enough to do the same later that night, since he was stubbornly not going to move from that spot. They made up for that in the morning since they all took a lazy, leisurely waking as part of their celebration of Ore's beginning twenty-eight years before then.

-o-o-o-

A message in the castle Family's whispered call came to the Ministry of Intelligence. "Rio and Amber, handle it. They aren't to know anything other than you're family to the Twins. He knows them." Ilena's order was somewhat cryptic, but they understood. They'd already received their full orders earlier that day. It was just her way to remind them of the things she felt were most important.

They rose and curtsied to her. "Yes, Mistress Ilena," Rio answered for them, then they were both putting on warm outerwear. At least this winter's day was one of the rare sunny ones. Rio made sure her boots were laced up tight. The snowfall had put enough snow on the ground it might get into them over the tops. Her sigh as they stepped out of the royal staff residential building froze in the air, turning into white mist. It definitely was reaching full winter temperatures. She tried hard not to think about that, though. She wasn't often sent outside and it was a nice enough day to enjoy it.

"Amber," she admitted, "I actually don't know my way around the castle yet. You'll have to do the tour. I'll learn it with him." She smiled wryly at herself.

Amber smiled back. "Okay. I can do that. I think I've swept every walkway possible in this small village." Rio chuckled at the humor.

They headed for the Pelican gate, where most of the people called for by the Crown entered the castle grounds. It was the secondary gate in the wall on the city side. Rio hadn't walked this pathway since she'd been brought to the castle at the beginning. She enjoyed seeing all the gardens, for all they were mostly bare–twig hedges and flat–earth garden beds. She decided she might like to walk it again in half a year when it was green and flowering. "Most of the castle grounds is like this, isn't it?" she asked Amber.

"Yes. For all there are a lot of large buildings with many rooms, they've tried to make it very open and pleasing to be here," Amber agreed. She looked around, then took them down a side passage. They arrived at a larger garden area surrounded by high hedges. She took them past an opening in those hedges, pausing so Rio could look in. It was just a large open area of deep snow. Large stone urns filled with dirt were set around the area as decoration. Presumably they held growing flowers when it wasn't winter. The center piece was a decorative fountain, not currently flowing.

"This is where they hold the high lords' teas, particularly when the Regent or King are invited," Amber explained. "It's off the main path so usually only those who are invited come this way." She closed her eyes half–way and added, "And if you don't belong, they frown and shoo you off. We can come today because in winter those teas are held in greenhouses or in ballrooms. ...If they're held at all."

"Ah," Rio could understand that.

A little later, Amber took Rio's arm in her hand and held her back. They were on a walkway between two office buildings that led into a more narrow courtyard than most. Very quietly Amber whispered, *Listen. If you hear footsteps, whispers, or even just breathing, you want to go by another way.* They stood still and listened very closely until they both agreed no one was there, then they scurried on through the courtyard.

Once they were far enough, Amber explained. "That's the favorite place for trapping. That can be both women and men. If a young woman traps you there you get scolded fiercely so they can feel better about themselves. If it's a young man, you get wooed in ways you don't want or need."

Rio shuddered. "Can we go around it, or even over the roof?"

Amber considered that. "Over the roof, maybe, but we have to go through there to get to the Pelican gate from almost anywhere." She pointed ahead of them and Rio could see the gate, with its guards on the outside with their spears in hand and their swords poking their long cloaks out in funny shapes behind them. "It's just before the people at the gate can see, so it's considered a safe zone for doing that sort of thing."

Rio frowned. "It isn't discouraged?"

"Oh, there are plenty of people who scold right back, and who get angry, but since it's random and they learn the patterns of the walking guards, it's hard to catch them and make it stop." Amber shrugged. "It's winter so it's less likely to happen right now, but with the sunshine we still needed to be careful. On our walk back they'll stay out of sight. They don't want to get a bad reputation early with new people."

"Ah," Rio nodded. They paused to step out of the way of a paige dressed in the livery of the castle and a young man who had the look of being very new to the castle. She blinked at him, then said, "Hey, wait!" The paige stopped, stopping the young man. "Are you Flandras? My brother Marcus said you'd be coming sometime today!"

The surprised young man bobbed his head at them. "I am. I didn't know Marcus had a sister at the castle."

"I'm to see him to his quarters," the paige let them know, since he was supposed to do his job expeditiously.

Amber and Rio turned to join them going back. "We'll come along, then," Amber said amicably. "Once you've shown him his quarters, we can show him around the castle." Rio nodded her agreement. Flandras seemed a bit uncomfortable but the paige just shrugged and got them on the move again. They let the paige do his usual tour requirement since he had it memorized, just keeping them company.

Flandras had on the Kouzanshi high–mountain brown cloak that was just as much coat because it had wide sleeves and heavy buckles down the front. His boots were fur lined and up to the knee instead of half of the calf. He had a large travel bag over his shoulder and a slightly smaller one in his hand, both likely containing everything that was his to bring from the university.

"Oh! You'll be with the other middle staff! That's high praise," Amber said as they arrived at a building and the paige headed for the main door. "What do you do?" she asked as they walked into the building.

"Statistics," Flandras answered, still a little uncomfortable. "Math."

Both girls shuddered. "That's hard. Marcus is struggling because the direction gets confused in his head. He can do it if he's really careful, but he's coming new to it. We write and memorize, but math isn't used so much. That must be why you were called up." Amber was nodding wisely and Rio agreed.

The paige shuddered as well. "I'm also hoping to not be called up to a math department. Will you be in the Ministry of Finance?"

Flandras shook his head. "I don't think so, but I'm not sure. I've been called to come, but not told for which department yet."

"Well, you'll get that assignment either sometime later today, when I've reported you've come, or by tomorrow morning at the latest. You get today to get used to the castle for sure," the paige reassured him. Flandras relaxed a little to hear that he wasn't going to be thrown into work just yet.

Rio took note of which floor and room the paige took Flandras to, but the girls stayed out in the hallway to respect his private space while he put his bags down and explored just a little. He discovered he'd have a roommate, who was out doing their work for the day since it was still in the middle of the afternoon. "Is it a good roommate for someone new?" Amber whisper–asked the paige.

The paige shrugged. "Likely it's sufficient. No one in this hall of the wing is very outgoing and they're all worked harder than they like." Flandras had arrived to hear the final comment and was looking at the paige with wide eyes. The paige gave him a small smile. "When all you do is fall asleep, wake up, and leave again, it's not all that bad."

Flandras gave a knowing smile. "I had roommates in Kouzanshi. I hardly saw them since I was mostly in my lab there. I think we shouldn't even bother to rent rooms there, except sometimes we need to sleep really soundly for a few days. The cot in the lab can only work for so long before the brain gives up because the body did weeks ago."

They laughed with him at that. "You'll not have to do that here, most likely ...unless you're put in the Ministry of Finance." The paige's voice dropped to a whisper, "That minister is under punishment by the Regent right now, so it's rather bad. It's good you don't think you're going there." Flandras' eyes were wide again and he shook his head, wishing that one off. "Well, I'll let these two young ladies take you on to the cafeteria. The cart arrives on the main floor in the atrium we came in from if you need a faster meal."

"Cart?" Flandras asked, but the paige was already trotting off.

Rio turned for the atrium, remembering how to get that far. "The kitchen paiges bring them every morning very early and every evening to leave them for people to eat from as they need. Plates and utensils are on them, too, on the middle rack. You dish up your plate, put the covers back over the food platters to keep them as warm as possible for the next person, and when you're done put the dirty dishes on the bottom rack. The whole of it gets covered in the winter to try to keep them warm, but it's hard. You'll want to learn what time it gets delivered to this wing to get warm food."

Amber teased, "You'll learn it if you listen for the running feet early in the morning. Everyone would rather have warm than not, but some get used to eating it lukewarm or cool and don't care, wanting to have the extra minutes of sleep."

Flandras grimaced. "That would be better than the forgetting and having to walk miles to the eating district." He paused to consider, then added, "Or making sandwiches on Common's Day and still be eating them stale on Knight's Day." They laughed with him again, agreeing that cold food carts might just be better than that.

They pointed out where the cart likely would be brought to and motioned to the chairs surrounding the atrium as the places to sit and eat at. "In your lap," Rio said dryly. Flandras' confusion cleared up. Then they were out the door and Amber was leading them towards the cafeteria.

"You'll want to memorize this, but if you can get someone in the building to walk there with you until you do, that works best," Amber said. "There are three cafeterias, each based on what level you are in the castle." She glanced at Rio, then explained a little more humbly, "That's because it's easier to get along with those of your same level. You really could eat at any of them, but the ones you'll find people to talk to about your sticky problems will be at the cafeteria for the middle–level staff. ...Especially if your sticky problems are in high–level mathematics."

"Ah," Flandras understood. They arrived there in not too long, since the cafeterias were built to be close to the residential buildings they supported.

Amber explained that, too, as they passed the various residential build-ings. One residence was for the middle–level staff of specific ministries, with wings for each one. Two were for middle–level married staff and were suites, not just single bedrooms. "That one for the young marrieds, that other for the older marrieds." A twinkle of a tease crinkled up the edges of her eyes. "Of course it swaps all the time which is which since no one likes to move out unless they're moved up."

Rio could tell they were headed even farther from the gate and in to-wards the center of the castle grounds. Amber turned them at a larger open courtyard and had them walk perpendicular to their original direction. Rio was sure she would be lost already by now if Amber wasn't directing their feet. They turned one more time to head back towards the Pelican gate, if Rio still had the general sense of direction correct. The outer castle wall was visible now and they followed it generally.

Amber pointed out the lower–level staff buildings, although they didn't walk through all of them, then the servant's buildings, then walked them past the smaller building they knew well. "This one is for those specifically called up by the royals to walk with them more closely. One whole wing of it has been given to Princess Ilena and her Ministry of Intelligence, housing her household as well. The Regent doesn't use the other side of it much, but there are people living there that Queen Mother Kata and King Sasou have called up to tasks here before Regent Rei came."

"Oh, that's what it is," Rio murmured. Amber gave a nod. Flandras gave that building a more introspective study as they walked on past it.

"And these are the residences of the high lords and their households," Amber said waving her hand at a rather grand collection of buildings. "They have suites of five rooms or more, often taking half of a wing, although it might be upstairs or down on a single side. They're the closest to the offices, where we're going next. These are the ones who need to be on call, or who are too lazy to go out to homes in the city every night and come back every morning. Or they're ones who've inherited their positions from their
434

great–grandfathers and they believe the suite is their's, not the Regent's." Her nose wrinkled up.

Rio stared at her. "I wouldn't have thought you'd have that much of Mistress in you," she pointed out.

Amber gaped at her, then laughed a little. "Well, in that instance, yes. But in my case, it's jealousy more than anything, I suspect, since that was learned when I was frustrated with my own level."

It was Rio's turn to gape a little. "And that was very honest. Very good! I think I'll take about an hour to recover from that one."

Amber glared at her a little, then tossed her head. "When it's you I can bite a little."

Rio laughed. "Yes, you can," she allowed kindly. Amber stared at her, then turned away, her cheeks going pinker than the cold was making them.

Flandras was lost, so Rio turned the conversation back to something he could follow. "You're to come this way tomorrow morning. Your first meeting will be in the Regent's office building. Ask for the Lotus office. Be there by nine o'clock." Having her internal map reoriented by passing by her own home and recognizing Flandras' residence shortly after, she could speak with a little more authority again.

Amber nodded. "Come through these wider passageways between the high lord's buildings. They all have names, but for now only remember visual landmarks." She pointed to the tall buildings beyond the residential ones. "Those are the office buildings. The one closest to the west wall is the one you want." She led them through the broad passageway, uncovered by anything but the bright blue sky.

"At every outside door are guards. You tell them you've been sent for and where the meeting is. They'll let you in and direct you. ...Ah, the gate guards did give you your badge, didn't they?" Rio asked.

Flandras put his hand to his chest. "I put it on when I dropped off my things in the room," he said.

"Good. Remember to wear it all the time. Until they get used to seeing your face, they'll ask for it every time. They want to know the people in the castle belong here." Rio was very sober. They didn't want him being taken to the prison or being kicked out.

"They did say," Flandras reassured them. "But, I noticed none of them are stopping me now?" They'd passed plenty of guards now, including at the outer door to the building he was housed in.

"They know the paige that took you to your quarters and they know us," Amber reassured him. "It's more when you're by yourself they'll ask. They know new people get the tour and don't ask."

"Well..., if we took you into the Royal office building they would. We've never been in there either," Rio cautioned.

"True," Amber said. "It's that one," she pointed to the most decorated of the buildings they'd come to, although they'd all been getting more and more so as they walked. "This door closest to us is closest to the office you're going to. Go up to the second floor, without delay or detour once you're on the stairs. The first floor is ministries that might snatch you up as an able body and then everyone will be in trouble." She looked directly into Flandras' eyes and soberly said, "You are the Regent's. There's a reason you're not in the aide's wing, though. Keep that part secret."

Flandras' eyes were wide again. Rio, just as soberly looked into his eyes as well. "You'll learn why tomorrow."

He finally swallowed and gave a nod. "What department will I say, then?"

"Continue to say you don't know until after your first meeting. You can ask them to tell you what you can say." Rio turned them all back towards the residential buildings. "Warm up in your room, put away your things, meet your roommate and ask him to show you where the cafeteria is again for dinner. Become a known face there. You'll likely be given your own small office."

Amber waved to the office buildings closest to the residential buildings. "Likely one in those."

Flandras nodded. He could already live that way. About half–way back to his new residence, he asked Rio quietly, "Are you really Marcus' sister?"

She gave him a small smile. "Yes, but not by blood. By adoption." Flandras gave a nod but stayed silent.

Amber kept up small conversation with him until they had him ensconced back in his room. "Ah, and if you get lost, just ask anyone. If you discover young ladies going in and out, you're in the wrong wing." She winked at Flandras who went a bit red. She put her finger to the side of her mouth and pondered, then said, "Oh, yes, and there's a monitor who'll throw you out if you're in the wrong wing, particularly at the wrong time of day. Just tell them you're new and blush really hard, like you will anyway. But they'll only be patient with that for about two times. Then they'll expect you to keep it straight."

"No problem," Flandras answered. "I'll probably run away the third time I see them... for all I'm likely to have my head in my math instead of on where my feet are going." They smiled at him, then took their leave.

"I think we'll need to be sure he's got a secret guard," Rio mused on their way through one of the smaller gardens back to their own building. "If only to remind him to turn left instead of right there at the last split."

Amber laughed into her hand. "Truly. Particularly when it's likely to be a right instead of a left at the offices."

Rio sighed and shook her head. She did wonder if Ilena was going to have him trained up to Paige so he could memorize like they could. She was just as glad the tour had only been living places and offices. She wasn't ready for the rest of the castle yet. That had only been the western half.

-o-o-o-

Rei didn't go straight to his seat in the Lower office when he arrived for the final security meeting of the year. Instead he went to the fireplace and rubbed his hands together in front of it. He was taken warmly from behind by arms that wrapped around him. A light kiss came on his cheek. "So cold already?" He sighed at Ilena. "Or is it nervousness?" she whispered.

"You know, in this hold, it's really obvious how tall I am, and how tall you are," he said, not answering either question.

She chuckled. "It's having a short wife that makes you forget."

Rei snorted. "Not to mention I keep seeing you in a chair."

"Well, there's that," she agreed.

"Or on a short horse," he laughed at her silently.

"Yeah," she let him go finally. "But I like them, so I get to disguise myself."

Rei turned to look her in the eyes. "He's here," she said quietly to him. "We'll meet with him after this meeting. Are you ready?" Rei already knew. He'd heard it said in the Family code. She'd already asked him if Flandras could have the time to get to know the castle and get settled. Still, the formal notification was okay, too.

She was spot–on for what was keeping him on his feet, too. Having to talk to Flandras was having to face the reality of war with Gael. He'd rather not. He still needed the break from too many stressors. Delegating it would be good, however. Then he could breathe for a while.

He took a deep breath, and gave her a nod. "We'll talk here first so I can know exactly what to bring up today."

"Okay." Ilena took his cloak and he moved out of it, letting her have it to hand to Henry. Henry hung it on a peg. Rei moved to the head seat at the short table.

"What's the fastest way to get messages into and out of Brulac?" he asked first.

Mitchel answered, "We're using a flag system right now. It's very common in Brulac for flags to fly from the tops of buildings. It's going to be broken soon, though, perhaps even before we can finish this. We've had a few reports that were garbled, and thus concerning."

"By letter mostly," Ilena answered. "I can't have my people using the secret code because Brulac knows about it now. They'll be listening for it."

One corner of her lips curled up. "Unless you *want* them to know my people have arrived."

Mitchel agreed. "Merchants can transport letters easier than spies can get in or out. So far they haven't broken our written code." Rei added that set of information to his board for Brulac.

Rei turned to Ore and Ilena. "I'm going to let Mizi go to Kouzanshi. I'm working on the timing, but I'm going to have Ore go with her. It's one of the first tests and incorrect messages I want to send to him." His eyes pinned them both. "We want both King Gastonne and his Minister of Intelligence to continue to be lulled by the thought I'm still very junior. The mouse knows that separating you two is difficult and should be even more difficult in the winter months. Showing them I'm still oblivious to that difficulty is important for now."

He focused on Ore. "I need you to go as my Messenger to all the northern garrisons to tell them the reason we're having the war games at the same time as the exhibition." He turned his attention to Garen. "You'll write up your statement to the same. Ore knows what more to tell them in secret if they ask for it." Ore indicated he understood.

Rei sat up straighter. "I'll be sending Kirk to the eastern, southern, and central garrisons during that same time, with the same message, to test and see if he can be another Messenger for me. On horseback he'll move faster than the carriage will, so he should be back about the same time. Who would you send?" Rei asked Ilena.

Ilena blinked, then considered the question's answer. "Marcus and Henry. I need them to be recruiting for the messenger service, since that's my next alternative to the whispered language. Plus all the garrisons know them so they can also pass on any gossip and information you need passed along. Zade doesn't know them yet, and they're *slightly* more expendable than my Messengers, should Zade decide to imprison them anyway. ...That is, if you'll have Ore meet with him this time?"

Rei didn't answer to that one. He wasn't there yet in his own thinking. Only the garrisons needed visits as of yet. "That would be fine. Then it can look like Ore's leaving the greater restraints with you to see you're kept tame in the castle, as if he's unsure I can do it." He looked at them with the fierceness of the hawk, letting *them* at least know he was planning on doing it himself this time, and properly. "I'll let you know, then, when I've put it into the schedule."

Rei had been purposefully being outwardly lax in the Rose Office this past month when it came to handling anyone. His firm hand could be seen in the castle as a whole, but he'd learned that some stayed blind when they only saw what little he was willing to show them directly. People's opinions always colored and hid truths. He wanted to know how much their mouse had seen and how they'd interpreted it.

"I've called for General Grosweiler to come back here ...ostensibly to work with you, Garen, on the war games project. I have things I want to talk to him about as well." Garen blinked and gave a nod.

Rei moved on quickly to his final summary topic. "I've received reports from all of the holdings that they understand their requirement for the census. Ilena's set of questions was added to by several other ministers so we modified the full set to not be egregious for the census takers. You'll receive yours later today, when the landed lords should also be receiving their copies. The garrisons have already set up schedules for soldiers to be out with the lords' assigned assistants for the project starting the first of Ante–Cold Solstice. I expect it to take Kouzanshi and Nijoushi the longest to get answers back to us.

"We'll summarize the data and send the specific summaries to the landed lords for their areas. Full summaries will be given to the ministries and Sasou. I'll be asking your ministry to be helping hands when we get to those summaries. I want them completed as quickly as possible. All of the Rosebud and Rose offices will also be involved." Ilena looked like she wanted to protest, or offer other non–ministry personnel for the project, but she'd already been in the meeting they'd had about financing the project. Rei just couldn't afford to hire on more for this one project than they already had.

The more he and Ilena had discussed both the census and the audit projects, the more they'd felt that something just wasn't right with how the region was working financially. The feel of the region was that it was doing well enough, thus there should be enough income in taxes and duties to Nijou. However, it was the regent that was having to pay a cost in not having enough personnel. He was concerned that it was symptomatic of something even worse brewing. That was on his plate for discussion in the next meeting.

He couldn't keep the worry frown off his face those thoughts brought him. He reviewed his notes and moved on to the next thing on his list for this meeting. Staying focused was best.

-o-o-o-

Flandras had *personally* been able to hear the master strategist of their age lay out how his mind worked. He was taking the walk to his new office from the Lotus office slowly so that he could bask in the awe, wanting to savor it before he became lost in the work he'd been given to do.

He'd dreamed of sitting at the feet of the second Touka king, the Strategist, whose battle strategies were still legendary. He'd poured over them so many times he had them memorized. Other Touka kings had similar moments in time. Flandras had heard stories of how Sasou had been while at Kishi Knight's school and he'd heard rumors of the youngest Touka's gifts. Just that much had made his heart yearn to sit and listen to them, to see if they also had the gifts of their forefathers. To have now finally heard it for himself was most certainly a dream come true, and he'd not been disappointed.

Flandras had to wonder if he'd been born just for this time. He'd been so driven to understand the world mathematically. His favorite stories had been the wars of the past. Playing with the mathematics of war had been his delight ever since he'd been blessed with an instructor that could keep up with his brain and teach him the math of statistics. When it had come time for him to pick a profession, he'd been recommended to Kishi Knight's school because of his ability to pick apart the wars to understand the strategy, but he'd loved the math too much to give that up.

Unexpected blessings had continued to drop into his lap. His visit to Kouzanshi university had been on a whim of frustration, wishing for any place that he could keep playing with what he loved. It had been the perfect environment for him. To have Ilena find him and be able to walk his talk with him had been truly a god–send. To have learned at the end she was also a Touka had been a golden moment following on the overwhelming heels of being called up to work the job he'd barely dreamed of working because it was so unlikely.

Yet, now that he'd met with Rei and Ilena, he had to wonder if some providence had been behind it all. Not only had he been able to turn his joy and strengths into useful skills, those skills were actually needed at this time to the royals of Ryokudo.

He was to confirm the pathway they were on, then to help fill in the holes Rei had openly shown still existed and those that Flandras found as he studied it. Just like the few who didn't act the expected way made things fall apart, so did blind spots in the people who were trying to move forward. Flandras would do his best or his own birth would become meaningless.

DANCE LESSONS FOR THIEVES

Ilena bowed to the couple in the middle of the room, then nodded at Marcus. "Ah," Rei said as Marcus wheeled Ilena towards the door, "Ilena ...where, or perhaps rather when, did you learn to dance?"

Ilena looked at him, a slightly sad smile on her face. "In the streets of Selicia, on the plains of Tarc, and in my spare time in Ryokudo." She paused, her head tipping. "One doesn't have to have musicians to dance, when one can hear the music within, and one doesn't have to move to understand the motions. ...Nor does one have to have a partner."

She looked back at them after opening the door. "It just helps." Marcus pushed her out of the room and the door closed behind them.

—CoT 545-3, p. 246.

The prank Ilena pulled on her Favorites when she began to collect people.

DANCE LESSONS FOR THIEVES

The Queen of Night, Ilena, arrived in Kouzanshi with the new Messenger in tow. The Queen's Guards met them there. "We're going to learn how to infiltrate high society next." She got three pairs of very wide open eyes. She shrugged at them. "*I'm* high society, so get used to it — fast." They didn't quite groan, but they did tease her mercilessly since she never *looked* high society.

-o-o-o-

The ballroom below them was a cacophony of orchestral music, conversations, and flowing skirts that swirled out and back in colorful blooms around the ladies as they danced around their more stick–like partners. Ilena almost couldn't contain her excitement and the boys were wide–eyed again as they stared.

"Stop looking at the value of what they're wearing and start memorizing the patterns of movement," she scolded them. That wasn't easy, but they eventually were focused down on single pairs of partners. She'd moved from the group movement to the patterns of the feet and how the arms flowed around them.

-o-o-o-

For two weeks almost every night was a trip to a ballroom somewhere. They did have to travel some so they also got to see area variations. "And she won't even let us snitch anything!" came the complaint as they were headed for the last one before her arrival at her home of Tokumade.

"You show me you can go dancing past your prize and filch it without them knowing and then you can do that," she glared at them.

They froze. "...Dancing ...past?"

"Yes. I'll be testing you when we get together again to see if you're prepared to hide among the guests as a proper guest yourselves. Review the entire scene again and again, practicing what you see on the dance floor and as one who isn't dancing until you can be one of them. Then we'll see if you get any sort of reward of that kind."

They paid extra attention that night, soaking up as much as they could of the scene as a whole. She didn't slack off either.

-o-o-o-

"What ball are *you* going to?" Pakyo asked roughly as he passed Ilena on his way from the stable to the house. He was actually curious, but he wasn't necessarily being kind.

"Eventually," Ilena answered shortly, her mind mostly lost to the movements of her memories that she was trying to get her body to replicate. She was completely unprepared for him to sweep her up as an impromptu partner.

"No idea you had it in you," she commented mildly as she suddenly found it much simpler to perform the movements.

"When did you learn it?" he asked her, now a little rough in his tone with suspicion.

"You're the one who took us this time," she answered calmly. "Have you settled yet on a bride?"

He looked at her silently for a while, still continuing the motions of the dance. Then he sneered, "Going to be jealous?"

"No. Supremely sympathetic. I'm sure I have no idea why."

He looked away with an irritated snort. "Orders to keep the family line going."

"From whom? The ghosts of the dead?" she asked in surprise.

He gave a sour look. "Queen."

"Ah," she looked down humbly and let him lead the dance in silence for a little longer. "Do you want me to prepare separate quarters for her?"

Pakyo decided to end the dance shortly thereafter, weary of having to think of a thing he wasn't interested in. He walked off without answering, but she knew she'd get an answer eventually. He just didn't know yet.

She bowed to him, then began the next dance on her list. It had been rather helpful to have had a partner, actually. She understood a little better now her own movements and what would be expected of her when she was really there.

-o-o-o-

"Alright, let's see what you can do," Ilena said firmly and sat on the city park bench. "Thayne, you're first and I'm your partner."

Thayne took a breath to get into character, then walked smoothly over, bowed over his hand and politely asked if she would dance with him. He froze on the "dance floor" just for a moment, not having picked his dance first. She raised an eyebrow, but he began to hum the tune to the dance he chose. She was pleasantly surprised by that addition.

After the first little bit, he stopped humming (though not dancing) to say, "I must say, dancing with a real partner is different. You've certainly learned quite well. Obviously there's something I'm missing. Will you tell me what it is?"

"You've not learned to lead. The minute muscle differences between alone and partnered can't be learned until you do have a partner. The male leads and the female follows, but it's not to fling the partner around. It's done very smoothly with very small muscle movements. Here. I'll lead briefly." She did until he gave a nod and she went back to her own role.

He had to struggle with it a bit, but when he got it, he got it for good. She gave a satisfied nod and they ended the dance with the proper obeisance.

The "twins" were a little better, since they'd practiced together. She waited to tease Henry as the female of the two until after she danced with both of them, just to make sure they hadn't figured it out on their own and practiced both sides.

Once they'd made it through the initial test, they practiced all of the dances together. Henry and Marcus traded out dancing follower so the boys could all practice dancing lead.

That was through the third dance. The fourth dance, two street women cut in smoothly and suddenly they were dancing three partners, with the boys relaxing in relief. Occasionally they had to scold their partners for trying to dance lead, not helping them.

They drew a large enough party crowd that when they were done with the ballroom dances it moved into country peasant dances and they got to learn those, too. Not a bad night in all, Ilena figured.

As the crowd disappeared in the early hours, someone called out, "So whose party was this? Who's paying for all this?" People disappeared fast until only Ilena and her three were left, sardonic smiles on their faces.

Ilena looked into the face of the person who'd apparently thought there was going to be a payment made for the drink. Eyes filled with concern and blinked at her. "You started this?"

"I was just practicing. Everyone else decided to make it a party. Who hired you? I didn't."

"B–but..., the money for the drink 'as to come from somewhere."

"Does it? When you lifted it to begin with to get the coin, you should've known well enough it wouldn't come from nightwalkers who are thieves for a living just like yourself. I think your coin is the education you've given yourself tonight. Please don't forget it."

The enterprising thief glanced at her boys again, and decided to retreat. "Find out who he lifted the bottles from," she ordered them. She'd repay them, but not enough to cover it all she was sure.

-o-o-o-

"Aren't you going to come dancing with us?" Three pairs of eyes glared at her accusingly. They were dressed as young noble lords and wore it well in her opinion.

"No. I'm watching you tonight as rearguard. This is your test. Don't lift anything tonight. You've got to have clean hands until we get to the final target."

"Oh, there really is a target in the end?" Henry asked snidely, not happy to be going without her.

"What are you wearing anyway?" Marcus asked.

"If I have to come rescue you, I'm your guard," she said. She was in formal pants and jacket that she'd had made up to be able to climb the walls in, so she could do both.

"Role reversal tonight is it?" Thayne asked dryly.

"Yes. And it's how we'll get in, too. Let's go."

They did marvelously that night and she didn't even have to go rescue them. They wouldn't admit it, but they also had fun flirting and discovered the joy of the dance. It helped that it was a ball for young ladies and lords instead of the stuffier older attendees they'd learned from. Ilena got her information that night and was satisfied.

-o-o-o-

"So..., when are we going to the real ball?" They were lounging on a roof almost a week later.

"Don't know," Ilena answered. They took a few minutes to figure it out, then tackled her.

"I swear, I'm going to stuff you into a dress sometime," Marcus scolded her. "Just to make you pay." She just laughed.

When they gave up the chase, Henry groaned. "And I'm going to make you lift four and give them all to me for making us learn all that without any payment at all."

She moved back and brushed his hair back from his face and pet him for a while. Softly she said, "I promise. You'll get your payment someday. You really don't have to steal the only thing they own of value and that you can't sell since everyone will know who it really belongs to.

"Stealing those things will get you thrown into prison faster than anything else you could sell, other than a lordling or ladyling themselves. Don't touch them. Promise me."

His eyes had gone to her sharply. "No, really," he said sarcastically.

"Really, Henry," she said back mildly. "Those baubles are their medallions and pins of office. Start learning your House and position signs all over again." They went back into their memories and slowly went pale and groaned. She sat with them quietly to comfort them.

"So, what did you really go to get?" Thayne asked quietly.

"The clues we needed to begin collecting my treasures. Only those level of folk know where to find the really excellent crafters, and that's the sort of gathering where they'll brag about their newest acquisitions." She gave them their next set of detailed orders. This time they'd be hunting.

People and Places

Ryokudo The country our main characters are from and royals of.

Ichijou The main palace of Ryokudo, residence of the King and Queen, on the southern coast in the eastern corner.

– King Sasou Touka (Age: 28.) Older brother to Rei, older adoptive brother to Ilena.

– Queen Aryana (Age: 27.) Sasou's wife. Zade's younger sister.

– Lord Michael Barret (Age: 37.) King Sasou's childhood guard, first aide, head nag, and Minister of Intelligence of Ryokudo.

– Parmenia (Age: 35.) Head Court Healer of Ichijou. Mizi and Ryan's superior before they moved to Nijou.

Ichijoutsu The bustling capital port city of Ryokudo that sits at the feet of Ichijou. Full of trade and people who smile because their kings work hard to make life simple and fulfilling for their subjects.

Region of Suiran The entire northern portion of Ryokudo. It's in the main dense woods with boggy soil, filling up the rolling hills that lead up to the north rocky mountains.

Tarc The Grand Duchy in the farthest northeast of Suiran, accessible through low rolling hills of trees that give way to grassland. Tarc is one wide expanse of highland grassland, populated by nomadic clans of horsemen.

– Zerak' (Age: 33.) Storm Clan Head. Right Hand Second of the Head Clan Heads. "First Prince" of Tarc. Grand Marshal of the Grand Duchy of Tarc. Older half–brother to Prota. Husband of Mir'nah. Strongest of the Tarc, the God of War to the Tarc.

– Mir'nah, Zerak's first (currently only) wife, head wife of the Storm Clan, friend of Mizi's.

– Prota (Age: 27.) Fox Clan Head. Left Hand Second of the Head Clan Heads. "Second Prince" of Tarc. Co-Steward of the Grand Duchy of Tarc. Younger half–brother to Zerak'. Husband of Nal'fa. Wisest of the Tarc.

– Nal'fa, Prota's first (currently only) wife, head wife of the Fox Clan, friend of Mizi's.

– Kalnar, Halter Clan Head. Oldest clan head of the Tarc, he is a moderate politically, and an ally of Ilena's.

– Ranir, Figurative Star Clan Head, husband of Fi'nah, gifted to her by Ilena.

– Fi'nah, Actual Star Clan Head, first (currently only) wife of Ranir. Appointed by Ilena with Rei's approval. Ilena's bond sister.

– Kir'tak, Foal Clan Head, husband of Bri'nah. Justinian helped them when he was in the Saddle Clan encampment while they were testing the Lord of Tarc.

– Bri'nah, Kir'tak's first (currently only) wife, head wife of the Foal Clan.

– Maroz, Grouse Clan Head. While he is under punishment for not properly leading his clan, he is living with Zerak' to learn how to properly be a clan head. His clan is divided between the Mouse and Grasshopper Clans to learn the Corrected Law properly. It is hoped they will be able to become a clan again after their lessons are over.

– Banak', P'rathna of Tarc Law. Rei's Tarc Advisor and Usuri of the Head Clan. Tarc historian of the Time of Chaos and Change.

Yosai The Earldom of the House of Durand. Lies to the east of Nijou and is often on the northern front of the northeast corner battles when they occur. A House allied with Rei because he "stole" the heir to walk behind him.

– Earl Durand (Age: 47.) Mina's father. Tasked with heading the training of the new lords called up to hold those lands damaged between Nakaba and Nijou.

– Countess Roselle (Age: 35.) One of Ilena's Captains, assigned to Yosai. Earl Durand's second wife. Stepmother to Mina.

Nijou The secondary castle of Ryokudo, the head seat of the Regent of Suiran. Originally it was the head seat of the smaller nation of Waldstaat before they submitted to Ryokudo's king. Set near the tri–corner border of Ryokudo, Tarc, and Brulac so they can quickly defend the contested location.

– Dowager Queen Kata Touka (Age: 53.) Sasou and Rei's mother. She lives in isolation within Nijou, having given the rulership of Ryokudo to Sasou when he reached a sufficient age and education to take over the throne. She was Regent of Suiran before Sasou sent Rei to take over the position.

– First Prince Rei Touka (Age: 19.) Regent of Suiran, younger brother to Sasou. Mizi's husband. Ilena's adoptive younger brother. Our secondary male protagonist.

– Count Andrew Marciel (Age: 28.) Rei's childhood guard, first aide and knight. Mina's husband.

– Sir Ramona "Mina" Durand (Age: 25.) Rei's second aide and knight, Andrew's wife. Heir to Yosai Earldom.

– Sir Tairn Malkin (Age: 28.) Rei's fourth knight and aide. One of Sasou's intelligence agents. Heir to Nakaba Earldom, Dane's older brother.

– Sir Dane Malkin (Age: 24.) Rei's fifth knight and aide. One of Ilena's agents. Youngest son of Earl Malkin, younger brother to Tairn.

– Viscount Aiden (Age: 51.) Rei's sixth aide. Called up to be the voice of neutrality, age, and wisdom within Rei's closest aides.

– Rutherford (Age: 40.) Rei's manservant since he was very young.

– General Garen (Age: 42.) General of the Nijou garrison. Trained into Ilena's intelligence network.

– Corporal David Tellius (Age: 23.) Assistant to the General of the Nijou garrison. One of Ilena's agents.

– General Sirius Grosweiler. Ryokudo field battle general with experience against Tarc and Brulac.

– Marquis Rotius, Suiran Minister of the Interior. A neutral minister of sound mind.

– Count Hulmer, Suiran Minister of Finance. A minister that is set against Touka but uses "reasonable" words to not sound like he is.

– Count Eadsley, Suiran Minister of Public Works. An impeccable minister who finds it extremely distasteful to have women in positions of political power or holding positions of office.

– Marquis Preston, Suiran Minister of Natural Resources and Trade. A busy–body who told his daughter to use underhanded tricks to try to become Rei's princess during the candidate testing.

– Baron Odle, A director in Nijou's court. He's been pleased that the Regent and his closest aides have been reasonable and helpful to him as he's tried to do his best.

– Vicount Finlay, A mid–level lord of the Nijou court that was trained in Ichijou and is known well enough there. Lord Aiden suggests that he become Ore's Voice, to train him to the Ichijou court requirements. Ore has him train Grandfather to the high court details instead.

– Miss Opal Preston (Age: 19) Marquis Preston's daughter, one of the final candidates for Rei's princess, but she caved to her father's requirement to use underhanded methods to be in that position. She's being trained to become an emissary to Selicia, where Rei needs to open relations, and where it's far enough away he doesn't have to see her anymore to be reminded of the debacle.

– Miss Contina (Age: 20) To be sent with Opal Preston as Opal's lady–in–waiting to Selicia for cutting into Mizi in Opal's behalf.

– Baron Ryan of Nijou (Age: 17.) Head Court Healer of Nijou. Mizi's superior. Chooses to become a trained Agent in Ilena's network.

– First Princess Mizi Touka (Age: 19.) Rei's wife. Adjunct to the Regent and Assistant over Petitioners. Court Healer of Nijou, assigned specifically to care for Rei's health. Our secondary female protagonist.

– Lady Brianna Welxom (Age: 50.) Rei's seventh aide. Mizi's head nurse.

– Leanna Wilcox (Age: 21.) Mizi's assistant for her role as Assistant over Petitioners. Married to the heir of Viscount Wilcox.

– Delia (Age: 20.) Mizi's hairdresser. Captain in Ilena's network assigned to be Rei's translator and teacher.

– Maria Reed (Age: 20.) Mizi's personal maid. Daughter of court Vicount Reed.

– Tanner (Age: 38.) Mizi's secretary. Mizi's hidden guardian assigned from Ilena's department.

– Sir Sam (Age: 38.) Mizi's head guard. Assigned to Mizi by Sasou. Leon's partner.

– Sir Leon (Age: 24.) Rei's eighth knight. Mizi's guard. Sam's partner

– Sir Brian Umber (Age: 25.) Rei's sixth knight. Mizi's guard and aide. Son of court Viscount Umber. Kirk's partner.

– Sir Kirk Leander (Age: 25.) Rei's seventh knight. Mizi's guard and aide. Youngest son of a landed baron, Baron Leander. Brian's partner.

– Second Prince Ore Melick (Age: 28.) Interim Grand Duke of Tarc. Rei's third aide and knight. Messenger of the Regent. Count Falcon's Hollow. Ilena's husband, partner, and guard. Suiran Assistant Minister of Intelligence. Father to Ilena's Mother at the head of the intelligence network. Queen's Consort and Queen's Knight in the House of the Queen of Night. Suiran Nightwalker King: Head of a House of nightwalkers who've made him their Head because they wanted him there. Marluk' to the Tarc. Our primary male protagonist.

– Lord Hayward, Co-Steward of the Grand Duchy of Tarc. Handles the books and works with Ilena and Ore in Nijou.

– Marquis Randolph Thorin (Age: 49.) Ore's secretary and Voice. Suiran Ministry of Intelligence Financial Officer. Known as Grandfather in the intelligence network. Leah's husband.

– Earl Petroi Somas (Age: 34.) Ilena's childhood guard and first knight. Ore's man–at–arms. Suiran Associate Minister of Intelligence over International Affairs. First Son in Ilena's intelligence network. Nijoushi Messenger of the Queen of Night. Thayne's partner.

– Vicount Thayne Melick (Age: 25.) Second knight of Ilena. Ore's man–at–arms. Suiran Associate Minister of Intelligence over National Affairs. Second Son in Ilena's intelligence network. Kouzanshi Messenger of and Queen's Guard for the Queen of Night. Petroi's partner.

– Jefferson (Age: 42.) Suiran Ministry of Intelligence Director, Eastern Affairs.

– Collin (Age: 38.) Suiran Ministry of Intelligence Director, Western Affairs.

– Baron Reynold Tennyson (Age: 31.) Tarc researcher. Suiran Ministry of Intelligence Director, Tarc Affairs. Grand Duchy of Tarc Historian: Chronicler of Tarc. Justinian's partner.

– Justinian (Age: 18.) Ore's manservant. Suiran Ministry of Intelligence Assistant, Tarc Affairs. Queen's Treasure. King's Assassin. Son of the Naluk' and Marluk' to the Tarc. Reynold's partner.

– Second Princess Ilena Polov Touka (Age: 25.) Interim Grand Duchess of Tarc. Adopted sister of Sasou and Rei. Suiran Minister of Intelligence. Ore's wife and partner. Countess of Falcon's Hollow. Mother: the Head of an information network on current events in the noble houses and cities of Suiran and beyond. Queen of Night: the Head of a nightwalker House she uses as an information network on current events in the underworld. Head of the House of the Southern Nijoushi district: Crafter's Mall. Naluk' to the Tarc. Our primary female protagonist.

– Marchioness Leah Undel (Age: 47.) Ilena's nurse and secretary. Grandmother in the intelligence network. Randolph's wife.

– Baron Henry Melick (Age: 22.) Third knight of Ilena and her personal guard. Suiran Ministry of Intelligence, Direct Assistant to the Minister. Twin and Third Son in Ilena's intelligence network. Queen's Guard for the Queen of Night. Marcus' partner.

– Baron Marcus Melick (Age: 21.) Fourth knight of Ilena and her personal guard. Suiran Ministry of Intelligence, Direct Assistant to the Minister. Twin and Fourth Son in Ilena's intelligence network. Queen's Guard for the Queen of Night. Henry's partner.

– Baroness Rio Melick (Age: 18.) Ilena's maid. Suiran Ministry of Intelligence Director, Internal Affairs. First Daughter in the intelligence network.

– Amber (Age: 19.) Suiran Ministry of Intelligence Assistant, Internal Affairs.

– Lord Mitchel Barkley (Age: 52.) Former Queen's Minister of Intelligence. Suiran Associate Minister of Intelligence, Brulac Affairs.

– Count Liam Melick (Age: 36.) Ilena's aide and hidden guard. Ilena's Voice and Voice of the Queen of Night. Suiran Ministry of Intelligence Assistant, in training. Assigned to Mitchel Barkley to learn his network and eventually be over it with Carl. Carl's partner.

– Carl Stern (Age: 30.) Suiran Ministry of Intelligence Assistant, in training. Mitchel's main contact with Kata's Brulac spy network. Liam's partner.

Nijoushi The capital city of Suiran, sitting at the more–protected western edge of the castle grounds.

– Landras, Nijoushi first lieutenant of the House of the Queen of Night. The face of loyalty to Ilena.

– Danel, Nijoushi second lieutenant of the House of the Queen of Night. The face of loyalty of the House to itself. Wounded in a battle in Tarc, pardoned for his bravery there ...posthumously?

– Barakka, Nijoushi third lieutenant of the House of the Queen of Night. The face of selfish loyalty: each member of the House to themselves.

– Raine Marciel (Age: 39.) Northern partner of the trading and merchant company Marciel and Crane Trading Company. Andrew's cousin. Ilena does almost exclusive business with him for the sake of her Falcon Studios. Ally of the Sage Seraph and the Queen of Night.

– Robert (Age: 33.) Third–level master stonesmith of Falcon Stoneworks Studio.

– Peter (Age: 20.) Most junior of Robert's apprentices, specializing in small detailed stonecarving.

– Balar (Age: 40.) Head of Falcon Construction Studio.

– Lady Seraphina (Age: 39.) Third–level mistress of Falcon Fabricworks Studio.

– Emerson, Second–level master of Falcon Leatherworks Studio

– Gold Lion (Flynn) Head of the House of the Gold Lion, nightwalker House of the Eastern Nijoushi district: The Northern Gardens. Main business is the prostitute houses.

– Sage Seraph (Brendan) Head of the House of the Sage Seraph, nightwalker House of the Northern Nijoushi district: Merchant Street. Main business is doing business with the legitimate businesses of the city.

– Black Ram (Russel Marciel) Younger brother to Raine, cousin to Andrew. Head of the House of the Black Ram, nightwalker House of the Western Nijoushi district: Traveler's Row. Main business is doing business with visitors to the city.

– Aron, Squad commander of the nightwalkers assigned to protect Ore while he was going around the clans in Tarc. First lieutenant of the House of the Suiran Nightwalker King in Nijoushi.

Falcon's Hollow A small holding and manor located in the bowl of a large hidden hollow south of Nijou. Granted to Ore upon being raised up to Court Count.

– Betty (Age: 53.) Steward of Falcon's Hollow. Assigned to take the office of Falcon's Hollow Steward to relieve Ilena's burdens.

– Foster (Age: 45.) Marshal of Falcon's Hollow. Thayne's father, Sallie's husband, Thom's adoptive father. Captain of Falcon's Hollow in Ilena's information network.

– Sallie (Age: 25.) Châtelaine of Falcon's Hollow. Thayne's step–mother, Foster's wife, Thom's mother.

– Roald (Age: 29.) Assistant Marshal of Falcon's Hollow. Captain–equivalent in the House of the Queen of Night.

– Cirock (Age: 41.) Captain in Ilena's information network over the area around Falcon's Hollow. Assists Foster when he needs to work with the people of the area.

– Edward (Age: 17.) Horseman apprentice to Ilena. Head stableboy.

– Thom (Age: 4.) Sallie's son, Foster's adopted son. At a young age he already has a strong affinity to horses. It's expected he'll follow in Ilena and Edward's footsteps.

Tokumade The prior Earldom of the House of Shicchi, the house of the line of the kings of Waldstaat. Lies to the central northeast of Suiran, west of Nijoushi.

Nakaba The Earldom of the House of Malkin. Lies in the center of the Region. An honorable House that is allied with Sasou and Rei.

– Earl Malkin (Age: 50.) Tairn and Dane's father. Tasked with managing the damaged lands between Nakaba and Nijoushi until the new lords are sufficiently trained. Owes Ilena two debts of life.

Kouzanshi The university city of Ryokudo, set up high in the rough mountains of the northwest corner of the country.

– Marquis Zade Yosuko (Age: 36.) Lord of Kouzanshi. Older brother of Queen Aryana. At odds with the Queen of Night for being a thorn in his side.

– Shiotsu (Age: 34.) Head of the Medical Department of the University of Kouzanshi. Ilena, Mizi, and Ryan's Professor of Medicine. Tiana's husband.

– Tiana (Age: 26.) Shiotsu's assistant and wife.

– Hana (Age: 21.) Chemist at the university. A friend of Mizi and Ryan's from when they were there to study, and a friend (and adopted student) of Ilena's.

– Julie Inule (Age: 21.) Grew up Kirk's half–sister. Studying to become the Nijou medic to the messenger birds of Ryokudo on their island of origination in the Inner Sea. Kirk's intended.

– Damas, Kouzanshi first lieutenant of the House of the Queen of Night. The face of loyalty to Ilena.

– Mandor, Kouzanshi second lieutenant of the House of the Queen of Night. The face of loyalty of the House to itself.

– Zeph, Kouzanshi third lieutenant of the House of the Queen of Night. The face of selfish loyalty: each member of the House to themselves.

Neighboring Nations

Gael Altherly's neighbor to their west. They've begun to invade Altherly, refusing any peace negotiations just within this year.

Altherly The nation west of Ryokudo. Rough rolling hills and a wide river divide the nations.

– King Roland, King of Altherly.

– Second Prince Airn Roland (Age: 16.) Sasou has agreed, under the table, to keep Airn safe while the war between Gael and Altherly becomes a full–blown sad reality. He's working his way east from Kouzanshi to Nijou now that the winter snows have settled into the mountains above Kouzanshi.

– Sir Erlic Yetherly (Age: 33.) Airn's senior aide.

– Sir Ian Ulmer (Age: 26.) Airn's personal guard.

Selicia The nation to the northwest of Ryokudo, accessible only through two harsh passes through the rocky mountains. Kata's sister, Tatiana Touka, was married to the third prince of Selicia, Raoul Polov. They were murdered in a coup in that nation about the same time as Kata's husband died.

– King Sandras (Age: 59.) King of Selicia.

– First Prince Naraj (Age: 37.) Visited at the time of Rei's wedding to negotiate an agreement to put down the Lord of Tarc and to broach reopening relations between Ryokudo and Selicia.

Brulac The nation east of Ryokudo. There are tall mountains between the two nations on the south end of the border, but only tall wooded hills separate them in the northeastern corner of Ryokudo.

– King Gastonne, King of Brulac. He has tried multiple times to win Kata as his wife. Kata believes Gastonne had her husband assassinated and has a vendetta against him. Sasou's opinion of him is very low: that he loves power and graft more than his people and as a corrupted King he needs to be removed. Ilena suspects that he was the hand behind all of the Lord of Tarc's moves. All three believe that he is in league with Gael with the expectation he'll invade Ryokudo while they're distracted helping Altherly.

Yamanzar Nation across the Inner Sea from Ryokudo. There is a small land access between the two nations, a bare roadway between a tall mountain and the sea. On the other side of that mountain is Brulac.

– King Rayis (Age: 41.) King of Yamanzar.

– First Prince Amiran (Age: 23.) The reason Mizi left Yamanzar. Since meeting the team of Mizi and Rei his goal has been to learn how to have the strength of honorable royalty. Alia's husband.

– First Princess Alia (Age: 20.) Amiran's wife.

– Hizaber (Age: 38.) Mizi's father. Leader of the Raionmure, a band of people hiding from the nobles of Yamanzar to save their lives.

– Darin (Age: 32.) Hizaber's first lieutenant.

– Zayn (Age: 21.) Assistant to Hizaber. Adopted Hizaber and follows him with great devotion.

www.ingramcontent.com/pod-product-compliance
Lightning Source LLC
Chambersburg PA
CBHW070231200726
48293CB00005B/1567